Bartell

April 1921

WORLD'S END

WORLD'S END

Upton Sinclair

The Literary Guild of America, Inc.
NEW YORK

CL

PRINTED IN U. S. A.

**PUBLISHED ON THE SAME DAY IN THE DOMINION OF CANADA BY
THE MACMILLAN COMPANY OF CANADA LIMITED**

Author's Note

In the course of this novel a number of well-known persons make their appearance, some of them living, some dead; they appear under their own names, and what is said about them is factually correct.

There are other characters which are fictitious, and in these cases the author has gone out of his way to avoid seeming to point at real persons. He has given them unlikely names, and hopes that no persons bearing such names exist. But it is impossible to make sure; therefore the writer states that, if any such coincidence occurs, it is accidental. This is not the customary "hedge clause" which the author of a *roman à clef* publishes for legal protection; it means what it says and is intended to be so taken.

Various European concerns engaged in the manufacture of munitions have been named in the story, and what has been said about them is also according to the records. There is one American firm, and that, with all its affairs, is imaginary. The writer has done his best to avoid seeming to indicate any actual American firm or family.

Contents

Book One: God's in His Heaven

I.	MUSIC MADE VISIBLE	1
II.	CÔTE D'AZUR	17
III.	PLAYGROUND OF EUROPE	35
IV.	CHRISTMAS-CARD CASTLE	54
V.	THE FACTS OF LIFE	74
VI.	ARMS AND THE MAN	91

Book Two: A Little Cloud

VII.	THE ISLES OF GREECE	119
VIII.	THIS REALM, THIS ENGLAND	137
IX.	GREEN AND PLEASANT LAND	156
X.	LA BELLE FRANCE	176
XI.	C'EST LA GUERRE	195

Book Three: Bella Gerant Alii

XII.	LOVED I NOT HONOUR MORE	227
XIII.	WOMEN MUST WEEP	247
XIV.	THE FURIES OF PAIN	265
XV.	AMOR INTER ARMA	285
XVI.	BUSINESS AS USUAL	305
XVII.	A MAN'S WORLD	322
XVIII.	AWAY FROM ALL THAT	340

Book Four: Land of the Pilgrims' Pride

XIX.	OLD COLONIAL	367
XX.	THE PIERIAN SPRING	383
XXI.	THE THOUGHTS OF YOUTH	401
XXII.	ABOVE THE BATTLE	419
XXIII.	MIDSUMMER-NIGHT'S DREAM	434
XXIV.	THE WORLD WELL LOST	452

Book Five:
They Have Sown the Wind

XXV.	THE BATTLE FLAGS ARE FURLED	479
XXVI.	THE PARLIAMENT OF MAN	494
XXVII.	THE FEDERATION OF THE WORLD	514
XXVIII.	THE RED PERIL	533
XXIX.	A FRIEND IN NEED	555
XXX.	OUT OF THE DEPTHS	575
XXXI.	IN THE ENEMY'S COUNTRY	597

Book Six:
They Shall Reap the Whirlwind

XXXII.	I HAVE SEEN THE FUTURE	615
XXXIII.	WOE TO THE CONQUERED	634
XXXIV.	YOUNG LOCHINVAR	650
XXXV.	I CAN NO OTHER	667
XXXVI.	THE CHOICE OF HERCULES	686
XXXVII.	PEACE IN OUR TIME	704
XXXVIII.	BATTLE OF THE STAGS	718

BOOK ONE

God's in His Heaven

1

Music Made Visible

THE American boy's name was Lanning Budd; people called him
Lanny, an agreeable name, easy to say. He had been born in Switzerland, and spent most of his life on the French Riviera; he had never
crossed the ocean, but considered himself American because his
mother and father were that. He had traveled a lot, and just now
was in a little village in the suburbs of Dresden, his mother having
left him while she went off on a yachting trip to the fiords of Norway. Lanny didn't mind, for he was used to being left in places, and
knew how to get along with people from other parts of the world.
He would eat their foods, pick up a smattering of their languages,
and hear stories about strange ways of life.

Lanny was thirteen, and growing fast, but much dancing had kept
his figure slender and graceful. His wavy brown hair was worn long,
that being the fashion for boys; when it dropped into his eyes, he
gave a toss of the head. His eyes also were brown, and looked out
with eagerness on whatever part of Europe he was in. Just now he
was sure that Hellerau was the most delightful of places, and surely
this day of the Festspiel was the most delightful of days.

Upon a high plateau stood a tall white temple with smooth round
pillars in front, and to it were drifting throngs of people who had
journeyed from places all over the earth where art was loved and
cherished; fashionable ones among them, but mostly art people,
writers and critics, musicians, actors, producers—celebrities in such
numbers that it was impossible to keep track of them. All Lanny's
life he had heard their names, and here they were in the flesh. With

two friends, a German boy slightly older than himself and an English boy older still, he wandered among the crowd in a state of eager delight.

"There he is!" one would whisper.

"Which?"

"The one with the pink flower."

"Who is he?"

One of the older boys would explain. Perhaps it was a great blond Russian named Stanislavsky; perhaps a carelessly dressed Englishman, Granville Barker. The boys would stare, but not too openly or too long. It was a place of courtesy, and celebrities were worshiped but not disturbed. To ask for an autograph was a crudity undreamed of in the Dalcroze school.

The three were on the alert for the king of celebrities, who had promised to be present. They spied him at some distance, talking with two ladies. Others also had spied him, and were doing as the boys did, walking slowly past, inclining their ears in the hope of catching a stray pearl of wit or wisdom; then stopping a little way off, watching with half-averted gaze.

"His whiskers look like gold," murmured Lanny.

"Whiskers?" queried Kurt, the German boy, who spoke English carefully and precisely. "I thought you say beard."

"Whiskers are beard and mustaches both," ventured Lanny, and then inquired: "Aren't they, Rick?"

"Whiskers stick out," opined the English boy, and added: "His are the color of the soil of Hellerau." It was true, for the ground was reddish yellow, and had glints of sunlight in it. "Hellerau means bright meadow," Kurt explained.

II

The king of celebrities was then in his middle fifties, and the breeze that blew on that elevated spot tossed his whiskers, which stuck out. Tall and erect, he had eyes as gay as the bluebells on the meadow and teeth like the petals of the daisies. He wore an English tweed suit of brown with reddish threads in it, and when he threw his head back and laughed—which he did every time he made a joke —all the flowers on the bright meadow danced.

The trio stared until they thought maybe it wasn't polite any more, and then turned their eyes away. "Do you suppose he'd answer if we spoke to him?" ventured Lanny.

"Oh, no!" exclaimed Kurt, the most strictly brought up of the three.

"What would we say?" demanded Rick.

"We might think up something. You try; you're English."

"English people don't ever speak without being introduced."

"Think of something anyhow," persisted Lanny. "It can't hurt to pretend."

Rick was fifteen, and his father was a baronet who preferred to be known as a designer of stage sets. "Mr. Shaw," he suggested, with Oxford accent and polished manner, "may I take the liberty of telling you how much I have enjoyed the reading of your prefaces?"

"That's what everybody says," declared Lanny. "He's sick of it. You try, Kurt."

Kurt clicked his heels and bowed; he was the son of an official in Silesia, and couldn't even imagine addressing anyone without doing that. "Mr. Shaw, we Germans count ourselves your discoverers, and it does us honor to welcome you to our soil."

"That's better," judged the American. "But maybe the Bürgermeister has already said it."

"You try it then," said Rick.

Lanny knew from his father and others that Americans said what they wanted to, and without too much ceremony. "Mr. Shaw," he announced, "we three boys are going to dance for you in a few minutes, and we're tickled to death about it."

"He'll know that's American, all right," admitted Rick. "Would you dare to do it?"

"I don't know," said Lanny. "He looks quite kind."

The king of celebrities had started to move toward the tall white temple, and Kurt glanced quickly at his watch. "*Herrgott!* Three minutes to curtain!"

He bolted, with the other two at his heels. Breathless, they dashed into the robing room, where the chorus master gazed at them sternly. "It is disgraceful to be late for the Festspiel," he declared.

But it didn't take three boys long to slip out of shirts and trousers, B.V.D.'s and sandals, and into their light dancing tunics. That they were out of breath was no matter, for there was the overture. They stole to their assigned positions on the darkened stage and squatted on the floor to wait until it was time for the rising of the curtain.

III

Orpheus, the singer, had descended into hell. He stood, his lyre in hand, confronting a host of furies with a baleful glare in their eyes. Infernal music pounded forth their protest. "Who is this mortal one now drawing near, bold to intrude on these awful abodes?"

Furies, it is well known, are dangerous; these trembled with their peculiar excitement, and could hardly be restrained. Their feet trod with eagerness to leap at the intruder, their hands reached out with longing to seize and rend him. The music crashed and rushed upward in a frenzied presto, it crashed and rushed down again, and bodies shook and swayed with the drive of it.

The spirits stood upon a slope within the entrance gates of Hell; tier upon tier of them, and in the dim blue light of infernal fires their naked arms and legs made, as it were, a mountain of motion. Their anger wove itself into patterns of menace, so that the gentle musician could hardly keep from shrinking. He touched his lyre, and soft strains floated forth; tinkling triplets like the shimmering of little waves in the moonlight. But the fiends would not hear. "No!" they thundered, with the hammer-strokes of arms and the trampling of feet. In vain the melodious pleading of the lyre! "Furies, specters, phantoms terrific, let your hearts have pity on my soul-tormenting pain."

The musician sang his story. He had lost his beloved Eurydice, who was somewhere in these realms of grief, and he must win her release. His strains poured forth until the hardest hearts were melted.

It was a triumph of love over anger, of beauty and grace over the evil forces which beset the lives of men.

The mountain of motion burst forth into silent song. The denizens of Hell were transformed into shades of the Elysian fields, and showers of blessings fell upon them out of the music. "On these meadows all are happy-hearted; only peace and rest are known." In the midst of the rejoicing came the shy Eurydice to meet her spouse. Rapture seized the limbs now shining in bright light; they wove patterns as intricate as the music, portraying not merely melody but complicated harmonies. Beautiful designs were brought before the eye, counterpoint was heightened through another sense. It was music made visible; and when the curtain had fallen upon the bliss of Orpheus and his bride, a storm of applause shook the auditorium. Men and women stood shouting their delight at the revelation of a new form of art.

Outside, upon the steps of the temple, they crowded about the creator of "Eurythmics." Emile Jaques-Dalcroze was his name, a stocky, solidly built man with the sharply pointed black beard and mustache of a Frenchman and the black Windsor tie which marked the artist of those days. He had taken the musical patterns of Gluck's *Orpheus* and reproduced them with the bodies and bare arms and legs of children; the art lovers would go forth to tell the world that here was something not only beautiful but healing, a way to train the young in grace and happiness, in efficiency and co-ordination of body and mind.

Critics, producers, teachers, all of them were devotees of an old religion, the worship of the Muses. They believed that humanity could be saved by beauty and grace; and what better symbol than the fable of the Greek singer who descended into Hell and with voice and golden lyre tamed the furies and the fiends? Sooner or later among the children at Hellerau would appear another Orpheus to charm the senses, inspire the soul, and tame the furies of greed and hate. Wars would be banished—and not merely those among nations, but that bitter struggle of the classes which was threatening to rend Europe. In the Dalcroze school children of the well-to-do classes danced side by side with those of workers from the factory suburbs. In the temple of the Muses were no classes, nations, or races; only humanity with its dream of beauty and joy.

Such was the faith of all art lovers of the year 1913; such was the creed being taught in the tall white temple upon the bright meadow. In these fortunate modern days the spread of civilization had become automatic and irresistible. Forty-two years had passed since Europe had had a major war, and it was evident to all that love and brotherhood were stealing into the hearts of the furies, and that Orpheus was conquering with his heaven-sent voice and golden lyre.

IV

All Lanny Budd's young life he had played around with music. Wherever he was taken, there was always a piano, and he had begun picking at the keys as soon as he was old enough to climb upon a stool. He remembered snatches of everything he heard, and as soon as he got home would lose himself in the task of reproducing them. Now he had discovered a place where he could play music with arms and legs and all the rest of him; where he could stand in front of a mirror and see music with his eyes! He was so excited about it that he could hardly wait to jump into his clothes in the morning before dancing downstairs.

At Hellerau they taught you an alphabet and a grammar of movement. With your arms you kept the time; a set of movements for three-part time, another for four, and so on. With your feet and body you indicated the duration of notes. It was a kind of rhythmic gymnastics, planned to train the body in quick and exact response to mental impressions. When you had mastered the movements for the different tempi, you went on to more complex problems; you would mark three-part time with your feet and four-part time with your arms. You would learn to analyze and reproduce complicated musical structures; expressing the rhythms of a three-part canon by singing one part, acting another with the arms, and a third with the feet.

To Lanny the lovely part about this school was that nobody

thought you were queer because you wanted to dance; everybody understood that music and motion went together. At home people danced, of course, but it was a formal procedure, for which you dressed especially and hired musicians who played a special kind of music, the least interesting, and everybody danced as nearly the same way as possible. If a little boy danced all over the lawn, or through the pine woods, or down on the beach—well, people might think it was "cute," but they wouldn't join him.

Lanny was getting to an age where people would be expecting him to acquire dignity. He couldn't go on capering around, at least not unless he was going to take it up as a career and make money out of it. But here was this school, to provide him with a label and a warrant, so to speak. His mother would say: "There's Lanny, doing his Dalcroze." Lady Eversham-Watson would put up her ivory and gold lorgnette and drawl: "Oh, chawming!" The Baroness de la Tourette would lift her hands with a dozen diamonds and emeralds on them and exclaim: "*Ravissant!*" "Dalcroze" was the rage.

So Lanny worked hard and learned all he could during these precious weeks while his mother was away on the yacht of the gentleman who had invented Bluebird Soap and introduced it into several million American kitchens. Lanny would steal into a room where a group of boys and girls were practicing; nobody objected if a graceful and slender lad fell in and tried the steps. If he had ideas of his own he would go off into a corner and work them out, and nobody would pay any attention, unless he was doing it unusually well. There was dancing all over the place, in bedrooms and through corridors and out on the grounds; everybody was so wrapped up in his work that there would have been no special excitement if Queen Titania and her court had appeared, marking with their fairy feet the swift measures of the *Midsummer-Night's Dream* overture.

V

Lanny Budd had made two special friendships that summer. Kurt Meissner came from Silesia, where his father was comptroller-general of a great estate, a responsible and honorable post. Kurt was the youngest of four sons, so he did not have to become a government official or an officer in the army; his wish to conduct and possibly to compose music was respected, and he was learning in the thorough German way all the instruments which he would have to use. He was a year older than Lanny and half a head taller; he had straw-colored hair clipped close, wore pince-nez, and was serious in disposition and formal in manners. If a lady so much as walked by he rose from his chair, and if she smiled he would click his heels and bow from the waist. What he liked about the Dalcroze system was that it *was* a system; something you could analyze and understand thoroughly. Kurt would always obey the rules, and be troubled by Lanny's free and easy American way of changing anything if he thought he could make it better.

The English boy had a complicated name, Eric Vivian Pomeroy-Nielson; but people had made it easy by changing it to Rick. He was going to be a baronet some day, and said it was deuced uncomfortable, being a sort of halfway stage between a gentleman and a member of the nobility. It was Rick's idea of manners never to take anything seriously, or rather never to admit that he did; he dressed casually, made jokes, spoke of "ridin' " and "shootin'," forgot to finish many of his sentences, and had chosen "putrid" as his favorite adjective. He had dark hair with a tendency to curl, which he explained by the remark: "I suppose a Jew left his visiting card on my family." But with all his pose, you would make a mistake about Eric Pomeroy-Nielson if you did not realize that he was learning everything he could about his chosen profession of theater: music, dancing, poetry, acting, elocution, stage decoration, painting—even that art, which he said was his father's claim to greatness, of getting introduced to rich persons and wangling their cash for the support of "little theaters."

Each of these boys had a contribution to make to the others. Kurt knew German music, from Bach to Mahler. Lanny knew a little of everything, from old sarabands to "Alexander's Ragtime Band," a recent "hit" from overseas. As for Rick, he had been to some new-fangled arts-and-crafts school and learned a repertoire of old Eng-

lish folk songs and dances. When he sang and the others danced the
songs of Purcell, with so many trills and turns, and sometimes a score
of notes to a syllable, it became just what the song proclaimed—
"sweet Flora's holiday."

All three of these lads had been brought up in contact with older
persons and were mature beyond their years. To Americans they
would have seemed like little old men. All three were the product of
ripe cultures, which took art seriously, using it to replace other
forms of adventure. All were planning art careers; their parents were
rich enough—not so rich as to be "putrid," but so that they could
choose their own activities. All three looked forward to a future in
which art would go on expanding like some miraculous flower. New
"sensations" would be rumored, and crowds of eager and curious
folk would rush from Paris to Munich to Vienna, from Prague to
Berlin to London—just as now they had come flocking to the tall
white temple on the bright meadow, to learn how children could be
taught efficiency of mind and body and prepared for that society of
cultivated and gracious aesthetes in which they were expecting to
pass their days.

On a wide plain just below Hellerau was an exercise ground of
the German army. Here almost every day large bodies of men
marched and wheeled, ran and fell down and got up again. Horses
galloped, guns and caissons rumbled and were swung about, unlim-
bered, and pointed at an imaginary foe. The sounds of all this floated
up to the tall white temple, and when the wind was right, the dust
came also. But the dancers and musicians paid little attention to it.
Men had marched and drilled upon the soil of Europe ever since history began; but now there had been forty-two years of peace, and
only the old people remembered war. So much progress had been
made in science and in international relations that few men could
contemplate the possibility of wholesale bloodshed in Europe. The
art lovers were not among those few.

VI

When the summer season at the school was over, Lanny went to join his mother. He had tears in his eyes when he left Hellerau; such a lovely place, the only church in which he had ever worshiped. He told himself that he would never forget it; he promised his teachers to come back, and in the end to become a teacher himself. He promised Rick to see him in England, because his mother went there every "season," and if he tried hard he could persuade her to take him along.

As for Kurt, he was traveling with Lanny to the French Riviera; for the German lad had an aunt who lived there, and he had suggested paying her a visit of a couple of weeks before his school began. He had said nothing to her about an American boy who lived near by, for it was possible that his stiff and formal relative would not approve of such a friend. There were many stratifications among the upper classes of Europe, and these furies had never yielded to the lure of Orpheus and his lute.

Kurt was like an older brother to Lanny, taking charge of the travel arrangements and the tickets, and showing off his country to the visitor. They had to change trains at Leipzig, and had supper in a sidewalk café, ordering cabbage soup and finding that the vegetable had been inhabited before it was cooked. "Better a worm in the cabbage than no meat," said Kurt, quoting the peasants of his country.

Lanny forgot his dismay when they heard a humming sound overhead and saw people looking up. There in the reddish light of the sinking sun was a giant silver fish, gliding slowly and majestically across the sky. A Zeppelin! It was an achievement dreamed of by man for thousands of years, and now at last brought to reality in an age of miracles. German ingenuity had done it, and Kurt talked about it proudly. That very year German airliners had begun speeding from one city to another, and soon they promised air traffic across all the seas. No end to the triumphs of invention, the spread of science and culture in the great capitals of Europe!

The boys settled themselves in the night express, and Lanny told his friend about "Beauty," whom they were to meet in Paris. "Her friends all call her that," said the boy, "and so do I. She was only nineteen when I was born." Kurt could add nineteen and thirteen and realize that Lanny's mother was still young.

"My father lives in America," the other continued; "but he comes to Europe several times every year. The name Budd doesn't mean much to a German, I suppose, but it's well known over there; it's somewhat like saying Krupp in Germany. Of course the munitions plants are much smaller in the States; but people say Colt, and Remington, and Winchester—and Budd."

Lanny made haste to add: "Don't think that my parents are so very rich. Robbie—that's my father—has half a dozen brothers and sisters, and he has uncles and aunts who have their own children. My mother divorced my father years ago, and Robbie now has a wife and three children in Connecticut, where the Budd plants are. So you see there are plenty to divide up with. My father has charge of the sales of Budd's on the Continent, and I've always thought I'd be his assistant. But now I think I've changed my mind—I like 'Dalcroze' so much."

VII

Beauty Budd did not come to the station; she seldom did things which involved boredom and strain. Lanny was such a bright boy, he knew quite well how to have his bags carried to a taxi, and what to tip, and the name of their regular hotel. His mother would be waiting in their suite, and it would be better that way, because she would be fresh and cool and lovely. It was her business to be that, for him as for all the world.

Kind nature had assigned that role to her. She had everything: hair which flowed in waves of twenty-two-carat gold; soft, delicate skin, regular white teeth, lovely features—not what is called a doll-baby face, but one full of gaiety and kindness. She was small and delicate, in short, a delight to look at, and people turned to take their share of that delight wherever she went. It had been that way ever since she was a child, and of course she couldn't help knowing about it. But it wasn't vanity, rather a warm glow that suffused her, a happiness in being able to make others happy—and a pity for women who didn't have the blessed gift which made life so easy.

Beauty took all possible care of her natural endowment; she made a philosophy of this, and would explain it if you were interested. "I've had my share of griefs. I wept, and discovered that I wept alone—and I don't happen to be of a solitary nature. I laugh, and have plenty of company." That was the argument. Wasn't a beautiful woman as much worth taking care of as a flower or a jewel? Why not dress her elegantly, put her in a charming setting, and make her an art-work in a world of art lovers?

Her name was an art-work also. She had been born Blackless, and christened Mabel, and neither name had pleased her. Lanny's father had given her two new ones, and all her friends had agreed that they suited her. Now she even signed her checks "Beauty Budd," and if she signed too many she did not worry, because making people happy must be worth what it cost.

Now Lanny's mother was blooming after a long sea trip among the fiords, having kept her complexion carefully veiled from the sun which refused to set. Her only worry was that she had gained several pounds and had to take them off by painful self-denial. She adored her lovely boy, and here he came hurrying into the room; they ran to each other like children, and hugged and kissed. Beauty held him off and gazed at him. "Oh, Lanny, how big you've grown!" she exclaimed; and then hugged him again.

The German boy stood waiting. Lanny introduced him, and she greeted him warmly, reading in his eyes astonishment and adoration —the thing she was used to from men, whether they were fourteen or five times that. They would stand awe-stricken, forget their manners, become her slaves forever—and that was the best thing that could happen to them. It gave them something to look up to and worship; it kept them from turning into beasts and barbarians, as they were so strongly inclined to do. Beauty had put on for this occasion a blue Chinese silk morning robe with large golden pheasants on it, very gorgeous; she had guessed what it might do to Lanny's new friend, and saw that it was doing it. She was charming to him, and if he adored her he would be nice to her son, and everybody would be that much happier.

"Tell me about Hellerau," she said; and of course they did, or Lanny did, because the German boy was still tongue-tied. Beauty had had a piano put in the drawing room, and she ran to it. "What do you want?" she asked, and Lanny said: "Anything," making it easy for her, because really she didn't know so very many pieces. She began to play a Chopin polonaise, and the two boys danced, and she was enraptured, and made them proud of themselves. Kurt, who had never before heard of a mother who was also a child, revised his ideas of Americans in one short morning. Such free, such easygoing, such delightful people!

The boys bathed and dressed and went downstairs for lunch. Beauty ordered fruit juice and a cucumber salad. "I begin to grow plump on nothing," she said. "It's the tragedy of my life. I didn't dare to drink a glass of milk at a *saeter.*"

"What is a *saeter?*" asked Lanny.

"It's a pasture high up on the mountainside. We would go ashore in the launch and drive up to them; the very old farmhouses are made of logs, and have holes in the roof instead of chimneys. They have many little storehouses, the roofs covered with turf, and you see flower gardens growing on top of them. One even had a small tree."

"I saw that once in Silesia," said Kurt. "The roots bind the roof tighter. But the branches have to be cut away every year."

"We had the grandest time on the yacht," continued Beauty. "Did Lanny ever tell you about old Mr. Hackabury? He comes from the town of Reubens, Indiana, and he makes Bluebird Soap, millions of cakes every day, or every week, or whatever it is—I'm no good at figures. He carries little sample cakes in his pocket and gives them to everybody. The peasants were grateful; they are a clean people."

The boys told her about the *Orpheus* festival, and Bernard Shaw and Granville Barker and Stanislavsky. "It's quite the loveliest place I've ever been to," declared Lanny. "I think I want to become a teacher of 'Dalcroze.' "

Beauty didn't laugh, as other mothers might have done. "Of course, dear," she answered. "Whatever you want; but Robbie may be disappointed." Kurt had never heard of parents being addressed by such names as Beauty and Robbie; he assumed it was an American custom, and it seemed to work well, though of course it would never do for Silesia.

They were having their pastry; and Beauty said: "You might like to stay over for an extra day. I'd like to have a chance to see more of Kurt, but I've accepted an invitation to spend a fortnight in England, and then go to Scotland for the shooting." Lanny was disappointed, but it didn't occur to him to show it, because he was used to seeing his mother in snatches like this; he understood that she had obligations to her many friends and couldn't be expected to stay and entertain one boy, or even two.

Kurt, also, was disappointed, having thought he was going to feast his eyes on this work of art, created in far-off America and perfected in France. He made up for lost time, and was so adoring, and at the same time respectful and punctilious, that Beauty decided he was an exceptionally fine lad and was glad that dear Lanny had such good judgment in the choice of friends. Lanny had written who Kurt's parents were, and also of the aunt in Cannes, the Frau Doktor Hofrat von und zu Nebenaltenberg. Beauty didn't know her, but felt sure that anybody with such a name must be socially acceptable.

VIII

In the afternoon they went to an exhibition of modern art. "Everybody" was talking about the Salon des Indépendants, and therefore Beauty had to be able to say that she had seen it. She had a quick step and a quick eye, and so was able to inspect the year's work of a thousand or more artists in fifteen or twenty minutes. After that she had a dress fitting; the business of being an art-work oneself didn't leave very much time for the art-works of others. Lanny's mother, flitting through life like a butterfly over a flower bed, was so charming and so gay that few would ever note how little honey she gathered.

She left the two boys to share the display between them. The painters and sculptors of a continent had turned their imaginations loose, and the boys wandered past wall after wall covered with their efforts. Each seemed to shriek: "Look at me! I am the ne plus ultra!" Few seemed willing to paint in the old accepted way, so as actually to reproduce something. Here faces were made into planes and conic sections; eyes and noses changed positions, trees became blue, skies green, and human complexions both. It was the epoch of the "Nude Descending the Staircase"; this nude consisted of spirals, zigzags which might have been lightning flashes, a tangle of lines resembling telephone wires after a cyclone. You couldn't form the least idea why it was a "nude," and wished you might know the artist and ask if it was a colossal spoof, or what.

There were plenty of recognizable nudes; they were shown in the morgue, on the battlefield or the operating table. There were women with great pendent paunches and breasts, men with limbs diseased or missing. You got the definite impression that the "independent" artists of the continent of Europe were a disturbed and tormented lot. Perhaps they lived in garrets and didn't get enough to eat; Lanny and Kurt, neither of whom had ever seen a garret or missed a meal, did not think of that explanation. They could only wonder why, in a world with creatures like Lanny's mother, painters should prefer ugly and repulsive subjects. There was something wrong; but the riddle couldn't be solved by the son of Beauty Budd nor yet by the son of the comptroller-general of Castle Stubendorf in Upper Silesia.

Beauty had an engagement for dinner, so the two boys went to a cinema, an art which was still in its rough-and-tumble days. The French equivalent of a custard pie was, it appeared, a bucket of paperhanger's paste; the paperhanger was mistaken for a lover by a jealous husband, and the pursuit and fighting ended with the pot of paste falling from a ladder onto the husband's head, to the hilarious delight of the husband-haters of Paris. In the orchestra pit a solitary man sat in front of a piano and a book of scores marked for different kinds of scenes—love, grief, or battle, whatever it might be. He would turn hastily to the proper page, and when the ladder was about to topple he was ready with the thunderstorm passage from the *William Tell* overture. Quite different from the Salon des Indépendants, and also from Hellerau; but the tastes of boys are catholic, and they laughed as loudly as the least cultured bourgeois in the place.

Next morning Beauty did not get up until nearly noon, so the boys drove about; Kurt had never been to Paris before, and Lanny, quite at home, showed him the landmarks and gave him history lessons. Later came a polo-playing American by the name of Harry Murchison, a scion of the plate-glass industry; he had a fancy car, and drove them out to Versailles, where they had lunch in a sidewalk café, and wandered through the gardens and forests, and saw the Little Trianon, and were told by a guide about Marie Antoinette and the Princesse de Lamballe and other fair ones of the vanished past—but none of them so fair as Beauty! Both Lanny and Kurt were a bit jealous of the handsome young American who sought to monopolize the mother; but she was kind and saw to the equal distribution of her favors.

When they were back in the hotel she had them show some "Dalcroze" to her friend while she dressed. Harry was taking her to the opera, it appeared; but first they had dinner, and then drove the boys to the station and saw them on the *rapide* for the Côte d'Azur. Beauty always had tears in her eyes at partings, and so did Lanny, and—unexpectedly—so did Kurt. Beauty kissed him good-by; and when the two boys were settled in their compartment and the train was under way, Kurt exclaimed: "Oh, Lanny, I just *love* your mother!"

Lanny was pleased, of course. "So does everybody," was his reply.

2

Côte d'Azur

I

ON THE eastern side of a little peninsula which juts out into the Mediterranean stood the tiny village of Juan-les-Pins, looking across a bay, the Golfe Juan, with the Estérel mountains in the background. On this lovely sheltered coast was a villa, with a tract of two or three acres, which Robbie Budd had given to Lanny's mother years ago. He had put it in trust so that she could not sell or even mortgage it, thus placing her in an odd position, with financial ups and downs that made no real difference. Just now "Juan," as it was called, was enjoying a mild prosperity; land was being divided up into *lotissements*, considerable sums were being offered, and Beauty had the thrill of being worth a hundred thousand francs. In due course would come a depression, and she would be "ruined," and sorrowful about it; then would come a terrific "boom," then another "slump"—and Beauty believing in each one. But always she and Lanny would have a home, which was the way Robbie intended it to be.

This had been Lanny's nest ever since he could recall. In its deeply shaded pine woods he had picked the spring flowers and learned the calls of birds. On its slowly shelving sand-beach he had paddled and learned to swim. Down the shore were boats of fishermen drawn up, and nets spread out to dry, and here was the most exciting kind of life for a child; all the strange creatures of the deep flapping and struggling, displaying the hues of the rainbow to the dazzling sun, with fisherboys to tell him which would bite and sting, and which could be carried home to Leese, the jolly peasant woman who was

17

their cook. Lanny had learned to prattle in three languages, and it was a long time before he was able to sort them out; English to his mother and father, French to many guests and occasional teachers, and Provençal to servants, peasants, and fisher-folk.

The house was built on the top of a rise, some way back from the sea. It was of pink stucco with pale blue shutters and a low roof of red tiles. It was in Spanish style, built round a lovely court with a fountain and flowers; there Lanny played when the mistral was blowing, as it sometimes did for a week on end. Along the road outside ran a high wall with a hedge of pink and white oleanders peering over it, and a wooden gate with a bell which tinkled inside the court, and on each side of the gate an aloe, having thick basal leaves and a tall spike with many flowers—"God's candelabra," they were called.

Here was a happy place for a boy, with no enemies and few dangers. His father taught him to swim in all sorts of water, and to float as peacefully and securely as a sea turtle. He learned to row and to sail, and to come in quickly when storms gave their first warnings. He learned so much about fishing, and about the nuts which the peasants gathered in the forests and the herbs which they found in the fields, that Beauty used to say, if they ever got really poor, Lanny would feed them. He learned also to make friends, and to share in so many occupations that he would never need to be bored.

His mother, being a lady of fashion, naturally worried now and then about the plebeian tastes of her only child, and when she was there would invite the children of her rich friends as playmates. And that was all right with Lanny, the rich children were interesting too; he would take them down the shore and introduce them to the fisher-boys, and presently they would be ruining their expensive clothes learning to cast a hand net for shrimp. They would plan a walking trip into the hills, and rest at the door of some peasant cottage, and when they came back would tell how they had learned to weave baskets. Beauty would say with a laugh that Robbie's forefathers had been farmers, though of course in Connecticut they weren't the same as peasants.

II

Lanny Budd had never been to school, in the ordinary sense of the word. For one thing, his mother so often took him on journeys; and for another, he taught himself as many things as it seemed safe to put into one small head. He remembered phrases of every language he heard, and that was saying a lot on the Riviera. He was forever picking at the piano, and if he saw people dance a new dance, he had learned it before they got through. All his mother had to do was to show him his letters, and presently he was reading every book in the house that had pictures. You might be surprised to hear that Beauty Budd considered herself a lady of literary tastes; it meant that she noted the names of the books she heard people talking about, bought them, read the first few pages, and then was too busy to look at them again. Sooner or later Lanny would get hold of them, and if he didn't understand them, he would start pestering somebody with questions.

A good part of his education had come from listening. All sorts of people came to the house, and a well-bred little boy would sit quietly in a chair and not say a word. As a rule, people would forget that he was there, and have no idea that he was stowing things away in his mind: society and fashion, what people wore and what they ate, where they went and whom they met; the aristocracy of Europe and its titles; the rich people and their stocks and bonds, dividends and profits; the new cars, the new restaurants; the theaters and what they were showing, the operas and the names of the singers; the books that people were talking about; the journalists, the politicians, the heads of states—everything that was successful and therefore important.

When they were alone, the child would start in on his mother. "Beauty, what is taffeta, and what do you mean by cutting it on the bias? What are penguins and why are they like French politicians? What were the Dreyfusards, and why did the abbé get so excited when he talked about them?" It was hard on a mother who had developed to a high degree the art of taking part in conversation without bothering too much about details. With Lanny she had to get things right, because he would remember and bring them up again.

He had developed at a very early age the habit of cherishing some profound remark that he had heard one of his elders make, and getting it off in other company. Of course it would cause a sensation; and of course an active-minded child did not fail to enjoy this, and to repeat the performance. He had the advantage that he was operating behind a screen; for the elders seldom realize how shrewd children are, how attentively they listen, and how quickly they seize upon whatever is of advantage to them. The elders would say anything in a little boy's presence—and then later they would be astonished to find that he knew about such matters!

The city of Cannes lay only a few miles from his home, and the mother would betake herself there for shopping, and to have her charms attended to. Lanny, having promised never to go away with anybody, would find himself a seat on a street bench, or in a sidewalk café; and sooner or later there would be someone taking an interest in a bright lad with wavy brown hair, lively brown eyes, rosy cheeks, and a shirt of gray oxford cloth open at the throat.

In this way he had met, during the winter before he went to Hellerau, Colonel Sandys Ashleigh-Sandys—do not pronounce the y's— late of His Majesty's Royal Highlanders in the Indian Northwest. The colonel had white mustaches and a complexion like yellow parchment; it was trouble with his liver. He wore a linen suit, comfortably cut. A member of the exclusive "British colony," he would have turned away from any grown person who ventured to address him without a proper introduction; but when the tables were crowded and a small boy invited him to a seat, he did not think it necessary to decline. When the boy began to chat with all the grace of a man of the world, the colonel was inwardly amused and outwardly the soul of courtesy.

Lanny chose to talk about the latest popular novel he was halfway through. The old martinet with parasites in his liver questioned him about his reading, and found that this benighted lad had never read a novel of Scott, had never even heard of Dickens, and all he knew about the plays of Shakespeare was the incidental music of *A Midsummer Night's Dream*, written by a Jewish fellow. Lanny asked so many questions, and was so serious in his comments, that before they parted the colonel offered to send him a one-volume edition of the poet which he happened to be able to spare. One condition would be imposed—the lad must promise to read every word in the book.

Lanny had no idea of the size of that promise. He gave it, and also his name and address, and a couple of days later there arrived by the post an elegant tome weighing several pounds. It was the sort of work which is meant to be set upon a drawing-room table and dusted every day but never opened. Lanny kept his pledge literally, he began at the title page and spent a month reading straight through, in a state of tense excitement. He wore his mother out at mealtimes, telling her about the lovely ladies who were accused of dreadful crimes which they had not committed. Just what the crimes were supposed to be was vague in Lanny's mind, and how was his mother to answer his questions? What did a man mean when he said he knew a hawk from a handsaw, and what were maidenheads and how did you break them?

Presently there was Lanny making himself swords out of laths and helmets out of newspapers, and teaching fishermen's children to fence and nearly poke one another's eyes out! Shouting: "Zounds!" and "Avaunt, traitor!" and "Lay on, Macduff!" down on the beach! Spouting poetry all over the place, like an actor—maybe he might turn out to be that—how was any woman to know what she had brought into the world? It was evident to her that this child's imagination was going to carry him to strange places and make him do uncomfortable things.

III

Lanny and Kurt, arriving at Cannes, parted company before they left the train. The German boy was to be met by his aunt; and this widow of the Court-Counselor von und zu Nebenaltenberg was a person with old-fashioned notions who would probably disapprove of Americans on general principles. The situation turned out to be even more difficult, for the aunt knew or professed to know all about "that Budd woman," as she called Beauty, and was shocked that her nephew had met such a person. She wouldn't say what it was—just one word: "*Unschicklich!*"

Kurt asked no questions. "Mrs. Budd has gone to Scotland for the shooting season," he remarked, casually. He sat erect in the stiff chair, facing the meager, severe old lady, telling her the news about the many members of their family. He ate a sound German luncheon of rye bread with slices of *Leberwurst* and *Schweizerkäse*, followed by a small *Apfelkuchen* and a cup of weak tea with milk. When the two had finished this meal, the aunt laid out the proper portions of food for her solitary maid, and then opened a cedar chest which stood between the windows of the dining room, and stowed all the remaining food therein, and carefully locked the chest with one of a bunch of keys which she carried at her waist. "You can't trust these native servants with anything," said the Frau Doktor Hofrat. Her husband had been dead for ten years, but she still wore black for him and of course carried his titles.

However, she was a woman of culture, and in due course asked about Hellerau, and Kurt told her. She was prejudiced against Jaques-Dalcroze because he had a French name and beard; but Gluck's music was *echt deutsch*, so the Frau Doktor Hofrat asked questions and wished that she might have seen the Festspiel. Only after Kurt had awakened her curiosity to the utmost did the budding diplomat mention that his American boy friend had a real gift, and might assist him to give a Dalcroze demonstration. He was a very well-bred and polite boy, Kurt assured his aunt; he was only thirteen, and probably knew nothing about the "*Unschicklichkeit*" of his mother. Furthermore, he was an artist, or going to be, and one should not judge persons of that sort by ordinary standards. Consider Wagner, for example. Concerning even Beethoven there had been rumors . . .

By such insidious devices Kurt won his aunt's permission to invite Lanny Budd for tea. A telegram was dispatched, and the Budd chauffeur drove Lanny over at the proper hour. He entered a plain, immaculate apartment, clicked his heels, bowed from the waist, and apologized for his German—which really wasn't so bad, because he had had two German tutors, each for several months. He ate only one tiny sandwich and one cooky, and declined a second cup of tea. Then while Kurt played the piano he gave demonstrations of what the Dalcroze people called "plastic counterpoint"; the elderly widow played folk songs which Lanny did not know, and he listened, and invented movements for them, and made intelligent comments while he did so. The Frau Doktor Hofrat did not tell him that she had once lost a little boy who had brown hair and eyes like his; but she invited him to come again, and gave her consent for Kurt to visit his home.

So all was well, and the youngsters were turned loose to enjoy life in their own fashion. The luncheon that Kurt had with Lanny wasn't any frugal German meal. Leese prepared a *mostele*, an especially good fish which the boys caught; also an omelet with fresh truffles, and then fresh figs with cream and cake; that was the way they lived at the Budds', and any peasant woman was happy to serve two handsome lads who had such good appetites and paid so many compliments to the food.

The two boys lived in bathing trunks, which sufficed for clothing in this free and easy playground of Europe. They walked out along the peninsula to the Cap d'Antibes, where you could dive off the rocks into thirty feet of water so clear that you expected to reach the bottom. They hauled a seine on the shallow beach and brought in shrimp and squid and crabs and other odd forms of life which had swarmed in these waters for ages and had been hauled out by Roman boys, Greek boys, Phoenicians, Saracens, Barbary corsairs—children of unnumbered races which had invaded this "Azure Coast" since the land had sunk and let the water in.

From his earliest days Lanny had lived in the presence of this long past. He had learned geography in the course of motor trips, and his history lessons had come from asking about old ruins. People didn't always know the answers, but there would be a guidebook in one of the pockets of the car, and you could look up Arles or Avignon or whatever it might be. Antibes, which lay on the other side of the promontory, had once been a Roman city, with baths and an arena and an aqueduct; it was fascinating to look at the remains and think about the lives of people long gone from the earth which once they had held with pride and confidence. Not long ago, there had been dug up a memorial tablet to the little "Septentrion child" who had "danced and pleased in the theater"; Lanny Budd might have been that child come back to life, and he wondered how his predecessor had lived and what had brought him to his untimely end.

The two boys of the year 1913, having no idea what their ends were to be, wandered happily over the hills and valleys which run back from this coast. There was an endless variety of scenes: swift rivers, deep gorges, broad valleys; olive groves and vineyards, forests of cork oak and eucalyptus, meadows full of flowers; crowded villages, with terraced land cultivated to the last precious inch; palaces of Carrara marble with elaborate gardens and flowering trees—so many things to look at and ask questions about! Kurt couldn't talk to the peasants, but Lanny would translate for him, and the women noted the bright blue eyes and yellow hair of the strange lad from the North, and had the same thought as Pope Gregory, who had inspected the war prisoners and remarked: "Not Angles, but angels."

IV

High above Antibes is an ancient monastery, with a church, Notre-Dame-de-Bon-Port, from which the sailors of Antibes, barefooted and wearing white shirts, carry an image of the Virgin in a procession, so as to enjoy her protection from storms. From here there is a view of all the seas, the white cities of the Riviera, and distant Italian mountains capped with snow. To this place the boys brought their lunch, and Lanny pointed out the landmarks: to the west the Estérels, mountains of blood-red porphyry, and to the east the large city of Nice, and beyond it Monaco on its rock. Directly below them, in the bay, French warships were anchored; it was their favorite resting place, and sailors swarmed in the little town.

The boys spent the afternoon on this height, talking not merely of the scenery, but of themselves and what they planned to make of their lives. So serious they were, and so conscientious! Kurt was an ethical person, and when he revealed the moral compulsions of his soul, Lanny was quite awe-stricken.

"Did you ever think how few really cultured persons there are in the world?" inquired the German boy. "There are whole races and nations with practically none, and in the rest just a handful, holding aloft the banner of good taste, among so many millions of Hottentots."

"What are Hottentots?" asked Lanny, naïvely.

Kurt explained that this was a way of referring to persons without culture or ideals. The great mass of men were like that, and civilization was kept going by the labors of a devoted few. "Suppose they were to fail—what then?"

"I never thought about it," admitted the other, worried.

"We should sink into barbarism again, into another dark age. That is why the mission of art is such a high one, to save humanity by teaching a true love of beauty and respect for culture."

Lanny thought that was a very wonderful way to look at it, and said so. Kurt went on:

"We who understand that have to discipline ourselves as if for a priesthood. We have to make the most of our powers, living an ordered life and not wasting ourselves as so many musicians have done. I have made up my mind to be one who lives a life of reason, like Bach or Brahms. Do you know about them?"

"Not very much," Lanny had to admit.

"Of course I don't know how much talent I may have——"

"Oh, I'm sure you have a wonderful talent, Kurt!"

"Whatever it is, I want to cherish it and put it to service. Have you thought about doing that with your life?"

"I'm afraid I never had any great thoughts like yours, Kurt. You see, my parents don't take things so seriously."

"Surely they have taught you some ethical standards!"

"Well, they told me to enjoy the beautiful things I came upon;

and of course to be polite to people, and kind, and learn what I can from them."

"That's all right, only it's not enough. One must have a wider vision, nobler aims."

"I see it, Kurt, and I appreciate your telling me about it."

"Of course, one doesn't talk about such things except to a few chosen persons, who are capable of understanding one's soul."

"I realize that," said Lanny, humbly; "I'll try to be worthy of the trust. I'll be a sort of disciple, if I may."

The older lad agreed to accept him on that basis. They would correspond and tell each other their deeper longings, not keeping them locked up, as one had to do in a world of shallow and thoughtless people. When the sun began to drop behind the Estérels and the pair started down the road, they felt that they had had a sort of religious experience, such as might have come to the monks who through many centuries had paced the corridors of that monastery.

V

It was Kurt's idea that his new disciple should be invited to visit the great Castle Stubendorf during the Christmas holidays; and to this end it was desirable that he should cultivate the esteem of the Frau Doktor Hofrat, whose recommendation would decide the matter. So Lanny came several times to the apartment in Cannes, and danced "Dalcroze" for some of the friends of the severe and strait-laced German lady. Never once did anyone mention his mother or his father, or any of his American associates; but the Frau Doktor Hofrat probed his mind, and made certain that he had a genuine respect for the contributions of the Fatherland to the world's culture. At Kurt's suggestion, Lanny borrowed a volume of Schiller's poetry, and struggled diligently with it and asked the old lady's help now and then.

She also interested herself in his musical education, which had been of a deplorably irregular character. Kurt, like his aunt before him, had had a sound German training in piano technique; a veritable military drill; arms and wrists stiff, knuckles depressed, second joint elevated, fingers pulled up and sharply pushed down. But poor Lanny had got a hodge-podge of everything that friends of his mother had been moved to recommend. First had come Professor Zimmalini, protégé of the mother-in-law of Baroness de la Tourette. Having been a pupil of a pupil of Leschetizsky, the professor laid great stress upon equality of the fingers; the wrists depressed, the knuckles arched, the fingers rounded, the elbows curved even in ordinary legato. Lanny had been taught that for a whole winter; but then had come the London season, and after that Biarritz, and by the time they returned to their home, the professor had moved to Paris.

So then Lanny had a spell of the Breithaupt method, at a still higher price. He was told about forearm rotary motion, the importance of relaxation, and the avoidance of devitalization. But the excitable French professor who taught him all this suddenly fell under the spell of a stout concert singer and went off to the Argentine as her accompanist. Now Beauty had heard about a Professor Baumeister, who had recently come to Cannes, and she had told Lanny in her offhand way to take lessons from him if he wanted to. But Lanny hadn't got around to thinking about it yet.

When the Frau Doktor Hofrat heard all this her orderly German soul was shocked. This poor child was playing the piano half a dozen ways at the same time; and the fact that he was perfectly happy while doing so made it even worse. She assured him that the Herr Professor Baumeister was no better than a musical anarchist, and recommended a friend who had once taught at Castle Stubendorf and would impart the official German technique. Lanny promised to put this recommendation before his mother, and thereby completed his conquest of Kurt's aunt. She took the two boys to a concert—the one extravagance she permitted herself.

When the time came for Kurt to leave, he told his disciple that the aunt had consented to write to her brother, endorsing Lanny as worthy of guesthood. The American boy was extraordinarily delighted about it, for by this time he had heard so much about the

castle and the wonders of life there that it had come to seem to him
a place out of Grimm's fairy tales. He would meet Kurt's family,
see how Kurt lived, and become acquainted with the environment
in which his friend's lofty ideals had been nurtured.

VI

Kurt went away, and Lanny settled down to reading German,
practicing finger drill, and teaching fisherboys to dance Dalcroze.
He was never lonely, for Leese and the housemaid Rosine loved him
as if he were their own. He knew that Beauty would come in the
end, and a month later she came, full of news and gaiety. Then, out
of the blue, came a telegram from Robbie, saying that he was leaving Milan and would arrive the next day.

That was the way with Lanny's father, who thought no more of
sailing for Europe than Beauty did of going in to Cannes to have a
fitting. He didn't bother to cable, for he might be taking a train
for Constantinople or St. Petersburg, and he couldn't know how
long he would be there. Post cards would come, sometimes from
Newcastle, Connecticut, sometimes from London or Budapest. "See
you soon," or something like that. The next thing would be a telegram, saying that he would arrive on such and such a train.

Robbie Budd was still under forty and was the sort of father
any boy would choose if he were consulted. He had played foot-.
ball, and still played at polo now and then, and was solid and firm
to the touch. He had abundant brown hair, like his son, and when
you saw him in bathing trunks you discovered that it was all over
his chest and thighs, like a Teddy bear's. From him Lanny had got
his merry brown eyes and rosy cheeks, also his happy disposition
and willingness to take things as they came.

Robbie liked to do everything that Lanny liked, or maybe it was
the other way around. He would sit at the piano and romp for
hours, with even worse technique than his son's. He was no good at
"classical" music, but he knew college songs, Negro songs, musical
comedy songs—everything American, some of it jolly and some sen-

timental. In the water he did not know what it was to tire; he would stay in half the day or night, and if he thought you were tiring, he would say: "Lie on your back," and would come under you and put his hands under your armpits, and begin to work with his feet, and it was as if a tugboat had taken hold of you. He had ordered two pairs of goggles, to be strapped around the head and fitted tight with rubber, so that he and Lanny could drop down and live among the fishes. Robbie would take one of the three-pointed spears used by the fishermen; he would stalk a big *mérou*, and when he struck there would be a battle that Lanny would talk about for days.

Robbie Budd made quantities of money—he never said how much, and perhaps never knew exactly—but he left a trail of it behind him. He liked the smiling faces of those who have suddenly been made prosperous. He needed a lot of people to help him, and that was the way he persuaded them—a little bit at a time, and collecting the service quickly, before the debt was forgotten!

He expected some day to have the help of his son at this money-making; and because, for all his gaiety and his cynicism, he was a far-seeing and careful man, he had devised a system of training for this, his first and most dearly loved child. It appeared quite casual and incidental, but it had been thought out and was frequently checked for results. Robbie Budd caused his son to think of the selling of small arms and ammunition as the most romantic and thrilling of all occupations; he surrounded it with mysteries and intrigues, and impressed upon the boy the basic lesson that everything concerned with it was a matter of most solemn secrecy. Never, never, was the son of a munitions salesman to let slip one word about his father's affairs to any person, anywhere, under any circumstances! "On the whole continent of Europe there is nobody I really trust but you, Lanny"—so the father would declare.

"Don't you trust Beauty?" the boy asked, and the answer was:

"She trusts other people. The more she tries to keep a secret, the quicker it gets out. But you will never dream of saying a word to anybody about your father's business; you will understand that any one of Beauty's rich and fashionable friends may be trying to find out where your father has gone, what contracts he's interested in, what cabinet minister or army officer he has taken for a motor ride."

"Never a hint, Robbie, believe me! I'll talk about the fishing, or the new tenor at the opera." Lanny had learned this lesson so thoroughly that he was able to recognize at once when the Conte di Pistola or the wife of the attaché of the Austrian embassy was trying to pump him. He would tell his father about it, and Robbie would laugh and say: "Oh, yes, they are working for Zaharoff."

Lanny wouldn't have to hear any more; Zaharoff—accent on the first syllable—was the gray wolf who was gobbling up the munitions plants of Europe one by one and who considered the placing of a contract with an American as an act of high treason. Ever since he was old enough to remember, Lanny had been hearing stories of his father's duels with this most dangerous of men. The things Lanny knew about him might have upset every chancellery in Europe, if there had been any way to get them published.

When Robbie stepped off the train—he had come all the way from Bulgaria—both Beauty and Lanny were there to welcome him. He gave the latter a bear hug and the former a friendly handshake. Having a wife in Connecticut, Robbie didn't stay at the house, but at the hotel near by. He and Lanny ran a race down to the boathouse to get into their swimming trunks, and when they were out in a boat, far enough from all prying ears, Robbie grinned and said: "Well, I landed that Bulgarian contract."

"How did you do it?"

"I made a mistake as to the day of the week."

"How did that help?" There were so many strange ways of landing contracts that the brightest boy in the world couldn't guess them.

"Well, I thought it was Thursday, and I bet a thousand dollars on it."

"And you lost?"

"It was last Friday. We went to a kiosk on the corner and bought a Friday newspaper; and of course they couldn't have had that on Thursday." The two exchanged grins.

Lanny could guess the story now; but he liked to hear it told in Robbie's way, so he asked: "You really paid the debt?"

"It was a debt of honor," said the father gravely. "Captain Borisoff is a fine fellow, and I'm under obligations to him. He turned in a report that Budd carbines are superior to any on the market. They really are, of course."

"Sure, I know," said the boy. They were both of them serious about that; it was one of the fixed laws of the universe that Americans could beat Europeans at anything, once they put their minds to it. Lanny was glad; for he was an American, even though he had never set foot upon the land of the pilgrims' pride. He was glad that his father was able to outwit Zaharoff and all the other wolves and tigers of the munitions industry. Americans were the most honest people in the world, but of course if they had to, they could think up just as many smart tricks as any Levantine trader with Greek blood and a Russian moniker!

VII

It might occur to you that all this was hardly the best kind of moral training for a child; but the fact was that Lanny managed to preserve a sort of gay innocence toward it. Other boys got their thrills out of the "pulps" and the movies, but Lanny Budd got his from this wonderful father, his diplomatic and conspiratorial aides, and the generals, cabinet ministers, financial tycoons, and social high lights whom the boy met and would continue to meet so long as he was Robbie Budd's son.

The father's attitude toward these people was suave, even cordial, but behind their backs he laughed at them. They were the *crème de la crème* of Europe; they lived a life of many formalities and solemnities, gave themselves fancy titles, covered themselves with orders and decorations, and looked upon an American munitions salesman as a crude commercial fellow. Robbie didn't pay them enough of a tribute to resent these pretensions; he would chuckle as he told his son about the absurdities and weaknesses of this great one and that.

He would refer to the stout Countess Wyecroft as a "puller-in," and to the elegant and monocled Marquis de Trompejeu as a pimp. "They'll all do anything if you pay them enough—and guarantee them against being caught!"

Robbie had constructed a complete suit of intellectual armor to protect himself and his business against criticism, and he made a smaller-sized suit for Lanny and taught him to wear it. "Men hate each other," he would say. "They insist upon fighting, and there's nothing you can do about it, except learn to defend yourself. No nation would survive for a year unless it kept itself in readiness to repel attacks from greedy and jealous rivals; and you have to keep your weapons up to date, because the other fellow's always improving his. From the beginning of time there was a duel between those who made shields and those who made swords and spears; nowadays it's war between the makers of armorplate and the makers of shells and torpedoes. This will go on as long as there's any sort of progress."

The munitions industry was the most important part of every nation, insisted the head salesman of Budd Gunmakers Corporation; the one upon which all others depended. Most people would admit that, but they had the notion that the makers of guns and shells ought to work only for their own country, and that there was something unpatriotic in supplying other nations with such products. "But that's just people's ignorance," said Robbie; "they don't realize that propellants"—it was the industry's way of speaking of the various kinds of powder—"deteriorate fast, and after a few years they're worthless. So you can't store up the product and feel safe; you have to keep your producing machinery in order, and how can you do it unless you give it something to do? Are you going to stay at war just to keep your munitions workers in practice?"

Back there in the state of Connecticut was an establishment which Budd's had been building for three generations. Lanny had never seen it, but many pictures had been shown him and many stories told. In the beginning was a Connecticut Yankee who first thought of the idea of making guns with interchangeable parts, exactly alike, so they could be replaced and manufactured wholesale. Lanny's great-grandfather had been one of those who took up the idea and helped the country to put down the Indians, conquer Mexico, preserve the Union, and free Cuba and the Philippines. "That's the kind of service the armament people render," said Robbie. "They do it when it's needed, and at the time everybody's mighty glad to have it done!"

America hadn't had a really big war for half a century, and so American armaments plants were small by European standards. American wages were so much higher that the only way to compete was to turn out a better product—and to persuade the customers that you were doing so. This last was Robbie's job, and he worked hard at it, but was never satisfied; he grumbled at Europe's inability to appreciate Yankee brains. Americans labored under another handicap, in that their plants used English inches as their standard of measurement, whereas Europe employed the metric system. Robbie had persuaded his father to install machinery of the latter sort, and he now had the duty of keeping that costly machinery running. The business he did never satisfied him; the contracts were "mere chicken-feed," he would say—but he was a well-fed and handsome chicken, all the same!

Some day Lanny would visit the Budd plant across the seas and learn its secrets. Meantime, he must get to know Europe, its different races and tribes and classes, what arms they needed, and how to get there with the right samples and grease the right palms. Said Robbie: "It's a serious matter to realize that thousands of workmen and their wives and children are dependent upon your business foresight. If Zaharoff had got the contract for the carbines from Bulgaria, it would have been British or French or Austrian workingmen who would have had the work and the wages, and not merely would workers' children in Connecticut have gone hungry, but storekeepers would have been bankrupted and farmers would have had no market for the food they grew." So it was not for himself and his family, but for a whole townful of people that Robbie Budd practiced the tricks of salesmanship, and lost large sums of money at poker or betting that it was Thursday when he knew it was Friday! Of course it was terrible that men went to war and killed one another; but for that you had to blame nature, not the Budd family. Robbie and his son would put on their goggles and drop down among the fishes for a while, and when they came up and sat on the rocks to rest, the man would talk about the life that went on in that strange dim world. Uncounted billions of microscopic creatures called plankton were produced in the sunshine at the surface, and tiny fish and shrimp and other creatures fed upon them. Larger fish devoured the small ones, and monsters like the sharks preyed upon these. All reproduced themselves incessantly, and this had gone on for tens of millions of years, with changes so slight that they were hardly to be noticed. Such was life, and you could no more change it than you could stop the rising and setting of the sun; you just had to understand the sun's behavior and adjust yourself to it.

This was a lesson which Robbie preached incessantly, so that to Lanny it became like the landscape and the climate, the music he heard and the food he ate. Robbie would enforce it with picturesque illustrations; he would bring up a lame fish that had had one of its fins bitten off, and he would say: "You see, he didn't keep up his armaments industry!"

Now Lanny heard more of this, and decided that he had better put off telling his father about becoming a Dalcroze dancer. And what about all those noble ideals which Kurt Meissner had revealed to him, and which had impressed him so greatly a month or so ago? What was the use of thinking about religion and self-dedication and all that, if men were shrimps and crabs, and nations were sharks and octopi? Here was a problem which men had been debating before Lanny Budd was born and which it would take him some time to settle!

3

Playground of Europe

I

BEAUTY stayed a couple of weeks, and so did Robbie, with the result that Lanny's life became what the newspapers call one continuous round of social gaieties. Beauty gave a tennis party, with afternoon tea, and a row of fashionable ladies decorating the sidelines. She gave a dinner party, with dancing on the loggia, and Venetian lanterns hanging, and an orchestra from Cannes. When they were not having or preparing things like these, they were motoring to the homes of friends up and down the coast, for motorboat races, or bridge, or fireworks, or whatever it might be.

Lanny had his part in these events. People who had heard about "Dalcroze" would ask for a demonstration, and he would oblige them without having to be begged. Lady Eversham-Watson put up her ivory and gold lorgnette and drawled: "Chawming!" and the Baroness de la Tourette lifted her hands with a dozen diamonds and emeralds on them and exclaimed: "*Ravissant!*"—all exactly as Lanny had foreseen. This attention and applause did not spoil him, because it was his plan to take up the role of teacher, and here was a beginning. He liked to please people, and everybody loved him for it; or at any rate they said they did, and Lanny took the world for the gay and delightful thing it strove so hard to appear.

It was a world of people who had money. Lanny had always taken it for granted that everybody had it. He had never known any poor people; or, to be more exact, he had never known about their poverty. The servants worked hard, but they were well paid and had plenty to eat and enjoyed working in the rich homes, knowing the rich people and gossiping about their ways. The Provençal peasants partook of nature's bounty, and were independent and free-spoken. The fishermen went to sea and caught fish; they had done that all their lives, and liked to do it, and were healthy, and drank wine and sang and danced. If now and then one was hurt, or lost his boat, a collection would be taken, and Lanny would tell Beauty about it and she would contribute.

The rich people had the function of exhibiting elegance and grace to the world, and the Côte d'Azur was a place set apart for that performance. It was the winter playground of Europe; the wealthy and fashionable came from all over the world and either built themselves homes or stayed in luxurious hotels, dressing in the latest fashions and displaying themselves on waterfront parade grounds such as the Boulevard de la Croisette in Cannes and the Promenade des Anglais in Nice. They danced and played baccarat and roulette, golf and tennis; they motored and sailed, and ate and drank in public, and lay about on the beaches under gaily striped umbrellas. Photographers took pictures of them, and newspapers and magazines all over the world paid high prices for them, and so the exhibition of elegance had become a large-scale business.

The ladies who lent their charms to this parade were spoken of as professional beauties, and they took their profession with the same seriousness as a physician takes the healing of bodies or a priest the saving of souls. It was an exacting occupation and left its devotees little time to think about anything else; during the exhibition periods, known as "seasons," they made it a rule to change their costumes four times a day, thus keeping the cameramen on the jump; during the "off seasons" they hardly got a chance to recuperate, because they had to spend their time planning with *couturiers* and *marchands de modes* and others to keep them at the head of the next procession.

It would seem as if a woman by the name of Beauty Budd had been especially cut out for such a career. And she might have had it, but for the fact that she was so poor. All she had was this home, and a thousand dollars a month which Robbie allowed her. He was strict with her; had made her promise not to incur debts, and never to gamble unless it was a business matter, with Robbie himself taking part. Of course you couldn't take that too literally; she had to play bridge, and couldn't very well insist upon paying cash for the clothes she ordered—the makers would have thought there was something wrong with her.

Thus in the view of Lanny Budd the meaning of "being poor" was that his lovely mother was outclassed in the race for attention. She would never be listed as one of the "ten best-dressed women of Paris." Fortunately she was of a happy disposition and did not let these hardships mar her life; she learned to make a joke of them, and also a virtue. She would talk about her unwillingness to "pay the price," a remark which some of her friends might have resented as a reflection upon themselves.

But these were matters beyond Lanny's understanding as yet. He would try to console his mother. "I'm glad you're poor. If you weren't, I wouldn't see even a little of you!"

She would hug him, and tears would come into the lovely blue eyes. "You're the best thing in the whole world, and I'm a foolish woman ever to think about anything else!"

"That's the way I'd like it!" Lanny would grin.

II

The reason why Robbie stayed so long on this trip was that he had another deal on, and Beauty was helping him. That was an aspect of their relationship which Lanny had learned about, and in which he also took part according to his abilities. Customers had to be met "socially," something far more effective than mere business acquaintanceship. In the latter case they would be thinking only about money, but in the former they would like you; at any rate they would pretend they did, and you would try to make it real. You had to "entertain" them, and for this purpose what could be more helpful than a woman with the charms of Beauty Budd? For this well-recognized part of the selling of munitions Robbie paid generously.

The Russian Minister of War would be planning to visit Paris with his wife. Robbie had scouts who kept him posted, and he would telegraph Beauty, who would at once inquire among her friends and find someone who knew either the minister or his wife, and would invite them down for a few days to warm their old bones. Beauty would meet them and make an engagement for tea, and wire Robbie, who would come in a shiny new car and take the tired old couple motoring, and show them the Corniche road, and maybe let them have a fling in the Casino at Monte Carlo.

Robbie's agents would have provided him with a regular dossier about such guests, including their tastes and their weaknesses. Beauty would have several duchesses and countesses at the tea party, and when the minister took his seat at the gaming table, Robbie would slip him a bundle of thousand-franc notes and tell him laughingly to take a "flier" for him. The old gentleman would do so, and if he lost Robbie would tell him to forget it, and if he won he would forget it without being told. Later, when Robbie would tell him news about the marvelous new sub-machine gun which Budd's were putting on the market, the minister would be deeply interested and would make a date for Robbie to demonstrate it in St. Petersburg.

When Robbie was leaving to keep that date, he would say to Beauty: "I can't motor to St. Petersburg. I'd get stuck like Napoleon in the snow." Yes, there was snow in Russia, impossible as it might seem in Juan-les-Pins, where everybody lay around on the beach absorbing sunshine. "That old car of yours is beginning to look shabby," he would add. "You better take mine. But don't let anybody swindle you on the old one; you ought to get five or six thousand francs for it at least." If Beauty protested that he was too generous, Robbie had a formula: "It goes on the expense account."

A marvelous phenomenon, the expense account of a munitions salesman, which could be stretched to include both his business and his pleasures. It included the newspaper man who brought the tip, and the detective who prepared the dossier. It included the car, and the chauffeur, and the gambling losses. It included the tea party and, strange to say, it might even include some of the duchesses and countesses—those who were so important that it was an honor for a Russian cabinet minister to meet them, instead of for them to meet a Russian cabinet minister.

Such subtle distinctions you had to know thoroughly if you wanted to land contracts. The great ladies knew their own value and the value of the service expected. If it was to get the wife and daughter of an American millionaire presented at the Court of St. James's, that might be worth a thousand pounds; but if it was just a matter of introducing you to a politician or a financier, that might be done for a thousand francs.

Of course there were members of the nobility who were not for sale. Some English milords were so rich they could afford to be dignified. Some of the old French families were poor as church mice, but chose to live in retirement, dress dowdily, and pray for the return of the Bourbon pretender. But the people Robbie Budd made use of belonged to the *grand monde;* their pleasure was to shine in public, and the ladies especially were frequently in debt and ravenous for money. Beauty made it her business to know them, and with her woman's tact she would find out what service they could render and what they would expect. Some were frank, and would name their price and be prepared to haggle over it; others took a high tone, and said they would do it to oblige dear, darling Beauty. These were the persons who got more.

Thus Lanny, opening his eyes to the world in which he was to live, came to realize that among the swarms of elegant and showy people who passed through his home there were all sorts and sizes, and each had to be treated differently. A few were friends whom his mother loved and trusted; others were there for business reasons, and might turn out to be "horrid people," who would go off and say mean things about her behind her back. When that happened she would cry, and Lanny would want to kick those false

friends the next time he met them. But that was another lesson of
the *grand monde* which you had to learn; you never kicked anybody, but on the contrary were as effusive as ever, and the most
you allowed yourself was a sly little thrust with a sharp stiletto of
wit.

III

The new deal was to be with Rumania, which was about to supply part of its army with automatic pistols; this had become necessary because Bulgaria had just done the same. Several countries in
southeastern Europe had fought two wars among themselves in the
past three years, and no one could guess when the next one would
start, or who would be fighting whom. Budd's was putting out for
the European trade a new eight-cartridge 7.65 mm. automatic
which it claimed was the best in the world. Of course Robbie always had to claim that, but in this case he told Lanny that he really
believed it.

He had in Paris a fellow by the name of "Bub" Smith, who had
been a cowboy and could shoot the head off a hatpin, and would
have done it while the hat was on a lady's head if there had been
any female willing to face a William Tell from Texas. Robbie had
arranged for this man to come whenever needed, because army
officers were generally so impressed by good marksmanship that
they would attribute it to the gun. Now he was going to bring Bub
to the Riviera to meet a certain Captain Bragescu, a member of the
commission which was making preliminary investigations prior to
the final tests in Bucharest. Robbie laughed about that phrase "preliminary investigations," which meant that the captain wanted to
look into Robbie's pocketbook before he looked into his pistol.

The captain arrived unannounced, just after Robbie and Beauty
had gone off to a dinner dance. A taxi drew up in front of "Bienvenu," the bell at the gate tinkled, and Rosine ushered into Lanny's
presence a mincing and elegant figure with mustaches dyed black
and twisted to sharp points, in a sky-blue military uniform fitting

tightly and drawn in at the waist so that you knew he was wearing corsets. You might have found it hard to believe that an army officer would have his cheeks painted and powdered and would smell strongly of perfume, but so it was.

Lanny was embarrassed, because he had on some old fishing togs and a fisherboy named Ruggiero was waiting for him down on the beach. But he welcomed the guest courteously, and explained where his father and mother had gone, and offered to telephone them at once. "Oh, no!" said Captain Bragescu. "I would not think of interfering with their engagement."

An idea occurred to Lanny. "I wonder if you'd be interested in seeing torch-fishing."

"What do you get?" asked the officer. It turned out that he had done a lot of fishing at home.

So Lanny ran down to the boathouse, where there were some of Robbie's old clothes and a warm sweater—for it turns cold on the Riviera the moment the sun disappears behind the Estérels. The captain took off his corsets, and proved to be not in the least effeminate. Down the beach they met an Italian fisherboy, a year or two older than Lanny, and strong as his work required. The Rumanian spoke good French, but had trouble with a mixture of Provençal and Ligurian, so Lanny had to help out.

While Ruggiero rowed the heavy boat out toward the Cap, the army officer told about the fishing he had seen in his boyhood, at the mouth of the Danube, for the huge sturgeon. It was a rather ghastly procedure, for they cut out the roe, containing seven million eggs, and then threw the fish back alive. This was the black caviar, the epicure's delight—but Lanny wouldn't enjoy it quite so much for a while.

The sea was smooth except for long swells, and when the torch was blazing you could see much farther into the depths than you could reach with the trident. Peering down among the rocks, you would see a *langouste* poking out his greenish-gray head. You would get the three-pronged spear poised above him and strike, and up he would come, snapping his heavy tail back and forth. He was pleasanter to have in the boat than an American lobster, because he had no big claws that might take off one of your fingers.

Also, there were fishes of many hues and sizes; they seemed to be dazzled by the light, and even an amateur like the captain could hit one now and then. Presently he saw a head underneath some waving branches of a sea plant; he struck, and was all but jerked into the water. "Look out!" shouted the fisherboy, and leaped to help him. It was fortunate the officer didn't have those corsets on, for now he needed every particle of muscle and wind he had.

They brought up a huge green moray, the largest of all the eels, and the most dangerous. Ruggiero gaffed him, but cried: "Don't haul him into the boat!" He clubbed and stabbed the creature until the life was all gone out of him, for he had teeth as sharp as razor blades. He was more than six feet long, and when you saw him down in the water you thought he was clad in elegant green velvet.

He had been esteemed as a food fish ever since the days of the ancient Romans; so the pair had a fine story to tell Beauty and Robbie in the morning. Lanny's reputation as an entertainer of customers was much enhanced; for Captain Bragescu might have thought that dinner dances were got up for business reasons, but he couldn't doubt that this eager lad really admired his prowess as a fisherman.

IV

Bub Smith showed up on the morning train; a stocky fellow with a funny flat face—his nose had been broken in a fall from a horse and there had been nobody to set it, so he just let it stay as it was. But there was nothing the matter with either his eyes or his hands. "I'm feeling fine this morning," he said; "I could shoot holes through the side of a barn." He looked at Lanny with a twinkle in his pale blue eyes; they were old pals, and Bub had taught Lanny cowboy songs. He was introduced to the army captain, and was just about speechless at the spectacle of a man with paint and powder on his face and corsets under his sky-blue uniform.

Well, they motored back into the hills, where there was a little valley with a heavy forest of eucalyptus, and a peasant who for a few francs would let them shoot holes in his trees. The chauffeur lugged a couple of heavy boxes out of the car, one with the 7.65 mm. automatics and the other with the cartridges; Bub took a cardboard target and tacked it onto a big tree about thirty paces away. Meantime Robbie was loading the pistols. "I want to show you how quickly it can be done," he said. Pretty soon Bub took his stand, and quick as a flash threw up his arm and fired. The shots came so fast it was just a whir, and there was the target with the central bull's eye shot clean out.

Captain Bragescu, of course, was enraptured by such a performance. Pierre, the chauffeur, ran and got the target for them. You could see parts of the circle made by each bullet, but there wasn't any hole that wasn't part of one big hole. "I'll take that back to Bucharest with me!" said the captain.

"Wait," replied Bub; "I'll make you a few more." So they tacked up another target, and Bub took a different gun and did it again; he was ready to do it as long as the ammunition held out.

But the officer was convinced. "*C'est bon*," he said. He wouldn't be too enthusiastic, for it was a matter of business, but he repeated several times: "*Oui, c'est bon.*"

He tried it himself, and spattered the target all over with his shots. Bub showed him how to swing up the gun, and how to keep it from jerking, and then he did better. Robbie took his turn. He knew all about shooting, of course, and apologized to the captain for being too good; it was just a matter of understanding this remarkable weapon, he said.

Then Lanny took his turn. The army weapon was too heavy for him, but he had brought along his own thirty-two. Lanny was pretty good, but nobody seemed really good after Bub Smith. When the captain learned that Bub had been a cowboy, he exclaimed:

"*Ça s'explique!* I have seen them in the cinema. We need men who can ride and shoot like that in Rumania. We are troubled with mountaineers who don't like to pay taxes."

V

They went home to lunch, and Beauty had some friends in; but you could see that Beauty herself was company enough for Bragescu. He could hardly take his eyes off this delicate creation in pink and cream and gold. She, being used to that sort of thing, was kind, but sedate and never the least bit flirtatious. Lanny always got plenty of motherly attention at such times. He was too young to understand these subtleties, but he played up to her all the same, and they made a sweet and sentimental pair.

It was the Baroness de la Tourette who was supposed to do the entertaining of the officer. Sophie Timmons had been her maiden name, and her father owned a chain of hardware factories in several towns of the Middle West. He sent his only daughter lots of money, but never enough for her husband the baron, who lived in Paris and had very expensive tastes. The baroness had one of those henna heads, and had what you might call a henna laugh; she talked fast and loud, half in French and half in English, and was considered to be the life of every party. Lanny was too young to observe that while she chattered her eyes would roam restlessly, as if her mind were not entirely on her work. She was his mother's best friend, and had a kind heart in spite of all her smartness.

The captain was taken off by Robbie to have the drawings of the Budd automatic pistol explained to him. Afterward they all went for a sail, and watched the sun sink into the Mediterranean; then they dressed and went to Cannes to dine at a fashionable resort, and later came home to play poker. Lanny was just getting into bed when he heard them come in and settle themselves at the table, and he peeked in at the door for a bit.

They made a pretty sight in front of the big open fire of crackling pine; the men in evening dress, except the Rumanian in a blue and gold dress uniform; the ladies in lovely soft dresses cut halfway down their smooth white backs. They had picked up friends at the restaurant, including Lord and Lady Eversham-Watson. She was another rich American who had married a title, but she had used better judgment; his lordship was a large, solid, and rather dull gentleman past middle age, but he admired his gay wife and liked to see her shine in company. She was a talkative little woman who managed him and made it acceptable by joking; her money came out of a Kentucky whisky known as "Petries' Peerless."

Lanny had never been taught to play poker, but had watched it sometimes. They might still be playing when he woke up in the morning, and would go on playing most of the day; he was used to the sight of Petries' Peerless and soda bottles on the side table, and half-empty glasses, and the not very pleasant odor of stale tobacco smoke, and little ashtrays filled with stubs. He was used to hearing how "rotten" his father was as a poker player, and would smile to himself, for this was one of the secrets which he shared with Robbie, who used as much skill in losing as other people did in trying to win.

Always to the right man, of course! This time Captain Bragescu would be the lucky one. Robbie, bland and smiling, would draw cards every time, and wait until the captain gave signs of having a strong hand, then raise him, and finally quit and drop his cards without showing them. After this had happened a few times the captain would realize that it was safe for him to bet heavily, and when Robbie would propose to raise the limit, he would agree. This would go on for hours, until the lucky officer had most of the chips piled in front of him, and would think that he owned the world. At the end Robbie would say: "It's amazing how you've mastered our American game." It was such a decent way to arrange a contract for guns that the captain could not fail to appreciate it. The guns were all right, of course, and the Rumanian army would be safe from the Bulgarians and able to capture the rebel mountaineers and collect the taxes.

VI

Robbie motored to Marseille to meet some member of his family who was coming from Egypt, and Beauty went to dance at a ball which a friend was giving in one of the white marble palaces on the heights above Nice. It would last until morning, and she would sleep there and return later. Lanny settled himself to the reading of a well-worn novel which somebody had picked up on a bookstall and left in the house.

It was a story about slum life on the outskirts of an American industrial town. The district was known as the "Cabbage Patch," and in it lived an Irish washerwoman with a brood of children, all dreadfully poor, but so honest and good that it touched your heart. Lanny, whose heart was always being touched by one thing or another, found this the dearest and sweetest of stories. By next morning he was nearly through with it and, sitting in the warm sunshine of the court, with narcissus beds around him and a huge bougainvillaea throwing a purple mantle over the kitchen porch, he yearned to have been born in a slum, so that he might be so generous and kindhearted and hard-working and helpful to everybody around him.

There came a tinkling of the bell, and Lanny went to the front gate and was confronted by his Uncle Jesse, his mother's brother. Jesse Blackless was a painter of a sort—that is to say, he had a small income and didn't have to work. He lived in a fishing village some distance to the west, a place where "nobody ever went," as Beauty phrased it. But it was just as well, because Jesse didn't seem to care about visitors, nor they about him; he lived alone in a cottage which he had fixed up in his own fashion. Lanny had been there once, when Uncle Jesse was sick and his sister felt it necessary to pay a duty call, taking along a basket of delicacies. That had been two or three years ago, and the boy had a vague memory of soiled dishes, a frying pan on the center table, and half a room filled with unframed paintings.

The artist was a man of forty or so, wearing a sport shirt open at the neck, a pair of linen trousers, not very well pressed, and tennis shoes dusty from his walk. He wore no hat, and his hair was gone entirely from the top, so that the brown dome was like a bronze Buddha's. He looked old for his years, and had many wrinkles around his eyes; when he smiled his mouth went a little crooked.

His manner was quizzical, which made you think he was laughing at you, which wasn't quite polite. Lanny didn't know what it was, but he had got the impression that there was something wrong about his Uncle Jesse; Beauty saw him rarely, and if Robbie spoke of him, it was in a way implying disapproval. All the boy knew definitely was that Uncle Jesse had had a studio in Paris, and that Beauty had been visiting him at the time she met Robbie and fell in love.

Lanny invited him into the court and got him a chair and, as Uncle Jesse looked hot after his walk, called Rosine to bring some wine. "Mother's gone to the ball at Mrs. Dagenham Price's," said the boy.

"She would," was Jesse's comment.

"Robbie's gone to Marseille," Lanny added.

"I suppose he's making lots of money."

"I suppose so." That was a subject Lanny did not discuss, so the conversation lagged.

But then Lanny recalled the Salon des Indépendants, and said he had been there. "Are they spoofing, or aren't they?" he asked.

"No doubt many of them are," said Uncle Jesse. "Poor devils, they have to get something to eat, and what do critics or buyers know about original work?"

Lanny had picked up ideas concerning the graphic arts, as well as all the others. Many painters lived along the Côte d'Azur and reproduced its charms; a few were famous, and now and then someone would persuade Beauty that it was a cultural action to invite one to a tea party, or perhaps be taken to his studio to inspect his work. Now and then she would "fall for" something that was especially praised, and these hung as showpieces in the home. The most regarded was a blazing sunrise painted by a certain van Gogh, who had lived at Arles, which you passed when you motored to Paris; in fact he had gone crazy there and had cut off one of his ears. Also there was a pond covered with shining water lilies by Monet. These canvases were becoming so valuable that Beauty was talking about having them insured, but it cost so much that she kept putting it off.

VII

There was, of course, a limit to the amount of time that a specialist in the art of painting cared to devote to exchanging ideas with a youngster; so presently the conversation lagged again. Uncle Jesse watched the bees and the hummingbirds in the flowers, and then his eyes happened to fall upon Lanny's book, which had been laid back up on the grass. "What are you reading?" he inquired.

Lanny handed him the volume, and he smiled one of those twisted smiles. "It was a best-seller many years ago."

"Have you read it?" inquired the boy.

"It's tripe," replied Uncle Jesse.

Lanny had to be polite at all hazards, so after a moment he said: "It interests me because it tells about the slums, which I don't know about."

"But wouldn't it be better," asked the uncle, "if you went and looked at them, instead of reading sentimental nonsense about them?"

"I'd be interested," replied the lad; "but of course there aren't any slums on the Riviera."

Uncle Jesse wanted to laugh again, but there was such an earnest look in his nephew's eyes that he checked himself. "It happens that I'm going to pay a visit in a slum this afternoon. Would you like to come?"

The boy was much excited. It was exactly what he had been longing for, though without having formulated it. A "cabbage patch" in Cannes—imagine such a thing! And a woman who lived there for the same noble and idealistic reasons that Lanny had been dreaming about! "This woman is poor," his uncle explained, "but she doesn't need to be. She is highly educated and could make money, but she prefers to live among the working people."

Leese gave them some lunch, and then they walked to the tram and rode cheaply into the city. When they got off, they walked into the "old town," picturesque and fascinating to tourists. They turned into a lane where the tall buildings came closer together at the top, and very little light got down. There are thousands of such tenements in towns all along the Mediterranean shore; built of stone, several stories high, and having been there for a hundred years or more. There will be steps in the street, and many turns, and archways, and courts with balconies above, and at the end perhaps a dead wall, or a glimpse of an old church, prompting the tourist to unsling his camera.

Of course Lanny knew that people lived in such tenements. Babies swarmed on the steps, with flies crawling over their sore eyes; chickens dodged beneath your feet, donkeys jostled you with their loads, and peddlers shouted their wares into your ears. But somehow when you were thinking about antiquities you forgot about human beings; things that are ancient and artistic are lifted into a different realm. The son of Beauty Budd might have walked through such "old towns" for years and never once had the idea of going inside for a visit. But now Uncle Jesse turned into one of the small doorways. It was dark inside, no electric light, not even gas; the steps felt as if they were made of rotten boards, and the odors seemed as old as the house. Doors were left ajar and fresh smells came out; food cooking, and clothes—"Let's hope they're in separate kettles," said the sardonic visitor. Babies squalled, and one very nearly got caught between their legs. Yes, it was a "cabbage patch"!

VIII

The man knocked on a door, a voice called, and they went in. There appeared to be only one room; it had one window, and a woman was sitting near it. She seemed to be old, and was wrapped in a shawl; the light made a silhouette of her face, which was emaciated, and yellow in hue, as happens when the blood goes out of the skins of these swarthy Mediterranean people. Her face lighted when she saw who it was, and she greeted Jesse Blackless in French and held out to his nephew a hand in which he could feel all the bones.

The woman's name was Barbara Pugliese; pronounced Italian fashion, Pool-yay-say. They were evidently old friends, but had not met for some time. Uncle Jesse was anxious about her cough, and she said it was about the same; she was well taken care of, since many here loved her, and brought her food. She asked about Jesse's health, and then about his painting; he said that nobody paid any attention to it, but it kept him out of mischief—but perhaps that was just his way of making a joke.

They talked part of the time in Italian, of which Lanny understood only a little; perhaps they thought he didn't understand any. He gathered that they knew the same persons, and talked about what these were doing. They discussed international affairs, and the diplomats and statesmen, of whom they thought badly—but so did most people in France, the boy had observed. He knew the names of many politicians, but was hazy about parties and doctrines.

His eyes roamed over the room. It was small, the furniture scanty and plain. There was a single bed, or perhaps it was just a cot, with a couple of worn blankets on it; a chest of drawers; a table with odds and ends piled on it, mostly papers and pamphlets; a lot of books on a trunk—apparently no other place for them; a curtain covering one corner, presumably with clothes behind it. This was how you lived in a slum!

Lanny found himself watching the woman again. He had never seen so much grief in a face. To him suffering was a theme for art, so he found himself remembering Christian martyrs as painted by the Italian primitives; he kept trying to recall one of the saints of Cimabue. The woman's voice was soft and her manner gentle, and he decided that she was truly a saint; yes, she lived in this terrible place out of pity for the poor, and must be an even more wonderful person than Mrs. Wiggs of the Cabbage Patch.

When they went out Lanny hoped that Uncle Jesse would tell him about her; but the painter was an unsatisfying sort of companion. All he said was: "Well, you've seen a slum."

"Yes, Uncle Jesse," replied the boy humbly. Presently he added: "Don't you think we ought to take her some food, or something?"

"It wouldn't do any good. She'd just give it away."

The man appeared to be wrapped up in his own thoughts, and Lanny hesitated to disturb him. But finally he asked: "Uncle Jesse, why do there have to be poor people like those?"

The other replied at once: "Because there are rich people like us." That was confusing to the boy, who had always been led to believe that it was the rich people who gave the poor people work; he knew of cases in which they had done it out of kindness, because they were sorry for the poor.

Lanny tried again. "Why doesn't somebody clean up places like that?"

"Because somebody is making money out of them."

"I don't mean the landlords," Lanny explained. "I mean the city officials."

"Maybe they're the landlords; or else they're collecting graft."

"In France, Uncle Jesse?" Lanny had been given to understand that that happened only in America.

The painter laughed one of his disagreeable laughs. "They don't publish it here," he said. They were in front of the Mairie, and he waved his hand toward it. "Go dig in there, and you'll find all you want." As they walked on, he added: "As much as in the munitions industry."

Of course Lanny couldn't discuss that, and perhaps his uncle knew it. Perhaps Uncle Jesse had argued too much in his life, and had grown tired of it. Anyhow, they had come to the tram, where their ways parted. The boy would ride home alone, because his uncle's home lay to the west, and a long way off. Lanny thanked him and said he had enjoyed the visit, and would think over what he had seen and heard. Uncle Jesse smiled another of his twisted smiles, and said: "Don't let it worry you."

IX

Walking from the tram in Juan, Lanny had got to the gate of his home when a car tooted behind him, and there was Robbie just arriving. They greeted each other, and Robbie said: "Where have you been?" When Lanny replied: "I went to Cannes with Uncle Jesse," the father's manner changed in an unexpected way.

"Does that fellow come here?" he demanded. The boy answered that it was the first time in a long while. Robbie took him into the house, and called Beauty into her room, and Lanny also, and shut the door.

It was the first time the boy had ever seen his father really angry. Lanny was put through a regular cross-examination, and when he told about Barbara Pugliese, his father exploded in bad language, and the boy learned some of the things that Uncle Jesse had not chosen to explain to him.

The woman was a prominent leader of the "syndicalist" movement. That was a long word, and Lanny didn't know what it meant, until Robbie said that for practical purposes it was the same as anarchism. The boy had heard enough about that, for every once in a while a bomb would go off and kill some ruler or prime minister or general, and perhaps some innocent bystanders. It had happened in Russia, in Austria, Spain, Italy, even in France; it was the work of embittered and deadly conspirators, nihilists, terrorists, men and women seeking to destroy all organized government. Only last year a band of them had been robbing banks in Paris and had fought a regular battle with the police. "There are no more depraved people living!" exclaimed the father.

Lanny broke in: "Oh, surely, Robbie, she isn't like that. She's so gentle and kind, she's like a saint."

Robbie turned upon the mother. "You see! That snake in the grass, imposing upon the credulity of a child!"

He couldn't blame Lanny, of course. He controlled his anger, and explained that these people were subtle and posed as being idealists, when in their hearts were hatred and jealousy; they poisoned the minds of the young and impressionable.

Beauty began to cry, so the father talked more quietly. "I have always left Lanny's upbringing to you, and I have no fault to find with what you've done, but this is one thing on which I have to put down my foot. The black sheep of your family—or perhaps I had better say the red sheep of your family—is certainly not going to corrupt our son."

"But, Robbie," sobbed the mother, "I hadn't the least idea that Jesse was going to call."

"All right," said Robbie. "Write him a note and tell him it's not to happen again and Lanny is to be let alone."

But that caused more weeping. "After all, he's my brother, Robbie. And he was kind to us; he was the only one who didn't raise a row."

"I've no quarrel with him, Beauty. All I want is for him to keep away from our son."

Beauty wiped her eyes and her nose; she knew that she looked ugly when she wept and she hated ugliness above all things. "Listen, Robbie, try to be reasonable. Jesse hasn't been here for half a year, and the last time he came Lanny didn't even know it. It will probably be as long before he'll be moved to come again. Can't we just tell Lanny not to have anything to do with him? I'm sure this child isn't interested in him."

"No, really, Robbie!" The boy hastened to support his mother. "If I'd had any idea that you objected, I'd have made some excuse and gone away."

So the father was persuaded to leave it that way; the lad gave his promise that never again would he let his Uncle Jesse take him anywhere, and there would be no more slumming tours with anybody. The concern of his father, who was usually so easygoing, made an indelible impression on the boy. Robbie behaved as if his son had been exposed to leprosy or bubonic plague; he probed Lanny's mental symptoms, looking for some infected spot which might be cut out before it had time to spread. Just what had Jesse Blackless said, and what had that Pugliese woman said?

Some inner voice told Lanny not to mention the remark about graft in the munitions industry; but he quoted his uncle's explanation of why there had to be poor people—because there were rich people.

"There's a sample of their poison!" exclaimed the father, and set out to provide Lanny with the proper antidote. "The reason there are poor is because most people are shiftless and lazy and don't save their money; they spend it on drink, or they gamble it away, and so of course they suffer. Envy of the good fortune of others is one of the commonest of human failings, and agitators play upon it, they make a business of preaching discontent and inciting the poor to revolt. That is a very great social danger, which many people fail to realize."

Robbie became a bit apologetic now for having lost his temper and scolded Lanny's mother in Lanny's presence. The reason was that it was his duty to protect a child's immature mind. Lanny, who adored his handsome and vigorous father, was grateful for this protection. It was a relief to him to be told what was true and thus be saved from confusion of mind. So in the end everything became all right again; storm clouds blew over, and tears were dried, and Beauty was beautiful as she was meant to be.

4

Christmas-Card Castle

I

THERE had come to the Frau Robert Budd a formal and stately letter, almost a legal document, from the comptroller-general of Castle Stubendorf in Silesia, saying in the German language that it would give him pleasure if *der junge Herr* Lanning Budd might be permitted to visit his home during the Christmas holidays. *Der junge Herr* danced with delight and carried the letter around in his pocket for days; the Frau Budd replied on fashionable notepaper that she was pleased to accept the kind invitation on behalf of her son. The hour arrived, and Lanny's *smoking* and his warm clothes were packed into two suitcases, and Leese prepared fried chicken and bread and butter sandwiches, just in case the dining car might run out of food. In a nice new traveling suit, and with a heavy overcoat and a French copy of Sienkiewicz's *With Fire and Sword*, Lanny was ready for an expedition to the North Pole.

Since Robbie had gone back to Connecticut, the mother bore the responsibility for this journey. All the way into Cannes she renewed her adjurations and Lanny his promises: he would never step from the train except at the proper stations; he would never allow anyone to persuade him to go anywhere; he would keep his money fastened with a safety pin in the inside pocket of his jacket; he would send a telegram from Vienna, and another from the station of the castle; and so on and so on. Lanny considered all this excessive, because he had just celebrated his fourteenth birthday and felt himself a man of the world.

He brushed away his tears, and saw Beauty and the chauffeur and the familiar Cannes station disappear. The sights of the Riviera sped by: Antibes, Nice, Monaco, Monte Carlo, Menton, and then suddenly it was Italy, and the customs men coming through the train, asking politely if you had anything to declare. Then the Italian shore, and the train plunging through short smoky tunnels, and out into sight of little blue bays and fisherboats with red sails. Presently came Genoa, a mass of tall buildings piled up on a steep shore. The train went inland and wound through a long valley, and ahead were the southern Alps shining white. In the morning they were in Austria, and everywhere was snow; the houses having steeply pitched roofs weighted with heavy stones and the inns having carved and gilded signs.

A wonderful invention, these international sleeping cars; among the many forces which were binding Europe together, mingling the nations, the cultures, the languages. There were no restrictions upon travel, except the price of the ticket; you paid and received a magical document which entitled you to go to whatever places you had chosen. On the way you met all sorts of people, and chatted with them freely, and told them about your affairs, and heard about theirs. To travel far enough was to acquire an education in the business, politics, manners, morals, and tongues of Europe.

II

As his first traveling companions the fates assigned to Lanny two elderly ladies whose accent told him they were Americans. From them he learned that in the land which he considered his own there was a state as well as a city of the name of Washington; this state lay far in the northwest and provided the world with quantities of lumber and canned salmon. In the city of Seattle these two ladies had taught classes of school children for a period of thirty years, and all that time had been saving for the great adventure of their lives, which was to spend a year in Europe, seeing everything they had been reading about all their lives. They were as naïve about it and as eager as if they had been pupils instead of teachers; when they learned that this polite boy had lived in Europe all his life, they put him in the teacher's seat.

At Genoa the ladies departed, and their places were taken by a Jewish gentleman with handsome dark eyes and wavy dark hair, carrying two large suitcases full of household gadgets. He spoke French and English of a sort, and he too was romantic, but in an oddly different way. The ladies from the land of lumber had been brought up where everything was crude and new, so their interest was in the old things of Europe, the strange types of architecture, the picturesque costumes of peasants. But this Jewish gentleman—his name was Robin, shortened from Rabinowich—had been brought up among old things, and found them dirty and stupid. His job was to travel all over this old Europe selling modern electrical contraptions.

"Look at me," said Mr. Robin; and Lanny did so. "I was raised in a village near Lodz, in a hut with a dirt floor. I went to school in another such hut, and sat and scratched my legs and tried to catch the fleas, and chanted long Hebrew texts of which I did not understand one word. I saw my old grandmother's head split open in a pogrom. But now I am a civilized man; I have a bath in the morning and put on clean clothes. I understand science, and do not have any more nonsense in my head, such as that I commit a sin if I eat meat and butter from the same dish. What I earn belongs to me, and I no longer fear that some official will rob me, or that hoodlums will beat me because my ancestors were what they call Christ-killers. So you see I am glad that things shall be new, and I do not have the least longing for any of the antiquities of this continent."

It was a novel point of view to Lanny; he looked out of the car window and saw Europe through the eyes of a Jewish "bagman." The nations were becoming standardized, their differences were disappearing. An office building was the same in whatever city it was erected; and so were the trams, the automobiles, the goods you bought in the shops. Said the salesman of electrical curling irons: "If you look at the people on this train, you will see that they are dressed much alike. The train itself is a standard product, and by means of it we travel from town to town selling products which are messengers of internationalism."

Lanny told where he was going, and how Kurt Meissner said that art was the greatest of international agents. Mr. Robin agreed with that. Lanny mentioned that he had a van Gogh in the dining room of his home, and it developed that Mr. Robin lived in Holland, and knew about that strange genius who had been able to sell only one painting in his whole lifetime, though now a single work brought hundreds of dollars. Said Mr. Robin: "How I wish that I knew such a genius now alive!"

This salesman of gadgets was a curious combination of shrewdness and naïveté. He would have got the better of you in a business deal, and then, if you had been his guest, he would have spent twice as much money on you. He was proud of how he had risen in the world, and happy to tell a little American boy all about it. He gave him his business card and said: "Come and see me if you ever come to Rotterdam." When he took up his heavy cases and departed,

Lanny thought well of the Jews and wondered why he didn't know more of them.

III

From Vienna the traveler enjoyed the society of a demure and sober little Fräulein a year or two younger than himself; she was returning from her music studies in Vienna, and had eyes exactly the color of bluebells and a golden pigtail at least two inches in diameter hanging down her back. Such a treasure was not entrusted to the chances of travel alone, and Fräulein Elsa had with her a governess who wore spectacles and sat so stiff and straight and stared so resolutely before her that Lanny decided to accompany Sienkiewicz to Poland of the seventeenth century, and share the military exploits of the roistering Pan Zagloba and the long-suffering Pan Longin Podbipienta.

But it is not easy to avoid speaking to people who are shut up in a little box with you all day long. With true German frugality the pair had their lunch, and it was difficult to eat it and not offer their traveling companion so much as one or two *Leibnitzkeks*. Lanny said politely: "No, thank you," but the ice was broken. The governess asked where the young gentleman was traveling to, and when he said he was to spend the holidays at Schloss Stubendorf, a transformation took place in her demeanor. "*Ach, so?*" cried she, and was all politeness, and a comical eagerness to find out whose guest he was to be. Lanny, too proud of himself to be a snob, hastened to say that he did not know the Graf or the Gräfin, but had met the youngest son of the comptroller-general and was to be the guest of his family.

That sufficed to make pliable the backbone of Fräulein Grobich. *Ja, wirklich*, the Herr Heinrich Karl Meissner had a post of great responsibility, and was a man of excellent family; the Fräulein knew all about him, because the husband of the Fräulein's sister had begun his career in the office of Schloss Stubendorf. She began to tell about the place, and her conversation was peppered with *Durchlauchts* and *Erlauchts*, *Hoheits* and *Hochwohlgeborens*. It was a great property, that of the Graf, and the young gentleman was fortunate in going there *zu Weihnachten*, because then the castle would be open and the great family would be visible. Fräulein Grobich was thrilled to be in the presence of one who was soon to be in the presence of the assembled *Adel* of Stubendorf.

She wanted to know how Lanny had met the son of the Herr Comptroller-General; when he said at Hellerau, the governess exclaimed: "*Ach, Elsa, der junge Herr hat den Dalcroze-Rhythmus studiert!*" This was permission to enter into conversation with the shy little girl; the bright blue eyes were turned upon him, and the soft well-modulated voice asked questions. Of course nothing pleased him more than to talk about Hellerau; he couldn't offer a demonstration in the crowded compartment, and his German was but a feeble stammering compared with the eloquence which filled his soul.

As for the soul of Fräulein Grobich, what filled it was a sound and proper German respect for rank and position, the phenomenon which was most to impress Lanny during his visit. What you heard about in Silesia was *Ordnung*. Everyone had his place, and knew what it was; each looked up to those above him with a correctly proportioned amount of reverence, unmingled with any trace of envy. As the guest of an important official, Lanny would share the dignity of his host. The shy little maid and her vigilant governess gave him the first taste of this agreeable treatment, and he was sorry when he had to say his *Lebewohls*.

IV

There was a local train waiting on a siding. It had only two cars, and Lanny had to crowd himself into a seat with a farmer who had been to town to sell some of his cattle. He had a large red face and much beer on his breath, and was extremely sociable, telling the little foreign boy about the crops of the district and its important landmarks. When he learned that the boy had come all the way from France to visit the son of Herr Comptroller-General Meissner, he was even more impressed than the governess, and tried to crowd himself up and leave more room for *"die Herrschaft,"* as he began to call the young stranger. From then on he waited for *die Herrschaft* to ask questions, so as to be sure he was not presuming.

The little train was winding up a valley; it had turned dark, and presently the farmer pointed out the lights of the castle on a distant height. There was a whole town built around it, said the farmer, and everything belonged to the Graf, who was referred to as *Seine Hochgeboren.* There were vast forests filled with stags and buffalo and wild boar which *Seine Hochgeboren* and his guests hunted. Six weeks ago *Seine Majestät der Kaiser* himself had visited the place, and there had been the greatest hunt that anyone in the district could remember. Now everything was covered with heavy snow and no more hunting was done; the creatures came to the feed racks, where hay was put out for them so that they would not starve.

Ja, gewiss, said the farmer, he knew the Herr Comptroller-General; he was the business manager of all these properties, and had several assistants, or heads of departments. He had four sons, of whom three were in the army. The farmer knew the *jungen Herrn* Kurt Meissner, a fine lad, he studied music, and would probably play at some of the festivals. Then Lanny was told about the noble family, the wife and the sons and daughters and brothers and sisters of *Seine Hochgeboren.* The farmer was a tenant of the estate, but it was so big that he did not get off until the second station beyond that of the castle. When they came to the latter, he insisted upon taking Lanny's bags and carrying them out to the platform for him; he bowed and touched his hat, and was still doing it when Kurt came running up and grabbed Lanny.

My, how happy those two lads were to see each other again; and how many handshakes and pats on the back they exchanged! Snow was falling, making a blur of the station lights. Kurt had a sleigh with a fine team of horses; he tucked Lanny in under a big fur robe and gave him a pair of mitts to put on, and away they went. They couldn't see much, but the horses knew the way, winding to the height on which the castle stood. Lanny talked about his trip, and Kurt about the festivities which were coming; so much news they had to pour out, and so many plans for their ten days together! Friendship and youth make a delightful combination.

Lanny saw dark masses of buildings with many lights; he got out and was taken indoors and presented to a large family of large people: the father stout, but erect and military, with close-cut gray hair and mustaches trimmed in imitation of his Kaiser's; the kind and comfortable mother, having a great bosom ornamented with a rope of pearls; two sons, tall blond fellows straight as ramrods, with hair cut close like Kurt's, clicking their heels and bowing formally; a sister a year older than Kurt, slender, fair-haired, still in the pigtail stage, but ready to become a temporary mother to a visiting stranger. There were other relatives, a large company, all full of the sentimentality of Christmas and eager to share it with their guest.

Kurt had grown an inch or two since Lanny saw him. He was going to be a fine, tall fellow like his brothers; would he wear a monocle and turn himself into a walking ramrod? Probably so, because he admired them, and would serve his term in the army. His rather severe face was pale, because he had been working hard. But his love of *Ordnung* would always be tempered with the sweetness of music, and he would be Lanny's friend and appreciate the gay, easygoing disposition which Lanny had got from both mother and father. So, at any rate, Kurt assured him when they were up in Kurt's den which they were to share. He was kind and affectionate, but very serious, and talked grandly about his work and purposes, his devotion to art, and to friendship, something which one did not undertake lightly, but with deliberation and moral purpose.

V

Next morning Lanny looked out of the window and saw the great Schloss, five or six stories high, its roofs and turrets covered with fresh snow, gleaming like a Christmas card in the light of the newly risen sun. The picture made him think of all the fairy tales and romances of knights and princesses that he had ever read. To a boy who had spent most of his life on the Riviera, the mere presence of snow was an adventure; to put on his big overcoat and the mitts that Kurt lent him and go out and run, and see his breath in the air, and throw snowballs and get tumbled in a snowbank—that was fairyland. To go back into the house and be served *Pfannkuchen* and broiled venison for breakfast, and be told that it had been shot by *Seine Majestät* himself—could you beat that for thrills?

The Graf Stubendorf and family were expected on the morning train from Berlin, and it would be better for the guest to see the castle before they arrived. So after breakfast the boys ran up the long drive through the park, and climbed the score of steps to the gray stone building; they were admitted by bowing servants in blue uniforms, white gaiters, and white gloves. There was an entrance hall three stories high, and a reception room as big as a theater. All the front of the castle had been built in the last century, but there was an old part in the rear which was six hundred years old and had been captured and recaptured in some of those cruel wars which Lanny had been reading about on the train.

The modern part was splendid with white and gold woodwork, and walls upholstered in hand-embroidered silk, and furniture with scarlet brocade. There was a great deal of heavy carved furniture, and the general atmosphere of a museum. The old part was the most interesting to Lanny, because there were a tower and a donjon keep, an armor room, and a refectory having a huge fireplace with a black pot hanging on a hook. Lanny wondered if Pan Zagloba had ever drunk wassail in that hall. He hefted huge halberds and battle-axes, and tried to imagine what the world must have been like when men went about armored like crabs and lobsters.

They walked about the environs of the castle. It was as the farmer had said, a town, the old part medieval and crowded, the new parts well laid out. Stubendorf was a *Gutsbezirk*, and the Graf was a state functionary, which meant, in effect, that he had his own court of justice, police force, and jail; the feudal system combined with modern plumbing and street paving. But this didn't occur to Lanny, who was living in a lovely fairy tale.

They came back in time to witness the arrival of *Seine Hochge-boren* and family. The great ones drove from the station in limousines; all the servants of the castle, a hundred or two, were lined up on the steps in costumes of long ago, the men on one side, the women on the other. The uniforms of the men bore indications of their rank, while the women had white aprons and lace fichus and white cotton stockings, and wore their hair in plaits down their backs. All were drilled once a week in a system of etiquette complete to the opening of doors.

The Graf Stubendorf was known in Germany as a poet and aesthete, and also as one of the Kaiser's intimates. He was a large man, stoutish and pasty, with a soft brown beard and gracious smile. His three sons were the orthodox military men with shaven heads and mustaches twisted to sharp points; they marched up the stairs in order of seniority, making grave acknowledgment of the bows of the servants. The mother, an elegant lady dressed in the latest Paris fashion, walked behind her sons, and the daughters walked behind her. Of course that may have been an accident; or it may have been because their Kaiser had prescribed the proper concerns of women—kitchen, children, and church—listed presumably in order of importance.

VI

In the afternoon the boys put on high boots and took repeating shotguns for hunting. Kurt's father had arranged it with the Oberforstmeister, an important personage in a green uniform with silver braid; he furnished them a Jäger, who would carry a rifle for their protection. It was not permitted to shoot roebuck or large game, but there were plenty of hare and pheasants in the forest.

They drove in the sleigh, following a wood road, slowly because of the fresh drifts of snow. They passed racks where the deer came to feed; the great stags lifted their heads and kept watch, but made no move to escape. They behaved like cattle, and it didn't seem much like hunting to go out and take post on a wooden platform, with a high-powered rifle and telescopic sight, and have beaters drive such creatures in front of you. When Lanny's father went after game it was in the Canadian wilderness, where the moose were not stall-fed; or out in the Rockies, where mountain sheep ran like the devil, leaping over boulders high up among the clouds.

Kurt said that would be fun, of course, but in Germany shooting was a privilege of the land owners, and the upper classes made a ceremony of it. The Jäger told them about the recent visit of the Kaiser. *Seine Majestät* had a special uniform, buff in color, and a splendid bird in his hat; he took his post on a high stand, and his entourage watched him shoot buffalo as they ran by, and boars, and stags, picking out the largest with the best heads. Afterward a pile of the game was made and the Kaiser had his picture taken, standing in front of it. A rather expensive sport, because it was estimated that to raise a single stag cost several thousand marks. But Kurt explained that none of it was wasted; the carcasses were distributed among those who had a right to them, and Lanny would eat his fill three times a day.

Lanny had never seen either buffalo or wild boars, and was greatly excited by the idea. The former was not the shaggy American bison, but smooth-skinned creatures that had been domesticated in Egypt and brought to Europe by the ancient Romans; now they ran wild in the forests and were very dangerous if wounded. As for the boars, they did not molest human beings—but still, it was well to have a rifle along.

After hunting through a great stretch of forest, they came upon a clearing with a tiny farm and a cottage that might have been the home of the witch in Grimm's fairy tales. They stopped to rest, and found no witch, but a peasant mother with half a dozen little ones, the boys with bullet heads and the girls with braided hair, all staring with wide blue eyes at *die Herrschaften*. There was only one room and a shed in back; the beds were shelves against the walls, and a good part of the room was taken up by a large stove, polished like a patent-leather shoe. Everything in the place had been manicured by this lean and toilworn woman, with tendons in her arms showing like whipcords. She was excited by the visit, and ran to get milk for *die Herrschaften,* as she called them over and over; she stood while they drank it, and apologized because she had nothing better, and because her husband was not at home, and because she had only a hard bench for them to sit on, and so forth. When they left, Lanny looked back and saw a pile of children's faces in the window of the hut, and it stayed with him as one of the sights of Germany.

They returned with a large bag of game, and a still larger appetite. They had a meal to match it, with half a dozen courses of meats and fowl. When they rose from the table they all took hands and danced gaily around it, crying *"Mahlzeit!"* Afterward they gathered round the piano and sang sentimental songs in melting voices, also Kurt and his guest were asked to show what they had learned at Hellerau. Lanny was *echt deutsch* that night, and stowed in his memory two lines of poetry which his friend quoted, to the effect that when you hear singing you may lie down in peace, because evil people have no songs.

VII

"Fröhliche Weihnachten," said everybody next morning, for it was the day before Christmas. The young people took a long sleigh ride and saw the country, and in the afternoon they played music, and Lanny danced with Kurt's sister. In the evening the Christmas celebration took place, and there were presents for all the family and the servants; not under the Christmas tree, but on separate little tables, covered with linen cloths. After the tree was lighted, the presents were given out. The Herr Comptroller said a few words, and shook hands with each of his servants, and they all kissed the hand of his wife. Everything was warmhearted, everybody wished happiness to everybody else, and they sang *"Stille Nacht"* with tears in their eyes.

Next morning they had a preliminary breakfast, eating a long kind of bun called *Dresdner Christstollen,* with raisins in it and sugar on top; also eggs, and many kinds of homemade jam, and coffee with hot milk. That was supposed to carry you until half-past ten, when you had the so-called "fork-breakfast." It appeared that ideas of diet reform which were spreading among Lanny's American friends had never been heard of in this Prussian province, and such things as *Hasenpfeffer*, fresh pork sausage, and several other kinds of meat could be eaten in great quantities in the morning.

Later on there was to be a celebration at the Schloss, and everybody dressed, the men in uniforms and decorations, and the ladies with their jewels, silks, and laces. They came in a happy solemn mood as to a church festival. For the tenants and employees it was the one time in the year when they might pass the portals of the great building which dominated their lives. They waited respectfully outside until the last of the dignitaries had entered and taken their places; then the crowd streamed into the great hall, the men taking off their hats before they ascended the steps, the peasant women with kerchiefs or shawls over their heads, curtsying to everybody. Those for whom there were no seats packed themselves around the walls.

Seine Hochgeboren and family came in by a private entrance, and everybody stood and said *"Fröhliche Weihnachten."* The pastor said a prayer, quite a long one, and they all stood again and sang a hymn, in such volume as to drown out the organ. The Graf gave them all Christmas greetings in a fatherly talk, full of assurances of concern for their welfare, and declaring the divine origin of *"deutsche Treu und Werde."* In their happy land, so favored by God, peace and order prevailed, and every man and woman cherished the sacred flame of loyalty in his heart. In this happy Christmas season they renewed their pledges to the Kaiser and Fatherland. The applause which followed seemed to indicate that *Seine Hochgeboren* was completely justified in his faith.

A great fir tree out of the forest stood in a corner of the hall, and there were presents for everyone, even to the toilworn peasant woman and the half dozen little ones who had stared at Lanny out of the window of the hut. Four men in uniform called the names on the packages and handed them out; but even with this procedure it took long to distribute them all. Not a person left the hall, and *Seine Hochgeboren* shook hands with each man and woman. Lanny was not bored, because these were Kurt's people, and he was interested to watch their faces and their costumes.

Next day the Comptroller-General went to report to his employer upon the state of affairs. He was invited to a smoker that evening, together with his eldest son. Other neighboring land owners came, and several of the higher officials of the estate, the chief of police, the head forester, and so on. Over pipes and beer they discussed the state of the country, both local and national, and the Graf honored them by reporting upon matters of importance on which he had special sources of information. The following evening Herr Meissner told his family what had gone on at this smoker, and gave his own views of the matters discussed. Everybody in the household listened respectfully to what the stout and imposing father said, and no one ventured to question anything. The guest from a foreign land could not understand all the long words, but listened attentively, and afterward had matters explained to him by Kurt.

Seine Hochgeboren had reported that other nations, jealous of German diligence and skill, had surrounded the Fatherland with a wall—*die Einkreisung*, was the phrase. Either that wall would be taken down by agreement, or it would have to be broken, because the Germans were a growing people, and would not be denied their place in the sun. The Graf had spoken of a dark cloud of barbarism in the eastern sky, and by that, of course, he meant Russia. The nobility and land owners of Upper Silesia got along well with their neighbors, the nobility and land owners of the Tsar's realm, and had no quarrel with them; but they were exasperated by the alliance with France, which was putting up huge sums of money for the arming of Russia. For what purpose? the Graf wished to know. There could be but one answer—a contemplated attack upon Germany.

Also, *Seine Hochgeboren* had talked about enemies within the Fatherland; he described them as rats, gnawing and nibbling. Of course he meant the Social-Democrats, said Herr Meissner. They had no strength in Stubendorf, where the good old ways prevailed; but in all the industrial districts they never ceased their hateful agitation, and at the next elections to the Reichstag they might win an actual majority. If that happened, steps would undoubtedly have to be taken to put them down by force.

Lanny was moved to tell his friend Kurt about his visit to the "cabbage patch" of Cannes. He didn't mention that he had an uncle who was a "red sheep"—that was too terrible a family secret; he said merely that somebody had taken him to meet a woman "Red," and he had been deceived into thinking that she was a good person. Kurt replied: "No doubt many of these agitators are sincere fanatics. Indeed, it's rather the fashion nowadays to say smart and cynical things against the government." He added: "There's more Socialist sentiment in Silesia than perhaps *Seine Hochgeboren* realizes; there are many coal mines in the province, and in the open portions are large industries and a lot of discontent among the workers."

Kurt talked in his usual lofty way about social problems. He said that art and culture would filter down from the cultivated classes and ultimately would civilize and regenerate the common people. He was especially certain that the artist must hold himself above the squabbles of politics. Solemnly he declared: "Just as knowledge is power, so is beauty; those who create it are masters of the Idea, which precedes everything in human affairs. As the idea of the chair comes before the making of the chair, so the idea of beauty, good-ness, justice, has to be nourished in creative minds. In the beginning was the Word"—and so on for a great many words.

Lanny did not know that all this was German philosophy with a capital P; that a learned professor in Königsberg had sat in his study with his eyes fixed upon a church steeple for twenty years, spinning mental cobwebs made of such high-sounding polysyllables. Lanny did not know that twenty-three centuries previously a wealthy gentleman of Athens of the name of Plato had walked up and down under a portico doing the same thing, and that his doctrines had spread to Alexandria, and from there had reached a Jewish enthusiast by the name of John. What Lanny thought was that his friend, Kurt Meissner, had worked up all this for himself, and he was quite overcome with awe.

VIII

The ten days passed rapidly, and one morning the two boys packed their belongings, said their farewells, and were driven to the station. They rode together to the junction, renewing their pledges of everlasting loyalty. At the junction their roads parted, and Kurt, whose train came first, made sure that his guest had his ticket in a safe place, and that the station master would see him aboard his train. Lanny watched Kurt depart; and then, because a cold wind was blowing, he went into the café of the station and ordered a cup of hot cocoa.

While he was sipping it and thinking over adventures the memory of which would always delight him, a man came into the room, looked around, and then came to Lanny's table. There were other tables, but the man appeared to be sociable, and Lanny was glad to chat with anyone in this agreeable country. The stranger said: "*Guten Morgen,*" and Lanny returned the greeting, and at the same time took the man in with a swift appraisal.

The stranger was small, rather dark, and sallow; his hat, tie, and overcoat were lacking in those touches of elegance which meant a "gentleman." He wore glasses, and his thin face had a worried look; his fingers were stained with tobacco. He ordered a glass of beer, and then remarked: "*Ein Fremder, nicht wahr?*" When Lanny replied that he was an American, the man began to speak somewhat hesitating English. He had seen Lanny with Kurt Meissner, and said that he knew Kurt; had Lanny been staying at the Schloss?

Lanny explained where he had been staying, and they talked about the visit. Lanny enjoyed nothing more than telling about what a good time he had had, and how kind everybody had been. The man seemed to know all about affairs at the castle. Ja, ja, he knew the Herr Comptroller-General, also his sons; they had gone back to the army. No time to be lost in the army; that very morning a company of light artillery had gone into the mountains for practice, the guns mounted on sleds, the troops on skis. Lanny said he had seen them getting off the train; wonderful how fast they had slid those guns off the flatcars. The stranger said that was part of the drill and was timed to the second. The Fatherland had many enemies and must ever be on the alert.

Lanny was interested to hear this from another German. Apparently it was the first thought in the mind of everyone in the country. He told the stranger about the political discussions which had taken place, and how Graf Stubendorf had warned his officials of the dark cloud hanging over the east and of the rats within which were gnawing and nibbling. "He must mean the Social-Democrats," said the stranger; and Lanny replied, yes, that was what Herr Meissner had explained to his family.

Lanny's father had carefully posted him as to the dangers of talking about the munitions industry; but it never occurred to the lad that there could be any reason for not discussing the patriotic sentiments of the defenders of the Fatherland. The stranger wanted to know exactly what *Seine Hochgeboren* had said, and where and how he had said it; so Lanny told about the smoker, and who had been present at it. *Seine Hochgeboren* had said that if the "rats" were to carry the Reichstag at the next elections, it might be necessary to put them down by force; the comptroller-general had agreed with this idea.

Lanny mentioned also the hunting, and what he had learned about the Kaiser's extraordinary prowess as a slaughterer of game. The stranger said that photographs of it had been published in the papers; there was one in a magazine which Lanny could buy on the newsstands. He would observe that the Kaiser kept his left arm behind him; one would always find that in any picture of him, for he had a withered arm and was very sensitive about it. Had they mentioned how he had a special knife and fork, made in one piece, so that he could eat with one hand? Lanny said, no, they hadn't told him things like that. A flicker of a smile crossed the little man's sallow face.

The stranger went on to set forth how in the castle they had prepared every day a special newspaper for the Kaiser, printed in gold. Lanny said that didn't sound as if it would be easy reading.

The other agreed; but it would never do for the All-Highest to read a common newspaper, such as any of his subjects could buy for ten pfennigs. Had they told him whether everybody in the room had to rise and click his heels when the Kaiser addressed that person?

There had come what seemed a note of sneering in the man's voice, and the boy became vaguely uneasy and changed the subject. He told how they had shot hare and pheasants in those wonderful forests; and about the farm with the cottage and the pretty children. Lanny said how much he had been impressed by the cleanness and order he had seen in that cottage, and in fact throughout the domain of the Graf, and by the evidences of loyalty and discipline. "Ach, yes!" replied the man. "You see, Napoleon never got here."

The youngster didn't know enough history to understand that remark, so the other explained that wherever the French armies had penetrated, they had distributed the lands among the peasants, and so had broken the feudal system. If Lanny had been in France, he must know how independent and free-spoken the peasants were; none of this bowing and kowtowing to the masters, the everlasting *Hoheits* and *Hochgeborens*. Lanny said that he had noted that difference.

"Perhaps I ought to tell you," continued the stranger, "that I am a journalist. I am indebted to you for some very useful information."

Lanny felt something fall inside and hit the pit of his stomach. "Oh!" he cried. "Surely you're not going to quote what I've been saying!"

"Don't worry," said the other, smiling. "I am a man of tact. I promise not to mention or indicate you in any way."

"But I was a guest there!" exclaimed Lanny. "I haven't the right to repeat what they told me. That would be shameful!"

"By your own account many persons heard what Stubendorf said. Any one of them might have told it to me. And as to Meissner——"

"It was in his own house!" cried the boy. "Nothing could be more private."

"He'll be saying it to many persons, and he won't have any idea how it came to my ears."

Lanny was so bewildered and embarrassed he didn't know what to answer. Such an ending for his holiday! The other, reading his face, continued apologetically: "You must understand that we journalists have to take our information where we find it. I am one of the editors of the *Arbeiterzeitung*, a Social-Democratic newspaper, and I have to consider the interests of the oppressed workers whom I serve."

Again something hit Lanny's stomach, even more heavily than before. "What interest can the workers . . . ?" he began; but then speech failed him.

Said the editor: "Our people take seriously their rights as citizens; but their opponents, it appears, do not share that view. The Comptroller-General of Schloss Stubendorf announces that if the workers win at the polls, the masters will not submit to the decision, but will resort to force and counter-revolution. Don't you see how very important that news will be to our readers?"

Lanny could not find words to answer.

"You came here as a guest," continued the other, "and you found everything lovely. There was nobody to take you behind the scenes and show you how this charming Christmas puppet show is worked. You are too young to form any idea of what it means to live in the Middle Ages; but I will give you facts which you can think about on your journey. You admire the fairy-story cottage in the forest and the pretty children—but nobody mentioned that the first of them might be the child of your host, the Herr Comptroller-General."

"Oh, surely not!" cried Lanny, outraged.

"He scattered his seed freely when he was younger. And I'll tell you more for your own welfare. You are a charming boy, and if ever you come for another visit, do not attract the attention of the Graf Stubendorf, or under any circumstances be left alone in the room with him."

Lanny, staring at his interlocutor, didn't know just what the man meant, but he knew it was something very bad, and the blood was climbing to his cheeks and forehead.

"I will not offend your young mind with the details. Suffice it to say that some men in the Kaiser's intimate circle have extremely evil ways of life. A few years ago there was a public scandal which forced one of the Kaiser's best friends to retire from public lif₋. Stubendorf is an exquisite fellow, highly sentimental, and thinks he is a poet; but I tell you that neither boys nor girls are safe in this feudal principality which has seemed to you like a set of Christmas cards."

There came a roaring outside the station, and the uniformed official came to the door. "*Der Zug, junger Herr,*" said he, with feudal politeness. The Social-Democratic editor rose quickly and went out by another door, while the station master took Lanny's bags and put him safely into the right car.

Lanny never learned the name of that editor, and never knew what he published. For a while his happiness was poisoned by the fear of a scandal; but nothing happened, so apparently the man had kept his promise. Lanny was ashamed of his lack of discretion and resolved never to tell anyone about the incident. A bitter and hateful fellow, that editor; repeating slanders, or perhaps making them up. Lanny decided that Social-Democrats had minds warped with envy, and must be fully as dangerous as anarchists. But all the same he couldn't help wondering if the stories were true—and whether perhaps it mightn't have been better if Napoleon had got to Stubendorf!

5

The Facts of Life

I

LANNY came home with the idea fixed in his head that he ought to go to school; he wanted to settle down to hard study and be disciplined and conscientious like those Germans. The idea somewhat alarmed his mother, and she asked, just what did he want to learn. Lanny presented a list: he wanted to understand what Kurt called philosophy, that is, what life was, and why it was, and how the Idea always preceded the Thing; second, he wanted to understand the long German words that he had heard, such as *Erscheinungsphänomenologie* and *Minderwertigkeitscomplexe;* third, he wanted to know how to calculate trajectories and the expansive forces of propellants, so as to understand Robbie when he was talking to the artillery experts; and, finally, he wanted to learn to multiply and divide numbers.

Beauty was puzzled; she didn't know any of these things herself, and wasn't sure if there was any school in the neighborhood where they were taught. She pointed out that if Lanny went away to boarding school, he wouldn't be on hand for the visits of his father; also he would miss a great deal of travel, which was another kind of education, wasn't it? So finally it was decided that the way to solve the problem was, first, to buy a large dictionary and a twenty-volume encyclopedia; and, second, to get a tutor who understood arithmetic.

So it came about that Mr. Ridgley Elphinstone entered into Lanny Budd's young life. Mr. Elphinstone was an Oxford student whose health had weakened, and he was living *en pension* in the village. Beauty was introduced to him at a bridge party, and when the hostess mentioned that the young man was poor, Beauty had the bright idea to inquire if he could teach arithmetic. He answered sadly that he had forgotten all he had ever known, but doubtless he could brush up; that was the way of all tutors, he explained, they got advance information as to what was expected, and they brushed up. Mr. Elphinstone came and made an inventory of Lanny's disordered stock of knowledge, and told Beauty that it might be difficult to make an educated man of him, but since he was going to have money, why did it matter?

After that Mr. Elphinstone came every morning, unless Lanny was otherwise engaged. He was a thin person of melancholy aspect, with dark Byronic hair and eyes, and spent his spare time composing poetry which he never showed to anyone. Apart from his code as an English gentleman, he appeared to have only one conviction, which was that nothing was certain, and anyhow it made no difference. His method of instruction was most agreeable; he would tell Lanny anything he wanted to know, and if neither of them knew it, they would look it up in the encyclopedia. Incidentally, Mr. Elphinstone fell in love with Beauty, which was as she expected; being poor but proud he never said anything, which made the most pleasant arrangement possible.

So far, Lanny's pronunciation of his own tongue had been modeled upon that of his father, who was a Connecticut Yankee. But the Oxford accent is most impressive, and the boy now lived in daily contact with it, so presently he was being heard to declare that he "had bean," and that he knew "we-ah" he was going, he saw "cle-ahly" what was his "gaoal." He would say that he "re-ahlized" that his education was "diff'rent," but that it was "mod'n," and he wanted it to be "thurrah." He developed aristocratic sentiments, and when he discussed politics would say: "We must not shut ahr eyes to the fact that it is necess'ry for someone to commahnd." If one of the boys invited him to play tennis he would reply: "Ah-i will luke and see the tah-eem." When Robbie returned he "tuke"

some amused "lukes" at his son, and informed him that the sound
of "oo" as in the word "loot" came from the quite unfashionable
North of England.

II

Among the guests at one of the tea parties was a Russian baron
of the name of Livens-Mazursky. The friend who brought him said
that he was rich and important, owned a newspaper in St. Petersburg, had diplomatic contacts, and would be a valuable person to
Robbie—all that sort of thing. He was of striking appearance, large,
with flourishing black whiskers, pale cheeks, and lips so red that
you wondered if he did not stain them. His eyes were prominent
and bright, and he talked with animation in whatever language the
company preferred. He spent his money freely, so everybody liked
him.

Baron Livens came to the house several times and seemed to take
an interest in the handsome boy. Lanny was used to that, many
people did it; also he was used to the ardent temperament of the
Russians and thought he would be helping the American munitions
industry by making friends with a brilliant man who had once been
a cavalry officer, and who seemed like a character stepping out of
With Fire and Sword.

One afternoon Lanny went with his mother to Cannes, and while
she did some shopping he went to a kiosk and got a magazine, and
sat down to read and wait for his mother in the lobby of one of the
fashionable hotels. Baron Livens happened in, and sat beside him,
and asked him what he was reading, chatted about magazines, and
finally told Lanny that he had some wonderful reproductions of
Russian paintings in his suite upstairs. So they went up in the lift,
and the baron ushered Lanny into a showy drawing room, and got
the prints, and they sat down at a table together to look at pictures.

Presently one of the man's arms was about Lanny, and that was
all right; but then he bent down and kissed the boy on the cheek.
All boys in those days had the experience of being kissed with
whiskers, and didn't like it. When the action was repeated, Lanny

shrank and said: "Please don't." But the baron held on to him, and Lanny became alarmed; he looked, and discovered a half-crazy stare in the man's eyes. A panic seized the boy and he cried: "Let me go!" Lanny had not forgotten what the Social-Democratic editor had told him about Graf Stubendorf; he had tried to imagine what he was being warned against, and now it flashed into his mind that this must be it! He struggled and started to scream, which frightened the man, so that he let go his hold, and Lanny sprang up and rushed to the door.

It was locked; and this discovery gave Lanny the wildest fright he had ever known. He shrieked at the top of his voice: "Help! Help! Let me out!" The baron tried to quiet him, but Lanny got a big upholstered chair between them, and yelled louder; until the man said: "Be quiet, you little fool, and then I'll open the door." "All right, open it," panted Lanny. When it was open he made the man step away from it, and then dashed out and down the stairs without waiting for the lift.

In the lobby he took a seat, pale and shivering; for a while he thought he was going to be nauseated. Then he saw the bewhiskered baron bringing the magazine which had been left behind. Lanny jumped up and kept backing away; he wouldn't let the Russian get near him. The man was agitated too, and tried to plead; it was all a misunderstanding, he had meant no harm, he had little boys of his own whom he loved, and Lanny reminded him of them.

Such was the situation when Beauty appeared. She saw that something had happened, and the baron tried to explain; the dear little boy had misunderstood him, it was a cruel accident, most embarrassing. Lanny wouldn't speak of it, he just wanted to get out of there. "Please, Beauty, please!" he said, so they went out to the street.

"Have you been hurt?" asked the frightened mother.

But Lanny said: "No, I got away from him." He wouldn't talk about it on the street, and then he wouldn't talk in the car, because Pierre, the chauffeur, could hear them. "Let's go home," he said, and sat holding his mother's hand as tightly as he could.

III

By the time they reached Bienvenu, Lanny had got over some of his agitation, and was wondering whether he could have been making a mistake. But when he told his mother about it she said, no, he had been in real danger; she would like to go and shoot that Russian beast. But she wouldn't tell the youngster what it was about; a kind of fog of embarrassment settled over them, and all Lanny got out of it was anxious monitions never to let any man touch him again, never to go anywhere with any man again—it appeared that he couldn't safely have anything to do with anybody except a few of his mother's intimates.

Beauty had to talk to somebody, and called in her friend Sophie, Baroness de la Tourette. Oh, yes, said that experienced woman of the world, everybody knew about Livens; but what could you do? Have him arrested? It would make a journalist's holiday, he would fight back and blacken you with scandals. Shoot him? Yes, but the French laws were rather strict; the jury would have to be made to weep, and lawyers who can do that charge a fortune. The thing to do was to make the child understand, so that it couldn't happen again.

"But what on earth can I say to him?" exclaimed Beauty.

"Do you mean you haven't given him a straight talk?" demanded her friend.

"I just can't bring myself to it, Sophie. He is so innocent——"

"Innocent, hell!" retorted Sophie Timmons, that henna blonde with the henna laugh; the daughter of a hardware manufacturer who was a piece of hardware herself. "He plays around with these peasant children—don't you suppose they watch the animals and talk about it? If you heard them you would pass out."

"Oh, my God!" lamented Beauty. "I wish there was no such thing as sex in the world!"

"Well, there's plenty of it on this 'Coast of Pleasure,' and your little one will soon be ready for his share. You'd better wake up."

"His father is the one who ought to tell him, Sophie."

"All right then, send a cablegram, 'Robbie come at once and tell Lanny the facts of life.'" They both laughed, but it didn't solve the problem. "Couldn't the tutor do it?" suggested the baroness finally. "I haven't the faintest notion what his ideas are."

"Well, at the worst I should think they'd be better than Livens'," responded the other, dryly.

The Baroness de la Tourette of course told the story all over the place, and Baron Livens-Mazursky found himself cut off from a number of calling lists; he suddenly decided to spend the rest of the winter at Capri, a place which was not so puritanical as Cannes. Lanny's mother repeated her warnings to the boy, with such solemnity that he began to acquire the psychology of a wild deer in the forest; he looked before he ventured into any dark places, and if he saw anyone, male or female, getting close to him he moved.

IV

But even the wild deer in the forest enjoys life, and Lanny couldn't be kept from wanting to talk to people and find out about them. Soon afterward came the Adventure of the Gigolo, which was the last straw, so Beauty declared. The story of Lanny's gigolo spread among the smart crowd up and down the Riviera, and every now and then someone would ask: "Well, Lanny, how's your gigolo getting along?" He knew they were making fun, but it didn't worry him, for his mind was firmly made up that his gigolo was really a very kind man, much more so than some of the persons who tried to win money from his mother at bridge.

It was another of those occasions when Beauty was having herself made more so. This time it was a ravishing evening gown of pale blue chiffon over cloth of silver, which was being "created" by M. Claire, the couturier in Nice, at a specially moderate price because of the advertising he would get. It meant long sessions of fitting in which Beauty got a bit dizzy, and Lanny preferred to sit out under the plane trees and watch the traffic go by, the fashionable people strolling, and the *bonnes* with the pretty children.

He sat on a bench, and along came a gentleman of thirty or so, wearing correct afternoon attire in the morning, and a neatly trimmed little black mustache and a cane with a ball of polished agate for a handle. He had an amiable expression, and perhaps recognized a similar one on the face of the boy. Certainly he could see that the boy was fashionably attired. It was now the height of the season, and the town was full of tall slender youths from England and America, wearing sports shirts, linen trousers, and tennis shoes or sandals.

The gentleman took a seat on the bench, and after a while stole a glance at the book in Lanny's lap. "*J'ai lou cela*," he remarked.

Which told Lanny right away that he was a countryman, a native of Provence. These people do not pronounce the *u* as do the French; the name of Lanny's town was not spoken in French fashion, or in Spanish, but "Jou-an." Lanny answered in Provençal, and the stranger's face lighted up. "Oh, you are not a foreigner?" Lanny explained that he was born in Switzerland and had lived most of his life in "Jou-an." The stranger said that he came from the mountain village of Charaze, where his parents were peasants.

That called for explanation; for the sons of peasants do not as a rule spend their mornings strolling under the plane trees of the Avenue de la Victoire, dressed in frock coat and striped trousers trimmed with black braid. M. Pinjon—that was his name—explained that he had risen in the world by becoming a professional dancer. Lanny said that he too was a dancer of a sort, and wished to learn all he could about that agreeable art. M. Pinjon said that what counted was that one had the spirit, the inner fire. Yes, assented Lanny; so few had that fire, which was the soul of every art. Kurt had said that, and Lanny remembered it and used it to excellent effect.

So you see the acquaintance started upon the very highest plane. Lanny was moved to tell about Hellerau, and the tall white temple loomed as a place of magic to which M. Pinjon might some day make a pilgrimage. Lanny described the technique of Eurythmics;

a little bit more and he would have been giving a demonstration on the sidewalk of the avenue.

V

Out of the fervor of his nature as an artist and a son of the warm South, M. Pinjon told the story of his life. He was a child of a large family, and the little plot of earth in Charaze was too small to sustain them all. So he, the youngest, had fared forth to make his fortune in the world, and for a while had not found it easy. He had lived in a wretched lodging—there was a "cabbage patch" also in Nice, and much refuse was dumped into the streets, and the smells were painful to a countryman who was used to thyme and lavender on the hillsides.

M. Pinjon had become a waiter, a menial position in a small café; but he had saved every sou, and bought himself this costume, patterned carefully after those he had observed in the *grand monde*. At home he had been a skillful dancer of the farandole, and had soon begun a study of modern dancing, no simple task, since twenty-eight forms of the tango were now being danced on the Riviera, besides such American innovations as the "turkey trot" and the "bunny hug."

Having cultivated his ten talents, M. Pinjon had obtained an opening in one of the casinos. He was what was called, somewhat unkindly, a "gigolo." True, there were evil men in the business, ready to take advantage of opportunities; but M. Pinjon was a serious person, a French peasant at heart, and his purpose in life was to save up a sufficiency of *livres* to purchase a bit of land which he had picked out near his ancestral home and there to live as his forefathers had done, cultivating the olive and the vine and saying prayers against the return of the Saracens.

Ladies came in great numbers to the casino; ladies who were lonely, mostly because they were middle-aged, and the men, whether old or young, preferred to dance with young partners. However, middle-aged ladies were reluctant to bid farewell to their youth, and to the enjoyment which we all crave. M. Pinjon spoke quite feelingly and at the same time instructively about the problem of the middle-aged lady. Why should she not dance—having nothing else to do? Since the men did not invite her, she was compelled to pay for partners, and it was in this way that M. Pinjon gained a modest living. He danced with strange ladies in a dignified and respectful way, and if they wished to be taught he helped them to improve their style.

He seemed anxious that this polite and intelligent boy should agree with him that this was a proper thing to do; and Lanny did agree with him. M. Pinjon came back to the subject of Dalcroze, and asked if there was a book about it. Lanny gave him the name of a book and he wrote it down. The boy was moved to add: "If you ever come to Juan, and will call at our home, I'll be glad to show you as much of it as I can." The dancer wrote down Lanny's address, and said he would surely not fail; he played the piccolo flute, and would bring it and render old Provençal tunes and Lanny would dance them.

At this point came Beauty, tired and a little cross after the ordeal of "fitting." Lanny introduced her to his new friend, and of course Beauty had to be polite, but at the same time most reserved, because she could perceive social subtleties which a boy couldn't, and this wasn't the first time that Lanny's habit of picking up strange persons had caused embarrassment. When they got into the car and were driving home, Lanny told her about his new friend, and—well, of course Beauty couldn't be angry with the child, but, oh, dear, oh, dear—she had to sink back into the cushions of the car and laugh. She thought how Sophie would laugh, and how Margy would laugh—that was Lady Eversham-Watson. And they did, of course; everybody did, except Lanny.

The worst of it was there was no way to keep the man from calling. The mother had to explain carefully to Lanny that there are certain social differences that just can't be overlooked. "You'll of course have to be polite to this poor fellow, but you mustn't ask him to call again, nor promise to go and see him dance at the casino. Above all, I won't meet him again."

M. Pinjon rode all the way from Nice in an autobus, his first free day. He brought his piccolo, and they sat out on the terrace, and he played shrill little tunes, "Magali," and the "Marche des Rois," and Lanny danced them, and the son of the warm South became inspired, and played faster and more gaily, and danced while he played. Beauty, who happened to be at home, peered through the blinds of a window now and then, and watched the dapper little man with the neat black mustache capering with such agility; she had to admit that it was a touching scene—out of the childhood of the world, as it were, before social classes came into being.

Afterward Rosine brought wine and cake. M. Pinjon was treated with every courtesy—except that he did not again see the face of the loveliest of grass widows. The Provençal chansons which tell of troubadours singing in castles and carrying away princesses somehow did not fit the circumstances of the year 1914 on the Côte d'Azur.

VI

After that episode Beauty Budd decided that she could no longer leave her child in ignorance of the facts of life. She sought out her friend Sophie, who had a new suggestion. There was in Nice an Austrian-Jewish physician of the name of Bauer-Siemans, practitioner of a method known as psychoanalysis, just now sweeping Europe and America. Ladies in the highest social circles discovered that they had inferiority complexes—that was the German jawbreaker *Minderwertigkeitscomplexe*, called "the Minkos" for short. Ladies and gentlemen talked quite blandly about their Oedipus fixations and their anal-erotic impulses; it was horrible, but at the same time fascinating. The thing that carried ladies off their feet was the fact that for ten dollars an hour you could employ a cultured and intelligent gentleman to hear you talk about yourself. It cost many times that to give a dinner party—and then you discovered that the gentlemen wanted to talk about *them*selves!

"I don't know how much I believe of that stuff," said the Baroness de la Tourette; "but at least the man knows the facts and won't mind talking about them."

"But will he want to bother with a child, Sophie?"

"Hand him an envelope with a hundred-franc note in it, and let nature do the rest," said the practical-minded baroness.

So Mrs. Budd telephoned and asked for an hour or two of the valuable time of Dr. Bauer-Siemans, and took Lanny with her and left him in the outer office while she told about the baron, and then the gigolo.

The psychoanalyst was a learned-looking gentleman having a high forehead topped with black wavy hair, and gold pince-nez which he took off now and then and used in making gestures. He spoke English with a not too heavy accent. "But why don't you talk to the boy yourself, Mrs. Budd?" he demanded.

More blood mounted to Beauty's already well-suffused cheeks. "I just can't, Doctor. I've tried, but I can't speak the words."

"You are an American?" he inquired.

"I am the daughter of a Baptist minister in New England."

"Ah, I see. Puritanism!" Dr. Bauer-Siemans said it as if it were "poliomyelitis" or "Addison's disease."

"It seems to be ingrained," said Beauty, lowering her lovely blue eyes.

"The purpose of psychoanalysis is to bring such repressions to the surface of consciousness, Mrs. Budd. So we get rid of them and acquire normal attitudes."

"What I want is for you to talk to Lanny," said the mother, hastily. "I would like you to consider it a professional matter, please." She handed over a scented envelope, not sealed but with the flap tucked in.

The doctor smiled. "We don't usually receive payment in advance," he said, and laid the envelope on the desk. "Leave the little fellow with me for an hour or so, and I'll tell him what he needs to know." So Beauty got up and went out; meantime the doctor glanced into the envelope, and saw that Lanny was entitled to a full dose of the facts of life.

VII

The boy found himself seated in a chair facing the desk of this strange professional gentleman. When he heard what he was there for, the blood began to climb into *his* cheeks; for Lanny, too, was a little Puritan, far from the home of his forefathers.

However, it wasn't really so bad; for the Baroness de la Tourette had been right. Lanny had not failed to see the animals, and the peasant boys had talked in the crudest language. His mind was a queer jumble of truth and nonsense, most of the latter supplied by his own speculations. The peasant boys had told him that men and women behaved like that also, but Lanny hadn't been able to believe it; when the doctor asked why not, he said: "It didn't seem dignified." The other smiled and replied: "We do many things which do not seem dignified, but we have to take nature as we find it."

The doctor's explanations were not by means of the bees and the flowers, but with the help of a medical book full of pictures. After Lanny had got over the first shock he found this absorbingly interesting; here were the things he had been wondering about, and someone who would give him straight answers. It was impossible for Lanny to imagine such desires or behavior on his own part, but the doctor said that he would very soon be coming to that period of life. He would find the time of love one of happiness, but also of danger and strain; there arose problems of two different natures, man's and woman's, learning to adjust themselves each to the other, and they needed all the knowledge that was to be had.

All this was sensible, and something which every boy ought to have; Lanny said so, and pleased the learned-looking doctor, who gave him the full course for which the mother had paid, and even a little extra. He took up a subject which had a great effect upon the future of both mother and son. "I understand that your mother is divorced," he remarked. "There are many problems for children of such a family."

"I suppose so," said Lanny innocently—for he was not aware of any problems in his own family.

"Understand, I'm not going to pry into your affairs; but if you choose to tell me things that will help me to guide you, it will be under the seal of confidence."

"Yes, sir," said Lanny. "Thank you very much."

"When families break up, sooner or later one party or the other remarries, or perhaps both do; so the child becomes a stepchild, which means adjustments that are far from easy."

"My father has remarried and has a family in Connecticut; but I have never been there."

"Possibly your father foresees difficulties. How long have your mother and father been divorced?"

"It was before I can remember. Ten years, I guess."

"Well, let me tell you things out of my experience. Your mother is a beautiful woman, and doubtless many men have wished to marry her. Perhaps she has refused because she doesn't want to make you unhappy. Has she ever talked to you about such matters?"

"No, sir."

"You have seen men in the company of your mother, of course."

"Yes, sir."

"You haven't liked it, perhaps?"

Lanny began to be disturbed. "I—I suppose I haven't liked it if they were with her too much," he admitted.

Dr. Bauer-Siemans smiled, and told him that a psychoanalyst talked to hundreds of men and women, and they all had patterns of behavior which one learned to recognize. "Often they are ashamed of these," he said, "and try to deny them, and we have to drag the truth out of them—for their own good, of course, since the first step toward rational behavior is to know our own selves. You understand what I am saying?"

"I think so, Doctor."

"Then face this question in your own heart." The doctor had his gold pince-nez in his hand, and used them as if to pin Lanny down. "Would you be jealous if your mother were to love some man?"

"Yes, sir—I'm afraid maybe I would."

"But ask yourself this: when the time comes that you fall in love with some woman—as you will before many years are past—will you expect your mother to be jealous of that woman?"

"Would she?" asked the boy, surprised.

"She may have a strong impulse to do it, and it will mean a moral struggle to put her son's welfare ahead of her own. My point is that you may have to face such a struggle—to put your mother's welfare ahead of yours. Do you think you could do it?"

"I suppose I could, if it was the right sort of man."

"Of course, if your mother fell in love with a worthless man, for example a drunkard, you would urge her against it, as any of her friends would. But you must face the fact that your mother is more apt to know what sort of man can make her happy than her son is."

"Yes, sir, I suppose so," admitted the son.

"Understand again, I know nothing about your mother's affairs. I am just discussing ordinary human behavior. The most likely situation is that your mother has a lover and is keeping it a secret from you because she thinks it would shock you."

The blood began a violent surge into Lanny's throat and cheeks. "Oh, no, sir! I don't think that can be!"

Aiming his gold pince-nez at Lanny's face, the other went on relentlessly. "It would be a wholly unnatural thing for a young woman like your mother to go for ten years without a love life. It wouldn't be good for her health, and still less for her happiness. It is far more likely that she has tried to find some man who can make her happy. So long as you were a little boy, it would be possible for her to keep this hidden from you. But from now on it will not be so easy. Sooner or later you may discover signs that your mother is in love with some man. When that happens, you have to know your duty, which is not to stand in her way, or to humiliate or embarrass her, but to say frankly and sensibly: 'Of course, I want you to be happy; I accept the situation, and will make myself agreeable to the man of your choice.' Will you remember that?"

"Yes, sir," said Lanny. But his voice was rather shaky.

VIII

Beauty had been wandering around in the shops, in a state of mind as if Lanny were having his tonsils out. A great relief to find him whole and sound, not blushing or crying or doing anything to embarrass her. "Dr. Bauer-Siemans is a well-informed man," he said with dignity. He was going to take it like that, an affair between men; his mother need not concern herself with it any further.

"Home, Pierre," said Beauty; and on the way they were silent.

Something was going on in Lanny's mind, a quite extraordinary process. There used to be a popular kind of puzzle, a picture in which a cat was hidden, a large cat filling a good part of the picture in such a way that you had a hard time to find it. But when once you had found it, it stood out so you could hardly see anything else; you couldn't imagine how you had ever looked at that picture without seeing the cat.

So now with Lanny Budd; he was looking at a picture, tracing one line and then another; until suddenly—there was a large cat grinning at him!

Farther out on the peninsula of Antibes, a mile or so from the Budd home, lived a young French painter, Marcel Detaze. He was several years younger than Beauty, a well-built, active man with a fair mustache and hair soft and fine, so that the wind blew it every way; he had grave features and dark melancholy eyes, in striking contrast with his hair. He lived in a cottage, having a peasant woman in now and then to cook him a meal and clean up. He painted the seascapes of that varied coast, loving the waves that lifted themselves in great green masses and crashed into white foam on the rocks; he painted them well, but his work wasn't known, and like so many young painters he had a problem to find room for all his canvases. Now and then he sold one, but most were stored in a shed, against the day when collectors would come bidding.

Beauty thought a great deal of Marcel's work, and had bought several specimens and hung them where her friends would see them. She watched his progress closely, and often when she came home from a walk would say: "I stopped at Marcel's; he's improving all the time." Or she would say: "I am going over to Marcel's; some of the others are coming to tea." There were half a dozen painters who had their studios within walking distance, and they would stop in and make comments on one another's work. It had never struck Lanny as strange that Béauty would go to meet a painter, instead of inviting him to her home to tea, as she did other men.

Many circumstances like that Lanny had never noticed, because he was a little boy, and the relationships of men and women were not prominent in his thoughts. But Dr. Bauer-Siemans had put the picture in front of him and told him to look for the cat; and there it was!

Marcel Detaze was Beauty's lover! She went over there to be with him, and she made up little tales because she wanted to keep the secret from Lanny. That was why the painter came so rarely to the house, and then only when there was other company; that was why he didn't come when Robbie was there, and why he had so little to do with Lanny—fearing perhaps to be drawn into intimacy and so betray something. Or perhaps he didn't like Lanny, because he thought that Lanny stood between Beauty and himself!

If the boy had found out this secret without warning it would have given him a painful shock. But now the learned doctor had told him how to take it—and he would have to obey. But not without a struggle! Lanny wanted his mother to himself; he had to bite his lip and resolve heroically that he would not hate that young French-man with the worn corduroy trousers and little blue cap. He painted the sea, but he didn't know how to swim, and like most French people on the Riviera he seemed to have the idea it would kill him to get caught out in the rain!

Well, the doctor had said that Beauty was to select her own lover, with no help from her son. So Lanny forced himself to admit that the painter was good-looking. Perhaps he had attracted Beauty because he was so different from her; he appeared as if nursing a secret sorrow. Lanny, having read a few romances, imagined the young painter in love with some lady of high degree in Paris—he had come from there—and Beauty taking pity on him and healing his broken heart. It would be like Lanny's mother to wish to heal some broken heart!

Another part of the "cat" was Beauty's relations with other men. There had been a stream of them through her life, ever since Lanny could remember. Many were rich, and some were prominent; some had come as customers of Robbie—officials, army officers, and so on —and had remained as friends. They would appear in elaborate uniforms or evening dress, and take Beauty to balls and parties; they would bring her expensive gifts which she would gently refuse to accept. They would gaze at her with adoration—this was something which Lanny had been aware of, because Beauty and her women friends made so many jokes about it.

For the first time Lanny understood a remark which he had heard his mother make; she would not "pay the price." She might have been rich, she might have had a title and lived in a palace and sailed about in a yacht like her friends, Mr. and Mrs. Hackabury; but she preferred to be true to her painter. Lanny decided that this was a truly romantic situation. Marcel was too poor to marry her; or perhaps they thought Robbie wouldn't like it. The boy suddenly realized that it was exciting to have such a beautiful mother and to share the secrets of her heart.

IX

The two, returning from the visit to the doctor, came to their home, and Lanny followed Beauty into her room. She sat down, and he went and knelt by her, and put his head against her and his arms around her waist. That way he couldn't see her face, nor she his, and it would be less embarrassing. "Beauty," he whispered, "I want to tell you something."

"Yes, dear?"

"I know about Marcel."

He felt her give a gasp. "Lanny—how"—and then: "That doctor?"

"He doesn't know—but I guessed it. I want to tell you, it's all right with me."

There was a pause; then to his astonishment, Beauty put her face in her hands and burst into tears. She sobbed and sobbed, and only after some time managed to blurt out: "Oh, Lanny, I was so afraid! I thought you'd hate me!"

"But why should I?" asked the boy. "We are going to understand each other, always—and be happy."

6

Arms and the Man

I

IT WAS February; springtime on the Riviera. The garden was carpeted with irises and anemones, and overhead the acacia trees were masses of gold. It was the height of the "season"; the boulevards blooming with gay parasols trimmed with lace and with large, floppy hats with flowers and fruits on them. On the beaches the ladies wore costumes so fragile that it seemed too bad to take them into the water, and many didn't. There was opera every night, and gambling in scores of casinos, and dancing to the music of "nigger bands"— thumping and pounding on the Côte d'Azur as if it were the Gold Coast of Africa.

There had come a postcard from Robbie in London, then another from Constantinople, and now a "wireless" from a steamship expected to dock in Marseille next day. Beauty having engagements, Pierre took Lanny in the car to meet him. It was the Route Nationale,

the main highway along the shore, becoming ever more crowded
with traffic, so that the authorities were talking about widening and
improving it; but to get things done took a long time in a land of
bureaucracy. The traveler passed scenes of great natural beauty, em-
bellished with advertisements of brandies, cigars, and mineral waters.
You wound upward into the Estérels, where the landscape was red
and the road dangerous. Then came the Maures, still rougher mountains; in the old days they had been full of bandits, but now disorder had been banished from the world, and bandits appeared only
in grand opera.

Pierre Bazoche was a swarthy, good-looking fellow of peasant
origin, who had entered the service of Mrs. Budd many years ago
and seemed unaffected by contact with wealth; he put on his uniform and drove the car whenever that was desired, and the rest of
the time he wore his smock and cut the dead wood which the mistral blew down. He spoke French with a strong accent of Provence,
and pretended that he didn't know English; but Lanny saw the
flicker of a smile now and then, which led him to believe that Pierre
was wiser than he let on. Like all French servants—those in the country, at any rate—he had adopted the family, and expressed his opinions with a freedom which gave surprise to visitors.

Pierre Bazoche and Lanny were fast friends, and chatted all the
way. The boy was curious about everything he saw, and the chauffeur was proud of his responsibility, having been cautioned many
times and made many promises. He could tell the legends of the district, while Lanny dispensed historical information from the guidebook. Toulon, the great French naval base: Lanny read statistics as
to the number of ships and their armament, and wondered if any of
it had come from Budd's.

The journey wasn't much more than a hundred miles, but cars
were not so fast in those days, nor was the highway built for speed.
When they got to the Quai du Port, the ship *Pharaoh* wasn't in sight
yet, so they went to a waterfront café and ate fried cuttlefish and
endives, and then strolled and watched the sights of one of the great
ports of the world, with ships and sailors from the seven seas. If the

pair had ventured into side streets, they would have found a "cabbage patch" of vast dimensions; but such places were dangerous, and they had promised to stay on the main avenues and never under any circumstances become separated.

II

The steamer was warped up to the quay, and there was Robbie waving, looking brown and handsome in a white linen suit. Presently they were settled in the back seat of the car, both of them beaming with happiness and the boy talking fast. Robbie wouldn't discuss business until they were alone, but Lanny told about his visit to Germany, including even the Social-Democratic editor, now six weeks in the past. Robbie took that seriously, and confirmed his son's idea that Social-Democrats were fully as reprehensible as anarchists; maybe they didn't use bombs, but they provided the soil in which bombs grew, the envy and hatred which caused unbalanced natures to resort to violence.

"I'm on another deal," the father said. "There's a big man staying on the Riviera and I have to convince him that the Budd ground-type air-cooled machine gun is the best." That was all he would say until next day, when he and his son went sailing. Out in the wide Golfe Juan, with little waves slapping the side of the boat, "That's my idea of privacy!" laughed the representative of Budd Gunmakers Corporation. Anchored here and there in the bay were the gray French warships, also keeping their own secrets. Lanny would keep his father's, as he had been so carefully trained to do.

There was another crisis in the affairs of Europe, Robbie reported; one of those underground wars in which diplomats wrestled with one another, making dire threats, always, of course, in polished French. It didn't mean much, in the father's opinion; the story of Europe was just one crisis after another. Three years back there had been a severe one over the Agadir question, and that had broken into the press; but now the wise and powerful ones were keeping matters to themselves, a far safer and more sensible way.

It was a game of bluffing, and one form it took was ordering the means to make good your threats; so came harvest-time for the munitions people. When Russia heard that Austria was equipping its army with field-guns that could shoot faster and farther, the Russians would understand that Austria was getting in position to demand that Russia should stop her arming of Serbia. So then, of course, the munitions people, who had sold field-guns to Russia and Serbia two years ago, would come hurrying to St. Petersburg and Belgrade to show what improvements they had been able to devise since that time.

It was most amusing, as Robbie told it. He knew personally most of the diplomats and statesmen and made it into a melodrama of greeds and jealousies, fears and hates. They were Robbie's oysters, which he opened and ate. Sometimes he had to buy them, and sometimes fool them, and sometimes frighten them by the perfectly real dangers of having their enemies grow too strong for them.

Robbie's talks to his son were history lessons, repeated until the lad understood them thoroughly. He told how in the last great war Germany had conquered France, and imposed a huge indemnity, and taken Alsace and Lorraine with their treasures of coal and iron ore. Now whenever French politicians wanted to gather votes, they made eloquent speeches about *la revanche,* and the French government had formed an alliance with Russia and loaned huge sums of money for the purchase of armaments. The secret undeclared wars now being waged were for support of the near-by smaller states. "The politicians of Rumania sell out to France and get a supply of French money and arms; so then the Germans hire a new set of Rumanian politicians, and when these get into power you hear reports that Rumania is buying Krupp guns." So Robbie, explaining the politics of Europe in the spring of 1914.

Britain sat on her safe little island and watched the strife, throwing her influence in support of the side which seemed weaker; it being the fixed policy of the British never to let any one nation get mastery of the Continent, but to help strengthen the most promising rival of the strongest. Just now Germany had made the mistake of building a fleet, so Britain was on the side of France and had made a secret deal to render aid if France was attacked by Germany. "That has been denied in the British Parliament," Robbie declared, "but the British diplomat's definition of a lie is an untrue statement made to a person who has a right to know the truth. Needless to say, there aren't many such persons!"

So the armaments industry was booming, and anybody who could produce guns that would shoot or shells that would explode could feel sure of a market. But an American firm was at a disadvantage, because it got practically no support from its own government. "When I go into a Balkan nation to bid against British or French, German or Austrian manufacturers, I have to beat not merely their salesmen and their bankers, but also their diplomats, who make threats and promises, demanding that the business shall come to their nationals. The American embassy will be good-natured but incompetent; and this injures not merely American businessmen and investors, but workingmen who suffer from unemployment and low wages because our government doesn't fight for its share of world trade."

This situation was now worse than ever, the father explained, because a college professor had got himself elected President of the United States, an impractical schoolmaster with a swarm of pacifist bees in his bonnet. As a result of his preachments American business was discouraged, and the country was on the way to a panic and hard times. Somehow or other the businessmen would have to take control of their country, said the representative of Budd Gunmakers.

III

Robbie mentioned to his son that the deal he had made with Rumania was in danger of falling through, and that he might have to go back to Bucharest to see about it. "Is it Bragescu?" asked Lanny —for he considered the captain as his man, in a way.

"No," replied the father. "Bragescu has played straight, at least so far as I can judge. But politicians have been pulling wires in the war department, and I've just learned that Zaharoff is behind it."

Once more this sinister figure was brought before Lanny's imagination. Zaharoff was "Vickers," the great munitions industry of Sheffield; and "Vickers" had the Maxim machine gun as their ace card. It wasn't as good as the Budd gun, but how could you prove it to officials who knew that their careers depended upon their remaining unconvinced? Robbie compared Zaharoff to a spider, sitting in the center of a web that reached into the capital of every country in the world; into legislatures, state and war departments, armies and navies, banks—to say nothing of all the interests that were bound up with munitions, such as chemicals, steel, coal, oil, and shipping.

Basil Zaharoff believed in the "rough stuff"; he had learned it in his youth and never seen reason to change. He had been born of Greek parents in Asia Minor, and as a youth had found his way to Constantinople, where he had been a fireman and a guide, both harmless-sounding occupations—until you learned that the former had meant starting fires for blackmail or burglary, while the latter had meant touting for every kind of vice. Zaharoff had become agent for a merchant of Athens, and in a London police court had pleaded guilty to misappropriating boxes of gum and sacks of gallnuts belonging to his employer.

Returning to Athens, he had represented a Swedish engineer named Nordenfeldt, who had invented a machine gun and a submarine. War was threatened between Greece and Turkey, and Zaharoff persuaded the Greek government that it could win the war by purchasing a submarine; then he went to Constantinople and pointed out to the Turkish government the grave peril in which they stood, with the result that they purchased two submarines. Said Robbie Budd: "Forty years' adherence to that simple technique has made him the armaments king of Europe."

New instruments of death were invented, one after another, and the Greek would seek out the inventor and take him into partnership. Robbie laughed and pointed out that a thing had to be invented only once, but it had to be sold many times, and that was why the ex-fireman always had the advantage over his partners. The toughest nut he had to crack was a Maine Yankee of the name of Hiram Maxim, who invented a machine gun better than the Nordenfeldt; the latter gun took four men to handle it, while the Maxim gun took only one and could shoot out the bull's eye of a target just as Bub Smith did with the Budd automatic.

Many were the stories concerning that duel between New England and the Levant; Robbie had got them directly from the mouth of his fellow-Yankee, and so had learned to fight the old Greek devil with his own Greek fire. More than once the devil had got Maxim's mechanics drunk on the eve of an important demonstration; it appeared that in those days it was impossible to find a mechanic who could have any money in his pocket without getting drunk. Later on, Maxim demonstrated his gun to high officers of the Austrian army, including the Emperor Francis Joseph, and wrote the Emperor's initials on the target with bullet holes. Basil Zaharoff stood outside the fence and watched this performance, and assured the assembled newspaper men that the gun which had performed this marvel was the Nordenfeldt—and the story thus went out to the world! Zaharoff explained to the army officers that the reason for Maxim's astonishing success was that Maxim was a master mechanic, and had made this gun by hand; it could not be produced in a factory because every part had to be exact to the hundredth part of a millimeter. This news held up the sale for a long time.

The result of the duel was that Zaharoff learned respect for the Maxim gun, while Maxim learned respect for Zaharoff. They combined their resources, and the Nordenfeldt gun was shelved. Later on Maxim and Zaharoff sold out for six and a half million dollars to the British Vickers; Zaharoff was taken into the concern, and soon became its master. The combination of British mechanical skill with Levantine salesmanship proved unbeatable; but that was all going to be changed, now that the president of Budd Gunmakers Corporation had been persuaded to let his youngest son come over to Europe and show what a Connecticut Yankee could do in the court of King Basil!

IV

When the head salesman of a large business enterprise took time
to explain such details to a boy, he pretended that he wanted to unbosom himself; but of course he was following out his plan of preparing the boy for his future career. Robbie Budd had for his son a
dream which was no modest one; and now and then he would drop a
hint of it—enough to take away the boy's breath.

Basil Zaharoff was sixty-five now, and couldn't last forever. Who
was going to take his place as master of the most important of all
trades? And where was the industry of the future to be situated? In
Sheffield, England? In the French village of Creusot? In the German
Ruhr, or at Skoda in Austria, or on the Volga, as the Russian Tsar
was daring to dream? Robbie Budd had picked out a far safer loca-
tion, up the Newcastle River in Connecticut. "It'll not be an extension of Budd's," he explained; "but a new and completely modern
plant. No enemy can ever get to it, and when it's in operation it will
mean three things: American workingmen will supply the world, an
American family will collect the money, and America will stand
behind its ramparts, able to defy all the other nations put together.
That's what we'll some day have to do, so why not get ready?"

Robbie went on to explain what Zaharoff was doing in France.
The country's armament trust was known as Schneider-Creusot, and
for years the old Greek devil had been intriguing to get control of
it and share the profits of the rearming of Russia. He had bought a
popular weekly paper so that he could tell the French people what
he wished to have believed. He had endowed a home for retired
French sailors and been awarded the rosette of the Legion of Honor.
He had bought a Belgian bank, so as to become a director in Schneider's; and when his rivals had kicked him out, he had proceeded to
tie up Europe in a net of intrigue in order to bring them to their
knees.

First, he had gone to Turkey, and as "Vickers, Limited" had signed
a contract to provide that country with warships and arsenals. This
had frightened Russia, whose dream was to get Constantinople; so

the old rascal had proceeded to that country, and pointed out to its officials the grave danger to them of remaining dependent upon foreign armaments. Zaharoff offered, through his British Vickers, to build a complete modern plant at Tsaritsyn on the Volga, and to lease all the Vickers patents and trade secrets to Russia. This, in turn, had frightened the French; for they could never be sure of the position of Britain in any future war, and if Russia got help from Britain, it would no longer need help from France. To make matters worse, Zaharoff had spread the story that the German Krupps were buying the Putilov arms plant in Russia. All this had broken the French nerve, and Schneider had had to give way and let Zaharoff have his share of the money which France had just loaned to Russia.

"That's why you have to watch the papers," said the father, and showed an item he had clipped that very day. Vickers had received orders from the Russian government for thirty-two million dollars' worth of armaments. "More than one-fourth the whole French loan!" sighed Robbie—deeply grieved because his country had no part in it. America's arms plants were pitifully small, and the business they could pick up in Europe was the crumbs that fell from a rich man's table. "But you and I are going to change all that!" said the salesman to his son.

V

They let down their anchor for a while and caught some fish, and Lanny told about Mr. Elphinstone, and got teased about his new English accent. Then Robbie mentioned that he had to go to Monte Carlo the following day, having an appointment with a Turkish pasha who was interested in buying ground-type, air-cooled machine guns. Robbie had found out that France was lending money to Turkey, with which to pay Zaharoff for his warships and arsenals; so the Turkish officials had plenty of cash. "It's a queer mix-up," Robbie said; "I'm not sure if I'll ever understand it. Even though the French are lending money to Turkey, they appear to distrust it, and don't want it armed too fast; but the Germans seem to want Turkey

armed—at French expense, of course. I am dealing with Turkish officials who are secretly in German pay, or so I have reason to believe."
Lanny said he was getting dizzy at that point.

"Yes, it's funny," the father agreed. "The minister I talked with
in Constantinople said that our guns were too cheap; they couldn't
possibly be good at that price. Of course he wanted me to put the
price higher, and give him a Rolls-Royce, or sell it to him second-
hand for a hundred dollars. Finally I was advised to take up the matter with another minister who is disporting himself at Monte Carlo."

"Oh, yes," said Lanny, "I saw him at the motorboat races; he wore
a large striped necktie and yellow suede shoes." The father smiled
and remarked that Oriental peoples all loved color.

Robbie told a sensational story about what had happened on board
the ship. A few hours before reaching Marseille, the door of his
cabin had been jimmied, and a portfolio of his papers, relating to this
Turkish deal, had been stolen. Fortunately the most secret letters,
which might have cost the life of that minister in Constantinople,
had been sewed up in the lining of Robbie's coat—he patted the spot.
But it was highly inconvenient to lose the drawings of the gun. "Of
course it was Zaharoff," the father added.

"You mean that he was on that ship?" asked Lanny.

The other laughed. "No; the old wolf did that sort of thing when
he was young, and belonged to the *tulumbadschi*, those firemen of
Constantinople who were really gangsters. But now he's an officer in
the Legion of Honor, and when he wants a burglary done he hires
somebody else."

Lanny was excited, of course. "You need a bodyguard!" he exclaimed; and then, a marvelous idea: "Oh, Robbie, why don't you
take me with you to Monte?"

The father laughed. "As a bodyguard?"

"If you have something you want taken care of, they wouldn't
suspect me; and I'd hang onto it, believe me!"

Lanny's fervor mounted, and he began a campaign. "Listen, Robbie, I stayed home and didn't go to school for fear I'd miss seeing
you; and then you come and only stay one day, and maybe you'll be

called to Bucharest as soon as you get through at Monte. But if you'll let me go with you I can see you a lot—you're not going to be with that Turk all day and night. When you are, I'll keep out of the way —I'll get things to read, or go to a movie, and I'll stay in the hotel room at night, honest I will. Please, Robbie, please, you really ought to have somebody with you, and if I'm ever to learn about the in- dustry—you just can't imagine what it'll mean to me. . . ."

And so on, until the father said: "All right." Lanny was so happy he stood on his head in the stern of the boat and kicked his bare legs in the air.

VI

Beauty insisted upon lending them her car, so that Pierre would go along to help take care of Lanny. They would have a Budd auto- matic in the car, and Pierre knew how to use it—he couldn't fail to learn in a household where boxes of cartridges lay around like choc- olates in other homes. Robbie laughed and said he didn't think Za- haroff had had any murder done for some years; but anyhow, it gave a fourteen-year-old boy more thrills than all the movies produced up to February 1914.

The road from Antibes to Nice is straight and flat, and there were advertising signs and a big racetrack, many motorcars, and in those days still a few carriages. When you pass Nice you travel on one of three roads, called *corniches*, which means "shelves"; if you wanted scenery you chose the highest shelf, and if you wanted to get there you chose the lowest, but in either case you kept tooting your horn, for no matter how carefully you made the turns, you could never tell what lunatic might come whirling around the next one.

Monaco is a tiny province with a ruler of its own. The "Prince" of those days was interested in oceanography, and had constructed a great aquarium; but this wasn't such a novelty to Lanny, who had learned to expel the air from his lungs and sink down to where the fishes live. "Monte," as the smart people call it, is a small town on a flat rocky height which juts out into the sea. There are terraces below it, carved out of the rock, and you can look over the water from your hotel windows; down below you hear incessant shooting, for next to playing roulette and baccarat, the favorite amusement of the visitors is killing pigeons. The tender-minded comfort themselves with the thought that somebody eats those that fall, and presumably the hawks end the troubles of those that fly away wounded.

Lanny had been here before, and there was nothing new to him in a street of fashionable shops and hotels. They went to the most expensive of the latter, and Robbie engaged a suite, and sent up his card to the Turkish dignitary, whose secretary came and requested in polished French that "M. Bood" would be so kind as to return in an hour, as the pasha was "in conference." Robbie said, certainly, and they went out to stroll in the beautiful gardens of the Casino, which have walks lined with palm trees and flowering shrubs. There was a little circle of flower beds, and as they came to it, Robbie said, in a low voice: "Here he comes."

"Who?" whispered Lanny; and the answer was: "The man we talked about in the boat."

The boy's heart gave a jump. He looked and saw a tall, gray-haired gentleman turning onto the other side of the circle. He paid no attention to them, so Lanny could take a good look.

Basil Zaharoff had been a vigorous man in his youth, but had grown heavy. He wore the garment of an Englishman on formal occasions, which is called a frock coat, cut large as if to hide his central bulk, and hanging down in back all the way to his knees; a smooth, black, and very ugly garment supposed to confer dignity upon its wearer. Added to it were striped trousers, shoes with spats, and on his head a tall cylinder of smooth black silk. The munitions king had a gray mustache and what was called an "imperial," a tuft of hair starting from the front of his chin, and hanging down three or four inches below it. He walked with a cane, stooping slightly, which made his hooked nose the most prominent thing about him and gave the odd impression that he was smelling his way.

"Having his constitutional," said Robbie, after Zaharoff had passed. Lanny took a rear view of the man who was worth so many millions, and had got them by having other men's papers stolen. "He comes here often," explained the father. "He stays at the hotel with his duquesa."

"He is married?" asked the boy, and Robbie told the strange story of this master of Europe who could not buy the one thing he most wanted.

Some twenty-five years ago, when the ex-fireman had got well under way as a salesman of munitions, he went to Spain on a deal, and met a seventeen-year-old duchess of that realm, owning almost as many names as Zaharoff now owned companies. Robbie, who liked to make fun of the pretensions of Europe, said that the only case he had ever heard of a person having more names was a runaway slave whom his great-uncle had rescued by way of the "underground railroad." The Spanish lady was María del Pilar Antonia Angela Patrocino Simón de Muguiro y Berute, Duquesa de Marqueni y Villafranca de los Caballeros. Legend had it that Zaharoff had met her on a sleeping car, by rescuing her from the cruelties of her husband on her wedding night. However that may be, it was certain that the husband had become violently insane, and was confined in a cell, and for twenty-five years Zaharoff and the lady had been living together, but couldn't marry because the Catholic Church, of which she was a devout member, does not permit divorce. It was usually possible to persuade the Church authorities to annul a marriage on some pretext, but it would have been embarrassing in this case, for the reason that the mad duke happened to be a cousin of King Alfonso.

The couple were devoted to each other, and Robbie said that might be one of the reasons for the business success of the ex-fireman; he was proof against traps which men bait for one another with women. The former peasant boy naturally felt honored to have the love of a duquesa, and she helped him to meet the right people. "Like you and Beauty!" remarked Lanny.

VII

Father and son went back to the hotel, and Robbie was invited upstairs to his pasha. Lanny had one of those little Tauchnitz novels in his pocket, and was going to sit quietly in a big armchair and read. But first, being young and full of curiosity, he stood looking about the entrance hall of this imitation palace where the millionaires of Europe came to seek their pleasures both greedy and cruel. Zaharoff came with his duquesa; Turkish pashas came with their boys; English milords, Indian maharajas, Russian grand dukes— Lanny knew, because his mother had met them. Battles were fought here, part of the underground war that Robbie talked about, for the ownership of armaments, of coal and steel and oil. . . .

Lanny's eyes, sweeping the lobby, saw a man in chauffeur's uniform come in at the front door, walk the length of the red plush carpet to the desk, and hand an envelope to the clerk. "M. Zaharoff," he said, and turned and retraced his steps to the door.

Zaharoff! Lanny's eyes followed the clerk and saw him turn and put the letter into one of the many pigeonholes which covered the wall behind him. Lanny marked the spot; for even a pigeonhole is of interest when it belongs to a munitions king.

Lanny hadn't known that his mind could work so fast. Perhaps it was something that had already reasoned itself out in his subconsciousness. Zaharoff had stolen Robbie's papers, including the drawings of the Budd ground-type air-cooled machine gun, essential to the making of deals. Somebody ought to punish the thief and teach him a lesson; as Robbie had put it in his playful way: "Fight the old Greek devil with his own Greek fire."

The clerk, who looked as if he had just been lifted out of a bandbox, was bored. He tapped his pencil on the polished mahogany top of the counter which separated him from the public; the midafternoon train had come in, and no automobiles were arriving. Two bellhops, in blue uniforms with rows of gold buttons, sat on a bench around a corner of the lobby, and poked each other in the ribs and tried to shove each other off their seats; the clerk moved over to where he could see them, and at his stern taps the bellhops straightened up and stared solemnly in front of them.

Around this corner sat a young lady who attended to the telephone switchboard; she too was mentally unoccupied—there being no gossip over the wires. The clerk moved toward her and spoke, and she smiled at him. Lanny moved to where he could see them; it was what the French call *le flirt*, and promised to last for a few moments. Lanny noted that the clerk had passed the point where he could see the pigeonholes.

The boy did not dart or do anything to reveal the excitement that had gripped him. He moved with due casualness to the far end of the counter, raised the part which was on hinges and served as a gate, and stepped behind it, just as if he belonged there. He went to the pigeonholes, took out the Zaharoff letter, and slipped it into his pocket. A bright idea occurring to him, he took a letter from another pigeonhole and slipped it into the Zaharoff hole. The clerk would think it was his own mistake. Still quietly, Lanny retraced his steps; he strolled over to one of the large overstuffed chairs of the lobby and took a seat. *Le flirt* continued.

VIII

It was Lanny Budd's first venture into crime, and he learned at once a number of its penalties. First of all, the nervous strain involved; his heart was pounding like that of a young bird, and his head was in a whirl. No longer did he have the least interest in a Tauchnitz novel or any other. He was looking about him furtively, to see if anybody hiding behind a pillar of the lobby had been watching him.

Second, he discovered that stealing involves lying, and that one lie requires others. What would he say if anyone had seen him? He had thought that the letter was in the pigeonhole of his own room. A mere mistake in numbers, that was all. But why had he not asked the clerk for the letter? Well, he had seen the clerk busy talking with the young lady. What were the chances that the clerk would know the name of Budd, and realize that Budd and Zaharoff were rivals for the armaments trade of the world?

Third, the moral confusion. Lanny had always been a good little boy, and had done what his parents asked him, and so had never had any serious pangs of conscience. But now—should he have done it or not? Did one bad turn deserve another? Should you really fight the devil with fire? After all, who was going to punish Zaharoff if Lanny didn't? The police? Robbie had said that Zaharoff could do anything with the police that he chose—was he not the richest man in France and an officer of the Legion of Honor?

Lanny wished that his father would come and decide the matter for him. But the father didn't come; he had a deal to discuss, and might be gone for a long time. If Lanny got hungry, he was to go to the restaurant of the hotel and have his supper. But Lanny didn't think he'd ever be hungry again. He sat and tried to figure out, was he ashamed of himself or was he proud? It was the famed New England conscience at work, a long way from home.

He tried to imagine what might be in that letter. His fancy went off on excursions wild as the *Arabian Nights*. The agent who had stolen Robbie's portfolio from the ship was waiting to tell what he had found, and where it was now hidden; Robbie and Lanny would go at once to the place, and with the help of the Budd automatic would retrieve the property. The shape of the envelope suggested that the letter might be from a lady. Perhaps a woman spy—Lanny knew about them from a recent American movie.

What might the handwriting reveal? After many cautious glances Lanny took out the letter and, keeping it covered by his book, studied the inscription. Yes, undoubtedly a woman's. Lanny held the book and letter up to his nose; still less doubt now. The old rascal, living in this fashionable hotel with his duquesa, was receiving assignation notes from another woman! Lanny knew about such doings, not merely from movies, but from gossip of his mother's friends. He had heard how politicians and others were trapped and plundered by blackmailers. Robbie would let Zaharoff know that he had this incriminating document in his hands, and Robbie's property would be returned to him by a messenger who would neither ask nor answer questions.

Persons came into the hotel, and others departed; Lanny watched them all. Some took seats and chatted, and Lanny tried to hear what they were saying; from now on he was surrounded by intrigues, and any chance phrase might reveal something. Two ladies sat near him, and talked about the races, and about a skirt cut in the new fashion, with slits on the side. They were shallow creatures, heedless of the undeclared war now going on in Europe. Lanny got up and moved to another chair.

Presently came a sight which he had been expecting. Through the revolving glass doors of the entrance strode a large figure in a voluminous black frock coat, with a black silk tower on his head. The doorman in gorgeous uniform was revolving the doors for him, lest he have to make even that much effort with his hands. The bellhops leaped to attention, the clerk stood like a statue of gentility, the conversation in the lobby fell to whispers, the whole world was in suspense as the munitions king strode down the pathway of red velvet, smelling his way with his prominent hooked nose.

He stopped at the desk. Lanny was too far away to hear a word that was spoken, but he could understand the pantomime just as well. The clerk turned and took a letter from a pigeonhole and handed it to the great man with a respectful bow and murmur. The great man looked at it, then handed it back to the clerk. The clerk looked at it and registered surprise. He turned hastily and began taking other letters from pigeonholes and looking at them. Finally he turned to the great man with more bows and murmurings. The great man stalked to the lift and disappeared.

IX

Robbie came at last; and Lanny said quickly: "Something has happened. I want to tell you about it." They went up to the room, and Lanny looked around, to be sure they were alone. "Here's a letter for Zaharoff," he said, and held it out to his father.

The other was puzzled. "How did you get it?"

"I took it out of his box downstairs. Nobody saw me."

Even before the father said a word, almost before he had time to comprehend the idea, Lanny knew that he shouldn't have done it; he wished he hadn't done it.

"You mean," said Robbie, "you stole this from the hotel desk?"

"Well, Robbie, he stole your papers, and I thought this might refer to them."

Robbie was looking at his son as if he couldn't quite grasp what he was hearing. It was most uncomfortable for Lanny, and the blood began burning in his cheeks. "Whatever put that into your head, son?"

"You did, Robbie. You said you would fight the old devil with his own Greek fire."

"Yes, Lanny—but to steal!"

"You have had papers stolen for you—at least I got that idea, Robbie. You told me you had got some papers belonging to that Prince Vanya, or whoever it was, in Russia."

"Yes, son; but that was different."

A subtle point, hard for a boy to get. There were things you hired servants to do, detectives and that sort of persons, whose business it was. But you wouldn't do these things yourself; your dignity was offended by the very thought of doing them. Lanny had stepped out of his class as a gentleman.

Robbie stood staring at the piece of fashionable stationery, addressed in a lady's handwriting; and the boy's unhappiness grew. "I honestly thought I'd be helping you," he pleaded.

The father said: "Yes, I know, of course. But you made a mistake."

Another pause, and Robbie inquired: "Do you know if Zaharoff has come back to the hotel?" When Lanny answered that he had, the father said: "I think you must take this letter to him."

"*Take* it, Robbie?"

"Tell him how you got it, and apologize."

"But, Robbie, how awful! What excuse can I give?"

"Don't give any excuse. Tell him the facts."

"Shall I tell him who I am?"

"That's a fact, isn't it?"

"Shall I tell him that you think he stole your papers?"

"That's a fact, too."

Lanny saw that his father was in an implacable mood; and, rattled as the boy was, he had sense enough to know what it meant. Robbie wished to teach him a lesson, so that he wouldn't turn into a thief. "All right," he said. "Whatever you say."

He took the letter and started toward the door. Then, an idea occurring to him, he turned. "Suppose he beats me?"

"I don't think he'll do that," replied the other. "You see, he's a coward."

<h2 style="text-align:center">X</h2>

Lanny went by the stairway, not wanting anybody to see him. He knew the room number. He knocked, and to a young man who came to the door he said: "I have a letter for M. Zaharoff."

"May I have it, please?" asked the man.

"I have to hand it to him personally."

The secretary took him in with practiced professional eye. "Will you give me your name?"

"I would rather give it to M. Zaharoff. Just tell him, please, that I have a letter which I must put into his hands. It'll only take a moment."

Perhaps the secretary saw about Lanny Budd those signs which are not easy to counterfeit, and which establish even a youngster as entitled to consideration. "Will you come in, please?" he said, and the lad entered a drawing room full of gilt and plush and silk embroidery and marble and ormolu—all things which fortify the self-esteem of possessors of wealth. Lanny waited, standing. He didn't feel at home and didn't expect to.

In a minute or two a door was opened, and the master of Europe came in. He had changed his ugly broadcloth coat for a smoking jacket of green flowered silk. He came about halfway and then said: "You have a message for me?" The boy was surprised by his voice, which was low and well modulated; his French was perfect.

"M. Zaharoff," said Lanny, with all the firmness he could summon, "this is a letter of yours which I stole. I have brought it to you with my apologies."

The old man was so surprised that he did not put out his hand for the letter. "You *stole* it?"

"My father told me that you caused his portfolio to be stolen, so I thought I would pay you back. But my father does not approve of that, so I am bringing the letter."

The old spider sensed a trembling in his web. Such a trembling may be caused by something that spiders eat, or again it may be caused by something that eats spiders. The cold blue eyes narrowed. "So your father thinks that I employ thieves?"

"He says that is your practice; but he doesn't want it to be mine."

"Did he tell you to tell me that?"

"He told me that whatever questions you asked me I was to answer with the facts."

This, obviously, was something which might be of importance. Wariness and concentration were in every feature of Basil Zaharoff He knew how to watch and think, and let the other person betray himself. But Lanny had said his say, and continued to hold the letter.

So finally the munitions king took it; but he did not look at it. "May I ask your name, young man?"

"My name is Lanning Prescott Budd."

"Of Budd Gunmakers Corporation?"

"That is my family, sir."

"Your father is Robert Budd, then?"

"Yes, sir."

Another silence; Lanny had the feeling that everything that had ever been in his soul was being read and judged. He felt sure that the prominent hooked nose was smelling him. "Have a seat, please," said the old man, at last.

Lanny seated himself on the front half of a chair, and the Greek sat near. He examined the letter, then opened it slowly. A smile relieved the concentration on his face, and he handed the document to the boy, saying: "Oblige me, please."

Lanny thought it was his duty to read it. It said, in French: "The Marquise des Pompailles requests the pleasure of the company of M. Zaharoff and the Duquesa de Villafranca to tea at five this afternoon to meet the Prince and Princess von Glitzenstein."

"A little late," said the munitions king dryly.

"I am sorry, sir," murmured Lanny, his face burning.

"We should not have gone," said the other. In all Lanny's imaginings, it had never occurred to him that an old Greek devil might have a sense of humor; but it was now plain that he did. His lips smiled; but oddly enough, Lanny felt that the blue eyes were not smiling. They still watched.

"Thank you, sir," said Lanny, returning the letter.

Another silence. Finally the old gentleman remarked: "So Robert Budd thinks I have had his portfolio stolen! May I inquire where this happened?"

"On board the steamer *Pharaoh*, sir."

"The thief has not yet reported to me; but as soon as he does, I promise that I will return the property unopened—just as you have done with mine. You will tell your father that?"

"Certainly, sir. Thank you." Lanny was quite solemn about it, and only afterward did he realize that Zaharoff had been "spoofing" him.

"And you won't feel that you have to intercept any more of my invitations?"

"No, sir."

"You are going to be an honorable and truthtelling young gentleman from now on?"

"I will try, sir," said Lanny.

"I, too, used to have the same thought upon occasions," said the munitions king. Was it wistfulness or was it humor in his soft voice? "However, I found that it would be necessary for me to retire from my present business—and unfortunately it is the only one I have."

Lanny didn't know how to reply, so there was another silence.

When Zaharoff spoke again, it was in a business-like tone. "Young man, you say that your father told you to state the facts."

"Yes, sir."

"Then tell me: does your father wish to see me?"

"Not that I know of, sir."

"You don't think that he sent you here for that purpose?"

Lanny was taken aback. "Oh, no, sir!" he exclaimed. Then realizing the full implication of the question, he decided to fight back. "My father once told me about Bismarck—who said that the way he fooled people was by telling them the truth."

The old man smiled again. "You are a clever lad," said he; "but don't let Bismarck fool you with nonsense like that. Do you think your father would object to seeing me?"

"I don't know why he should, sir."

Zaharoff had in his hand the letter from the Marquise des Pompailles. He went to the escritoire and sat down and did some writing on it. Then he handed this to the boy, saying: "Read it again." Lanny saw that Zaharoff had marked out some of the words and written others over them. He read:

"M. Basil Zaharoff requests the pleasure of the company of M. Robert Budd and his son to tea this afternoon to discuss the problems of the armaments industry."

XI

The duquesa did not appear for the occasion. The waiter who brought the tray poured whisky and soda for the two gentlemen, and tea for Lanny; then he retired with quick bows.

The peasant boy from Asia Minor had become a citizen of whatever country he was in; so now he was an American businessman, using American business language. He sat erect and spoke with decision. He said that while he had never met Mr. Budd, he had watched him from a distance and admired him. Zaharoff himself had been a "hustler" in his time, although the Americans had not yet taught him that word. He said that the leaders of the armaments industry ought to understand one another, because theirs was the only trade in which competitors helped instead of harming. The more armaments one nation got, the more the other nations were compelled to get. "We are all boosters for one another, Mr. Budd."

It was flattering to be called one of the leaders of the armaments industry, but Robbie tried not to feel too exalted. He said that the future of the industry had never looked so bright to him as it did just then; they could all afford to be "bullish." The other replied that he could say even more than that; they were going to have to learn to go into a new element, the air. Robbie agreed with this also. Basil Zaharoff forgot now and then that he was an American, and set down his glass and rubbed his hands together, slowly and thoughtfully.

He soon made it clear why he had asked for a conference. He looked at Robbie and then at Lanny, and said: "I suppose this bright little man never talks about his father's affairs?" Robbie answered that whatever mistakes the little man might make, he would never make that one.

Tactfully, and with many flatteries, the Greek trader declared that he had conceived a great admiration for the methods of New England Yankees. He wanted to do for Mr. Budd what he had done nearly forty years ago for the Maine Yankee named Maxim. He gave Mr. Budd to understand that he was prepared to make him an excellent proposition; he added that he meant those words in the most generous sense; he made a gesture of baring his heart.

Robbie answered with equal courtesy that he appreciated this honor, but was unfortunately compelled to decline it. No, it was not merely that he was under contract; it was a question of home ties and loyalties. Zaharoff interrupted him, urging him to think carefully; his offer would not merely satisfy Mr. Budd, but even surprise him. The business he was doing at present would be small indeed compared to what he could do if he would join forces with Vickers, Limited. The whole world was open to them——

"Mr. Zaharoff," said the younger man, "you must understand that Budds have been making small arms for some eighty years, and it's a matter of prestige with us. I am not just a munitions salesman, but a member of a family."

"Ah, yes," said the old gentleman. "Ah, yes!" Had this young fellow meant to give him a sword prick? "Family dignity is an important thing. But I wonder"—he paused and closed his eyes, doing his wondering intensely—"if there might be the possibility of a combination—some stock that might be purchased . . . ?"

"There is stock on the market," replied Robbie; "but not very much, I imagine."

"What I meant is if your family might see the advantage . . . ? We have Vickers in most of the countries of Europe, and why not in the States? Do you think that members of your family might care to sell?"

Their eyes met; it was the climax of a duel. "My guess is, Mr. Zaharoff, they would rather buy Vickers than sell Budd's."

"Ah, indeed!" replied the munitions king. Not by the flicker of an eyelash would he show surprise. "That would be a large transaction, Mr. Budd."

It was David defying Goliath; for of course Budd's was a pygmy compared to Vickers. "We can leave it open for the moment," said Robbie, blandly. "As it happens, my son and I have one advantage which we have not earned. I am under forty, and he is fourteen."

Never was war more politely declared, nor a declaration of war more gracefully accepted. "Ah, yes," said the munitions king— whose duquesa had no sons, only two daughters. "Perhaps I have made a mistake and devoted myself to the wrong industry, Mr. Budd. I should have been finding out how to prolong life, instead of how to destroy it. Perhaps thirty years from now, you may decide that you have made the same mistake." The speaker paused for a moment, and then added: "If there is any life left then."

A man who wishes to succeed in the world of action has to keep his mind fixed upon what he is doing; he has to like what he is doing, and not be plagued with doubts and scruples. But somewhere in the depths of the soul of every man lurk weaknesses, watching for a chance to slip past the censor who guards our conduct. Was it because this naïve little boy had broken into the munitions king's life with his odd problem of conscience? Or had the father touched some chord by his reference to age? Anyhow, the master of Europe was moved to lift a corner of the mask he wore. Said he:

"Have you noticed, Mr. Budd, the strange situation in which we find ourselves? We spend our lives manufacturing articles of commerce, and every now and then we are seized by the painful thought that these articles may be used."

Robbie smiled. If a civilized man has to face the secrets of his soul, let him by all means do it with humor. "It appears," he suggested, "the ideal society would be one in which men devoted their energies to producing things which they never intended to use."

"But unfortunately, Mr. Budd, when one has perfected something, the impulse to try it out is strong. I have here a torpedo"—the munitions salesman held it up before the mind's eye—"to the devising of which my great establishment has devoted twenty years. Some say that it will put the battleship out of business. Others say no. Am I to go to my grave not knowing the answer?"

Robbie felt called upon to smile again, but not to answer.

"And this new project upon which we are all working, Mr. Budd—that of dropping bombs from the air! Will that be tried? Shall we have to take our armies and navies into the skies? And ask yourself this: Suppose some nation should decide that its real enemies are the makers of munitions? Suppose that instead of dropping bombs upon battleships and fortresses, they should take to dropping them upon de luxe hotels?"

The mask was up, and Lanny knew what his father meant when he said that Zaharoff was a coward. The magnate who was supposed to hold the fate of Europe in his hands had shrunk, and had become a tormented old man whose hands trembled and who wanted to break down and beg people not to go to war—or perhaps beg God to forgive him if they did.

But when Lanny made this remark to his father afterward, the father laughed. He said: "Don't fool yourself, kid! The old hellion will fight us twice as hard for the next contract."

BOOK TWO

A Little Cloud

7

The Isles of Greece

ROBBIE went to Bucharest, and then back to Connecticut, and the vacant place in Lanny's life was taken by Mr. and Mrs. Ezra Hackabury and their yacht *Bluebird*.

They arrived several days late, because they had a bad passage across the Atlantic. But their friends didn't have to worry, for they had sent frequent messages. The message from Madeira said: "Ezra sick." The message from Gibraltar said: "Ezra sicker." The one from Marseille said: "Ezra no better." When finally the *Bluebird* showed up in the Golfe Juan and the soap manufacturer and his wife were brought ashore, he had to be helped out of the launch by two of his sailors in white ducks. He was a large, florid-faced man, and when the color went out of his skin it made you think of that celebrated painting—futurist, cubist, or whatever it was—"The Woman Who Swallowed the Mustard-Pot."

They got him into the car, and then to Bienvenu. He asked them to put him in a lawn swing, so as to "taper him off"; he insisted that the columns of the veranda were trying to hit him. He was one of those fellows who make jokes even when they have to moan and groan them. He was afraid to take even a drink of water, because the drops turned to rubber and bounced out of his stomach. All he wanted was to lie down and repeat, over and over: "Jesus, how I hate the sea!"

Nobody could have afforded a better contrast to Mr. Hackabury than the lady he had chosen for his partner. The sea and the wind hadn't disturbed so much as one glossy black hair of her head. Her

119

skin was white and soft, her coloring was of pastel shades which she never changed; in fact, she didn't have to do a thing for herself, so the other women enviously declared. She didn't have to be witty, hardly even to speak; she just had to be still, cool, and statuesque, and now and then smile a faint mysterious smile. At once the men all started to compare her to Mona Lisa and throw themselves at her feet. She was somewhat under thirty, at the height of her charms; she knew it, and was kind in a pitying way to this large, crude Middle Westerner who had had his sixty-third birthday and who made soap for several million kitchens in order to provide her with the background and setting she required.

Edna Hackabury, née Slazens, was the daughter of a clerk in the office of an American newspaper in Paris. Being poor and the possessor of a striking figure, she had served as a model for several painters, one of them Jesse Blackless, Beauty's brother. She had married a painter, and when he became a drunkard, had divorced him. It was Beauty Budd who had helped to make a match for her with a retired widower, traveling in Europe with a man secretary and looking for diversion after a lifetime of immersion in soap.

Edna's beauty had swept the manufacturer off his feet; he had married her as quickly as the French laws permitted, and had taken her on a honeymoon to Egypt, and then back to the town called Reubens, Indiana. Reubens had been awe-stricken by this elegant creature from Paris, but Edna had not reciprocated its sentiments; she hadn't the remotest intention of living there. She stayed just long enough to be polite, and to make sure that her three stepsons, all married men with families, understood the soap business and would work hard to provide her with the money she required. Then she began pointing out to her husband the folly of wasting their lives in this "hole" when there were so many wonderful things to be enjoyed in other parts of the world.

So they set forth, and when they got to New York, Edna tactfully broached the idea that, instead of traveling in vulgar promiscuity on steamships and trains, they should get a yacht, and be able to invite their chosen friends to whatever place might take their fancy. Ezra was staggered; he was a bad sailor, and hadn't the least notion why it was "vulgar" to meet a lot of other people. But his wife assured him that he would soon get his sea legs, and that when he met the right people, he would lose interest in the wrong ones. The money was his, wasn't it? Why not get some fun out of it, instead of leaving it to children and grandchildren who wouldn't have the least idea what to do with it?

So the Hackaburys went shopping for yachts. You could buy one all ready-made, it appeared, with officers and crew and even a supply of fuel oil and canned goods. They found a Wall Street "plunger" who had plunged too deep, and they had bought him out, and sailed to Europe in lovely spring weather, and attended the Cowes regatta of 1913 in near-royal style. This was the summer that Lanny had spent at Hellerau; the Hackaburys had explored the fiords of Norway, taking Lord and Lady Eversham-Watson, and the Baroness de la Tourette and her friend Eddie Patterson, a rich young American who lived all over Europe; also Beauty Budd and her painter friend, Marcel Detaze, and a couple of unattached Englishmen of the best families to dance, play cards, and make conversation.

At first it had seemed shocking to Ezra Hackabury to have as guests two couples who weren't married, but who visited each other's cabin and stayed. But his wife told him this was a provincial prejudice on his part; it was quite "the thing" among the best people. The baroness was the victim of an unhappy marriage, while Beauty was poor, and of course couldn't marry her painter; however, she was dear and sweet and very good company, and had helped Edna to meet her Ezra, for which they both owed a debt of gratitude which they must do their best to repay. The considerate thing would be for Ezra to buy a couple of Marcel's seascapes and hang them in the saloon of the *Bluebird*. Ezra did so.

II

The cruise proved such a success that another had been arranged, and the guests were arriving with their mountains of luggage, ready to set out for the eastern Mediterranean. Edna and Beauty had one of their heart-to-heart talks, and Beauty told about Baron Livens and Dr. Bauer-Siemans, and how cleverly Lanny had guessed about Marcel. Edna said: "How perfectly dear of him!" She was a long-time friend of that polite little boy, and at once suggested that he should go along on the cruise. "He never gets in anybody's way, and it'll be educational for him." Beauty said she was sure he would love it; and the mistress of the yacht added: "We can put him in the cabin with Ezra."

It was going to be a delightful adventure for all of them. Marcel Detaze was looking forward to painting the Isles of Greece, where burning Sappho loved and sung. The poetry of Byron being famous, as well as that of Sappho, everybody looked upon the region as one of glamour, and the guidebooks all agreed that it was a paradise in early spring. Everybody was pleased except poor Ezra, who knew only one fact: that every isle was surrounded by water. "The sea is insane," he kept saying. At first he refused to go; but when he saw tears in his wife's beautiful dark eyes, he said: "Well, not till I've had some food."

The soapman's appetite came back with a rush, and next day he was able to move about the garden, and the day after that he wanted to explore the Cap d'Antibes; no, not a drive, but a walk, actually a walk of several miles. The only person who was capable of such a feat was Lanny, who took charge of the one-time farm-boy and answered his questions about how the country people lived here, and what they ate, and what things cost.

The pair sat on the rocks of the Cap and looked at the water, and Mr. Hackabury admitted that it was fine from that vantage point; the coloring varied from pale green in the shallows to deep purple in the distance, and on the bottom were many-colored veils and palm fronds waving like slow-motion pictures. "Could you catch those fish?" asked Mr. Hackabury; and then: "Are they good to eat?" and: "What do the fishermen get for them in the market?" He looked at the anchored vessels of the French navy, and said: "I hate war and everything about it. How can your father stand to be thinking about guns all the time?"

He told Lanny about the soap business; where the fats came from and how they were treated, and the new "straight-line" machinery which turned out cakes of soap faster than you could count them. He told about the selling, a highly competitive business; making the public want your kind was a game which would take you a lifetime to learn and was full of amusing quirks. In fact, Ezra Hackabury selling kitchen soap sounded remarkably like Robbie Budd selling machine guns.

Also Mr. Hackabury talked about America; he thought it was terrible that a boy had never seen his own country. "They are a different people," he said, "and don't let anybody fool you, they are better." Lanny said his father thought so too, and had told him a lot about Yankee mechanics and farmers, how capable and hard-headed they were, and yet how kind. The soapman told about life in a small village, which Reubens had been when he was a boy. Everybody was independent, and a man got what he worked for and no more; people were not worldly, the stranger was welcomed and not suspected and snubbed. Pretty soon the lilacs and honeysuckle would be in bloom.

"Yes," said Lanny, "I've seen them. Mrs. Chattersworth, who lives up on the heights above Cannes, has some in her gardens, and they do very well."

To this the other replied: "I suppose they'll live here if they have to, but they won't like it."

In short, the old gentleman was homesick. He said that back in Reubens were fellows who had grown up with him, and would now be pitching horseshoes on the south side of a big red barn where the snow melted early. Lanny had never heard about pitching horseshoes and asked what it was. "I know where the peasants have their horses shod," said he. "I'll take you there and maybe we can buy some shoes."

So that's what they did next morning. Since Pierre was driving the ladies for shopping, Mr. Hackabury rented a car, and they were taken to the blacksmith's place, and to the man's bewilderment Mr. Hackabury paid him three times too much for some clean new shoes, and gave him several little cakes of soap besides. When the ladies came home after lunch to dress for a tea party, they found that this oddly assorted couple had picked out a shady corner of the lawn, and Mr. Hackabury with his coat off was showing Lanny the subtle art of projecting horseshoes through the air so that they fell close to a stake.

III

In short, there sprang up one of those friendships which Lanny was always forming with persons older than himself. Such persons liked to talk, and Lanny liked to listen; they liked to teach, and he liked to learn. So when the stores were all on board the yacht, and the passengers packed and ready to follow, Mr. Hackabury took his new friend aside. "See here, Lanny; do you like motoring?" When Lanny replied that he did, the soapman said: "I've been studying the guidebooks, and I have a scheme. We'll motor to Naples and pick up the yacht there, and so I'll escape two or three days and nights of seasickness."

Lanny said: "Fine," and the owner of the yacht made the announcement to his surprised guests. He proposed to hire a car; but Beauty said there would be no one to use her car while she was away, and she would feel a lot safer if they had Pierre to drive them.

So for three days and nights the boy stayed with this homesick manufacturer, and absorbed a lifetime's lore about the civilization of Indiana. Ezra told the story of his life, from the time he had raised his first calf, an orphan which he had fed with his fingers by dipping them in the milk. A drunken hobo who worked on the farm at harvest-time had shown Ezra's father how to make a good quality of soap, and presently Ezra was making it for the neighbors, earning pocket money. He began saving pocket money to buy machinery to make more soap, and that was the way a great business had started.

For fifty years now Ezra Hackabury had lived with his nose in soap. Before he was twenty-one the people of the village of Reubens, seeing his diligence, had helped to finance the erection of a brick factory, and all these persons were now well-to-do and able to play golf at the country club. The soapman quoted from Scripture: "Seest thou a man diligent in his business? He shall stand before kings." Ezra hadn't done that, but he said: "I reckon I might if I put my mind to it."

There was a box of soap in the car, having a bright bluebird on the box, and one on the wrapper of each cake. The soapman had chosen this symbol because the bluebird was the prettiest and cleanest thing he had seen in his boyhood, and the people of the Middle West all understood his idea. Later on a fellow had written a play of the same name, which Ezra regarded as an infringement and an indignity. People assumed that he had named the soap for the play, but of course the fact was the other way around, said the manufacturer.

The box in the car contained little sample cakes. Mr. Hackabury was never without some in his pocket, his contribution to the spread of civilization in backward lands. Every time a motorcar stopped in Italy, a swarm of ragged urchins would gather and clamor for pennies; the American millionaire would pull out a fistful of his Bluebird packages, and the children would grab them eagerly, and either smell or taste them, and then register disillusionment. Lanny said: "Most of them probably don't know what soap is for." Mr. Hackabury answered: "It's terrible, the poverty of these old nations."

That was his attitude to all the sights of Italy, which he was seeing for the first time. He thought only of the modern conveniences which were not at hand; of the machinery he would like to install, and the business he could do. He wasn't the least bit interested in getting out and looking at the windows of an old church; all that was superstition, of a variety which he called "Cath'lic." When they came to Pisa and saw the leaning tower, he said: "What's the use? With modern steel they could make it lean even more, but it don't do anybody any good."

So it went, the whole trip. Carrara with its famous marble quarries reminded Mr. Hackabury of the new postoffice they were building in Reubens; he had a picture postcard of it. When he saw a dog lying in the road, he was reminded of the hound with which he had hunted coons when he was a boy. When the soapman saw a peasant digging in hard soil, he told about Asa Cantle, who was making a good living raising angleworms to be planted in soil to keep it aerated. There were a million things we could learn about nature that would make life easier for everybody on earth. Ezra told as many of them as there was time for.

They could watch the sea part of the time, and it stayed smooth as the millpond from which the Bluebird soap factory derived its power. But Mr. Hackabury was not to be fooled—he was sure that when they got on it they would find it was heaving and sinking. "The food ain't so good in these Eye-talian inns," he said, "but what I eat I keep. And anyhow, we can say we've seen the country."

IV

They bade farewell to Pierre and the motorcar, and went on board the yacht, which put to sea. The smells improved—but the treacherous element behaved just as Mr. Hackabury had said, and he took to his cabin and did not appear again until they were under the shelter of the rocky Peloponnesus.

Meanwhile a new friendship opened up for Lanny Budd. On the deck sat Marcel Detaze before his easel, wearing his picturesque little blue cap and his old corduroy trousers; he had sketched out a view of the Bay of Naples with Capri for a background, and a fisherboat with a black sail crossing the dying sun. Marcel worked on this for days, trying to get the thing which he called "atmosphere," which made the difference between a work of art and a daub. "Do you know Turner's atmosphere?" he asked of Lanny. "Do you know Corot's?"

Marcel was one of those painters who don't mind talking while they work. So Lanny drew up a camp chair and watched every stroke of the brush, and received lectures on technique. Every painter has his own style, and if you took a microscope to the brushwork, you could tell one from another. The despair of Marcel was the infinity of nature; a sunset like this shifted its tints every moment, and which would you choose? You had to get the effects of distance, and you had to make a flat surface appear endless; you had to turn a dead mineral substance into a thousand other things —not to mention the soul of the painter who was looking at them all. "No landscape exists until the painter makes it," said Marcel.

When his work wasn't going right, he was restless, and wanted to pace the deck. Lanny liked to walk too, so they kept each other company. The boy was so used to being with grown people, it didn't occur to him as surprising that a serious-minded artist should give so much time to him. Only gradually he realized that Marcel was availing himself of this opportunity to make friends. Hitherto he had had to hide from Lanny, but now he was taking him into the family—Marcel's family.

The boy was pleased to find the painter a person who worked so hard at his job. Marcel deliberately refused to learn to play cards, and while the others stayed up half the night, he went to bed, like Lanny, and, like Lanny, was fresh in the morning. He would get up early to watch the pearly tints in the sky, and when he told Lanny about this, the lad got up early too, and heard a discourse on color, and learned the names of many shades, and something about how paints are mixed. Lanny began to think that maybe he was missing his true vocation; he wondered what his father and mother would say if he were to get himself an easel and a palette and join one of the art classes which painters conducted on the Côte d'Azur.

This relationship between Lanny and Marcel seemed strange to a Middle Western American, but not in the least to a Frenchman.

The painter was prepared to become an extra father to Lanny, if this was permitted, and it was. The boy observed what was going on between Marcel and his mother, and realized that the man was trying to persuade her to give less of her time and energy to these fashionable people, and more of it to him. Marcel thought that Beauty was wearing herself out running about to social functions, depriving herself of sleep, and being so excited that she hardly took time to eat. Every now and then these "smart" ladies would find themselves threatened with a breakdown, and would have to go away and take baths or cures or what not to restore themselves. "It's a silly way of life," declared the hard-working man of art.

V

A cold wind was blowing from the snow-covered Mount Olympus, and the yacht sought shelter behind the long island called Euboea. Here was a wide channel, blue and still and warm; Mr. Hackabury said: "This is all I ever want to see of the Isles of Greece, and let's stay right here."

The channel ran for a hundred and fifty miles, and they would steam to a new place and anchor, and the party would be rowed ashore to some bedraggled village, and would climb a hill, and there would be the ruins of an ancient building, the stones once white now mottled and grayish, a great column lying in the dust, the segments which composed it having come apart, so that it looked like a row of enormous cheese boxes laid end to end. Sheep grazed among the ruins, and the bronzed old shepherd had built himself a hut of brush, pointed at the top like an Indian tepee.

Marcel had a guidebook, and would read about the temple which had stood there, and who had built it. Most of the company would be bored, and wander off in pairs and chat about their own affairs. One ruin was just like another to them. But the painter knew the differences of styles and periods, and would point these out to Lanny; so came a new stage in the boy's education. He had never known much about Greece, but now he became excited. Something wonderful had been here, more than two thousand years ago. A great people had lived, and had dreamed lovely things, such as Lanny caught gleams of in music and tried to catch and express in a dance. Now those splendid people were gone, and it was sad; when you stood among their old marbles and watched the sun going down across the blue-shadowed bay, feelings of infinite melancholy stole over you; you felt that you too were dying and being forgotten.

Marcel had a book with verses and inscriptions of these ancient ones. Invariably the verses were sad, as if the people had foreseen the fate which was to befall them. "Perhaps they had seen ruins of earlier people," suggested Lanny; and the painter said: "Civilizations rise and fall, and nobody has been able to find out what kills them."

"Do you suppose that can happen to us?" asked Lanny, a bit awe-stricken; and when the painter said that he believed it would happen, the boy watched the sun go down, with shivers that were not entirely from the north winds.

Marcel Detaze developed a great interest in this newly adopted son. The rest of the company were well-bred people, whom it was pleasant to travel with, but they were conventional and had little understanding of what went on in the soul of an artist. But this boy knew instinctively; something in him leaped in response to an art emotion. So Marcel would supplement the guidebook with everything he knew about Greek art, and he found that Lanny remembered what he heard. Later on, when they visited Athens, the boy found an English bookstore with books about ancient Greece, and so was able to read the history which had provided English statesmen with their examples, and the mythology which had provided English poets with their similes, for three or four hundred years.

Marcel and Lanny and Mr. Hackabury did the walking for the party. The latter had no interest in ruins, but he toiled up the slopes because he didn't want to put on more weight. While the younger pair examined columns Ionic or Corinthian, Mr. Hackabury would wander off and talk in sign language to the shepherds. Once he bought a lamb; not because he wanted it, but because of his curiosity as to prices current in this country. He put out a handful of coins, and pointed, and the shepherd took one small piece of silver. Ezra gave him some soap for good measure, and tucked the lamb under his arm and carried it to the ship. When the ladies heard that they were to have it for dinner, they said it was a horrid idea; they were used to eating roast meat, but not to seeing the creature first!

VI

Warm sunshine and peace settled over the Aegean Sea, and the *Bluebird* ventured forth to explore the islands famed in song and story. They are the tops of sunken chains of mountains, and to the unpoetic they look much alike; the fact that Phoebus Apollo was born on one and Sappho on another didn't mean much to modern society ladies. What counted was the fact that they had no harbors, and you had to be rowed ashore, and there was nothing to see but houses of plastered stone, and men with white starched skirts like ballet dancers. Swarms of children followed you, staring as if at a circus parade, and it was not very interesting to buy laces and sponges which you didn't need, or to eat pistachio nuts when you weren't hungry. Having once drunk coffee out of copper pots with long handles, and discovered that it was sticky and sweet, you decided that it was pleasanter on deck dancing to the music of a phonograph or trying to win back the money you lost at bridge the night before. Ezra, in his capacity as host, would propose a party to visit one of the "hanging monasteries," but his wife would say that she was tired and would prefer to rest and read a novel; one of the gentlemen would say that he would stay and keep her company; others would follow suit, and so it would come to the usual trio of sightseers, Ezra, Marcel, and Lanny.

There were several little dramas going on among these guests, which Lanny Budd was too young to understand or even suspect.

Of the two young Englishmen who had been brought along, one was named Fashynge; he had no special occupation, but was welcomed because he was a good dancer and cardplayer, and had the right sort of conversation, difficult for anybody to understand unless he knew a certain small set of people, their personal peculiarities, what had happened to them, and what they thought was funny. Society ladies like to have such men about, and Cedric Fashynge devoted himself to Beauty Budd, uninvited and without asking any return. Marcel said he was an ass, but probably a harmless one. Lady Eversham-Watson was attracted by him, and Beauty would playfully tell "Ceddy" to dance with Margy and do this and that with her; but "Ceddy" didn't obey—and anyhow, his lordship was always about, seeing to it that his wife received every attention that she required.

The other Englishman was older and more serious; Captain Andrew Fontenoy Fitz-Laing was his name, abridged to "Fitzy." He had got a bullet through his hip in some obscure skirmish with the Afghans, and would wince now and then when he got up out of his chair suddenly, but would say casually that it was "nothing." He was tall and erect, and had a fine golden mustache and fair pink skin about which the ladies teased him. He had the devil in his blue eyes, so Beauty declared; and anybody who watched them closely would see them turn in the direction of Edna Hackabury. If Edna's black eyes happened to encounter them, there would take place a slow deepening of color in the alabaster cheeks and throat of the soap manufacturer's wife. Of the eleven passengers on the yacht, there were only two who had not observed this phenomenon—Lanny and the soap manufacturer.

It had been going on for quite a while, for Fitzy had been on the cruise to Norway. Having a much worse hip at that time, he had not been able to go ashore and visit the *saeters*, so Edna had often stayed to keep him company. He had been among the guests who had accompanied the Hackaburys on their return to the States the previous fall, and had been with them at Key West and the Bahamas, and also crossing the Atlantic. This had been fortunate,

for otherwise Edna would have had no company at all while they
were at sea.

VII

They went to Athens—partly because everybody would ask if
they had been there, and partly in order to refuel. The port is called
the Piraeus, and there isn't much of a harbor—the tugs just turned
the *Bluebird* around and set her against a stone pier, and there were
the venders of laces and sponges, and swarms of hackmen clamoring
in various tongues to drive them to town. The weather was pleasant,
and they let themselves be driven about the avenues of a small city,
and saw that there was a museum, and on a height some distance
away ruins which the hackman said were the Parthenon. Did anybody want to look at any more ruins?

Marcel and Lanny did; and Mr. Hackabury went along for company. They rode up on the backs of donkeys, in the company of
thin American schoolteachers and stout German tourists. Ezra sat
down to rest while the younger pair wandered among these noble
remnants, which had been blasted by a powder explosion during a
siege, and from which Lord Elgin had taken all the beautiful statu-
ary. Marcel told what gods had been worshiped here and what arts
practiced, more than twenty centuries before. Now it was a shrine
to lovers of beauty; not long ago Isadora Duncan had danced here,
and when the police had wished to stop her she had told them it was
her way of praying.

They had planned to stay all day, and study diligently; but the old
gentleman called to them and said he guessed he'd have to go down;
he didn't feel quite right; maybe it was a touch of the sun, or something he had eaten. He told them to stay, but they insisted on going
with him—they could just as well come back next day.

So they drove to the boat, and went on board. Ezra went to his
cabin, and Marcel and Lanny stayed on the afterdeck, telling Beauty
and some of the others about the sights they had seen. They were interrupted by shouts from inside the yacht, and loud, crashing noises.

Lanny, the most agile among them, was the first to dash into the saloon and down the corridor from which the sounds came.

He saw an extraordinary spectacle—the owner of the yacht, having apparently recovered his health, had taken from the wall a red-painted fire ax, and with it was vigorously chopping at the lock of one of the cabin doors. "Open up!" he would shout; then, without waiting for anyone to obey, he would give another mighty whack. A steward in white duck jacket, and a deckhand, also in white, stood staring with wide eyes; the first mate came running, and then Lanny, Marcel, Lanny's mother, Lord Eversham-Watson, the baroness—all crowding into the corridor and standing speechless.

Two or three more whacks and the door gave way, and the owner of the *Bluebird* stood gazing inside. The others couldn't see—they kept away from the ax, whose wielder was panting heavily. For a few moments this hard breathing was the only sound; then he commanded: "Come on out!" No answer from within the cabin, and he shouted more fiercely: "Come out; or do you want me to drag you?"

From inside came the voice of Captain Fitz-Laing: "Put the ax down."

"Oh, I'm not going to hit you," replied Ezra. "I just wanted to see you. Come on out, you dirty skunk."

Fitzy came limping through the doorway, his handsome face very pale, his clothing in disarray. He passed the large and powerful soapman, watching him guardedly. The others made way for him, and he went down the corridor.

"You saw him, now take a look at her," said the man with the ax. He was speaking, not to his guests, but to the members of the crew; several others had come, and the owner of the yacht ordered them to the doorway, insisting: "You have seen her? I shall need you for witnesses." Thus directed, they peered into the cabin, from which came now the sounds of Edna Hackabury's weeping.

"You know her?" demanded Ezra, relentlessly. He set his ax against the wall, and took from his pocket a pencil and some paper.

"I want your names and addresses, some place where I can reach you," he said. From one man after another he got this information and wrote it down carefully, while the sobbing inside the cabin went on, and the guests stood, helpless with embarrassment, not saying a word.

"Now then," said Ezra, when he had what he needed, "I'm through." He turned to the group of guests. "I'll leave you this floating whorehouse," he declared. "Take it any place you please. I'm going back to God's country, where people still have a sense of decency."

There came a scream from the cabin, and Edna rushed out, half undressed as she was, and flung herself at her husband. "No, Ezra, no!" She started to plead that she hadn't meant it—she had been too much tempted—she would never do it again—he must forgive her. But he said: "I don't know you," and pushed her away and went on down the corridor.

The first person he had to pass was Lanny, and he stopped and put his hand on the lad's head. "I'm sorry you had to see this, son," he remarked, kindly. "You're in a tough spot. I hope you get out of it some day." He walked by the others without looking at them, and went into the cabin he had been sharing with Lanny and started throwing his belongings into a couple of suitcases. His wife followed him, weeping hysterically. She groveled at his feet, she begged and besought him; but each time he shoved her out of the way. When he had what he needed in the suitcases, he took one in each hand and strode out of the cabin and up the companionway, crossed the gangway to the shore, stepped into one of the waiting hacks— and that was the last they saw of him.

VIII

Doubtless things like that have happened in the Isles of Greece on many occasions, both ancient and modern; but none of these people had ever seen it, and they found it more exciting than looking at ruins or buying picture post cards of the Parthenon. The ladies gathered in poor Edna's cabin, and did what they could to console her, telling her that she had got rid of a great burden, and ought to be thankful. Ceddie Fashynge and Eddie Patterson went out and found Captain Andrew Fontenoy Fitz-Laing bracing himself with a few drinks in a café, and brought him back to the *Bluebird*.

When they had time to think matters over, they realized that it wasn't so bad; they had got rid of a dreadful bore, who in a crisis had shown himself a ruffian as well. Edna and Fitzy would no longer have to hide and cower. The latter, being a gentleman, would of course offer to marry her; but unfortunately he had nothing but his army pay, and couldn't keep a wife on that. Perhaps the soapman would make a settlement; anyhow, if he stuck by his word and left her the yacht, it would make a tidy nest egg.

The question was, what should they do next? They had been having such a jolly time, and it would be a shame to end it. Fortunately there was a person on board who could afford to keep the cruise going, and that was Eversham-Watson—or rather, his wife. Prompted by her, he said he would see them back to Cowes, which they had chosen as the place for the ending of their cruise. "The honor of England is at stake," said his lordship; his bright and chirrupy little American wife had told him that, and he said it—solemnly and heavily, so that it sounded like a political speech instead of a joke.

Everybody wanted to get away from the Piraeus, before the madman from Indiana changed his mind and came back and turned them out. Edna gave the order to put to sea and she moved into Fitzy's cabin—it was necessary, really, since the door of her own was split to pieces and the carpenter had to make a new one. There were now three pairs of happy lovers on the yacht, to say nothing of one married couple who had learned to get along reasonably well. There was no longer anything to be concealed, and nobody to embarrass anybody else.

Lanny had a cabin to himself now, and if he missed his elderly friend, he did not tell anyone. He was left to speculate by himself about the strange scene he had witnessed; for nobody on board seemed to want to talk to him about it. Despite his having acquired a complete supply of the facts of life, his mother was greatly embarrassed, and considered that Mr. Hackabury had committed an outrage in allowing a child to witness such a scandal. All Beauty said was that the soap manufacturer had shown himself a crude and boorish person; "one of those men who think they can buy a woman's heart and hold it like a chattel."

All the party seemed to sympathize with Edna, except Marcel Detaze. From remarks he made to Beauty, Lanny gathered that he had his own ideas; but he didn't explain them to Lanny, and the boy was shrewd enough to realize that he must never under any circumstances come between Marcel and his mother, and had better not even know if there was any difference between them.

The *Bluebird* steamed south to Crete and then to the coast of Africa. The weather was hot, the sea blue and still, no one seasick, and no cloud in anyone's sky. They had hundreds of records for the phonograph, and played American ragtime and danced under the awnings which covered the after part of the deck. When they came to Tunis, and the ruins of what had been Carthage, they were in the midst of a long siege of poker; but the yacht stopped to get fresh fruits and vegetables, so Marcel and Lanny went ashore, and saw strange dark men wearing white hoods, and women going about completely veiled, with eyes black as sloes peering out seductively. They saw another sunset over broken shafts of marble, and Marcel told about Hannibal who had driven the elephants across the Alps, and Cato who had said every day all his life that Carthage must be destroyed. Lanny hadn't known that ancient history was so interesting, and went looking for a bookstore in Tunis, something hard to find.

Then Algiers, and they all went ashore and paid strange musicians and dancers to entertain them. They hired camels and rode into the interior, and saw date-palms growing, and poked into native houses, and Marcel sat for hours making sketches which he would use by and by. Lanny stuck to him, asking questions and learning about lines and shadows. The boy had now decided that he liked painting best of all the arts; for dancing was being ruined, nobody cared for

anything but hugging each other and moving around in a slow kind
of stupefied stagger.

But painting was something you could do by yourself. Lanny
dreamed of some day achieving what Marcel had given up in despair
—to convey, on canvas, that sense of melancholy which came over
them, watching a sunset behind the ruins of old civilizations, and
thinking about the men who had lived in those days and tried to
make the world more beautiful. You wanted to call to those men to
come back. You couldn't bear to know that they would never hear
you; that they were gone, and all their dreams, their music and dancing, their temples and the gods who had dwelt in them! Some day
you also would be gone, and other men would stand and call to you,
and you, too, would not hear.

8

This Realm, This England

I

THE harbor of Cowes lies on the sheltered side of the Isle of
Wight, and is the headquarters of the Royal Yacht Squadron and
scene of the great regatta every summer. Here came the *Bluebird* at
the beginning of May, in time for the pleasant weather and the opening of the London "season."

The gay company broke up. Edna Hackabury received a com-
munication from a firm of solicitors representing her husband, and
went up to the city to learn her fate. Beauty Budd was going to
visit the Eversham-Watsons at their town house. Marcel Detaze was

returning to his studio on the Cap d'Antibes, to put upon canvas his memories of Africa and Greece. The plan had been for Lanny to return with him; but here was a letter from Eric Vivian Pomeroy-Nielson, to whom Lanny had written from Athens. Rick begged: "Oh, please don't go away without seeing me! I'll come to town to meet you, and we'll go to the opera and the Russian ballet. Pretty soon school will be over, and you can come to the country with me. Kurt Meissner is coming, and we'll have a grand time."

Kurt wrote from his school. He had worked hard and won prizes, and his father had promised him a reward. He had an uncle who was an official in a rubber company and had business in London, and was willing to take him along, to see the Russian ballet, and to hear the symphony orchestra and the opera, and to learn all he could about English music. So of course Lanny began begging to stay, and Lady Eversham-Watson said: "Why not? The dear little fellow can enjoy himself at our country place as long as he pleases, and if he wants to come to town, there will be someone to bring him."

If you have ever drunk Kentucky Bourbon, you have probably contributed to the fortune of Margy Petries; if you have ever read a magazine in the English language, you have surely not escaped the self-praises of "Petries' Peerless." Lord Eversham-Watson had met the creator of this beverage at one of the racing meets, and had been invited to come to the bluegrass country and see how they raised horses. He had come, and seen, and conquered, or so he had thought; but that was because he didn't know Kentucky girls. Margy was one of those talkative little women who make you think they are shallow, but underneath have a sleepless determination to have their own way. His lordship—"Bumbles" to his friends—was heavy and slow, and liked to be comfortable; Margy was his second wife, and all he demanded was that she shouldn't go too far with other men. She had paid his debts, and he let her spend the rest of her father's money for whatever she fancied.

As a result, here was an old English country house that you could really live in. All the rooms had been rearranged and everybody had a bathtub. The old furniture, dingy, smelling of the Wars of the

Roses—so Margy said, though she had the vaguest idea what or when they were—had been sold as antiques, and everything was now bright chintz or satin, with color schemes that said, gather ye rosebuds while ye may. There were light wicker chairs and tables, and twin beds for fashionable young wives. Old tapestries in the billiard room had been replaced with a weird device called "batik," and there was a bar in the smoking room, patronized mainly by the ladies, and having decorations out of a children's nursery tale. The rugs were woven in futurist patterns, and on them lay two Russian wolfhounds with snow-white silky hair; when these noble creatures went out in wet weather they donned waterproof garments of a soft gray color edged with scarlet and fastened with two leather straps in front and another about the middle.

If you were a guest at Southcourt you could have anything there was in the Empire; all you had to do was to indicate your wish to one of the silent servants. This silence was to Lanny the most curious aspect of life in England; for in Provence the servants talked to you whenever they felt like it, and laughed and joked; but here they never spoke unless it was part of a ritual, such as to ask whether you wanted China or Ceylon tea, and white or Demerara sugar. If you spoke an unnecessary word to them, they would answer so briefly that you felt you were being rebuked for a breach of form. They wanted you to assume that they did not exist; and if one of them forgot something, or did it wrong, the usually placid "Bumbles" would storm at the unfortunate creature in a manner that shocked Lanny Budd far more than it did the creature.

You weren't supposed to notice this, and if you didn't, you would find Southcourt a delightful place to stay. There were plenty of horses, and generally somebody wanting to ride. There was a comfortable library, and Margy had not bothered to change the books. The pleasantest part of life at an English country house was the way you were let alone to do what you pleased. The rule of silence applied only to house servants; the gardener would talk to you about flowers, and the kennelman about dogs, and the stableman about horses. The place was in Sussex, and there were rolling hills, now fresh with spring grass; Lanny had thought of England as a small island, but there seemed to be great tracts of land that nobody wanted to use except for sheep. The shepherds, too, didn't mind talking—the only trouble was they used so many strange words.

II

Somebody was motoring to town, and Lanny went along. Automobiles were becoming faster and more dependable every year, also more luxurious. It had suddenly occurred to many persons at once that they didn't need to ride in the open, with a gale blowing on them, and ladies' hats having to be tied on with many yards of chiffon. No, they were now enclosing cars like little rooms. The one Lanny rode in was called a "sporting saloon," and consisted of a square black box in the rear, with a long black cylinder in front for the engine; it was heavy and the tires were small, but Lanny had never seen anything so elegant, and it was marvelous to come rolling into London in your own private parlor. The chauffeur sat out in the wind, and wore goggles, and his cap was fastened to them, and a high tight collar made him sit up straight and stiff. He drove on the left side of the road, and Lanny couldn't get over the idea that somebody would forget about that and run into them.

Rick came to town to spend Saturday and Sunday, and they fell into each other's arms. He was English, but being a devotee of the arts, he didn't mind letting a friend know that he was glad to see him. Rick was such a handsome fellow, with dark eyes and hair very wavy; he had a slender figure, elegant manners, and fastidious tastes —Lanny was quite overwhelmed by him, and proud to introduce him to his friends.

And what a lot they had to talk about! Lanny had been to Silesia, and to Greece and Africa, while Rick had been coming in week-ends to theaters and operas. They were both at the growing age, and measured each other, and tried each other's muscles, and danced a bit, and played odds and ends of music, and chatted about the Russian ballet which was to open next week, and they would make a date for the Saturday matinees and get their tickets right away. This was at the town house of the Eversham-Watsons, where Beauty was staying, and also Edna Hackabury. The latter had been to see her husband's solicitors, and had been informed that he had filed suit for divorce in Indiana. If Mrs. Hackabury contested the action, she would undoubtedly lose and get nothing; if she agreed not to contest, Mr. Hackabury would give her the choice of the following: the yacht, to be placed in escrow and to become her property on the day the decree was final; or an income of ten thousand dollars a year for life.

Edna had been making inquiries, and learned that yachts were a standard commodity, bringing good prices, so she was all for proposition number one. But her military gentleman announced that his rights as a future husband were not going to be put in escrow. He said if Edna got the price of the yacht she would spend it on clothes and parties in a year; whereas Bluebird Soap stood close to British consols in the estimation of "the City," and two thousand pounds a year was a sum on which a retired army officer and his spouse could live comfortably in some not too fashionable part of the Riviera. So it was settled; and Edna's friends agreed that she was fairly lucky. She had her clothes for the present season, and would be "top-notch" for that long. She must put on a bold front and not let anything get her down.

There was gossip, of course; you couldn't keep such a story from the journalists, who flutter like hummingbirds over the social flower beds, sticking their long noses into everything. There were paragraphs of the sort known as "spicy": a yacht that was in the social as well as the marine register, and an owner in the role of infuriated husband chopping down a cabin door with an ax intended for a different sort of fire. No names were given, but "everybody" knew who it was, and ladies whispered and put up their lorgnettes when the soapman's wife and her slightly lame captain came strolling across the greensward at Ranelagh. Edna wore a genuine Paquin creation —it was a "Paquin year," and the famed woman dressmaker had set off the American's soft white skin and raven-black hair with a strik-

ing ensemble of the same bold contrasts. Picture a dashing wide
black hat with three saucy corners, and with aigrettes sticking in
several directions like broom-tails; a black riding jacket and white
blouse with rolling collar and tie like a man's; a huge muff of black
fur with tails nearly to the ankles; a tall white cane like a shepherd's crook; and on a leash the world's wonder, one of those priceless Japanese Chin dogs famed for their resemblance to a chrysanthe-
mum—a black "butterfly" head with a white blaze over the skull,
and long white hair almost to the ground, and a tail curved exactly
like the petals of a great flower. That was "swank" of the season of
1914; it was *vif*, it was *chic*, it was *la grande tenue*.

III

The social whirl was now in full career. There were two or three
smart dances every night; also people had taken to dancing at teas
and at supper parties after the theater. The Argentine tango was the
rage, also the maxixe—"a slide, a swing, and a throw away." In short,
the town had gone dance-crazy, and some of the fetes were of mag-
nificence such as you read about in the days of Marie Antoinette.
The Duchess of Winterton turned the garden of her town house
into a dancing pavilion, with a board platform and the shrubs and
trees sticking through holes. With a rustic bandstand and colored
lanterns at night it was a scene from the Vienna woods—but no
waltzes, no, the music of a famous "nigger-band."

A half-grown boy wasn't invited to such affairs, but there were
plenty of other things he could do to keep "in the swim." He could
walk bȳ Rotten Row, and see the great ladies and gentlemen of fashion in their riding costumes, and crowds of people lined up to stare,
separated from them only by a wooden railing. He could go to hear
the "bell-ringing" for the Queen's birthday. He could see the coach-
ing parade; the smart gentlemen, and even one smart lady, driving
fancy turnouts with four horses, an array of guests, and two grooms
sitting in back as stiff as statues. He could attend the military tourna-
ment at Olympia, and see a score of riders charging at a long hurdle

from opposite directions, all leaping over it at the same moment, passing each other in the air so close that the knees of the riders often touched.

Also Lanny was invited to ride on a coach with his mother's friends to the races on Derby Day. That was the time you really saw England. Three or four hundred thousand people came out to Epsom Downs, on trains, in carriages or motorcars, or in the huge motorbusses which were the new feature of the town. The roads were packed all day long, first going and then coming; Epsom was described as a vast garage, and people said that soon there would be no horses at the Derby except those in the races. The common people were out for a holiday, and ate and drank and laughed and shouted without regard to etiquette. The people of fashion were there to be looked at, and they put on the finest show that money could buy.

Everybody agreed that the styles for that summer of 1914 were the most extreme since the Restoration, the Grand Monarque, the Third Empire—whatever period of history sounded most impressive. Svelte contours were gone, and fluffiness was the rule; waists were becoming slimmer, side panniers were coming back, flounces were multiplied beyond reason; skirts were tight—a cause of embarrassment to ladies ascending the steps of motorcars and coaches, and the moralists commented sternly upon the unseemly exhibitions which resulted. They complained also that the distinction between evening and day frocks was almost lost; really, flesh-pink chiffon was too *intime* for open air! Fete and race gowns were cut low at the throat, and materials worn over the arms were so diaphanous that they were hardly to be seen at all.

Those who aimed to be really smart did not heed the moralists, but they had to heed the weather; so with these scanty costumes went capes. Everyone agreed that it was a renaissance of the cape; Venetian capes, Cavalier capes, *manteaux militaires*, all made of the most exquisite materials, of silk and satin brocade, sometimes embroidered with great flowers, painted ninons and delicate doublures; the linings were velvet, always of the brightest colors, and the capes were weighted down with diamonds or other jewels, and held across the figure by straps of plaid silk or chiffon, with jeweled buckles of butterfly or flower design.

In short, the fancy of the dressmakers had been turned loose for many months, and the product was set up conspicuously on the tops of coaches or in open motorcars for the crowds to inspect. If they liked it they said so, and if they didn't they said it even louder. Fashionable society tittered over the misadventure of the Dowager Duchess of Gunpowder, a stout old lady who arrayed herself in pink taffeta, with a wide hat of soft straw covered with pink chiffon and roses, known as a "Watteau confection." In a traffic jam her carriage was halted, and some navvies working by the road leaned on their shovels and had a good long look at the show. "Wot ho, Bill!" one of them shouted. "Wot price mutton dressed as lamb!"

Inside the racetrack the big busses were lined all the way down the straight. The weather was fine, and everybody happy. The royal family put in an early appearance, and the King and Queen stood in the royal box and received a hearty ovation. "Bumbles" pointed out to Lanny the precautions taken to keep the suffragettes from interfering with the race; for last year one of them had dashed out and thrown herself under the horses' hoofs and got killed—"the daughter of a very good family, too," said his lordship, with disgust. To keep that from happening a second time the track had been lined with three sets of railings, and police and soldiers were watching all the way around. Every Derby receives a name, and this one was dubbed "the silent Derby," because a French horse won and two outsiders were placed; the favorites were nowhere, so that everybody lost money except the bookies.

IV

At the next week-end came the art lover Rick, and they saw the Russians in *Le Coq d'Or* by Rimsky-Korsakov. They saw the foolish King Dodon with a tall gold crown and a great black beard to his waist, and a huge warrior in chain mail, with a curved sword half as big as himself and shining like a bass tuba. This was the Tsar's own ballet troupe, trained for the dance since early childhood, and all London raved over them. Lanny's enthusiasm for dancing came back, and he and Rick exhausted themselves trying to reproduce those amazing Muscovite leaps.

Also, they went to hear Chaliapin, an enormous blond man with a voice that filled the firmament. They went to see Westminster Abbey, and found a fashionable wedding going on; they heard the clamor of high-toned bells, and got a glimpse of the bridal pair emerging, one in a cloud of tulle, the other with a pale, peaked face, dwarfed by a tall black cylinder on top. Rick didn't seem to think very highly of the old families which ruled his country; he said the groom was probably dim-witted, while the bride would be the daughter of a brewer or a South African diamond king.

Later on came the Trooping of the King's Colours on the Horse Guards' Parade, the occasion being the King's "official birthday": a gorgeous ceremony with a troop of horsemen wearing huge bearskin hats. The King rode at their head, a frail-looking gentleman with dark brown mustaches and beard closely trimmed. They had mounted one of those bearskins on top of him, also a uniform much too large for him, loaded with gold epaulets and a belt, a wide blue sash, and a variety of stars and orders. The young Prince of Wales looked still more uncomfortable, having a pathetic thin face and a sword which he would have had a hard time brandishing.

They made the Queen colonel-in-chief of a regiment; her uniform was blue, all over gold in front, and her hat was of fur with a blue bag hanging from it, and a tall white pompon standing up a foot in the air. Lanny had seen in an American magazine a picture of a drum major in such a costume. He said that to Rick, who replied that the influence of this royal family was a very bad thing for England. "They give themselves up entirely to the tailoring and dressmaking business," said the severe young art lover. "Their friends are the big money snobs. If an artist receives honors, it is some painter of fashionable portraits. Titles are entirely a question of finance; you pay so much cash into the party treasury, and become Sir Snuffley Snooks or the Marquess of Paleale." In short, Sir Alfred Pomeroy-Nielson having got no honors for his efforts to promote little theaters in England, his eldest son thought ill of the government.

"Go and see it in action," he advised. So Lanny went on a week-day to Westminster, and was admitted to the visitors' gallery of the House of Commons, now covered with heavy wire net on account of suffragettes' attempts to throw themselves over the railing. Lanny looked down upon the members of the House, mostly wearing top hats, except for the Labour non-conformists. The front-benchers sprawled with their feet upon the bench in front of them. Any of the members, when they didn't like what was said, shouted loudly. The Labour men hated the Tories, the Tories hated the Liberals, and the Irish hated everybody. A fierce controversy was under way over the question of self-government for Ireland; the Ulstermen were swearing they would never be ruled by Catholics, and Sir Edward Carson was organizing an army and threatening civil war. In short, the Mother of Parliaments was hardly setting the best of examples to her children all over the world.

V

There were two "Courts," at which fashionable American ladies dreamed of being presented; but not Beauty Budd, a divorced woman. The same applied to the "state ball," and to the levee at St. James's Palace. But there were plenty of private balls—it was becoming the fashion to give them at West End hotels, where there was room enough for everybody you knew. There would be dinner parties in advance. Margy, Lady Eversham-Watson, was having one at the Savoy; Lanny Budd, so proud of his beautiful blond mother, saw her in a state of exaltation, being got ready for this grand occasion, and her friends Margy and Sophie in the same state of mind and body.

Lanny knew a lot about women's costumes, being a little ladies' man, and hearing them talking all the time, and going with them to be fitted, or seeing it done at home. Just as lovers of painting hoped to find a genius whom they could buy up cheap, so women like Beauty Budd, forced to economize, dreamed of finding a seamstress of talent who would make them something as good as the great establishments could turn out. And when they got it, was it really good? They would torment themselves, and would ask even a boy who loved beautiful things, and knew the names of materials and ways of cutting them, and what colors went together.

Here was Beauty ready to be launched in a costume about which her son had been hearing talk for weeks: a ball dress of pink tulle, with simili diamonds put on the skirt in three-tier pleated flounces. The corsage was a little coat of heavy guipure lace embroidered with amethysts and gold. It was cut in that ultra style which had caused an old gentleman at a dinner party to say that he couldn't express an opinion of the ladies' costumes because he hadn't looked under the table. The plump and creamy-white bust of Beauty appeared on the point of emerging from the corsage, like Venus from the waves, all that prevented it being two little straps made of flat links of gold. The tiny dancing slippers were of tissue of gold incrusted with gems, and the high heels took you back to Empire days, having flower designs worked on them in jewels.

"Well, how do you like me?" asked the mother, and Lanny said he liked her well enough to dance with her all night if she needed him. She gave him eager little pats on the head, but he mustn't kiss her because of her powder.

Then he had to admire the costume of the Baroness de la Tourette, likewise completed after labors and consultations. Sophie's crown of henna hair topped a gown of brocade; roses and rose leaves in silver on a ground of rich blue, very supple, and draped graciously—so said its creator, a *couturier* who was on hand to approve the final effect, and who rubbed his hands together with delight. The gown had a narrow train from the waist, to be held up for dancing, and a deep belt of dark blue velvet, with pleatings of silver lace carried to make kimono sleeves. There was a Cavalier cape of fine old Brussels lace weighted with embroidery of diamonds and gold; and slippers of stamped velvet to match, also embroidered with diamonds. The only difference was that Sophie's were real, while Beauty's were not, and would people notice the difference? It was terrible to feel yourself just an imitation.

But Sophie, good soul, said: "Nonsense! None of the richest people wear their valuable gems any more. They keep them stored in vaults and wear replicas."

"Yes, of course," said Beauty. "But then everybody knows they have the real ones; and everybody knows I haven't!"

"Forget it!" commanded the hardware manufacturer's daughter. "You've got what not one in a hundred has, and most of them would give their eyeteeth for." Kind Sophie said things like that.

Beauty put one more dab of powder on her little white nose, and there was Harry Murchison waiting for her, tall, well set up, looking like a fashion plate. Lanny watched them get into the rich young American's motorcar, and went back into the house, reckoning the months before he, too, would have a full-dress suit and an opera hat, and be able to take his mother to balls at the Savoy Hotel!

VI

Lanny, left alone, went out for a walk. He liked to walk anywhere, but especially in the streets of London. At this time of year it didn't get dark until after nine o'clock, and meantime there were mists and haze and pastel colors in the sky. Lanny would walk by the Serpentine River in Hyde Park, and watch the beautiful black and white swans; he would walk along the Embankment, observing the clouds across the river, and the tugs and launches gliding over the dull gray surface. Sometimes he would climb to the top of one of those new motorbusses, from which for thruppence you could see everything there was in London—seven million people, and nobody had ever counted how many houses, or how many cabs, carriages, and automobiles.

The city had been laid out by ancient Saxon or Roman cows, and rarely had their paths been straight. One village had run into another, all higgledy-piggledy; and where was Bandbox Lane High

Court, or Old Pine Hill New Corners?—you might be within a quarter of a mile of the place, but you couldn't find a soul who had ever heard of it. Few streets had the same name for any distance; you would start walking on the Strand, and presently it was Fleet Street, and then it was Ludgate Hill, Cannon Street, Fenchurch, Aldgate—and like as not would evaporate and disappear entirely. The same peculiarity was shared by the old buildings; you would go down a corridor, and descend three steps, and turn to the left, pass three doors and climb a winding stairway, turn to the right, walk a dozen steps—and knock on a door which hadn't been opened for a hundred years.

Lanny felt in an adventurous mood that evening and started off in a new direction. For a while he was on a wide thoroughfare, with motorcars taking people to the theaters, and crowds looking into windows of gaily decorated shops. Then little by little the neighborhood changed; the shops became poorer, the men wore caps, and the women dingy shawls. The street began to ramble, and Lanny did the same; he was keeping in a general easterly direction, but that didn't mean anything special, for he had never heard of the East End of London. He had the general idea that the seven million population was composed mainly of ladies and gentlemen such as he had seen in Mayfair, with their servants and tradespeople, and a sprinkling of saucy flower girls, lively newsboys, and picturesque old beggars trying to sell you "a box o' lights."

But now Lanny had walked through a looking glass, or plunged down a shaft to the center of the earth, or to the bottom of the sea; he had taken a drug, or fallen into a trance—something or other that had transported him into a new world. He couldn't believe his eyes, and walked on, fascinated, staring; it just couldn't be real, there couldn't be such creatures on earth! English men and women were tall, and stood up straight, and took bold strides, and had long thin faces, sometimes a little too long, especially the women—Robbie impolitely called them horse-faces! Both men and women whom Lanny had met had rosy complexions, sometimes alarmingly so, suggestive of apoplexy. But suddenly here were creatures squat and stooped, that shambled instead of walking; their legs were short and their arms long—they looked like apes more than human beings! Features crooked, teeth missing, complexions sallow or pasty—no, this couldn't be England!

And the clothes they had on! Lanny had never seen such rags, never dreamed they existed on earth. Clothes that were not fitted to the human form, but dangled as on scarecrows, and when they threatened to fall to pieces were fastened with pins or bits of string, or even pieces of wood. They were filthy with every sort of grime and grease, and gave out the musty acrid smell of stale human sweat; the sum total of it filled the streets and polluted the winds that blew from the North Sea.

And the swarms of these creatures! Where did they come from, and where could they go? The sidewalks were crowded, so that you had to jostle your way. There were no longer any motorcars or carriages, and few horse-drawn vehicles, only pushcarts, called "barrows." Many had things to sell, things that must surely have been gathered out of dustbins: old rags of clothing, as bad as what the people had on; worn, badly patched shoes set in rows along the curb; the cheapest vegetables, wilted and bruised; stinking fish, scraps of meat turned purple or black, old rusty pans, chipped and damaged crockery, all the rubbish of the world. Shops had it spread out in front, and shopkeepers stood watching, while dingy women with bedraggled skirts pulled things about and smelled and chaffered and argued. Tired workingmen sat on the steps, puffing at pipes. Babies swarmed everywhere, ghostly death's-head children suckled on gin. There were innumerable garbage cans, and hardly one without some human creature digging in it for food.

Every other place, it seemed, was a pub. Murmurs and sometimes uproar came from within, and now and then a drunken man would push back the swinging doors and stagger forth—bringing with him a reek of alcohol, and more of that dreadful animal stench, and shouts and curses in a language bearing odd resemblances to the one that Lanny used. He would listen and try to puzzle out the words. A young woman with a ragged straw hat, pulling herself loose from a man: "Blymee, I 'ave ter git the dyner fer me bybee!" What was that? And two fellows coming out of a pub wiping big mustaches on coatsleeves and carrying on an argument, one shouting at the other: "Ow, gow an' be a Sowcialist!"

VII

The sun had gone down behind Lanny's back, and twilight was letting down its veils over this strange nightmare. One who thought of being a painter might have noted interesting effects of darkness and shadow; somber brick tenements, three or four stories high, blackened with the smoke of centuries; forests of chimney pots pouring out new blackness all the time; sodden human figures, shawl-clad and hunched, growing dimmer in the twilight, blending into the shadows of walls and doorways and dustbins full of trash. But Lanny wasn't thinking about art; he was overcome with more direct, more human emotions. That there should be a world like this, so near to the glittering hotel where his mother and her friends were dancing in their jeweled gowns and slippers! That there should be human beings of English blood, sunk to this state of squalor!

Lanny was beginning to be uneasy. This slum appeared to be endless, and he didn't know how to get out of it. He had been told that any time he lost his way, he should ask a "bobby," but there appeared to be none in this lost world, and Lanny didn't know if it was safe to speak to any of these lost people. The men seemed to be looking at him with hostile eyes, and the leering women frightened him no less. "Two bob to you, mytey!" a girl would say, holding out her hands with what she meant for a seductive gesture. Starved children followed him, beggars whined and showed their sores and crippled limbs; he hurried on, being afraid to take out his purse.

Darkness was falling fast. The shopping district of the slum came to an end, and Lanny, trying to find a better neighborhood, followed a street that widened out. There were sheds, and gravel under foot; dimly he could see benches, and people sitting on them—the same terrible ape figures in stinking rags, men and women and children:

a baby laid on its back, and no one even troubling to put a cover on it; whole families huddled near together; a bearded man with his head back, snoring, a woman curled up against him; a man and a woman lying in each other's arms.

A raw wind had sprung up, and Lanny felt chilly, even while he was walking; but these people sat or lay, never moving. Could it be that they had no place to go? The boy had observed human forms curled up alongside dustbins and sheds, and had supposed they must be drunk; but could it be that they slept out all night?

He pressed on, still more hurriedly; he was beginning to be really afraid now. He had broken his promise to his mother, never to go anywhere except where plenty of people were to be seen. He was in a dark street, and the figures that passed were slinking and furtive, and many seemed to be watching him. He saw two women fighting, shrieking at each other, pulling hair; children stood watching them, apathetic and silent.

It was a street of tenements, but now and then came a pub, with lights and sounds of roistering. A man came out, and as he swung the doors open, the light fell on Lanny. The stranger fell in beside him on the narrow sidewalk. " 'Ullo, little tyke!" said he.

Lanny thought he ought to be polite. "Hello," he replied; and the fellow doubtless noted something different about his accent. "Whur yer bound fer, mytey?" he demanded.

"I don't know," replied Lanny, hesitatingly. "I'm afraid maybe I'm lost."

"Ho! Little toff!" exclaimed the other. "Little toff come inter the slums lookin' fer mayflowers, eh, wot?" He was a burly fellow, and in the light of the pub the boy had seen that his face was grimy, as if he were a coal heaver; or perhaps it was several days' growth of beard. His breath reeked of alcohol. "Listen, mytey," he said, leaning over cajolingly, "gimme a bob, will yer? Me throat is so dry it burns up, it fair do."

This was a problem for the boy. If he took out his purse the fellow would probably grab it. "I'm sorry, I haven't any money with me," said he.

"Garn!" snarled the other, turning ugly at once. "A toff don't go withaht no brass."

They had come to a dark place in the street, and Lanny had just decided to make a dash for it, when to his terror the man grabbed him by the arm. "Cough up!" he commanded.

Lanny struggled; then, finding that the fellow's grip was too strong, he screamed: "Help! Help!"

"Shut yer bloomin' fyce," growled the man, "or I'll bryke every bone in yer body!" He fetched the boy a cuff on the side of the head. It was the first time that Lanny had ever been struck in his whole life, and it had a terrifying effect on him; he became frantic, he twisted and struggled, harder than ever, and shouted at the top of his lungs.

The ruffian began to drag him toward a dark opening leading into a court. Lanny's cries brought people to doors and windows, but not one moved a hand to help him; they just stood and looked. They were interested, but not concerned—as if it were a Punch and Judy show.

But suddenly a door in the court was flung open, and a light streamed upon the scene. A young woman emerged, wild-looking, with tousled black hair and a blouse open at the throat and hanging out at the waist, as if she had put it on in a hurry. When she saw the man and his victim, she darted toward them. "Wot yer doin', Slicer?"

The answer was, "Shut yer silly fyce!" But the girl began shouting louder: " 'Ave yer gone barmy, ye bleedin' fool? Carnt yer see the kid's a toff? An' right in front of yer own drum!" When the man continued to drag Lanny into the court, she rushed at him like a wildcat. "Cut it, I sye! Yer'll 'ave the tecs 'ere, an' we'll all do a stretch!"

He called her a "bitch," and she told the world in return that he was a "muckworm." When he still wouldn't give up, she began clawing at his face in a fury. He had to take one hand to push her away, and that gave Lanny his chance; with a frantic effort he tore himself loose and dashed for the street.

The crowd gave way; it wasn't theirs to stop him. The man came pounding behind, cursing; but Lanny hadn't been climbing mountains and swimming in the Golfe Juan and practicing Muscovite leaps for nothing. He was built like a deer, whereas the man was heavy and clumsy, and presently he gave up. But the boy didn't stop until he had got to a thoroughfare thronged with long-bearded Jews and curly-headed babies, and having signs that said: "Whitechapel High Street."

Then a blue uniform, the one sight that could really bring an end to Lanny's terror. The London bobby didn't carry weapons, like the French gendarme, but he was a symbol of the Empire. Lanny waited until he got back his breath and could speak normally, then he approached and said: "Please, would you tell me how to get to the tube?"

The bobby had a large blue helmet, with a strap across his chin. He answered like an automaton: "First t'right, second t'left." He said it very fast, and when Lanny said: "I beg pardon?" he said it again, even faster than before.

The boy thought it over, and then dropped a delicate hint: "Please, might I walk with you if you're going that way?" It was obviously not the right accent for Whitechapel, and the "copper" looked him over more carefully, and then said: "Right you are, guv'nor."

They walked together in silent state. When they parted, Lanny wasn't sure if the symbol of the Empire would accept a tip, but he took a chance, and held out a shilling which he had denied to "Slicer." The symbol took it with one hand and with the other touched his helmet. "Kew!" said he. The visitor had already had it explained to him that this was the second half of "Thank you," doing duty for the whole.

VIII

Lanny decided to say nothing to his mother about his misadventure. It would only worry her, and do no good; he had learned his lesson, and wouldn't repeat the mistake. He brooded all by himself over the state of the people of East London. When he went to call for his mother at a tea party in Kensington Gardens, the sight of exquisite ladies on the greensward under the trees made him think of the families that were lying out on benches all night because they had no place to go. Instead of snow-white tulle and pink mousseline de soie, he saw filthy and loathsome rags; instead of the fragrant concentrations of the flower gardens' of Provence, he smelled the stink of rotting bodies and the reek of gin.

They drove to Ascot on the second day of the races, the day of the gold vase. It was known as a "black and white" Ascot, because of the costumes decreed by the fashion dictators. He saw black and white striped taffeta dresses with black and white parasols to match. He listened to the chatter of his mother and her friends, commenting upon the fashion parade—froufrou hats, broché effects, corsage prolonged into polonaise, shot silk draped as tunic, butterfly wing confection, black liseré straw, poufs of tea-rose taffeta, bandeau hats and plume towers, cothurns of lizard-green suede—and all the while he would be seeing babies lying on benches with only rags to cover them. He watched the royal procession, the King and Queen riding across the turf amid thunderous cheers from the crowd, and he thought: "I wonder if they know about it!"

The person he took into his confidence was Rick; and Rick said that people knew if they chose to know, but mostly they didn't. He said those conditions were as old as England. The politicians talked about remedying them, but when they got elected they thought about getting elected again. He said it was a problem of educating those slum people; of raising the tone of the intellectual and art life of the country. He took Lanny to a matinee of a play by Bernard Shaw which was the rage that season, and dealt with a flower girl who talked just the sort of Cockney that Lanny had heard during his descent into hell. A professor of phonetics succeeded in correcting her accent, making her into a regular lady of Mayfair. It was most amusing—and it seemed to be in line with Rick's suggestion.

Kurt Meissner arrived, and he, too, was taken into the discussion.

Said Kurt: "We don't leave our poor to the mercies of the wage market. The Germans are efficient, and provide decent housing for the workers, and insurance against sickness, old age, and unemployment." Kurt was perhaps a little too well satisfied with conditions in his country, and too contemptuous of British slackness. Rick, who was willing to make any number of sarcastic remarks about his native land, wasn't so pleased to hear them from a foreigner. Rick and Kurt didn't get along so well in London as they had in Hellerau.

Lanny talked about the question of poverty with his mother also, and Beauty assured him that the kind English people were not overlooking the problem. He would soon see proof of it; the twenty-fourth of June was known as "Alexandra Day," and the fashionable ladies of England honored their Queen Mother by putting on their daintiest white frocks and hats with many flowers and going out on the streets of the cities to sell artificial pink roses for the benefit of the overcrowded hospitals. Lanny saw his mother, the loveliest sight in Piccadilly Circus, taking in silver coins hand over fist; he had to drive three times in one of Lord Eversham-Watson's cars to keep her supplied with stock in trade. He hoped that he might be able to provide accommodations for all those babies who were sleeping outdoors on benches.

9

Green and Pleasant Land

I

THE home of Sir Alfred Pomeroy-Nielson was called "The Reaches," and was close to the Thames River some way below

Oxford. It was a very old place, and not much had been done to modernize it, because, as Rick explained, his father was too poor; they had all they could do to keep the place, and not much left for their beloved arts. There was a little bit of everything in the architecture of the house: an old tower, a peaked roof with gables, mullioned windows, a crenelated wall, a venerable archway through which you drove to the porte-cochere. The structures were jammed one against another, and topping them all were chimney pots, sometimes three or four in a row. This meant that all the year except summer the maidservants were busy carrying coal scuttles; and since there was very little running water, when they had finished with scuttles they carried pails.

But, of course, in summertime everybody went to the river, crossing a beautiful sloping lawn under an archway of aged oaks. It was a new kind of swimming for Lanny, and he thought he could never get enough of it. The boys lived in bathing suits, and "punted" in a long flat-bottomed boat with a ten-foot pole. It was a nice friendly little river, neither wide nor deep. Boathouses lined it, and gaily decorated motorboats went by, and long thin shells, with oarsmen practicing for the coming races. It was a holiday thoroughfare, and there was laughter and singing; the three musketeers of the arts sang all the songs they knew.

Rick had a sister, two years older than himself, and therefore too old for either of the visitors; but she had friends with younger sisters, so there was a troop of English girls bright-cheeked and jolly, interested in everything the boys were doing, and sharing their sports. Lanny was just at the age where he was preparing to discover that girls were wonderful, and here they were.

Sir Alfred Pomeroy-Nielson was a middle-aged gentleman, tall and slender, with handsome dark mustaches turning gray, sharp features, a hawk's nose, and keen dark eyes. He had a Spanish mother, and maybe a trace of Jewish blood, as Rick had said. He was a lover of all the arts and friend of all the artists. He knew many rich people, and acted as a sort of go-between for the bohemian world; telling the "swells" what was what in art and helping the struggling geniuses to find patrons. An impecunious playwright would bring him a blank-verse tragedy, and Sir Alfred would decide that it was a masterpiece, and would design a group of magnificent sets for it; then he would set out to find a backer, and when he failed he would declare that England was going to the dogs. He had very high standards, and would relieve his disappointments by composing sharp epigrams.

It was a free and easy world which he had made for himself within his castle. The most extreme opinions were freely voiced, and it was everybody's pride not to be shocked. But at the same time it would be better not to commit any lapse of table etiquette, and when you took off your bathing suit you put on the right sort of clothes. This made an odd mixture of convention and scorn for convention, and a boy with American parents had now and then to ask his friend for guidance. Rick would give it with an apology. "The older people try to be mod'n, but they really aren't quite up to it."

Kurt Meissner found even greater difficulties, because he was stiff and serious and couldn't get used to the idea of saying things that you didn't entirely mean. "In a Pickwickian sense," was the English phrase, and what was a youth from a province of Prussia to make of it? Kurt was puzzled by their habit of running down their own country; what they said about the state of England was what Kurt himself believed, but he couldn't get used to the idea of Englishmen saying it. They would even discuss the desirability of getting rid of their royal family. "The Prince of Wales is going to turn out to be another dancing boy," Sir Alfred would remark blandly; "a ladies' man like his grandfather."

And then the suffragettes! The son of the comptroller-general of Castle Stubendorf had read in the newspapers about maniacal creatures who were pouring acids into letter boxes and chaining themselves to the railings of the House of Commons in order to prove their fitness to have the vote; but never in his wildest moment had it occurred to him that he might be called upon to sit at dinner table with one of these creatures, and to take her punting upon the Thames! But here was Mildred Noggyns, nineteen years old, the daughter of a former undersecretary in the government; pretty, but pale and rather grim, only three weeks out of Holloway gaol after having chopped a hole in the painted face of the Velásquez Venus, most highly prized treasure of the National Gallery. And talking quite calmly about it, discussing the "cat-and-mouse act," by which the authorities were combating hunger strikes; they let you out of jail when they thought you were near dying, and took you back again as soon as you had picked up a bit.

Rick's sister, Jocelyn, abetted her; and of course these saucy ladies soon found out what was in the haughty soul of the Junker from Silesia, and it became their delight to tease him beyond endurance. They wouldn't let him help them into a punt. "No, thank you, all that nonsense is over, chivalry, and bowing and scraping before women; we're quite able to get into punts by ourselves, and we'll do our share of handling the pole, if you please. And what do you mean when you say that man is gregarious, and that man is a spiritual being, and so on? Do you refer to lordly males like yourself, or do you deign to include the females? And if you include us, why don't you say so? Of course, we know it's just a way of speaking, but it's a benighted way devised by men, and we object to it."

"Yes, Miss Noggyns," Kurt would reply, "but unfortunately I have not learned any word in your language which expresses the concept 'man and woman.'" When the feminist lady proposed that they should create such a word, Kurt replied, gravely: "I have found it hard enough to learn the English language as it exists, without presuming to add anything to it."

II

The three boys discussed the matter among themselves. Kurt thought that the revolt of women meant the breakdown of English society; it was like the "war of the members" in one of the fables of Aesop. Lanny hoped that, if women got the vote, society might be kinder and there wouldn't be so much talk about war. Rick said: "It won't make much difference, one way or the other; the women'll

divide about as the men do, and there'll be more votes to count."
Generally when these three argued they had different opinions—and
when they finished, they still had them.

Of course they talked about girls, and what was called the "sex
problem." No one of the three had as yet had a sex experience. Kurt
said that he had had opportunities; the peasant girls were often willing enough, and looked upon it as an honor that a gentleman would
do them; but Kurt had the idea of saving himself for a great and
worthy love. Lanny remembered what the Social-Democratic editor
had said about Kurt's father, but of course he wouldn't breathe a
word of that.

Rick said, rather casually: "If a sex experience comes my way I'll
probably take it; I think people make more fuss about it than is
necessary—especially since methods of birth control are generally
known. It seems to me the women are waking up and will attend to
changing our ideas."

"I'd hate to put Miss Mildred Noggyns in charge of *my* ideas."
replied Kurt; and they all laughed.

Lanny, desiring to contribute something to the conversation, told
about his unpleasant experience with Baron Livens-Mazursky. Rick,
young man of the world, said that homosexuality was spreading, it
was one of the consequences of the false morality of Puritanism.
"There's a plague of it in our public schools," he declared. "The
boys hide their share from the masters, and the masters hide their
share from the boys, or think they do."

This was one time that Kurt didn't try to prove that Germany
was superior to England. "It's bad in our army," he said. Lanny decided to tell how he had unwittingly got into conversation with a
Social-Democratic editor in a railway station, and the man had repeated evil rumors about high-up persons. "Such an editor would
believe the worst about our ruling classes," said Kurt.

They talked also about something that had happened the other
day in Sarajevo, capital of the province of Bosnia; the Austrian arch-
duke, heir to the throne of the Empire, had been on an official tour
with his wife, and the two of them had been murdered while riding

in their motorcar. Rick and Lanny had heard their elders discussing
it, but hadn't paid much attention; Kurt now explained that Bosnia
was a province of Austria inhabited mostly by Slavs, an inferior and
disorderly people. "They are always agitating against the Austrian
authorities," he said, "and the Serbians across the border encourage
them. The murder was committed by students, and naturally the
Austrians will have to take strong measures to punish the conspirators."

The other two were interested in the story, but as something far
off that didn't mean much to them. It was politics; and they were
all agreed that politics was an activity which artists were in duty
bound to look upon with contempt. All three were dedicated to the
service of the ideal. "*Im Ganzen, Guten, Wahren resolut zu leben*"
—so Goethe had taught, and Kurt repeated it to the other two. The
diplomats in the Balkans would continue to squabble, but men of
superior mind would pass over such headlines in the newspapers,
and give their attention to the reviews of Ravel's *Daphnis and Chloe*,
then being superbly danced by the Russian ballet.

III

Another event of the moment was the Royal Regatta at Henley-
on-Thames. Amateur oarsmen from many parts of the world assembled, and the river was put upon the map for three days. There were
two American crews among them, so Lanny had a chance to feel
patriotic. The finals were rowed on Saturday, and Lanny's mother
came with a motoring party from London, and met the family who
were hosts to her boy. Of course these free and "mod'n" people
didn't concern themselves about her divorce, and she was lovely in
her simple white frock, of what the French call *mousseline de com-
munion*, and a jardiniere hat with pink hedge roses held in place by
a white chiffon veil several yards in length. At her throat was a
diamond bow brooch that also looked simple—unless you knew that
it was set in platinum.

Harry Murchison drove the party, and had servants following in another car, to set up tables and spread an elaborate "breakfast" on the lawn of The Reaches. It was a festivity without a single flaw— unless you counted the fact that wasps persisted in getting stuck in the jam. Afterwards they motored to Henley, and the Pomeroy- Nielsons invited them to a private enclosure of one of the rowing clubs, from which they had a view of the finish. The course had been marked off with piles driven, and booms, and there were no launches and no high wind to trouble the oarsmen, as you had on the big rivers of America: just a nice friendly sort of tea-party place, so that oarsmen rowing down the course could hear the conversa- tion of spectators on both banks. On one side was a towpath, on which the crowd ran or bicycled; on the other side, behind the booms, were punts and rowboats crowded together like sampans on a Chinese river.

It was a gay scene; the men wore blazers with the colors of their rowing clubs, while the ladies in their bright gowns lolled upon silken cushions. Of course you wouldn't expect an English crowd to roar and cheer like an American one. "Well rowed, Harvard!" would be the proper expression of enthusiasm. It happened that the final in the eight-oar event for the Grand Challenge Cup was rowed by two American crews, one composed of Harvard under- graduates, and the other of Harvard graduates; so there were many crimson flags and nasal New England accents. Oddly enough, the race was rowed on the Fourth of July, so the Americans had to be careful not to give offense to their well-mannered hosts.

Only one thing marred a perfect day for Lanny Budd: that was the attention which Harry Murchison was so obviously paying to his mother. It was Harry who helped her out of the motorcar, and Harry who helped her in again, and it happened to be Harry who caught her when one of her fancy high-heeled slippers caused her ankle to turn. He was a good-looking and agreeable fellow, and the Pomeroy-Nielsons could have no reason to criticize his interest in an unattached woman—but that would be because they didn't know about Marcel Detaze. But Lanny thought of Marcel down there at the Cap, painting diligently; he must be lonely, and wondering when

his Beauty would get through with the social whirl and return to
the life of art and love.

She was going back to France right after this race—but not going
home yet. She had been invited to spend a fortnight with Mrs. Emily
Chattersworth, an American friend who lived on the Riviera in winter and in a château near Paris in summer. From a bit of conversation Lanny now gathered that Harry Murchison was motoring her
there, and would be in Paris and take her to a fête champêtre.
Lanny couldn't get away from the disturbing thought: was this too-
agreeable heir of a plate-glass factory in Pennsylvania trying to win
the love of his mother? And if so, where did Marcel come in? Had
Beauty begun to tire of her painter? A whole new set of problems
for a youngster who was supposed to have learned all the facts of
life!

IV

Among the girls who came to The Reaches was the daughter of
an army officer by the name of Rosemary Codwilliger, which you
pronounced Culliver. She had hazel eyes and smooth thick hair the
color of straw, and very regular, rather grave features—she might
have served as model for a girlish Minerva, goddess of wisdom. She
was a year older than Lanny, and took a maternal attitude toward
him, which he liked, being a mother's boy. Rosemary was fascinated
by "Dalcroze," and would watch Lanny and Rick and imitate what
they did, and was very good at it. She had been to the Riviera and
knew the places Lanny knew, so they had plenty to talk about.

When the young couples strolled apart, it would be Rosemary
and Lanny. They were sitting near the river, watching the last tints
of the fading day; a single very bright star, and no sound on the
river, but up at the house Kurt Meissner playing the slow movement
of Mozart's D minor piano concerto. A lovely melody, tender and
touching, floated down to them; it died to a whisper, rose again, and
then again, in different forms, an infinite variety. It whispered of
love and beauty, it captivated the soul and led it into a heaven of
ecstasy, pure yet passionate.

It was one of those rare moments in which new possibilities of the spirit seem to be unveiled; and when at last the music died away, neither of them moved for a while. Lanny felt the girl's hand touching his; he returned the pressure gently, and again they were still. A faint breeze stirred tiny ripples on the surface of the water, and caused the evening star's reflection to shiver and tremble. In the soul of Lanny something of the same kind began to happen, the strangest, indescribable sense of delight pervading his being. He leaned closer to the girl, who seemed to feel the same way.

The music had begun again. Kurt was playing something that Lanny didn't know. It sounded like Beethoven; slow and mournful, a lament for mankind and the suffering men inflict upon one another. But the magic of art turns sorrow into beauty, pain into ecstasy; the young people were flooded with an emotion which caused their two hands to tighten and tremble, and tears to start down their cheeks. When the music died again, Lanny whispered: "Oh, that was so sweet!" Not a brilliant observation, but the tones of his voice were eloquent.

Rosemary's reply startled him. "You may kiss me, Lanny."

He hadn't known that he wanted to kiss her; probably he wouldn't have dared to think of it. But he realized at once that it would be pleasant to kiss her—very gently, respectfully, of course. So he planned; but when he touched his lips to hers, her arms folded about him, and they clung together in a long embrace. Those strange thrills became more intense, they suffused the boy's whole being. He seemed to know what all the music of the world was about, what it was trying to express. He wanted nothing but to stay there, perfectly still, and have Kurt go on playing sweet, sad melodies.

Somebody came along, interrupting them, so they got up and went into the house. Lanny's cheeks were flushed, but Rosemary was as cool and serene as the girlish Minerva, goddess of wisdom. Whenever she looked at Lanny she smiled, a gentle smile, at once a reassurance and a pledge of happiness to come.

So after that, whenever circumstances permitted, those two wandered off by themselves. As soon as they were alone, their hands would come together; and when they found a sheltered spot, or darkness to protect them, their arms would be about each other and their lips would meet. They never went any further; Lanny would have been shocked by the idea, and the girl did not invite it. They were at a stage where happiness came easily, and in satisfactory abundance.

It was long before Lanny admitted to himself that these thrills had anything to do with that puzzling thing called "sex" that people were always talking about. No, this was something rare and exalted, a secret bliss which they alone had discovered, and concerning which they would breathe no whisper to anyone else. At least that is what Lanny said, and Rosemary smiled her wise, motherly smile, and said: "You dear!"

They both kept the secret; and when the time came for Lanny to go back to town, the girl told him it would be just "*au revoir.*" "My mother is talking about the Riviera for next winter," she said. "We'll write to each other, and surely not forget how happy we've been."

Lanny answered: "I'll think of it every time I listen to music or play it. And that will be often!"

V

One other adventure before the boy left that green and pleasant land. Kurt had gone up to London to meet his uncle's friends. Rick had to do some studying; owing to his preoccupation with the arts, he had failed in his mathematics and had to stand an examination in the fall. Lanny read for a while, and then went for a walk.

It was delightful country, with a great variety of prospects; the land owners had a right to bar you from their property, but they generally didn't, and there were lanes and footpaths, with stiles over the fences, and little dells with streams running through them. Summer was at its height; the sun, not having long to stay, did its best by shining for long hours, and the green things made the most of their opportunity, crowding to the light. A very different world from Provence; greener trees, and landscapes more intimate and friendly, warmer to the heart if not to the thermometer.

Lanny rambled, turning wherever he saw anything that interested him, and not caring where he went; he knew the names of villages near The Reaches, and anybody could tell him the way. When it was time to go back, he trusted to luck. He found himself on the edge of a patch of woodland, with a fence as you entered, and a stile to enable you to step over it; he sat there to rest, and saw a figure moving on another path, which crossed his at the farther edge of the patch of woods. It was a girl, and Lanny couldn't see clearly, but it appeared that she was carrying something over her shoulder; then, as he watched, she suddenly disappeared and he didn't see her again. He was puzzled, because there seemed to be no drop in the ground. Could it be that the girl had fallen?

His curiosity was aroused, and he climbed over the stile and went toward the place. Sure enough, there was the girl lying flat on the ground, and a sack of turnips, some of them having spilled out when she fell. Lanny ran toward her, and saw that she was about of his own age, barefooted, wearing a torn and dirty old skirt and blouse; her hair hadn't been combed, and she was far from prepossessing. It looked as if she had fainted; anyhow, there she lay, and Lanny noticed that her skin was bloodless and that she was emaciated to a painful degree. He might have decided that she was drunk, but instead he guessed that she hadn't had enough to eat.

He had heard somewhere that when people fainted you dashed cold water in their faces and slapped their hands. He tried the latter, but perhaps didn't put enough energy into it. He looked and saw buildings some distance beyond the wood, and ran toward them and found a row of cottages close together, of the sort which look picturesque in old etchings. They might have been as old as Queen Anne, or as Elizabeth; they had low thatched roofs, small windows, and doorways not quite regular, and so low that even Lanny had to bend his head to enter. He saw a woman in front of them and ran to her, calling that there was a girl lying out there on the ground. The woman was tousle-headed and red-faced, and she said, dully:

"It'll be that Higgs gel, over thurr," and pointed to one of the cottages.

Lanny ran to the place and knocked on the door. It was opened after a while by a woman with straggly hair and only three teeth visible. The English poor, whenever they had a toothache, simply pulled the tooth out; no doubt many a woman who looked like this one had been hanged or burned for a witch. "Aye, it'll be Madge," she said, with no great excitement. She got him some water in a pail, and he went running with it.

By dint of throwing handfuls in the girl's face he got her eyes open by the time the woman arrived. They lifted her to her feet and the woman helped her to the cottage, while Lanny lugged the turnips. Stooping under the doorway, they laid the girl on the bed, which consisted of a mattress stuffed with straw on a board frame. The girl's skin was transparent and looked like wax; she closed her eyes, and Lanny couldn't be sure whether she had fainted again or not.

"Hadn't you better give her something to eat?" he asked; and the reply was: "There's nowt in the house." This bewildered him. "But what do you do?" he demanded, and the woman said, dully: "The man'll bring summat when he comes, belike."

That didn't satisfy this good Samaritan. He wanted to know if there wasn't some place where he could purchase food, and the woman told him where to find a shop. It proved to be a miserable place, with flyspecked peppermints and gumdrops in the window. He bought a loaf of bread, a tin of beans, and a rusty one of salmon, his guess at a balanced diet. When he got back to the cottage he found that there was no tin-opener, and he had to break into the tins with a knife and a block of wood. When he put the food before the girl, she wolfed it like a famished animal, leaving only part of the bread.

Lanny looked about him. He had read a poem called "The Cottar's Saturday Night." He hadn't been quite sure what a "cottar" was, but now he was in the home of one. It didn't bear much resemblance to the poem. A dark-colored clay had been stuffed into chinks of the walls, and the floor was of planks, very old and worn. The fireplace was black with the smoke of ages. There was another bed like the one the girl was lying on, and a table apparently knocked together by amateur hands, and three stools, each with three peg legs. There was also a row of shelves with a few pans and dishes, and some ancient clothing hanging on the walls, and a water bucket on the floor. That was about all.

One place on the floor was wet, and the woman saw Lanny's eyes resting upon it. "It's the roof," said she. "The blurry landlord won't have it fixed." Lanny asked who was the landlord, and the reply was: "Sir Alfred." It gave the boy a start. "Sir Alfred Pomeroy-Nielson?" The woman answered: "Aye, he's the stingy one, he'll do nowt for ye, not if the house was to blow down."

VI

So Lanny had something to think about on his short walk to The Reaches. He wasn't sure if he ought to mention the matter to his hosts, but he decided that they'd be apt to hear about it, and would think it unnatural that he had kept silence. Lanny went to Rick and told him; good old Rick, who never got embarrassed about anything. Rick said: "It's that good-for-nothing old laborer, Higgs. He's a sot that spends every penny he can get his hands on for drink. What can you do for such a family? The pater's been talking of getting rid of him for a long time, and he should have done it." Rick added that he'd tell his father; but he didn't invite Lanny to the conference. Lanny had an uncomfortable feeling, as if he had opened a closed door and a family skeleton had tumbled out.

The Pomeroy-Nielsons thanked him for his good deed, and Rick took the trouble to explain matters further. The land on which those cottages stood belonged to the family, but the tenants worked for other people. "Most of them are behind with their rent," said Rick, "because the pater's reluctant to press them as other landlords do. The old tenements are nothing but a nuisance, and he has often thought of razing them and plowing the land." The son of the fam-

ily added, with one of his dry smiles, that of course that wouldn't
go very far toward solving the housing question; but you couldn't
expect a man to be an authority on both art and economics.

Lady Pomeroy-Nielson was a stoutish, motherly person who
looked after the boys and made them change their shoes when they
got wet. She was kind, and told Lanny that she would take the poor
child a basket of food. "But I fear it won't do much good," she
added, "unless I stay and see it eaten. That Higgs is a rough fellow,
and he'll take anything he can get his hands on and sell it for a
drink."

Rick discussed with his guest the problem of poverty in England's green and pleasant land. He declared that when human beings got below a certain level, it was very difficult to help them;
drink and drugs took the place of food and they finished themselves
off. Lanny said his father had explained that to him, but he had
thought it applied only to city slums; it had never occurred to him
that there might be slums in the country. Rick said there could be
little difference between country and city; if there was an over-
supply of labor in one it shifted immediately to the other. In the
hop-picking season, hundreds of thousands of people from London's
East End spread out over the country looking for work, and if they
found conditions a bit better on the land, some of them would stay.

It was an insoluble problem—as Rick, and Rick's father, and
Lanny's father agreed; but all the same Lanny couldn't forget the
feel of the pitiful thin body that he had lifted, the waxen skin, and
the frantic look in the girl's eyes when food was held out to her.
Nor could he drive from his mind the impolite thought that, if he
were an English landed gentleman, he would have his lovely green
lawn a trifle less perfectly manicured, and spend the money on keeping the roofs of his cottages in repair.

VII

There had come a cablegram from Robbie; he was sailing from
New York on the *Lusitania*, and would be at the Hotel Cecil on a

certain day. Of course a summons from Robbie took precedence over all other affairs. Lanny went to town the night before, and telephoned the steamship office to find out at what hour the steamer was due. The boy was sitting in the lobby, reading a book, but looking up every few minutes, and when the familiar sturdy figure appeared in the doorway, he sprang up to welcome his father. It was a hot July morning, and perspiration glistened on Robbie's forehead, but he looked well and vigorous as always, and everything he wore was fresh and spotless.

It had been four or five months since his last trip, and they had a lot of news to swap. At lunch Lanny told about Greece and Africa, and the scene on board the *Bluebird*. Then he told about his adventures in the slums of London and of Berkshire. The father said: "That's the curse of England. The most depressing thing I ever saw in my life was the people of London's slums spread out on Hampstead Heath on a bank holiday; men and women lying together on the ground in broad daylight."

Robbie Budd had come on an interesting errand. The firm had completed a new gun on high-angle mountings, to be used for protection against airplanes; the season's best-seller in the armaments trade, he predicted. It would mean another battle with Zaharoff, because Vickers already had one, but it wasn't nearly so good and couldn't be fired so fast. "Are we going to wipe him out?" asked the boy eagerly; and Robbie said they would if there was such a thing as justice in the world. He said this with one of his boyish grins, and added his fear that there wouldn't be any in England for Budd's.

They made themselves comfortable in their suite. Robbie got a bottle of whisky out of his suitcase, and ordered soda and ice—the London hotels were quite "American" now, and ice was one of the signs. For Lanny there was ginger beer, the father having asked him to wait many years before he touched liquor, or smoked, or learned to play poker. He said he wished he had waited longer himself. Lanny was interested to note in how many ways parents expected their children to be wiser than themselves.

Robbie telephoned the manager of Budd's London office, and while waiting for him to arrive, they talked about the English and their Empire. Lanny knew the country now and took a personal interest in it, but he found that his father didn't share his enthusiasm. Robbie had been in business competition with the English, which was different from being a guest in their well-conducted homes. "They are sharp traders," he said, "and that's all right, but what gets your goat is the mask of righteousness they put on; nobody else sells armaments for the love of Jesus Christ." The Empire, he added, was run by a little group of insiders in "the City"—the financial district. "There are no harder-fisted traders anywhere; power for themselves is what they are out for, and they'll destroy the rest of the world to get and keep it."

Lanny had got the impression that they liked Americans; but Robbie said: "Not so. All that talk about 'Hands across the sea,' don't let it fool you for a moment. They're jealous of us, and the best thing they can think of about us is that we're three thousand miles away."

Lanny told about a talk with Sir Alfred, in which the baronet had deplored the great amount of graft in American political life, and had expressed satisfaction because they had nothing of the sort in Britain. "They have a lot more," said the munitions salesman, "only they call it by polite names. In our country when the political bosses want to fill their campaign chest, they put up some rich man for a high office—a 'fat cat' they call him—and he pays the bills and gets elected for a term of years. In England the man pays a much bigger sum into the party campaign chest, and he's made a marquess or a lord, and he and his descendants will govern the Empire forever after—but that isn't corruption, that's 'nobility'!"

You could see the effect of such a system in the armaments industry, Robbie went on to explain; and he didn't have to do any guessing, he was where he could watch the machinery working. "I've come to England with a better gun than Vickers is making; but will the British Empire get that gun? I'm going to do my best, but I'll make a private wager that it'll be the Germans who come across first. The reason is Zaharoff and his associates. They're the best blood, so called, in England. On the board of Vickers are four marquesses and dukes, twenty knights, and fifty viscounts and barons. The Empire will do exactly what they say—and there won't be any 'graft' involved."

VIII

Robbie went about his important affairs, while Lanny learned to know the pictures in the National Gallery. Also he met Kurt's uncle, a stout and florid gentleman who told him about rubber plantations in the Dutch East Indies, and took them to lunch at a place where they could have a *rijstafel*. Rick came to town over the week-end, and they went to the opera and concerts, and to a cricket match. They had lunch with Robbie, who was glad Lanny had picked two such intelligent fellows as friends; he said he would take them to a place that would give them a thrill—the War Planes Review now being held on Salisbury Plain. Robbie had been invited by an army captain who had to do with his negotiations.

The boys were delighted, of course. They had been hearing a lot about the picturesque idea of battles fought in the air. The four of them were up early in the morning, and took a train for Salisbury, some eighty miles west of London, where Captain Finchley had a car to meet them and bring them to the camp. They spent the whole day wandering about seeing the sights. The Royal Flying Corps had put up sheds for seventy planes, and most of them were in the air or lined up on the field, a spectacle the like of which had never before been seen. The officers, of course, were proud of the enterprise and might of Britain.

The largest and newest of the machines was a Farman, and the men dubbed it "the mechanical cow." It was a frail-looking structure, a biplane spreading nearly forty feet across, the wing frames of light spruce and the surface of canvas, well coated and waterproofed. The flier sat in the open, and of course a mighty gale blew around him when he was in the air, so he was muffled up and wore a big helmet. The principal service expected of him was to obtain information as to enemy troop movements and the position of artillery; some planes were provided with wireless sets, others with photographic apparatus. That lone fellow up there was going to be pretty busy, for he also had a carbine and a couple of revolvers with which to defend himself; or he might have an explosive bomb attached to a wire cable, the idea being to get above an enemy plane and run the cable over him.

Many planes were diving and swooping, acquiring the needed skill. Some were learning a new art called "flying in formation"; others were practicing dropping objects upon stationary targets. The visitors watched them until their eyes ached, and the backs of their necks. Every now and then a new plane would take off, and the moment when it left the ground always came to the beholder as a fresh miracle: man's dream of ages realized, the conquest of the last of the elements. The visitors were introduced to some of the pilots, well-padded fellows who of course made it a matter of pride to take it all in the day's work; going up was no miracle to them, and flying around was, to tell the truth, a good deal of a bore, once you got the hang of it. One place in the sky was exactly like another, and the ground beneath was no more exciting than your parlor rug. They were practicing night flying—and that, they admitted, was something that kept you awake. Also, they were very proud because they had succeeded in "looping the loop" in a biplane, for the first time in history.

Lanny was interested to see the effect of all this upon his English friend. Eric Vivian Pomeroy-Nielson, young man of the world whose "note" was sophistication and whose motto was *nil admirari*, was stirred to eloquence by the idea of military aviation. He remarked to Lanny's father that after all England wasn't as backward as the Americans might have thought. He began asking technical questions of Captain Finchley and the fliers; he wanted to know if it wouldn't be possible to mount a machine gun in a plane, and they told him that the French were trying it. "That would be a fight to put a man on his mettle!" exclaimed Rick; a surprising remark from a youth who had been heard to speak of army men as "troglodytes."

Captain Finchley was pleased by this enthusiasm. "I wish more English boys felt that way," he remarked; "the failure of the recent recruiting is a cause of deep concern to all friends of the Empire." Robbie Budd took the occasion to speak about the effect which this new kind of warfare was bound to have upon the position of Englishmen. It deprived them of the advantage of their island solitude. Planes were now flying the Channel, and the Americans had even devised a sort of catapult that could launch a plane from a ship. It was certain that in the next war bombs would be dropped upon munitions centers and factories; and guns that could be fired at planes and airships would surely have to be mounted at vital points. Lanny understood that his father was giving a sales talk—Captain Finchley was on the board which had to decide about the Budd gun with high-angle mountings. Robbie had told his son the previous evening that they were trying to "stall" him; they wouldn't say they would buy the gun, yet they were obviously worried by the idea of his taking it anywhere else.

IX

On their way back to town in the evening the four talked about what they had seen, and the likelihood of these dangerous contrivances being actually put to the test. Kurt Meissner was worried by a letter he had received from home; the situation in the Balkans was more serious than anybody in England seemed to realize. Robbie said, yes, but it was always that way; the English were an easygoing people and left problems for others to solve as much as possible. This was just one more crisis.

"But," exclaimed Kurt, "do the English or anybody else expect the Austrians to let Serbian hooligans incite the murder of Austrian rulers on Austrian soil?"

"The diplomats will get together and stop it," Robbie told him soothingly. Nothing to worry about.

"But it is said that the Russians are backing the Serbs!"

"I know; they're always shoving one another about. The Russians say: 'You let my Serbian friends alone.' The Germans say: 'You let my Austrian friends alone.' The French say: 'You let my Russian friends alone'—so it goes. They've been making faces at one another for hundreds of years."

"I know it, Mr. Budd—but they've been going to war, too."

"The world has been changing so fast that it no longer pays to go to war, Kurt. The nations couldn't finance a war; it would bankrupt them all."

"But," argued Kurt, "when people get angry enough, they don't stop to calculate."

"The masses don't, but they don't have the say any more. It's the financiers who decide, and they're first-class calculators. What's happened is, we've made weapons so destructive that nobody dares use them. Just to have them is enough." Robbie paused for a moment, and smiled. "Did Lanny ever tell you about his meeting with Zaharoff? The old man was worried by the thought that his armaments might some day be put to use; I suggested to him that the ideal of civilization was to spend all our energies making things we never meant to use." Robbie chuckled, and they all chuckled with him, though a bit dubiously.

A few days later Lanny set out for France to join his mother, and Robbie was packing up his Budd gun, preparatory to taking it to Germany, in an effort to wake the British up—or so he confided to his son. On that day King George was reviewing the might of the British navy off Spithead. His flagship was the *Iron Duke,* a dreadnought that could shoot away fifty thousand dollars in a single minute. Included in its armament were two twelve-pounder guns with high-angle mountings against airplanes. On that day . . .

It was the twentieth of July 1914.

10

La Belle France

I

MRS. EMILY CHATTERSWORTH was the widow of a New York banker who had once held great power, controlling railroads and trust companies and what not; he had become involved in some Congressional investigation—it had been a long time ago, and nobody remembered just what it was, but the newspapers had exhibited bad manners, and the banker had decided that his native land was lacking in refinement. His widow had inherited his fortune and, being still good-looking, was described by Sophie, Baroness de la Tourette, as "an island entirely surrounded by French suitors." Perhaps the country's laws regarding the property rights of married women were unsatisfactory to Mrs. Emily; anyhow, she had remained for years the sole mistress of Les Forêts, as her country estate was called.

The château was in French Renaissance style, a four-story structure of gray stone, built at the head of a little artificial lake. There was an esplanade in front, resembling the docks of a port, complete with several small lighthouses; when the lights were turned on at night the effect was impressive. At the front of the house, beyond the entrance drive, was a garden, the central feature of which was a great fleur-de-lis made of gold and purple flowers. Surrounding the place were smooth lawns shaded by chestnut trees, and beyond them were dark forests of beeches, for which the place had been named. In them were deer and pheasants, and in the kennels were dogs used for hunting in the fall. Among other interesting things was an orchid house, in which you might examine the strange and costly products of the jungles of South America, for as long as you could stand the moist heat in which they throve.

The rooms of this château were splendid, and had tapestries and works of art which connoisseurs came to study. Mrs. Emily knew what she had, and spoke of them with authority. She lived and entertained in the French manner, conducting what was called a salon—an arduous undertaking, a career all in itself. It meant inviting a number of celebrated men at regular intervals and giving them a chance to air their wit and erudition before others. Each one of these personages was conscious of his own importance, and resentful of the pretended importance of his rivals; to know who could get along with whom, and to reconcile all the vanities and jealousies, took skill and energy enough for a diplomat guarding the fate of nations.

Beauty Budd had very few pretensions to wit, and still fewer to erudition, but she possessed a treasure appreciated in any drawing room—she was easy to look at. She also possessed a full supply of womanly tact, and was naturally kind, and didn't quarrel with other ladies or try to take away their men. The weaker sex was supposed to do little talking at a salon; as among the fowls, it was the males who displayed the gorgeous plumage and made the loud noises. The company did not break up into groups, as was the custom in English and American drawing rooms. There would be a super-celebrity who would set the theme and do most of the expounding; the other celebrities would say their say, and the function of the hostess was to supervise and shepherd the conversation. The other ladies listened, and did not interrupt unless they were quite sure they had something supremely witty that could be uttered in a sentence or two. Generally they thought of it too late, and for that misfortune the French had a phrase, *esprit de l'escalier*, that is to say, staircase wit.

Of course it was not possible for an American woman, however wealthy, to have a really first-class salon in France. The fashionables and the intellectuals of that land were clannish, and it took a full lifetime to learn the subtleties of their differentiations. There were royalist salons and republican salons, Catholic salons and free-thought salons, literary and art salons, each its own little world, with but slight interest in foreigners. However, an American could provide a way for her fellow-countrymen to meet such Frenchmen as were international-minded, and Mrs. Emily, a handsome and stately lady, was conscientious about performing this service.

She would give dinner parties, also in the French manner, the hostess sitting midway between the ends of the table, putting the most important guest directly across from her, and then shading off to persons of least importance, who sat at the ends. There was a French phrase for that too, *le bout de table*. At dinner parties you did not chat with the person on either hand, but listened to those whose importance had been indicated by their seating. One of these was privileged to hold forth for a few minutes on any subject, and then he was expected to let the hostess indicate another performer. A cultivated people had been centuries evolving this routine, and to them it was extremely important.

II

There wasn't much place for children in Les Forêts, and they were rarely invited. But Mrs. Emily had met Lanny on the Riviera, and knew that he could be counted upon to wipe his feet before treading the heavy red velvet carpets which covered the entrance hall and went up the central stairway. He would stand for a long time looking at a painting in silence, and if he asked a question it would be an intelligent one. He never interrupted the conversation of his elders, and had listened to so many conversations that he was almost an elder himself. Mrs. Emily had suggested to Beauty that he might come and stay until they both were ready to return to Juan-les-Pins.

So here was Lanny, playing tennis with the children of the steward who managed the estate, swimming in the lake, riding the fine, high-strung horses, playing not too loudly upon a sonorous piano, and reading in a library where a pale and black-clad scholar had spent a lifetime cataloguing and watching over treasures. Here was a person worth listening to, and glad to have an audience. A week with M. Priedieu meant as much to Lanny Budd as a term in college. The old gentleman helped to orientate him in the world of books, making known to him the writers from whom he could find out about other writers; it was like giving him a map of the forests, so that he could go out and explore for himself.

Another educational influence was Mrs. Emily's mother, who was history. She had been a "Baltimore belle," and told how beautiful she used to be and how the beaux had swarmed about her. Now she was in her mid-seventies, and had lovely golden curls which looked quite natural; Lanny was surprised when his mother told him how once the sprightly old lady had rocked with laughter and thrown her curls into her plate of soup. She was painted all pink and white over her many wrinkles, and was automatically driven to exercise charm upon anything that came along in trousers.

Lanny fell under her spell, and she told him how her daughter Emily had been born amid the sounds of battle; the Fifth New York regiment, marching through Baltimore on its way to defend Washington at the outbreak of the American Civil War, had fired upon the citizens. "That fixes her age at fifty-three, so she doesn't like to have it told on her, and you must keep it a secret; but Emily herself won't be able to keep it much longer unless she consents to dye her hair. Dear me, how I do rattle on!" said Mrs. Sally Lee Sibley; and she added: "What a hideous and ruinous thing that war was, and how lucky we are who don't have to see such things!"

Lanny was moved to tell how yesterday he had heard Prince Skobelkov remark that Russia ought to bring war on right now, because his country was ready and could never be more so. The old lady looked at the boy in horror and whispered: "Oh, no, no! Don't let anybody say such a thing! Oh, what wicked people!" Mrs. Sally Lee Sibley lived in Europe because it was her fate, but privately she hated it.

III

Of course a half-grown boy was not invited to a salon or to formal dinner parties; but there were house guests, and callers in great numbers, and Lanny met them, and listened to conversations about the state of Europe, in which persons who were on the inside of affairs talked freely, being among those who had a right to know. There was a Russian military mission in Paris, and the famous general, Prince Skobelkov, was a member of it; he found time to motor out and have tea, even in the midst of a world-shaking crisis. Also the French Senator Bidou-Lascelles, who said, in American poker language: "Germany is trying to use Austria to bluff Russia, and this will go on indefinitely unless we call the bluff." The Prince assented, and added: "Our official information is that Austria is unprepared, and will prove a weak ally."

Lanny listened, and thought that he didn't like these two old men. The Russian was large, red-faced, and tightly laced up, and spoke French explosively. The senator was baldheaded and paunchy, with a white imperial that waggled somewhat absurdly; he was an ardent Catholic, and fought for his Church party in the Senate, but to Lanny he didn't seem religious, but rather a little gnome plotting dreadful things. Lanny recollected the beautiful Austrian country through which he had passed, the mountain cottages with steep roofs to shed the snow, and the inns with fancy gilded signs. He thought of Kurt Meissner, and his brothers who were in the German army. Kurt was to come to Paris in a few days, to meet his "rubber" uncle and return home with him. Lanny had thought of having him invited to Les Forêts, but decided that it wouldn't do, with people voicing opinions like these.

Mrs. Emily had thrown her estate open for a charity bazaar, and booths had been set up, decorated with bunting and huge quantities of flowers. Everybody donated things to be sold, and the crowds came and bought them. It appeared that there were vast numbers of persons who had money enough to wear fashionable clothes, but couldn't get into the right society. Here they would have a chance, not merely to look at the *gratin*, as the inner circle was called, but even to speak to them.

It was a scheme devised to turn the weaknesses of human nature to a useful purpose. There were "cabbage patches" in Paris, too, and the poor who lived in them sometimes fell ill, and had to be cared for in hospitals, and this was the established way to raise the money. The most aloof of the great ladies of society offered themselves as bait, duchesses and countesses of the old nobility putting themselves on exhibition, and you might have the honor of addressing them. But you weren't to expect to have it cheaply, for the prices were graded according to those laws of precedence which ruled at dinner parties. A cousin of the Russian Tsar was in charge of the booth where Mrs. Emily's orchids were sold, and for the commonest of them you would have to part with a hundred-franc note, or twenty American dollars. Along with it you would get a charming smile from a regal person, and if you paid double the price asked, she might even hold out a hand to be kissed.

This was like a debut party for Lanny; he was to act as a sort of page, and run errands for the ladies, and he had on long trousers for the first time—a neat white linen suit made especially for the occasion. He felt extremely self-conscious, but knew he mustn't show it; he strolled about the soft green lawns and was introduced to many persons, and made himself helpful in every way he could think of. The grounds presented a gay picture; so many ladies with striped parasols and hats full of flowers and feathers and even whole birds.

Beauty was selling little bouquets, as she had done in London; she was notable in pale yellow taffeta embroidered with large green berries; the corsage prolonged into a polonaise, and the skirt of soft white muslin, cut narrow. With a throat low and sleeves short, Beauty made the most of her numerous charms and was in a state of exaltation, as always when there were many people about and she knew they were admiring her; she had a smile for everybody, and a happy greeting, especially for gentlemen whom she discovered without a boutonnière. She would extend one seductively, saying:

"*Pour les pauvres.*" When they asked the price she would say: "All you have," and when they handed her a ten-franc note, she would thank them soulfully, and they would have to forget about the change, because she didn't have any.

Harry Murchison was there, following her everywhere with his eyes. He was a fair mark for the ladies, for he was known as a rich American, and handsome; they lured him to the booths, and he would buy whatever they offered, and then take it to another booth to be sold again by ladies equally charming. They made a game out of the whole thing—it could be nothing but that, of course, because there were persons here who could have built hospitals for all the poor of Paris if they had wanted to. But what they wanted was to dress up and display themselves. They sat at little tables and had Mrs. Emily's uniformed servants bring them tea and little cakes; they sipped and nibbled while they chatted, and paid double prices for what they got, and if there were any tips, these also went *pour les pauvres.*

IV

A day or two later there was a more exclusive tea party; Mrs. Emily's friends were invited to meet a famous writer. He was no stranger to Lanny Budd, because he had a villa at Antibes, and came there often, and went around wearing little round skullcaps of silk or velvet, always of a bright color and always different—he must have had a hundred of them. He was an old gentleman, tall and thin, with a large head and a long face, like a horse's. His name was Thibault, but he went by his pen name of Anatole France. Everybody talked about his books, but Lanny had got the impression that they were not for the young.

Now he came in a blue velvet coat and a large brown felt hat. He descended slowly from a motorcar, and was escorted to the shade of a great chestnut tree; once he was seated in a lawn chair, all the ladies and gentlemen brought their chairs where they could sit and look and listen. As soon as he got started, everyone else was silent;

they had come to hear him, and he knew it, and they knew it, and
he knew that they knew it, and so on. Had he rehearsed in his mind
what he was going to say? Very probably; but nobody minded that.
He poured out for them a stream of ironic remarks, in an even tone,
with a serious mien except for a twinkle in the bright old eyes. Now
and then he would put his fingers together in front of him, and
move them as if he were telling off the points in his mind.

Most of his talk was too subtle for a youngster. M. France had
read everything that was old, and his mind was a storehouse of
anecdotes and allusions to history, religion, and art; it was as if you
were wandering through a museum so crowded that you hardly had
room to move or time to see anything properly. Possibly there was
only one person in the company who could understand everything
the great man was saying, and that was M. Priedieu, the pale, ascetic
librarian, who stood humbly on the outskirts and was not introduced. Lanny thought there was pain in his face, he being a reverent
scholar, whereas M. France made mockery of everything he touched.

Somebody started to ask him a question beginning: "What do
you think—?" and he answered quickly: "I am trying to cure
myself of the habit of thinking, which is a great infirmity. May God
preserve you from it, as He has preserved His greatest saints, and
those whom He loves and destines to eternal felicity!"

Sooner or later the conversation of French ladies and gentlemen
was apt to turn to the subject of love. On this also it appeared that
the elderly author was skeptical. A saucy young lady asked him
something about love in South America, and he made a laughing
reply, and the company was vastly amused. Lanny didn't understand
it, but afterward he gathered that M. France had once taken a
lecture trip to the Argentine, and on the steamer had met a young
actress; he had traveled with her, introducing her as his wife. Later,
when he returned to France, he did not want her as a wife, but the
young lady was disposed to insist, and there resulted a considerable
scandal.

Also Lanny heard about a wealthy lady of Paris to whom this
story had caused great distress. Madame de Caillavet was her name,

and she was credited with having made the fame and fortune of Anatole France, setting up a salon for the display of his talents and driving this most indolent person to the task of writing books. She and her husband had maintained with France the relationship known as *la vie à trois*—life in threes, instead of pairs. No one had objected to that, but the Argentine actress had made four, and everyone considered her *de trop*.

Madame de Caillavet was dead now, so Anatole France no longer had a salon. Perhaps that was why it was possible for an American hostess to lure him to a tea party. After he had taken his departure, they all gossiped about him, saying as many malicious things as he himself had said about Cicero, Cleopatra, St. Cyprian, Joan of Arc, King Louis XV, the Empress Catherine of Russia, and many other personages of history whom he had quoted. However, all agreed that he was an extremely diverting person; they had been so well entertained that for two hours they had forgotten the disturbing news that the Austrian government had delivered to the Serbian government an ultimatum which practically required the abdication of the latter and the taking over of its police functions by Austrian officials.

V

Beauty went motoring with Harry Murchison. She was gone all day, and came back looking flushed and happy, and Lanny went to her room to chat. They would have little snatches like that—she would tell him where she had been, and the nice things that Prince This and Ambassador That had said to her.

But this time she wanted to talk about Harry. He was such an obliging and generous fellow, and his family in Pennsylvania was a very old one; he had an ancestor who had been a member of the First Continental Congress. Harry liked Lanny very much, calling him the best-mannered boy he had ever met; but he thought it was too bad for him not to have a chance to know his own country. "That's what Mr. Hackabury said, too," remarked the boy.

But Beauty didn't want to talk about soap just then; she was interested in plate glass. "Tell me," she persisted, "do you really like him?"

"Why, yes, I think he's all right." Lanny was a bit reserved.

But then came a knockout. "How would you feel if I was to marry him?"

The boy would have had to be a highly trained diplomat to hide the dismay which smote him. The blood mounted to his cheeks, and he stared at his mother until she dropped her eyes. "Oh, Beauty!" he exclaimed. "What about Marcel?"

"Come sit here by me, dear," she said. "It's not easy to explain such things to one so young. Marcel has never expected to marry me. He has no money and he knows that I have none."

"But I don't understand. Would Robbie stop giving you money if you married?"

"No, dear, I don't mean that. But I can't always live on what Robbie gives me."

"But why not, Beauty? Aren't we getting along all right?"

"You don't know about my affairs. I have an awful lot of debts; they drive me to distraction."

"But why can't we go and live quietly at Bienvenu and not spend so much money?"

"I can't shut myself up like that, Lanny—I'm just not made for it. I'd have to give up all my friends, I couldn't travel anywhere, I couldn't entertain. And you wouldn't have any education—you wouldn't see the world as you've been doing——"

"Oh, please don't do it on my account!" the boy broke in. "I'd be perfectly happy to stay home and read books and play the piano."

"You think you would, dear; but that's because you don't know enough about life. People like us have to have money and opportunities—so many things you will find that you want."

"If I do, I can go to work and get them for myself, can't I?"

Beauty didn't answer; for of course that wasn't the real point; she was thinking about what she herself wanted right now. After a while Lanny ventured, in a low voice: "Marcel will be so unhappy!"

"Marcel has his art, dear. He's perfectly content to live in a hut and paint pictures all day."

"Maybe he is, so long as you are there. But doesn't he miss you right now?"

"Are you so fond of him, Lanny?"

"I thought that was what you wanted!" the boy burst out. "I thought that was the way to be fair to you!"

"It was, dear; and it was sweet. I appreciate it more than I've ever told you. But there are circumstances that I cannot control."

There was a pause, and the mother began to talk about Harry Murchison again. He had been in love with her for quite a while, and had been begging her to marry him; his love was a true and unselfish one. He was an unusually fine man, and could offer her things that others couldn't—not merely his money, but protection, and help in managing her affairs, in dealing with other people, who so often took advantage of her trustfulness and her lack of business knowledge.

"Harry has a lovely home in Pennsylvania, and we can go there to live, or we can travel—whatever we please. He's prepared to do everything he can for you; you can go to school if you like, or have a tutor—you can take Mr. Elphinstone to America with you, if you wish."

But Lanny didn't care anything about Mr. Elphinstone; he didn't care anything about America. He loved their home at Juan, the friends he had there and the things he did there. "Tell me, Beauty," he persisted, "don't you love Marcel any more?"

"In a way," she answered; "but"—then she stopped, embarrassed.

"Has he done something that isn't fair to you?"

The boy saw the beginning of tears in his mother's eyes. "Lanny, I don't think it's right for you to take up notions like that, and cross-question me and try to pin me down——"

"But I'm only trying to understand, Beauty!"

"You can't understand, because you aren't old enough, and these things are complicated and difficult. It's hard for a woman to know her own heart, to say nothing of trying to explain it to her son."

"Well, I wish very much that you'd do what you can," said Lanny, gravely. Something told him that this was a crisis in their lives; and how he wished he could grow up suddenly! "Can you love two men at the same time, Beauty?"

"That is what I've been asking myself for a long while. Apparently I can." Beauty hadn't intended to make any such confession, but she was in a state of inner turmoil, and it was her nature to blurt things out. "My love for Marcel has always been that of a mother; I've thought of him as a helpless child that needed me."

"Well, doesn't he still need you? And if he does, what is going to become of him?"

Tears were making their way onto Beauty's tender cheeks. She didn't answer, and Lanny wondered if it was because she had no answer. He was afraid of hurting his mother; but also he was afraid of seeing her hurt Marcel. He had watched them both on the yacht, and impressions of their love had been indelibly graven upon his mind. Marcel adored her; and what would he do without her?

"Tell me this, Beauty, have you told Harry you will marry him?"

"No, I haven't exactly said that; but he wants me so much——"

"Well, I don't think you ought to make up your mind to such a step in a hurry. If it's debts, you ought to talk to Robbie about them."

"Oh, no, Lanny! I promised him I wouldn't have any debts."

"Well, don't you think you ought to wait and talk to Marcel at least?" Lanny was growing up rapidly in the face of this crisis.

"Oh, I couldn't do that!"

"But what do you expect to do? Just walk off and leave him? Would that be fair, Beauty? It seems to me it would be dreadfully unkind!"

His mother was staring at him, greatly disconcerted. "Lanny, you oughtn't to talk to me like that. I'm your mother!"

"You're the best mother in the world," declared the boy, with ardor. "But I don't want to see you do something that'll make us all unhappy. Please, Beauty, don't promise Harry till we've had time to think about it. Some day you may see me making some mistake, and then you'll be begging me to wait."

Beauty began sobbing. "Oh, Lanny, I'm in such an awful mess! Harry will be so upset—I've kept him waiting too long!"

"Let him wait, all the same," he insisted. He found himself suddenly taking the position of head of the family. "We just can't decide such a thing all at once." Then, after a pause: "Tell me—does Harry know about Marcel?"

"Yes, he knows, of course."

"But does he know how—how serious it is?"

"He doesn't care, Lanny! He's in love with me."

"Well, he oughtn't to be—at least, I mean, he oughtn't try to take you away from us!"

VI

Lanny Budd, in the middle of his fifteenth year, had to sit down and figure out this complicated man and woman business. He had been collecting data from various persons, over a large section of Europe. They hadn't left him to find out about it in his own way, they had forced it upon him: Baron Livens-Mazursky, Dr. Bauer-Siemans, the Social-Democratic editor, Beauty, Marcel and Harry, Edna and Ezra Hackabury, Miss Noggyns and Rosemary, Sophie and her lover—Lanny had seen them embracing one evening on the deck of the *Bluebird*—Mrs. Emily, who had a leading French art critic as her *ami*, old M. France and his Madame de Caillavet and his Argentine actress—to say nothing of his jokes about the leading ladies and gentlemen of history, rather horrid persons, some of them. King Louis XV had said to one of his courtiers that one woman was the same as another, only first she must be bathed and then have her teeth attended to.

In this world into which Lanny Budd had been born, love was a game which people played for their amusement; a pastime on about the same level as bridge or baccarat, horse racing or polo. It was, incidentally, a duel between men and women, in which each tried to achieve prestige in the eyes of the other; that was what the salons were for, the dinner parties, the fashionable clothes, the fine houses, the works of art. Lanny couldn't have formulated that, but he observed the facts, and in a time of stress understanding came to him.

Concealment was an important aspect of nearly all love, as Lanny had observed it; and this seemed to indicate that many people disapproved of the practice—the church people, for example. He had never been to church, except for a fashionable wedding, or to look at stained-glass windows and architecture. But he knew that many society people professed to be religious, and now and then they repented of their love affairs and became actively pious. This was one of the most familiar aspects of life in France, and in French fiction. Sophie's mother-in-law, an elderly lady of the old nobility with a worthless and dissipated son, lived alone, wore black, kept herself surrounded by priests and nuns, and prayed day and night for the soul of the prodigal.

Of course, there were married persons who managed to stay together and raise families. Robbie was apparently that sort; he never went after women, so far as Lanny had heard; but he seldom referred to his family in Connecticut, so it hardly existed for the boy. Apparently the Pomeroy-Nielsons also got along with each other; but Lanny had heard so much of extramarital adventures, he somehow took it for granted that if you came to know a person well enough, you'd find some hidden *affaire*.

The fashionable people had a code under which they did what they pleased, and he had never heard any of them question this right. But evidently the outside world did question it, and that seemed to put the fashionable ones in a trying position. They had always to guard against a thing called "a scandal." Lanny had commented upon this to Rick, who explained that "a scandal" was having your *affaire* get into newspapers. Because of the libel laws, this could happen only if it was dragged into court. In English country houses, everybody would know that Lord Black and Lady White were lovers, and all hostesses would put them in adjoining rooms; but never a word would be said about it, except among the "right" people, and it was an unforgivable offense to betray another person's love affair or do anything that would bring publicity upon it.

Lanny had been officially taught the "facts of life," and so was beginning to know his way about in society. He had come to know who was whose, so to speak, and at the same time he knew that he wasn't supposed to know—unless the persons themselves allowed him to. There were things he mustn't say to them, and others he must never say to anyone. The persons he met might be doing something very evil, but if there hadn't been "a scandal," they would be received in society, and it wasn't his privilege to set up a code and try to enforce it.

It had never before occurred to Lanny to find any serious fault with his darling Beauty. But now his quick mind could not fail to put two and two together. For years he had been hearing her tell her friends that she refused to "pay the price"; and now, how could he keep from believing that she was changing her mind? It was painful to have to face the idea that his adored mother might be selling herself to a handsome young millionaire in order to be able to have her gowns made by Paquin or Poiret, and to wear long ropes of genuine pearls as her friend Emily Chattersworth did! He told himself that there must be some reason why she was no longer happy with Marcel. The only thing he could think of was the painter's efforts to keep her from gambling, and from running into debt and losing her sleep. But Lanny had decided that Marcel was right about that.

VII

"I must go and see Isadora," said Mrs. Emily. "Maybe Lanny would like to go along."

Lanny cried: "Oh, thank you! I'd love it—more than anything." For years he had been hearing about Isadora, and once he had seen her at a lawn party at Cannes, but he had never had an opportunity to meet her or even to see her dance. People raved about her in such terms that to the boy she was a fabulous being.

Harry Murchison telephoned, and when Beauty told him about the proposed trip, he begged to be allowed to drive them. Mrs. Emily gave her consent; it appeared that she was promoting the affair between Harry and Beauty, giving the latter what she considered sensible advice.

They set out, Lanny riding in the front seat beside the young scion of plate glass, who laid himself out to be agreeable. But Lanny was hard to please; he was polite, but reserved; he knew quite well that he wasn't being wooed for his own beautiful eyes. Harry Murchison was well dressed and dignified, and had been to college and all that, but his best friend couldn't have claimed that he was a brilliant talker. When it came to questions of art and the imagination, he would listen for a while, trying to find something to say that was safe.

For example, Harry had seen Isadora Duncan dance; and what could he say about it? He said that she danced on an empty stage, and with bare feet, and that people in Pittsburgh had considered that decidedly *risqué*. He said that she had an orchestra, and danced "classical" music—as if anybody had imagined her dancing a cakewalk! If you made him search his memory he might add that she had blue velvet curtains at the back of the stage, and wore draperies of different colors according to the music, and that people clapped and shouted and made her come on again and again.

But imagine Marcel Detaze talking about Isadora! In the first place, he would know what was unique in her art, and how it was related to other dancing. He would know the difference between free gestures and any sort of conventionalized form. He would know the names of the compositions she danced, and what they expressed —poignant grief, joy of nature, revolt against fate, springtime awakening—and as Marcel told you about them he would grieve, rejoice, revolt, or awaken. He would use many gestures, he would make you realize the feat that was being performed—one small woman's figure, alone and without the aid of scenery, embodying the deepest experiences of the human soul; struck down with grief, lifted up in ecstasy, sweeping across the stage in such a tumult that you felt you were watching a great procession.

In short, Lanny was all for French temperament, as against American common sense. Of course, plate glass was useful, perhaps even necessary to civilization; but what did Harry Murchison have to do with it, except that he happened to be the grandson of a man who had known about it? Harry got big dividend checks, and would get bigger ones when his father and mother died; but that was all. He had sense enough to find Pittsburgh smoky and boring, and had come to Paris in search of culture and beauty. And that was all right—only let him find some other beauty than that upon which Lanny and Marcel had staked their claims!

Mrs. Emily in the back seat was telling about the *affaires* of Isadora, and Lanny turned his head to listen. The dancer was another person who had been experimenting with the sex life. She was a "free lover"—a new term to Lanny. He gathered its meaning to be that she refused to conceal what she did. Defying the dreadful thing called "scandal," she had had two children, one by a son of Ellen Terry, the actress, and the other by an American millionaire whom she called "Lohengrin." The smart world could not overlook such an opportunity for entertaining itself, and delighted in a story that Isadora had once offered to have a child by Bernard Shaw, saying that such a child would have her beauty and his brains; to which the skeptical playwright had replied: "Suppose it should have my beauty and your brains?"

The jealous fates would not permit a woman to believe too much in happiness, or to practice what she preached. Early in the previous year a dreadful tragedy had befallen those two lovely children. They had been left in an automobile, and apparently the chauffeur had failed to set the brakes properly. The car had rolled down hill, crashed into a bridge, and plunged into deep water; the children had been taken out dead. The distracted mother had wandered over Europe, hardly knowing what she did; but now her friend "Lohengrin" had taken charge of her, and had purchased a great hotel in the environs of Paris, and Isadora was trying to restore herself to life by teaching other people's children to dance—and incidentally, so Mrs. Emily revealed, by having another child of her own.

VIII

The hotel at Bellevue was a large place with several hundred rooms; a commonplace building, but with lovely gardens sloping to the river, and from the terrace in front of it a view over the whole of Paris. The dining room had been turned into the dancing room, and there were Isadora's blue velvet curtains. Tiers of seats had been built on each side, where the pupils sat while the lessons were given on the floor. The teachers were the older pupils; the school had been going for only a few months, but already they had been able to give a festival at the Trocadéro and rouse an audience to transports of delight.

Isadora Duncan was a not very large woman, with abundant dark brown hair, regular features, a gentle, sad expression, and a figure of loveliness and grace. She had come from California, unknown and without resources, except her genius, and had created an art which held vast audiences spellbound in all the capitals of Europe and America. Even now, expecting a baby in a few days, she would step forward to show her troop of children some gesture; she would make a few simple movements against the background of her blue curtains, and something magical would happen, a spirit would be revealed, an intimation of glory. Even reclining on a couch, making motions with arms and hands, Isadora was noble and inspiring.

The music of a piano sounded and a group of children swung into action, eager, alert, radiating joy. Lanny Budd's whole being leaped with them. It took him back to Hellerau, but it was different, more spontaneous, lacking the basis of drill. In "Dalcroze" there was science; but these children caught a spirit—and Lanny, too, had that spirit; he knew instantly what they were doing. He could hardly keep his seat; for dancing is not something to be watched, it is something to be done.

Afterward they had lunch in the garden, the visitors, the teachers, and the children. "Lohengrin" was pouring out this prodigality, and to Lanny the place seemed a sort of artists' heaven. The children, boys and girls of all ages, wore tunics of bright colors; they lived on vegetarian foods, but it didn't keep them from having bright cheeks and eyes, and hearts full of love for Isadora, and for the beauty they were helping to create. Lanny exclaimed: "Oh, I'd like to come here, Beauty! Do you suppose Isadora would take me?"

"Perhaps she would," said Beauty; and Mrs. Emily said she would ask her, if they meant it. Mrs. Emily had helped Isadora to become known, and the lovely white feet had danced more than once on the lawn under the chestnut trees at Les Forêts.

But suddenly Lanny thought, was he free just then to think about dancing? Didn't he have to stay with Beauty, and watch over her, and try to save poor Marcel from having his happiness ruined? Oh, this accursed sex problem!

Artists came to Bellevue, and sat upon a platform in the center of the hall and made sketches of the dancing children. At Meudon, not far away, was the studio of a famous sculptor, Auguste Rodin; a sturdy son of the people with a great spade beard, broad features, and ponderous form. He was an old man now, becoming feeble, but he could still make wonderful sketches. He sat near Lanny and, when the dancing was over, talked about the loveliness of it, and wished he could have had such models for all his work—models who lived, and moved, and brought harmony before the eyes in a thousand shifting forms. Lanny thought that this old man himself had been able to make marble and bronze live and move; he tried to say it, and the sculptor put his big hand on the boy's head, and told him to come to the studio some day and see the works which had not yet been given to the world.

Driving into Paris, the ladies talked about Rodin, who also was providing evidence about the love life! He was getting into his dotage, and had fallen prey to an American woman, married to a

Frenchman who bore one of the oldest and proudest names in history. "But that doesn't keep them from being bad characters," said Mrs. Emily. She told how this pair had preyed upon the old artist and got him to sign away much of his precious work.

"Oh, dear, oh, dear!" exclaimed Beauty Budd. "What pitiful creatures men are!" She meant it for Harry, of course; but Lanny heard it and agreed. People wished to take love as a source of pleasure, but it seemed to bring them torment. The primrose path had thorns in it, and as time passed these thorns became dry and hard and sharper than a serpent's tooth.

They came into Paris at the hour when the shops and factories were closing, and the streets swarming with people. The crowds did not seem to be hurrying as usual; they would form groups and stand talking together. The newsboys were shouting everywhere, and the headlines on the papers were big enough so that motorists could read without stopping. LA GUERRE! was the gist of them all. Austria had that day declared war upon Serbia! And what was Russia going to do? What would Germany do? And France? And England? People stared at one another, unable to grasp the awful thing that was crashing upon the world.

11

C'est la Guerre

I

BEAUTIFUL flowers bloomed in the garden that was Europe. They spread wide petals to the sunshine, trusting the security of the warm and sheltered place. Over them fluttered butterflies, also

of splendid hues and delicate structure, loving the sunlight, floating
upon peace and stillness. But suddenly came a tempest, harsh and
blind, tearing the fragile wings of the butterflies, hurling them
against the branches of trees or into the sodden ground; ripping the
petals off the flowers, stripping the foliage, leaving bare wrecked
limbs to mock the lovers of beauty. So it was with Lanny Budd
during the next dreadful week, and so with all the persons he knew,
and with countless millions of others, from Land's End to
Vladivostok, from Archangel to the Cape of Good Hope. It was
the worst week in the history of Europe—and there were many more
to follow.

Lanny had been expecting his friend Kurt Meissner in Paris;
but several days before had come a letter from Kurt, written on a
Channel steamer, saying that his father had telegraphed him to
return home at once, taking the first boat by way of the Hook of
Holland. Kurt had been worried, thinking there must be illness in
his family; but now Lanny understood what had happened—Herr
Meissner had known what was coming. In London and Paris one
heard many stories about Germans who had received such warnings,
and had taken measures for their personal safety or their financial
advantage. Here and there one had even passed on a discreet "tip"
to an American friend.

Lanny and his mother came to Paris, and Robbie showed up there
on the morning after Austria declared war. He wouldn't lack
advance information, be sure! He said that a salesman of armaments
wouldn't have to do any more traveling now; the governments
would find him wherever he was. The thing had come which Robbie
had said couldn't possibly come; but it didn't take him long to
adjust himself to it. "All right, it's what Europe wants, let them
have it." Budd's would continue to turn out products, and anybody
could buy them who came with the cash. Somebody had been telling Robbie about Shaw's *Major Barbara*, so now he talked impressively about "the Creed of the Armorer."

It was good to have Robbie at hand in a time like this; self-
possessed as ever, a firm rock of counsel, also a checkbook open to

friends in trouble. He and Beauty and Lanny settled down to a conference; and presently Harry Murchison came into it—forcing himself in, by taking his problem to Robbie. They had met once before and were on friendly terms, Harry being the sort of fellow that Robbie approved.

"Mr. Budd," said he, "I don't know why you and Beauty parted, and I'm not interested; but I know you're still her friend, and she listens to you, and I wish you'd give her sensible advice. I want to marry her—right now—today—and take her out of this hell that's starting here. She can have a new life in America; I'll do most anything she asks, give her anything she can think of. As for Lanny, I'll take care of him, or you can—I like the boy, and we'll be the best of friends if he'll let me. Surely that's a fair offer!"

Robbie thought it was; and so the whole situation was forced into the open. Lanny talked to his father, not merely about Marcel, but about Baron Livens-Mazursky, and Dr. Bauer-Siemans, and the Hackaburys, and Isadora, and Anatole France, and all the rest; he had to make Robbie understand how he came to know so much about love, and why he was taking it upon himself to keep a French painter from losing his beautiful blond mistress. Robbie didn't have much use for either Frenchmen or painters, but he was very much for Lanny, and couldn't help being tickled by this odd situation, a sensitive, idealistic kid undertaking to make a hero out of his mother's lover—and seeming very likely to get away with it. It was clear that Beauty was still half in love with her painter; the other half in love with the idea of becoming a respectable American lady, wife of a man who could give her security and position. Which would she choose?

II

It was a time for showdowns. In the crash of kingdoms and empires, human blunders and failures shrank to smaller proportions. Beauty took her son into a room apart, and told him a story which so far she had kept from nearly everyone she knew. She couldn't look him in the eyes, and blushed intensely—her throat, her cheeks, her forehead. "Your father and I have never been married, Lanny. The story that we are divorced is one that I made up to protect you and me. I didn't want people to know that you are illegitimate, and make it a handicap to your life."

She rushed on to pour out the details, defending both herself and Robbie. They had met in Paris when they were very young, and they had loved each other truly, and had planned to marry. But Beauty had been an artist's model, and had been painted in the nude. Lanny would understand that, he knew what art was; one of the pictures had been exhibited in a salon, and was much admired. But some malicious person had sent a photograph of it to Robbie's father, the head of an old and proud family of Puritan New England. It had meant only one thing to him, that Beauty was an indecent woman; he was a harsh and domineering man, and was he going to have his son marrying a painter's model, and having her picture in the newspapers naked instead of in the usual bridal costume? That was what he said, and he laid down the law: if Robbie married such a woman his father would disown and disinherit him.

Robbie wanted to do it, even so, but Beauty wouldn't let him; she loved him and wouldn't wreck his life. They had lived together without marriage; the father had consented to ignore his son's mistress, something not so unusual, even for Puritans in New England. It was hard on Lanny, but they hadn't meant for him to happen—Lanny had been an accident, said his mother at the climax of her confusion and blushes.

She had thought she would never have the courage to tell this story to her son; she took it for granted that he would receive it with shame, and perhaps with anger toward her. But Lanny had by now seen so much of lawless love, and heard about so much more, that the distinctions were blurred in his mind. He said it didn't worry him to be illegitimate; it hadn't hurt his health, and it wouldn't hurt his feelings if somebody called him a bastard—he had read about them in Shakespeare and had got the impression that they were a lively lot. What did give him shivers was the idea of having been an "accident." "Where would I have been, and what would I have been, if you and Robbie hadn't had me?"

Tears came into the mother's bright blue eyes; she saw that he was trying to spare her; he was being a darling, as usual. She hastened to explain the situation which now confronted her, the reasons why her decision was so important. If she were to marry Harry Murchison, that would cover all her past and make her a "respectable" woman; it wouldn't make Lanny legitimate, but it would keep anybody from bothering about it—and anyhow Robbie intended to acknowledge him as his son.

Lanny could understand all that; but he said: "What good will it do you to be respectable if you aren't happy?"

"But, Lanny!" she exclaimed. "I mean to be happy with Harry."

"Maybe," said he; "but I don't believe you'll ever forget that you left Marcel without any cause. Suppose he goes and jumps off the Cap?"

"Oh, Lanny, he won't do that!"

"How can you be sure? And then, suppose that France mobilizes? Marcel will have to go to war, won't he?"

Beauty turned pale; that was the horror she couldn't bring herself to face. The boy, seeing that he had the advantage, pushed harder. "Could you bear to leave him if you knew he had gone to fight for his country?" All Beauty could do was to bury her face in her arms and weep. Lanny said: "You better wait and see what happens."

III

They wouldn't have to wait long. Surely nobody could complain of the slowness of events at the end of July 1914! First it was Russia mobilizing one and a quarter million men; then it was the German Kaiser serving an ultimatum to the effect that Russia had to cease mobilizing. Paris buzzed like a beehive at swarming time; for France was Russia's ally and was bound to go to war if Russia was attacked.

Robbie had said that the governments would find him, and they did. By one means or another, word spread that the representative of Budd's was staying at the Hotel Crillon, in a front suite with a pleasant view up the Champs-Élysées. Military gentlemen representing most of the governments of Europe came to enjoy that view, and partake of the array of drinks which Robbie had upon the sideboard in his reception room—all going onto the expense account of a munitions salesman. The immaculately uniformed gentlemen came to find out what stocks Budd's had on hand at present—of guns and ammunition, of course, not of whiskies, brandies, and liqueurs.

Robbie would smile suavely, and say that he regretted that Budd's was such a very small plant, and had practically no stocks on hand. "You know how it is, I begged your General So-and-So to place an order last year. I warned you all what was coming."

"Yes, we know," the military gentlemen would reply, sorrowfully. "If the decision had rested with us, we should have been prepared. But the politicians, the parliaments"—they would shrug their shoulders. "What could we do?"

Robbie knew all about politicians and parliaments; in his country they were called Congress and had steadily refused to vote what the safety of the country required. Now, of course, there would be a quick change, the purse strings would be loosened. The policy of Budd's was fixed; it was "first come, first served" to all the world. The terms in this present crisis would be fifty percent of the purchase price to be placed in escrow with the First National Bank of Newcastle, Connecticut, before the order was accepted; the balance to be placed in escrow a week before the completion of the order, to be paid against bills of lading when shipment was made. Munitions makers had grown suddenly exacting, it appeared. Robbie added confidentially—to everyone—that he had cabled his firm recommending an immediate increase of fifty percent in its entire schedule of prices: this to meet inevitable rises in the cost of materials and labor.

The visitors would depart; and while the next lot cooled their heels in the lobby, the salesman would take off the heavy alligator-skin belt which he always wore, slip a catch, and draw out several long strips of parchment with fine writing on them. He would sit at his portable typewriter, the newest contraption created by Yankee ingenuity, and would study the parchment strips and proceed to type out a cablegram in code.

That secret code had been one of the thrills of Lanny's life for several years. It was changed every time Robbie made a trip, and there were only two copies of it in existence; the other was in the possession of Robbie's father. The one other person who knew about it was the confidential clerk who devised it, and who did the decoding for the president of the company. The belt in which Robbie kept his own copy was never off his person except when he was in the bathtub or in swimming; usually he swam from a boat, and before he sank down among the fishes he would make sure there were no agents of foreign governments near by.

Robbie had talked quite a lot about ciphers and codes. Any cipher could be "broken" by an expert; but a code was safe, because it gave purely arbitrary meanings to words. The smartest expert could hardly find out that "Agamemnon" meant Turkey, or that "hippo-griff" meant the premier of Rumania. Robbie would use the cable company's code-book for the ordinary phrases of his message: "I have promised immediate delivery," or "I advise acceptance," and so on; but crucial words, such as names of countries, of individuals he was dealing with and the goods they were ordering, were in the private code. These precautions had been adopted after a deal had been lost because Zaharoff had a man in the office of Budd Gun-makers and was getting copies of Robbie's messages.

Seeing how overwhelmed his father was, Lanny asked if he could help; and the father said: "It's too bad you don't know how to type."

"I can find the letters on the keyboard," replied the boy, "and you don't hit 'em so fast yourself."

"You'll find it's pretty poor fun."

"If I'm really helping you, I'll think it's the best fun there is."

So Robbie wrote his cablegram in English, and showed the boy how to look up phrases in the regular code-book, and underlined those words which would be in his own list. While Robbie interviewed a friend of Captain Bragescu, just arrived from Rumania, Lanny worked patiently by the "hunt and peck" method, producing a long string of ten-letter words: "California Independed Hilarioust Scorpionly Necessands," and so on. Lanny's grandfather, who had tried hard not to let him be born, and who so far had refused to recognize the failure of that effort, would learn from this painstaking service that the government of Holland was anxious over the possibility of invasion, and would pay thirty percent premium for delivery of twenty thousand carbines during the month of August.

By the time Robbie's interview was concluded, the message was ready, and he went over it and found only two or three errors, and said it was a great help; which of course made the boy as proud as Punch. Robbie burned the original message, and let the ashes drop into the toilet bowl. Then Lanny asked: "Do you ever add anything out of code?"

"Sometimes," replied the father. "Why?"

"Just say: 'Lanny coded this.'"

Robbie chuckled, but he said: "Wait till he sells the guns and gets the money!"

IV

The cablegram dispatched, the pair went for a stroll, to get some fresh air into their lungs before lunch. The other delegations could wait, said Robbie; no sense in killing yourself—anyhow, Budd's was loaded up with orders; in the past couple of weeks they had accumulated a "backlog" for six months. For years Robbie had been urging the family to expand the plant; Robbie's eldest brother, Lawford, who was in charge of production, had opposed it, but finally their father had adopted Robbie's program. Now he wouldn't have to worry any more.

"What's he worrying about?" asked Lanny, and Robbie answered: "Bankers! Once you let Wall Street get its claws into you, you cease to be a family institution."

It was Friday, the last day of July. Newsboys were shouting

la guerre again. Germany had declared martial law. She was going to war with somebody, and it could only be with France's ally. People appeared to have lost interest in the ordinary tasks; they stopped on street corners, or in front of bistros, kiosks, and tobacco shops, to talk about the meaning of events. People spoke to you who wouldn't ordinarily have done so. "They're scared," said Robbie. "That brings human beings together."

There came the sound of drums; a regiment marching—toward the east, of course. The soldiers sweated under a load of equipment; rifle and bayonet, knapsack, a big blanket roll, a canteen, even a little spade. Their blue coats were long and heavy, their red trousers big and baggy. The crowds came running, but they didn't cheer. Neither the soldiers nor the people looked happy. "Is France mobilizing?" asked Lanny, and his father replied: "Troops would be moving toward the frontier in any case."

They returned to the Crillon, and while they were at lunch a cablegram was brought to Robbie. "From Newcastle," he said. It was in code, of course, and Lanny exclaimed eagerly: "Oh, let me try it!" The father said: "O.K."

When they went upstairs Robbie took off the magic belt, and Lanny shut himself in his bedroom with cablegram and code-book, leaving the father free for more interviews. The cablegram conveyed the information that Turkey was twenty-four hours overdue upon the first payment for ground-type air-cooled machine guns ordered. Might it not be wise to cancel the deal and dispose of the guns to the British army? Robbie was to advise immediately what increased price he thought the British would pay.

It sounded so important that Lanny took the decoded message to his father, and Robbie cut short his interview and got busy on the telephone to locate a member of the British military mission then holding consultations with the French Ministry of War. Lanny went back to put into code the words: "Advise cancellation Turkey am making inquiries Britain."

A man like Robbie Budd would normally have a secretary with him; but Robbie was active, and had always preferred to handle his own affairs and write his own letters to his father. Now he was caught in a sudden hurricane, and less willing than ever to trust anybody. So there was a chance for a fourteen-year-old boy to step into a secretary's job—for which he was not without some preparation.

Robbie checked the message and found it all right. He put on his magic belt and went down to take a taxi for an appointment with the British officer. Lanny filed the cablegram, and then went to the street and bought the latest newspaper. When he came back he found there was a letter for his mother—in the familiar handwriting of Marcel Detaze, and postmarked Juan-les-Pins. It was an unusually thick letter, and Lanny didn't have to guess that Marcel would be pouring out his soul. He took it up to his mother's suite. He would rest for a while from being a code expert, and resume his role as consultant upon affairs of the heart.

V

Beauty had been to lunch with her friend Emily Chattersworth, and was loaded up with "sensible" advice on the problem which was exercising her. But when she saw that letter, all the labors of her friend were undone. She paled and caught her breath, and her hands trembled while she read. When she had finished the long letter, she sat staring in front of her, biting her lip as if enduring pain.

Lanny had an impulse to say: "May I read it?" But he feared that wouldn't be polite, and merely asked: "Is he in trouble, Beauty?"

"He is uncertain about everything," she answered, and then started to read him the letter, which was in French, and began "*Chérie.*" Before she got very far, her voice broke, and she handed him the sheets, saying: "You have to know about it."

Lanny read: "I have been hoping every day to hear from you and to see you, but now I fear it will be too late. It looks as if there will be mobilization, and I cannot come to Paris because it would look like running away. I cannot be sure, but I expect my class will be called among the first. If I go, I will write you. I do not know where I shall be, but you can write me in care of my regiment.

"I keep reminding myself that you are an American, and I cannot be sure how you will feel about what is happening. But you know that I am a Frenchman and can have no doubt who is right in this unwanted conflict. It is cruel that our happiness has to be broken, and that millions of other women will be stricken with grief. It is perhaps a minor tragedy that men of talent have to be dragged from their task of making beauty, and instead must destroy it upon the battlefield. But it is our fate, and if the summons comes, I shall not permit myself to be weakened by repining. In this I hope for your help.

"One sad idea has been haunting my mind. It may be that Lanny's father will wish to take him out of this hell which Europe is about to become. It may be that you will wish to go with your son. I have thought about it day and night, and what it is my duty to say to you. I have written half a dozen letters and torn them up. I have pleaded with you for the right of our love; and then I have decided that I was being selfish, thinking about my own welfare while making myself believe I was thinking about yours. I have written a letter of renunciation, in the name of true, unselfish love, and then decided that I would seem cold, when in reality I was so trembling with grief and longing that my hand could hardly control the pen.

"If I could have one hour's talk with you, I could make it all clear. I expected that as my right, and you gave me to think that I was to have it. But you kept postponing your coming—and I felt that you must have known about this crisis, and the prospect of my being called to the defense of my country. This is not said in complaint, but merely to make plain my situation.

"In what you are about to read, I beg you to remember our hours of ecstasy. Remember our tears that mingled, and all the pulses of our hearts. Everything that I have ever been to you, I am today, and will be forever, if fate spares me. I love you; my being trembles when I think of you, my courage dissolves, I curse war, mankind, fate, and God Himself, that gives us such bliss and then tears it away. I feel all that, and I am all that. But also I am a citizen of France, with a duty there is no escaping. Also I am a rational man, knowing what the world is, and what can happen to a woman in it. I say: 'What have you to offer to this woman, or to any woman born to the pleasant things of life?'

"There are times when I feel that I know about the value of my own work. I say: 'It is good, and some day the world will know that it is good.' But then I remember how van Gogh succeeded in selling only one painting in his lifetime, and that to his brother. So I ask myself: 'Have I anything more than he had?' I tell myself there are hundreds, perhaps thousands of painters, each as sure of his own merits as I am of mine; and very few of them can be right. Who can say there is any sure guarantee that genuine merit will be recognized in the world? Why may it not be suffocated by indifference, just as life may be annihilated in the blast of war?

"I tell myself that if you go to America, you will almost certainly marry there, and I shall never see you again. Grief overwhelms me; but then reason speaks, reminding me that my life may be snuffed out in a few days—or worse, that I may be mutilated, and made into something you had better not see or know about. I say: 'If she takes her dear son to America, that will be the happiest path for her and for him. Her wise American friends must be telling her that. What right have I to add to the ache of her heart?'

"It may be, Chérie, that all this is fantasy. If so, call it a lover's nightmare, and laugh at it. But it is better to write something foolish than not to let you know my heart. If I am called, what I write thereafter will be under the eyes of an army censor. I beg you to learn not to worry about me, it is the destiny of the men of our time. France must be saved from the insolence of an autocrat, and whatever comes to each individual is his to endure. My love, my blessings go with you, and my prayers for your happiness."

Tears had come into Lanny's eyes as he read, and were trickling down his cheeks. When he was through he, too, sat staring before him, not seeing anything, not knowing anything to say. He didn't think that Marcel believed in prayers, or in blessings. Was it just a manner of speaking, or was it a cry wrung from him when his own forces were not enough to meet his need? Maybe he would be glad to go to war, and to get killed, as a way of escape from his grief.

"It's her own affair," Robbie had said to his son. "It's a mistake to urge people to any course, because then they hold you responsible for the consequences. Let her make her own decision." So the boy didn't say a word, just let the tears trickle.

"Oh, Lanny, what shall I do?" whispered Beauty, at last. When he didn't answer, she began to sob. "It's monstrous that a man like Marcel should be dragged away to war!"

"He doesn't have to be dragged," said the boy. "Don't you see that he would go anyway? We can't help that part of it. Most of the women of France will have that to endure." Robbie had said this, and the boy knew it was right.

But Beauty was a different kind of woman, belonging to the class which wasn't supposed to suffer. So far she had refused to do so. That was why it seemed such a perfect solution of the problem to flee to America, in the care of a capable man who had no part in Europe's hates and slaughters. That was undoubtedly the sensible way—as Robbie and Emily and all her friends kept assuring her. How provoking and unreasonable that a woman who had given her heart couldn't get it back without finding it all bleeding and torn!

"Tell me, what shall I do?" she repeated.

"Robbie doesn't want me to say any more about it," the boy answered. "You know what I think."

"Harry is coming to take me to dinner," persisted the mother. "What am I to say to him?"

The boy remembered what his father had told him during the *affaire* Zaharoff. "Tell him the facts, Beauty."

VI

Lanny returned to his other job. Robbie wrote out a long message to his father, advising him that Turkish officials were deeply involved in intrigues with Germany and the outcome might be a blockade of all Turkish ports. The British military mission advised that Britain would certainly want all the ground-type air-cooled machine guns it could get. Robbie advised against charging a higher price, except as part of a general boost in the price schedule. He recommended this latter more urgently than ever. Future quotations should be subject to increase depending upon raw-material prices certain to jump enormously.

A long message which would take a good part of the afternoon; Robbie hated to put it off on the youngster, but Lanny said he had never done anything he enjoyed more. He would stick right there and make himself an expert, and when Robbie was willing to send a message without checking it, he would be as proud as if he'd got the tiny red ribbon of the Legion of Honor.

So they went to work, Lanny at his table, and the father talking to harassed and exhausted military men. This went on until after seven o'clock, when Robbie said they'd eat, no matter what happened to Europe. "Let's go to a place where real Parisians eat," he suggested. "Fellow I know will be there."

They got into a taxi, and he gave an address on the Rue Montmartre. "We're to meet a journalist; a man who has worthwhile connections, and often brings me tips. I give him a couple of hundred-franc notes. It's the custom of the country."

It was a place Lanny had never heard of before. There were many tables on the sidewalk, but Robbie passed these by and strolled inside; he looked about, and went toward a table where sat a little man with heavy dark mustache and beard, pince-nez on a black silk cord, and a black tie. The man jumped up when he saw him. "Ah, M. Bood!" he exclaimed, trying to say it American fashion, but not succeeding.

"*Bon jour, M. Pastier,*" replied Robbie, and introduced Lanny: "*Mon secrétaire.*" The man looked puzzled; for not many businessmen have secretaries fourteen years old. Robbie laughed, and added: "*Aussi mon fils.*"

"*Ah, votre fils!*" exclaimed the Frenchman, exuberantly, and shook hands with the lad. "*C'est le* crown prince, *hein?*"

"*Je l'espeer,*" replied Robbie; his French was no better than M. Pastier's American.

The other invited them to sit down. They ordered, and Robbie included a large bottle of wine, knowing that his acquaintance would assist them. The Frenchman was a voluble talker, and impressed Lanny greatly. The boy was too young to realize that persons in this profession sometimes pretend to know more than they can know. To listen to him you would have thought he was the intimate friend of all the prominent members of the cabinet, and had talked with several of them that afternoon.

He reported that Germany had been making desperate efforts to detach France from her Russian engagements. "The German ambassador pleaded with friends of mine at the Quai d'Orsay. 'There is and should be no need for two highly civilized nations to engage in strife. Russia is a barbarous state, a Tatar empire, essentially Asiatic.' So they argue. They would prefer to devour us at a second meal," added the Frenchman, his black eyes shining.

"*Naturellement,*" said Robbie.

"But we have an alliance; the word of France has been given! Imagine, if you can, the insolence of these Teutons—they demand of us the fortresses of Toul and Verdun, as guarantees of our abandonment of the Russian alliance. Is it probable that we built them for that?"

"*Pas probable,*" assented the American.

"When the French people hear that, they will rise as one man!" exclaimed the journalist, and illustrated with a vigorous rising of both arms.

"What will your workers do, your Socialists?" asked Robbie. It was a question which troubled everybody.

The other said: "Look," and indicated with his eyes. "Over there at that table by the window. The question is being settled tonight."

The American saw eight or ten men sitting at dinner, talking among themselves. They might have been journalists like M. Pastier, or perhaps doctors or lawyers. At the head of the table was a large stoutish man with a heavy gray beard, a broad face, and grand-fatherly appearance. "Jaurès," whispered the Frenchman.

Lanny had heard the name; he knew it was one of the Socialist leaders, and that he made eloquent speeches in the Chamber of Depu-ties. What Lanny saw was a heavy-set old gentleman with baggy clothes, talking excitedly, with many gestures. "They are Socialist editors and deputies," explained M. Pastier. "They have just returned from the conference at Brussels."

The three watched for a while, and others in the restaurant did the same. The Socialists were men of the people, deciding the affairs of the people, and there was no need for them to hide themselves. Lanny decided that their leader must be a kind old gentleman, but he looked exhausted and harassed.

"It is a grave problem for them," explained the journalist; "for they are internationalists, and against war. But Jaurès spoke plainly to the Germans at Brussels—if they obey their Kaiser and march, there will be nothing for the French workers to do but defend their *patrie*. Have you seen *L'Humanité* this morning?"

"I don't patronize it," said Robbie.

"Jaurès speaks of 'Man's irremediable need to save his family and his country even through armed nationalism.'"

"Too bad he didn't discover that before he began advocating the general strike in case of war!"

"Jaurès is an honest man; I say it, even though I have opposed him. I have known him for many years. Would you be interested to meet him?"

"No, thanks," said Robbie, coldly. "He's a bit out of my line." He led the conversation to the chances of British intervention in the expected war. He had his reasons for wanting to know about that; it would be worth many hundred-franc notes to Budd Gunmakers.

After dinner father and son strolled along the boulevards and looked at the crowds. When they got to the Crillon, there was an-other cablegram. Lanny began insisting that he wasn't at all tired;

surely he could work till bedtime, and so on—when the telephone
rang, and Robbie answered. "What?" he cried, and then: "*Mon
Dieu!*" and: "What will that mean?" He listened for a while, then
hung up the receiver and said: "Jaurès has been shot!"

It was the boy's turn to exclaim and question. "Right where we
left him," said the father. "Fellow on the street pushed the window
curtains aside and put a couple of bullets into the back of his head."

"He's dead?"

"So Pastier reports."

"Who did it, Robbie?"

"Some patriot, they suppose; somebody who thought he was going to oppose the war."

"What will happen now?"

Robbie shrugged his shoulders, almost as if he had been a Frenchman. "It's just one life. If war starts, there'll be a million others.
C'est la guerre, as the French say. Pastier says that Germany's expected to declare war on Russia tomorrow; and if so, France is in."

VII

It was hard upon a young fellow who had just assumed an important and responsible position to have to be distracted by the sex
problem. Lanny learned how it interferes with business, and all the
other serious things of life; he said a plague upon it—for the first
time in his life, but not for the last. Here he was, the next morning,
comfortably fixed by the window in his bedroom, with the code
material and a long message from Connecticut, badly delayed by
congestion of the cables. But instead of looking up the word "marketless," he was sitting lost in thought, and presently interrupting
his father's reading of the mail. "Robbie, don't you think one of us
ought to see Beauty for a few minutes?"

"Anything special?" asked the other, absentmindedly.

"Harry told her last night that she'd have to make up her mind,
or he's going back to the States without her. She says it's an ultimatum."

"Well, there's a lot of ultimatums being served right now. One more hardly counts."

"Don't joke, Robbie. She's terribly upset."

"What's she doing?"

"Just sitting staring in front of her."

"Has she got a looking glass?"

Lanny saw that his father was determined to keep out of it; so he looked up the word "marketless." But before he started on the word "lightening," he interrupted again. "Robbie, does it often happen that a woman thinks she is in love with two men and can't decide which?"

"Yes," said the father, "it happens to both men and women." He put down the letter he was reading and added: "It happened to me, when I had to decide whether I was going to get married or not." It was the first time Robbie had ever spoken of that event to his son, and the boy waited to see if he'd say more. "I had to make up my mind, and I did. And now Beauty has to do it. It won't hurt her to sit staring in front of her. She's owed it to herself for a long while to do some serious thinking."

So Lanny looked up "lightening," and three or four words more. But he couldn't help trying once again. "Robbie, you don't want me to give Beauty advice; but I've already given her some, and I know it's counting with her. You don't think it was good advice?"

"It wasn't what I'd give her; but it may be right for her. She's a sentimental person, and it seems she's very much in love with that painter fellow."

"Oh, really she is, Robbie. I watched them all the time on the yacht. Anybody could see it."

"But he's a lot younger than she is; and that's going to make a tragedy some day."

"You mean, Marcel will stop loving her?"

"Not entirely, perhaps; he'll be torn in half, just the way she is now."

"You mean he'll get interested in some younger woman?"

"I mean he'll have to be a saint if he doesn't; and I haven't met any saints among French painters."

"You ought to know Marcel better, Robbie. He is one of the very best men I ever have met."

"I'm taking your word for him. But there's a lot you still must learn, son. Beauty would be poor—that is, by the standards of everyone she knows or wants to know. And that's awful hard on the affections. It gets worse and worse as you get older, too."

"You think it's right for people to marry for money, then?"

"I think there's an awful lot of bunk talked on the subject. People fool themselves, and try to fool other people. I've watched marriages, scores of them, and I know that money was the important element in most. It was dressed up in fine words, of course; it was called 'family,' and 'social position,' and 'culture,' and 'refinement.' "

"But aren't those things real?"

"Sure they are. Each is like a fine house; it's built on a foundation—and the foundation is money. If you build a house without any foundation, it doesn't last long."

"I see," said the boy. It impressed him greatly, like everything his father said.

"Don't let anybody fool you about money, son. The people who talk that nonsense don't believe it themselves. They tell you that money won't buy this, that, and the other thing. I tell you that money will buy an awful lot, especially if you're a good shopper. You get my point?"

"Oh, sure, Robbie."

"Take Edna Hackabury. Money bought her a yacht, and the yacht got her a lot of friends. Now she's lost her yacht, and she and her captain will have to live on two thousand pounds a year; and how many of her old friends will come to see her? She'll be embarrassed if they do, because she can't keep up with them. She'll find that she's forced to get some cheaper friends."

"I know, Robbie, there are people like that; but others are interested in art, and music, and books, and so on."

"That's quite true; and I'm glad to see that you prefer such friends. But when those friends grow old, and their blood flows slower, they'll want a warm fire, and money will buy the fire. Money won't buy them appreciation of books, but it will buy them books, and what's the use of appreciation if you haven't anything to use it on? No, son, the only way to be happy without money is to go and live in a tub, like Diogenes, or be a Hindu with a rag around your loins and a bowl to beg for rice. Even then you can't live unless other people have cared enough for money to grow rice, and to market and transport it."

"Then you don't think there's anything we can do for Beauty?"

"What I think, son, is that one or the other of us has got to work at that code; because this is a time of crisis, and a whole lot of women have worse troubles than trying to make up their minds which man they want."

VIII

That was the first of August; and early in the day came the news that Germany had declared war on Russia. Soon afterward it was reported that both Germany and France had ordered general mobilization.

The temper of Paris changed in an hour. Previously everything had been hushed; people anxious, frightened, horrified. But now the die was cast. It was war! That hateful Kaiser with his waxed mustaches, those military men who surrounded him, strutting and blustering—they had thrown Europe into the furnace. At least, that was the way the Paris crowds saw it; and business came to an end for the day, everybody rushed into the streets. Bugles sounding everywhere, drums rolling, crowds marching and cheering. They were singing the "Marseillaise" on every street corner; and "Malbrouck s'en va-t-en guerre"—to which Americans sing "For He's a Jolly Good Fellow"; also the "Carmagnole," which Americans do not know— all the old revolutionary songs of France, now become patriotic and respectable.

Lanny finished his secretarial labors and went out to see the sights, the most stirring any boy could have imagined. Pink mobilization orders posted on kiosks and walls; young men assembling and marching to the trains; women and girls running beside them, singing, weeping hysterically, or laughing, borne up by the excitement of the throngs; people throwing flowers at them, putting roses in the soldiers' red caps, in the hair of the girls. And the regiments marching to the railroad stations, or being loaded into trucks—it wouldn't be long before you could no longer find a taxicab or even a horse in Paris.

And then back to the Hotel Crillon. The Champs-Élysées, that wide avenue, and the great open spaces, the Place de la Concorde, the Place du Carrousel, now like military encampments; regiments marching, horses galloping, artillery rumbling, people singing, shouting: "*La guerre! La guerre!*"

Inside the hotel another kind of tumult, for it appeared that there were thousands of Americans in Paris, and they all wanted to get out quickly. Many were caught without funds; they wanted food and shelter, railroad tickets, steamer accommodations, everything all at once. They had been reading about a new kind of warfare, and had visions of squadrons of German airplanes dropping bombs upon Paris that afternoon. It seemed that every person who had ever met Robbie Budd was now asking him for advice, for the loan of money, for his influence in getting something from the embassy, from the consulate, from railroad and steamship and travel bureaus.

When they couldn't get hold of Robbie, they would go to his former wife, who had always been able to get anything from him. Beauty, who wanted to sit and stare in front of her and think, who wanted to weep without anybody seeing her ruined complexion, had to put on a few dabs of paint and powder, and her lovely blue Chinese morning robe with large golden pheasants on it, and receive her friends, and the friends of her friend Emily and her friend Sophie and her friend Margy, and tell them what Robbie said, that there wasn't any immediate danger, that the embassy would advance money as soon as they had time to hear from Washington, that Robbie himself couldn't possibly do anything, he was besieged by military men trying to buy things which he didn't have and couldn't make for months yet.

They even fell upon Robbie's newly appointed secretary, to ask what he knew and what he thought. Lanny had never had such an exciting time; it was like going to war himself. He would run to his father with something he thought especially urgent, and there would be that solid rock of a man, hearty, serene, smiling. He'd say: "Remember, son, there've been lots of wars in this old Europe, and this will pass like the others." He'd say: "Remember, some of these are real friends, and some are spongers who won't ever repay the money they're trying to borrow." He'd see Lanny standing at the window, watching the troops march by and the flags flying, listening to the drums beating and the crowds shouting; he'd see the color mounting in the boy's cheeks and the light shining in his eyes, and he'd say: "Remember, kiddo, this isn't your war. Don't make any mistake and take it into your heart. You're an American!"

IX

That was the line the father was going to take. Budd's didn't engage in any wars; Budd's made munitions, and played no favorites. The father found time, in the midst of excitements and confusions, to hammer that fact in and rivet it. "I'll have to go back to Newcastle, to try to straighten out my father and brothers; and I don't want my son to step into anybody's bear trap. Remember, there never was a war in which the right was all on one side. And remember that in every war both sides lie like hell. That's half the battle—keeping up the spirits of your own crowd, and getting allies to help you. Truth is whatever you can get believed. Remember it every time you pick up a newspaper."

The father went on to prove his case. He told how Bismarck had forged a telegram in order to get the Franco-Prussian war started when he was ready for it. He told about the intrigues of the Tsar's government, the most despotic and corrupt in Europe. He explained how the great financial interests, the steel cartels, the oil and electrical trusts, and the banks which financed them, controlled both France and Germany. They owned properties in both countries, and would see that those properties were protected; they would make billions of profits, and buy new properties, and be more than ever masters, however the war might end.

"And that's all right," continued the father; "that's their business; only remember it isn't yours. Remember that among their properties are all the big newspapers. Find out who owns the one you read." Robbie took up several that were lying on the table. "This is the de Wendels'," he said; "the Comité des Forges—the steel trust that runs French politics. This one is Schneider-Creusot. And here's your old friend Zaharoff!"

The father opened one paper, and asked: "Did you get this little story?" He pointed to an account of a state ceremony which had taken place on the previous day—Zaharoff had been promoted to commander of the Legion of Honor. A strange bit of irony, that it should have happened the day that Jaurès was shot! "I don't hold any brief for Socialist tub-thumpers," said Robbie; "but he was perhaps honest, as you heard Pastier say. They shoot him, and they give one of their highest honors to an old Levantine trader who would sell the whole country tomorrow for a hundred million francs."

Practically all the Americans in Paris sympathized with France, because they believed that France had wanted peace, and because it was a republic. But Robbie wouldn't leave it at that. What counted nowadays was business, and the oil, steel, and munitions men of France wanted what all the others wanted. "Is it peace when you lend billions of francs to Russia, and force them to spend the money for arms to fight Germany?"

"I suppose you're right," the boy had to admit.

"Put yourself in the place of the German people—your friend Kurt, and his family, and millions like them. They look to their eastern border——"

"A dark cloud of barbarism, the Graf Stubendorf called it," Lanny remembered suddenly.

"Russian diplomacy has one purpose—to get Constantinople, and that means to keep Germany from getting it. Russia is called a steam roller, and it's built to roll westward; the French paid for it, and taught the Russians how to run it. Of course the Germans will fight like hell to stop it."

"Who do you think's going to win, Robbie?" Purely as a sporting proposition, it got a boy keyed up.

"Nobody on earth can say. The French are setting out for Berlin, and the Germans for Paris; they'll meet, and there'll be a smash, and one side or the other will crumple. The only thing you can be sure of is that it won't be a long war."

"How long?"

"Three or four months. Both sides would go bankrupt if it lasted longer."

"And what will England do?"

"I could make a pile of money if I knew. The men who have to make the decision are running around like a lot of ants when you turn over a stone. If England had said she'd defend France, there wouldn't have been any war. But that's the trouble with countries that have parliaments, they can't make up their minds to anything—not until it's too late."

X

Harry Murchison had put down his money and engaged a stateroom for two on a steamer sailing the next day; also a berth for Lanny in another stateroom. He had done this before the rush began, and now it was a part of his "ultimatum." He and Beauty could be married that night; or they could be married by the captain of the steamer. Harry came two or three times during the day to plead his cause and argue against the folly of hesitation. He would lock the door so that nobody could interrupt them, and he wouldn't let her answer the telephone; he was a young man who had been used to having his own way most of his life. He hadn't much consideration for Beauty's feelings; he said that she was somewhat hysterical right now, and didn't really know her own mind. Once the die was cast, the marriage words spoken, she'd settle down and be glad somebody had acted for her.

It was the technique known in America as "high-pressure salesmanship." Beauty would beg for time, but Harry would insist: "I've got to sail on that steamer. There's going to be an awful lot of plate glass smashed in the next few months, and I've got to be in Pittsburgh to see about replacing it."

"Don't leave me, Harry," the tormented woman pleaded. "Surely you can put it off one more week."

"If you don't go now you mayn't be able to go until the war's over. Call up the steamship company and see what they tell you. Everything is booked for months ahead, and there's talk of our government having to send steamers to get Americans out of Europe."

Robbie decided suddenly that he had better go too. Cablegrams were being delayed and censorship might stop them entirely. He told Harry that if Beauty rejected the chance, he'd take her half of the stateroom. "But don't let her know it!" he hastened to add. "If she goes, I'll manage to get on board somehow." Robbie was a friend of all the steamship people, and knew discreet ways to arrange matters. "They can put a cot in the captain's cabin," he remarked, smiling.

It was a trying position for Lanny, not knowing whether his future was to be on the French Riviera or in a smoky valley of steel and coal three thousand miles to the west. He made no complaint for himself, but he did think that the cards were being stacked against Marcel. It was an elementary principle of justice that both sides should be represented in any court. Lanny had a strong impulse to represent the painter, but Robbie had asked him to keep his hands off, and Robbie's wish was a command.

In between codings and decodings, Lanny would go to see his mother, and tell her that he loved her—that was about all he could say. Toward evening he found Mrs. Emily with her; and these two fashionable ladies had tears running down their cheeks. It wasn't because of Beauty's problems, nor was it the million Frenchwomen left at home to face the thought of bereavement. It was a terrible story which Mrs. Emily had brought. While troops were marching and crowds shouting and singing in all the streets, fate had chosen to strike another blow at Isadora Duncan. She had lain in agony for many hours, trying to bear her baby; and at last when it was placed in her arms, she had felt it suddenly beginning to turn cold. She screamed, and the attendants came running and tried to save it, but in vain; in a few minutes the spark of life had expired, and that unhappy woman was desolate again.

"Oh, my God, what has happened to the world?" whispered Lanny's mother. It certainly seemed as if some devil had got hold of affairs, at least temporarily. Everybody had been so happy, the playground of Europe had seemed such a delightful place—and here it was being turned into a charnel house, a sepulcher not even whited.

"I see those pitiful men marching away," said Mrs. Emily, "and I think how the hospitals and the graves will be filled with them, and it just seems more than a woman can bear."

"I know," said Beauty; "it's one of the reasons why I'm so tempted to flee from France."

"If the Germans break through," said the other woman, "my home lies directly in their path."

"Surely the Germans wouldn't harm that beautiful place!" exclaimed Lanny's mother. But then right away she remembered having heard how the Turks used the Parthenon to store powder in!

XI

Robbie and his son went to dinner. Beauty declined their invitation; she couldn't eat anything, she said. They guessed that Harry was coming again. The time was getting short; if she was going she had a lot of packing to do. Apparently she was, for Mrs. Emily had given her another talking to. Also Robbie had been with her—and Robbie was not following the course he had advised for his son.

Father and son came back to the hotel, and there were more delayed cables. But Beauty phoned; she wanted very much to talk to Lanny—just a few minutes, she promised—and Robbie said all right, he'd go on with the decoding himself.

Beauty was pale, seeming more distraught than ever; she was walking up and down the room, twisting her hands together. "Marcel has gone to war," she announced.

There was a telegram lying on the table, and Lanny read it. "I have been called to the colors. God bless you. Love." No high-pressure salesmanship here!

"Lanny I've got to make up my mind now!" exclaimed the mother. "I've got to decide our whole future."

"Yes, Beauty," said the boy, quietly.

"I want to think about your happiness, as well as my own."

"Don't bother about me, Beauty. I'm going to make the best of whatever you decide. If you're Harry's wife, I'll make myself agreeable and never give you any worry."

"It'll mean that you go to live in America. Will you like that?"

"I don't know, because I don't know what I'll find; but I'll get along."

"Tell me what you really prefer."

Lanny hesitated. "Robbie doesn't want me to interfere, Beauty."

"I know; but I'm asking. I have to think about both of us. If you had your choice—if you had nothing to consider but your own wishes—where would you go?"

Lanny thought for a while. His father could hardly object to his answering a straight question like that. Finally he said: "I'd go back to Juan."

"You like it there so well?"

"I've always been happy there. That's my home."

"But now there's going to be war. It mayn't be safe any more."

"Those French warships will stay in the Golfe, I imagine; and it isn't likely anybody's going to lick the British and French fleets."

"But Italy has some sort of a treaty with Germany and Austria. Doesn't she have to help them fight?"

"Italy has just announced that she will take a 'defensive attitude.' Robbie says that means they'll wait, and see which side offers them the most. That's bound to be England, because she has money."

"Our friends all talk about going back to America. It'll be lonely at Juan."

"Maybe for you," said the boy. "But you know how it is—I never did see enough of my mother. We could read, and play music, and swim, and wait for Marcel to come back." Lanny stopped, not being sure if it was fair for him to mention that aspect of the matter.

The mother's voice trembled as she said: "He may never come back, Lanny."

"There's a chance, of course. But Robbie says the war won't last long. And Marcel may never see any fighting—Robbie thinks the Provençal regiments will be kept on the Italian border, at least till they're sure what Italy's going to do. And then again, Marcel might come back wounded, and we'd both want to take care of him. It wouldn't be nice to know that he was hurt, and in need of help, and we couldn't give it."

"I know, Lanny, I know." The tears were starting again in the beautiful blue eyes. "That's what has been tearing my heart in half." She sat with her hands clasped tightly together, and the boy watched her lips trembling. "That's really what you want to do, isn't it, Lanny?"

"You asked me to tell you."

"I know. I couldn't decide it all by myself. If I do what you say, I may be a forlorn and desolate old woman. You won't get tired of me?"

"You can bet I won't."

"And you'll stand by Marcel? You'll help us, whatever hard things may come?"

"Indeed I will."

"You'll be a French boy, Lanny—not an American."

"I'll be a bit of everything, as I am now. That hasn't hurt me." He tried to conceal his joy, but didn't succeed altogether. "You really mean it, Beauty?"

"I mean it. Or, rather, I'll let you mean it for me. I'm a weak and foolish woman, Lanny. I oughtn't to have got into this jam at all. You'll have to take charge of me and make me behave myself."

"Well, I've wanted to sometimes," admitted the youngster. He wasn't sure whether he ought to laugh or cry. "Oh, Beauty, I really think it's the right thing to do!"

"All right, I'll believe you. I'll have to write a note to Harry. I just haven't the courage to see him again."

"That's all right—he ought to stop worrying you. He really hasn't any claim to you."

"He has, Lanny—more than you can guess. But I'll tell him it's all over—and we'll never see Pittsburgh."

"I can get along without so much smoke," declared the boy.

"I think I'd better tell Robbie first," said the mother. "Maybe he can help to break the shock to Harry. He'll tell him I'm not really as good as I look!"

"Harry won't suffer so much," said the young man of the world. "There'll be plenty of girls on the steamer willing to marry him."

"He's a dear, kind fellow, Lanny—you're not in a position to appreciate him. I'll write him, and he can sail tomorrow, and you and I will go to Juan right away. I'll save and pay my debts, and give up trying to shine in society—do you think there'll ever be any more society in Europe, Lanny?"

So it was settled at last; and so it was done. Robbie and Harry sailed the next day—with nobody to see them off. Beauty was packing up her many belongings, with the help of the maid whom she had engaged for her Paris sojourn, but whom she was not taking to the Riviera. Lanny was helping all he could, and writing a letter to Rick, and also one to Marcel, which he hoped would some day be delivered by the postal service of the French army. The army was rather preoccupied on that particular day—since it happened to be the one which the Kaiser's troops had chosen for the invading of Luxembourg and France.

BOOK THREE

Bella Gerant Alii

12

Loved I Not Honour More

I

THE August sun on the Riviera is a blinding white glare and a baking heat. In it the grapes ripen to deepest purple and olives fill themselves to bursting with golden oil. Men and women born and raised in the Midi have skins filled with dark pigments to protect them, and they can work in the fields without damage to their complexions. But to a blond daughter of chill and foggy New England the excess of light and heat assumed an aspect hostile and menacing; an enemy seeking to dry the juices out of her nerves, cover her fair skin with scaly brown spots, and deprive her of those charms by which and for which she had been living.

So Beauty Budd had to hide in the protection of a shuttered house, and have an electric fan to blow away the heat from her body. She rarely went out until after sundown, and since there was no one to look at her during the day, she yielded gradually to the temptation of not taking too much trouble. She would wear her old dressing gowns to save the new ones, and let her son see her with hair straggling. She got little exercise, there being nothing for her to do in a house with servants.

The result was that terror which haunts the lives of society ladies, the monster known as *embonpoint*, a most insidious enemy, who keeps watch at the gates of one's being like a cat at a gopher hole. It never sleeps, and never forgets, but stays on the job, ready to take advantage of every moment of weakness or carelessness. It creeps upon you one milligram at a time—for the advances of this enemy are not measured in space but in avoirdupois. With it, everything is gain and nothing loss; what it wins it keeps. The battle with this unfairest of fiends became the chief concern of Beauty's life, and the principal topic of her conversation in the bosom of her family.

No use looking to the government for help. During the course of the war the inhabitants of the great cities would be rationed, and those of whole countries such as Germany and Britain; but over the warm valleys of the Riviera roamed cattle, turning grass into rich cream, and there were vast cellars and caves filled with barrels of olive oil, and new supplies forming in billions of tiny black globes on the gnarled and ancient trees. Figs were ripening, bees were busy making honey—in short, war or no war, a lady who received a thousand dollars' worth of credit every month in the invulnerable currency of the United States of America could have delivered at her door unlimited quantities of oleaginous and saccharine materials.

Nor could the trapped soul expect help from the servants who waited upon her. Leese, the cook, was fat and hearty, and Rosine, the maid, would become so in due course, and both of them were set in the conviction that this was the proper way for women to be. "*C'est la nature*," was the formula of all the people of the South of France for all the weaknesses of the flesh. They looked with dismay upon the fashion of Anglo-Saxon ladies to keep themselves in a semi-starved condition under the impression that this was the way to be beautiful; they would loudly insist that the practice was responsible for whatever headache, *crise de nerfs*, or other malaise such ladies might experience. Leese fried her fish and her rice in olive oil, and her desserts were mixed with cream; she would set a little island of butter afloat in the center of each plate of potage, and crown every sort of sweet with a rosette or curlicue of fat emulsified and made into snow-white bubbles of air. If she was asked not to do these things, she would exercise an old family servant's right to forget.

So in desperation Beauty turned to her son. "Lanny, don't let me have so much cream!" she would cry. She adopted the European practice of hot milk with coffee; and Lanny would watch while she poured a little cream over her fresh figs, and would then keep the pitcher on his side of the table. "No more now," he would say when he caught her casting a glance at the tiny Sèvres pitcher. But the boy's efforts were thwarted by the mother's practice of keeping a box of chocolates in her room. She would nibble them between meals; and very soon it became evident that the cunning monster of *embonpoint* could utilize the bean of a sterculiaceous tree exactly as well as the mammary secretion of *Bos domestica*. Beauty would be in a state of bewilderment about it. "Why, I hardly eat anything at all!" she would exclaim.

II

The explanation of all this was obvious. Beauty Budd was a social being, who could not live without the stimulus of rivalry. When she was going out among people, she would be all keyed up, and when food was put before her, she would be so absorbed in conversation that she would take only absentminded nibbles. But when she was shut up in the house alone, or with people upon whom she did not need to "make an impression," then, alas, she had time to realize that she was hungry. Not even the thought of a world at war, and the sufferings of millions of men, could save her from that moral decline.

There were friends she might have seen; but in the tumult of fear which had seized the world she preferred to keep to herself. All the Americans in France were hating the Germans; but Beauty hated war with such intensity that she didn't care who won, if only the fighting would end. As for Lanny, he was doing what his father advised, keeping himself neutral. This being the case, they couldn't even speak to their own servants about the terror that was sweeping down upon Paris.

Lanny had to be "society" to his adored mother. He would invite her to a *thé dansant;* putting a record on the phonograph, and letting her show him the fine points of the fashionable dances. He in turn would teach her "Dalcroze," and make her do "plastic counterpoint"; she would be required to "feel" the music, and they would experiment and argue, and have a very good time. Then he would invite her to a concert, in which they would be both performers and audience; they would play duets, and he would make her work at it. No fun just playing the same things over; if you were going to get anywhere you had to be able to read. He would put a score before her and exhort and scold like a music master.

When Beauty was exhausted from that, he wouldn't let her lie down by the box of chocolates; no, it was time for their swim. When she got into her suit, he would walk behind her to the beach and survey the shapely white calves, and worry her by saying: "They are undoubtedly getting thicker!" The water was warm, and Beauty would want to float and relax, and let him swim around her; but no again, he would challenge her to a race along the shore. He would splash and make her chase him. But he never did succeed in persuading her to put on Robbie's goggles and sink down among the fishes.

They would read aloud, taking turns. Beauty couldn't concentrate upon a book very long, she was too restless—or else too sleepy. But when she had someone to read to her, that was a form of social life. She would interrupt and talk about the story, and have the stimulus of another person's reactions. In course of the years many books had accumulated in the house; friends had given them, or Beauty had bought them on people's recommendation, but had seldom found time to look at them. But now they would enjoy the company of M. France, whom they had met so recently. Lanny found *Le Lys Rouge* on the shelves, a fashionable love story treated with touches of the worldling's playful mockery. It had been his popular success, and proved a success with Beauty. It took her back to the happy days, the élite of the world enjoying the impulses of what they politely termed their hearts—the glands having not as yet been publicly discovered. Without difficulty Beauty saw herself in the role of a heroine who had become involved with three men, and couldn't figure out what to do. Having visited in Florence, she recalled the lovely landscapes, and they discussed the art treasures and art ideas in the book.

Lanny remembered that M. Priedieu, the librarian, had spoken about Stendhal. A copy of *La Chartreuse de Parme* had got onto the shelves, they had no idea how. Once more Beauty saw herself as a heroine, a woman for whom love excused all things. She was enraptured by detailed and precise analysis of the great passion. "Oh, that is exactly right!" she would exclaim, and the reading would stop while she told Lanny about men and women, and how they behaved when they were happy in love, or when they were sad; of different types of lovers, and what they said, and whether they meant it or not; how it felt to be disappointed, and to be jealous, and to be thwarted; how love and hatred became mixed and intertangled; the part that vanity played, and love of domination, and love of self, and love of the world and its applause. Beauty Budd had had a great deal of experience, and the subject was one of unending fascination.

Perhaps not all moralists would have approved this kind of conversation between a mother and a son. But she had told Lanny in Paris that if they came back to Juan, he would be a French boy. So he would have to know the arts of love, if only to protect himself. There were dangerous kinds of women, who could wreck the happiness of a man, old or young, and care not a flip of the fan about it. One should know how to tell the good ones from the bad—and generally, alas, it was not possible until it was too late.

There was another purpose, too; Beauty was defending herself, and Marcel, and Harry, or rather what she had done to Harry. Perhaps her conscience troubled her, for she talked often about the plate-glass man, and what might be happening to him in Pittsburgh. Love was bewildering, and many times you wouldn't be happy if you did and wouldn't be if you didn't. You might make a resolve to go off by yourself and have nothing more to do with love; but men had refused to let Beauty do it, and some day soon women would be refusing to let Lanny do it.

After which they would go back to Henri Beyle, soldier, diplomat, and man of the world, who had written under the pen name of Stendhal, and who would tell them how love had fared in the midst of the last World War—just a hundred years earlier, not so long ago in Europe's long story.

III

There came post cards from Marcel Detaze; he was well, busy, and happy to know they were safe at home. He was not permitted to say where he was, but gave the number of his regiment and battalion. The censoring of mail was strict, but no censor in France would object to a painter's declaring that he loved his beautiful blond mistress or to her replying that the sentiments were reciprocated. Beauty fed her soul upon these messages—plus Robbie's assurance that the war couldn't last more than three or four months. Maybe Marcel wasn't going to see any fighting; he would come home with a story of interesting adventure, and life would begin again where it had left off.

Everybody they had met in Paris, and everybody they met now, was confident that the French armies were going to hold the Germans while the Russian steam roller hurtled over Prussia and captured Berlin. The French military authorities had been so confident that they had planned a giant movement of their forces through Alsace and Lorraine; they would break the German lines at the south, then, sweeping north, cut the communications of the enemy advancing through Belgium and northern France. The papers told about the beginning of this counterattack and what it was intended to do; then suddenly they fell silent, and the next reports of fighting in this district came from places in France. Those who understood military affairs knew what this meant—that the armies of *la patrie* had sustained a grave defeat.

As to what was happening farther north, not all the censorship in the land could hide the facts from the public. One had only to take a map and mark on it the places where fighting was reported, and he would see that it was the German steam roller which was hurtling —and at the rate of ten or twenty miles a day. The little Belgian army was fighting desperately, but was being swept aside; its forts were being pulverized by heavy artillery, and towns and villages in the path of the invasion were being wrecked and burned. The still smaller British army which had been landed at the Channel ports

was apparently meeting the same fate. The Kaiser was on his way
to Paris!

IV

There came a letter from Sophie, Baroness de la Tourette. That
very lively lady had been having an adventure, and wrote about it
in detail—being shut up in a room in a fourth-class hotel in Paris,
much bored with nothing to do. She had gone to spend the month
of August with friends at a country place on the river Maas, which
flows through the heart of Belgium. Sophie was a nonpolitical person, entirely devoted to having a good time; she rarely looked at
newspapers, and when she heard people talking about war threats,
she paid no attention, being unable to take seriously the idea that
anybody would disturb the comfort of a person of her social position.

The ladies she was visiting shared her attitude. News traveled
slowly in the country; and when at last they heard that the Germans
had crossed the frontier, they did not worry; the army would be
going to France, and it might be interesting to watch it pass. Only
when they heard the sound of heavy guns did they realize that they
might be in danger, and then it was too late; a troop of Uhlans with
long lances came galloping up the driveway, and the automobiles
and horses on the place were seized. Soon afterward arrived several
limousines, and elegant officers descended, and with bowing and
heel-clicking informed the ladies of the regrettable need to take the
château for a temporary staff headquarters. They all had wasp
waists, and wore monocles, long gray coats, gold bracelets, and
shiny belts and boots; their manners were impeccable, and they
spoke excellent English, and seemed to be well pleased with a lady
who was introduced as Miss Sophie Timmons from the far-off state
of Ohio.

Her friends had suddenly realized that under the law, being married to a Frenchman, she was French and might be interned for the
period of the war. That night she sent her maid to the village and

succeeded in hiring a cart and an elderly bony white horse; taking only a suitcase, she and the maid and a peasant driver had set out toward Brussels. There was fighting everywhere to the south and east of them, and the roads were crowded with refugees driving dogcarts, trundling handcarts, or carrying their belongings on their backs. More than once they had had to sit for long periods by the roadside to let the German armies pass, and the woman's letter was full of amazed horror at the perfection of the Kaiser's war machine. For a solid hour she watched motorized artillery rolling by: heavy siege guns, light field-pieces, wicked-looking rapid-firers; caissons, trucks loaded with shells, and baggage trains, pontoon trains, field kitchens. "My dear, they have been getting ready for this all our lifetime!" wrote the Baroness de la Tourette.

She watched the marching men in their dull field-gray uniforms, so much more sensible than the conspicuous blue and red of the French. The Germans tramped in close, almost solid ranks, forever and ever and ever—in one village they told Sophie of an unbroken procession for more than thirty hours. "And so many with cigars in their mouths!" she wrote. "I wondered, had they been pillaging the shops."

The fugitives slept in their cart for fear it might be stolen; and after two days and nights they reached Brussels, which the Germans had not yet taken. From there they got to Ostend, where the British were landing troops, and then by boat to Boulogne, and to Paris by train. "You should see this city!" wrote Sophie. "Everybody has gone that can get away. The government has taken all the horses and trucks. Maybe the taxicabs have been hired by refugees—I'm hoping that a few will come back. All the big hotels are closed—the men employees are in the army. The Place de la Concorde is full of soldiers sleeping upon straw. The strangest thing is that gold and silver coins have disappeared entirely; they say people are hoarding them, and you can't get any change because there's only paper money. I am waiting for a chance to come south without having to walk. I hope the Germans do not get here first. It would be embarrassing to meet those officers again!"

V

When Marcel departed to join the army, he had brought the keys of his cottage to the servants at Bienvenu and left them for Madame Budd. The servants being French, the occasion had not been casual; they had wept and called upon God to protect him, which in turn had brought tears to the eyes of Monsieur. He had said that it was *pour la patrie*, and that they should take care of the precious Madame, if and when she returned; after those wicked Germans had been driven from the soil of France, they would all live happy forever after, as in the fairy tales.

Leese and Rosine of course knew all about the love affair. To them it was romance, delight, the wine and perfume of life; they lived upon it as women in the United States were learning to live upon the romances, real and imaginary, of the movie stars of Hollywood. Beauty's servants talked about it, not merely among themselves, but with all the other servants of the neighborhood; everybody watched, everybody shared the tenderness, the delight; everybody said, what a shame the young painter was so poor!

Now Beauty received a card from Marcel, saying that, if anything should happen to him, he wanted her to have his paintings. "I don't know if they will ever be worth anything," he wrote; "but you have been kind to them, while to my relatives they mean nothing. Perhaps it might be well to move them to your house, where they would be safer. Do what you please about this."

Beauty, watching for every hint in his messages, clasped her hand to her heart. "Lanny, do you suppose that means he's going to some post of danger?"

"I don't know why it should," said the boy. "We have our own paintings insured, and certainly we ought to take care of his."

Beauty had been going to the little house and sitting there, remembering the times when she had been so happy, and reproaching herself because she had not appreciated her blessings. Now she went with Lanny to carry out Marcel's commission. There were more than a hundred canvases, each tacked upon a wooden frame, and stacked in a sort of shed-room at the rear of the house. One by one Lanny brought them out and studied them—all those aspects of Mediterranean sea and shore which he knew better than anything else. He exclaimed over the loveliness of them; he was ready to set himself up as an art critic against all the world. Beauty wiped the tears from her eyes and exclaimed over the wickedness of a war that had taken such a lover, and stopped such work, and even made it impossible for Sophie to come to the Riviera unless she walked!

There was a group of paintings from the trip to Norway. Lanny had never seen these or heard of them, for it had been before he was told about Marcel. The boy had heard so much about this cold and shining country, and here it was by the magic of art. Here was more than fiords and mountains and *saeters* and ancient farmhouses with openings in the roofs instead of chimneys; here was the soul of these things, old, yet forever new, so long as men loved beauty and marveled at its self-renewal. Here, also, was Greece with its memories, and Africa with its grim desert men, muffled and silent. The *Bluebird* was being made over into a hospital ship right now; but its two cruises with the soap king would live—"well, as long as I do," said Lanny.

VI

The whereabouts of Marcel was supposed to be a secret, upon the preserving of which the safety of *la patrie* depended. But when you take thousands of young men from a neighborhood and put them into encampments not more than a hundred miles away, it soon becomes what the French call *un secret de Polichinelle*, something which everybody knows. The truck drivers talked when they came to the towns for supplies, and pretty soon Leese and Rosine were able to inform the family that the painter's regiment was on guard duty in the Alpes Maritimes.

Italy had declared for neutrality in this war; but it could not be forgotten that she had been a member of the so-called Triple Alliance with Germany and Austria. There was a powerful Italian party known as the Triplicists, who wanted to carry out the pledges, and in these days of quick political overturns France dared not leave her Provençal border unguarded. So Marcel had for a while what the British called a "cushy" job. But the trouble was that as the menace of the German steam roller increased, more and more men were being grabbed up and rushed to the north. Right away Beauty decided that she must visit that camp. She didn't wait to write, not knowing if the censor would let such a letter pass; she would just go to the place and lay siege to whatever authorities might be in command. Beauty had arts which she trusted, but which could not be exercised by mail.

The difficulty lay with transportation. They had their car, but Pierre Bazoche was in the army—oddly enough he was a sergeant, and gave orders to the beloved of his former employer. This seemed to the employer among the atrocities of war, but it amused Lanny, and he was sure it wouldn't worry Marcel. Pierre was a capable fellow, and his orders were doubtless proper.

Leese could always find among her innumerable relatives a man or woman to do anything that was needed, and she now produced an elderly truck driver of the flower farms of the Cap d'Antibes, who could be spared for this journey of romantic interest. He was washed and made presentable in Pierre's uniform, and managed to solve the problem of getting the *essence*, which had suddenly grown scarce and high in price, being needed in huge quantities to move the troops and guns for the saving of Paris.

Lanny sat in the front seat and made friends with old Claude Santoze, who was dark and hook-nosed, and doubtless descended from the Saracen invaders. His black hair was grizzling, and he had half a dozen children at home, but he wanted nothing so much as a chance to fight, and wanted to talk about the war and what Lanny knew about it. The youngster put on the mantle of authority, having a purpose of his own, which was to persuade Claude to say that a boy so intelligent and sensible was old enough to learn to drive a car, and that he, Claude, was willing for a suitable fee to take the time off to teach him.

Having accomplished this much, Lanny moved into the back seat and began a campaign with his mother. He could sail a boat, and run a motorboat, and why was a car any different? Like all boys of his time, Lanny was fascinated by machinery, and listened to the talk of motor owners and drivers and asked all the questions he dared. Now even the women of France were learning to drive, and surely the son of Robbie Budd, maker of machines, ought to be allowed to try. So in the end Beauty said yes; it was one of her characteristics that she found it so hard to say anything else.

VII

They were traveling up the valley of the river Var, amid scenery which took their minds off their troubles. Before many hours they were winding along the sides of mountains, and could only hope that the descendant of the Saracens was as alert as he looked. The chill of autumn was in the air, and the wind blew delightful odors from the pine forests. They were in what seemed a wilderness, when they came suddenly upon the encampment; Beauty was surprised, for she had taken it for granted that soldiers in wartime slept like rabbits in holes in the ground. She had not realized that they would have a town, with excellent one-story wooden buildings and regular streets laid out.

The exercising of feminine charm was going to be difficult. There was a barrier across the road, and the men on duty could not be cajoled into raising it for a car whose occupants had no credentials. The lady would have to submit her request in writing; so they drove back to a tiny village which had what called itself an *auberge*, and Beauty hired the only two bedrooms it contained. There she penned a note—could you guess to whom? Respectfully and with due formality she addressed herself to Sergeant Pierre Bazoche—the bright idea having occurred to her that a person of rank might be able to pull more wires than a humble private, even though a man of genius. Beauty informed the sergeant that she was the fiancée of Private Detaze, and requested the sergeant's kind offices to obtain a leave of absence for the private.

Lanny handed this in at the barrier, and after that there was nothing to do but wait. It was dark before the answer came, in the shape of the sergeant himself, looking distinguished in his long blue coat and baggy red pants, but not presuming on his new status. He lifted his képi and bowed, and said that he was delighted to see them both. Like everybody else, his first wish was to know about the terrible events in the north; could it be that Paris was in danger? Could it be that the capital had been moved to Bordeaux? Only afterwards did he mention the matter which was so close to Beauty's heart. Nothing could be done that night, but he was taking steps to arrange matters in the morning so that Madame's wishes might be granted.

How were Beauty and her son going to spend an evening in that wretched village, with only a few huts of woodsmen and charcoal burners, and only candles in their rooms? Lanny had an original suggestion, fitting his own disposition: why not sit in the public room and talk with whoever might come in? The possibility of such a proceeding would never have crossed the mind of Beauty Budd; but the boy argued they would be nothing but peasant fellows, with whom he had chatted off and on all his days. If there was a lady in the room, they would surely mind their conversation. They would sip their wine, play their dominoes, sing their songs. If they were soldiers, they would want to be told about the war, like Pierre. They were Marcel's comrades, and one of them might some day save his life.

That settled it. Beauty decided that she wanted to know them all! So the two had their supper at one of the rough wooden tables in the little drinking place; fried rabbit and onions and dried olives and bread and cheese and sour wine. When they were through they did not leave, but called for a set of dominoes; and when the soldiers came straggling in—what a sensation! Lanny talked with them, and the whisper passed around: *"Des Américains!"* Ah, yes, that accounted for it; in that wonderful land of millionaires and cinema stars it must be the custom for rich and divinely beautiful blond ladies to sit in public rooms and chat with common soldiers. Before long Lanny revealed why they were there, and the sensation was magnified. *Sapristi! C'est la fiancée de Marcel Detaze! Il est peintre! Il est bon enfant! C'est un diable heureux!*

It happened just as Lanny said it would; they all wanted to know about the war. Here were rich people, who had traveled, had been in Paris when the war broke out—what had they seen? And a friend who had been in Belgium—what had *she* seen? Was it true, Madame, that the Germans were cutting off the hands of Belgian children? That they were spearing babies upon their bayonets and carrying them on the march? Beauty reported that her friend had not mentioned any such sights. She did not express opinions of her own. They were not there to make pro-German propaganda, nor to excite disaffection among the troops!

VIII

In the course of the next morning came Marcel; young, erect, and happy, walking upon air. He caught Beauty in his arms and kissed her, right there in front of an audience, including Lanny, and mine host with long gray mustaches, and several mule teams with drivers, all grinning. Romance had come to the Alpes Maritimes! The men could not have been more interested if it had been a company of movie stars to put them into a picture.

The military life agreed with Marcel; why shouldn't it? asked he—in that bracing mountain air, at the most delightful season of the year, living outdoors, marching and drilling, eating wholesome food, and not a care in the world, except the absence of his beloved. "*Regardez!*" he cried, and pointed to the mountains. "I will have something new to paint!" He showed Lanny the far snowy peaks, and the valleys filled with mist. "There's a new kind of atmosphere," he said, and wanted to start on it right away. He had just come from sentry duty; on that mountain to the east he paced back and forth many hours at a stretch; it was good, because it gave him time to think and to work out his philosophy of life—and of love, he added. When Beauty spoke of danger, he laughed; he and the Italian sentries exchanged cigarettes and witticisms—"Jokes and smokes," said Marcel, who was brushing up his English.

They had lunch in the *auberge*, and Marcel was like all the other soldiers, he wanted to talk about nothing but the war. "Did you bring me any papers?" Yes, Lanny had had that kind thought, and Marcel wanted to see them at once. The boy could see that his mother's feelings were hurt; the painter could actually look at an old newspaper when he had Beauty Budd in front of him! But that's what has to be expected, thought she. "Man's love is of man's life a thing apart; 'Tis woman's whole existence."

Worse than that: before the lunch was over, Marcel revealed that he wasn't content with this idyllic existence in the mountains; he was pining to get up to the north, into the hell of death and destruction. He undertook to defend this attitude, even though he saw that it brought tears to the eyes of his beautiful blond mistress. "*La patrie est en danger!*" It was the war cry of the French Revolution, and now, more than a hundred years later, it was shaking the soul of Marcel Detaze. How could any Frenchman know that the goose-step was trampling the banks of the river Marne, only a few miles from Paris, and not desire to rush there, and interpose his body between the most beautiful city in the world and the most hateful of enemies?

Lanny knew that they wanted to be alone; their every glance revealed it, and he said that he would take a walk and see all he could of those grand mountains. Marcel pointed to the west and said: "All France is that way." Then he pointed to the east and added: "All that is forbidden."

So Lanny walked to the west, and when he was tired he sat and talked to a shepherd on a hillside; he drank the clear icy water of a mountain stream, and saw the trout darting here and there, and a great bird, perhaps an eagle, sailing overhead, and large grouse called capercaillie whirring through the pine forests. When he came back, toward dark, he saw by the faces of the lovers that they were happy, and by the quivering gray mustaches of the *aubergiste* and the smiles of his stout wife that all the world loved a lover. Madame had prepared a sort of wedding cake for the occasion, and it was washed down with wine by mule drivers and soldiers who sang love songs, for all the world like a grand opera chorus. *"Nous partons, courage; courage aux soldats."*

IX

When they got home again they found that the Baroness de la Tourette had returned to Cannes; she and her maid had managed to crowd into a train, sitting up the whole night—but that was a small matter after the hardships they had been through. Sophie had tales to tell about Paris under what had so nearly been a siege. The German army of invasion had come swinging down on the city, turning like the spokes of a wheel with far-off Verdun as the hub. But when they got close to Paris they veered to the east, apparently planning to enclose the French armies at Verdun and the other fortifications. The minds of their commanders were obsessed by the memory of Sedan; if they could make such a wholesale capture, they could end this war as they had ended the last.

There is around Paris a convergence of waters known as "the seven rivers"; gentle streams, meandering through wooded lands with towns and villages along the banks, and many bridges. The Marne flows into the Seine just before it enters the city at the east. It was along the former river that the German von Kluck contemptuously exposed the right wing of his army; and General Gallieni assembled all the taxicabs and trucks in a great metropolis, rushed his reserves to the front, and hurled them against the enemy forces.

You saw hardly any young men in Paris during those fateful days of the battle of the Marne. The older men and women and children listened to the thunder of the guns that did not cease day or night; they sat upon the parapets of the river, and saw the wreckage of trees and buildings, of everything that would float, including the bodies of dead animals—the human bodies were being fished out before they got into the city. Overhead came now and then a sight of irresistible fascination, an aeroplane soaring, spying out the troop movements, or possibly bringing bombs. The enemy plane was known as a *Taube*—an odd fantasy, to turn the dove of peace into a cruel instrument of slaughter. Already they had dropped explosives upon Antwerp and killed many women and children. Nevertheless, curiosity was too great, and everywhere in the open places you saw crowds gazing into the sky.

The sound of the guns receded, and by this the people knew that one of the great battles of history had been fought and won. But they did not shout or celebrate; Paris knew what a victory cost, and waited for the taxicabs to bring back their loads of wounded and their news about the dead. The Germans were thrown back upon the Aisne, thirty miles farther north; so the flight of refugees from Paris stopped—and at last it became possible for a lady of title to get to the Riviera without having to walk.

With Sophie came Eddie Patterson, her amiable friend whose distinction in life was that he had chosen the right grandfather. The old gentleman had once engineered through the legislature of his state a franchise to build a railroad bridge; now he drew a royalty from the railroad of one cent for every passenger who crossed the river. Eddie was an amateur billiard player with various medals and cups, and was also fond of motorboating. He talked of giving his fastest boat to the French government to be used in hunting submarines; he would soon see it cruising the Golfe Juan day and night with a four-pounder gun bolted onto the bow.

Eddie Patterson was a slender and rather stoop-shouldered fellow who talked hardheadedly, and had never given any indication of having a flighty mind; but now he had somehow worked himself into a furious rage against the Germans and was talking about volunteering for some kind of service. Sophie was in a panic about it, and of course appealed for the help of her friend Beauty Budd, who agreed with her that men were crazy, and that none of them ever really appreciated a woman's love.

At any hour of the day or night Sophie and Eddie would get into an argument. "All that talk about German atrocities is just propaganda," the baroness would announce. "Haven't I been there and

seen? Of course the Germans shoot civilians who fire at them from
the windows of houses. And maybe they are holding the mayors of
Belgian towns as hostages; but isn't that always done in wartime?
Isn't it according to international law?" Sophie talked as if she were
a leading authority on the subject, and Eddie would answer with an
impolite American word: "Bunk!" After listening to a few such discussions, Lanny made up his mind that neither of them really knew
very much about it, but were just repeating what they read in the
papers. Since there were hardly any but French and English papers
to be had, a person like himself who wanted to be neutral had a hard
time of it.

X

What women have to do is to keep their restless and frantic men
entertained. So Lanny would be pressed into service to take Eddie
Patterson fishing, or tempt him into roaming the hills to explore ancient Roman and Saracen ruins. But truly it was impossible to get
away from the war anywhere in France.

Once they stopped to watch the distilling of lavender, high up on
a wind-swept plateau. There were odd-looking contrivances on
wheels, with an iron belly full of fire, and a rounded dome on top
from which ran a long spout, making them look like fantastic birds.
A crew of women and older men were harvesting the plants, tend-
ing the fires, and collecting the essence in barrels. Pretty soon Lanny
was talking with them, and they became more concerned to ask him
questions than to earn their daily bread. Americans were rich and
were bound to know more than poor peasants of the Midi. "What
do you think, Messieurs? Will *les Allemands* be driven from our
soil? And how long will it take? And what do you think the Italians will do? Surely they could not attack us, their cousins, almost
their brothers!"

On Lanny's own Cap d'Antibes the principal industry was growing flowers for perfumes, and in winter this is done under glass. It
was estimated that there were more than a million glass frames upon
that promontory; and naturally those people who owned them were

troubled to hear about bombs being dropped from the sky, and about strange deadly craft rising from the sea and launching torpedoes. Such things sounded fabulous, but they must be real, because often you could see war vessels patrolling, and now and then a seaplane scouting, and there were notices in all public places for fishermen and others to report at once any unusual sight on the sea.

Now came the flower growers, wanting to talk about *les affaires*. What did these foreign gentry think about the chances of enemy bombing of the Cap? What would be the effect, supposing that a stray torpedo were to hit the rocks? Would it have force enough to shatter those million glass frames? And what did it mean that people who were supposed to be civilized, who had come to the Riviera by the tens of thousands, as the Germans had done—many great steamers loaded with them every winter—should now go away and repay their hosts in this dreadful manner?

There came a letter from Mrs. Emily Chattersworth, who had fled from Les Forêts when the Germans came near, and after the great battle had returned to see what had become of her home. "I suppose I can count myself fortunate," she wrote, "because only half a dozen shells struck the house, and they were not of the biggest. Apparently they didn't get their heavy guns this far, and the French retired without offering much resistance. The Uhlans came first, and they must have had an art specialist with them, because they packed up the best tapestries and most valuable pictures, and took them all. They dumped a lot of furniture out of the windows —I don't know whether that was pure vandalism or whether they were planning to build breastworks. They did use the billiard table for that purpose, setting it up on edge; it didn't work very well, for there are many bullet holes through it. They used the main rooms for surgical work, and just outside the window are piles of bloody boots and clothing cut from the wounded. They raided the cellars, of course, and the place is a litter of broken bottles. In the center of my beautiful fleur-de-lis in the front garden is a shell hole and a wrecked gun caisson with pieces of human flesh still sticking to it.

"But what breaks my heart is the fate of my glorious forests.

There was a whole German division concealed in them, and the French set fire to the woods in many places; the enemy came out fighting and were slaughtered wholesale. The woods are still burning and will never be the same in our lifetime. The stench from thousands of bodies which have not yet been found loads the air at night and is the most awful thing one could imagine. I do not know if I can ever endure to live in the place again. I can only pray that the barbarians will not have a second chance at it. The opinion of our friends here is that they are through and will be entirely out of France in another month or two."

So there was more ammunition for Eddie Patterson! One by one the militarists among the Americans were joining up; some in the Foreign Legion, others in the ambulance service, many women for hospital work. The French aviation service was popular among the adventurous-minded young men—but to Sophie this was the most horrible idea of all, for those man-birds were hunting one another in the skies, and the casualties among them were appalling. In the first days all France had been electrified by the deed of one flier, who had driven his plane straight through the gasbag of a Zeppelin, and out at the other side. The mass of hydrogen had exploded and the huge airship had crashed, an inferno of flame; the aviator, of course, had shared its fate.

Beauty Budd would fling her arms about her boy and cry: "Oh, Lanny, don't ever let them get you into a war!" And then one day she received a letter which made her heart stand still:

"Chérie: Your visit shines as the most precious jewel of my memory. The news which I have to tell will make you sad, I fear—but be courageous for my sake. Your coming was the occasion of my having the opportunity to make the acquaintance of my commandant, and being able to volunteer for special service. I am being sent elsewhere to receive training, concerning which it is not permissible for me to write. For the present you may address me in care of l'École Supérieure d'Aéronautique at Vincennes.

"Your love is the sunshine of my life, and knows neither clouds nor night. I adore you. Marcel."

13

Women Must Weep

I

IT WAS going to be some time before Lanny Budd would see his father again. The warring nations would have their "missions" in New York for the purpose of buying military supplies; Robbie's headquarters would be there, and he would make a great deal of money. The various governments would float bonds in the United States, and persons who believed in their financial stability would buy the bonds, and the money would be spent for everything that was needed by armies. Robbie explained these matters in his letters, and said that England and France had placed enough orders with Budd's to justify great enlargements of the plant.

Robbie wrote cautiously, being aware that mail would be read by the French censor. "Remember what I told you about your own attitude, and do not let anybody sway you from it. This is the most important thing for your life." That was enough for Lanny; he did his best to resist the tug of forces about him. Robbie sent magazines and papers with articles that would give him a balanced view; not marking the articles—that would have made it too easy for the censor—but writing him a few days later to read pages so-and-so.

"One thing I was wrong about," the father admitted. "This war is going to last longer than I thought." When Lanny read that, the giant armies were locked in an embrace of death on the river Aisne; the French trying to drive the Germans still farther back, the Germans trying to hold on. They fought all day, and at night food and ammunition were brought up in *camions* and carts, and the armies went on fighting. Battles lasted not days but weeks, and you could hardly say when one ended and the next began. The troops charged and retreated and charged again, fighting over ground already laid waste. They dug themselves in, and when rain filled up the trenches they stayed in them, because it was better to be wet than dead.

It was the same on the eastern front also. The Russian steam roller had made some headway against the Austrians, but in East Prussia it had got stuck in the swampy lands about the Masurian Lakes. The Russians had been surrounded and slaughtered wholesale; but many had got away, and fresh armies had come up and they were pushing back and forth across the border, one great battle after another.

It was going to be that way for a long time—the fiercest fighting, inspired by the bitterest hatreds that Europe had known for centuries. Each nation was going to mobilize its resources from every part of the world; resources of man power, of money, of goods, and of intellectual and moral factors. Each side was doing everything in its power to make the other odious, and neither was going to have any patience with those who were lukewarm or doubting. A mother and son from America who wanted to keep themselves neutral would be buffeted about like birds in a thunderstorm.

II

Traveling by himself to a new post of duty, Marcel was free of censorship for a day or two. He wrote on the train and mailed in Paris an eloquent and passionate love letter, inspired by their recent day and night together. It filled Beauty with joy but also with anguish, for it told her that this treasure of her heart was going to one of the most terrible of all posts of danger. He was to receive several weeks of intensive training to enable him to act as observer in a stationary balloon.

He had suggested this post as one for which his career as a painter fitted him especially. His ability to distinguish shades of color would enable him to detect camouflage. He had studied landscapes from mountain tops, and could see things that the ordinary eye would miss. "You must learn to be happy in the thought that I shall be of real use to my country"—so he wrote, and perhaps really believed it, being a man. What Beauty did was to crumple the letter in her hands, and sink down with her face upon it and wet it with her tears.

After that there was little peace in Bienvenu. Beauty went about with death written on her face; Lanny would hear her sobbing in the night, and would go to her room and try to comfort her. "You chose a Frenchman, Beauty. You can't expect him to be anything else." The boy had been reading an anthology of English poetry, which Mr. Elphinstone had left behind when he went home to try to get into the army. Being young, Lanny sought to comfort his mother with noble sentiments expressed in immortal words. "I could not love thee, dear, so much, Loved I not honour more."

So he quoted; but it only seemed to make Beauty mad. "What do you mean, 'honour'? It's nothing but the desire of powerful men to rule over others. It's a trick to get millions of people to follow them and die for their glory."

Going about the house brooding, did Beauty Budd regret the choice she had made? If so, she didn't say it to Lanny. What she told him was that life was a thing too cruel to be endured. It could not be that there was a God—the idea was crazy. We were being mocked by some devil, or by a swarm of them—a separate devil in the heart of every man who sought to kill his fellows.

Beauty's good friend Sophie and her young man, Eddie Patterson, rallied to her support. They brought with them an elderly retired Swiss diplomat who bore the distinguished name of Rochambeau; having been behind the scenes of Europe most of his life, he was not to be deceived by any propaganda, and could not be offended by the antimilitarist utterances of a self-centered American lady. These four played bridge; they played with a kind of desperation, all day and most of the night, stopping only when Leese put a meal upon the table and tapped a little tune on the Chinese gongs that hung by the dining-room door. They played for very small stakes, but took their game with the utmost seriousness, having their different systems of play, and discussing each hand, what they had done and whether some other way might not have been better. They never mentioned, and they tried never to think, how men were being mangled with shot and shell while these fine points of bidding and leading and signaling were being settled.

A convenient arrangement for Lanny, because it set him free to read. Also he could play tennis with boys and girls of the near-by villas, and keep the household supplied with seafood. But he had to promise not to go sailing upon the bay, because of Beauty's fear that a German submarine might rise up without warning and torpedo the pleasure boats in the Golfe Juan.

III

Lanny kept up a correspondence with his friend Rick, and learned once more how difficult was going to be the role of neutral in this war. Rick said that the way the Germans were behaving in Belgium deprived them of all claim to be considered as civilized men. Rick hadn't been as much impressed by Kurt's long words as had Lanny, and he said that anyhow, what was the use of fancy-sounding philosophy if you didn't make it count in everyday affairs? Rick said furthermore that from now on America's safety depended on the British fleet, and the quicker the Americans realized it the better for them and for the world.

Lanny was at a disadvantage in these arguments, because he was afraid that if he repeated what his father had told him, the censor wouldn't allow the letter to pass. So he just mentioned what he was reading, and the sights he was seeing. The French had what was called an "aérohydro," a plane that could land upon water, and one of them, having sprung an oil leak, had come down by the quay at Juan; Lanny had watched it being repaired, and then had seen it depart. It carried a machine gun, a Hotchkiss—Lanny knew all the types of guns, as other boys knew automobiles. Rick in return told about the London busses being made over into "transports" for troops, and about crowds of clerks and businessmen drilling in

Hyde Park, still in their civilian clothes, and with only sticks for guns.

But Rick's principal interest was in the air. He wrote a lot about having met one of the fliers with whom they had talked at Salisbury Plain; this officer had fought a pistol duel in the sky, and had got his German. The British, too, were putting machine guns in their planes; but it was a problem, for most planes had the propeller in front, and that was where you wanted to shoot if you were following an enemy. The idea now was to shoot through the propeller, and the British had devised one with flanges which would turn aside whatever bullets struck its blades.

"That's the service I'm going into," said Rick. "But I've promised the pater to wait until next year. The age requirement is eighteen, but a lot of the fellows do a little fibbing. I could, because I'm tall. It is hard to do any studying in times like these. No doubt it's easier for an American."

Lanny corresponded also with Rosemary Codwilliger—pronounced Culliver. He always felt funny when he wrote that name; but he knew that many English names were queer, especially the fashionable ones; the owners carefully preserved this queerness as a form of distinction, as one way of showing that they didn't care a hang whether anybody agreed with them about the way to spell, or to pronounce, or to do anything else. It did not occur to Lanny that people like that might be difficult to get along with in other ways; all he remembered was that Rosemary was delightful to look at, and how sweet it had been to sit with his arms around her in the moonlight.

He didn't write anything about that. They exchanged placid and friendly letters that would make proper reading for both censors and parents. She said that her father was commanding a regiment somewhere in France, and that her mother's nephew, the Honorable Gerald Smithtotten, had been killed after holding the Condé Canal near Mons against seven enemy attacks. "This war is rather hard on our best families," explained the daughter of Captain Codwilliger, "because they have to show themselves on the parapets or whatever it is, to set an example for the men. I want to take up nursing, but mother keeps begging me to finish this year's school. Mothers always think that we are a lot younger than we are really. Are American mothers like that?"

IV

Lanny could not help thinking about Kurt all the time, and wondering what he was doing and thinking. Of course Kurt would be patriotic. Would he blame Lanny for not taking the side of Germany? What reason would he give? Lanny wished he could find out; but of course no letters were allowed to come or go between countries at war.

One day it happened that Lanny was poking into a bureau drawer where he kept handkerchiefs and a fishing reel and some cartridges and photographs and old letters and what not. He picked up a business card and read: "*Johannes Robin, Agent, Maatschappij voor Electrische Specialiteiten, Rotterdam.*" What a lot had happened in the world since Lanny had talked with that Jewish gentleman on the train last Christmas! "I wonder if I'll ever see him again," the boy reflected.

He remembered that he had intended to write to Mr. Robin; and this brought another idea, that possibly the salesman of gadgets might be willing to mail a letter to Kurt for him. Lanny had learned, from the conversation of his mother's friends, that one could communicate with Germans in this way; it was against the law, but much business was still being carried on by way of neutral countries. "It couldn't do Mr. Robin any harm," the boy decided, "because I won't say anything the censor can object to; I won't even need to say that I'm in France."

He sat himself down and composed a letter to his friend in Germany. To set the German censors straight he began:

"My father has told me that it's an American's duty to keep neutral, and I am doing it. I don't want to lose touch with you, so I write to say that I am at home, and that my mother and I are well.

My father is back in Connecticut. I am studying hard, reading the best books I can get, and not forgetting the ideals of the nobler life. I am also practicing sight reading, although my piano technique is still mixed up. I have no teachers at present, but my mother has met a young American college man who came over on a cattle boat for the adventure and now thinks he may stay for a while because he has become interested in a young lady who lives near us. He may want to earn some money, so may teach me what he learned at college, if he has not forgotten it. Please give my sincere regards to all the members of your family, and write your affectionate friend, Lanny."

Certainly that letter could do no injury to any nation at war; and Lanny wrote the salesman in Rotterdam, recalling their meeting on the train and hoping that this would find Mr. Robin well, and that his business had not been too greatly injured by the war. Lanny explained that here was a letter to the friend he had visited in Silesia. Mr. Robin was welcome to read the letter, and Lanny assured him that it contained no war secrets; Mr. Robin would be at liberty to test the paper with lemon juice or with heat—Lanny had been reading and hearing about spies and the way they operated. He hoped that this request would not embarrass Mr. Robin in any way; if it did, he was at liberty to destroy the letter; otherwise would he please mail it in a plain envelope addressed to Kurt Meissner at Schloss Stubendorf, Upper Silesia.

Lanny posted the two letters in the same envelope, and then waited. In due course came a reply from Mr. Robin, cordial as Lanny had expected. Mr. Robin was pleased to take his word about the letter, and would mail future letters if so desired. He recalled his fellow-traveler with pleasure and hoped to meet him again some day. No, the war had not injured his business; on the contrary, he had been able to expand it along new lines, not so different from those of Lanny's father. Mr. Robin told about his family; he had two little boys, one ten and the other eight, and he took the liberty of enclosing a snapshot, so that Lanny might feel that he knew them.

Lanny studied the picture, which had been taken in the summer-time, and showed the family standing at the entrance to a pergola, with a Belgian shepherd dog lying on the ground in front of them. Mr. Robin had on an outing shirt with a soft collar such as Lanny himself wore; Mrs. Robin was stoutish and kind-looking, and the two little boys gazed soberly at Lanny, as if they had known that he was going to be seeing them, and wondered what sort of fellow he might be. They had dark wavy hair like their father, and large, gentle eyes; on the back their names were written, Hans and Freddi, and the information that the former played the violin and the latter the clarinet. Lanny thought once more that he liked the Jews, and asked his mother why they didn't know any. Beauty replied that she hadn't happened to meet them; Robbie didn't like them any too much.

A couple of weeks later came a letter postmarked Switzerland, without the name of any sender. It proved to be from Kurt—evidently he too had some friend whom he trusted. It was in the same cautious tone as Lanny's. "I am glad to hear about an American's attitude to present events. You will of course understand that my point of view is different. You are fortunate in being able to go on with your music studies. For me it has become necessary to make preparations for a more active career. Whatever happens, I will always think of you with warm friendship. My soul remains what it has always been, and I count upon yours. I will write you when I can and hope that you will do the same. The members of my family are well at present. All, as you can imagine, are very busy. Those who are at home join me in kindest regards. Kurt."

Lanny showed this to his mother, and she agreed that Kurt must be preparing for some sort of military service. He was only sixteen, but then the Germans were thorough and began young. His brothers, no doubt, were in the fighting now. Lanny tried to read between the lines; that sentence about his friend's soul meant to tell him, over the censor's shoulder, that even though Kurt went to war, he would still believe in the importance of the ideal, and in art as an

instrument for uplifting mankind. The war was not going to make
any difference in their friendship.

V

Since Kurt was counting upon Lanny's soul, Lanny must be
worthy of it. He decided that he spent too much time reading love
stories, and should begin at once upon something uplifting. He was
wondering what to choose, when he happened to hear M. Rochambeau, the retired diplomat, remark that the priests and bishops who
were blessing the instruments of slaughter in the various nations
were not very well representing the spirit of Jesus. Lanny reflected
that he had seen many pictures of Jesus, and of Jesus's mother, and
of apostles and angels and saints and what not, yet he knew very
little about the Christian religion. Both his mother and his father
had had it forced upon them in their youth, and hated it. But as a
matter of art education, shouldn't Lanny read up on it?

He asked the white-haired and courtly ex-diplomat where he
could find out what Jesus had said, and was reminded that the words
were set down in some old books called the Gospels. M. Rochambeau didn't happen to own a copy, and Beauty's friends, of whom
the boy made inquiry, found the idea amusing. Finally Lanny found
in a bookstore a copy of this ancient work.

Winter was coming now. In Flanders and through northern
France a million men were lying out in the open, in trenches and
shell holes half full of filthy water which froze at night. They were
devoured by vermin and half paralyzed by cold, eating bread and
canned meat, when it could be brought to them over roads which
had been turned into quagmires. All day and night bullets whistled
above them and shells came down out of the sky, blowing bodies to
fragments and burying others under loads of mud. The wounded
had to lie where they fell until death released them, or night made
it possible for their fellows to drag them back into the trenches.

And with this going on a few hundred miles away, Lanny was

reading the story of Jesus, four times over, with variations. He was deeply touched by it each time, and wept over the way that poor man had been treated, and loved him for the kind and gentle things he had said. If somebody had happened along to speak for one of the religious sects—almost any of them—that person might have made a convert. As it was, Lanny had no one to consult but a worldly-wise ex-diplomat, who told him that if he wanted to follow Jesus he would have to do it in his own heart, because none of the churches were traveling in that path or near it.

So Lanny didn't go to church. Instead he studied arithmetic, algebra, and modern history with his new tutor, Jerry Pendleton, a happy-go-lucky fellow whom Beauty Budd had met in the way she met most persons, at a party for tea and dancing; she liked him because he had red hair, a gay disposition, and good manners. He had come to Europe with a chum, working their way, and had got caught, first by the war, and then by a mademoiselle whose mother conducted the *pension* at which he was staying. Instead of going back to finish his senior year in a fresh-water college, Jerry had lingered on, and a job as tutor presented itself as a happy solution of several problems.

The young man's account of education in the United States was not exactly favorable; he said that the main thing you learned was how to get along with other fellows, and with girls. He confessed, as Mr. Elphinstone had done, that he had forgotten all the subjects he was going to teach, but he and Lanny could read together, and there was that magnificent encyclopedia which could never go wrong. Jerry would at least keep the kid out of mischief—and at the same time Mrs. Budd could give him kindly advice about the most bewildering love affair he had ever run into. Mlle. Cerise, it appeared, was being brought up in French fashion, which meant that she couldn't see a young man without her mother being close by, and he couldn't even bring her to one of Mrs. Budd's tea parties without a chaperon. At home you took a girl motoring, or if you didn't have a car, you bicycled and had a picnic in the woods; but here they were all nuns until after they were married—and then, apparently, you could pick them up in the gambling rooms at the casino.

"Not quite all of them," said Beauty, beginning the education of her son's tutor.

VI

Once again, for a day, Marcel Detaze was free from the censor. He was on his way to his post of duty, and poured out his heart to his beloved. This time he didn't hide from her the dangers to which he was going. The hour had come when she had to steel her soul.

Marcel was gay, as always; that was the way you had to take life, if you didn't mean to let it get you down. Make a work of art of it; put your best into it; play your little part, and be ready to quit before the audience got tired of you. Marcel described a "sausage balloon" as a grotesque and amusing object, in rebellion against the men who had created it and obstinately trying to break out of their control. It was huge and fat, and assumed changing shapes, and danced and cavorted in the air. A net of cords imprisoned it, and a steel cable bound it to the earth. The cable was on a pulley, and two stout horses or oxen plodding across a field let the balloon up or pulled it down.

All this for the sake of an observer who sat in a bulletproof basket underneath the balloon, equipped with field glasses and measuring instruments, and a telephone set. It was his task to spy out enemy entrenchments, and the movements of troops and guns. He had to have a keen eyesight, and be trained to recognize the difference between branches growing on trees and the same when cut down and made into a screen for a heavy gun. He had to know Birnam Wood when it was removed to Dunsinane. Also, he had to be a man who had traveled to the fiords of Norway and the Isles of Greece without getting seasick; for the winds which blew off the North Sea would toss him around like a whole yachtful of soap kings—so wrote the painter, who had been sorry for poor Ezra Hackabury, but couldn't help finding him funny.

Of course such a balloon would be a target for the enemy. Airplanes would come darting out of the clouds at a hundred miles an hour, spitting fire as they came. "We have guns on the ground to stop them," wrote Marcel; "guns with high-angle mountings designed especially to shoot at planes, but I fear they are not very good yet, and Lanny should tell his father to invent better ones for my protection. The shells from these guns make white puffs of smoke when they explode, so that the gunner can correct his aim. The English call the guns 'Archies,' and I am told that this comes from some music-hall character who said: 'Archibald, certainly not!' It is wonderful, the humor with which the English fellows take this messy business. I have had one as an instructor and he has explained their jokes to me. The heavy shells which make an enormous cloud of black smoke they call 'Jack Johnsons,' because of a Negro prize fighter who is dangerous. Also they call them 'black Marias' and 'coal boxes.' Doubtless there will be new names by the time I get to the front."

Beauty broke down and couldn't read any more. It seemed to her horrible that men should make jokes about death and destruction. Of course they laughed so that they might not have to weep; but Beauty could weep, and she did. She was certain that her lover was gone forever, and her hopes died a new death every time she thought of him. Lanny, talking with M. Rochambeau, learned that his mother had cause for fear, because the job which Marcel had chosen represented just about the peak of peril in this war. A single correct observation followed by a well-placed shell might put a battery of guns out of action; so the enemy waged incessant warfare upon the stationary balloons. This far the French had managed to keep the mastery of the air, but the fighting was incessant and the death rate high. "Women must weep," a poet in Lanny's anthology had said.

VII

Mrs. Emily Chattersworth wrote the news. Learning of the dreadful sufferings of the wounded after the great battle of the Aisne, she had lent the Château Les Forêts to the government for a hospital. Then she had been moved to go and see what was being done, and had been so shocked by the sight of mangled bodies brought in by the hundreds, and the efforts of exhausted doctors and nurses to help them, that she had abandoned her career as *salonnière* and taken up that of hospital director. Now she was helping to organize a society in Paris for the aid of the wounded and was asking all her friends for help and contributions. Would Beauty Budd do something? Mrs. Emily said that Marcel might some day be brought to Les Forêts; and of course that fetched Beauty. Despite her vow to economize and pay her debts, she sent a check to her friend.

Then Lanny began to observe a curious phenomenon. Having given her lover, and then her money, Beauty could no longer refuse to give her heart. So far she had been hating war; but now little by little she took to hating Germans. Of course she didn't know about *Weltpolitik*, and didn't try to discuss it; Beauty was personal, and recalled the hordes of Teutons who had come flocking to the Riviera in recent winters. The hotelkeepers had welcomed them, because they spent money; but Beauty hadn't welcomed them, because she loved the quiet of her retreat and they invaded it. The women were enormous and had voices like Valkyries; the men had jowls, and rolls of fat on the backs of their necks, and huge bellies and buttocks which they displayed indecently to the winter sunshine. They drank and ate sausages in public, made ugly guttural noises—and now, as it turned out, they had all the time been spying and intriguing, preparing huge engines of destruction and death!

Yes, Beauty decided, she hated all Germans; and this made for disharmony in the little island of peace which she had created at Bienvenu. Sophie didn't want to hate the Germans because it might start her Eddie off to be a hero, like Marcel. M. Rochambeau didn't want it because he was old and tired, and liable to heart attacks if he let himself get excited. "Dear lady," he would plead, "we in this crowded continent have been hating each other for so many centuries—pray do not bring us any more fuel for our fires." The re-

tired diplomat's voice was gentle, and his manner that of some
elderly prelate.

Lanny agreed that things were going to be harder for him if his
mother became warlike. He would remind her of Kurt, and of great
Germans like Goethe and Schiller and Beethoven, who belonged to
all Europe. He would repeat to her the things which Robbie had told
him—and of which the father kept reminding him, in carefully veiled
language. When Beauty burst out that Robbie was thinking of the
money he was going to make out of this war, Lanny was a bit
shocked, and withdrew into himself. It wouldn't do to remind his
mother that it was Robbie's money on which they were both living,
and which she was giving to Mrs. Emily.

VIII

Jerry Pendleton was being a good companion. He liked to do the
things that Lanny liked, and they climbed the hills and played tennis and swam and fished, and Jerry cultivated the mother of Mlle.
Cerise by bringing in more seafood than the *pension* could consume.
They enjoyed torch-fishing especially, and made themselves expert
spearsmen, and got many a green moray, but never one as big as
Captain Bragescu's. One night a strange adventure befell them—
oddly enough the very thing that Beauty had been worried about,
and for which everybody had laughed at her. It was to be that
way all through the war; truth would outrun fiction, and if anybody said that a thing couldn't happen, then right away it did.

A still night, something not so common in the month of December, and two young fellows in fishing togs and sweaters, because it
was cold in spite of the lack of wind. They had a torch set in the
bow of the boat, blazing brightly, and were lying, one on each side,
with their heads over the gunwales, looking down into the crystal-
clear water. The sea growths waved gently to and fro, and it was
like some enchanted land; the *langoustes* poked their heads out from
the rocks, and fish idled here and there, many of them camouflaged,
just like the Germans. Lanny thought about Marcel, doing the same

kind of work, but high in the air instead of on top of the sea.
The Cannes lighthouse was flashing red and green. Not many
lights on the shore, for the night life of the Golfe Juan was dimmed
that winter. Not many sounds, just the murmur of distant traffic,
and now and then the put-put of a motorboat. But suddenly a
strange sort of splashing, the movement of a great bulk of water,
and a series of waves rushing toward them, rocking their little boat
so that they could no longer look into the depths. They stared
toward the sound, shading their eyes from the torchlight, and gradually made out something, a dim shape. Impossible to believe it and
equally impossible to doubt it—a round boxlike object arisen from
the depths of the sea, and lying there, quite still!

"A submarine!" whispered Lanny; and his companion exclaimed:
"Put out the torch!" Lanny was nearer, and grabbed it and plunged
it into the water. A hissing sound, then silence and darkness, and
the rowboat rocking in the swells.

The two listened, their hearts thumping. "They must have seen
us," Jerry whispered. They waited and wondered what to do. They
had both read stories about submarines sinking vessels, and not even
bothering to save the crews. This might be an enemy one, or again
it might be French or British.

Sounds travel clearly over smooth water. They heard footsteps,
people moving; then came splashing and, unmistakably, the sound
of muffled oars. "They're coming after us!" exclaimed Lanny; and
his tutor grabbed their oars and began to row for dear life for the
shore, less than a hundred feet away.

Would the people on the submarine turn on a searchlight and
open fire on them? It was something they both thought of, and they
had a good right to be scared. But nothing of the sort happened.
They got to the shore and crept out of the boat; then, safe behind
rocks, they listened again, and heard the muffled oars, undoubtedly
coming nearer—but a little farther down the shore. Very plainly
they heard the rowing stop, and after a minute or less it began
again—the boat, or whatever it was, was going back to the submarine.

"They came to get somebody," whispered Jerry.

"Or else to put somebody ashore."

"It must be an enemy. No French boat would behave like that." A moment later the tutor added: "Somebody on shore may be looking for us." That called for no argument, and the pair got up and started to climb toward the road.

"Look here," whispered Jerry, suddenly; "this may be very serious, and we ought to tell the police or the military. If anybody was put ashore, he'd be armed, and he'd mean business."

"That's right," answered the younger boy, in a delightful state of excitement.

"Do you know where there'd be a telephone?"

"In almost any of the villas along the road."

"Well, let's go quietly; and if anyone tries to stop us we'll bolt— you go one way and I'll go another. They can hardly get us both in the dark."

They tiptoed down the road, and presently came to a house with lights, and asked permission to telephone the nearest police station. The police ordered them to wait right there, which they were glad to do, and meanwhile told their story to a family of English people who were greatly excited. A car with gendarmes arrived soon, and another with military men a little later. They took the Americans down to the shore and asked them a hundred questions. There was no sign of any submarine, only Lanny's boat, which the tide was about to float away. Launches came, and men searched the shore, finding no trace of anything—but would there have been, on those masses of rocks? The two young fellows managed to convince the authorities of their good faith, and one of the army men said that it must have been an Austrian submarine from the Adriatic.

That was all they said. A curtain of silence fell about the matter; nothing was published—but there was a lot of patrolling by torpedo boats and "aérohydros" in the neighborhood. M. Rochambeau, who knew about military matters, said that the enemy's purpose must have been to put ashore some important agent who was too well known to come in with a neutral passport. Doubtless he would have a place of refuge prepared. The secret service of the Allies would be trying to find out who he was and what he had come for.

Besides the open war of arms, there was this underground war of spying and sabotage always going on; both sides had their agents in all the services of the enemy, and were spending fortunes to corrupt and undermine. The French had gathered up the known enemy aliens in the Midi and interned them on the Île Ste.-Marguerite, which lay just offshore from Cannes, and had been the peaceful home of some fifty nuns, and a place where tourists came to sit under the big pine trees and have tea. But of course there must be many Germans at large in France, posing as Swiss, or Danes, or citizens of the United States, or what not; they would be watching troop movements, perhaps planning to blow up railroad bridges, or to put bombs upon merchant vessels, or even warships. If they were caught, you wouldn't hear anything about it; they would be taken to some military fortress, and stood against a wall blindfolded and shot through the heart.

IX

The dread news came for which Beauty had been waiting many weeks. It was written by a comrade of Marcel's, a "ground man" whom he had pledged to this duty. The comrade regretted to inform Madame Budd that her friend had been severely injured; his "kite balloon" had been attacked by two enemy planes, and had been hauled down, but not quickly enough; some fifteen meters above ground it had caught fire, and Marcel had leaped out, and had been badly smashed up, also burned. He had been taken to the base hospital at Beauvais, and the writer could not say as to his present condition.

After her first collapse, Beauty's one idea was to get to him; she couldn't stop sobbing, and was in the grip of a sort of convulsion of shuddering—but she must go, she must go—right now, come on! She wouldn't even wait to put clothes into a suitcase. She had visions of her lover mutilated, defaced—he would be in agony, he might be dying at that moment. "Oh, God, my God, help me, help my poor Marcel!"

It happened that Jerry and M. Rochambeau were in the house, as well as Lanny. They tried to comfort her, but what could they say? They tried to restrain her, but she wouldn't listen to reason. "You must find out if you can get on the train," argued the diplomat. But her answer was that she would motor. "Then you must arrange to get *essence*"—but she said: "I'll find a way—I'll pay what it costs—you can always get things if you pay."

"But, my dear lady, you may not be able to get near the town—it's in the war zone, and they never allow relatives or visitors."

"I'll find a way. I'll go to Paris and lay siege to the government."

"There are many persons laying siege to the government right now—including the Germans."

"I'm going to help Marcel. I'll find a way—I'll take a job as nurse with Emily Chattersworth. She'll get me there somehow. Who will come with me?"

Lanny had learned to drive a car, but hardly well enough for this trip. Jerry Pendleton was a first-class driver, and knew how to fix carburetors and those other miserable devices that were always getting out of order. Jerry would go; and the terrified maids would rush to pile some clothes into suitcases—warm things, for Madame was declaring hysterically that if they wouldn't let her into the town she would sleep in the car, or in the open like the soldiers. None of her pretty things—but then she changed her mind, if she had to call on government officials she would have to look her best—nothing showy, but that simplicity which is the apex of art, and which costs in accordance. A strange thing to see a woman, so choked with her own sobs that she could hardly make herself understood, at the same time trying to decide what sort of dress was proper to wear in approaching the war minister of a government in such dire peril of its existence that it had had to move to a remote port by the sea!

Lanny packed his suitcase, taking a warm sweater and the overcoat he had worn in Silesia; a good suit also, because he too might have to interview officials. Beauty sent a wire to Mrs. Emily, asking her to use her influence; M. Rochambeau sent a telegram to an official of his acquaintance who could arrange it if any man could. "Only woman can do the impossible," added the old gentleman, parodying Goethe.

They piled robes and blankets into the car, filling up the seat alongside Beauty, who sat now, a mask of horror, gazing into a life-long nightmare. They drove to the *pension* where Jerry stayed, and he ran upstairs and threw some of his things into a bag. Downstairs were Mlle. Cerise and her mother and her aunt, all shocked by the news. The red-headed tutor grabbed the proper young French lady and kissed her first on one cheek and then on the other. "*Adieu! Au revoir!*" he cried, and fled.

"*Ah, ces Américains!*" exclaimed the mother.

"*Un peuple tout à fait fou!*" added the aunt.

It was practically an engagement.

14

The Furies of Pain

I

THE little town of Beauvais lies about fifty miles to the north of Paris. It is something over a thousand years old, and has an ancient cathedral, and battlements now made into boulevards. It was like Paris, in that the Germans had got there almost, but not quite. Its inhabitants had heard the thunder of guns, and were still hearing it, day and night, a distant storm where the sun came up. Thunderstorms are capricious, and whether this one would return was a subject of hourly speculation. People studied the bulletins in front of the ancient Hôtel de Ville and hoped that what they read was true.

To keep the storm away, everybody was working day and night. The Chemin de Fer du Nord passed through the town, which had become a base: soldiers detraining, guns and ammunition being unloaded, depots established to store food and fodder and pass them up to the front, everything that would be needed if the line was to hold and the enemy be driven back. No use to expect comfort in such a place; count yourself lucky that you were alive.

Beauty Budd was here because she belonged to that class of people who are accustomed to have their own way. She had met cabinet ministers at tea parties and salons, she had given a generous check for the aid of the French wounded, she bore the name of a munitions family now being importuned to expand their plant and help to save *la patrie*. So when she appeared at the door of an official, the secretary bowed and escorted her in; the official said: "Certainly, Madame," and signed the document and had it stamped.

So the car with the red-headed college boy chauffeur had been passed by sentries on the edge of Beauvais, and the harassed authorities of the town did their best to make things agreeable for a lady whose grief added dignity to her numerous charms. "Yes, Madame, we will do our best to find your friend; but it will not be easy, because we have no general records." There was another battle going on; the grumbling guns were making hundreds of new cases every hour, and they were dumped here because there was no time to take them farther.

"We will go ourselves and search," said Madame; and when they told her that all the buildings in the town which could be spared had been turned into hospitals, she asked: "Can you give me a list?" The boys drove her to one place after another, and she would stand waiting while a clerk looked through a register of the living and another of the dead; her hands would be clenched and her lips trembling, and the two escorts at her side would be ready to catch her if she started to fall.

At last they found the name of Marcel Detaze; in a dingy old inn, so crowded with cots in the corridors that there was barely room to get through. It was Milton's "Stygian cave forlorn, 'Mongst horrid shapes, and shrieks, and sights unholy." Beauty Budd, accustomed to every luxury, was plunged into this inferno, ill-lighted, clamorous with cries and groans, stinking of blood and suppurating wounds and disinfectants. Ambulances and carts were unloading new cases on the sidewalk; sometimes they were dead before a place could be found for them, and then they were carted to open graves outside the city.

II

Marcel was alive. That was all Beauty had asked for. They could not tell her much about him. His legs had been broken and had been set. His back was injured, they didn't know how badly. He doubtless had internal injuries. His burns had been dressed; very painful, of course, but they did not think he would be blind. "We have no time, Madame," they said. "We do not sleep, we are exhausted."

Beauty could see that it was true; doctors and nurses and attendants, all were pale and had dark rings under their eyes, and some of them staggered. "*C'est la guerre, Madame.*" "I know, I know," said Beauty.

They took her to where he lay upon a cot, with a dozen other men in the same room. There would have been no way of recognizing him; his head was a mass of bandages, only an opening for his mouth and nose, and these appeared to be open sores. She had to kneel by him and whisper: "Is it you, Marcel?" He did not stir; just murmured: "Yes." She said: "Darling, I have come to help you." When she put her ear to his lips, she heard faintly: "Let me die." There was something wrong with his voice, but she made out the words: "Don't try to save me. I would be a monster."

Beauty had never been taught anything about psychology; only what she had picked up by watching people she knew. She had never heard of a "death-wish," and if anyone had spoken of autohypnosis she would have wondered if it was a gadget for a motorcar. But she had her share of common sense, and perceived right away that she had to take command of Marcel's mind. She had to make him want to live. She had to find what might be an ear under the mass of bandages, make sure that the sounds were going into it, and then say, firmly and slowly:

"Marcel, I love you. I love your soul, and I don't care what has happened to your body. I mean to stand by you and pull you through. You have got to live for my sake. No matter what it costs, you must stand it, and see it through. Do you hear me, Marcel?"

"I hear you."

"All right then. Don't say no to me. You must do it because I want you to. For the sake of our love. I want to take you away from here, and nurse you, and you will get over this. But first you have to make up your mind to it. You have to want to live. You have to love me enough. Do you understand me?"

"It is not fair to you——"

"That is for me to say. Don't argue with me. Don't waste your strength. You belong to me, and you have no right to leave me, to deprive me of your love. I don't care what you say, I don't want to hear it—I want you. Whatever there is of you that the doctors can save—that much is mine, and you must not take it from me. You can live only if you try to, and I ask you to do that. I want your promise. I want you to say it and mean it. I have to go out and make arrangements to take you to Paris; but I can't go till I know that you will fight, and not give up. You told me to have courage, Marcel. Now I have it, and you have to repay me. Do you understand?"

"I understand."

"I want your promise. I want to know that if I go out to get help, you will fight with everything that's in you to keep alive, to keep your hope and courage, for my sake, and for our love. There's no use talking about love if you're not willing to do that much for it. Answer me that you will."

She put her ear to the opening again, and heard a whisper: "All right." She touched him gently on the shoulder, not knowing what part of him might be a wound, and said: "Wait for me. I'll come back just as quickly as I can make arrangements. Anything else I can do?"

"Water," he said. She didn't know how to give it to him, for she was afraid to lift his head, and she had no tube, and no one to ask. She dipped her handkerchief into a glass and squeezed a little into his mouth, and kept that up until he said it was enough.

III

The doctors made no objection to having a patient taken off their hands. They said he couldn't be crowded into an automobile, that would surely kill him; and there was no ambulance available. It was a question of making changes in Beauty's own car, one of the new and fashionable kind called a "limousine," a square black box. It might be possible to take out two of the seats, the right-hand ones, and make a place to lay a narrow mattress on the floor. Then Jerry made a suggestion—why not put a board platform on top of the two seats, with a mattress on that?

They drove to a garage; there was nobody but the wife of the proprietor and an elderly mechanic, both greatly startled by the idea of cutting out a piece of the back of a luxury car, so that a wounded soldier could be slid into it. The windshield was large, and the mechanic thought he might be able to remove that. Beauty said: "Break it if necessary. We can have it replaced in Paris." Jerry took the proprietress aside and spoke magic words: *"C'est l'ami de cette belle dame."*

"Ah, c'est l'amour!" That explained everything, and they went to work with enthusiasm. Love will find out the way! They managed to get the windshield off without too great harm, and they put some boards together and made a platform, and the proprietress brought an old mattress, and Lanny worked at it with his pocket knife, cutting it down to the right size. *"Ah, ces Américains!"*

While all this was being done, Beauty was out looking for a telephone, to call a surgeon she knew in Paris, and arrange for Marcel to be received at a private hospital. When she got back, the platform

was in place, and the mattress on top of it, a reasonably good place
for a wounded man to lie for the time it would take to get him to
the big city.

Two tired attendants carried the patient down and slid him onto
the mattress without damage. Beauty distributed money to everyone who helped them, and Jerry gave them cigarettes, which they
wanted even more at the moment. It was dark when they set out,
but no matter—Marcel was alive, and Beauty sat in the rear seat,
which brought her head about level with his ear, and for two hours
she whispered: "Marcel, I love you, and you are going to live for
my sake." She found a thousand variations of it, and Lanny listened,
and learned things about love. He was in a cramped position—they
had taken out some of the bags and tied them onto the rear of the
car, and Lanny was squatting on the floor at his mother's knees, underneath Marcel's mattress. He couldn't see anything, but he could
hear, and he learned that love is not all pleasure, but can be agony
and heartache, martyrdom and sacrifice. He learned what the clergyman was talking about in the marriage service: "For better for
worse, for richer for poorer, in sickness and in health, to love and
to cherish, till death us do part."

IV

The human body is a complicated engine with many miles of elastic
pipes large and small. In order that the engine may develop the maximum horsepower per pound of weight, the pipes are made of fragile
materials, and the framework which encloses and supports them is
porous and brittle. When you take such a contraption fifty feet up
in the air and explode a mass of hydrogen gas above it, and let it
crash onto hard ground, you produce in a second or two results
which surgeons and nurses may need a long time to remedy.

There were no physicians in Paris who were not overworked,
and no hospital which was not crowded; but the lady with the magical name of Budd used her influence, and Robbie, getting the news
by cable from his son, replied: "Spare no expense." So Marcel was

X-rayed and investigated, and his burns were treated according to the modern technique of cleaning away damaged tissues. After several days of watching, the doctors said that he would live, if he did not become discouraged by the ordeals he would have to undergo, and if his *amour propre* was not too greatly wounded by the certainty of looking like a scarecrow.

It was up to Beauty. She could have that scarecrow if she wanted it, and she did. There were no more thoughts about Pittsburgh now; she had made her bed and she would lie in it—right here in a private room in a *maison de santé*. She got herself some nurse's uniforms and made a job of it; the people of the place were only too glad, having plenty to do without this difficult case. She had a cot in one corner of the room, and for weeks hardly ever left it; she took no chance of Marcel's *amour propre* breaking loose and causing him to throw himself out of the window. She would be right there, to keep reminding him that he belonged to her, and that her property sense was strong.

Troops of little demons came and sat upon the metal bars which made the head and foot of Marcel's bed. His physical eyes were swathed in bandages, but he saw them plainly with his mind's eye. Some had round shaven heads with *Pickelhauben* on; some had sharp-pointed mustaches which they twisted and turned up at the ends; others were just regular devils with horns and red tails. They came in relays, and pinched the painter's wounded flesh and poked needles into it; they twisted his broken joints, they pulled and strained his damaged pipes—in short, they gave him no peace day or night. The sweat would stand out on him—wherever he had enough skin left for that to happen. He would writhe, and do his best not to groan, because of that poor woman who sat there in anguish of soul, talking to him when he couldn't listen, trying to help him when there wasn't any help. When you are in pain you are alone.

There were the burns that kept having to be dressed; there were bones that had been set wrong and had to be broken again; he was always being transported to the operating room for more probing and poking. The doctors could give him opiates, of course, but

there was a limit, if they intended to keep him alive. He just had to
stand it; he had to learn to live with pain and make a game of it.
The doctors would help him by making jokes, and letting him make
them. He took to calling them "plumbers," and threatening to get
an American one, because the French ones didn't know their business. They answered that they would know it a lot better before
this war was over. Beauty could hardly stand such jokes, but she
toughened herself. "*C'est la guerre.*"

V

The youth and his youthful tutor had rooms in a hotel near by.
The walls had white wainscoting and pink flowered silk above it,
and the chairs were upholstered to match. The elevators looked as
if they were made of gold, and were of open grillwork, so that you
could watch people rising up or sinking down. An elderly official
in a grand uniform set the front doors to revolving for them, and
young women musicians in red coats and gold braid played Hungar-
ian dances while they ate their meals. It was a life of unimaginable
luxury for Jerry Pendleton, whose father owned a couple of drug
stores in a town of Kansas.

They got some books and faithfully studied every morning. After
lunch they walked, and looked at pictures and the other sights of
Paris, and then went to relieve Lanny's mother so that she could
have a nap. The pair were a comfort to Marcel; for men have to be
together, it appears; they just can't stand women all the time. Men
understand why you have to get out into the world, in spite of
danger and death. When Marcel was able to listen, he enjoyed hearing about American college life, including football; and about a trip
on a cattle boat, and then tramping over Europe, sleeping in hay-
stacks. He wished that he had thought of something so original
when he was a youth.

Also, of course, he had to know about the war. Beauty had hoped
never to hear of it again, but she had to read the news to him, and

learn to think about strategy instead of broken bodies. Those two armies had locked themselves together, like wild stags which have got their horns caught and are doomed to butt each other around the forest until both of them drop. All that bitter winter the armies would thrust here and yield there, until gradually they got settled down into the earth. The Germans constructed an elaborate set of entrenchments, line behind line; to the defense of these lines they would bring up everything they had, and Britain and France would do the same on the other side of "no man's land." Each army was frantically getting ready for the spring "push" that was to end the war—so the experts all said, only they differed as to what the ending would be.

Winters in Paris are disagreeable, and people of means do not stay if they can help it. But Beauty hardly ever went out, and the boys didn't mind, because they were young and everything was new and delightful. They saw motion pictures, French and American; they went to plays, and Jerry improved his French. They had a piano in their suite—for Robbie wrote that he was making a pile of money, and Lanny might have anything he wanted, provided he did not smoke or drink or go with prostitutes.

Friends came to see Beauty and Marcel: Emily Chattersworth, very serious now, completely wrapped up in the affairs of her *blessés;* Sophie and her Eddie, she trying so hard to keep her man entertained and hoping that the sight of poor Marcel might teach him the cruelty and wickedness of fighting. But it didn't work that way; men seemed to be drawn to death like moths into the flame; they thought of vengeance rather than of safety. Lanny wrote to Rick, telling what had happened, and it surely did not act as a deterrent with the English boy; he longed all the more to get up there in the air and hunt a *Taube.*

The time came when the sufferer's burns were healed enough so that the bandages could be taken off. That was a time of fresh trials for Beauty—the doctors had to warn her, she must be prepared for the worst, and not let Marcel see any trace of horror in her face. He wouldn't have a mirror, but of course he would put his fingers to his face and feel what was there. His friends must help him get used to it, and make him believe that it made no difference to them.

Beauty, who had been named for her looks, and valued hers and others' very high among the gifts of life, had chosen a man who possessed fine blond hair and mustaches, grave, melancholy features, and an expression of romantic tenderness. Now he had no hair at all, just a red scalp, and his face was a flaming scar. His lips were gone on one side, so that he could only make a pretense at articulating the letters b and p. Out of the gaping wound his teeth grinned hideously, and the gum of the lower jaw was all exposed. Some day a facial surgeon might replace the lip, so the doctors assured him. Fortunately his eyesight was uninjured, but one of his upper eyelids was gone, and most of his ears.

Beauty had to go and look at that mask, and smile affectionately, and say that it didn't matter a bit. Marcel's right hand was well enough to be kissed, and that was where she kissed him. Since he liked so much to make jokes, she told him that she would take up needlework, like other old ladies, and learn to patch up his skin. Seriously she insisted that it was his soul she cared about, and that wasn't changed. After saying all this, she went off to the little room which she had to dress in, and there wept hysterically, cursing God and the Kaiser.

Lanny and Jerry, duly warned, went in armed with cheerfulness. "Well, do you think you can stand me?" asked the victim; and Lanny said: "Don't be silly, Marcel. You know we'd like you in sections if you came that way."

Jerry added: "I read an article about what the surgeons are doing, making new faces. Gosh, it takes your breath away!"

"They've taken away pretty nearly everything but my breath," replied the painter.

Lanny said: "They've left your eyes and your hands, and you'll go back to the Cap and paint better than ever." That was the way to talk!

VI

What was Beauty going to make of this blow which fate had dealt her? She believed in happiness and talked about it as a right. A minister's daughter, raised in a stuffy, uncultured home, she had learned to loathe incessant droning of hymns and preaching of tiresome duty; she had fled from it, and still avoided every mention of its symbols. But suddenly all those hated things had sprung as it were out of the earth, had seized her and bound her with chains which there could be no breaking.

Lanny was all tenderness and kindness, and when she wanted to weep he was there to console her. In his presence she wept for Marcel; he never knew that she went alone and wept for herself. Over and over she fought this bitter battle. No use trying to get away from it—her bridges were burned. She couldn't desert this wreck of a man, and whatever happiness she found would have to be by his side. She who was so dainty had had to accustom herself to blood and stenches; and now she would have to eat and sleep and walk and talk in the presence of what ordinary people see only in nightmares.

Even from her devoted son she must hide her rage at this fate. Even to herself she was ashamed to admit that she regretted her bargain and dreamed of a happiness she might have had in a far-off land of plenty and peace. She had to force herself to be loyal to her choice; but this moral compulsion was associated in her mind with a dull and stolid religion, full of phrases which seemed to have been designed to take the gaiety and charm out of existence. Mabel Blackless, seventeen years old and bursting with the joy of life, hadn't wanted to lay her burdens at the foot of the cross, or to have any redeeming blood spilled for her; she had wanted to see Paris, and had borrowed money and run away to join her brother.

And now it seemed that she was back where she had come from; teaching herself to carry the cross. Her best friends mustn't know about it, because if they did they would pity her, and to be pitied was unendurable. She must tie herself down once for all! In that mood she went out one day and told her story to the *maire* of the *arrondissement*, and arranged for him to come to the hospital. She went back and told Marcel what she had done, and refused to hear any of his objections, pretending to have her feelings hurt by them. With two of the nurses for witnesses, they were married under the French civil law.

Did Marcel guess what was in her heart? She had to fight him, and lie vigorously; how else would he be persuaded to go on living? She and her son and her son's tutor had to make real to themselves the game they played. It wasn't hard for Lanny, because art counted for so much with him; also, it was wartime, and everybody was full of fervors, and wounds were a medal or badge of glory. The marriage made Beauty a "respectable woman" for the first time; but oddly enough it meant a social comedown, the name of Budd being one of power. She would have to get busy and boost Marcel's paintings, and make herself "somebody" again!

VII

The first thing was to contrive something for him to wear over his face. Hero or no hero, he couldn't bear to let anybody look at that mask of horror. He would cover the top of his head with a skullcap, and across his forehead would hang a close-fitting silk veil, with small holes for eyes and nose. Beauty went out and got some pink silk lingerie material, but he wouldn't wear pink; he wanted gray, so that it wouldn't show the dust; they compromised on white when Beauty said that she would make a lot of them and wash them with her own hands. She made a pattern, and after that had something to keep her fingers busy while she sat by his bedside.

It was springtime before he was able to move about, and they took him back to Juan in the car, making a two-day journey of it, so as not to put any strain on him. He looked not so bad with his skullcap and veil; the world was getting used to the sight of *mutilés* —and not yet tired of them. Jerry supported him on one side and Lanny on the other, and they got him into Bienvenu without mishap.

Oh, the glory of that sunshine in the little court; the almost over-powering scent of orange blossoms and jasmine in the evening, and the song of the nightingales! Here were three women to adore him and wait upon him, and nobody to disturb him; here Beauty meant him to spend the rest of his days in peace, and paint whatever wonderful things he might have in him. She was going to give up all her frivolous life—save only such contacts as might help in a campaign to win recognition for genius.

There were just a few painter friends Marcel wanted to see, and these would come to him, and bring their work for him to look at—or if it was too big, Lanny would bring it in the car. The patient was soon able to sit up and read, and there were plenty of books and magazines. Often they read aloud; Jerry came and tutored Lanny, and Marcel would listen and improve his English. They had music; and when he grew stronger he walked about the place. The furies of pain would never let him entirely alone, but he learned to outwit them. He was a more silent man than he used to be; there were things going on inside him about which he did not tell and did not wish to be asked by anyone.

VIII

The military deadlock at the front continued. All winter long the Allies had spent their forces trying to take trenches defended by machine guns—a weapon of which the Germans had managed to get the biggest supply. It was something that Robbie Budd had helped to teach them—and which he had tried in vain to teach the French and British. He couldn't write freely about it now, but there were hints in his letters, and Lanny knew what they meant, having been so often entertained by his father's comic portrayals of the British War Office officials with whom he had been trying to do business. So haughty they were, so ineffable, almost godlike in their self-satisfaction—and so dumb! No vulgar American could tell them anything; and now dapper young officers strolled out in front of their troops, waving their swagger sticks, and the German sharp-shooters knocked them over like partridges off tree limbs. It was sublime, but it wasn't going to win this war of machines.

All the nations had come to realize that they were facing a long struggle. Old M. Rochambeau, who came often to see Beauty and her husband, used a terrible phrase, "a war of attrition." It was like the game of checkers in which you had one more man than your enemy, so every time you swapped with him, you increased your advantage. "Yes, dear lady," said the ex-diplomat, in answer to Beauty's exclamation of horror, "that is the basis on which military strategy is being calculated, and no one stops to ask what you or I think about it."

Man power plus manufacturing power was what would count. Britain had sacrificed her little professional army in order to save the Channel ports, and now she was rushing a new army into readiness, a volunteer army of a million men. There would be a second million, and as many more as needed; they would be shipped to some part of the fighting line, and swapped for Germans, man for man, or as near to it as possible.

The Turkish politicians had been bought into the war on the German side; which meant that the Black Sea was shut off, and nothing could be sent into Russia's southern ports. So a British expedition had been sent to take the Dardanelles. Rick informed Lanny that a cousin of his was going as a private in one of these regiments; Rosemary wrote that her father had been promoted to the rank of colonel, and was to command this same regiment. Rosemary had extracted a promise from her mother to be allowed to study nursing after one more year, and perhaps she would some day be on one of those ships. She promised that she would wave to Lanny as she went by!

It wasn't long before Italy was bought by the Allies, and that was important to people who lived in Provence. It lifted a fear from their souls, and freed the regiments guarding the southeastern border. "You see," said Marcel to his wife, "I saved a few months by volunteering!" It had been a sore point, that he had gone out of his way to get himself smashed up. Now she could congratulate herself that it had been done quickly!

IX

Marcel's paintings had been stored in the spare room of the villa, and now he would set them up one by one and look at them. He wanted to see what sort of painter he had really been, in those days that now seemed a different lifetime. Lanny and Jerry and M. Rochambeau would join him, and make comments, more or less expert. Lanny and his tutor thought they were marvelous, but the painter took to shaking his head more and more. No, they weren't much; it was too easy to do things like that; there was no soul in them. Lanny protested; but the old diplomat said: "You've become a different man."

It was something which happened now and then to painters, poets, musicians. Sometimes it amounted to a transformation. Verdi had changed his style entirely in his middle years; Tolstoy had decided that his greatest novels were useless, even corrupting. Van Gogh had painted everything gloomy and grim in Holland, and then had come to the Midi and exploded in a burst of color. "You will start work all over," said the old gentleman; "find some new way to say what you feel."

People who didn't understand art—people like Marcel's wife, for example—were going to have an unhappy time while he was groping his way into that new stage of life. He became restless and discontented; he found fault with everybody and everything; his life had come to nothing. He took to going out at night, when people couldn't stare at his mask, and wandering about the roads on the Cap. Beauty was exasperated, but she dared not show it; she was haunted by the idea that if she made him unhappy he might try to get back into the army, or else in some fit of melancholia he might seek to release her from her burden by jumping off the rocks. She had never forgotten Lanny's suggestion of that possibility, at the time when she was thinking about Pittsburgh, Pennsylvania.

She ordered built for her genius a little studio in an out of the way corner of the place; north light, and all modern conveniences, including a storeroom for his canvases; the whole place of stone, entirely fireproof. She got him a new easel, and a pneumatic cushion for his chair, to spare his sore bones. There was everything ready for him—everything but his own spirit. He would go to the place and sit and brood. He would spend much time stretching canvases on frames, and would sit and dab paint on them, and finally would take them out behind the studio and burn them, saying that he was no good any more. What he wanted to say couldn't be said in any medium known.

Blazing hot summer had come. It was before the Riviera had been discovered as a summer resort, but Lanny, now fifteen, went about all day in bathing trunks and loved it. Marcel sat in his studio in the same costume—with nobody to look at his scarred and battered body. He had taken to staying by himself; he painted or read all day, and ate his meals alone, and only came out after dark. Then he would take a long walk, or if there were visitors he cared about, he would sit on the veranda in the dark with them. Or he would sit alone and listen to Lanny playing the piano.

X

The war had lasted a year. Some thought it was a stalemate, and others thought that Germany was winning. She held her line in France, and let the Allies waste themselves pounding at it while she broke the Russian armies. She had launched gas warfare, a new device filling the world with dismay. She was answering the British blockade by submarine warfare; British waters were a "military area," and all vessels in them liable to be sunk without warning.

In May had come the attack upon the *Lusitania*, the incident which excited the greatest horror in the United States. This great passenger liner, with more than two thousand persons on board, was passing the Irish coast in a calm sea: two o'clock in the afternoon, and the passengers had come from lunch, and were walking the

decks, or playing cards, reading or chatting, when a submarine
rose from the depths and launched a torpedo, blowing a hole in the
huge vessel's side. The sea rushed in and sank her in a few minutes,
drowning some twelve hundred persons, including more than a hundred babies.

When Americans read about the sinking of merchant vessels,
British or neutral, and the drowning of the crews, they didn't know
any of the people, and their imagination didn't have much to take
hold of. But here were people "everybody" knew—society people,
rich people, some of them prominent and popular—writers like
Justus Miles Forman and Elbert Hubbard, theatrical people like
Charles Frohman and Charles Klein, millionaires like the Vander-
bilts. Their friends had gone to the pier in New York to see them
off, or to the pier to welcome them—and then they read this horror
story. When the boatloads of survivors were brought in, the papers
of the world were filled with accounts of families torn apart, of
fathers and mothers giving their lives to save their little ones, of
quiet heroism and serenity in the face of death.

Americans in France felt the shock even more intensely, for
nearly everyone had friends, American or English, on board. Two
of Mrs. Emily's oldest friends had given their lives to save children
not their own. The sister of Edna Hackabury, now Mrs. Fitz-Laing,
was among those of whom no word was heard. Beauty counted half
a dozen persons of her acquaintance on the passenger list, and found
only two on the list of survivors. Not much of the spirit of "neutrality" was left in the minds of ladies and gentlemen who discussed
such matters over their afternoon tea.

Thus America was dragged into the center of the world debate.
President Wilson protested, and the German government answered
that submarines could not give warning without risking destruction,
and manifestly could not take off passengers and crew. The *Lusitania* had carried cartridges—so Germany charged, and the British
denied it, and how was the truth to be known? The Germans agreed
to sink no more such vessels, but they did not keep the promise. All
passenger vessels carried cargo, and most merchant vessels carried

passengers, and how could a submarine under war conditions make certain? The Germans demanded that President Wilson should resist the British attempt to starve the German people and should insist that American ships be allowed to carry to Germany food which Germany had bought and paid for. When President Wilson wrote letters denouncing German barbarity, the Allies were delighted; when he wrote letters denouncing British violations of American trade rights, all sympathizers with the Allies denounced him.

For a year Robbie had kept writing to his son, never failing to warn him against losing his head. Robbie was determined that no Budd should be drawn into Europe's quarrels; Budds were businessmen, and did not let themselves be used to pull anybody's chestnuts out of the fire. Robbie had been on the inside, and knew that every one of these nations was thinking about its own aggrandizement. Twice it happened that an employee was coming to France, and Robbie took the trouble to write a long letter and have it mailed in Paris, so that it wouldn't be opened by a censor. "Study and think and improve your mind, and keep it clear of all this fog of hatred and propaganda." Lanny did his best to obey—but it is not pleasant to differ from everybody you meet.

XI

For several months Marcel worked at his painting and burned up everything he produced. Lanny got up the courage to protest, and got his mother to back him. One day when he was at the studio he began begging to be allowed to see what was on the easel, covered up with a cloth. He was so much interested in his stepfather's development that he could learn even from his failures. "Please, Marcel! Right now!"

The painter said it was nothing, just a joke; he had been avoiding an hour of boredom. But that made Lanny beg all the harder—he was bored too, he said. So finally Marcel let him take off the cloth. He looked, and laughed out loud, and was so delighted that he danced around.

Marcel had painted himself lying on that bed in the hospital, head swathed in bandages, two frightened eyes looking out; and all around him on the bed crowded the little furies of pain, as he had watched them for so many months. It happened that Mr. Robin had sent Lanny a copy of a German weekly magazine, containing pictures of some of the national heroes, and Marcel had turned them into a swarm of little demons with instruments of torture in their claws. There was the stiff Prussian officer with his lean face, sharp nose, and monocle; there was Hindenburg with his shaven head and bull's neck; there was the Kaiser with his bristling mustaches; there was the professor with bushy beard and stern dogmatic face. The whole of German *Kultur* was there, and it was amazing, the different kinds of malice that Marcel had managed to pack into those faces, and still keep them funny.

Lanny argued harder than ever. If it gave him so much pleasure, why shouldn't the family share it? So they took it up to the house, where Jerry did a war dance, and M. Rochambeau forgot his usual gravity, and even Beauty laughed. Lanny said it ought to be shown somewhere, but Marcel said, nonsense, it was just a caricature, he didn't wish to be known as a cartoonist. But the elderly diplomat came to Lanny's support; he said there was a lot of German propaganda all over the world, and why shouldn't the French use their genius for ridicule? The four of them wrung this concession from the stubborn man of art—they might have a photograph of it and send copies to their friends.

They got a real photographer and had a big one made, and wrote on the bottom of the negative: "Soldier in Pain." Lanny sent one to his father, and one to Rick—whose father was now in charge of precautions against spies and saboteurs in his part of England. Beauty sent one to several of her friends; and the first thing she knew came a telegram from Mrs. Emily, saying that one of the big weekly papers in Paris offered two hundred francs for the right to reproduce the painting. When this magazine appeared there came a cablegram from one of the big New York newspapers offering a hundred dollars for the American rights; and on top of that a concern which was making picture post cards asked Marcel's price to let them use it.

The New York paper came out with a story about the painter, saying that he had been in an air crash, and this was his own experience. Marcel was annoyed for a while; he hated that sort of publicity. But to Beauty it was marvelous; it set everybody to talking about her husband, and visitors came to the house again, and she had an excuse to get out her pretty clothes. She had a vision of her husband becoming a famous and highly paid magazine illustrator; but Marcel said, to hell with it, and jammed his red silk skullcap down on his head and stalked off to the studio to brood there. So Beauty had to run to him, and fall on her knees and admit that she was a cheap and silly creature, and that Marcel was to paint whatever he wanted, and needn't see a single one of the curiosity seekers —they would disconnect the bell at the gate if he wished it.

However, Lanny managed to get his way about one thing; Marcel promised not to burn any more of his work. On this point the boy collected historical facts from painter friends and retailed them to his stepfather. "We have all Michelangelo's sketches, and Leonardo's, and Rembrandt's, and Rodin's—so we can follow their minds, and learn what they were thinking and trying. We learn from what they rejected as well as from what they kept." So it was agreed that everything Marcel did from that time on was to be put away on shelves in the storeroom; and, furthermore, Lanny might be allowed to see something now and then—but no more publicity.

15

Amor inter Arma

I

JUST before Christmas, Mrs. Emily Chattersworth returned to Cannes, and opened her winter home. She needed a rest, so she told her friends; but she didn't take it for long. There were too many wounded French soldiers all over the Midi; tens of thousands of them, and many as bad as Marcel. The casino at Juan—a small place at that time—had been turned into a hospital, as had all sorts of public buildings throughout France. But there was never room enough, never help enough. Frenchwomen, who as a rule confined their activities to their own homes, were now organizing hospitals and relief depots; and of course they were glad to have help from anyone who would give it.

So it wasn't long before Mrs. Emily was agitating and organizing, making her American friends on the Riviera ashamed of wasting their time playing bridge and dancing; she told them stories about men deprived of hands and feet and eyes and what not, and facing the problem of how to keep alive. In the end, impatient of delays, Mrs. Emily turned her own home into an institution for what was called "re-education": teaching new occupations to men so crippled they could no longer practice their former ones. A man who had lost his right hand would learn to do something with a hook, and men who had lost their legs would learn to make baskets or brooms. Mrs. Emily moved herself into what had been a maid's room, and filled up her whole mansion with her "pupils," and when that wasn't enough, put up tents on her lawns.

The wife of Marcel Detaze was especially exposed to this vigorous lady's attacks. "Don't you care about anybody's husband but your own?" Beauty was ashamed to give the wrong answer, and after she had made sure that Marcel was occupied with his painting, Lanny would drive her up to Sept Chênes, as the place was called, and give what help she could. She didn't know how to make brooms or baskets, and as a "re-educator" she wasn't very much, but she was the world's wonder when it came to uplifting the souls of men. Suffering had dealt kindly with her, and added a touch of mystery to her loveliness, and when she came into the room all the *mutilés* would stop looking at brooms and baskets, and if she said something to a poor devil he would remember it the rest of the day. After what she had been through with Marcel, she didn't mind seeing scars of war, and she learned to get the same thrill which in the old days she had got from entering a ballroom and having "important" people stare at her and ask who she was.

It was good for Lanny too, because the world he was going to live in was not to be composed exclusively of "important" persons, manifesting grace and charm at enormous expense. Going to Mrs. Emily's was a kind of "slumming" which not even Robbie could have objected to; and Lanny had an advantage over his mother in that he knew Provençal, and could chat with these peasants and fishermen as he had done all his life. Several of them were the same persons he had known, fathers or older brothers of the children he had played with.

And oddest circumstance of all—Lanny's gigolo! That happy and graceful dancing man whom he had picked up in Nice, and who had come to Bienvenu and spent an afternoon playing the piccolo flute and demonstrating the steps of the farandole! Here he was, drawing a harsh breath now and then, because he had got trapped in a dugout full of fumes from a shell; and surely he would never dance again, because his right leg was gone just below the hip. Instead he was learning to carve little dancing figures out of wood, and when he was through with that form of education, he would go back to his father's farm, where there was wood in plenty, and the organization which Mrs. Emily had formed would try to sell his toys for the Christmas trade. M. Pinjon was the same kindly and gentle dreamer that Lanny recalled, and the boy had the satisfaction of seeing his mother willing to talk to him now, and hearing her admit that he was a good creature, who doubtless had done no harm to anyone in his life.

II

One of Mrs. Emily's bright ideas was that men who had hands and eyes but no feet might learn to paint. Of course it was late in life for them to begin, but then look at Gauguin, look at van Gogh —you just could never tell where you might find a genius. Might it not be possible for Marcel to come now and then and give a lesson to these pitiful souls?

Marcel was coming to care less and less for people. Even the best of them made him aware of his own condition, and it was only when he was alone and buried in his work that life was bearable to him. But he heard Beauty talking for hours at a time about Emily Chattersworth, and of course this work came close to his heart. He too was a *mutilé*, and a comrade of all the others. He couldn't teach anything, because he couldn't talk; even Mrs. Emily had a hard time understanding him, unless Beauty sat by and said some of the words over again. But he offered to come and entertain them by making sketches on a blackboard—for example, those little German devils that seemed to amuse people. Somebody else might explain and comment on the work as he did it.

So they drove up to Sept Chênes one evening. Mrs. Emily had set up a blackboard, and had got one of her patients to do the talking, a journalist who had lost the fingers of his right hand and was learning to write with his left. He was an amusing talker, and Marcel with his skullcap and veil was a figure of mystery. He was clever and quick at sketching, and his Prussian devils made the audience roar. The deaf ones could see them, and the blind ones could hear about them. If the lecturer missed a point, Marcel would write a word or two on the board. It wasn't long before the men were shouting what they wanted next, and Marcel would draw that. He had been at the front long enough to know the little touches that made things real to his comrades.

He drew a heroic figure of the *poilu. Poil* means your hair, and is a symbol of your power. The *poilu* was a mighty fellow, and wore a red military *képi,* with a depression in the round top like a saucer. When Marcel drew a rough wooden cross in a field, and hung one of those battered caps on top of it, every man in the room knew what that meant, for he had seen thousands of them. The *poilu* wore a long coat, and when he was marching he buttoned back the front flaps to make room for his legs, so when you saw that, you knew he was on the march. If his face was set grimly, you knew he was going to say: *"Nous les aurons,"* that is: "We'll have them, we'll get them."

What he was going to get was the *boche.* That was another word of the war. The British called him "Jerry," and the Yanks, when they came along, would call him "Heinie," and sometimes "Fritzie"; but to the *poilu* he was *le boche,* and when Marcel drew him, he made him not ugly or hateful, just stupid and discouraged, and that too seemed right to *anciens combattants.* When Marcel desired to draw something hateful, it wore a long coat to the ankles, tightly drawn in at the waist, and a monocle, and a gold bracelet, and an expression of monstrous insolence.

III

That visit was important to the painter because it gave him a place to go. With these poor devils he need never be ashamed, never humiliated. He would return now and then to entertain them; or he would go and just talk with them, or rather, let them talk to him. One of them had been with Marcel's own regiment in the Alpes Maritimes, and from him Marcel learned that his comrades had been moved to the front in the Vosges mountains, and what had happened to them there.

The men wouldn't talk to strangers about the war; it was too terrible, it would discourage people. But among themselves it was all right, and Marcel's mutilated face was a passport to all hearts. He heard about winter fighting in heavy snow, with the trenches only a few yards apart, so that you could hear the enemy talking, and shout abuse and defiance at him; if you lifted your cap an inch above the parapet, it would be riddled with bullets in a second or two. Shelling was incessant, day and night, and hand grenades were thrown; only a few sentries stayed to watch, while the rest hid in dugouts underground. Great tracts in the forest had been reduced to splinters, and in the *poste de secours*, a shelter dug half under the hillside, a dozen doctors had been killed in the course of a year. No going about at all in the daytime; yet you could hear the church bells ringing in a village behind the lines. One of the stories was about a man who picked up an old hand organ in one of the buildings wrecked by shells, and brought it up one rainy night to one of the *cagnas*, or dugouts, and stood outside in the rain playing it, and men began singing, hundreds of them all over the place, even with the shells falling around. "Sidi Brahim," they sang.

Among other things, Lanny learned what had happened to his mother's former chauffeur and handy man, Sergeant Pierre Bazoche. He had taken part in one of those innumerable attempts that came to nothing. Line after line of men had charged across an exposed place on a hillside, and just lay where they fell. There was no way to get to them; those who were not killed at once died slowly—but in any case they stayed all winter, and the smell of them made an invisible cloud that drifted slowly over the trenches, sometimes to the poilus and sometimes to the boches.

After talks like that Marcel would go back and paint. He made a painting that he called "Fear," and for a while he didn't want anybody to see it; perhaps it was a confession of something in himself. He was so proud, so serene, and full of ardor for his beloved France —could it be that he had ever been terrified? The truth is that this complicated arrangement of pipes and tissues that comprise a man is so fragile, so soft and easily damaged, that nature has provided an automatic impulse to protect it. There are parts of it that can hurt so abominably—and in truth you would have difficulty in naming any part that you would care to have struck by a little steel cylinder moving at the rate of half a mile per second. The boches had this same feeling, and many Catholics among them carried on their persons magic formulas containing detailed specifications. "May God preserve me against all manner of arms and weapons, shot and cannon, long or short swords, knives or daggers, or carbines, halberds, or any thing that cuts or pierces, against thrusts of rapiers, long and short rifles, or guns, and suchlike, which have been forged since the birth of Christ; against all kinds of metal, be it iron or steel, brass or lead, ore or wood." The poor devils lay dead upon the field with these prayers in their pockets.

Marcel painted a dim, mysterious form, the upper part of a human being, you couldn't be sure whether it was man or woman; it was shrouded in a sort of dark hood, and you saw only the face, and at first only the eyes, which had a faint glow, and were staring at you with a look that seized your own. The face was not distorted, the expression was subtler than that, it was a soul which had been acquainted with fear for a long time; and not just a physical fear, but a moral horror at a society in which men inflicted such things upon one another.

At least, that is what M. Rochambeau said after he had looked at the picture for a long time. He said it was quite extraordinary, and certainly none of the persons who saw it ever forgot it. But Marcel put it away. He said it wasn't a picture for wartime—not until the enemy could see it too!

IV

The British had failed in their efforts to take the Dardanelles, largely because they couldn't decide whether the taking was worth the cost. Now they were starting an advance from Salonika, a harbor in the north of Greece. That country had a pro-German king, and those beautiful islands which the *Bluebird* had visited had become lurking places of submarines seeking to destroy British commerce and the troopships which came heavily loaded from India and Australia. The entire Mediterranean was the scene of unresting naval war, and Lanny didn't need to look at war maps, because he had been to the places and had pictures of them in his eager mind.

When he and Jerry went fishing they watched every ship that passed—and there were great numbers—knowing that at any moment there might be an explosion and a pillar of black smoke. They never happened to see that, but they heard firing more than once, and ran to a high point of the Cap and with field glasses watched a sinking ship, and saw motorboats hurrying out to bring off survivors. Up and down the coast people told stories of hospital ships sunk with all on board, of loaded troopships torpedoed, of submarines rammed, or sunk by a well-aimed shot, or getting entangled in the chains and nets now set in front of harbors.

The fighting at Gallipoli had one important consequence for Lanny. The father of Rosemary Codwilliger was wounded, and in a hospital in Malta; this made the mother decide to spend the winter on the Riviera, where he could join her when he was able to be moved. "She says she's in need of a rest," wrote the girl, "but I think it's to get me out of the notion of nursing. She's afraid I'll get to know people outside our social circle."

The family wanted a quiet place, Rosemary added, and it happened that the Baroness Sophie had a little villa on the Cap, not the one she lived in. Lanny sent a snapshot of it to the girl, and as a result her family rented the place and set a date for their arrival; the mother, a widowed aunt, Rosemary herself, and her father whenever the doctors and the submarines would let him.

Lanny was sixteen now, and old enough to know that he was interested in girls. This grave and sweet English lass had captured his imagination, and he looked back upon the river Thames and its green and pleasant land as one of his happiest memories. He had met other girls on the Riviera, and had swum and boated and danced with them, but principally they interested him because they reminded him of Rosemary.

A year and a half had passed, and now she was coming, and Lanny hoped to be included in her social circle. His mother was a respectable married woman, and his stepfather had all but given his life in the war which was England's. Lanny had never met Rosemary's mother or aunt, but he hoped for success with them as in the case of the Frau Doktor Hofrat von und zu Nebenaltenberg—who now, by the way, was among the Germans interned on the Île Ste.-Marguerite, which Lanny could view from the veranda of his home.

The boy had told his mother about the English girl and how much he liked her; it would have been cruelty to withhold such news from Beauty, to whom it was the most interesting of subjects. She warned him not to expect too much from the English, because they were a peculiar people, rigidly bound by their own conventions. With Americans they were apt to go so far and no farther.

Just now Beauty had another love affair on her hands, that of Jerry Pendleton, who clamored for advice about French girls. He was finding in one of them such an odd mixture of fervor and reserve; and such a complication of mothers and aunts! Did Mrs. Detaze think that an American could be happy with a French wife? And would such a wife be happy in America? The situation was complicated by the fact that Jerry didn't know what he wanted to do with himself. He had come away fully determined to escape the drug store business; he dreamed of being a newspaperman, perhaps a foreign correspondent. But what would he do with a wife under those circumstances? Lanny's tutor, torn between his destinies, was much like Beauty having to choose between Pittsburgh and the Cap d'Antibes. Lanny's lessons suffered during the discussions—but he could always go and read the encyclopedia.

V

The three ladies and a maid arrived, and Lanny was at the train to meet them and take them to the villa. He had the keys, and knew the place and showed it to them. He had lived on the Cap all his life, and could tell them about the shops and services and other practical matters. Also he knew about servants—the innumerable relatives of

Leese were available and the ladies had only to choose. The most exclusive English family could hardly reject the assistance of such a polite and agreeable youth.

Mrs. Codwilliger was a tall, thin-faced lady from whom Lanny might have learned how Rosemary would look when she was forty; but he didn't. She and her sister, tall and still thinner, were the daughters of Lord Dewthorpe, and estimated themselves accordingly. But when Lanny's mother offered to call, they could not say no; and when they heard the romantic story of the painter who stayed in his studio alone, never appearing in public without a veil, their deep English instincts of self-sufficiency were touched. When Lanny offered to lend them several of his stepfather's seascapes to remedy the rather crude taste in art of the baroness, they had to admit that the habitability of their home had been increased.

Rosemary was a year older than Lanny, which meant that she was now a young lady. As it happened, she was a very grand one, belonging to a set which managed to impress other people—they "got away with it," to use the American slang. The youth was prepared to worship her at a distance. But they strolled off, and sat where they could see the moonlight flung across the water in showers of brilliant fire. There was a distant sound of music from the great hotel—all the lovely things which they remembered on the banks of the Thames.

So Lanny was moved, very timidly, to draw closer to this delightful being, and she did not seem to mind. When he gently touched her hand she did not draw it away, and presently they resumed, quite naturally and simply, the relation they had had in the old days. He put his arm about her, and after a while he kissed her, and they sat dissolved in the well-remembered bliss. But this time it did not stop at the same point.

Rosemary Codwilliger was a friend and admirer of that ardent suffragette, Miss Noggyns, who had so upset Kurt Meissner at The Reaches. With the coming of the war these redoubtable ladies had dropped their agitation, but they expected to have their demands granted before the war was over; and what were they going to do with their new freedom? That they would go into Parliament, attend the universities, and move into all the professions—such things went without saying. But what would they do about love and sex and marriage? What would they do about the so-called "double standard," which permitted men to have premarital sex relations without social disgrace, but denied that privilege to women?

Obviously, there were two alternatives. Women could adopt the double standard, or they could demand that men conform to the single standard. It soon appeared that the latter was very difficult, whereas the former was easy. The subject was made more complex by the possibility that not all women were alike; what might be pleasing to some might not be to all. In magazines, pamphlets, and books of the "feminist" movement these questions were vehemently debated, and the ideas were tried out by numbers of persons, with results not always according to schedule.

Rosemary's young mind was a ferment of these theories. First of all, she had been taught, you must be frank. You couldn't be so with the old people, of course; but young people in love, or thinking of being in love, had to be honest with each other and try to understand each other; love had to be a give and take, each respecting the other's personality, and so on. The problems of sex had apparently been changed by the discovery of birth control, which Mr. Bernard Shaw called "the most revolutionary discovery of the nineteenth century." Since you no longer needed to have babies, the question to be considered was whether love would bring happiness to the lovers.

Rosemary was blond, with features regular and a manner gentle and serene. In many ways she reminded Lanny of his mother, and perhaps that was why she had drawn him so strongly. He was a mother's boy, used to being told what to do, and Rosemary was prepared to deal with him on that basis—it was, apparently, what they all meant by "women's rights." Anyway, they sat in a remote and well-shadowed part of the garden, with arms around each other; and it seemed unavoidable that they should talk of intimate matters. Lanny told about love problems which puzzled him, and Rosemary imparted ideas which she had gathered from a weekly journal called the *Freewoman.*

When Lanny had listened to Kurt Meissner's expositions of German philosophy, he had attributed it all to Kurt's wonderful brain; so now he thought that Rosemary had worked out the theory of sexual equality for herself. Of course he was deeply impressed, and at first rather frightened. But after these ideas had been discussed for two or three evenings, they no longer seemed so strange; the boy who had become a man within the last year began to wonder whether all those words about freedom and happiness might possibly apply to him and his lovely friend. This had an alarming effect; a wave of excitement swept over him, and his teeth began to chatter and his hands to shake uncontrollably.

"What's the matter, Lanny?" asked the girl.

He didn't dare to answer at first, but finally he told her: "I'm afraid maybe I'm falling in love with you." It was all as if it had never happened in the world before.

"Well, why not, Lanny?" she asked, gently.

"You mean—you really wouldn't mind?"

"You know I think you are a very dear boy."

So he kissed her on the lips—more ardently than ever before. They sat clasped together, and a clamor arose in him. He pressed her to him, and when she submitted, he began to fondle her more and more intimately. He knew then that the experience had come to him about which he had heard everybody talking, and which had been such a mystery in his thoughts.

The girl stayed his trembling hands. "You mustn't, Lanny. It wouldn't be safe." Then she whispered: "I'll have to go to the house first, and get something."

So they got up and walked. Lanny found his knees shaking, which perplexed him greatly. It must be what the French novelists call *la grande passion!* He waited some distance from the house while Rosemary went in—as it happened, there was company and no one paid any heed to her. Presently she came back, and they lost themselves in a secluded part of the garden, and there she taught him those things about which he had been so curious. At first his agitation was painful, but presently he was dissolved in a flood of bliss, which seemed to justify the theories of the "new women." If he was happy and she was happy, why should the vague and remote "world" of their elders concern itself with their affairs?

VI

It wasn't long before Lanny told his mother about this affair. Impossible not to, because she asked pointed questions, and it would have been hurting her feelings to evade. Beauty's reaction to the disclosure was a peculiar one. She had been what you might call a practicing feminist, but without any theories; she had had her own way about love, but always with the proper feeling that she was doing wrong. It was hard to explain, but that feeling seemed necessary; you knew it was wrong, and that made it right. But to assert that it was right was a shocking boldness. And when a girl was only seventeen! "Was she virgin?" asked Beauty, and added with distaste: "Certainly she didn't act like it." Lanny didn't know and couldn't make inquiries.

Beauty couldn't altogether dislike Rosemary, but she never got over the idea that there was something alarming about her—a portent of a new world that Beauty didn't understand. The mother's feeling was that her dear little boy had been seduced, and that he was much too young. She took the problem to her husband, but failed to get him excited. "Nature knows a lot more about that than you do," said the painter, and went on painting.

Springtime again on the Riviera, to Lanny the most delightful he had ever known. The flesh of woman was revealed to him, and the discovery transfused everything else in his life. The world and every common sight to him did seem appareled in celestial light, the glory and the freshness of a dream. Now for the first time he knew what music was about, and poetry, and dancing, not to mention the birds and the butterflies. The flowers had the colors of Rosemary, and she had their perfume. She was to him a being of magic, and when he was with her he never wanted to take his eyes from her, and when he wasn't with her he wished he was.

Of course he couldn't be with her all the time; because "what would people say?" The "world" did matter after all, it appeared. Cool and serene, Rosemary took charge. Lanny must go on with his studying, and not make her feel that she was a bad influence. When they boated and swam and played tennis, they must be with other young people, for appearance' sake; and the same in the evening—there must be some sort of pretext, a dance, a party, a sail—the young people all understood that, they all had the same desires, and would stroll away in couples, casually and innocently. They protected one another, a conspiracy of the new against the old.

Did Rosemary succeed in fooling her mother and her aunt? In those early days of the revolt of youth the old were in a peculiar state of emotional paralysis. They didn't dare to know; it was too awful to let themselves know—and yet of course they did. They would look at the young with fright in their eyes, and seldom dare to speak—for what could they say? Rosemary had given her answer in advance—she wanted to go out and earn her own living. Girls were nursing, they were even getting jobs in munitions factories, wearing black overalls and filling shells with explosives. They were going out on the streets delivering tirades, calling on men to enlist, pinning white feathers on those who looked as if they ought to. And the things they were reading, and left around the house, careless of who might see them!

It had been prior to the outbreak of the war that Rosemary had fallen under the spell of one of those suffragettes—a teacher, it was. Still a child, with pigtails down her back, she had walked into the National Gallery with a hand ax concealed under her skirt, and at a prearranged signal had passed it to one of those notorious women who hadn't dared bring it in herself, because she was known and might be searched. And that not a crazy whim or a lark, but a means of reforming the world! Something they took up as a religion, for which they were willing to die! You might put them in jail, but they would only try to starve themselves to death; you wanted to say to the devil with them and let them do it, but you didn't dare.

VII

The German high command had made up its collective mind that in order to win the war they had to break through on the western front, and they had picked the fortress of Verdun as the place. This was the head of the original French defenses, the part which had not given way; a complex of fortifications covering various heights along both banks of the river Meuse. Now that the war had been going on for a year and a half, the technique of taking such fortifications had become well settled. You had to bring up enough heavy guns, and pile enough ammunition behind them, to reduce the enemy entrenchments to dust and rubble; then you put down what was called a "creeping barrage" of shells which exploded in small fragments, to destroy the men who had been hiding underground and who came up after your heavy bombardment. The "creeping barrage" moved forward, just ahead of your lines of infantry, which could thus advance in comparative safety, and take what was left of the trenches, an operation known as "mopping up." The enemy would have line after line of trenches, and you had to repeat this same procedure and hope to break through finally and turn a "war of position" into a "war of movement."

To stop such an attack, the French gunners had to be better than the Germans, and have more shells. The French airmen had to keep the mastery and bring in more information as to what was happening. But more than anything else, the plain everyday poilu had to crawl into his rabbit warrens, and those of him who were left alive had to pop up at the right moment, and hide in whatever shell holes might be left and shoot enough of the advancing Germans to discourage the rest. That was all there was to it, you just had to outstay the enemy. When you had fired all your cartridges, you got more from a dead comrade in the same shell hole. If the night passed and nobody brought you food, you starved. If it rained, you lay in the mud, and if the mud froze, you tried to keep your hands alive so that you could shoot.

The Verdun area covered a hundred square miles or so, and during the fighting it was turned into a chaos of shell craters and nothing else. Places like Fort Douaumont were taken and retaken a half-dozen times, and the living fought among the dead of both sides. The main battle began in February of 1916 and lasted until July without cessation, and after that off and on for a year. The Germans brought sixty-four divisions, which was more than a million men. The French fired more than ten million shells from field guns, and nearly two million from medium and heavy guns.

The German Crown Prince was in command, and that was one more reason for the French wanting to win. The whole world watched and waited while the armies staggered back and forth. A break-through might mean the German conquest of France, and nobody knew that better than the poilu; he invented for himself a chant, which became a sort of incantation, a spell to rouse the souls of men perishing of wounds and exhaustion, who yet would kill one more enemy before dying. *"Passeront pas, passeront pas!"* they sang or gasped. "They shall not pass."

VIII

Such were the events some three hundred miles to the north of Lanny Budd while he was playing with love in springtime. He couldn't keep the war from troubling his conscience, but there was nothing he could do about it—especially not so long as he was under pledge to keep neutral. He was the one person of that sort he knew. Eddie Patterson was now driving an ambulance behind the lines at Verdun, and so his Sophie no longer had any motive for not hating the Germans, and she was hating them. All Lanny could say was: "Excuse me, I promised my father not to talk about the war."

Budd's were now making small arms and ammunition in large quantities, and exclusively for the Allies. There was no way to make

any for the Germans; the British blockade was too tight, and anyhow the British and French were on hand to buy everything you
could produce, paying top prices on the nail. The big Wall Street
banks took British and French bonds and sold them to the American
public, and Budd's got the cash. Under Robbie's contract he was entitled to a commission on every deal. He would spend this money
freely and gaily, as always; but he was a stubborn fellow, and
nobody was going to get him to say that any nation of Europe—
and that included the British Empire—was ever right about anything
Robbie had been on the inside, and knew they were all wrong.

Out of this came the first little rift between Lanny and his girl-
friend. Rosemary wasn't satisfied to have him hold his tongue; she
began to pin him down and ask what he really thought. When he
repeated his formula, she wanted to know: "What are you, a man
or a dummy? Do you have to think everything your father thinks?
If I thought what my parents think, would I be here with you?"
Lanny was troubled, because he had taken it for granted that this
delightful young woman was as gentle as she looked. But apparently
a sharp tongue was part of the equipment of every "feminist," and
first among "women's rights" was the right to tell her man what she
thought of him.

Both British and French were bitter against the Americans, because they were not taking part in the war, but just making money
out of it, and at the same time making objections to the blockade.
Nearly all the Americans in France felt the same way, and were
ashamed of their country. The conversation at Bienvenu was all
along that line; and while Marcel was careful not to say anything in
Lanny's presence, the boy knew that Marcel blamed Robbie because
he was making money out of the French and at the same time with-
holding his sympathy from them. The painter was eaten up with
anxiety all during the battle of Verdun; he would burst out with
some expression of loathing for the "Huns," and Lanny wouldn't
say anything, and it would appear that a chill had fallen in the home.
The relationship of stepfather and stepson is a complicated one at
best, and this wasn't the best.

The boy would go off and try to think out by himself the problems of the war. He would remember things that Robbie had told him
about the trickery of Allied diplomacy. Right now it was being said
in America that the Allies had made secret treaties dividing up the
spoils of the war they hadn't won; worse yet, they had promised the
same territory to different peoples. Robbie would send articles about
such matters to his son, finding ways to get them by the censor—and
the consequence of knowing about such things was that the boy no
longer fitted anywhere in France.

IX

Marcel painted a picture of the poilu, the savior of *la patrie*. He
tried to put into it all his love for the men with whom he had
trained and fought. When he was done, he said it wasn't good
enough, he hadn't got what he wanted; but his friends thought differently; the painting was shown at a salon in Paris, and made a hit,
and was taken up and reproduced in posters. Beauty thought that
her husband would get satisfaction out of that service to his country; but nothing could please him, it appeared. He didn't want to
be a popular painter—and anyhow, art was futility in a time like this.

So came a crisis in the affairs of this married pair. How rarely
does it happen that two human creatures, with all their differences,
weaknesses, moods can get along without quarreling! Beauty was
carrying her cross, in the best evangelical church fashion; she was
pouring out her own redemptive blood in the secrecy of her heart.
But she couldn't be happy in her tragic situation, and the bitterness
which she repressed was bound to escape at some spots in her life.
She couldn't restrain her annoyance at this contrary attitude of
Marcel. Why should a man go to the trouble of making pictures,
and then not want to have people see them, even quarrel with those
who wanted a chance to admire them? Why was it necessary to say
something contrary every time his work was praised? In vain did
Lanny, budding young critic, try to make plain to his mother that a
true artist is wrestling with a vision of something higher and better,

and cannot endure to be admired for what he knows is less than his best.

Out of this clash of temperaments came a terrible thing: Lanny came home one evening from his love-making to find his mother lying on her bed sobbing. Her husband had broached to her the idea of going back into the army. He had the crazy notion that he ought to be helping to hold the line at Verdun; he was a trained man, and France needed every one. He was as good as ever, he ininsisted; he could march, and had tried long walks to make sure. He could handle a gun—the only thing wrong was that he was ugly, but out there in mud and powder smoke who would care?

Beauty had had a fit of hysterics and called him some bad names, an ingrate, a fool, and so on. If she meant no more to him than that, he would have to go—but he would never see her again. "I did it once, Marcel, but I won't do it a second time."

She really meant it, so she declared to her son. She had reached the limit of endurance. If Marcel went, *la patrie* could take care of him next time in some soldiers' home. She said it with hardness in her face that was a new thing to Lanny; one does not wrestle with duty for long periods without going back to the moods and even the facial expressions of one's Puritan forefathers. But five minutes later Beauty broke down; her lips were trembling, and she was asking whether perhaps it was her impatience and lack of art sense which were making the painter dissatisfied with his lot.

So there was no peace in this woman's soul until midsummer, when the German attacks on the great fortress slowed up. By that time she had managed to get her man started upon another project —to paint a portrait of her. It is a use that every painter makes sooner or later of the woman he loves; if Marcel had it in him to do any portrait, she would be it. Beauty had changed, and what Marcel saw was the woman of anguish who had prayed to his soul, the woman of pity who talked to crippled soldiers and helped them to want to live.

She put on one of her nurse's uniforms and went over to the studio and sat for hours every day; an old story to her. Marcel painted her sitting in a chair with her hands folded, and all the grief of France in her face. "Sister of Mercy," he was going to call her; and Beauty didn't have to act, because of the terror in her heart. She couldn't tell what turn the next great battle might take. She could only urge Marcel to take his time and get it perfect; she wanted him to have something he really believed in—so that he would stay a painter instead of a poilu!

X

Lanny's young dream of love died early in the month of May, and it wasn't a merry month for him. At that time the thoughts of English people on the Riviera turned to their lovely green island with its chilly breezes. Furthermore it developed that Rosemary's father had to be examined by surgeons at home; he was brought to Marseille, and from there north, and Lanny never met him.

"Darling, we shall see each other again," said the girl. "You'll come to England, or I'll be coming here."

"I'll wait for you—always," said Lanny, fervently. "I want you to marry me, Rosemary."

She looked startled. "Oh, Lanny, I don't think we can marry. I wouldn't count on that if I were you."

The boy was startled in turn. "But why not?"

"We're much too young to think about it. I don't want to marry for a long time."

"I can wait, Rosemary."

"Darling, don't think about it, please. It wouldn't be fair to you." Seeing the bewilderment in his face, she added: "It would make my parents so terribly unhappy if I were to marry outside our own sort of people."

"But—but"—he had trouble in finding words. "Wouldn't it make them unhappy to know about our love?"

"They aren't going to know about that; and it's quite a different thing. Marriage is so serious; you have children, and property settlements, and all that bother; and there'd be the question whether

our children were to be Americans or English. You might want to
go to America to live——"

"I'm really not much of an American, Rosemary. I've never been
there, and may never go."

"You can't be sure; and my people wouldn't be sure. They'd make
an awful fuss, I know."

"Many English people marry Americans," argued the boy. "Lord
Eversham-Watson—I visited them, and they seemed quite happy."

"I know, darling, it's done; and don't have your blessed feelings
hurt—you know I love you, and we've been so happy, and will be
some more. But if we tie ourselves down, and get our families to
arguing and all that—it would be a frightful bore."

Lanny was imperfectly educated in modern ideas, and couldn't
get the thing clear in his mind. He wanted his adored one all the
time, and couldn't imagine that she might not want him. Why was
she so concerned about her family in this one matter, and so indifferent, even defiant, in others? He asked her to explain it, and she
tried, groping to put into words things that were instinctive and
unformulated. It appeared that young ladies of the English govern-
ing classes who joined the movement for equal rights wanted certain
definite things, like being able to write M.P. after their names, and
to have divorce on equal terms with men; but they didn't mean to
interfere with the system whereby their families governed the realm.
They accepted the idea that when the time came for marriage
each should adopt some honored name with a peculiar spelling, and
become the mistress of some beautiful old country house and the
mother of future viscounts and barons, or at the least admirals and
cabinet ministers.

"It mayn't be so easy to find an upper-class Englishman," remarked the boy; "the way they're getting killed off in this war."

"There'll be some left," answered the girl, easily. She had only to
look in the mirror to know that she had special advantages.

Lanny pondered some more, and then inquired: "Is it because I
don't take sides in the war?"

"That's just a bit of it, Lanny. It helps me to realize that we shouldn't be happy; our ideas are so different, and our interests. Whatever happens to England, I have to be for her, and so will my children when I have them."

"They are apt to go just so far and no farther," Beauty had told her son. When he parted from Rosemary Codwilliger, pronounced Culliver, it was with tears and sighs on both sides, and a perfectly clear understanding that he might have a sweet and lovely mistress for an indefinite time, provided that he would come where she was, and do what she asked him to do. When Lanny told his mother about it, and she told Marcel, the painter remarked that the boy had been used as a guinea pig in a scientific experiment. When he learned that the boy was unhappy, he added that scientific experiments were not conducted for the benefit of the guinea pigs.

16

Business as Usual

I

WHEN the German army came to Les Forêts, old M. Priedieu, the librarian, had stayed to guard his employer's treasures. He had stood by, pale with horror, while drunken hussars cut the valuable pictures from the walls, rolled up the tapestries, dumped the venerable leather-covered chairs out of the windows, and swept the priceless books from the shelves in pure wantonness. They didn't do any physical harm to the white-haired old man, but they so wounded his sensibilities that he took to his bed, and a few days later died quietly in his sleep.

But his spirit lived on in Lanny Budd. All the boy's life he would remember what the grave old scholar had told him about the love of books. This was something that no misfortune or sorrow could take from a man, and its possessor had a refuge from all the evils of the world. Montesquieu had said that to love reading was to exchange hours of boredom for hours of delight; Laharpe had said that a book is a friend that never deceives. The librarian of Les Forêts had advised Lanny to seek the friendship of the French classic authors and let them teach him dignity, grace, and perfection of form.

Now misfortune and sorrow had come; love had dallied with Lanny Budd for a while and then tossed him away. The crisis found him without companionship, because Jerry Pendleton had come to an arrangement with his *belle amie* to wait for him, and had gone back to Kansas to complete his education. In this plight Lanny sought the friendship of one Jean Racine, who had died more than two hundred years previously but lived on by the magic of the printed page. He took disordered emotions and converted them into well-made dramas, in which exalted beings stalked the scene and poured out their sufferings in verses so eloquent that a youth of sixteen was moved to seek lonely places by the sea or in the forest and declaim them to tritons or hamadryads.

Also Lanny won the friendship of a severe and stern spirit by the name of Pierre Corneille, who had made over the French theater, and had had no easy time of it in his life. The aristocratic personages who had sprung from his brain, full panoplied in pride and owing fealty to duty alone, reminded a sensitive youth that the life of man had never been easy, and that fate appeared to have other purposes than to feed pleasure to avid lips. Since one had to die sooner or later, let it be magnificently, to the accompaniment of verses that had the sweep of an orchestra:

> *Je suis jeune, il est vrai; mais aux âmes bien nées*
> *La valeur n'attend point le nombre des années.*

After Lanny had read *Le Cid* and *Horace* and *Cinna*, he remembered the great hours he had spent among the Isles of Greece, and that these people also could be had in friendship by the magic of the printed word. M. Priedieu had told him about Sophocles, and Lanny got a French translation of the seven plays and read them aloud to his stepfather. Together they indulged in more speculation about the Greek view of life, which had begun with the worship of sensuous beauty and ended with a confrontation of dreadful and inexplicable doom. For what had this gay and eager people been brought into being on those bright and sunny shores, to leave behind them only broken marble columns, and a few thousand melodious verses embodying proud resignation and despair?

As a result of these influences, encountered at the most impressionable age, Lanny Budd became conservative in his taste in the arts. He liked a writer to have something to say, and to say it with clarity and precision; he liked a musician to reveal his ideas in music, and not in program notes; he liked a painter to produce works that bore some resemblance to something. He disliked loud noises and confusion, and obscurity cultivated as a form of exclusiveness. All of which meant that Lanny was out-of-date before he had got fairly started in life.

I I

Inspired by sublime examples, the painter gave his stepson useful advice concerning love. It was good to do with it, but also good to be able to do without it. In this, as in other affairs, one must be master of one's self. There were a thousand reasons why love might fail, and one must have resources within and be able to meet the shocks of fate. Lanny knew that Marcel spoke with authority—this lover who had had to leave his love and go to war; this worshiper of beauty who now had to speak through a veil in order that his friends might not see his ugliness. When Marcel said that Lanny too might some day hear a call that would take him away from music and art and love—the youth trembled in the depths of his soul.

Lanny talked about these problems of love and happiness with his mother also. Strict moralists might have been shocked that

Beauty was willing to know about her son's too early entanglement, and to sanction it; but her course had this compensation, that when the youth was in trouble, now or later, he came to her and had the benefit of her experience.

She tried now to explain to him things that she didn't understand very well herself. No, she didn't think that Rosemary was heartless; it was evident that the girl had taken up the ideas of older women, who perhaps had suffered too much in a man's world, and had revolted from it and gone to extremes in the effort to protect themselves. Beauty told her son that kind and good people frequently had to suffer for those who were not so. Just so Kurt Meissner and other kind and good Germans might suffer for those cruel and arrogant ones who had dragged the nation into an awful calamity.

That was another problem with which Lanny wrestled frequently. Was Europe really going to be another Greece, and destroy itself by internecine wars? Would travelers some day come to Juan and to Cannes, and see the remains of lovely villas like Bienvenu and splendid palaces like Sept Chênes, and dig in the ruins and speculate concerning the lives of those who had built them, and the hostile fate which had driven them upon a course of self-destruction?

Lanny had written several times to Kurt, through the kind agency of the Jewish salesman of electrical gadgets, now engaged in buying from the United States such devices as magnetos for automobiles and airplanes, and reshipping them to Germany. Lanny wrote Kurt about the tenderness of Racine and the stern pride of Corneille and the moral sublimity of Sophocles; and Kurt replied that his friend was fortunate in being able to devote himself to these lofty themes. He, Kurt Meissner, was now taking up practical duties, and soon would be engaged in what he considered the most important work in the world. Lanny had no difficulty in understanding that his German friend was going into the war, and didn't wish, or perhaps wouldn't be allowed, to say where or when or how.

Lanny had to think of Kurt as fighting, and he had to do the same for Rick, who had finished his final year of school and was soon to have his heart's desire. "Sophocles is fine," wrote the English youth on a post card, "but I am reading Blériot"—that being the type of airplane the British were using. Rick didn't say where he was, but Rosemary had brought news about him, and Lanny knew that his friend was in touch with that Captain Finchley whom they had met at the review on Salisbury Plain, and was expecting to go to the camp which this officer now commanded. Lanny knew that the training was intensive and quick, for the need of the Allies for young fliers was desperate. A cousin of Rosemary's had been sent out after only some twenty hours of practice flying, and on his very first flight in France had been shot down by a German outfit. Kurt and Rick were going to fight each other; and suppose they were to meet up in the air!

Lanny took upon himself the duty of serving, at least in his own thoughts, as mediator between these two. It was obvious that when such high-minded youths disagreed so bitterly, there must be truth on both sides and a middle ground where sooner or later they would have to meet. This cruel war must come to an end, and when it did, there would be needed a friend who could speak to both of them and bring them together again.

III

No easy matter to keep that attitude, surrounded as Lanny was with persons whose hatred of Germans kept heating itself up like a furnace fire. Lanny would try to make a compromise by saying that the German rulers were wicked men, while the poor German people were deceived; but his mother said, no, they were a bloodthirsty race, they rejoiced in the infliction of suffering; you could never have got English sailors to send ships to the bottom and leave women and children to drown. Lanny saw that it was useless to argue; he went on playing the music of Mozart and Beethoven, who spoke directly to his soul. He knew they were not bloodthirsty, and neither were the people who had loved and cherished them and made them part of a national tradition.

No, there was something wrong with the world's thinking, and the young fellow's expanding mind kept trying to find out what it was. He wished very much that he might have the help of his father, whom he had not seen for two years. He was often tempted to write and ask Robbie to come to him; but he remembered the deadly submarines lurking all around France and Britain, and he would write: "I'm getting along O.K., and we'll have a lot to talk about when this is over."

Everybody was saying that it was bound to be over in a few months more. Never had wishes been father to so many thoughts. Each new offensive was going to be the final break-through; the Germans would be driven out of France, and the morale of the deceived people would crack. The German authorities kept saying the same thing, except that it was the French line that would crack, and Paris that would be taken. Both sides went on calling their young men, training them as fast as possible, and rushing them into the line; manufacturing enormous quantities of shells and using them in earth-shaking bombardments to prepare for infantry attacks. The battle of Ypres was opened by the British firing a hundred and ten million dollars' worth of ammunition.

The Germans had offered poison gas as their contribution to the progress of military science; and now it was the British turn to have a new idea. Early in the war an English officer had realized the impossibility of making infantry advances against machine guns, and had thought of some kind of steel fortress, heavy enough to be bulletproof, and moving on a caterpillar tread, so that it could go over shell holes and trenches. With a fleet of those to clean out machine-gun nests, it might at last be possible to restore the "war of movement."

It was nearly a year before the British officer could get anything done about his idea; and when after another year it was tried, it wasn't tried thoroughly; there weren't enough tanks and they weren't used as he had planned. All that fitted in exactly with the picture of the British War Office which Robbie had sketched for his son long before the conflict started.

Since Lanny couldn't talk about these matters with his father, he took M. Rochambeau as a substitute. This fine and sensitive old gentleman represented a nation which had maintained its freedom for four hundred years in the heart of warring Europe. It was because of the mountains, he said; and also because they were so fortunate as not to have any gold or oil. M. Rochambeau had surveyed Europe from a high watchtower; he pointed out that most of the Swiss were German-speaking, and French and Germans there had learned to live together in peace, and some day Europe must profit by their example. There would have to be a federation of states like the Swiss cantons, with a central government having power to enforce law and order. This was a vital idea, and Lanny stowed it away among others which he would need.

IV

Three years had passed since Robert Budd had forbidden Lanny to talk with his Uncle Jesse Blackless, and during that period the painter had come perhaps half a dozen times to call upon his sister. When Lanny happened to encounter him, the boy said a polite "How do you do, Uncle Jesse?" and then betook himself elsewhere. He had no reason to be particularly interested in this rather odd-looking relative, and never thought about him except when he showed up. There were so many worthwhile things in the world that Lanny did no more than wonder vaguely what might be so shocking and dangerous about his uncle's ideas.

Jesse and Marcel knew each other. Marcel didn't think much of Jesse as a painter, but they had friends in common, and both were interested in what was going on in the art world. So now when the older man came he went down to Marcel's studio and sat for a while, and Lanny went fishing or swimming.

Did Robbie's prohibition against his son's talking with Uncle Jesse include also talking about him? It was a subtle point of law, which Lanny would have asked Robbie about if it had been possible. On one occasion, after Jesse had called, the stepfather remarked: "Your uncle and your father ought to meet each other now. They could get along much better."

Lanny had to say something, so he asked: "How come?"

"They feel the same way about the war. Jesse can't see any difference at all between French and Germans."

"I don't think that's exactly true of Robbie," said the boy, hesitatingly—for he didn't like to talk about his father in this connection. He added: "I've never understood my uncle's ideas, but I know how Robbie despises them."

"It's a case of extremes meeting, I suppose," remarked the other. "Jesse is an out-and-out revolutionist. He blames all the trouble on big financiers trying to grab colonies and trade. He says they use the governments for their own purposes; they start wars when they want something, and stop them when they've got it."

"Well, it looks like this one might have run away with them," commented the boy.

"Jesse says not so," replied the other. "He thinks the British oil men want Mesopotamia, and they've promised Constantinople to Russia, and Syria to France. Also they want to sink the German fleet. After that their oil will be safe, and they'll make peace."

"Do you believe anything like that, Marcel?"

The voice that came from behind the white silk veil had a touch of grimness. "I'd hate having to think that I'd had my face burned off to help Royal Dutch Shell increase the value of its shares!"

V

Lanny wrote to his father: "I am finding it hard to think as you want me to." And of course Robbie understood that. He had met Americans returned from France, and seen how bitter they were against the Germans; he knew how many of the young fellows had joined the French Foreign Legion, or the Lafayette Escadrille, a group of American fliers fighting for France. One day Lanny received a long typewritten letter from his father, postmarked Paris.

He understood that it had been brought across by some friend or employee.

"If I were with you," wrote the father, "I could answer all the things that people are telling you. As it is, I have to ask you to believe that I have the answers. You know that I have sources of information and do not say that I know something unless I do. I am making this emphatic because your happiness and indeed your whole future may be at stake, and I could never forgive myself if you were to get caught in the sticky flypaper which is now being set for the feet of Americans. If I thought there was any chance of this happening to you I would come at once and take you away."

After that solemn preamble, the head of the European sales department of Budd Gunmakers went on to remind his son that this was a war of profits. "I am making them myself," he said. "Budd's couldn't help making them unless we gave the plant away. People come and stuff them into our pockets. But I don't sell them the right to do my thinking for me.

"Germany is trying to break her way to the east, mainly to get oil, the first necessity of modern machine industry. There is oil in Rumania and the Caucasus, and more in Mesopotamia and Persia. Look up these places on the map, so as to know what I'm telling you. England, Russia, and France all have a share, while Germany has none. That's what all the shooting is about; and I am begging you to paste this up on your looking glass, or some place where you will see it every day. It's an oil man's war, and they are all patriotic, because if they lose the war they'll lose the oil. But the steel men and the coal men have worked out international cartels, so they don't have to be patriotic. They have ways of communicating across no man's land, and they do. I'm a steel man, and they talk to me, and so I get news that will never be printed."

What the steel men were doing, Robbie explained, was selling to both sides, and getting the whole world into their debt. Robbie's own income for this year of 1916 would be five times what it had been before the war, and the profits of the biggest American powder and chemical concern would be multiplied by ten. "The gentle-man whom you met with me in Monte Carlo is keeping very quiet nowadays; he doesn't want to attract attention to what he is doing, which is stuffing money into all the hiding places he can find. I would wager that his profits before this slaughter is over will be a quarter of a billion dollars. He has put himself in the same position as ourselves—he couldn't help making money if he wanted to."

But that wasn't all. These international industrialists had taken entire charge of the war so far as their own properties were con-cerned. The military men were allowed to destroy whatever else they pleased, but nothing belonging to Krupp and Thyssen and Stinnes, the German munitions kings who had French connections and investments, or anything belonging to Schneider and the de Wendels, masters of the Comité des Forges, who had German con-nections and investments. Any army man who attempted to win the war by that forbidden method would be sent to some part of the fighting zone that was less dangerous for the steel kings and more dangerous for him.

Said the father: "I could tell you a hundred different facts which I know, and which all fit into one pattern. The great source of steel for both France and Germany is in Lorraine, called the Briey basin; get your map and look it up, and you will see that the battle line runs right through it. On one side the Germans are getting twenty or thirty million tons of ore every year and smelting it into steel, and on the other side the French are doing the same. On the French side the profits are going to François de Wendel, President of the Comité des Forges and member of the Chamber of Deputies; on the other side they are going to his brother Charles Wendel, naturalized German subject and member of the Reichstag. Those huge blast furnaces and smelters are in plain sight; but no aviators even tried to bomb them until recently. Then one single attempt was made, and the lieutenant who had charge of it was an employee of the Comité des Forges. Surprisingly, the attempt was a failure."

Robbie went on to explain that the same thing was happening to the four or five million tons of iron ore which Germany was getting from Sweden; the Danish line which brought this ore to Germany had never lost a vessel, in that service or any other, and the Swedish railroads which carried the ore burned British coal. "If it hadn't been for this," wrote the father, "Germany would have been out of the war a year ago. It's not too much to say that every man who died at Verdun, and everyone who has died since then, has been a sacrifice to those businessmen who own the newspapers and the politicians of France. That is why I tell you, if you are going to be patriotic, let it be for the American steel kings, of whom you may some day be one. Don't be patriotic for Schneider and the de Wendels, nor for Deterding, nor for Zaharoff!"

V I

Lanny kept that letter and studied it, and thought about it as hard as he knew how. He did not fail to note the curious thing that Marcel had commented upon, the similarity of his father's views with those of the outlawed uncle. The uncle and the father agreed upon the same set of facts, and they even drew the same conclusion —that nobody ought to be patriotic. The point where they split was that Robbie said you had to stuff your pockets, because you couldn't help it; whereas Uncle Jesse—Lanny wasn't sure what he wanted, but apparently it was to empty Robbie's pockets!

Lanny took this letter to his mother, and it threw her into a panic. Politics and high finance didn't mean much to her, but she thought about the effect of such news upon her husband, and made Lanny promise not to mention it to him. Just now he was putting the finishing touches on his "Sister of Mercy," and was much absorbed in it. If the French weren't winning the war, at least they weren't losing it, so Marcel could be what his wife called "rational." As it happened, it was in that Briey district that he had been sitting in a kite balloon, surveying those blast furnaces and smelters which were the source of the enemy's fighting power. He had been praying for the day when France might have enough planes to destroy them. If now the terrible idea was suggested to him that *la patrie* had the power, but was kept from using it by traitors, who could guess what frenzy might seize him?

So Lanny took the letter to his adviser in international affairs, M. Rochambeau. This old gentleman represented a small nation which was forced to buy its oil at market prices, and had never engaged in attempts to despoil its neighbors; therefore he could contemplate problems of high finance from the point of view of the eighth and tenth commandments. When Lanny expressed his bewilderment at the seeming agreement between his conservative father and his revolutionary uncle, the retired diplomat answered with his quiet smile that every businessman was something of a revolutionist, whether he knew it or not. Each demanded his profits, and sought the removal of any factor that menaced his trade or privileges.

Lanny, whose mind was questioning everything and wondering about his own relation to it, was thinking a great deal about whether he wanted to follow in his father's footsteps and become the munitions king of America, or whether he wanted to play around with the arts. And now he heard this old gentleman, who knew the world and met it with suavity, point out the difference between business and art. One might look at a Rembrandt picture, or near a Beethoven symphony, without depriving others of the privilege; but one couldn't become an oil king without taking oil away from others.

Said Lanny: "My father argues that the businessman creates wealth without limit."

Replied the other: "The only thing that I have observed to be without limit is the businessman's desire for profits. He has to have raw materials, and he has to have patents, and if he has too many competitors, his profits vanish."

"But Robbie argues that if he invents a machine gun"—the boy stopped suddenly, as if doubting his own argument.

"Every invention has an intellectual element," conceded the other. "But the machine gun is obviously intended to limit the privileges and possessions of other men. Just now it is being used by the oil kings to make it impossible to get any oil except on their terms. And isn't that a sort of revolution?"

Having thus disposed of Robert Budd as a "Red," the elderly ex-diplomat went on to deal with him as a pacifist; remarking, with the same gentle smile, that it had been long since kings were men of brawn, riding at the head of their retainers and splitting skulls with a battle-ax. The invention of machinery had produced a new kind of men, who sat in offices and dictated orders which put other men at work. If they felt that their interests required war they would have it; but they themselves would remain safe.

"Do you know any Latin?" asked M. Rochambeau; and when the answer was no, he quoted a verse of the poet Ovid, beginning: "Let others make war." The old gentleman suggested that these words might serve one of the great munitions families on its coat of arms. "*Bella gerant alii!*" He was too polite to name the Budd family, but Lanny got the point, and reflected that if his father had heard this conversation, he might have put M. Rochambeau on the prohibited list along with Uncle Jesse!

VII

Rosemary was back in England, and wrote now and then, letters cool and casual as herself. "I enjoyed our meeting so much," she said—just like that! You could hear Miss Noggyns or some other of those feminist ladies telling her: "Don't take it too seriously. That's the way women are made to suffer. Let the men do the suffering!"

So Lanny learned his own lessons. Don't wear your heart on your sleeve; don't make yourself too cheap. Among the fashionable young people at Juan was an American girl who gave evidence of being willing to console him; she was pretty, and svelte, as they all kept themselves, and her silks and satins and lawns and what not were cut to the latest pattern; she cast seductive glances at a handsome playmate, just emerged into manhood and conscious of it, blushing easily, and with strange messages flashing along his nerves. The world was at war, and nothing was certain, and young and old were learning to take their pleasures as they found them.

But Lanny had dreams of shining and wonderful things in love.

He thought it over, and told his mother about this too willing miss, and Beauty asked: "Is she interested in what you are thinking? Does she say anything that appeals to you especially?" When the boy admitted that she hadn't so far, Beauty said: "Then what will you talk about? How will you keep from being bored?"

So he would go off and lose himself in his piano practice. He could find highly exciting things in music and poetry. His anthology contained a poem by Bobby Burns, who spoke with authority concerning sexual prodigality: "But, och! it hardens a' within, An' petrifies the feelin'." Lanny resolved to wait awhile, and maybe Rosemary would find that she missed him more than she had expected.

She wrote about Rick, who had finished his training and left for France. He had had two days' leave and had come home, looking splendid in his khaki uniform. He had been so happy at getting what he wanted. Not a word about sadness in going away, and Lanny understood that there hadn't been many words—that was the English way. "Cheerio! Business as usual!"

A few days later a card came from Rick himself. No address on it, except the number of his unit in the Royal Flying Corps. "Fine setup here. Wish I could write you all about it. Jolly lot of fellows. Hope I can keep up with them. Write me the news. How's old Sophocles? And when are the Americans coming in? Rick."

Lanny could picture these jolly fellows in their camp a few miles behind the lines. It would be about the same as the one he had visited on the rolling Salisbury Plain. Eager young chaps with cheeks of bright red; smooth-shaven, except for now and then a dapper little mustache; no "side," provided you belonged in the right class; taking whatever came with a laugh; willing to die a hundred deaths but not to shed one tear. The English magazines were full of pictures of them, some smiling, some grave, all handsome; each with a string of old English names: "Lieutenant Granville Fortescue Somers, R.F.C. Killed in action, Vimy. Oct. 17, 1916." So it went.

VIII

There was mourning all around Lanny Budd; women in black everywhere on the streets. Women in terror, trembling every time they heard a knock at the door; afraid to look at a newspaper with its stories of wholesale slaughter. Poor Sophie de la Tourette was visiting Sept Chênes to help re-educate the victims; not really caring much about them, but feeling that she had to do something, because Eddie was doing something, everybody was doing it, you had to or you'd go crazy.

Letters came from the ambulance driver; his baroness brought them to Beauty, and Lanny had a chance to read them. The exciting occupation was having an unexpected effect upon a rather dull young American whose only previous achievements had been in billiard matches and motorboat races. He wanted Sophie to share his adventures, and wrote quite vivid prose.

He was sleeping in a half-demolished barn, and the French peasants' manure pile had become a leading feature of his life, the least unpleasant of the smells of war. He was living on bully beef, and a can of chicken from Chicago made a holiday. In front of him were the French trenches, and behind him the French artillery, and he tried to count the number of shots per minute, but it couldn't be done because they overlapped. You were on duty for a twenty-four-hour stretch, and the ambulance would be ordered out at any moment of the day or night. You drove without lights, in mud anywhere from three inches to three feet deep, and you heard all the familiar jokes about seeing a cap lying in the road and stooping to pick it up, and finding that there was a man under it, walking to town, or perhaps riding horseback. Keeping an ambulance right side up on such a road was really a lot of fun, and trying to see the shell holes at night made you wish you had a pet cat along. Sometimes the shell holes were made especially for your ambulance, and that was something you made bets about with your *brancardier*. You wore a helmet, "just in case."

"Have you seen Old Bill?" inquired Eddie, and enclosed one of Captain Bairnsfather's cartoons, with which the English at the front were teaching themselves to laugh at calamity. "Old Bill" was a Cockney with a large mustache and a serious expression; he was shown crouching in a shell hole with bombs going off all around him, and saying to his companion, angrily: "Well, if you knows of a better 'ole, go to it." And there was the elderly colonel who had come home for a brief leave and found that he couldn't get along outside the trenches. He had had one dug in his garden, and was sitting out in it on a rainy night, half covered with water, and with an umbrella over his head.

That was the sporting way to take war. The Americans living in France became ashamed of themselves and of their country. You just couldn't stay amid all that grief and desperate agony, and go on playing cards and dancing, going to the dressmaker and the hairdresser as you had done in the old days. It grew harder and harder for Lanny, and now and then he would find himself thinking: "I'll have to ask Robbie to turn me loose."

He helped himself a little by reading German books and playing German music, and remembering Kurt and the other warmhearted people he had met at Schloss Stubendorf. He hadn't heard from Kurt for quite a while, and could only wonder, did it mean that he had gone to the front and been killed, or had he too become disgusted with Americans—because they didn't do anything to stop the Allied blockade which was starving the women and children of the Fatherland? Lanny wrote another letter, in care of Mr. Robin, and received a reply from the oldest of the two little Robins:

"Dear Mister Lanny Budd: My papa has maled the letter that you sended. I am lerning to right the English but not so good. I have the picture that you sended my papa and feel that I know you and hope that I meat you when no more it is war. Yours respectful Hansi Robin. P.S. I am twelve and I practice now Beethoven's D-major romance for violin."

IX

The end of the year 1916 was a time of bitter discouragement for the Allied cause. Rumania had come into the war and been conquered. Russia was practically out, and Italy had accomplished little. The French armies were discouraged by having been too many times marched into barbed-wire entanglements and mowed down by machine guns. And on top of all that came the resumption of unrestricted submarine warfare. The German high command had made up their minds that even if America came in, the destruction of Allied commerce would be so great that Britain would be brought to her knees before America could do anything effective. At the end of January notice was given that all shipping in British and French waters, and in the Mediterranean, was subject to attack without warning. In January the total destruction of shipping was 285,000 tons; in the following April it rose to 852,000.

It was plain to everybody that Britain could not stand that rate of loss, and the American people had to face the question whether they were willing to see the British Empire replaced by a German one. At least everybody whom Lanny knew said that was the question, and no use fooling yourself. The youth found it a hard problem to think about, and wished more than ever to have his father at hand. He read bits of the speeches which President Wilson made, and the notes which he wrote to the German government, and it seemed to him that the only way he could comply with his father's orders was to start a new and determined campaign of sight reading at the piano.

The U-boats began sinking American ships; and then came the publication of an intercepted letter from the German government, inviting the Mexicans to enter the war on the German side, and promising them a handsome reward, including Texas, Arizona, and New Mexico. That helped Americans to understand what the war was about, and there was a general movement of the country to get ready.

An exciting time for Americans in France, and for none more

than Lanny. Would his father expect him to be neutral now?
Or was he going to be free to feel the way everybody else did,
and the way he wanted to—or at least thought he wanted to? Kurt
Meissner seemed farther away, and the voices of Mozart and
Beethoven grew fainter; France was all around, and its questioning
was incessant: "Why don't you Americans help us?" Lanny heard
it so often that he didn't go out any more, but became a sort of
youthful hermit, swimming and fishing by himself, and reading
books about other times and places. He wrote his father concerning
these troubles, and added: "Tell me if America is coming in, and
if so what I am to do."

Then one day late in March came a cablegram—one of the
old-style ones such as Lanny had not received for more than two
years and a half. "Sailing for Paris tomorrow wish you to join me
there will wire upon arrival Robert Budd."

17

A Man's World

I

LANNY spent a whole week thinking about submarines. It was
the time when the German campaign reached its high point; they
were sinking thirty thousand tons a day, and one of every four
vessels which left the British Isles never returned. Lanny didn't
have to imagine a submarine rising from the sea—he had seen it.
From eyewitnesses he had heard how torpedoes exploded, and
people rushed into lifeboats, and men gave their lives to save

women and children. Robbie was the sort of man who would do that, and Lanny felt as if he were tossing a coin every hour for his father's life.

At last a telegram from Le Havre. Thank God, he was on land! He was writing; and next day Lanny received the most important letter of his young life. Robbie was proposing to take him to Connecticut!

"I think the time has come when you ought to know your own country," wrote the father. "It appears certain that we are going into the war, and whatever part you take ought to be in America. My wife invites you to stay with us this summer; I will get you a tutor and you will study hard, and be able to enter prep school this fall and get ready for college." That meant Yale, which was Robbie's own college, and that of his forefathers for a hundred years or more.

There was a letter for Beauty also. Robbie hoped she would agree with him that a lad ought to have a chance to know his own people. Beauty had now had him to herself for thirty-two months —Robbie had an arithmetical mind. He said that if the war lasted, it would be better for Lanny to be in Connecticut, where Robbie could arrange for him to render service in the production of munitions. "You may put your mind at ease on one subject," he wrote. "Lanny will not go into the trenches. He is too valuable to me, and I will be valuable to the government." *Bella gerant alii!*

"What do you want to do?" asked the mother, after they had shared these letters.

"Well, of course, I'd like to see America," said the youth; and the mother's heart sank. Such a lovely safe nest she had made here, but of course he wouldn't stay in it; the last thing in the world that men wanted appeared to be safety.

"I suppose I'll have to give you up," she said. "The cards are all stacked against a woman."

"Don't worry, Beauty, I'll take good care of myself, and come back when the war's over. I don't think I'll want to live anywhere but here."

"You'll meet some girl over there, and she'll tell you what to do."

"I'm going to get tough," replied the boy; but he didn't look it.

"I knew this had to come, Lanny. But I hoped Robbie would wait till the sea was safe."

"Plenty of people are getting through; and he and I are pretty good swimmers." Lanny thought for a moment, then added: "I wonder what he's going to do about telling his friends the bad news about me."

"He told his wife about us both before they were married. I imagine he'll tell other people that you're his son, and let it go at that. Don't let it worry you."

"If anybody doesn't want me around," said the boy, "I can always go somewhere else. Shall you miss me too terribly, Beauty?"

"It'll be all right if I know you're happy. I ought to tell you a bit of news that I've just learned—I'm going to have a baby."

"Oh, gosh!" A wide smile spread over Lanny's face. "That's grand, Beauty! It will tickle Marcel, won't it?"

"Frenchmen are like that," she answered.

"All men are, aren't they?" After a while he inquired: "Was it another accident, or did you decide to do it?"

"Marcel and I decided."

"It's a grand place to bring up a child, Beauty—I can tell you that." He kissed her on both cheeks until she cried with happiness and sorrow mingled.

II

It seemed cruel that a youth should be so excited at the idea of leaving his mother; but he couldn't help it, and she understood. To be with Robbie in Paris, and travel on a great steamer, and see that city of New York which he knew from motion pictures, and the marvelous plant of Budd's, the economic foundation of his life. It was a center of his imaginings, a forge of Vulcan a million times magnified, a Fafnir and Fasolt cave where monstrous forces were generated. And to meet that mysterious family, so many of them that you couldn't keep their names straight, and all different and queer. Robbie didn't often talk about them, but behaved as if they were a dark secret. Or perhaps it was Lanny who was the dark secret!

He packed the few things he would take with him; that required only a couple of hours, and he was ready to go on the evening train. Beauty broke down and wept—it was such short notice. He was a mother's darling; and who else would love him as she had? The world was cruel, so many wicked people in it, women especially—she understood their hearts, the cold and selfish ones, the gold diggers, the harpies! So many things she ought to have taught him, and now it was too late, he couldn't remember them; he was crazy with eagerness to get out into that world which seemed to her so full of pain. She gave him many warnings, extracted many promises—and all the time aware that she was boring him a little.

Lanny had a good-by talk with Marcel, and this was more to the point. Marcel had left his family, respectable bourgeois in a provincial town; they had wanted him to be a lawyer, perhaps a judge, and instead he had come to Paris to dab paint on canvas. They gave him a small allowance, but didn't pretend to like his work. "You are lucky," Marcel said; "your parents are sympathetic, they'll stand by you even if you don't succeed. But don't be surprised if you don't like your relatives. Don't bare your heart to the hawks."

"What makes you say that?" asked the boy, puzzled.

"Rich people are pretty much the same all over the world. They believe in money, and if you don't make money they think there's something wrong with you. If you don't see life as they do, they take it as a criticism, and right away you're an outsider. If I were taking you to meet my family, that's how I'd have to warn you."

"Well, I'll write and let you know what I find, Marcel."

"If you like it, all right. I'm just putting you on guard. You've had a happy life so far, everything has been easy—but it can hardly be like that all the way through."

"Anyhow," remarked the boy, "Robbie says that America's going to help France."

"Tell them to hurry," replied the painter. "My poor country is bleeding at every vein."

III

Lanny was seventeen, and had grown nearly a foot in those thirty-two months since he had seen his father. For many youths it is an awkward age, but he was strongly knit, brown with sunshine and red with well-nourished blood. He came running from the train to welcome Robbie, and there was something in the sight of him which made the man's heart turn over. Flesh of my flesh— but better than I am, without my scars and my painful secrets! So Robbie thought, as the lad seized him and kissed him on both cheeks. There was a trace of down on Lanny's lips, light brown and soft; his eyes were clear and his look eager.

He wanted to know everything about his father in the first moment. That grand rock of a man, that everybody could depend on; he would solve all the problems, relieve all the anxieties—all in the first moment! Robbie looked just the same as ever; he was in his early forties, and his vigor was still unimpaired; whatever clouds might be in his moral sky showed no trace. He looked handsome in brown tweeds, with tie and shoes to match; Lanny, whose suit was gray, decided at once that he would look better in brown.

"Well, what do you think about the war?" The first question every man asked then.

The father looked grave immediately. "We're going in; not a doubt of it."

"And are you going to support it?"

"What can I do? What can anybody do?"

It was nearing the end of March. Relations with Germany had been severed for many weeks, and President Wilson had declared a state of what he called "armed neutrality." America was going to arm its merchant vessels, and in the meantime Germany was going on sinking them, day after day. Shipping was delayed, the vessels in American harbors were afraid to venture out.

"What can we do?" repeated Robbie. "The only alternative is to declare an embargo, and abandon our European trade entirely."

"What would that do?"

"It would bring a panic in a week. Budd's would have to shut down, and throw twenty thousand men out of work."

Driving to their hotel in a horse-drawn cab, Robbie explained this situation. A large-scale manufacturing enterprise was geared to a certain schedule. A quantity of finished goods came off the conveyors every day, and was boxed and put into freight cars or trucks—or, in the case of Budd's, which had its own river frontage, onto ships. Vessels were loaded and moved away, making room for others. If for any reason that schedule was interrupted, the plant would be blockaded, because its warehouses could hold only a few days' output. The same thing would happen at the other end, because raw materials came on a fixed schedule—they had been ordered and had to be taken and paid for, but there was place to store only a limited supply; they were supposed to go through the plant and be moved on.

That, said Robbie, was the situation not merely with steel mills and munitions plants, but with meat packing and flour milling, making boots and saddles, automobiles and trucks, anything you could think of. Rightly or wrongly, wisely or unwisely, American business had geared itself to the task of supplying the need of the nations of Europe. American finance had geared itself to taking and marketing their bonds. If all this were suddenly stopped, there would be such a breakdown as had never been known in the world before—"ten or twenty million men out of work," declared the representative of Budd Gunmakers Corporation.

Lanny had heard many persons express disapproval of those who were making money out of this war; Kurt, and Rick, and Beauty, Sophie, Marcel, and M. Rochambeau. But when he listened to his father, all that vanished like mist before the morning sun. He saw

right away that things had to be like this; if you were going to
have machinery, and produce goods on a big scale, you had to
do it in a fixed way. The artists and dreamers and moralists were
just talking about things they didn't understand.

At least that was the way it seemed until Lanny got off by himself. Then he began to have troubles in his thinking. Robbie was
all for Budd's, and defended the right of Budd's to get all the
business it could, and to keep its workers employed. But Robbie
didn't like Zaharoff, and had a tendency to resent the business that
Vickers got. Robbie blamed Schneider-Creusot because it sold
goods to neutral countries which resold them to Germany; he
objected to the French de Wendels' protecting their properties in
Germany. But suppose that Budd's had owned plants in Germany—
wouldn't Robbie be trying to take care of them, and pointing out
the harm it would do if they were bombed?

In short, wasn't there as much to be said for one set of businessmen as for another? As much for Germans as for British or French
or Americans? Lanny felt in duty bound to be fair to his friend
Kurt, and to Kurt's family who had been so kind to him. He could
not forget having heard Herr Meissner using these very same
arguments about the need of German manufacturers to get raw
materials and to win foreign markets, in order to keep their workers
employed and their plants running on schedule. It was extremely
puzzling; but Lanny didn't say much about it, because for two
years and a half he had been learning to keep his ideas to himself.
In wartime it appeared that nobody wanted to see both sides of
any question.

IV

Of course the father and son didn't spend all their time discussing
world politics. Lanny had to tell about Beauty and Marcel; about
the painter's wounds, and his way of life, and his work; about the
new baby they were going to have, on purpose—a somewhat rare
event nowadays, so Robbie remarked. And about Sophie and her
Eddie Patterson and his ambulance driving; about Mrs. Emily and

Les Forêts, and old M. Priedieu and how he had died; about Sept Chênes, and the war victims who were being re-educated, including Lanny's gigolo, who would never jig again. And about Mr. Robin, and the letters to Kurt, and the little Robins, and the Jews, and didn't Robbie like them, and why not? And about Rosemary—a large subject in herself; and Rick and his flying—as soon as Lanny learned that he was to have a few days in Paris he got off a card to Rick, on the chance that he might be able to get a day's leave and visit his friend.

Robbie would ask questions, and Lanny would think of details he had left out. There was Marcel's painting; he was getting better and better, everybody agreed; he was doing an old peasant woman who grew roses on the Cap, and had lost three sons, one after another, and it showed in her face, and still more in the portrait that Marcel was making of her. The one he had done of Beauty, called "Sister of Mercy," was to be shown at a salon in the Petit Palais, and one of the things Lanny wanted to do was to find out about it. If Robbie went to view it he would find a new woman, one much more serious, and really sad. "Of course she's not that way all the time," added the boy; "but that's how Marcel sees things. He can't forgive fate for what it's done to his face—nor for what it's doing to France."

Robbie also had things to tell. For the most part they had to do with business; for he was not one of those persons who have states of soul which require explanation. He had been making money hand over fist, and it kept him in good humor; he found it pleasant, not only for himself, but for many other people. He was troubled because Lanny's wants were so modest in that regard; he seemed to think they ought to celebrate their reunion by buying something handsome. The only thing Lanny could think of was one of Marcel's paintings to take to America. But Robbie didn't think that would be such a good idea—no use to say anything about a stepfather right at the outset!

Lanny told how seriously Beauty was taking the re-education of the *mutilés*, and so Robbie sent her a check for a couple of thousand dollars, telling her she might use it for that purpose if she pleased. He added a friendly message for Mrs. Emily, knowing that Beauty would take it to her; in this way the money would win credit for Beauty with that socially powerful lady. Robbie explained this procedure, so that his son might learn how to make his way in the world. No use to have money unless you knew how to use it, and how to handle people. There were some to whom you gave it with a careless gesture, and others to whom you doled it out carefully.

Robbie remarked with a smile that there had been personal reasons for his opposition to America's entering the war; Budd's would now begin manufacturing for the United States government, and Robbie would get no commissions on that. "It will be a great satisfaction to my brother Lawford," he added. "It has pained him to see me making more money than himself."

Lanny was going to meet this brother, so the time had come for Robbie to tell about him. "He will be polite to you, but don't expect him to be anything more, because nature hasn't made him that way. He's all right if you let him alone; but unfortunately I haven't—not since the day I was born, and attracted too much attention in the nursery. I was better-looking than he, and mother made too much fuss over me."

Robbie spoke playfully, but made it plain that there was something of a feud between his older brother and himself. When Robbie had come of age, he had offered to learn the selling end of the business, and the father had given him a chance, working on commission, plus an expense account. This latter had made much trouble, because Lawford objected to one item or another; when Robbie lost money to Captain Bragescu, his brother called it paying his gambling debts at the company's expense!

"And then came this war," said Robbie. "That was my good fortune, but surely not my fault. It resulted in my having an income two or three times his own—and he works hard running the plant, while I don't have to do another lick of work in my life unless I feel like it."

V

Just before Lanny left the Riviera a world-shaking event took place—the Russian revolution and the overthrow of the Tsar. Everybody was speculating as to what it meant, and what would be its effect upon the war. Most people in France believed it would help the Allies; the Russians would fight harder, now that they were free. But Robbie said that Russia was out, because of graft, incompetence, and the breakdown of her railroads. He said that freight had been landed from hundreds of steamers at Archangel in the far north, and at Vladivostok on the Pacific, and there was no way to get it to the war zones. Tens of millions of dollars' worth of goods was piled along the railroad tracks for miles, without more than a single tarpaulin to cover the boxes. Included in the stacks were Budd machine guns, and of course they were rusting and would soon be useless; meanwhile the Russian peasant-soldiers were expected to defend themselves with clubs and march to the attack with five men to one rifle.

"What is going to happen," said Robbie, "is breakdown and chaos; the country may be pillaged, or the Germans may take it. The German troops will be moved to the west, and may well be in Paris before the Americans can raise an army or get it across the ocean. That is what the German General Staff is reckoning on."

The father revealed the purpose which had brought him to Europe. The War Department of the United States government had sent an emissary to the president of Budd's, asking him to consider proposals for the licensing of Budd patents to various firms such as Vickers and Schneider, which were working day and night making munitions for the Allied governments. Under such licenses they would be permitted to make Budd machine guns, Budd anti-aircraft guns, and so on, paying a royalty to be agreed upon. If America should enter the war, Budd's itself would no longer be in position to manufacture for European nations, and it was desirable that our Allies should have the benefit of Yankee ingenuity and skill.

This question of patent licensing had been a subject of controversy inside the Budd organization for years. Foreign governments were always proposing it, offering handsome royalties. Robbie had opposed the policy, while Lawford had favored it, and each had labored to persuade the father to his point of view. The older brother insisted that it was dangerous to expand the plant any further; they would have to borrow money—and then some day the pacifists would impose a scheme of disarmament, Budd's wouldn't be able to meet its obligations, and some Wall Street banking syndicate would gobble it up. Robbie, on the other hand, argued that European manufacturers would make the most generous offers and sign on as many dotted lines as you prepared for them; but who was going to watch them, and know how many shell fuses they really made?

Lanny got from this a clearer realization of the situation between his father and his oldest uncle. The uncle was morose and jealous, and a dispute which had begun in the nursery had been transferred to the office of the company. Lawford opposed everything that Robbie advocated, and attributed selfish motives to him; as for Robbie, he seemed convinced that the chief motive of the brother's life was not to let Robbie have his way in anything. Now the War Department had stepped in and given Lawford a victory. Licenses would be issued to several European munitions firms, and in order to salve Robbie's feelings, his father had sent him to do the negotiating.

VI

Robbie telephoned to the home of Basil Zaharoff, which was on the Avenue Hoche. Lanny was in the room and heard one-half the conversation; the munitions king said something which caused Robbie to smile, and reply: "Yes, but he's not so little now." Robbie turned his eyes on Lanny as he listened. "Very well," he said. "He'll be happy to come, I'm sure."

The father hung up the receiver and remarked: "The old devil asked if I had that very intelligent little boy with me. He says to bring you along. Want to go?"

"Do I!" exclaimed the intelligent little boy. "But what does he want with me?"

"Don't let your vanity be flattered. We've got something he wants, and he'd like to make it a social matter, not one of business. Watch him and see how an old Levantine trader works."

"Doesn't he have an office?" inquired the boy.

"His office is where he happens to be. People find it worth while to come to him."

Lanny dressed for this special occasion, and late in the afternoon of a day which promised spring they drove to 53, Avenue Hoche, just off the Parc Monceau. It was one of a row of stately houses, with nothing to make it conspicuous; a home for a gentleman who didn't want to attract attention to himself, but wanted to stay hidden and work out plans to appeal to other men's fears and greeds. A discreet and velvet-footed man in black opened the door, and escorted them into the reception room, which had furniture and paintings in excellent taste—no doubt the duquesa's. Presently they were invited to a drawing room on the second floor, where the first thing they saw was an elaborate silver tea service ready for action. The windows were open, and a soft breeze stirred the curtains, and birds sang in trees just outside. Presently the munitions king entered, looking grayer and more worn—one does not make a quarter of a billion dollars without some cares.

He had hardly finished greeting them when a lady entered behind him. Had she heard the story of the boy who had had such an odd idea about helping his father's business? Or was it the special importance of the contracts which Robert Budd was bringing? Anyhow, here she came, and Zaharoff said: "The Duquesa de Villafranca," with a tone of quiet pride. The duquesa bowed but did not give her hand; she said, very kindly: "How do you do, Messieurs?" and seated herself at the tea table.

She had been only seventeen when she had met this munitions salesman, and they had been waiting twenty-seven years for her lunatic husband to die. She was a rather small and inconspicuous person, gracious, but even more reserved than her companion. His blue eyes were watching the visitors, and her dark eyes for the most part watched him. She had the olive complexion of a Spaniard, and wore a teagown of purple, with a double rope of pearls nearly to her waist. "You have had a dangerous journey, M. Budd," she remarked.

"Many men are facing danger these days, Madame," replied Robbie.

"Do you think that your country will help us to end this dreadful war?"

"I think so; and if we come in, we shall do our best."

"It will have to be done quickly," put in the munitions king; to which Robbie answered that large bodies took time to get in motion, but when they moved, it was with force.

They talked about the military situation. Zaharoff set forth the extreme importance to civilization of overcoming the German menace. He told about what he had done to set up Venizelos in Greece and bring that country in on the side of the Allies; he didn't say how much money he had spent, but that he had moved heaven and earth.

"Greece is my native land," he said. "Love of Greece has been the first passion of my life, and hatred of Turkish cruelty and fanaticism has been the second." As he talked about these matters his voice trembled a little, and Lanny thought, was all that playacting? If so, it was a remarkable performance. But Robbie told him afterward that it was genuine; the munitions king did really hate the Turks, and had spent millions buying newspapers and politicians, pulling wires against King Constantine and his German wife. Zaharoff had gone in for oil, and wanted Mesopotamia for his British companies. He used his money for things which the Allied governments wanted done, but which were too discreditable for them to do directly.

VII

Presently they were talking about President Wilson, who had said that Americans were "too proud to fight," and had been re-elected with the slogan, "He kept us out of war." Robbie explained the Presbyterian temperament, which would find some high moral basis for whatever it decided to do, and would then do it under divine direction. Now this President was talking about "war for democracy," and Zaharoff asked if that was supposed to be a moral slogan.

Robbie replied: "The founders of our nation didn't believe in democracy, M. Zaharoff, but it is supposed to be good politics now."

"Well, I should want to write the definition somewhat carefully." The old man smiled one of those strange smiles, in which his watchful eyes never took part.

"It is playing with fire," said the other, unsmiling. "We have seen in Russia what it may lead to, and not even Wilson wishes the war to end that way."

"God forbid!" exclaimed the munitions king; and no one could doubt the sincerity of that.

When you are having a lady of ancient lineage to pour tea for you, it is necessary to pay some attention to her. So presently Robbie remarked: "That is a lovely tea service you have, Duquesa."

"It is an heirloom of my family," replied María del Pilar Antonia Angela Patrocino Simón de Muguiro y Berute, Duquesa de Marqueni y Villafranca de los Caballeros.

"I had a gold one," put in the host. "But I have given it to the government, to help save the franc."

Was there just the trace of a frown on the gentle visage of the Spanish king's cousin? She had been laboring for a quarter of a century to make a gentleman out of a Levantine trader; and perhaps it cannot be done in one lifetime; perhaps in the midst of wars and revolutions one must excuse lapses from a much-burdened mind.

After they had had their tea, the old man remarked: "And now about that matter of business, Mr. Budd."

The hostess rose. "I am sure you gentlemen don't want an audience for your conference," she said; and added sweetly to Lanny: "Wouldn't you like to come and see my beautiful tulips?"

Of course Lanny went, and so lost his chance to observe the old trader in action. He was taken into a fine garden, and introduced to a pair of snow-white poodles, beautifully groomed and shaved to resemble lions. He learned about the tulips, which were just unfolding their beauties: the *bizarres*, which are yellow marked with purple and red; the *byblo'emen*, which are white marked with violet or purple; also a new kind from Turkestan. The Dutch people had cultivated them for centuries, and once they had been the basis of a great financial boom.

"Do you really love flowers?" asked the duquesa; and Lanny told about Bienvenu, and the court full of daffodils and bougain-villaea where he did his reading. He was used to ladies with titles, and not awed by them. He suspected that one who had the munitions king for a companion didn't feel entirely safe or happy, so he was moved to be kind. He mentioned Mrs. Emily, and found that the duquesa knew her, and had aided her war work; so Lanny told what she was doing at Sept Chênes, and added the story of M. Pinjon, the gigolo, which the duquesa found *sympathique*. She remarked that she would like to send a present to that poor man; since he played the flute, perhaps he might like to have a good one.

Time passed, and the two men of business did not appear. Lanny didn't want to be a nuisance to his hostess, who must have other things to do than to entertain a casually met youth. He told her he was used to getting along by himself, and she offered to take him to the library. He had seen many large rooms in fine homes, having walls lined with volumes de luxe which were rarely touched save to be dusted. The munitions king's were all behind glass, but on the table were magazines, and he said he would be happy with those. So the gentle lady excused herself. Lanny understood that she was far too rich to ask him to call again; and besides, maybe this was all just a matter of business, as Robbie had said!

VIII

At last the two emerged from their conference; both suave as ever—but you couldn't tell anything from that. The father and son strolled down the street, and Lanny said: "Well, what happened?"

Robbie answered, with one of his grins: "I thought he was going to cry, but he didn't quite."

"Why should he cry?" The boy knew that he was supposed to be naïve, so that his father would have the fun of telling it.

"I hurt his feelings by suggesting that we should require observers in the Vickers plants, to check their production under our licenses."

"Is he going to let you?"

"He said it was a very serious matter to admit strangers to a munitions factory in wartime. I answered that they wouldn't be strangers very long; he would know how to become acquainted with them." Robbie began to laugh; he enjoyed nothing more than such a battle over property rights—especially when he held the good cards close to his chest. "They really need our patents," he said; "and, believe me, they won't get them without paying. Why should they?"

Lanny didn't know any reason, and said so.

"Well, the old devil thought he knew a number of them. He was horrified at the schedule of royalties I put before him; he said he had been given to understand that America wanted to help the Allies, not to bleed them to death, or drive them to bankruptcy. I said I hadn't heard of any bankruptcies among the hundred and eighty Vickers companies in England, or the two hundred and sixty of them abroad. He said they had cut their prices to the bone as a patriotic duty to the British and French governments. I told him it was generally understood that his companies were getting the full twenty percent profit allowed them by British law.

You can see it wasn't a conversation for a duquesa to hear. Was she nice to you?"

"Very," said Lanny. "I liked her."

"Oh, sure," said the father. "But you can't like the consort of a wolf beyond a certain point."

Lanny saw that his father was not going to like Basil Zaharoff under any circumstances. He said so, and Robbie replied that a wolf didn't want to be liked; what he wanted was to eat, and when it was a question of dividing up food with him, you had to have a sharp-pointed goad in hand. "We have paid out good American money, financing inventions and perfecting complicated machines. We're not going to give those secrets to Zaharoff, not even in return for a tea party and a smile from a duquesa. We're going to have our share of the profits, paid right on the barrel-head, and I'm sent here to tell him so, and to put before him a contract which our lawyers have constructed like a wolf trap. I said that very politely, but in plain language."

"And what did you decide?"

"Oh, I left him the contracts, and he'll weep over them tonight, and tomorrow morning I'm to see his French factotum, Pietri, and he'll plead and argue, and demand this change and that, and I'll tell him to take it as it's written, or the Allies can get along with a poorer grade of machine guns."

"Will they, Robbie?"

"Just stick by me the next few days, son, and learn how we businessmen pull wires. If they turn down my contracts, I know half a dozen journalists in Paris and London who will make a story out of it for a reasonable fee. I can find a way to have the merits of the Budd products brought to the attention of a dignified and upright member of Parliament, who wouldn't take a bribe for anything, but will endeavor to protect his country against the greed of munitions magnates and the bungling of War Office bureaucrats."

IX

Robbie's next conference was with Bub Smith, the ex-cowboy with the broken nose who had come down to Juan three or four years previously and demonstrated the Budd automatic for Captain Bragescu. Bub had given up his job in Paris to work for Robbie, and had made a couple of trips to America in spite of the submarines. It was he who had brought letters for Lanny into France.

Now Robbie told his son that Bub had proved himself an "ace" at confidential work, and was going to have the job of keeping track of the lessees of Budd patents. "Of course Zaharoff himself is a man of honor," said Robbie, with a smile. "But there's always the possibility that some of the men who run his companies might be tempted to try tricks. Bub is to watch the French plants for me."

"Can one man keep track of them all?" asked the youth.

"I mean that he'll be the one to watch the watchers."

Robbie went on to explain that it wasn't possible to carry on an industry without workers; and there were always some of these glad to give information in exchange for a *pourboire.* Bub would build an organization for knowing what was going on in munitions factories.

"Isn't it a rather dangerous job?" asked Lanny. "I mean, mayn't they take him for a spy?"

"He'll have a letter from me, and the embassy will identify him."

"And won't the munitions people find out about him?"

"Oh, sure. They know we're bound to watch them."

"That won't hurt their feelings?"

Robbie was amused. "In our business you don't have feelings— you have cash."

18

Away from All That

A TELEPHONE call for Lanny at the Crillon. He answered, and let out a whoop. "Where are you? Oh, glory! Come right up." He hung up the receiver. "It's Rick! He got leave!" Lanny rushed out to the lift, to wait for his friend; grabbed him and hugged him, then held him off at arm's length and examined him. "Gee, Rick, you look grand!"

The young flying officer had grown to man's stature. His khaki uniform was cut double in front, making a sort of breastplate of cloth; on the left breast was a white badge, indicating that he had a flying certificate, and high up on both sleeves were eagle wings. His skin was bronzed and his cheeks rosy; flying hadn't hurt him. With his wavy black hair cut close and a brown service cap on top he was a handsome fellow; and so happy over this visit—they were going to see Paris together, and Paris was the world!

"Gee, Rick, how did you manage it?"

"I had done some extra duty, so I had it coming."

"How long have you got?"

"Till tomorrow night."

"And how is it, Rick?"

"Oh, not so bad."

"You've been fighting?"

"I've got two boches that I'm sure of."

"You havent been hurt?"

"I had one spill—turned over in mud; but fortunately it was soft."

Lanny led him to the room, and Robbie was glad to see him, of course; he set up the drinks, and Rick took one—they all drank in the air force, too much, he said, it was the only way they could keep going. Lanny drank soda, but said nothing about it. He sat, devouring that gallant figure with his eyes; so proud of his friend, thinking that he, Lanny, would never do anything as exciting and wonderful as that; his father wouldn't let him, his father wanted him to stay at home and make munitions for other men to use. But at least he could hear about it, and live it vicariously. He asked a stream of questions, and Rick answered casually, not much about himself, but about the squadron and what they were doing.

Of course Rick knew what was in his younger friend's mind, the adoration, the hero-worship; and of course it pleased him. But he wouldn't give a sign of it, he'd take it just as he took the job; nothing special, all in the day's work.

Rick could tell now what the censor wouldn't let him put on paper. He was stationed with General Allenby's Third Army, which lay in front of Vimy Ridge. He belonged to what was called the "corps wing," the group of fliers who served a particular body of troops. Observation planes equipped with two-way radios, or with photographic apparatus, went out to observe enemy positions, and fighting planes went along to protect them. Rick flew a machine known as a "Sopwith one-and-a-half strutter." It was a single-seater, such planes being lighter and faster, and the competition of the German Fokkers had forced it. Both sides now had what were called "interrupter gears"; that is, the action of the machine gun was synchronized with the propeller, so that the stream of bullets went through the whirling blades without hitting. So you didn't have to aim your gun, but just your plane; your job was to get on the other fellow's tail, and see him straight through your sights, and then cut loose. You would see two fighting planes maneuvering for position, darting this way and that, diving, rolling over, executing every sort of twist and turn. That sight was seen over Paris pretty nearly every day, and Lanny hadn't missed it.

His friend told many things about this strange new job of fighting in the air. In the sector where he flew, it was hard to distinguish the trenches, for the entire ground was a chaos of shell-craters. He flew at a speed of ninety miles an hour, and at a height of twelve hundred and fifty feet. When you came down suddenly from that height, you had headache, earache, even toothache, but it all passed away in three or four hours. The most curious thing was that you could hear the whine of the bullet before it reached you, and if you ducked quickly you might dodge it. Somehow that gave Lanny the biggest thrill of anything he had heard about the war; a mile and a half a minute, a quarter of a mile above the earth, and playing tag with bullets!

II

England and France were getting ready for the big spring "push"; everybody knew where it was to be, but it was a matter of good form not to name places. "Be silent," read the signs all over Paris; "enemy ears are listening." Rick said the air push was on all the time; the two sides were struggling incessantly for mastery. The English had held it pretty much through 1916; now it was a local matter, varying from place to place and from week to week. The Fokkers were fast, and their men fought like demons. The problem of the English was to train fliers quickly enough; they were used up faster than they could be sent across.

Rick stopped after he had said that; for it wasn't good form to reveal anything discouraging. But now and then he would mention a name. "Aubrey Valliance—you remember that fellow with the straw-colored hair you raced with, swimming? He was downed last week, poor chap. We don't know what happened—he just didn't come back." Lanny got the picture of those bright-cheeked English schoolboys, eighteen or nineteen, some younger, having told a fib about their ages. They would volunteer, and have a few tests of eyesight and sense of balance, and then be rushed to a training camp, listen to a few lectures, go up a few times with an instructor to be taught the rudiments, then go up alone and practice this and that, maybe a week, maybe less, thirty hours of flying, or even as few as twenty—and then off to France.

"Replacements," they were called; half a dozen would arrive in a truck at night and be introduced to their fellows; you hardly had time to remember their names. They would look on the bulletin board and see themselves scheduled to fly at dawn. They would have a drink, and a handshake, or maybe a salute. They would say: "Very good, sir," and step into their seats; the propellers would begin to roar, and away they would go, one after another. Maybe eight would go out, and only six would come back; you would wait, and listen, trying not to show your concern; after a certain period there was no use thinking about them any more, for the plane had only so much petrol, and no way to get any more. If the chap was down in enemy territory, you wouldn't know whether he was alive or dead; unless he had put up an extra-good fight, in which case an enemy flier might bring a bundle containing his boots and cap and pocketbook, and drop them onto the camp.

"Don't you ever get afraid, Rick?" asked Lanny. That was after Robbie had gone out to keep his engagements, and the two were alone.

Rick hesitated. "I guess I do; but it's no good thinking about. You've a job to do, and that's that."

Lanny recalled Mrs. Emily Chattersworth's mother, that very old lady who had told about the American Civil War. One of her stories had to do with a young Confederate officer whose knees were shaking before a battle, and someone accused him of being scared. "Of course I'm scared," he said; "if you were half as scared as I am you'd have run away long ago."

Rick said that was about it. He said that now and then there was some youngster whose nerves came near to breaking, and you had to figure out how to buck him up and get him started. The hardest job was that of the ground officer who had to send chaps out, knowing they weren't fit; but there was no choice, they had to keep up with the Germans. Apparently things weren't any better with them, because the score was about even. You'd soon know if they had the edge.

III

The pair went for a walk on the boulevards. Paris in wartime; every sort of uniform you could imagine, and Rick pointing them out to his friend: English Tommies out for a lark; Australians and New Zealanders, tall fellows with looped-up hats; Highlanders in kilts—the Germans called them "ladies from hell"; Italians in green; French zouaves with baggy knee-pants; African colonials, who fought fiercely, but looked bewildered in a great city. The poilus had a new uniform of gray-blue; the picturesque *képi rouge* and the baggy red pants had offered too good a target.

The two had lunch together; war bread, and very small portions of sugar, but anything else you could pay for. It was a special occasion, and Lanny wanted to spend all he had. He liked to be seen with this handsome young officer; his pacifist impulses weakened when put to such a test. He talked about Kurt, wishing he might be with them, instead of being on the other side of no man's land— or perhaps up in the air, fighting Rick! "I know he's in the army, but I've no idea where," said Lanny.

"We wouldn't get along so well," said the Englishman. "I always had the idea that German culture was a lot of wind and bluff." Rick went on like that at some length, saying that the reputation of Goethe was due to the fact of the Germans' wanting so badly to have a world poet; Goethe wasn't really so much. Lanny listened, thinking his own thoughts. If Kurt were here, would he say that Shakespeare was a barbarian, or something like that? It was going to take a long time to wipe the bitterness of this war out of the hearts of men. If America came in, what would happen to Lanny's own heart?

There is a saying: "Speak of angels and they flap their wings." The two friends came back from their stroll, and there was a letter for Lanny with a Swiss stamp on it, forwarded from Juan. "Kurt!" he exclaimed, and opened it quickly. His eyes ran over it. "He's been wounded!" Then he read aloud:

"Dear Lanny: It has been a long time since I have written. I have been very busy, and circumstances do not permit me to unbosom myself. Please believe that our friendship is not going to be ended, even by the news which I now read from abroad. I am now in hospital. It is not serious and I hope soon to be well again. It may not be possible for me to write for some time, so this is just to say Hello, and hope that you will not let anything interrupt your musical studies and the reading of the world's great poets. Ever your friend, Kurt."

The envelope showed that it had been opened by the censor. It was always a gamble whether any particular sentence might cause a letter to be destroyed. You had to read between the lines. The "news from abroad" of course meant America's coming into the war—which seemed certain, President Wilson having summoned a special session of Congress to meet in a few days. Kurt was telling Lanny that he hoped he wouldn't take part in fighting Germany.

"We mustn't let ourselves hate him, Rick," said the American.

The other answered: "The fighting men don't hate one another—not very often. What we hate is the damnable *Kultur* which has produced all these atrocities; also the rulers who impose it upon a credulous people."

Lanny could accept that; but would Kurt accept it? That was going to be a problem!

IV

Robbie was in the midst of conferences with the representatives of a half a dozen armaments concerns; but he found an hour to go with the pair to the exposition at the Petit Palais. It was a matter of *amour propre* with the French that not even a world war should stop the development of genius in their country; art lovers would come to see what was new in taste and culture even though bombs might be raining upon them from the sky. The younger painters of France were most of them putting camouflage on guns and ships;

but they had found time for sketches of war scenes. The older ones had gone on with their work, like Archimedes making scientific discoveries during the siege of Syracuse.

Battle pictures, of course, had always been found in every salon. Painters loved to portray thrilling conflicts: horses trampling men, sabers flashing, carbines spitting flame. Now there was a new kind of war, hard to know how to deal with. So much of it was fought at long distances, and with great machines—and how were you to make them dramatic? How were you to keep a picture of an airplane or a machine gun from looking like a photograph in *L'Illustration?* A general on horseback was an established figure of *la gloire;* but what could you do with a man in a tank or a submarine?

The answer of Marcel Detaze had been to go off in solitude and paint the figure of a woman in sorrow. Whether men were mutilated by sabers or by shrapnel made little difference to the wives and sweethearts of France; so said this young painter, and apparently the art lovers agreed with him. "Sister of Mercy" had been hung in an excellent position, and there were always people standing in front of it, and their faces showed that Marcel had conveyed something to their souls. Lanny listened to their comments, and little thrills crept up and down his spine. Even Robbie was moved; yes, the fellow had talent, you didn't have to be a "highbrow" to be sure of it.

Too bad that Beauty couldn't be on hand to share the sensation. She would have taken her friends, and stood and listened to what the crowds were saying; presently somebody would have glanced at her, and then at the picture, and then back at her again, in excitement and a little awe, and the blood would have started climbing to Beauty's cheeks, and even to her forehead; it would have been one of life's great moments. Call it vanity, but she was like that; "professional beauties" were amateur actresses, performing upon a larger stage with the help of newspapers and illustrated magazines. "I'll send her a ticket and tell her to come," said Robbie, who found her foibles diverting.

A further idea occurred to him, and he said to his son: "Do you remember what Beauty once told you about a painting that made my father angry?" Yes, that was one of the things Lanny wasn't going to forget—not in this incarnation! He said so, and Robbie inquired: "Would you be interested to see it?"

The youth was staggered. Somehow the idea seemed rather horrible. And with Rick along too! But he told himself that this was an old-fashioned attitude, unworthy of a connoisseur of art. Surely Rick would feel that way about it. So Lanny replied: "I would, of course."

"I've been told where it was. If it's been sold, maybe you can find out where it's gone." Robbie gave the name of one of the fashionable dealers on the Rue de la Paix, and told him to ask for the "Lady with a Blue Veil," by Oscar Deroulé. "You don't have to say that you know anything about it," added the father.

The two fellows set out. Lanny had to make some explanation, for of course Rick would recognize the portrait. Lanny couldn't say that he was an illegitimate son, and that this painting was to blame for it—no, that would be too much for even the coldest-blooded connoisseur! He said: "My mother posed for several painters when she was young, and I guess my father thinks I'm old enough to know about it now."

"Well, you surely can't blame the painters," was Rick's consoling reply.

V

The decorous and black-clad picture dealer found nothing out of the way in the fact that two young gentlemen wanted to see the "Lady with a Blue Veil" by Oscar Deroulé. It was his business to show pictures; a clerk went down some stairs and brought it up, and set it on a stand for them to look at, and then went to attend to another customer. So they had it to themselves, and no need to repress their feelings. "Oh, my God!" exclaimed Rick; and Lanny's heart hit him several blows underneath his throat.

There was Mabel Blackless, as she was in those days, just ripened into womanhood, a creature of such loveliness as made men catch their breath. The painter who had done her was a lover of the flesh, and had set himself to exploiting its lusciousness; the creams and whites and pinks, the velvety texture, the soft curves, the delicately changing shadows. Beauty was seated upon a silk-covered couch, half supported by one arm. There was a light blue veil across her hips, and the shower of her hair fell over one shoulder, half hiding a breast; she was in bright sunlight, and the fine strands gleamed like gold—not such an easy thing for a painter to get.

These were the modern days—they always are—and when a woman went swimming at Juan, she put on a fairly light bathing suit, and when it was wet it clung tightly, so really there wasn't so much in the picture that Lanny didn't know already. One thing he had never seen was her breasts, with nipples of delicate pink; he couldn't help thinking: "So that is where I was nourished!" He thought: "God, what a strange thing life is!" He confronted once more that most bewildering of ideas: "I was her accident! If it hadn't happened, where would I have been?"

He looked at the date in the corner of the painting; it was 1899, and he knew it was just before Robbie had come along and started him upon his strange journey into the present. Now, by the magic of art, the son could stand and look at the past; but no magic would enable him to look into the future, and know what he was going to do with his own power to create life. Were there baby souls waiting in the unknown, for him to decide whether or not they were to be?

His friend saw how deeply stirred he was; the blood had a way of mounting into Lanny's cheeks, just as you saw recorded in the portrait of his mother. Rick tried to ease him down by discussing the work from the technical point of view. Finally he allowed himself to remark: "If I owned that painting I don't think I'd ever marry. I'd expect too much!"

Lanny's reply was: "I think I'm the one who ought to own it." He recalled his father's wish to buy him something; and now he knew what it was going to be. When the dealer rejoined them he inquired: "What is the price of this painting?"

The man looked at him, and then pretended to look on the back of the painting. The artist was not a well-known one, and the price was thirty-two hundred francs, or six hundred and forty dollars. "I will take it," Lanny said. "I will pay you two hundred francs down, and if you send the painting to the Hotel Crillon this evening, I will have the rest." The dealer knew then that he should have asked a higher price, but it was too late.

When Lanny told his father what he had done, the latter was much amused. "Do you want to take it to America?"

Lanny laughed in turn. "I thought Beauty and I ought to have it. I'll send it to her, and she can stick it away with Marcel's work."

"It's a queer sort of a present," said Robbie, "but if it's what you want, O.K. There are half a dozen paintings of Beauty somewhere in the world, and you might hunt them up." Then the shrewd businessman added: "Buy options for two years, and you'll get some bargains that'll surprise you. The franc has been pegged, but it won't hold after the war!"

VI

The tongues of the two young men were loosened and they talked about love. Lanny told of his happiness with Rosemary, now almost a year past. He didn't have a right to say how far they had gone—but he found that Rosemary had told Rick's sister, and she in turn had told Rick. These young people had few secrets; their "emancipation" took the form of voluminous talk, and it was a mark of enlightenment to employ the plainest words.

When Lanny said he hadn't been able to be interested in any other girl, Rick told him it was hard luck that he had aimed too high. "I mean," he added, hastily, "from the English point of view. Her family puts on a lot of side. Of course, it's all bally rot; perhaps we'll sack the lot of them before this war is over."

Lanny told what his father had said to Zaharoff, that it might end as it had in Russia; to which Rick replied in his free and easy way that he'd take his chances with a new deal. He informed his friend

that the Codwilliger family was planning for Rosemary to marry
the oldest grandson of the very old Earl of Sandhaven; the grandson was the future heir, since his father had been killed in the same
siege of Gallipoli where Rosemary's father had been wounded.
Lanny could see how useless it was for him to hope—that is, of
course, from the English point of view. He gathered the impression
that he had been greatly honored by having had the future mother
of an earl for a temporary sweetheart.

It was Rick's turn to open his heart. "I've been meaning to tell
you, Lanny—I'm married."

"*What?*" cried the other, amazed.

"The night before I left for France. It's quite a long story. If
you want to hear it——"

"Oh, do I, Rick!"

The baronet's son had come to London to enlist in the Royal
Flying Corps, and at the home of one of his school friends had met
a girl just his age, a student at a college not far from his training
camp. They had hit it off together, and used to meet whenever
Rick had free time. "We talked about love," he said, "and I told
her I'd never had a girl. Of course all the chaps want to have one
before they go to the front—and all the girls want to have them, it
seems. She said she'd try it with me, and we were both quite happy
—only of course there wasn't very much time."

Rick paused. "And then?" said Lanny.

"Well, I knew I was going across in a week or so; and Nina—her
name is Nina Putney—told me she wanted to have a baby. I mightn't
come back—lots of the fellows have been downed on their first
flight."

"I know," said Lanny.

"I said: 'What will you do, alone?' And she said: 'I know what
I want. I can take care of it somehow.' She has a sister who's an
interior decorator, and would take her in. You know people don't
pay so much attention to illegitimacy in wartime; they make excuses. And Nina broke down—she said she had to have something
to remember me by. I couldn't very well say no."

"Is she going to have it?"

"So she writes me."

"You married her before that?"

"I thought I ought to tell the pater; if he was going to have a grandchild, he'd want to be sure about it. He looked up the family and found out they were all right—I mean, what he calls all right—so then he said we ought to get married. So we got a special license and went over to the church, the night before I reported for duty."

"Oh, Rick, what a story! Do you think she's a girl you'll be happy with?"

"I suppose we've as good a chance as most couples. Nina's game, and says she'll never hold me to it. She swears she wasn't trying to rope me in, and if I ever say it, she'll drop me flat." The young flying officer smiled a rather wry smile.

"You're supposed to be something of a catch, aren't you, Rick—I mean from the English point of view?"

Rick could talk about the social position of the Codwilliger family, but not of the Pomeroy-Nielsons. "The pater says we'll lose The Reaches if they keep piling war taxes on him. And what price a baronet if you have to live in lodgings?"

VII

Lanny was excited, of course. He wanted to know about Nina, and what she looked like—Rick had a little picture, which showed a slender, birdlike person with an eager, intense expression. Lanny admired her, and Rick was pleased. Lanny asked what she was studying, and about her family—her father was a barrister, but not a successful one; she would be one of these new women who had careers of their own, kept their own names, and so on. None of this clinging sort.

Lanny said that his father was taking him to London soon. Could he meet her? Rick said: "Of course."

"Could I give her a present, do you suppose? Would she like some picture that we could pick up for her?"

"You'd better wait," laughed the other, "and see what happens to me. If I'm put out, you'd better give her a baby basket."

"I'll give her both!" Lanny had recently become aware of the fact that his father had a pile of money.

"No Caliph of Bagdad business!" countered his friend. "You pick out a book that may keep her from being lonely, and write something in it, so she can remember you when you marry an oil princess in Connecticut."

"There isn't any oil in Connecticut, Rick."

"Well, nutmegs then. Your father says it's called the Nutmeg State. You'll make a whole crop of new princesses out of this war. They'll be bored, and they'll be crazy about you because you speak French, and dance, and have culture—you'll rank with a marquis or a Russian grand duke in exile."

Lanny was amused by this picture of himself in New England. He wanted to say: "They'll find out that I'm a bastard." But his lips were sealed.

Half a day, a night, and another day; never had thirty hours moved with such speed! They went to the Comédie Française, and sat in a box; they had a meal at midnight, and Robbie ordered an extra bottle of wine. They strolled on the boulevards in the morning, luxuriating in the sunshine, watching the crowds and gazing at the fine things for sale. Lanny bought a stock of chocolates, the one thing Rick admitted the chaps in the air force would appreciate. They picked up an old-fashioned open carriage with a bony but lively horse, and were driven about the Bois and the main boulevards, looking at historic buildings and remembering what they could of events. Rick knew a little about everything; he had all his old assurance, his worldly manner which impressed his younger friend so greatly.

Robbie came back to the hotel, feeling good, because Zaharoff's factotum had given way, and the other companies were giving way, and Robbie was collecting signatures on dotted lines. Lanny had to ask him not to be too exultant until Rick was gone. "You know how it is, he's giving his life, maybe, while we're making money."

"All right," said the salesman, with one of his chuckles. "I'll be good; but you tell Rick that if his old man wants to sell The Reaches, you'll buy it!" No use asking Robbie to shed any tears over the English aristocracy. They had had their day, and now the American businessmen were to have theirs. Gangway!

However, Robbie was very decent when the time for parting came. He had a big package delivered to Rick's room, and told him not to open it until he got back to camp. He told Lanny it contained cigarettes; the baronet's son would be the darling of the corps wing for a time. Robbie shook hands with him, and said "Cheerio," in the approved English fashion.

Lanny went to the train, and had tears in his eyes, he just couldn't help it. It would have been very bad form for Rick to have them; he said: "Thanks, old chap, you've been perfectly bully to me." And then: "Take care of yourself, and don't let the subs get you."

"Write me a post card every now and then," pleaded Lanny. "You know how it is, if I don't hear from you, I'll worry."

"Don't do that," said Rick. "Whatever comes, that's what comes." It was the nearest a modern man could approach to having a philosophy.

"Well, look out for the Fokkers—get them first!"

"Right-o!" The whistle blew, and Rick bolted, just in time for the train and for the honor of the Royal Flying Corps. Lanny stood, with tears flowing freely. "Good-by, Rick! Good-by!" His voice died into a sort of sob as the train moved on, and the face of Eric Vivian Pomeroy-Nielson disappeared, perhaps forever. That was the dreadful thing about wartime, you couldn't part from anybody without the thought: "I'll probably not see him again!"

VIII

The youth kept talking about this depressing idea until it worried his father. "You know, kid," he remarked, "you just can't be too soft in this world. It's painful to think of people getting killed, and I don't know the answer, except that maybe we put too much value on human life; we try to make more out of it than nature allows. This is certain, if you're too sensitive, and suffer too much, you wreck your own happiness, and maybe your health, and then what are you worth to yourself or anybody else?"

That was something to think about, and the youngster put his mind on it. What was the use of practicing the arts, of understanding and loving them, if you didn't dare let yourself feel? Manifestly, the purpose of art was to awaken feelings; but Robbie said you had to put them to sleep, or at any rate retire into a cave with them. Build yourself like a tortoise, with a hard shell around you, so that the world couldn't get hold of you to make you suffer!

Lanny voiced that, and the reply was: "Maybe it's a bad time for art right now. As I read history I see these periods come pretty frequently and last a long time, so you have to arm yourself somehow; unless, of course, you want to be a martyr, and die on a cross, or something like that. It makes good melodrama, or maybe great tragedy, but it's doggone uncomfortable while it's happening."

They were in their room, packing to leave for England; and Robbie said: "Sit down and let me tell you something I heard today." He lowered his voice, as if he thought that someone might be hiding in their room. Enemy ears are listening!

"Your friend is going off to fight the German Fokkers, and you're unhappy because they may get him. He's told you the Fokkers are fast and light, and that helps them, and may doom him. Do you know why they are so fast and light?'

"He says they're putting aluminum into them."

"Exactly. And where do they get it? What's it made from?"

"It's made out of bauxite, I know."

"And has Germany got any?"

"I don't know, Robbie."

"Few people know things like that; they don't teach them in the schools. Germany has very little, and she wants it badly, and pays high prices for it. Do you know who has it?"

"Well, I know that France has a lot, because Eddie Patterson drove me to the place where it's being mined." Lanny remembered this trip to a town called Brignolles, back from the coast; the reddish mineral was blasted from tunnels in a mountain, and brought down to the valley in great steel buckets rolling on a continuous wire cable. Lanny and his friend had been admitted to the place and had watched the stuff being dumped into lines of freight cars. It had been Lanny's first actual sight of big industry—unless you included the perfume factories in Grasse, where peasant women sat half buried in millions of rose leaves, amid an odor so powerful that a little of it sent you out with a headache.

Robbie went on with his story. "To make bauxite into aluminum takes electric power. Those lines of freight cars that you saw were taken to Switzerland, which has cheap power from its mountain streams. There the aluminum is made; and then it goes—can you guess?"

"To Germany?"

"It goes to whatever country bids the highest price for it; and Germany is in the market. So if your friend is brought down by a faster airplane, you'll know the reason. Also you'll know why your father keeps urging you not to tear your heart out over this war."

"But, Robbie!" The son's voice rose with excitement. "Something ought to be done about a thing like that!"

"Who's going to do it?"

"But it's treason!"

"It's business."

"Who are the people that are doing it?"

"A big concern, with a lot of stockholders; its shares are on the market, anybody can buy them who has the money. If you look up the board of directors, you'll find familiar names—that is, if you follow such things. You find Lord Booby, and you say: 'Zaharoff!' You see the Duc de Pumpkin, and you say: 'Schneider,' or perhaps 'de Wendel.' You see Isaac Steinberg, or some such name, and you say: 'Rothschild.' They have their directors in hundreds of different companies, all tied together in a big net—steel, oil, coal, chemicals, shipping, and, above all, banks. When you see those names, you might as well butt your brains out against a stone wall as try to stop them, or even to expose them—because they own the newspapers."

"But, Robbie," protested the youth, "doesn't it make any difference to those men whether the Germans take France?"

"They're building big industry, and they'll own it and run it. Whatever government comes in will have to have money, and will make terms with them, and business will go on as it's always done. It's a steam roller; and what I'm telling my son is, be on it and not under it!"

IX

The English and the French had made for themselves a sort of chicken run across the English Channel; a wide lane, fenced with heavy steel netting hung from two lines of buoys, and protected by mines. Back and forth through that lane went the troopships, the hospital ships, the freighters, the packet boats with passengers. Up and down the lines patrolled torpedo boats and destroyers, mine sweepers and trawlers; lookouts swept the sea with glasses, and gunners stood by their quick-firers, ready at a moment's notice to swing them into action. Overhead were airplanes humming, and silver blimps slowly gliding. The submarine campaign was at its peak, and the Allies were going back to the ancient system of convoys for merchant ships. They were doing it here, with fleets of slow-moving vessels laden with coal for France, escorted by armed trawlers.

At night the destroyers raced up and down, their searchlights flashing, making the scene bright almost as day. But the packet boats showed no lights, and passengers were not allowed on deck; you went on board after dark, and were escorted to your stateroom, and advised to sleep with your clothes on, and be sure to practice adjusting the life preserver which was overhead in your berth. Your porthole was sealed tightly with a dark cover, and to open it or show a light was a prison offense. You heard the sounds of departure, and felt the vibration of the screw and the tossing of the vessel. You slept, if your nerves were sound, and when you woke up you were in England, if your luck was reasonably good.

London in wartime was full of bustle, serious but not afraid. "Never say die," was the motto. England would follow her usual rule of losing every battle but the last. The theaters and the cinemas were crowded. Everybody was at work, both men and women; hours were long and wages high; the people of the slums had enough to eat for the first time in their lives. Lanny wondered: was that the solution to the problem of poverty and unemployment—to put everybody at work trying to blow some other people up?

Robbie had important men waiting to see him. There was no way for Lanny to help him; no more codes or ciphers now—whatever cablegrams you sent had to be in plain words, and signed by your full name; better not use any words the censor didn't know, and not too many figures. Robbie told a story about a man who tried to cable that he had purchased 12,462,873 sables; the military intelligence department got busy to find out how he had managed to get more sables than there were in the world.

Lanny had two young ladies to call on. Rosemary first, of course. She had got her heart's desire, and was working as a nurse. They called her a "student," but there wasn't much difference in these days, you went right to work, and learned by doing. She was in a big hospital which until recently had been a school. Her hours were long, and leave was hard to get; but when you are the granddaughter of an earl, you can manage things in England, even in wartime.

Toward sundown he went to meet her, expecting to see her in a nurse's costume of white; but she had changed to a blue chiffon dress and a little straw hat with blue cornflowers in it. The sight of her started something to tingling inside him. How lovely life could be, even with death ruling the world!

They walked in a near-by park, and she tried her best to be cool and matter of fact. But there was something between her and this young American that wasn't easy to control. They sat on a bench, and Lanny looked at her, and saw that she was afraid to meet his eyes, and that her lips were trembling.

"Have you missed me a little, Rosemary?"

"More than a little."

"I haven't been able to think about anybody else."

"Let's not talk about it, Lanny."

So he chatted for a while, telling her about Rick's brief holiday in Paris. He talked about his coming trip to America, and the reasons for it. "My father says we're surely coming into the war." Congress was then in session, and a fierce debate was going on; there might be a vote at any hour.

"Better late than never," replied Rosemary. The English in those days had become extremely impatient with the letter-writing of President Wilson.

"You mustn't blame me for it," said he. "But if we do come in, things will change quickly." He waited a reasonable time, then asked, with a smile: "If we do, Rosemary, will that make any difference in the way your parents feel about us colonials?"

"All that's so complicated, Lanny. Let's talk about nice agreeable things."

"The nicest agreeable thing I know is sitting on a park bench with the twilight falling about her and an evening star right in front of her eyes, and I haven't the least desire to talk about anything else. Tell me, darling: has there been any other man in your heart in the past eleven months?"

"There are hundreds of them, Lanny. I'm trying to help our poor boys back to life—or ease them out of it not too horribly."

"I know, dear," he said. "I've lived in the house with a war casualty for more than two years. But one can't work all the time, surely; one has to have a little fun."

Lanny didn't know England very well. He knew that the "lower orders" lay around in the parks in broad daylight; but just how dark did it have to be for a member of the nobility to permit a young man to take her hand, or put his arm around her on a park bench? He tried gently, and she did not repel him. Presently they were sitting close together, and the old mysterious spell renewed itself. Perhaps an hour passed; then he said: "Can't we go somewhere, Rosemary?"

Robbie had said: "Take her to one of the cheaper hotels; they don't ask questions." Robbie was practical on the subject of sex, as upon all others. He said there were three things a young fellow had to look out for: he mustn't get any girl into trouble; he mustn't get mixed up with any married woman unless he was sure the husband didn't care; and he mustn't get any disease. When Lanny had reassured him on these points, he said: "If you don't show up tonight, I won't worry."

X

So Lanny and Rosemary went strolling; and when they came to a place where they weren't apt to meet any of their fashionable friends, they went in, and he registered as Mr. and Mrs. Brown, and paid in advance, and no questions were asked. When they lay in the embrace which was so full of rapture for them both, they forgot the sordid surroundings, they forgot everything except that their time was short. Lanny was going out to face the submarines on the open ocean, and Rosemary was going to France, where the screaming shells paid no heed to a red cross on a woman's arm.

"Gather ye rosebuds while ye may, Old time is still a flying." Thus the English poet. The German has said: *"Pflücket die Rose, Eh' sie verblüht."* So there was one thing about which the two nations could agree. In countless cheap hotels in Berlin, as in London, the advice was being followed; and the wartime custom was no different in Paris—if you could accept the testimony of Napoleon Bonaparte, who had stood on the field of Eylau, observing the heaps of the slaughtered and remarking: "One night in Paris will remedy all that."

Their happiness was long-enduring, and nothing in the outside world was permitted to disturb it. Not even loud banging noises, all over the city—one of them very close by. Lanny made a joke of it: "I hope that's not some morals police force after us." The girl explained that those were anti-aircraft warnings, made by "maroons," a kind of harmless bomb made of heavy paper wrapped with twine.

They lay still in the dark and listened. Presently came louder explosions, and some of them were near, too. "Anti-aircraft guns,"
said Rosemary; she knew all the sounds. There came dull, heavy
crashes, and she told him those were the bombs. "You don't have
to worry unless it's a direct hit."

"You surely can't worry if it is," said Lanny. It was his first
time under fire, and he wanted to take it in the English manner.

"About as much risk as in a thunderstorm," said Rosemary. "The
silly fools think they can frighten us by wrecking a house here and
there and killing half a dozen harmless people in their beds."

"I suppose those'll be planes?" asked the youth.

"From occupied Belgium. The Zepps have stopped coming entirely."

The uproar grew louder, and presently there was a sharp cracking sound, and some of the glass in the window of their room fell
onto the floor. That was getting sort of close! "A piece of shrapnel,"
said Rosemary. "They don't have much force, because the air resistance stops them."

"You know all about it!" smiled Lanny.

"Naturally; I help to fix people up. I'll have some new cases in
the morning."

"None tonight, I hope, dear."

"Kiss me, Lanny. If we're going to die, let it be that way."

The uproar died away even more suddenly than it had come;
they slept awhile, and early in the morning, when they got up,
Lanny found a fragment of a shell near the broken window. It
wasn't much more than an inch square, but had unpleasantly jagged
edges. He said: "I'll keep it for a souvenir, unless you want it."

"We get plenty of them," replied the student nurse.

"Maybe it's a Budd." He knew, of course, that the British were
using Budd shrapnel. "I'll see if my father can tell."

"They gather up the pieces and use them again," explained Rosemary.

That was her casual way. She told him to phone her or wire her as to when he would be sailing. She didn't know if she could get another leave, but she would try.

They went outside, and heard newsboys shouting, and saw posters in large letters: "U.S.A. IN WAR!" "AMERICA JOINS!" While the scion of Budd Gunmakers had been gathering rosebuds with the granddaughter of Lord Dewthorpe, the Senate of the United States had voted a declaration to the effect that a condition of war already existed between that country and Germany.

XI

It was a pleasant time to be in London. There were celebrations in the streets, and the usually self-contained islanders were hunting for some American, so that they could shake him by the hand and say: "Thanks, old chap, this is grand, we're all brothers now, and when will you be coming over?" Lanny asked his father if this would help him in getting contracts; Robbie said they'd expect him to give the patents now—but no such instructions had come from Newcastle, Connecticut!

Lanny went to call on Nina Putney, still a student in college in spite of being married. He took her to lunch, and they had a long talk. She was a brunette, slender and delicate, with sensitive, finely cut features. She seemed more like a French girl than an English one; she was like Lanny, eager and somewhat impetuous; she said what she felt, and then perhaps wished she hadn't. The two could get along easily, because they shared the same adoration, and wanted to talk about it.

Nina told about her meeting with the most wonderful of would-be fliers, whose dream had since come true. He might be in the air now—oh, God, at this moment he might be in a death duel with one of the German Fokkers, so light and fast because they were made of aluminum manufactured in Switzerland from French bauxite! Lanny didn't tell the young bride about that; but a shadow hung over their meeting, and what could he say? He couldn't deny the mortal danger, or that it would last, day after day. No comfort that an airman came back alive, because he would be going out again so soon.

Business as usual! Lanny and Nina promised to write to each other, for Rick's sake, and she would tell him whatever news she got. America would hurry up, and this dreadful war would be won, and they would all live happy ever after. So, good-by, Nina, and take good care of that baby, and you're to have a basket, and remember, Budd's will stand back of you!

Robbie said he'd have all his affairs wound up in a couple of days, and no use to linger and be a target even for Budd shrapnel. He had engaged a stateroom, and Lanny, the lady-killer, might gather as many rosebuds as possible in that brief interim. He phoned to Rosemary, and she said, yes, she'd get away once more, even if they fined her for it. They went to the same hotel and got the same room—the pane of glass patched with brown paper. Once more they were happy, after the fashion that war permits—*amor inter arma;* concentrating on one moment, refusing to let the mind roam or the eye peer into the future.

In the morning, clinging to him, the girl said: "Lanny, you've been a darling, and I'll never forget you. Write me, and let me know how things go, and I'll do the same."

No more than that. She wouldn't talk about marriage; she would go on patching broken English bodies, and he would visit the home of his fathers, and come back as a soldier, or perhaps to sell armaments—who could say? "Good-by, dear; and do help us to win!"

So Lanny was through; and it was a good time to be leaving. The British were beginning their spring offensive, which would be drowned in mud and hung on barbed wire and mowed down by machine guns in the usual depressing way. The French had a new commander, Nivelle, and he would lead them into a slaughter that would bring the troops to the verge of mutiny. Away from all that!

They took a boat train at night, and went on board a steamship in darkness and silence. They knew they were being towed out into a harbor, and that tugs were pulling steel nets with buoys out of the way. But they couldn't see a thing, because the deck was covered with a shroud of burlap. They sat outside for a long while, listening to the sounds of the sea and conversing in whispers; not much chance to sleep, and nothing you could do. Everyone tried hard to seem unconcerned. Some men shut themselves up in their cabins and drank themselves insensitive; others played cards in the saloon and pretended not to care about death.

"Westward the star of empire takes its way," said Robbie. He was telling his son that they were off to God's country, the place to stay in, to believe in. He was telling him not to miss the grand-daughter of an earl too much; there were plenty of delightful demo-cratic maidens at home. He was saying that Europe was worn out; it would owe all its money to America, and collecting it would be fun. Yes, they were sitting pretty—unless by chance there should come a pale streak of foam out there on the starlit ocean, and a shattering explosion beneath them!

BOOK FOUR

Land of the Pilgrims' Pride

19

Old Colonial

I

THE city of Newcastle, Connecticut, lies at the mouth of the Newcastle River, and has a comfortable harbor, not muddy except in springtime. It has a highway bridge across the harbor, and beyond it a railroad bridge, both having "draws" so that ships may go up. The Budd plant lies above the bridges, and has a railroad spur running into it. Above the plant are salt marshes, which the progenitor of the family had the forethought to buy for a few dollars an acre. Everybody called him crazy at the time, but as a result of his forethought his descendants had both land and landings, by the simple process of putting a steam dredge at work running channels into the marsh and piling earth on both sides. In the year 1917 you could not have bought an acre of this salt marsh for ten thousand dollars.

As a result, the city had only one direction in which to grow; which meant that rents were high and working-class districts crowded. The families which had owned farms in that direction had either sold them, and moved away and been forgotten, or else they had leased the land, in which case they constituted the aristocracy of Newcastle, owning stock in banks and department stores, water and gas and electric companies, street railways and telephones. As a further result, Newcastle had remained a small city, and many of the workers in Budd's lived in near-by towns and came to the plant on "trolley cars."

In fact only a small part of Budd's itself was at Newcastle. Farther up the river were dams, and here the company made cartridges and fuses. The dams had locks, and motor barges took raw materials up and brought finished products down. This enabled Lanny's grandfather to say that he disapproved of the modern tendency toward congestion in great cities. Also it enabled him to get much cheaper labor.

In the state of Ohio, once known as the "Western Reserve" and settled largely by people from Connecticut, the Budds had a powder plant. In the state of Massachusetts they had recently bought a six-story cotton mill with a dam and power plant, the concern having gone into bankruptcy because of competition in Georgia and the Carolinas; this plant was now making hand grenades. In a somewhat smaller furniture factory they were setting up a cartridge plant. In the salt marshes of Newcastle ground was being made for new structures which would enable them to double their output of machine guns. So it went; the government was advancing the money to concerns which had the skill and could turn out instruments of war quickly.

All these deals had been arranged and plans laid months in advance, and many contracts were signed before war had been declared or funds voted by Congress. By the time Lanny arrived at Newcastle, all the men of the Budd family were under heavy pressure, working day and night, and talking about nothing but the war and the contribution they were making to it. Nearly everyone in the town was in the same mental state, and this afforded an opportunity for a stranger to slip in unobserved, and have time to adjust himself to an unknown world. Nobody would bother him; indeed, unless he made a noise they would hardly know he was there.

II

Until recently Robbie and his family had occupied an old Colonial house in the residential part of Newcastle. But there was a transformation going on all over New England. Motorcars had become so dependable, and hard-surfaced roads so good, that it was getting to be the fashion to buy a farm and turn it into a country estate; your friends did the same, and collectively built a country club

with a golf course, and thus had the advantages of town and country life. You got blooded rams, bulls, and boars; you produced milk
and strawberries and asparagus. You were called a "gentleman
farmer," and not merely had fresh air, space, and privacy, but you
tried to make it pay, and if you succeeded you bragged to all your
friends.

The population of such districts consisted of a "gentry," and a
great number of tenants and servants, all contented and respectable,
and all voting Tory, though it was called "Republican." What
Lanny saw of "New" England turned out to be much like Old
England. The scenery resembled that "green and pleasant land,"
where he had enjoyed long walks in the springtime three years ago.
There were country lanes and stone walls and small streams with
mill dams, and old farmhouses and churches that were shown as
landmarks. To be sure, some of the trees were different, high-arching
white elms and flowering dogwood soon to be in party costume;
also, the dialect of the country people was different—but these were
details.

The new house of the Robbie Budds stood at the head of an archway of elms more than a hundred years old. The farmhouse orig-
inally on the spot had been moved to one side and made into a
garage with chauffeur's and gardener's quarters above. A new house
had been built, modern inside, but keeping the "old Colonial" pattern. It had two stories and a half, and what was called a "gambrel"
roof, starting at a steep pitch, and, when it got halfway up, finishing
at a flatter pitch. In front of the house were big white columns
which went above the second story; at one side were smaller columns over a porte-cochere.

Inside, the house was plain, everything painted white. The furniture was of a sort Lanny had never seen before; it also was "old
Colonial," and he was to hear conversation about it, and learn the
difference between "highboys" and "lowboys," and what a "court
cupboard" was, and a "wing-chair," and a "ball and claw." Everything in the house had its proper place and to move it was bad manners. This had been explained to Lanny by his father; Esther had

strict ideas of propriety. He should not play the piano loudly, at
least not without asking if he would disturb anyone. He would
make things easier if he would go to church with the family.
Above all, he must be careful not to speak plainly about anything
having to do with the relationship of men and women; Esther tried
her best to be "modern" but she just couldn't, and it was better not
to put any strain upon her. Lanny promised.

III

He had seen pictures of her, so he knew her when he saw her
standing at the head of the stairs, with the big grandfather's clock
behind her. It was an important moment for her as well as for him,
and both of them realized it. She was becoming a stepmother, one
of the most difficult of human relationships; she was taking a
stranger into her perfectly ordered home, one from a culture foreign to hers and greatly suspected. He was young and he was weak,
yet he had a power which could not be disregarded, having entered
her husband's life ahead of her and sunk deep roots into his heart.

Esther Remson Budd was thirty-five at this time. She was a daughter of the president of the First National Bank of Newcastle, a Budd
institution. She had lived most of her life in the town, and her ideas
of Europe were derived from a summer of travel with teachers and
members of her class in a young ladies' finishing school. She was
one of the most conscientious of women, and gave earnest thought
to being just and upright. She was not cold, but made herself seem
so by subjecting to careful consideration everything she did and
said. She was charitable, and active in the affairs of the First Congregational Church, in which her father-in-law taught a men's Bible
class every Sunday morning. She guided her three children lovingly
but strictly, and did her best to use wisely the powers which wealth
and social position gave her.

To Esther at the age of twenty-one Robbie Budd had been a figure of romance. He went abroad frequently, met important people,
and came home with contracts, the report of which spread widely—

for hardly a person in that town could prosper except as Budd's prospered, and when Robbie sold automatics to Rumania, the merchants of Newcastle ordered a fresh stock of goods, and Esther's father bought her an electric coupé, a sort of showcase to drive about town in. Everybody she knew wanted her to marry Robbie; most of the girls had tried and failed, and knew there was some mystery, some story of a broken heart.

The time came when Robbie took Esther for a long drive and told her about the mysterious woman in France, the artists' model who had been painted in the nude by several men—a strange kind of promiscuity, wholly outside the possibilities of Newcastle, which in its heart was still a Puritan village. There was a child, but the woman refused to marry him and wreck his life. He had ended the unhappy affair, which was then about five years old; he had done so because he saw it preyed upon his father's mind, it could not possibly be fitted into the lessons imparted to the men's Bible class. Robbie would ask Esther to marry him, but only after she knew about this situation, and understood that he had a son and would not disown him.

The two families were working busily to make this match. Did the president of Budd's give his friend, the president of the First National Bank, some hint of the problem? Or did the latter guess what might have happened to a handsome and wealthy young businessman in Paris? Anyhow, Esther's father had a talk with her, of a sort unusual in Puritan New England. He told her the facts of life as concerning future husbands. Among the so-called "eligible" men of the town, those slightly older than herself and able to support her in the position to which she had been accustomed, she would have difficulty in finding one who had not had to do with some woman. The difference between Robbie Budd and most others was that they didn't consider it necessary to tell their future brides about the wild oats they had sown.

Esther asked for time to think all this over, and in the end she and Robbie were married. It had been thirteen years now, and they had three children, and Esther was as near to happiness as any of the "young matrons" she knew. Robbie played golf while his wife went to church, and he drank more liquor than she considered wise; but he was indifferent to the charms of the country club's seductresses, he let her have her way entirely with the children, and he gave her more money than she had use for. On the whole she could count herself a fortunate wife.

But now came this one wild oat of her husband, to be transplanted into her garden and to grow there. She was compelled to face the circumstances which had brought this about. If Lanny was going into an army, it obviously ought to be the American army; and if he came to America, and was denied his father's home, that would be a repudiation and an affront. To say that Robbie had had a previous marriage in France was one of those conventional lies that were hardly lies at all. Women would smile behind their fans, and whisper; but after all there has to be a statute of limitations on scandals.

IV

So Esther was standing at the top of the white-paneled staircase with the grandfather's clock behind her. She was tall and rather slender; she held herself erect, and was quiet and grave in manner. She had straight brown hair, drawn back from a high forehead in defiance of fashion's edicts. Her nose was a little too long and thin, but the rest of her features were regular and her smile kindly. Her brown eyes appraised Lanny, and she kissed him on the cheek. She had made up her just mind that she was going to treat him exactly like her own children, and Robbie had told Lanny that he was to call her "Mother."

She took him into her sitting room to get acquainted. He liked to talk, and was eager and friendly about it. He had been on a steamship which had been in peril of the submarines; he told how the passengers had behaved when they had struck a floating ice cake. He had been in London when it was bombed, and had a bit of shrapnel which had come through the window of a hotel room. (Of course he didn't say who had been in that room with him.) Esther, listening and watching, decided that he was intelligent, and if anything went wrong it could be explained to him. The load upon her mind grew lighter.

She took him to his room, which was in the rear. It was small, but had its own bath, and was alongside the rooms of her two boys. The walls were of pale blue, and the blankets on the single bed were the same. The rug in front of it was made by winding a long soft rope of braided rags into a spiral; his new mother explained that this was a "round-rug," and was an antique. She showed him the "highboy" in which he was to keep his shirts and such belongings. Esther knew the story of each old piece of furniture, which she had "picked up" on trips here and there in the country. Each of these adventures was important to her. As an art lover, Lanny could see that the pieces were well proportioned, and they must have been well made to be in use after a hundred years.

Outside it was warm, and the window of the room was open. There was a cherry tree close by, getting ready to bloom. A bird was singing in it with extraordinary vigor, and Lanny commented on this. Esther said it was a mocking-bird which came every season, and had arrived only a few days ago; not many of them reached New England. Lanny told about the nightingale which made its nest in the court at Bienvenu, and was treated as a member of the family. He had tried to write out all the notes it had sung, and now he would do the same for the mocking-bird. His new mother said this task would keep him busy. The mocking-bird said: "Kerchy, kerchy, kerchy, kerchy." Then it stopped and caught its breath and said: "You pay. You pay. You pay."

V

For months thereafter one of Lanny's adventures would be meeting his relatives. First came his two half-brothers, who attended a private school in town, and were taken every morning and called for in the afternoon. Robert junior was twelve, and Percy eleven; they were handsome boys, who knew how to move quietly about a well-ordered home. Of course they were curious about this new arrival from foreign parts. They took him out at once to show him their Belgian hares; also Prince, their fine German shepherd dog, which they called a "police dog," and which Lanny knew as an "Alsatian." Prince was formally introduced, and looked the new-comer over warily, smelled him thoroughly, and finally wagged his tail. That was important.

Then came Bess, who was nine; her school was near by, but she had a singing lesson that afternoon, and the chauffeur went for her after he had brought the boys. Bess was like her mother, tall for her years and slender, with the same thin nose and sober brown eyes. But she had not yet learned restraint; eagerness transformed her features. When she heard that Lanny had been where the sub-marines were she cried: "Oh, tell us about it!" She hung on every word, and Lanny found himself a young Marco Polo. "Oh, what did you do?" And: "What did you say?" And: "Weren't you dreadfully frightened?"

Lanny relived his own childhood through this half-sister. She asked him questions about his home and what he did there; about the war and the people he knew who had been in it; about the Christmas-card castle in Germany; about Greece, and the ruins, of which there were pictures in her school; about England, and the boat race, and the poor girl who hadn't had enough to eat, and the aviator who at this moment might be up in the air shooting at Ger-man planes with a machine gun—was it made by Budd's?

Not one detail escaped her; she would prove it if he left anything out the next time he told the story. And the teller became her hero, her idol; it was a case of love at first sight. He played the piano for her, he showed her how to dance "Dalcroze," and taught her the words of old songs. He made the French language come alive for her. The hour in the distant future when Bessie Budd first had to admit that this wonderful half-brother of hers was anything less than perfect would mark one of the tragedies of her stormy life.

VI

Comically different was Lanny's first meeting with his grand-father, Samuel Budd, which took place by appointment on the second evening after his arrival. Robbie escorted him to the old gentleman's home; impossible to subject a youth to such an ordeal alone. On the way the father told him what to do; not to talk too much, but to answer questions politely, and listen attentively. "It would have been better for me if I had always followed those rules," he said, with a trace of bitterness.

Robbie was driving and they were alone; so he could speak frankly, and it was time to do so. "People are what circumstances have made them, and they don't change very much after they are grown. Your grandfather is a stubborn person, as much so as the bricks of which his house is built, and you might as well butt your head against one as the other."

"I don't want to butt him," said the boy, both amused and wor-ried. "Tell me exactly what to do."

"Well, the first thing is to get clear that you are the fruit of sin."

From this remark Lanny realized that the quarrel which had wrecked his mother's life and separated him from his father was still going on, and that the wounds of it were festering in Robbie's heart. "Surely," the youth protested, "he can't blame me for what hap-pened then!"

"He will tell you about visiting the iniquity of the fathers upon the children unto the third and fourth generation."

"Who says that, Robbie?"

"It's somewhere in the Old Testament."

Lanny thought and then asked: "Just what does he want me to do?"

"He'll tell you that himself. All you have to do is to listen."

Another pause. Finally the son was moved to say: "I suppose he didn't want me to come to Newcastle?"

"He has agreed to accept you as one of his grandsons. And I think it is important that he should be made to do it."

"Well, whatever you say. I want to please you. But if you're doing it for my sake, you don't have to."

"I'm doing it for my own," said the other, grimly.

"It's been so many years, Robbie. Doesn't that count with him at all?"

"In the sight of the Lord a thousand years are as a day."

Most of the persons Lanny had met in his young life never said anything about the Lord, except as a metaphor or an expletive. Several had said in his hearing that they didn't believe any such Being existed. But now the thought came to Lanny that his father differed from these persons. Robbie believed that the Lord existed, and he didn't like Him.

VII

The president of Budd Gunmakers Corporation had been born in a red brick mansion on the residence boulevard which skirted the edge of Newcastle. He had lived in it all his life, and meant to die in it, regardless of automobiles, country clubs, and other changes of fashion. His butler had been his father's butler, and wasn't going to be changed, even though he was becoming tottery. There were electric lights in the house, but they were hung in old chandeliers. The hand-carved French walnut bookcases were oiled and polished until they shone, and behind their glass doors Lanny caught glimpses of books which he would have liked to examine. He knew this was a very old mansion, and that political as well as business history had been made in it; but it seemed strangely ugly and depressing.

The master was in his study, the ancient butler said, and Robbie led his son at once to the room. At a desk absorbed in some papers sat a man of seventy, solidly built and heavy, as if he did not exercise; partly bald, and having a considerable tuft of whitish gray hair underneath his chin, a style which Lanny had never seen before. He wore gold spectacles, and had creases between his heavy

gray eyebrows, which gave him a stern expression, cultivated perhaps for business purposes. From his desk it appeared that he had
carried home with him the burden of winning a war.

"Well, young man?" he said, looking up. He did not rise, and apparently didn't plan even to shake hands.

But to Lanny it seemed that a gentleman ought to shake hands
with his grandfather when he met him for the first time; so he went
straight to the desk and held out his hand, forcing the other to take
it. "How do you do, Grandfather?" he said; and as the answer appeared to come slowly he went on: "I have heard a great deal about
you, and I'm happy to meet you at last."

"Thank you," said the old gentleman, surprised by this cordiality.

"Everybody has been most kind to me, Grandfather," continued
Lanny, as if he thought his progenitor might be worrying about it.

"I am glad," said the other.

Lanny waited, and so did the old man; they gazed at each other,
a sort of duel of eyes. Robbie had told him not to talk; but something came to Lanny suddenly, a sort of inspiration. This old
munitions maker wasn't happy. He had to live in an ugly old house
and be burdened day and night with cares. He had an enormous
lot of power which other people were trying to get away from
him, and that made him suspicious, it forced him to be hard. But
he wasn't hard; underneath he was kind, and all you had to do
was to be kind to him, and not ask anything from him.

Lanny decided to follow that hunch. "Grandfather," he announced, "I think I am going to like America very much. I liked
England, and I've been surprised to find everything here so much
like England."

"Indeed, young man?"

"The best part of England, I mean. I hope I shan't see anything
like their terrible slums."

The elderly industrialist rose to the bait. "Our working people
are getting double wages now. You will see them wearing silk
socks and shirts, and buying themselves cars on the installment plan.
They will soon be our masters."

"I was told the same thing in England, sir. People complain about the taxes there. The owners of the great estates say that they are going to have to break them up. Do you think that will happen in this country?"

"Apparently we plan to finance our share of the war by means of loans," replied the president of Budd's. "It is a dangerous procedure."

"M. Zaharoff talked about that. He doesn't seem to object to war loans of any size. Maybe it is because he is getting so large a share of the proceeds."

"Ahem! Yes," said the grandfather. "I am happy to say that Budd's have not conducted their affairs on the same fly-by-night basis as Zaharoff."

The art of conversation is highly esteemed in France, and Lanny had acquired it. He had heard the worldly-wise Baroness de la Tourette declare that the one certain way to interest a man was to get him to talking about his own affairs. A beginning having been made in this case, Lanny went on to remark: "I find that Budd's have a very good reputation abroad, sir."

"Humph! They want our products just now."

"Yes, sir; but I mean with persons who are disinterested."

"Who, for example?"

"Well, M. Rochambeau. He spent a good part of his life in the Swiss diplomatic service, so he's very well informed. He has been most helpful to me during the two and a half years that I haven't been seeing Robbie. Anything I didn't understand about world affairs he was always kind enough to explain to me."

"You were fortunate."

"Yes, Grandfather. Before that there was M. Priedieu, the librarian at Mrs. Chattersworth's château. He helped to form my literary taste."

"What books did he give you, may I ask?"

"Stendhal and Montaigne, Corneille and Racine, and of course Molière."

"All French writers," said the deacon of the First Congregational

Church. "May I inquire whether any of your advisers ever mentioned a book called the Bible?"

"Oh, yes, sir. M. Rochambeau told me that I should study the New Testament. I had some difficulty in finding a copy on the Riviera."

"Did you read it?"

"Every word of it, sir."

"And what did you get out of it?"

"It moved me deeply; in fact it made me cry, four different times. You know it tells the same story four times over."

"I am aware of it," said the old gentleman, dryly. "Have you read the Old Testament?"

"No, sir; that is one of the unfortunate gaps in my education. They tell me you are conducting a Bible class."

"Every Sunday morning at ten o'clock. I am dealing with the First Book of Samuel, and would be pleased to have my grandson enroll."

"Thank you. I will surely come. M. Rochambeau tells me that the best Jewish literature is found in the Old Testament."

"It is much more than Jewish literature, young man. Do not forget that it is the Word of Almighty God, your heavenly Father."

VIII

All that time Robbie Budd had been sitting in silence, occupied with keeping his emotions from showing in his face. Of course he knew that this youngster had had a lot of practice in dealing with elderly gentlemen. Colonels and generals, cabinet ministers, senators, diplomats, bankers, they had come to Bienvenu, and sometimes it had happened that a boy had to make conversation until his mother got her nose powdered; or perhaps he had taken them for a sail, or for a walk, to show them the charms of the Cap. All this experience he had now put to use, apparently with success; for here sat the leader of the men's Bible class of the First Congregational Church of Newcastle, Connecticut, who was supposed to be saving the world for democracy, and had before him a portfolio of important papers contributory to that end; but he put his heavy fist on them, and set to work to save the soul of a seventeen-year-old bastard from a semi-heathen part of the world where you had difficulty in finding a copy of the sacred Word of God.

To this almost-lost soul he explained that the Scripture was a source, not merely of church doctrine, but of church polity; and that officers of the church—including Deacon Budd—were to be thought of as exemplars of Christian doctrine, from whom others might understand the nature of Conversion and the reality of Salvation. The deacon reached into the corner of his desk and produced a small pamphlet, yellowed with age, entitled *A Brief Digest of the Boston Confession of Faith.* "This," said he, "was composed by your great-great-grandfather for popular use as a simple statement of our basic faith. In it you will find clearly set forth that central truth of our religion—that there is no Salvation save in the blood of the Cross. For that guilt incurred by Adam's sin passed on into humanity together with the colossal iniquity of the accumulated sins through the ages has made all men hopelessly evil in God's sight, and deserving His just punishment of spiritual death. Outraged by human sin, the wrath of God has only been appeased by the atoning blood shed by His Son upon the Cross, and only by faith in the blood of Christ can any man find Salvation. No righteousness of life, no good deeds or kindly words, no service of fellow-men can offer any hope of Salvation. It is belief in that redeeming blood poured out on Calvary that alone can win God's forgiveness and save us from eternal death. I recommend the pamphlet as your introduction to the study of the true Old Gospel."

"Yes, Grandfather," said Lanny. He was deeply impressed. As in the case of Kurt explaining the intricacies of German philosophy, Lanny could not be sure how many of these striking ideas had been created by his remarkable progenitors.

Having thus performed his duty as a guardian of sound doctrine, the old gentleman allowed himself to unbend. "Your father tells me that you had a pleasant voyage."

"Oh, yes," replied the youth, brightening. "It couldn't have been pleasanter—except for the collision with an iceberg. Did Robbie tell you about that?"

"He overlooked it."

"It was such a small iceberg, I suppose it would be better to speak of it as a cake of ice. But it gave us quite a bump, and the ship came to a stop. Of course everybody's mind had been on submarines from the moment we left England, so they all thought we had been torpedoed, and there was a panic among the passengers."

"Indeed?"

"The strangest thing you could imagine, sir. I never saw people behave like that before. The women became hysterical, especially those in the third class. Those that had babies grabbed them up and rushed into the first-class saloon, and they all piled their babies in the middle of the floor. No one could imagine why they did that; I asked some of them afterwards, and they said they didn't know; some woman put her baby there, and the rest of them thought that must be the place for babies, so they laid them down there, and the babies were all squalling, and the women screaming, some of them on their knees praying, and some clamoring for the officers to save them—so much noise that the officers couldn't tell them that it was all right."

"A curious experience. And now, young man, may I ask what you plan to do with yourself in this new country?"

"Surely, Grandfather. Robbie wishes me to prepare for St. Thomas's, and he's going to get me a tutor."

"Do you really intend to work?"

"I always work hard when I get down to it. I wanted to be able to read music at sight, and I have stayed at it until I can read most anything."

"These are serious times, and few of us have time for music."

"I'm going to learn whatever my tutor wishes, Grandfather."

"Very well; I'll look to hear good reports."

There was a pause. Then the old man turned to his son. "Robert," said he, "I've been looking into this vanadium contract, and it strikes me as a plain hold-up."

"No doubt," said Robbie. "But we're getting our costs plus ten percent, so we don't have to worry."

"I don't like to pass a swindle like this on to the government."

"Well, the dealers have their story. Everybody's holding up everybody all along the line."

"I think you'd better go down to New York and inquire around."

"If you say so. I have to go anyhow, on account of that new bomb-sight design."

"It seems to be standing the tests?"

They went on for quite a while, talking technical details. Lanny was used to such talk, and managed to learn something. In this case he learned that an elderly businessman who got his church doctrine and polity from eighteen hundred years ago, and his chin whiskers and chandeliers from at least a hundred years ago, would change a bomb-sight or the formula for a steel alloy the moment his research men showed him evidence of an improvement.

At last the grandfather said: "All right. I have to get back to work."

"You're carrying too much of a load, Father," ventured Robbie. "You ought to leave some of these decisions to us young fellows."

"We'll be over the peak before long. I'll hold up this vanadium deal for a day, and you run up to New York. Good-by, young man"—this to Lanny—"and see that you come to my Bible class."

"Surely, Grandfather," replied the youth. But already the elder's eyes were turning toward that pile of papers on his desk.

The other two went out and got into the car, and Robbie started to drive. Lanny waited for him to speak; then he discovered that the vibration of the seat was not from the engine, but was his father shaking with laughter.

"Did I do the right thing, Robbie?"

"Grand, kid, perfectly grand!" Robbie shook some more, and then asked: "Whatever put it into your head to talk?"

"Did I say too much?"

"It was elegant conversation—but what made you think of it?"

"Well, I'll tell you. I just decided that people aren't kind enough to each other."

The father thought that over. "Maybe it was worth trying," he admitted.

20

The Pierian Spring

I

NORMAN HENRY HARPER was the name of Lanny's tutor. He didn't in the least resemble the elegant and easygoing Mr. Elphinstone, nor yet the happy-go-lucky Jerry Pendleton. He was a professional man, and performed his duties with dignity. He prepared young men to pass examinations. He already knew about the examinations; he found out about each young man as quickly as possible, and then, presto—A plus B equals C—the young man had passed the examination. To the resolution of this formula Mr. Harper devoted his exclusive attention; his equipment and procedure were streamlined, constructed upon scientific principles, as much so as a Budd machine gun.

Nor was this comparison fantastic; on the contrary, the more you considered it, the more apposite it appeared. Experts on military science had been writing for decades about the perpetual war going on between gunmakers and armorplate makers; and in the same way there were educators, whose business it was to cram knowledge into the minds of youth, and there was youth, perversely resisting this process, seeking every device to "get by."

The educators had invented examinations, and the students were trying to circumvent them. Being provided by their parents with large sums of money, it was natural that they should use it to get expert help in this never-ceasing war. And so had developed the profession of tutoring.

This was America that Lanny had come to live in, and he wanted to know all about it. He listened to what Mr. Harper said, and afterwards put his mind on it and tried to figure out what it meant. A young man wanted to get into "prep school" as quickly as possible, in order that he might get through "prep school" as quickly as possible, in order that he might get into college as quickly as possible, in order that he might get out of college as quickly as possible. Mr. Harper didn't say any of that—for the reason that it didn't need saying. If it wasn't so, what was he here for?

Mr. Harper was about forty years of age, a brisk and business-like person who might have been one of the Budd salesmen; he was getting bald, and plastered what hairs were left very carefully over the top of his head. For about half his life he had been studying college entrance examinations. It would be an exaggeration to say that he could tell you every question which had been asked in any college of the United States during twenty years; but his knowledge approached that encyclopedic character. He knew the personalities of the different professors, and what exam questions they had used for the last few years, and so he could make a pretty good guess what questions were due for another turn. He would hold up his hand in the middle of a conversation; no, no use to know that, they never asked anything like that.

Just recently had come a revolution in Mr. Harper's profession. The educational authorities had got together and set up a body called the College Entrance Examination Board, which was going to hold uniform examinations all over the country, good for any college the student might select. There were a quarter of a million college students, and six times as many high school students, so of course they had to be handled on a mass-production basis. It was part of the process of standardizing America; everybody was eating corn flakes out of the same kind of package, and all students of the year 1917 were going to get into college because they had read Washington Irving's *Alhambra* and George Washington's Farewell Address.

Lanny Budd was, so Mr. Harper declared, the most complicated problem he had ever tackled; he became quite enthusiastic over him, like a surgeon over an abdominal tumor with fascinating complications. From the point of view of the College Entrance Examination Board, Lanny quite literally didn't know anything. One by one the youth brought his burnt offerings and his wave offerings to the educational high priest and saw them rejected. Music? No, there are no credits for music. Greek dramatists? They teach those after you get into college, if at all. The same with Stendhal and Montaigne and Corneille and so on. Molière, now, they use *Le Bourgeois Gentilhomme*—are you sure you remember the plot? Advanced French will count three units out of the fifteen you must have— but are you sure you can pass advanced French?

"Well, I've spoken French all my life," said Lanny, bewildered.

"I know; but you won't be asked to speak it, and very few of your examiners could understand you if you did. How do you say 'a tired child'?"

"*Un enfant fatigué.*"

"And how do you say 'a beautiful day'?"

"*Un beau jour.*"

"Well, now, why do you put one adjective ahead of the noun and the other after it?"

The uneducated youth looked blank. "I really don't know," said he. "I just do it."

"Exactly. But the examination paper will ask you to state the rule, or give the list of exceptions, or whatever it may be. And what will you do?"

"I guess I'll have to go back to France," said Lanny.

II

Mr. Harper decided that by heroic efforts it might be possible for this eccentric pupil to be got ready for the third year of prep school in the fall. Private academies were not so crowded as public high schools, and were better able to handle exceptional cases. But the first thing was to buckle down to plane and solid geometry, and to ancient and medieval history. Yes, said Mr. Harper, Sophocles and Euripides might help, but what really counted was facts. If a candidate were to tell a board of examiners that the Greek spirit was basically one of tragedy, how would they know whether he was spoofing them? But if he said that the naval battle of Salamis was won in the year 480 B.C. by the Athenian Themistocles, there was something that couldn't be faked.

"All right," Lanny said, "I'll go to it." That was what his father wanted, and his grandfather, and his stepmother; that was the test of character, the way to get on in America. So he put his textbooks on the little table by the open window of his room, with the door shut so that nobody would disturb him, and set to work to ram the contents of those books into his mind—names, places, and dates, and no foolish unprofitable flights of the imagination; rules, formulas, and facts, and no superfluous emotions of pity or terror.

The only company he had was the mocking-bird. This slender and delicate creature, gray with a little white, liked to sit on the topmost spray of the cherry tree and pour out its astonishing volume of song. A mystery when it slept; for no matter how late Lanny might work, it was singing in the moonlight, and if he opened his eyes at dawn, it was already under full steam. It imitated the cries of all the other birds; it said "meeauw" like the catbird, and "flicker, flicker, flicker," like the big yellow-hammer. But mostly it improvised. Of course it said no words, because it couldn't form the consonants; but as you listened you were impelled to make up words to correspond to its rhythm and melody. Sometimes they came tripping fast: "Sicady, sicady, sicady, sicady."

Then the singer would stop, and and say very deliberately: "Peanuts first. Peanuts first."

Lanny was so determined to make good that he wanted to study all the time; but Esther wouldn't have that. In the middle of the afternoon, after Mr. Harper had come and heard him recite and had laid out the next day's work—then he must quit, and go with the other young people for tennis, and for what he now learned to call a "swim" instead of a "bathe." Five days in the week he could work, mornings and evenings; and on Saturdays there would be a picnic, or a sailing party, and in the evening a dance. He had so many cousins of all degrees that he wouldn't have to go out of the family for company and diversion.

They were an astonishing lot of people, these Budds. The earlier generations had married young, and the women had accepted all the children the Lord had sent them—ten, or sometimes twenty, and then the women would die off, and the men would start again. In these modern days, of course, everything was changed; one or two children was the rule, and a woman like Esther, who had three, felt that she had gone out of her way to serve the community. But still there were a great many Budds, and others with Budd for their first or middle name. Grandfather Samuel had six daughters and four sons living; Samuel's oldest brother, a farmer, was still thriving at the age of eighty, and had had seventeen children, and most of them still alive, preaching and practicing the Word of the Lord their God, that their days might be long in the land which the Lord their God had given them.

Most of those who were not preaching the Word were employed by Budd Gunmakers Corporation in one capacity or another, and just now were working at the task of making the days of the Germans as short as possible. The Germans had their own God, who was working just as hard for his side—so Lanny read in a German magazine which the kind Mr. Robin took the trouble to send him. How these Gods adjusted matters up in their heaven was a problem which was too much for Lanny, so he put his mind on the dates of ancient Greek and Roman wars.

III

On Sunday mornings the earnest student would dress himself
in a freshly pressed palm beach suit and panama hat, and at five
minutes before ten o'clock would be among those who thronged
into the First Congregational Church. This building occupied a
prominent position on the central "square" of Newcastle; a large,
two-story structure, built of wood and painted white, with a high-
pitched roof and rows of second-story windows resembling those
of a private residence. What told you it was a church was the
steeple which rose from the front center; a square tower, with a
round cylinder on top of that, then a smaller cube and then a very
sharp and tall pyramid on that. Topping all was a lightning rod;
but no cross—that would have meant idolatry, the "Whore of
Babylon"—in short, a Catholic church. There were stairs inside the
steeple, and windows so that you could look out as you climbed.
Robbie said the original purpose was so that the townsmen could
keep watch against the Pequot Indians; but there was a twinkle in
his eye, so Lanny wasn't sure.

The men's Bible class was one of the features of Newcastle life.
It is not in every town that you can meet the leading captain of
industry face to face once a week, and have a chance to ask him a
question. So many took advantage of this opportunity that the
class was held in the main body of the church. Many of the leading
businessmen attended, most of the Budd executives old and young,
and everyone who hoped ever to be an executive. It was a business
as well as a cultural event.

Did the teacher of this remarkable class have any cynical ideas
as to what caused so many hard-working citizens of his town to
give up their golf and tennis and listen to the expounding of ancient
Jewish morality and Swiss and Scottish theology? Doubtless he did,
for his faith in his Lord and Master did not extend to the too many
children of this Almighty One. It was enough for Samuel Budd
that they came; having them at his mercy for one hour, he pounded
the sacred message into them. If they did not take their chance,

it was because the Lord had predestined them to everlasting damnation, for reasons which were satisfactory to Him and into which no mortal had any business trying to pry. If they chose to sit with blank faces and occupy their minds with how to get a raise in salary, or how to get their wives invited to the Budd homes, or what make of new car they were going to purchase—that also had been arranged by an inscrutable Divine Providence, and all that a deacon of the stern old faith could do was to quote the texts which the Lord had provided, together with such interpretations as the Holy Spirit saw fit to reveal to him at ten o'clock on Sunday morning.

IV

The regular service followed the men's Bible class; which meant that the ladies had an extra hour in which to curl their hair and set on top of it their delicate confections of straw and artificial flowers. The war hadn't changed the fashions, nor the fact that there were fashions; all that elegance which had fled from Paris and London was now in Newcastle. The chauffeurs drove back to the homes for the ladies, and they entered with primness and piety, but now and then a sidelong glance to be sure that gentlemen standing in the sunshine on the steps were properly attentive.

That little heathen, Lanny Budd, had never attended a church service before, except for a wedding or a funeral; but he did not reveal that fact. The rule was the same as for a dinner party: watch your hostess and do what she does. He stood up and sang a hymn, from a book which Esther put into his hand, the number of the hymn having been announced twice by the minister. Then he bowed his head and closed his eyes while the Reverend Mr. Saddleback prayed. "Thou knowest, O Lord," was his opening formula; after which he proceeded to tell the Lord many things which the Lord knew, but which the congregation presumably didn't. Also he asked the Lord to do many things for the congregation, and it seemed to Lanny that the Lord must know about these already.

A well-trained choir sang a florid and elaborate anthem, this being Newcastle's substitute for grand opera. A collection was taken up, and Grandfather Budd passed the plate among the richest pew holders up front, and kept an eagle eye upon the bills which they dropped in. Finally Mr. Saddleback preached a sermon. Lanny had hoped that he would explain some of the difficult points of Fundamentalist doctrine, but instead he explained the will of the Lord with regard to Kaiser Wilhelm and his *Kultur*. "And surely your blood of your lives will I require; at the hand of every beast will I require it, and at the hand of man; at the hand of every man's brother will I require the life of man. Whoso sheddeth man's blood, by man shall his blood be shed. And I, behold, I establish my covenant with you, and with your seed after you." The Reverend Mr. Saddleback turned his pulpit into a Sinai, and thundered such awful words, and they seemed a direct message to Budd Gunmakers Corporation, which in the spring of that year 1917 had enlisted all its lathes and grinding machines, its jigs and dies and other tools, in the allied services of the United States government and the Lord God Almighty.

V

Lanny took time off to write letters home and tell his mother and Marcel how things were going with him. To cheer them up he went into detail about the martial fervors which surrounded him. Beauty sent him affectionate replies, and told him that Marcel was painting a portrait of Emily Chattersworth, and wouldn't let her pay him for it; it was his thanks for what she was doing for the poilus. Marcel was in a state of increasing suspense and dread, because of the failure of the French offensive in Champagne, in which his old regiment had been nearly wiped out. Beauty couldn't say much about it, but doubtless Robbie would have inside news; and he did.

Also Lanny wrote to Rick and to his wife. From the former he had a cheerful post card, beginning "Old Top," as usual. From

Nina he learned that Rick had made a dangerous forced landing, but fortunately behind the English lines; he was a highly skilled flier now, what they called an "ace." Also Nina said that the baby was real and was making itself known. She told him about her examinations, and he told about those for which he was being prepared. In his letters he permitted himself to have a little fun with them.

He wrote the Robin boys in the same strain, and they told him about their school work, which for some strange reason they loved. He wondered if it was a characteristic of the Jews that they enjoyed hard labor; if so, it gave them an unfair advantage over other races. Lanny found that they bore that reputation in Newcastle; they had little stores in the working-class districts of the town, and kept them open until late hours, and now and then were fined for selling things on the Sabbath—the Puritan Sabbath, that is. They sent their children to the schools, where they persisted in winning prizes; there were so many of them crowding into Harvard that they had been put on an unadmitted quota. Members of the New England aristocracy would say to their complacent sons: "If you don't buck up and work, I'll send you to Harvard to compete with the Jews." Lanny wrote that to the Robins, knowing that it would make them chirp.

The salesman of electrical apparatus in Rotterdam forwarded another of Lanny's letters to Kurt; a very careful one, in which Lanny told all about his studies, but didn't mention the U.S.A. He just said: "I have gone to visit my father's home. Write me there." Kurt knew about Newcastle; and in due course a letter came, by way of Switzerland, as usual. Kurt said that he was well, and had gone back to his duties, and was glad to hear that his friend was keeping his mind on matters of permanent interest and benefit. That was all; but Lanny could read between those lines, and understand that even though Kurt was now fighting America, he didn't want Lanny to be fighting Germany!

Midsummer; and Nina wrote again. Rick had had a week's leave, and had come home; she had been to The Reaches with him—and, oh, so happy they had been! So happy they might be all their lives, if only this cruel slaughter would end! The baronet and his wife had been kind to her, and Rick was a darling—they had boated and bathed and played croquet. And the heavenly nights, with music on the river, and starlight trembling on the water, and love in their hearts! It all came over Lanny in a wave of melancholy longing; he too had had love in his heart, and had it still—but the granddaughter of Lord Dewthorpe was the poorest of correspondents, and her letters were skimpy, matter of fact, and wholly lacking in charm. Taking care of wounded men all day left one tired and unromantic, it appeared. Old England had had too much of war, and now it was New England's turn.

VI

Perhaps the letter from Nina, and Lanny's continual thinking about it, may have had something to do with the strange experience which befell him a few nights later. When Lanny went to bed he was tired in both mind and body, and usually fell asleep at once, and rarely wakened until the maid tapped on his door. But now something roused him; at least, he insisted that he was awake, fully awake, and no amount of questioning by others could shake his certainty. He lay there, and it seemed that the first faint gray of dawn was stealing into the room—just enough light so that you could know it was a room, and that there were objects in it. The mocking-bird hadn't noticed the light, and the crickets had gone to sleep, and the stillness caught Lanny's attention; it seemed abnormal.

Then a weird feeling began to steal over him. Something was happening, he didn't know what it was, but fear of it began to stir in his soul, and his skin began to creep and draw tight, so it seemed. Lanny stared into the darkness, and it appeared to be taking form, and he began to wonder whether the light was daylight or something else; it seemed to be shaping itself into a mass at the foot of his bed, and the mass began to move, and suddenly Lanny realized it was Rick. A pale gray figure, just luminous enough so that it could be clearly seen; Rick in his flier's uniform, all stained with mud. On his face was a grave, rather mournful expression, and across his forehead a large red gash.

It came to Lanny in a sort of inner flash: Rick is dead! He raised his head a little and stared at the figure, and a cold chill went over him, and his teeth began to chatter, and his eyes popped wide, trying to see better. "Rick!" he whispered, half under his breath; but maybe that was a mistake, for right away the figure began to fade. Lanny cried again, half in fright and half in longing: "Rick! Speak to me!"

But the pale form faded away—or rather it seemed to spread itself over the room, and when it did, Lanny could see that it was the beginning of dawn and that objects were slowly looming in the room. All at once the mocking-bird tuned up and the other little birds outside began to say: "Cheep, cheep," and "Twitter, twitter." Lanny lay sick with horror, saying to himself soundlessly: "Rick is dead! Rick is dead!"

He did not go to sleep again. He lay till the sun was nearly up, and then put on his clothes and went into the garden and walked up and down, trying to get himself together before he had to meet the rest of the family. He tried to argue with himself; but there was no making headway against that inner voice. It was the first great loss of his life. He had to wrestle it out with himself—and he knew that he hated this war, and all wars, now and forever; just as Beauty had done in the beginning, and as Robbie still did in the depths of his heart, though he had stopped saying it.

VII

Impossible that Robbie and Esther should not notice his distraught condition. He said that he had slept badly—he didn't want to discuss the matter before the children. But after they had gone to their play he told his father and stepmother. As he had expected, Esther hated the idea. Hers was a practical mind and her beliefs in super-

normal phenomena were limited to those which had been ratified
and approved by biblical exegesis. The visit of Emmaus was all
right, because it was in the Bible; but for there to be an apparition
in the year 1917—and in her home!—that could be nothing but
superstition. Only Negroes, and maybe Catholics, let themselves
be troubled by such notions. "You just had a dream, Lanny!"
insisted his father's wife.

"I was exactly as wide awake as I am right now," he answered.
"I feel sure something dreadful has happened to Rick."

He wanted to cable Nina; and Robbie said he would send it—his
name being known would speed matters with the censors. He
promised to attend to it the moment he reached the office, and to
prepay a reply, because Nina didn't have much money. "What
news about Rick?" he sent; and in course of the afternoon his
secretary called the house and read Lanny the reply: "Rick reported
well last week's letter."

Of course, Lanny said, that didn't tell him anything. He insisted
upon a second message being sent, with reply prepaid: "Advise immediately if trouble." For two days Lanny waited, doing his utmost
to keep his mind upon his studies, so as not to forfeit the respect of
his stepmother and her friends. Then came another cablegram from
Nina: "Rick badly hurt great pain may not live prayers."

Somehow it was that last word which broke Lanny down and
made him cry like a baby. He was quite sure that Nina was not a
religious person; she was looking forward to being a scientist—but
now the same thing had happened to her that had happened to
Beauty in those dreadful hours when Marcel's life hung upon a
thread. She was praying; she was even moved to cable for Lanny's
help!

Could Lanny pray? He wasn't sure. He had listened to the Reverend Mr. Saddleback praying and had been inclined to take the
procedure with a trace of humor. But now he would be glad to
have anybody's help to keep Rick alive.

Esther, of course, was much affected by what had happened; in

this crisis their two so different natures came to a temporary understanding. Her pride was humbled, and she had to admit that there
were more things in heaven and earth than were dreamt of in her
philosophy. If something in Rick's soul had been able to travel from
France to Connecticut, why might not something from Lanny's go
back to France? As it happened, prayers for the sick and afflicted
were in accord with the doctrines of Esther's church; so why
should not the congregation be requested to pray for a wounded
English officer—especially since their own boys were not yet being
killed?

"Spare no expense in helping Rick," cabled the practical Robbie.
"Keep me advised by wire." He arranged for Nina to have unlimited
credit for cabling—you can do that kind of thing when you are one
of the princes of industry. Nina replied that her husband was in a
base hospital abroad, and she could not get to him; they just had to
wait—and pray.

It was some time before she herself knew the story and could
write it to Lanny. The English troops had been making an attack,
and Rick had been assigned to the defense of another plane which
was doing "contact flying"—that is, observing the advance of the
troops, and sending information by wireless so that the artillery
barrage could keep just in front of them. Rick had been attacked
by three German planes and had been shot through the knee; he
was forced to make a landing behind the enemy's lines, and his
plane overturned—that was when he had got the gashed forehead.
The attack being under way, the Germans had not found him; he
had dragged himself into a shell hole and hidden, and for two days
and nights had lain, conscious only part of the time, hoping that
the British might advance and find him. This had happened—but
meantime his wound had become infected, and he was suffering
dreadfully; it was a question whether his leg could be saved, or
whether he could survive having it amputated.

VIII

Men were being killed by thousands every day; but still the work of the world had to go on. Lanny had to wipe the tears from his eyes, shut from his mind the thought of his friend's suffering, and acquire information about the conquests of King Alexander the Great. Hosts of men had been mutilated in those wars; not with machine-gun bullets, but with arrows and spears, just as painful, and as liable to cause infection. All history was one river of blood— and who could live if he spent his time weeping upon its banks?

Lanny had managed to become interested in his job. He was young, and nothing could be entirely a bore. Mr. Harper came every day and heard him recite, and was pleased with his progress, and told Esther, so the youth enjoyed a glow of satisfaction. He was making good; he was taking the curse off himself—and he was getting an education. "Drink deep," a poet had sung of the Pierian spring. Here in America it had been dammed and piped, and the water was metered and duly paid for at a fixed price; you turned a spigot, and drew so many quarts at a time, and when you had drunk it five days a week for ten weeks, that was called a "unit." Ancient history, one unit; medieval history, one unit; algebra one, geometry one; elementary French two, advanced French three, and so on.

Lanny read the announcement, made by the Yale authorities, that the university would now require military training. The slogan "For God, for Country, and for Yale" would become "Yale for God and Country." But Robbie said not to worry, this war wasn't going to last forever, and after Yale had won it, everything could go on as before. Mr. Harper insisted that a unit would always be a unit; it was the indestructible particle of the educational world. So Lanny memorized the dates of Charles Martel the Hammer, and of Charlemagne and the Holy Roman Empire.

No more apparitions came to him. He learned by the more expensive medium of the cable that Rick was still alive; then that he had been brought to England; then that he was having an operation, and then a second—he was going to be one of those cases which constitute a sort of endowment for surgeons and hospitals. Lanny, of course, had written Nina all about his vision; Rick admitted that when he had crashed he had thought about Lanny—because Lanny was so afraid of crashes, and had told him about Marcel's.

Later on Nina wrote that Rick was back at his father's home, and she was helping to take care of him. "Write him affectionate things and cheer him up," she said. The knee is a difficult place to heal, and if Rick was ever to walk again, it would be with a steel brace on his leg. Poor, proud, defiant, impatient aesthete, he was going to be a pitiful, nerve-shaken cripple; his wife would be one of those devoted souls—millions of them all over Europe—who were glad to get even part of a husband back again, and have that much safe from the slaughterman's ax.

IX

Every time Lanny went swimming or boating, he saw great towering iron chimneys, pouring out billowing clouds of smoke. At night, if he sat on the front porch, he saw down the vista of the elm trees a dull red glare in the sky. That was Budd's; that was the plant, the source of all Lanny's good things, and one of the places where the war was being won. From earliest childhood he had listened to discourses about its functions and ownership—those precious pieces of paper called stock certificates, which guaranteed safety and comfort to whoever held them, and to his children and his children's children. Robbie, man of business and of money, had been wont to preach little sermons, playful yet serious; he would see a ragged old beggar slouching along in rain or snow, and would say: "There, but for the plant, go you!"

Of course Lanny wanted to see it, and Robbie promised to arrange it. As soon as they heard the proposal, Junior and Percy put in their clamors; they had seen it before, but no one could see it enough. And then Bess, loudest of all—why did she have to be left out of everything? Bess had heard about votes for women, and de-

clared that she believed in them from now on. Hadn't she just had
her tenth birthday party, and got better marks than either of her
brothers in school? The father said, all right, he would have one
of his secretaries take Saturday morning off and escort the four of
them.

They drove through the great steel gates of the plant, guarded
now by armed men, for there had been explosions in American munitions plants, and German agents were known to be active. They
were led from one huge building to another, and saw white-hot
steel being poured from giant ladles amid blinding showers of
sparks; they saw golden ingots being rolled into sheets, or cut by
screaming saws, or pounded and squeezed in huge presses. The clat-
ter and clamor was deafening to a stranger. Their escort said that
munitions were noisy at two periods of their career, the beginning
and the end; he said that men got used to both, sooner or later. The
foreman on the floor could tell in a moment if anything went
wrong, because one of the familiar sounds was missing or out of
tune.

They were taken through rooms as big as railroad sheds, in which
traveling cranes overhead brought heavy parts, and electric motor
trucks brought other parts, and men working in long lines assembled heavy machine guns, which were on wheels. A gallery ran
about the rooms, from which you could look down upon the
crowded floor, and it seemed a place of hopeless confusion; but the
secretary assured them that every motion made by one of those human ants had been studied for weeks in a laboratory, and that the
movements of each piece of machinery were timed to the second.

They walked through long rooms like corridors, in which such
things as time fuses for anti-aircraft shells were made. Women and
girls sat at a table which the children thought must surely be the
longest in the world; on top of it was an endless belt, gliding silently.
The object being manufactured started from nothing, and each
worker added a bit, or maybe just turned a screw, until, at the far
end, the completed products were slid onto trays, and taken by
truck to a part of the plant where shrapnel shells were loaded. That

place was remote, and visitors were not permitted there—not even members of the family.

Lanny was interested in time fuses, but still more interested in women and girls. He saw that they all wore uniforms, and that the motions of their hands were swift and unvarying; most of them never took their eyes from the job, and if they did, it was only for the fraction of a second—even when there was a good-looking young man in the line of vision. They were riveted to this task for seven hours and forty minutes every day, with twenty minutes for lunch, and Lanny wondered what it did to their minds and bodies. The secretary assured him that all this had been studied by experts, and the speed of the belt precisely adjusted so that no one would become weary. It was a pleasant thing to hear, but Lanny would have been interested to ask the girls.

Of course he might have gone out at night, in the parts of the town where the picture theaters and the bright lights were, and it would have been easy to "pick up" one of them and get her to talking. But Lanny wasn't roaming the streets at night; he was studying and earning credits with his family, as well as with St. Thomas's prep school. All he would know about the Budd plant was what a friendly but discreet young secretary saw fit to tell him. This was wartime, and every department was working in three eight-hour shifts. Those who couldn't stand the pace went elsewhere.

X

Lanny took his ideas and impressions home and thought them over in his leisure hours. He was proud of that large institution which his forefathers had built; he understood Robbie's dream, that some day his oldest son might become the master of it. Lanny put the question to himself: "Do I want to do that?" The time to decide was now; for what was the sense of shutting himself up in a room and learning the dates of old wars if his business was going to be with new ones?

It seemed to him that, if he meant to become a maker of munitions, he ought to go into the plant and begin learning from his father and his overburdened grandfather all about steel and aluminum and the new alloys which were being created in the laboratories; about slow-burning and quick-burning powders, and the ways of grinding which made the subtle differences; the various raw materials, their prices and sources of supply; money, and how it was handled and kept; and, above all, men, how to judge them, how to get out of them the best work they were capable of performing. This was the education which a captain of industry had to acquire. It was grim, tough work, and it did something to those who undertook it.

First of all Lanny ought to make up his mind on the subject of war. Did he agree with his father that men would go on fighting forever and ever, because that was their nature and nothing could change it? Did he agree with his grandfather that God had ordained every war, and that what happened on this earth was of little importance compared with eternity? Was he going to adopt either of those beliefs—or just drift along, believing one thing when his father talked to him, and another when he saw Rick's image at the foot of the bed?

One thing seemed plain: if you were going to be happy in any job, you had to believe in that job. Robbie said it was enough to know that the money was coming in; but Lanny was watching his father more closely, and becoming sure that he was far from happy. Robbie was by nature sociable, and liked to say what he thought; but now he kept silence. His heart was unwarmed by all this blaze of patriotic excitement which possessed the country, the newspapers full of propaganda, the streets blaring music and the oratory of "four-minute men" and salesmen of "liberty bonds." The airplanes were going to be driven by "liberty motors," and you ate "liberty steak" and "liberty cabbage" instead of hamburgers and sauerkraut. Robbie hated such nonsense; he hated still more to see the country and its resources being used for what he said were the purposes of British imperialism.

This attitude didn't make for contentment either in his work or in his home. As it happened, Robbie's wife was growing more martial-minded every day; she was believing the atrocity stories, putting her money into liberty bonds, helping to organize the women of Newcastle for community singing, for rolling bandages, nursing, whatever doings were called for by patriotic societies and government officials. It happened that President Wilson was the son of a Presbyterian minister, and that Esther's mother was the daughter of one. Esther read the President's golden words and believed every one of them; when Robbie would remark that the British ruling classes were the shrewdest propagandists in the world, a sudden chill would fall at the breakfast table.

21

The Thoughts of Youth

I

LANNY didn't meet his grandfather again for quite a while. He saw him in church, but made no attempt to catch his eye; just dropped his dollar bill into the plate and knew that his good deed had been credited for that day. The old gentleman was absorbed in the task which the Lord had assigned him, and he stayed in his big mansion, with an old-maid niece to run it, and rarely went anywhere except to his office. But he managed to keep track of the members of his big family, and if they were doing anything of which he disapproved, he let them know it. "Silence means consent," remarked Robbie, with a smile.

He added: "I showed him Mr. Harper's report on your progress."

"What did he say?"

"He grunted and said you were a clever lad, but a chatterbox. Of course that's not to be taken too seriously. It's not according to his nature to give praise."

Lanny met others of his uncles and aunts; sometimes in church, sometimes when they came to the house and stayed to meals. Robbie would tell him about these people—always when the two were alone, because Robbie's view of his relatives was often touched with mischief. They were a cranky lot; an old family which had had money for generations and could indulge their whims however extravagant. Some were satisfied to stay in harness, and make more money, even though they had no need of it; but others took up special duties, such as endowing missionaries and having the Bible translated into Torgut or Bashkir or some other unlikely language; or exploring the river Orinoco and bringing home black orchids; or traveling to Southern Arabia and making friends with a sheik, and purchasing blooded horses to drive about town and to breed from.

Great-Uncle Theophrastus Budd came calling on his way home from a convention of reformers. He was the eldest of the brothers of Grandfather Budd, and was known as a philanthropist; his cause was euthanasia, which meant the painless ending of the lives of the aged. He was getting pretty aged himself, and Robbie said that his heirs were waiting for him to practice what he preached. Great-Aunt Sophronia, an old maid, lived in an ancient house with many cats, and when Lanny went to call at her request, he found her in the attic with a dustcloth over her hair, sorting out family treasures in an old trunk. She had found moths in it, and was hunting them with a fly-spat, and invited Lanny to help her, which he did, and found it a pleasant diversion. This old lady had a sense of humor, and told her new grandnephew that some years ago she had lost interest in life, and had found to her surprise that this had made her quite happy.

These odd people had a way of quarreling bitterly and never making up. Uncle Andrew Budd and his wife had lived in the same

house for thirty years and never spoken. Cousin Timothy and
Cousin Rufus couldn't agree upon the division of their family farm,
so they had cut it in halves and lived as neighbors, but did not visit.
Aunt Agatha, Robbie's eldest sister, went off and took up residence
in a hotel, and forbade the clerk at the desk ever to announce any
person by the name of Budd. That was New England, Robbie
said; a sort of ingrown place, self-centered, opinionated, proud.

II

One whom Lanny met only in the most formal manner was his
Uncle Lawford. The meeting took place in church, where members of the family would exchange greetings in the aisles, or as they
walked to their cars. When an occasion arose, Esther said: "Lawford, this is Lanning, Robbie's son." And Uncle Lawford shook
hands and inquired: "How do you do?"—politely, as became two
children of the Lord meeting in His holy place. That was all.

He was a peculiar-looking man, heavily built, with broad square
shoulders and rather short bandy legs. He was close to fifty, and
his gray hair was thin on top; he had a square bulging forehead, and
on his face a look that Robbie said was "sour," but to Lanny it
seemed as if someone had just said something to hurt Uncle Lawford's feelings. Robbie said that was perhaps the case; Lawford
couldn't stand the least opposition in anything, and Robbie's way
of making jokes annoyed him beyond endurance.

These two might have let each other alone, but business affairs
wouldn't permit that. Every policy that Robbie advocated was opposed by the older brother. The father had the final say, and if he
came to Robbie's view, Lawford would withdraw into himself. He
was "vice-president in charge of production," and was vigilant and
competent, but he took the job as a dog does a bone—going off into
a corner by himself, and growling at any other dog that comes near.

Lanny said: "If I had anything to do with Budd's, I'd be bound
to run into him, wouldn't I?"

"I'm afraid so; but I'd back you, and I think we'd win."

"Suppose Grandfather Budd should die—how would that work out?"

"It'll be up to the stockholders; there'll be a hunt for proxies."

"Do members of the family own most of the stock?"

"Not outright, the plant's grown too big. But we have enough to keep control, especially with our friends in the town."

Lanny went off and thought about all that. To follow his father's occupation would mean to take up these ancient grudges and make himself the object of these festering hates. Did he want to do it? Or did he want to hurt his father by refusing to do it?

III

Important to the youth was his meeting with his Great-Great-Uncle Eli Budd, youngest and only surviving uncle of Grandfather Samuel. He lived in a town of the interior called Norton, and was eighty-three, and still hale. He sent word that he wanted to meet his new kinsman, and since he was the head of the family, his wish was a command. Lanny was to motor there on Saturday morning, and come back on Sunday evening; and Esther told him not merely how to behave, but where on the trip he would see a famous old "overhang" house, and an old mill which Esther's grandfather had built, and a churchyard with the headstone of the progenitor of all the Budds. "The churchyards are among the most interesting places in New England," said Lanny's stepmother.

The main street of the village of Norton was broad, and deeply shaded with great elms; its residences were white, and none had fences or hedges, but stood in a continuous well-kept lawn, with elms and oaks and maples averting the summer's glare. They were dignified old houses with well-proportioned Colonial doorways, and no unseemly noises ever disturbed their peace inside or out. In one of them the old gentleman lived with his second wife, some thirty years younger than himself, and one unmarried daughter—there were many such in New England, because so many of the young men went away. The family lived frugally, upon a small income, because this retired preacher valued independence more than any-thing else in the world. "The Budds will all tell you how to live if you will let them," he said to Lanny, with a dry smile.

He was a man of more than six feet, his frame slender and un-bowed. His hair was snow-white and long, his face smooth-shaven, with a large Roman nose and deeply graven lines about the mouth. His neck was long and the cords stood out on it, and the skin was like withered brown parchment. But his eyes were still keen, and his step though slow was steady. He had learned how to live, and to limit his desires and keep his spirit serene.

Lanny felt as soon as he entered the house that here was a place ruled by love. Great-Great-Aunt Bethesda was a Quaker, gentle, quiet, like a little gray dove. She said: "Has thee had a pleasant trip?"—and this was something new to Lanny, and awakened his curiosity. He knew that the old gentleman was a Unitarian, and that this had been a scandal in its time, and still was to Grandfather Samuel, and perhaps to Stepmother Esther. One glance about was enough to tell him that Eli was a scholar, for the walls were lined with books that had been read and lived with.

Sitting in this patriarch's study, Lanny was invited to talk about himself, and didn't mind doing it. He was able to guess what would interest his relatives: the natural beauty of the place where he had lived, and the cultivated persons he had met, especially the old ones, such as M. Anatole France, and M. Priedieu, and M. Rochambeau. Eli Budd questioned him about his reading; and when Lanny named names, he didn't say: "All French writers." He had read them him-self, and made comments on them, and was able to discover from Lanny's remarks that he had understood what was in them.

Between these two there took place that chemical process of the soul whereby two become one, not gradually, but all at once. They had lived three thousand miles apart, yet they had developed this affinity. The seventeen-year-old one told his difficulties and his problems, and the eighty-three-year-old one renewed his youth, and spoke words which seemed a sort of divination. Said he:

"Do not let other people invade your personality. Remember that every human being is a unique phenomenon, and worth developing. You will meet many who have no resources of their own, and who will try to fasten themselves upon you. You will find others eager to tell you what to do and think and be. But it is better to go apart and learn to be yourself."

Great-Great-Uncle Eli was a "transcendentalist," having known many of the old New England group. There is something in us all, he said, that is greater than ourselves, that works through us and can be used in the making of character. The central core of life is personality. To respect the personality of others is the beginning of virtue, and to enforce respect for it is the first duty of the individual toward all forms of government, all organizations and systems which men contrive to enslave and limit their fellows.

I V

Youth and age went out and strolled in the calm of twilight, and again in the freshness of the morning. They sat and ate the frugal meals which two gentle ladies prepared for them. But most of the time they just wanted to sit in the book-walled study and talk. Lanny had never heard anyone whose conversation satisfied him so completely, and old Eli saw his spirit reborn in this new Budd from across the sea.

Lanny told about his mother, and about Marcel; about Rick and his family, and about Kurt; he even told about Rosemary, and the old clergyman was not shocked; he said that customs in sexual matters varied in different parts of the world, and what suited some did not suit others. "The blood of youth is hot," he said, "and impatience sets traps for us, and prepares regrets that sometimes last all our lives. The important thing is not to wrong any woman—and that is no easy matter, for women are great demanders, and do not scruple to invade the personality." Great-Great-Uncle Eli smiled, but Lanny knew he was serious.

Free-thinker that this old man was, he was nevertheless a product of the Puritan conscience, and wanted men and women to become

pure in heart. As Lanny listened, he began to recall a certain afternoon upon the heights by the church of Notre-Dame-de-Bon-Port.
His friend Kurt Meissner had not merely voiced the same ethical
ideas, but had justified them by the same metaphysical concepts.
Lanny mentioned that to the ex-clergyman, who said there was
nothing strange about it, because New England transcendentalism
had stemmed directly from German philosophical idealism. Interesting to see a son of New England bringing home another load of it,
a century later!

Eli bade Lanny have the courage of his vision. Without it men
would be dull clods, and life would become blind greed and empty
pleasure-seeking. "God save the Budds if they were never anything
but munitions makers and salesmen!" exclaimed Eli; and these words
pierced to the center of Lanny's being. When the time came for
him to depart, this gentle yet hardy old man gave him a volume
of Emerson's essays inscribed by that great teacher's fine and sensitive hand. Emerson had been merely a name to Lanny; but he
promised to read the book, and did so.

V

Lanny drove up to Sand Hill, where St. Thomas's Academy is
situated, and took his examinations with success. The fact that the
name of Budd was signed to all his papers was not supposed to have
anything to do with his passing; nor the fact that one of the school's
largest brownstone buildings had been paid for out of the profits
which Budd Gunmakers had derived from the American Civil War,
and another from the profits of the Spanish-American War. St.
Thomas's was a part of the Budd tradition, and the family's right to
send its sons there was hereditary. Lanny asked his father about the
matter of his not being quite properly a Budd, and Robbie said he
had entered him as his son, and that was that; it wasn't the custom
to send over to France for marriage certificates.

The beautiful old buildings stood in a park having lawns and shade
trees like an English estate. They were of dull old red brick with

Boston ivy on the walls, making a safe home for millions of spiders and bugs. In one of the dormitories Lanny shared a comfortable room and bath with a cousin whom he had met on the tennis courts, but with whom he had little else in common.

Lanny had played with boys, but always a few at a time; he had never before been part of a horde. He discovered that a horde is something different, a being with a personality of its own. Being young and eager, he was curious about it, and every hour was a fresh adventure. He awoke to the ringing of an electric bell, went to breakfast to another ringing, and thereafter moved through the day as an electrically controlled robot. He acquired knowledge in weighed and measured portions; memorized facts and recited them, forgot many of them until the end of the month, relearned them for a "test," forgot them again until the end of a term, relearned them once more for "exam"—and then forgot them forever and ever, amen.

In addition to this part of his life, scheduled and ordained by the school authorities, the horde had its own life which it lived during off hours. This life centered upon three things: athletic prowess, class politics, and sex. If you could run, jump, or play football or baseball, your success was probable; if you could talk realistically about girls, that would help; if your family was notably rich and famous, and if you had Anglo-Saxon features, good clothes, and easy manners, all problems were solved. Entering the third year, Lanny was jumping into the midst of school politics, and had to be looked over and judged quickly. His cousin, belonging to a fashionable set, was ready to initiate him, and would be provoked if Lanny didn't display proper respect for the fine points upon which his friends based their judgments. "Be careful, or they'll set you down for a 'queerie,'" said this mentor.

VI

Robbie had asked Lanny not to play football, saying that he was too lightly built for this rough game. It was another of those cases

in which the father expected him to be wiser than himself. Robbie
didn't want Lanny to smoke or drink. He was willing for him to
have a girl now and then, but wanted him to be "choosy" about it.
He had wished Lanny to attend his grandfather's Bible class and his
stepmother's church—even though Robbie himself wouldn't do it,
and paid a price for refusing. All this was hard to fathom.

As it happened, Lanny could run, and liked to, and he was a good
tennis player, so he would never be entirely a "queerie." But he had
many handicaps to success at St. Thomas's. He had just come from
abroad, and that made him an object of curiosity. He pronounced
French correctly, which could only be taken as an affectation. He
had read a great many books, and his masters discovered this fact
and brought it out in class, hoping to waken a desire for culture in
these "young barbarians all at play." That was hard on Lanny.

His first disillusionment came with the discovery that class sessions at St. Thomas's were rather dull. They consisted mainly of the
recitation of lessons studied the night before, and if you had studied
well, you were bored listening to other fellows who had studied
badly, and you were only mildly entertained by their efforts to "get
by" with a wisecrack. Rarely was there any intelligent discussion in
class; rarely anything taught about which either masters or pupils
were deeply concerned. They were preparing for college, and all
instruction was aimed like a gun at a target; they learned names,
dates, theorems, verb forms, rules, and exceptions—everything definite and specific, that could be measured and counted.

Lanny found that he was expected to assemble now and then
with his cousin's "set." These were called "bull sessions," and there
would be some talk about the prospects of beating Groton or St.
Paul's at football, and some about the wire-pulling of a rival set;
but sooner or later the talk would turn to sex. Lanny was no Puritan—on the contrary, he was here to study the Puritans; and what
troubled him was that the element of mutuality or idealism appeared to be lacking in their relations with girls. Shrewd and observant young men of the world, they knew how to deal with
"gold diggers," "salamanders," and other deadly females of the

species. Both boys and girls appeared to regard the love market as they would later in life the stock market—a place where you got something for nothing.

One of the characteristics of the horde is that it does not allow you to be different; it persecutes those who do not conform to its ideas and obey its taboos. There was a sensitive younger lad named Benny Cartright, whose father was a well-known portrait painter; he found out that Lanny was interested in this subject, and would cling to him and ask yearning questions about the art world abroad. There was a son of Mrs. Bascome, well-known suffrage lecturer; this youth wore horn-rimmed spectacles and was opposed to war on principle. More than a year ago Robbie had told his son about the secret treaties of the Allies, in which they had distributed the spoils of war among themselves; now these treaties were published in the New York *Evening Post,* and this chap Bascome brought them to Lanny in the form of a pamphlet.

So, despite his cousin's warnings, Lanny became more queer, and this was in due course reported back to the family. The grown-ups also were a horde, and watched the young and spied upon them— just as the masters in this school were expected to do. St. Thomas's had a "rule book," and your attention would be called to section nine, paragraph six; if you disregarded the warning, attention would be called more sternly, and if a third warning had no effect, you might be "sequestered."

Among the masters at St. Thomas's was one who taught English, a slender and ascetic young man who was trying to write poetry in his off hours. By accident he discovered that Lanny had not merely read the Greek dramatists but had visited that country. They talked about it after class, and from this developed a liking, and Lanny was invited to the master's room on several occasions. This was a form of queerness with which the horde had never before had to deal, and they didn't know quite what to make of it. They applied to it a rather awful term out of their varied assortment of slang; they said that Budd was "sucking up to" the somewhat pathetic Mr. Algernon Baldwin—who got only eight hundred dollars a year for his earnest labors in this school, and had an invalid mother to take care of.

VII

There came a cablegram from Juan, making a happy little jingle, though this was probably not intentional: "Girl both well Marcel." Later came a letter—since one could not count upon the cable these days. Beauty had a lovely little baby girl, and had named her Marceline. The painter was exceedingly proud of himself, after the fashion of fathers. He had persuaded Beauty to the unprecedented course of nursing the baby herself; a matter of hygiene and morality upon which he laid much stress. He had got the idea out of Rousseau.

Then came a letter from Mrs. Eric Vivian Pomeroy-Nielson, announcing that she was the mother of a baby boy. Said Nina: "I won't say much about him, because everything about new babies has been said a million times already. I send a picture." So Lanny had a pair to set up on his bureau; he wrote to each of the mothers about the other, suggesting that they get in touch and start making a match.

Nina revealed that poor Rick had had another operation, his third; still hoping to get rid of pain in what was left of his knee. They were living at The Reaches. Sir Alfred was helping with war work, and riding around to places most of the time. They were saving food, because the submarine blockade was pinching England badly.

Lanny went home for Thanksgiving and read this letter to his father, who said that the submarines were being countered by the system of convoying ships. The U-boats didn't dare show themselves in the neighborhood of destroyers, because of the effectiveness of depth bombs. So with the help of the combined navies great fleets of vessels were crossing the Atlantic in safety. The top men at Budd's knew all about it, having to adjust their system of loading to the sailing dates of convoys.

Father and son talked also about the second Russian revolution, which had just occurred. The government of Kerensky, trying to go on with the war, had been overthrown by a group called Bolsheviks—a Russian word which nobody had ever heard before. These were out-and-out revolutionists, confiscating all property and socializing industry. Robbie said this overturn was the most terrible blow the Allies had yet received; it meant that Germany had won half the war, and the job of the United States had been doubled. "It may mean even more than that," he added. "Those forces of hatred and destruction exist everywhere, and they're bound to try the same thing in other countries."

"Do you suppose there are Bolsheviks in this country, Robbie?"

"Thousands of them; they're not all Russians, either. Your Uncle Jesse Blackless is some such crackpot. That's why I was determined he shouldn't get hold of you."

"You mean he's an active Red?"

"He used to be, and this may stir him up again. He may be behind these mutinies which have been happening in the French army."

"But that's crazy, Robbie. Don't they know the Germans would march straight in and take the country?"

"I suppose they figure that the same sort of agitation is going on among the German troops. If that fire once got to blazing, it might spread everywhere."

"Gosh! Do you suppose we have such people in Budd's?"

"If there are, they keep pretty quiet. Father and Lawford have ways to keep track of agitators."

"You mean we have spies?"

"Nobody can expect to run an industry unless he knows what's going on in it. This thing in Russia has set all the agitators crazy." Robbie thought for a moment, then added: "Those secret treaties of the Allies have put a powerful weapon into their hands. They say to the workers: 'Look what you're fighting for! Look what's being done to you!'"

"But you said that too, Robbie!"

"I know; but it's one thing for you and me to know such facts, and another for them to be in the hands of revolutionists and criminals."

"There's a chap in school who has a copy of those treaties and talks about them a lot. He says everything that you do."

"Watch out for him," replied the father—his sense of humor failing him for once. "Some older and shrewder persons may be using him. These are dangerous times, and you have to watch your step."

VIII

Lanny went back to school, and it wasn't long before he walked into the very trap against which his father had warned him. There was a Mrs. Riccardi, a well-to-do society lady of the town of Sand Hill who sometimes gave musicales in her home. She found out that Lanny had studied "Dalcroze," and begged him to come and tell her friends about it. Lanny brought Jack Bascome and Benny Cartright to this affair, and it wasn't long before Bascome was talking against the war to Mrs. Riccardi. He told her about the secret treaties, and gave her the pamphlet, and she passed it on to others. Of course rumors of this were bound to spread. The country was at war, and people who found fault with France and England were lending aid and comfort to the enemy, whether they realized it or not.

On a Sunday evening Lanny and his two "queeries," Benny and Jack, went by invitation to the home of this wealthy lady, and there was Mr. Baldwin, and another schoolmaster of aesthetic tastes, and several other persons, including a young Methodist preacher with the unfashionable name of Smathers. Lanny had never heard of him, but learned that he had been pastor of a church in Newcastle—in the working-class part of the city, known as "beyond the tracks." He was a gentle, mild-voiced person, and in the course of the evening Lanny learned that he had got into the newspapers when there had been a strike of the workers in the Budd plants, and he had helped to organize a relief kitchen for the wives and children, and had made speeches and been chased down an alley and clubbed by mounted police.

Of course Lanny ought to have known better than to ask questions of such a man. The man tried to avoid answering them, saying that he didn't wish to give offense to a member of the Budd family; but that was a challenge to Lanny's integrity; he had to declare that he couldn't possibly be offended by the truth. So Mr. Smathers said, all right, if he asked for it he could have it. The other members of the company gathered round to hear what this "radical" young minister might have to say to a son and heir of Budd Gunmakers.

What Mr. Smathers said was that Budd's didn't allow their workers to organize. They had refused to let the strikers speak on the streets and had suppressed their papers; they had had the town council pass a law forbidding the distribution of handbills. Later on they had shut down the strike headquarters and had the leaders arrested on various charges. They had brought in an army of guards, whom they had made into "deputy sheriffs," and provided with arms and ammunition—made by the Budd workers for their own undoing. So the strike had been broken, and now no one could talk union in any Budd plant; workers who breathed a word of it were instantly fired.

Could all that be true? asked Lanny; and the Reverend Mr. Smathers replied that everybody in Newcastle knew that it was true. The businessmen justified it by saying that it was necessary to keep the workers from being led into violence. "What that means," said the minister, "is that large-scale private industry will destroy what we in America call political democracy, and our liberties are doomed. It seems to me that is something about which American citizens ought to be making up their minds."

Lanny could only thank Mr. Smathers for speaking frankly, and say that he had lived abroad, and hadn't even heard about the strike, which had taken place in the summer of 1913, while he was at Hellerau. Strange to think of such things going on at the very time that he was learning to enact the role of one of Gluck's furies! Such a graceful and charming fury he had been—and taking it for granted that tragic and cruel things happened only in operas and dramas, and that you were doing your duty to mankind when you learned to enact them beautifully!

Lanny didn't tell Mr. Smathers how his father had admitted to him that Budd's maintained a spy system. Nor did he say what he knew about his Uncle Lawford, who had had the handling of that strike. A somber person was this "vice-president in charge of production"; both he and the president of the company would know that whatever they did to protect Budd's and its profits was the will of the Almighty, and that whoever opposed them was an agent of Satan—or perhaps of Lenin and Trotsky, two personal devils who had suddenly leaped onto the front pages of American newspapers.

IX

Of course those who had been present that evening went out and talked about it. From the point of view of a hostess it had been a great success; people would be eager to come to a home where such dramatic incidents took place. The reports spread in ever-widening circles, and did not follow the laws which govern sound and water waves, but grew louder and bigger as they traveled. So came a new experience for the new pupil of St. Thomas's Academy.

One morning he was called from class to the office of the headmaster, Mr. Scott. This gentleman was tall and gray-haired, firm but kind in manner. With him were two severe-looking gentlemen whose clothes made them known as persons of importance. One was large and heavy, with scanty hair, and was introduced as Mr. Tarbell; Lanny learned afterwards that he was an important banker from the state capital, chairman of the board of trustees of the school. The other was a young businessman of the keen, go-getter type, an official in one of the big insurance companies. Mr. Pettyman was his name, and he also was a trustee.

Lanny was quickly made aware that this was a grave occasion. They had come, said the headmaster, to make inquiries about Mr. Baldwin, concerning whom certain reports were being circulated:

they wished Lanny to tell them all he knew about this master.

The request brought the blood to Lanny's cheeks. "Mr. Baldwin is a gentleman of the very highest type," he said, quickly. "He has been most kind to me, and has given me a great deal of help."

"I am pleased to hear you say that," replied the headmaster. "Is there anything you could report that would do him harm?"

"I'm quite sure there is not, sir."

"Then I know you will be glad to answer any questions these gentlemen may ask you."

Lanny wasn't exactly glad, but he realized at once that if he hesitated, or seemed to be lacking in frankness, it would be taken as counting against his friend.

Mr. Tarbell, the banker, spoke in a slow and heavy voice. "It is being reported that Mr. Baldwin has talked in a way to indicate that he is out of sympathy with the war. Has he said anything of the sort to you?"

"Do you mean privately, or in class?"

"I mean either."

"In class I have never heard him mention the war. Privately he has sometimes agreed with things I have said to him."

"What have you said to him?"

"I have said it's a war for profits, and that for this reason I find it hard to give it any support."

"What reason can you have for saying that it's a war for profits?"

"I have seen the evidence, sir."

"Indeed! Who has shown it to you?"

"My father, for one."

The banker from Hartford appeared taken aback. "Your father has said that in so many words?"

"He has said it a hundred times. He wrote it to me continually while I was living in France. He warned me on no account to let myself forget that it's a war to protect big French and British interests, and that many of them are trading with the enemy, and protecting their own properties to the injury of their country."

"Ahem!" said Mr. Tarbell. Words seemed to have failed him.

"And what is more," persisted Lanny, "Zaharoff admitted as much in my presence."

"Who is Zaharoff?"

It was Lanny's turn to be surprised. "Zaharoff is the richest man in the world, sir."

"Indeed! Is he richer than Rockefeller?"

"He controls most of the armament plants of Europe, and my father says this war has made him the richest man in the world. Now he is keen for the war to continue—'*jusqu'au bout*,' he said. My father had a letter from Lord Riddell the other day, saying that was Zaharoff's phrase."

"And this man admits that his motive is profits?"

"Not in those words, sir, but it was the clear sense of many things he said."

"You know him personally, you mean?"

"I was in his home in Paris last March, with my father, and they talked about the war a great deal, as businessmen and makers of munitions."

X

The banker dropped the embarrassing subject of a war for profits. He said it had been reported that Mr. Baldwin had attended a social gathering in Sand Hill, at which there had been a great deal of Bolshevik talk by a notorious preacher named Smathers. Had Lanny been there? Lanny said he had been at Mrs. Riccardi's, if that was the place that was meant. He had heard no such talk; he had come away thinking that the Reverend Mr. Smathers was a saint, which was something different from a Bolshevik, as he understood it.

"But didn't he criticize Budd Gunmakers Corporation and its conduct of the strike?"

"He told what had happened—but only after I had asked him to."

"Do you accept what he told you?"

"I have in mind to ask my father about it, but I haven't seen him since that time."

"Did Mr. Baldwin take any part in that conversation?"

"I don't recall that he did. I think he listened, like most of the others."

"And did he say anything to you about it afterwards?"

"No, sir. He was probably afraid of embarrassing me."

"Did he know that Mr. Smathers was to be there?"

"I have no idea about that, sir. I was invited by Mrs. Riccardi, and I didn't know who else was coming."

"There were other pupils of St. Thomas's present?"

"Yes, sir."

"Who were they?"

Lanny hesitated. "I would rather not say anything about my fellow-pupils, sir. I have said that I would tell you about Mr. Baldwin."

The young go-getter, Mr. Pettyman, took up the questioning. He wanted to know about the master's ideas, and what was the basis of Lanny's intimacy with him. Lanny replied that Mr. Baldwin was a lover of poetry, and had written some fine verses, and had given them to Lanny to read. He had lent him books. What books? Lanny named a volume of Santayana. It was a foreign-sounding name, and evidently Mr. Pettyman hadn't heard of it, so Lanny mentioned that the writer had been a professor of philosophy at Harvard.

In a kind and fatherly way the banker reminded the impetuous lad that the nation was at war. "Our boys are going overseas to die in a cause which may not be perfect—but how often do you meet absolute perfection in this world? There has never been a war in which some persons didn't profiteer at the expense of the government. The same thing happened in the Civil War, but that didn't keep it from being a war to preserve the Union."

"I know," said Lanny. "My father has told me about that also. He says that was how J. P. Morgan made the start of his fortune— by selling condemned rifles to the Union government."

So ended the questioning of Lanny Budd. He didn't realize what an awful thing he had said until later, when he told his father about it, and Robbie manifested surprise mixed with amusement. Mr. Tar-

bell's great bank was known as a "Morgan bank," and the House of
Morgan was just then the apex of dignity and power in the financial world—it was handling the purchases of the Allied governments,
expending about three thousand million dollars of their money in
the United States!

22

Above the Battle

I

LANNY came home for Christmas. The war was not allowed
to interfere with this festival; a big tree was set up in the home, and
elaborate decorations were hung. Everybody spent a lot of time
thinking what presents to give to relatives who obviously didn't
need anything. Lanny, a stranger, sought the advice of his stepmother, and they went to the town's largest bookstore and tried to
guess what sort of book each person might care for. By this method
the well-to-do got reading matter enough to occupy their time for
the rest of the year.

Lanny remembered his Christmas at Schloss Stubendorf, where
people ate enormously, but were frugal in other spending. Here in
New England it was the other way around—it wasn't quite good
form to stuff your stomach, but Yankee ingenuity had been expended in devising toys to please the children of the rich, and adults
were swamped under a flood of goods incredibly perfect in
workmanship. On Christmas morning the base of the tree was piled
with packages wrapped in multicolored paper and tied with ribbons. Pipes and cigars, bedroom slippers, silk dressing gowns, neck-

ries—these were standard for the men—while ladies received jewels, wristwatches, silk stockings, veils and scarves, handbags and vanity cases, elaborately decorated boxes of chocolates and candied fruits —everyone had such quantities of these things that it was rather a bore opening parcels, and you could read in their faces the thought: "What on earth am I going to do with all this?"

Robert junior and Percy were two friendly and quite normal boys, living rather repressed lives at home. Esther considered all forms of extravagance as bad taste, and tried to teach this to her children; but she was fighting the current of her time, in which everything grew more elaborate and expensive, and a vast propaganda for spending was maintained by thousands of interested agencies. Here came this flood of goods, bearing the cards of uncles and aunts and cousins and school friends and even employees; the boys became surfeited, and couldn't really appreciate anything.

Lanny had his share of goods and of bewilderment. Good heavens, three sweaters—when already he had several hanging in his clothes closet! More neckties, more handkerchiefs, more hair brushes; an alligator-skin belt that was too heavy for comfort; newly published books that some clerk in a store had said would appeal to a youth. And in the midst of all that superfluity, a gift from Great-Great-Uncle Eli—a much worn copy of Thoreau's *Walden*, appearing as misplaced as its author would have been in this fashionable company. Henry David Thoreau, telling you how to live in a hut on a diet of cornmeal mush and beans, in order to have your spirit free and your time not in pawn to commercialism! Old New England and new New England met in the Budd family drawing room, and neither was much interested in the other.

II

Lanny had sent his great-great-uncle the handsomest book he could find in the local store, a "de luxe" copy of *Don Quixote* with the Doré illustrations. There came now an invitation to spend a week-end with the old gentleman, and to bring Bess along. Esther wasn't entirely pleased by the intimacy between her daughter and her stepson, but Lanny promised to drive very, very carefully on the snow-covered roads, and Bess was so thrilled and Robbie so pleased that the mother couldn't forbid the visit.

Between Lanny and his stepmother lay a temperamental gulf that nothing could ever bridge. Lanny was guided by his love of beauty, whereas Esther had to think carefully about everything she felt or did, and bring it into conformity with rigid standards. A few times in the afternoon she had come in to find her stepson playing the piano in a loud and extravagant manner, completely absorbed in it; Esther had stood and listened, uneasy in her mind. She had never heard such music, at least not in a drawing room, and to her it was disorderly and unwholesome. Impossible to believe that anyone could let himself go like that and not sooner or later misbehave in other ways.

Bess with her excitability had been something of a "problem child" to her mother; and now came this youth from abroad to stimulate that tendency. Bess would listen to his playing with a rapt expression, as if transported to some strange land where her mother had never been. Bess wanted to play like Lanny, she wanted to dance like him—and wear a one-piece bathing suit in a drawing room while doing it! She chattered about the places her romantic half-brother had visited, the people he had met, the sights he had seen, the stories he told her. Books on child training which Esther conscientiously read all agreed that you shouldn't be saying "Don't! Don't"—and so Esther didn't. But uneasiness troubled her heart.

On that lovely winter ride, snugly wrapped in fur robes, Lanny told the child about the wonderful old gentleman she was going to meet. Great-Great-Uncle Eli had once helped slaves to escape; his friend Thoreau had gone to jail for refusing to pay taxes to a slave-catching government, and when the poet Emerson had come and asked: "Henry, what are you doing here?" Henry had answered: "Waldo, what are you doing out of here?" Some of them had gone to live in a colony called Brook Farm, in order to be independent and have more wholesome lives. "What is a colony?" demanded

Bess; and then: "Oh, what fun! Are there any colonies now? Could we go and live in one, do you suppose?"

These two reincarnations of New England idealism arrived in the village of Norton in the proper mood to appreciate their venerable relative. The sweet little Quaker wife and the spinster daughter made them at home, and Bess sat for hours at the old man's feet. She couldn't understand all his long words, but she knew that what he said was good. When the two young people drove home again they had this new bond between them, as if some ancient prophet had anointed them with holy oil.

III

The last winter of the war was the darkest and most dreadful. For three years and a half all the ingenuities of man and the resources of science had been devoted to the ends of destruction. Both sides now had many kinds of poison gases: some which penetrated the clothing and tormented the skin, some which destroyed the lungs, some which blinded men, or made them vomit unceasingly. These gases were put into shells, and whole battlefronts were drenched with them. The Germans had flame throwers, which killed the man who used them as well as those in front. The British and French had tanks, "big Willies" and "little Willies," which advanced in front of the troops, spitting fire and death.

The poet's vision had come to reality, and there rained a ghastly dew from the nations' airy navies grappling in the central blue. Squadrons of swift fighting craft darted here and there; they swooped from the clouds and machine-gunned the marching troops; they raided behind the lines and dropped bombs upon railroads and ammunition dumps. The Zepps were fought with explosive bullets, and so great was the peril that the crews of two vessels destroyed them at home in order to avoid going out in them.

Everything had become bigger and more deadly than ever before. The Germans constructed enormous siege guns, known as "Big Berthas," and set them up in a forest behind Laon, and were firing shells into Paris from a distance of seventy-five miles. At first people had refused to believe such a thing possible; but now they were being fired every twenty minutes, and on Good Friday one of their shells struck a church and killed and wounded nearly two hundred persons, many of them women and children.

For the U-boats there were depth bombs, and nets across all the principal harbors and channels. The Americans were furnishing seventy thousand mines, which were being laid in a chain across the northern entrance to the North Sea, from the Orkney Islands to the coast of Norway, a distance of nearly three hundred miles. That made one for every twenty feet. Also the British had devised the "Q-boats"—old tramp steamers with concealed armor sent out to wander in the danger zones. A submarine would rise and open fire with shells—for they tried to save their torpedoes for bigger craft. Some of the men of the "Q-boat," the "panic-crew," would take to the boats; the "sub" would come closer to complete her job—and suddenly portions of the steamer sides would drop down, disclosing six-inch guns which would open deadly fire.

America was getting ready, upon a scale and with a speed never before known in history. You could feel the spirit of the country hardening in the face of world-wide danger. People talked about the war to the exclusion of everything else; even at St. Thomas's, even at the "bull sessions," the fellows discussed what was going on, and what part they hoped to have in it. The draft age was twenty-one, but you could volunteer younger, and now and then some upper classman would pack up his belongings and move to an officers' training camp.

Lanny was now eighteen, and his father worried over the possibility that his emotional temperament might take fire. Whenever the youth came home over Sunday, Robbie would sound him out to see if the bacteria of propaganda had found lodgment in his mind; if so, he would be subjected to a swift prophylaxis. "Did you ever hear of Lord Palmerston?" the father would inquire. "He was Prime Minister of England during our Civil War, and he said: 'England has no enduring friendships. She only has enduring interests.'"

Robbie and Esther didn't agree about England, or about America either, and Robbie's rule was to let her say anything she pleased, uncontradicted. He did the same thing with his friends; of course they all knew that he had special opportunities to get information, and their curiosity was aroused, but all he would say was that he made weapons for those who wanted to fight and had the cash. Now and then old Samuel would caution his son: "Tend to business and let fools shoot off their mouths." No one ever found out what the president of Budd Gunmakers thought about this war; all they knew was that he made munitions twenty-four hours every day, including the Lord's.

As a result of all this Lanny wasn't entirely happy through the war period. People weren't satisfied to let you think your own thoughts; they considered it their duty to probe you, to cross-examine you, and if you were wrong to try to set you right. At school the fellows decided that Lanny was lacking in appreciation of the land where his fathers died; his fashionable cousin told him so, and they agreed to have different roommates the following year. At the same time Lanny was deprived of the companionship of Mr. Baldwin, for the young master had been advised to confine his teaching to the subject of literature, and to avoid contacts with his pupils outside the classroom.

IV

There came a letter which gave Lanny an extraordinary thrill. The envelope was addressed by typewriter, with no sender's name, but with a United States stamp and a New York postmark; inside was a long missive from Kurt Meissner! At first Lanny wondered, had Kurt come to New York; but then he realized that his friend must have known somebody in a neutral country who was coming.

Anyhow, here was a real letter, the first Lanny had had from Germany since the outbreak of the war. Kurt gave the news about himself and his family. He was a captain of artillery, and had been twice wounded, once with a bullet through the thigh, and the second time having pieces of ribs torn out by a shell fragment. He was not at liberty to give the name of his unit or where it was stationed; only that he was writing from a billet in a town behind the front, while having a few days' recuperation. All three of his brothers had been in the war; one had been killed during the early invasion of East Prussia, and another was now at home recovering from a wound. Kurt's father had an important government post. His sister had married an officer, and was a widow with two babies.

Kurt told about the state of his soul, which was uncomplicated, and oddly like that of Marcel and of Rick. The country was at war, and it was necessary for a man to put aside everything else, and to help to overcome an arrogant and treacherous foe. Kurt said he was as much interested in music and philosophy as ever, but his duties as an artillery officer left him little time to think about these subjects. After the Fatherland had emerged victorious, as surely it must and would, he would hope to hear that his American friend had been able to go on with his studies.

This led to the main purpose of the letter, which was to plead with Lanny to resist the subtle wiles of the British propaganda machine. Kurt wasn't afraid that his friend might get physically hurt, for it was obvious that the British would be driven into the sea and the French would lose Paris long before the Americans could take any effective part in this war. But Kurt didn't want his friend's mind distorted and warped by the agents of British imperialism. These people, who had grabbed most of the desirable parts of the earth, now thought they had a chance to destroy the German fleet, build their Cape-to-Cairo railroad, keep the Germans from building the Berlin-to-Bagdad railroad, and in every way thwart the efforts of a vigorous and capable race to find their place in the sun.

It was to be expected that France would hate Germany and make war upon her, because the French were a jealous people, and thought of Germans as their hereditary enemies; they were pursuing their futile dream of getting Alsace-Lorraine with its treasures of coal and iron. But Englishmen were blood kinsmen to the Germans, and their war upon Germany was fratricide; the crime of using black and brown and yellow troops to destroy the highest culture in Europe would outlaw its perpetrators forever. Now the desperate British militarists were spending their wealth circulating a mass of lies about Germany's war methods and war aims; what a tragedy that Americans, a free people, with three thousand miles of ocean between them and Europe's quarrels, had swallowed all this propaganda, and were wasting their money and their labor helping Britain to grab more territory and harness more peoples to her imperial chariot!

Lanny took that letter to his father, and they read it together, and Robbie pointed out how its arguments resembled those which you could read every day in the Newcastle *Daily Courier*—but with everything turned around! Each saw his own side, and was blind to the other fellow's. "You write Kurt and tell him that you are going on with your studies," said the father; and added: "Phrase it carefully, because you can't tell who may read a letter nowadays."

V

Now and then Lanny would write to his mother, reciting his adventures in the land of the pilgrims' pride: all the strange kinds of people he was meeting, and how different it was from Provence. Knowing how Beauty was interested in human beings, he went into detail about his stepmother: a good woman, but so inhibited—a word Lanny had learned from the conversation of Sophie, Baroness de la Tourette, who was very different from Esther Remson Budd, and would have been a scandal if she had ever come to Newcastle. Lanny left no doubt that he preferred Juan as a home, but he was doing his job here as his father wished.

Beauty wrote once or twice a month, nice gossipy letters. Baby Marceline was thriving upon her natural diet, and Beauty herself was well, and as happy as one could expect to be in these sad days. More and more widows on the streets, more and more *mutilés* for Emily Chattersworth to crowd into her place. Prices were rising, and fear was universal—Beauty said she couldn't write all the alarming things that were reported. Everywhere an American went he heard one question: "When are your soldiers coming?" The Germans were preparing an enormous offensive by which they hoped to end the war; and poor France had scraped the bottom of the national pot for man power. There just weren't any more young men, hardly any middle-aged ones; you didn't see them on the streets, you didn't see them in the fields. "Oh, Lanny, I am praying to God it may be over before you grow up!"

Marcel would send a message, or scribble a line or two on the bottom of the page. Marcel didn't discuss the war, or his own problems; he would say something about the state of Lanny's soul: "Remember you are an artist, and don't let the Puritans frighten you." He would say: "I am painting a *chasseur* parting from his mother; it looks like this"—and he would give a little pencil sketch. He would say: "*Seine Majestät* is worried," and make a comic drawing of the figure most hated in France. Lanny treasured these sketches, and showed them to his father, but not to anyone else. His stepmother would of course disapprove of his having a stepfather; if Lanny's mother had been a woman with a sense of propriety she would have expiated her sin by living a celibate life.

But Beauty had been born without that sense. Beauty had a husband of a sort, and was making the most of him. She talked about his work upon every occasion, fought for it, and intrigued to get it shown and recognized—a custom in France, and possibly not unknown in other lands. When some critic called Marcel Detaze a painter with a future, Beauty purchased all the copies of that paper she could find, and cut out the article and sent it to her friends. Marcel still didn't care for being "promoted," but his wife had won the right to do what she could.

Her main struggle was to keep him from going back into the army. She would say, over and over: "The Americans are coming, Marcel! They are making a real army! They mean to finish it!" She would find things in the British and American papers and magazines and bring them to him. She wrote to Robbie, asking him to tell her what was going on, in such a way that Marcel would be convinced, and so be willing to stay at home and leave the saving of France to men who didn't happen to be geniuses.

VI

The new masters of Russia, the Bolsheviks, made peace with the Germans at Brest-Litovsk, an action regarded as treason by almost everybody in the Allied lands. It set the Germans free in the east, and enabled them for the first time to have an actual superiority of numbers on the western front. Their long-prepared offensive was launched in the middle of March; first against the British on the Somme, a front of nearly fifty miles. They brought up masses of artillery, and mountains of smoke shells and gas shells; they overwhelmed the British and drove them back with a loss of some three hundred thousand men. They attacked again farther north, and pushed the weakened British lines almost to the sea. Then they fell upon the French, and drove them again to the river Marne, close to Paris, as in the early days of the war.

This desperate fighting lasted for about three months, and all that while the French people lived in an agony of suspense, waiting hour by hour for news of the collapse which seemed inevitable. Frenchmen and Britons were dying by hundreds every hour, sometimes by thousands; and hopes were dying even faster—among them those of poor, tormented Beauty.

The first news came to Lanny by mail; no use to cable, since there was nothing to be done. "Marcel has gone," wrote the mother. "He stole away at night, leaving a letter on my pillow. I made it too hard for him, I suppose; he couldn't face any more scenes. Do not worry about me, I have got myself together. I've been living this over and over for the past two years, and never really believed I could escape it. Now I don't torment myself with hope; now I know I shall never see him again. They will take him into the army, and he will die fighting. I have to reconcile myself to the fact that one cannot have happiness in these times.

"Of course I have little Marceline," the letter went on. "That is why she was brought into the world, because in my secret heart I knew what was coming. I am still nursing her, but I have been going over to Sept Chênes every afternoon. There are such pitiful cases. I don't know what to think about the war, or what to expect. It seems impossible that the Germans can ever be driven out of France. Shall I have to watch the spectacle of American boys coming over and being sacrificed for nothing? Have I got to live to see my only son drawn into it? Am I going to hear the same phrases from you that I listened to from Marcel's lips?"

While Lanny was reading that letter, he knew that Marcel must be in the thick of the fighting. He was a trained man, and the fact that part of his face was gone wouldn't count in a time like this. They would give him a uniform and a gun, assign him to a regiment, and put him into one of the *camions* that were being rushed to the front.

And so it turned out. Marcel wrote letters to his wife, full of quiet certainty and peace; he was doing the thing that he had to do, that he was made to do. He wrote about the sights he had seen in Paris; about the men in his outfit, some too old and some too young, some veterans just out of hospital. He wasn't allowed to tell where he was going, but presently he was there, and the boche was in front of him, and still advancing, and had to be stopped.

And that was the end. There came no more letters. The enemy advanced, and was not stopped—at least not yet. Of course there remained the possibility that Marcel might have been taken prisoner; his friends had to wait until the war was over, and then wait some more; but they never heard from him. Later on Lanny made inquiries, and learned that Marcel's company had been defending one of those trenches which had been turned into shell holes; presumably he had stayed there, firing his rifle as long as he could hold it and see the enemy. He had been buried in an unmarked grave, along with many of his comrades; his dust would enrich the soil of *la patrie,* and his soul would inspire new generations of Frenchmen with a love of beauty, and with pity for the blunders and sorrows of mankind.

VII

Lanny came home for a week-end, and found a surprise letter. He had failed to let Jerry Pendleton know he was in the United States, so the letter had crossed the ocean and come back. His old tutor had been picked in one of the early drafts and trained in Camp Funston. Now he was a sergeant, a machine-gun expert giving special training to a group in Camp Devens and expecting soon to move on, to a destination not supposed to be mentioned in soldiers' letters. But Jerry said: "I'm going to see Cerise if I have to bust a gut"—which wasn't exactly keeping military secrets!

Lanny was greatly excited, for he had heard a lot about Camp Devens; it was where some of his classmates had gone, and others were planning to go at the end of the term. It was in Massachusetts, some three hours' drive from Newcastle. "Oh, Robbie, can't I go and see him? Right away, before he sails!"

"Send a wire and find out if he's still there," said the father. Lanny did so, and the reply came in a jiffy: "Delighted advise coming quickly visitors one to five any day." Jerry, economical fellow, had got in his exact ten words.

Lanny was all in a fuss. He must go the next day, which was Sunday. Wouldn't Robbie go with him? Jerry Pendleton was a grand chap, and perhaps was using the Budd gun, and might be able to tell Robbie things. The father said, all right, they'd make an excursion of it. Esther said to take the boys. Of course Bess started her clamor, and Robbie said: "Send Jerry a telegram to prepare tea for five!"

New England was beautiful at that time of year; the spring flowers up in the woods, and the trees a shimmering pale green. The rivers ran brown with floods from the distant hills, but the bridges were strong, and most of the roads were paved. The young people chattered with excitement, having heard a lot about this marvelous "cantonment," as it was officially called. There were sixteen of them scattered over the United States, and they had grown like the beanstalk in the fairy tale—last June there had been nothing, and two months later there had been accommodations, complete with all modern improvements, for six or seven hundred thousand men.

They arrived at the gates of the new city at one, and found their host waiting for them. The army was proud of its great feat, and visitors were made welcome. Jerry was bronzed by the sun and seemed taller, certainly he was broader, and a fine advertisement for military training; handsome in his khaki uniform with leggings and his service hat with a flat brim and strap. He was serious, and proud of the place, showing it off as if he owned it. It was a regular city, with avenues named A, B, C, and cross streets 1, 2, 3. Its buildings were mostly one-story, all alike, of unpainted pine siding; there were fourteen hundred buildings in Camp Devens, and the stuff had all been cut to a pattern. Jerry said that when the carpenters got going they aimed to make a record of one building every hour, and boasted of a world's record when they averaged one every fifteen minutes.

Now forty thousand doughboys swarmed all over the place: keen, clean-cut fellows, all smooth-shaven—and all having had chicken and mashed potatoes for their Sunday dinner. Another world's record was being made, an army without liquor; since it had put in the plumbing before anything else, there wasn't any disease and wasn't going to be. All this the machine-gun expert told them while standing on the running board of the car, guiding Robbie through the traffic of trucks, motorcycles, and mule wagons which were like old prairie schooners with khaki tops.

Jerry took them to his own building, which he said he had in strict privacy with some thirty other men. The long room had a low ceiling, and a pleasant smell of fresh pinewood. Everything was as clean as in a hospital; the cots were of black steel and the floors were swept and scrubbed daily. Jerry showed them the messroom, where they had better food than most of the men had ever seen in their lives. He took them to the drill grounds, where you could watch thousands of men exercising—"and believe me, we get plenty of it," said the red-headed sergeant.

"Yes," he added, "the machine guns are Budd's." He took them to the place where he gave instruction with real trenches, and rocks and trees and brush for cover. Jerry showed some of the drill, and sang a doughboy song: "Keep your head down, Fritzie boy!"

He and Robbie had technical details to talk about, while the young people stood and listened in awe. Yes, it was a grand gun; Jerry doubted if anybody in Europe had one as good. "I've studied some of them," he explained. "I have to teach something about them, because a soldier never knows what he may run into on the battlefield."

This man's army was learning fast, and it was going to do the job. Its training was all for attack, the sergeant affirmed. "We aren't going over there to sit in trenches. We teach the men how to capture positions, and to go on from there to the next one."

"The Germans have pretty good machine guns," cautioned Robbie.

"We expect to flatten them out with artillery, and then get them with hand grenades. There's one thing they lack, and that's a lifetime's practice at throwing a baseball. Most of our fellows can land a grenade onto a target the first throw. Every time you hit the nigger you get a good seegar!" Jerry grinned, and added: "I don't know if you ever went to a county fair in Kansas."

VIII

All the time Lanny kept thinking: "Marcel ought to be here and see this!"—a thought which had a tendency to diminish the pleasure of his visit. It was gratifying to meet an old friend, and find him bronzed and handsome, astonishingly matured and full of vigor; but when you thought how he might be three months from now— like Marcel, or Rick, or Lanny's gigolo—the crowded cantonment took on a different aspect. They watched those proud, upstanding fellows marching on the drill ground, and Lanny saw a troubled look on his half-sister's face, and guessed that she was thinking the same thoughts. She was only ten years old, but children always

know when there is dissension in a home, and Bess understood how
her father felt about this war, and how Lanny felt.

On their way home the two boys prattled gaily about the wonders they had seen. They were Budds, and made machine guns, and
in their fancy used them freely. They had learned to make sounds
in imitation of the weapon's chatter, and as the car rolled along
they discovered solid ranks of Germans charging out of some
farmer's woodlot, and mowed them down without the slightest
qualm. They wanted to know all about the men they had seen being entrained from the cantonment; what embarkation camp they
were taken to, and what kind of transports they boarded, the time
it took to get to France, the chances of a submarine sinking them.

Their father didn't worry about them, because they were too
young to get into this mess. But he wanted to be sure that Lanny
hadn't been seduced by all the glamour. Making war is an ancient
practice of mankind, and it is always impressive to see a job done
with vigor and speed. So Robbie waited for something to come out
of his eldest's thoughtful mood; and when it did, he got a pleasant
surprise.

Said Lanny: "Do you suppose that when school's over you could
find me some job in the plant for the summer?"

"What sort of a job, son?"

"Anything where I could be useful, and learn something about
the business."

"You really think that would interest you?"

"Well, everybody's doing something, and a fellow doesn't feel
comfortable just to be playing round."

"If you make a good record at school, Lanny, nobody's going to
question your right to a summer vacation."

"If they knew how little real work I have to do, they might. And
if you're going to tell a draft board that I'm needed to make munitions, hadn't I better know something about it?"

"It'll be two years and a half before you have to consider that
problem."

"I read that they're thinking of lowering the draft age. So if you don't want me in, you'd better get busy and fix up an alibi."

"We'll think about it," replied the father; and added, with a smile: "It would make something of a hit with the president of Budd's!"

23

Midsummer-Night's Dream

I

EXAMINATIONS came at St. Thomas's, and Lanny passed with good grades, and checked off his list several subjects about which he would never have to think again.

He had now spent fourteen months in Connecticut; and during that period more than a million Americans had been ferried across to France. Jerry Pendleton and fifty thousand other sergeants were ready to try out the idea that German machine-gun nests could be wiped out by baseball players throwing Budd hand grenades. During the fourteen months' period the plants had been working day and night without let-up. Smoke billowed from their chimneys, the workers toiled like swarms of ants, and the products were piled by the million in warehouses in France and behind the fighting front. The doughboys had had a sort of tryout at the battle of Cantigny, and now were being moved into position to stop the German advance on Paris.

Such was the news in the papers when Lanny sat down to discuss with his father the problem of how to spend the summer. He still wanted to go into the plant; and when Robbie asked his ideas, he said: "Why shouldn't I take a job like anybody else, and see how it feels to put in an eight-hour day?"

"Beginning at the bottom of the ladder?" smiled the father.

"Isn't that the accepted way?"

"Accepted by the fiction editors. You'd be set down in one corner of one room, and learn six motions of your hands, and do them say eight hundred times a day for three months. You would learn that it is very fatiguing."

"I thought I might learn something about the people I was working with."

"You'd learn that nine out of ten of them don't know anything but their six motions, and don't care about those. You'd learn that they are making a lot of money, and don't know what to do with it except to buy fancy shirts and socks and a second-hand car. You can learn all that by going down on Center Street any evening."

This was discouraging. "I didn't like to suggest going into the office, Robbie, because I don't know anything, and I saw that everybody was so busy."

"Both those things are true. But, first, tell me what's in your mind. Do you want to become a Budd executive, and live out by the country club? Or would you rather learn my business in Europe? In other words, do you want to make munitions or sell them?"

"I thought I ought to know both jobs, Robbie."

"You have to know something about both if you're going to know either; but they are highly specialized, and you have to concentrate. It's like choosing your major and minor subjects when you go to college."

"Well, you're asking if I want to be with you, or with Uncle Lawford. You know what I'll say to that."

"Then why not start in my office, and see everything in the plant from there, as I do?"

"Can you make sure I won't get in the way?"

"I'll make mighty darn sure of it," said the father. "If you get in my way, I'll tell you, and if you get in other people's way, they'll tell you."

"That's fair enough."

"All right then; here's my idea for the summer: have a desk in my room, and sit there and study munitions instead of sines and cosines or the names of English kings. When I interview callers you listen, and when I dictate letters, you get the correspondence and follow it back until you understand the deal. Study contracts and specifications, prices and discounts; get the blueprints, and what you don't understand ask me about. Learn the formulas for steel, and when you know enough to understand what you're seeing, go down to the shop and watch the process. When you know the parts of a gun, take it apart and see if you can put it together again. Go to the testing grounds and watch it work—all sorts of things like that."

Lanny listened in a glow. "Gee, Robbie, that's too much!"

"How far you get will depend on you. This much ought to be certain—in three months you'll know whether you're really interested and want to go on. Is that a deal?"

"You bet it is!"

"I'll tell my secretaries to give you whatever papers you ask for, and you'll make it your business to turn them back to the person you got them from. You mustn't touch the files yourself, because there can't be any blundering in them. If there's anything else you want, ask me, because everybody in the place is working under heavy pressure, and they wouldn't like you if you tripped them up. One thing you know already—you won't ever breathe a word to anybody about what you learn on this job."

II

For a while Lanny was like a sailorman who has dug up an old chest full of Spanish doubloons and jewels; he couldn't get enough of looking at them and running them through his hands. All those mysterious things that he had heard his father discussing with army

officers and ministers of war were now unveiled to him. One of the
first that came along was a lot of reports from the firms abroad
that had leased Budd patents for the duration of the war; also the
secret reports that Bub Smith was sending on the same subject. It
was like being turned loose amid the private papers of Sherlock
Holmes! Lanny dreamed of the day when he might be able to call
Robbie's attention to some discrepancy in the reports of Zaharoff's
companies, something that Robbie himself had overlooked in the
rush of affairs. But he never had that luck.

His new job brought him the honor of an invitation to dine at
his grandfather's. He and Robbie went together, and the old gentleman said: "Well, young man, I hear you have kept your promise."
Just that, and no more.

They talked about the war developments, and ate a New England
boiled dinner served by an old-maid servant under the direction of
an old-maid relative. Later in the evening the grandfather said:
"Well, young man, you have attended my Bible class. Have you
learned anything?" Lanny said that he had; and at once the other
launched on a discourse having to do with the one certainty of
Salvation through Faith. He talked for five minutes or more; and
then he turned to Robbie and remarked: "Well, number 17-B gun
seems to be holding up pretty well in France."

Lanny was so absorbed in his new researches that he wanted to
get to the office early, and wanted to stay at night when something
kept his father. But Esther intervened again, and Robbie agreed—a
growing youth ought not to work more than an eight-hour day,
and Lanny ought to get some tennis and a swim in the pool at the
country club before dinner. So it was ordered; and so the way was
prepared for another stage in a young man's expanding career.

The Newcastle Country Club had purchased two large farms and
built a one-story red brick clubhouse, close enough to town so that
businessmen could motor out now and then for a round of golf before dinner on summer evenings. Besides the Budd people, there
were officials of other manufacturing concerns, of utilities and
banks and the bigger stores; several doctors and lawyers, the local

newspaper publisher, and a few gentlemen of no special calling. The ladies came in the afternoon to play bridge, and in the evenings there were dances, and now and then some entertainment to relieve the boredom of people who knew one another too well. When you have lived all your life in a town, it may seem dull and commonplace; but when you are young, and a stranger, the commonest varieties of gossip take on the aspect of lessons in human nature.

There were several "sets" in this club: groups of persons who considered themselves superior to others, whether because they were richer, or because their families were older, or because they drank less, or because they drank more. There were a few who regarded themselves as clever; they were younger, and had the ideas called "modern." Since the western part of Connecticut is a suburb of New York, there were "smart" people, who did what they pleased and made cynical remarks about the "mores" of their grandfathers. You couldn't very well keep them out of a club, because some of them belonged to the "best" families.

Of course such a group would be interested in a handsome youth who had lived abroad, and spoke French fluently, and could talk about Cannes and Paris and London, Henley and Ascot and Longchamps. He played the piano, he danced well, and if he did not smoke or drink, that made him all the more an object of curiosity; the bored ladies imagined that he must be virginal, and they made themselves agreeable, and worried because he insisted upon staying in a dull office and couldn't be lured away for a *tête-à-tête*.

It was the practice of the club to give dramatic performances during the summer, in an open-air theater built in a woodland glade. There was a "dramatics committee," and hot arguments as to what sort of plays should be given. The smart crowd wanted modern things, full of talk about sex; the conservatives demanded and got something sentimental and sweet, suitable for the young people. In view of the conditions prevailing, they had given a war play called *Lilac Time*, which had been the success of the previous season in New York.

This summer everybody was supposed to be absorbed in war work. The businessmen went to their offices early and stayed late. The women spent their spare time rolling bandages, knitting socks and sweaters, or attending committee meetings where such activities were planned. But there were a few whom these efforts did not satisfy; perhaps their hearts were not in the killing of their fellow human beings, or in arousing the killing impulse in others. One could not say this, in the midst of all the patriotic fervors; what one said was that the cultural life of the community must not be allowed to lapse altogether, and that overworked executives who were forgoing their customary month of vacation ought to have some gracious form of entertainment.

So it was that the dramatics committee had summoned its courage and undertaken a production of *A Midsummer-Night's Dream*, which provides a variety of outdoor diversions and has charming music. The committee cast about for players suited to the various roles, and invited Lanny to become one of two lovelorn gentlemen who wander through a forest in the neighborhood of Athens. No one on the committee knew that Lanny himself had been a lovelorn gentleman for a couple of years. He still was—for only a few days ago he had received a letter from his erstwhile sweetheart, mentioning casually in the course of other news that she was about to be married to the grandson of the Earl of Sandhaven, who had been recalled from the "Mespot" front and was now attached to the War Office in London.

Lanny said he didn't think he'd have time to rehearse a play; but the committee assured him that the work would be done in the evening—of necessity, since the part of the Duke of Athens was to be played by a stately vice-president of the First National Bank, and the part of Bottom was entrusted to a member of the town's busiest law firm. Lanny's family gave their approval, and thereafter he dined at the club with other members of the cast, and on the stage of the open-air theater he alternately pursued and repulsed a beautiful damsel whose father managed the waterworks of the city of Newcastle. To his rival for her favor he recited:

"Lysander, keep thy Hermia; I will none:
If e'er I loved her, all that love is gone."

Lanny could say this well, because he had only to imagine that Lysander was the heir to an English earldom, and that Hermia's last name was Codwilliger, pronounced Culliver.

III

America is the land of mass production and standardization; whatever it is that you want done, you will find somebody ready to do it according to the latest improved methods—if you have the price. If you want to raise funds for charity by means of amateur theatricals, you will discover that there are firms which specialize in showing you exactly how to do it. They will send you a director to take charge; they will rent you scenery and costumes, or provide experts to make them; they will advise you what play to give, and if you choose a modern one they will arrange about the copyright; they will have tickets and programs printed—in short they will do everything to smooth the development of whatever histrionic talent may be latent in Osawatomie, Kansas, or Deadwood Gulch, South Dakota.

The director of the Newcastle Country Club production of *A Midsummer-Night's Dream* came from New York; a tall young man of aesthetic appearance, wearing spectacles, and hair a bit longer than was usual in the town. He had an absentminded manner and a habit of making oddly humorous remarks. He took a liking to Lanny, and told him about a part of New York called Greenwich Village, where young people interested in the arts forgathered, writing plays on a little oatmeal and producing them on a shoestring. Walter Hayden was a discreet person, who valued his job, and never exercised his sense of humor upon anything in Newcastle; but he made general remarks to Lanny about the odd position of a stage director whose actors were all rich people accustomed to doing what they pleased, so that only by the exercise of patience and tact could things be got a little less than terrible.

After the first two or three rehearsals, there began to spread in the polite assemblage an uneasy sense that something was lacking in the Newcastle Country Club version of *A Midsummer-Night's Dream*. One of the "swank" young matrons found an opportunity to draw Lanny aside and ask whether he did not think it barely possible that Adelaide Hitchcock was less than completely adapted to the role of Puck? Adelaide was a lovely young girl with a wealth of wavy brown hair and large soulful brown eyes which turned quite often in the direction of Lanny Budd. She had a shapely figure, and everything that was needed to make a fairy, so long as she stood silent and motionless; but when she spoke her lines there was no life in them, and when she came onto the stage it was as a young lady entering a drawing room, and not in the least as a dancing sprite, the incarnation of mischief.

Now if Lanny had been more at home in Connecticut, he would have stopped to reflect that the Hitchcock family was prominent in his father's city, and that Adelaide's mother was first cousin to Lanny's stepmother. But he was thinking about art, and he said that in his opinion Adelaide with wings on her shoulders would make a great addition to the train of Queen Titania; but for the part of Puck they needed a boy or girl who could act; and if it was a girl, it ought to be one with a boyish figure, without hips.

They talked about various members of the younger set and couldn't think of anybody. Lanny asked if there wasn't some teacher of dancing in the town who could make a suggestion; then suddenly Mrs. Jessup recalled that she had seen a play given by the students at the high school, and in it was a girl who had "stolen the show" by the extraordinary verve of her acting. Lanny said: "Why don't you bring her here and let the members meet her?" Again he showed that he was not at home in Connecticut; for in this old-fashioned city the daughters of the aristocracy did not attend the free high schools, and girls who attended these schools were rarely invited to country clubs.

Mrs. Jessup went off to find this girl, whose name was Gracyn

Phillipson and whose mother was an interior decorator, having a little shop and her living rooms above it. Before Mrs. Jessup went, she told her friends that Lanny had made the suggestion, thus giving him full credit for what happened. Later on it would be said that she was an "intriguer," and had manipulated matters to this end; but how could Lanny know about that?

IV

Gracyn Phillipson came to the club late the next afternoon, and Lanny was there as he had promised. One glance, and you could see that she was made for the role of Puck; a tiny, slender figure, with no hips that you would notice; a quick, eager manner, a voice full of laughter, and feet that danced of themselves. To be sure she was a brunette, and Lanny had somehow thought of fairies as blond; but when you came to consult the authorities, you couldn't find anything definite on the point.

Several of Mrs. Jessup's smart friends, having been told that Lanny Budd was interested in this young lady, had assembled to meet her. As the quickest way to bring out her "points," someone asked her to dance. A record was put on the phonograph, and of course it was up to a gallant youth to escort her onto the floor. If he had been discreet, he would have found some other partner for her and would have sat and studied her with a cold professional eye. But Lanny had a weakness for dancing, and it may be that the intriguers were taking advantage of that.

Anyhow, there were the two young persons on the floor, and an extraordinary thing happened. Lanny hadn't had a real dance since coming to the land of the pilgrims' pride, and he had missed it. The dancing that was done at the club was so subdued that it amounted to little more than taking a lady in your arms and walking about the room with her, backing her for a while and then reversing and letting her back you. People did this to the pounding of ragtime music which exercised a hypnotic effect, so that you might have been watching a roomful of automatons, electrically controlled so that they didn't bump into one another as they wove here and there.

But if you are young and full of fire you can dance fast and freely to any music. You can take three steps while others are taking one; you can bend and turn and leap—in short you can express the joy that is in you. And if you have in front of you a girl who is the very soul of motion, who watches you with excitement in her eyes, and reads in your face what you are going to do—that is something to wake you up and get you going. A few tentative steps, a few quick words, and the two bodies were swaying together, they were bringing grace and charm into being—they were creating a dance.

The watching ladies of course had seen dancing on the stage; there was a thing known as "society dancing," all the rage just then. But that dancing was carefully rehearsed; whereas these two young creatures had never seen each other before, and you could see that they were inventing something to express their pleasure in the meeting. It was stimulating, indeed it was almost improper—and that is what it became when the story started on its thousand-legged way through the city of Newcastle.

Was Gracyn Phillipson really what she seemed to Lanny that afternoon? Did joy really bubble up in her like water in a mountain spring? Lanny gave no thought to the question, and would have had no means of getting the answer. If Gracyn was acting—well, it meant that she was an actress. And surely nobody was expecting her to write *A Midsummer-Night's Dream*.

After the dancing there was tea, and this alert young creature revealed that it was the hope of her life to get on the stage. Mrs. Jessup had told her about the play that the club was producing, and she said that she would be tremendously honored by a chance to appear in it. Yes, she knew a little about the part of Puck; she had loved Shakespeare since childhood. Miss Phillipson didn't exactly say that she carried an assortment of Shakespearean roles about in her head; and of course there was the possibility that she had sat up most of the night learning Puck.

Anyhow, when Mrs. Jessup said: "Could you give us an idea of how you would do it?" the answer came promptly: "I'd be glad to, if it wouldn't bore you." No shyness, no inhibition; she was an actress. Right there in the main room of the clubhouse, with other ladies sipping tea or playing bridge, and gentlemen passing through with their golf bags, Gracyn Phillipson enacted the scene in which Puck replies to the orders of King Oberon to torment the lovers: "My fairy lord, this must be done with haste."

Presently came the place where Demetrius enters, wandering in the forest. Lanny being Demetrius, Gracyn gave him a sign, and he recited his challenge to his rival. Puck answered in the rival's voice, taunting him:

> "Thou coward, art thou bragging .to the stars,
> Telling the bushes that thou look'st for wars,
> And wilt not come?"

Gracyn managed to produce the voice of an angry man from somewhere in her throat. She put such energy and conviction into the playful scene that ladies at the tables put down their tea cups or cards, and gentlemen rested their golf bags against the wall and stood and listened. Everybody could see at once that this was an actress; but why on earth was she exhibiting herself at the Newcastle Country Club?

V

Rumor with its thousand tongues took up the tidings that Robbie Budd's son had interested himself in a high-school girl, and was trying to oust Adelaide Hitchcock from the role of Puck and to put his *protégée* in her place. He had had this *protégée* at the club and had danced with her and played a scene with her, and now the dramatics committee was requested to give her a chance to show what she could do. Lanny was calling it a matter of "art"; the thousand tongues each said that word with a different accent, indicative of subtle shadings of incredulity and amusement. "Art, indeed! Art, no less! Art, if you please! Art, art—to be sure, oh, yes, naturally, I don't think!"

The rumor came to Adelaide Hitchcock in the first half-hour. She rushed to her mother in tears. Oh, the insult, the humiliation— making her ridiculous before the whole town, ruining her for life! "I told them I was no actress; but they said I could do it, they made me go and learn all those silly verses and take all that trouble getting fitted with a dress!"

Of course the mother hastened to the telephone and called her cousin. "What on earth is this, Esther? Has your stepson gone out of his mind? What a scandal—bringing this creature to the club and making a spectacle of himself before the world?"

Esther had made a strict resolve that if ever there was anything serious to be said to Lanny, it would be said by his father; so now she told Robbie what she had heard. She took the precaution of adding: "Better not mention me. Just say that you've heard it."

Robbie led his son to his study after dinner and said: "What's ʳhis about you and an actress, kid?"

Lanny was astonished by the speed with which rumor could operate, with the help of a universal telephone system. "Gosh!" said he. "I never met the girl till this afternoon, and I never heard of her till yesterday."

"Who told you about her?"

"Mrs. Chris Jessup."

"Oh, I see!" said the father. "Tell me what happened."

Lanny told, and it was interesting to compare notes and discover how a tale could grow in two or three hours. Robbie couldn't keep from laughing; then he said: "It would be better if you didn't have anything to do with this fight. You see, Molly Jessup and Esther have been in each other's hair of late; it had to do with the chairmanship of some committee or other."

"Oh, I'm sorry, Robbie! I had no idea of that."

"It's the kind of thing you get in for the moment you have anything to do with women's affairs. Just sort of lay off this Miss Pillwiggle, or whatever her name is, and let the women fight it out."

"It'll be rather awkward," said the young man. "I've expressed the opinion that she can act; and now people will be asking me about it, and what shall I say?"

"Well, of course, I wouldn't want you to violate your artistic conscience," replied the father, gravely. "But it seems to me that when you find you've spilled some fat into a hot fire, you're justified in stepping back a bit."

It was Lanny's turn to laugh. Then he said: "Strictly between you and me, Robbie, Adelaide is a stick."

"Yes, son; but there are many kinds of sticks, and she's an important one."

"A gold stick?"

"More than that—a mace of office, or perhaps a totem."

VI

The dramatics committee assembled, and Miss Gracyn Phillipson, alias Pillwiggle, showed how she would propose to enact the role of Puck, alias Robin Goodfellow. After the demonstration had been completed, the committee asked the advice of Mr. Walter Hayden, and this experienced director of the rich replied that it was his practice to leave such decisions to the members; he would give his professional opinion only upon formal request. This having been solemnly voted, Mr. Hayden said that Miss Adelaide Hitchcock was endowed with gifts to make a very lovely fairy with wings on her shoulders; whereas Miss Phillipson was an actress and something of a find, who might some day reflect credit upon her native city.

Adelaide declined to put wings on her shoulders, and went away in a huff, declaring that she would never darken the doors of the country club again. The rehearsals went forward, and every evening for the next ten Lanny watched Gracyn Phillipson manifest enraptured gaiety upon the dimly lighted stage of a woodland theater. Every evening he staggered about in mock confusion, seeking to capture her, and crying:

"Nay, then, thou mock'st me. Thou shalt buy this dear,
If ever I thy face by daylight see."

He hardly knew her as a human being; he was under the spell of
the play, a victim of enchantment, and she the fairy creature who
poured into his eyes the magic juice which transformed the world.
"But, my good lord, I wot not by what power!—"

The long-awaited evening came, and Gracyn was trembling so
that she was pitiful. But the moment she danced onto the stage
something took hold of her—"I am that merry wanderer of the
night!" She swept through the part in triumph, and lifted an
amateur performance into something unique. The audience gave
her a polite ovation.

Then next day—and the spell was broken. Lanny was an appren-
tice salesman of armaments, and Gracyn was a poor girl whose
mother kept a shop and lived over it. The members of the club
had had an evening's diversion, the Red Cross had got a thousand
dollars, Lanny had made some enemies and Gracyn some friends;
at least so she thought, but she waited in vain for another invitation
to the club, and the painful realization dawned upon her that it took
more than talent to crash those golden gates.

It was too bad that Lanny had to justify the gossips. Now that
it was no longer a question of "art," he had no excuse for seeing
this young female. But he was interested enough to come and take
her driving in his car, and investigate her as a human being. He
discovered a quivering creature devoured by ambition, a prey alternately to hopes and fears. She wanted to get on the stage; how
was it to be done? Go to New York, of course. Mr. Hayden had
promised her introductions; but wasn't that just politeness? Didn't
he do that to young actresses in every town he visited? Already he
was on another job—and doubtless telling a stage-struck amateur
that she had talent.

So far in Newcastle Lanny had lived a restricted life and hadn't
met a single person outside his own class. But the impulse to get
interested in strangers was still alive in him; and now he met

Gracyn's friends, a group of young people with feeble and pathetic yearnings for beauty, and having no idea where to find it. Several were working in factories during the summer months, earning money to go to college; others had taken commercial courses in school, and now were taking jobs in offices, knowing themselves doomed to the dull round of business life. Most of them had never seen a great painting, or a "show" except vaudeville and cheap "road shows," or heard music except jazz dances and the bellowing of a movie theater organ.

And now came Lanny Budd, an Oberon, master of magic. Lanny could sit at the little upright piano in the Phillipson home and, without stopping to think for a moment, could cause ecstasy to flow out of the astonished instrument; could weave patterns of beauty, build towering structures of gorgeous sound. He would play snatches of Chabrier's *España*—and Gracyn, who knew nothing about Spanish dancing except for pictures of girls with tambourines, would listen and catch the mood. She would say: "Play it again"; the young people would pull the chairs out of the way and she would make up dance steps while he watched her over his shoulder. Among the country-club crowd everybody had so much and was bored with everything; whereas here they had so little and were so pathetically grateful for a crumb of culture and beauty.

VII

Lanny took to being out frequently in the evening; and of course the watchful Esther did not fail to make note of it. Once more, she would say nothing to her stepson but only to his father. Robbie didn't feel the same way about a young man enjoying his evenings, provided he had done his job during the day; but Robbie understood his wife and tried to please her, and said he would speak to the boy.

What he said was: "I hope you're not getting in too deep with that girl, Lanny."

"Oh, it's quite innocent, I assure you, Robbie. Her mother sits

in one room and paints watercolor designs for house decorations;
I play the piano and Gracyn dances and her young friends watch.
Then we make cheese sandwiches, and twice we've had beer, and
felt bohemian, really devilish."

"Couldn't you do that with some of our own crowd?"

"It just happens that I haven't met any of them who take my
music or dancing seriously."

"They are a rather frozen-up lot, I suppose."

"The trouble with most of them is they have no conversation."

Robbie repressed a smile, and asked: "Aren't you ever alone with
the girl?"

"I've taken her driving two or three times; that's the only way
she'd ever see the country. But we talk about the theater; I've told
her books to study, and she has done it. Her whole heart is set on
being an actress."

"It's a dog's life for a woman, son."

"I suppose so; but if you're really in love with art, you don't
mind hard work."

"What usually happens is that a woman thinks she's in love with
art, but really it's with a man. You mustn't get her into trouble."

"Oh, no, Robbie; it won't be anything like that, I assure you.
I've made up my mind that I'm through with love until I've got
my education, and know what I want to be and do. I had some
talk with Mr. Baldwin, my master at St. Thomas's, and he convinced me that that's the wisest way to live."

"Maybe so," said the cautious father; "but sometimes the women
won't let you, and it's hard to say no. You find you've got your
foot in a trap before you realize it."

So Lanny had to go off and consider in his mind: was he the
least bit in love with Gracyn Phillipson, or she with him? He was
sure that if he had been thinking of falling in love, he'd have
chosen some girl like Adelaide, who was soft and warm, and
obviously made to melt in your arms. It would have been a wiser
choice, because his parents would have been pleased, and her
parents, and they would have a lovely church wedding with brides-

maids and orange blossoms and yards and yards of white veils
spread all around her like a pedestal. But he hadn't been thinking
about love, he had been interested in acting, and in music and
dancing and poetry and the other arts that Shakespeare had woven
into an immortal fairy tale. Gracyn was boylike and frank and
interested in the same things, and they had made a pleasant friendship on that basis.

If she'd been thinking about anything else, she'd have let him
know it. Or would she? She was an actress; and might it be that
she was acting the part of boylike frankness? Acting is a tricky
business, and a woman might fool herself as well as others. Gracyn
wanted a start in life, and could surely not be unaware of the fact
that Lanny might give it to her. His father could get her a start if
he chose to take the trouble. Gracyn must have thought of this;
and would she think that Lanny was careless and indifferent to her
needs? Would she be too proud to hint at it, or take advantage of
their friendship? If so, she must be a fine person, and Lanny was
putting her to a severe test.

VIII

He took her driving the next evening, that being the only way
she could ever see the country. They followed the river drive, and
a full moon was strewing its showers of light over the water;
fireflies were flickering, and the world was lovely, as well as
mysterious. Over in France the doughboys had begun their long-
expected drive, and the newspapers were full of their exploits;
which lent a strange quality to any happiness you felt—as if it were
something you had no right to, and that might disappear while
you held it in your hands.

"Gracyn," said Lanny, "I've been thinking that if you're going
to get a job this season, you ought to be in New York now. while
the managers are getting their fall productions ready."

"I know, Lanny; but I can't!"

"What I thought was, I'd ask my father to back you to the

extent of a trip there. He saw your performance and liked it a lot."

"Oh, Lanny!" The girl caught her breath. "Oh, I couldn't let you do that!"

"It wouldn't break him."

"I know—but I haven't the right——"

"You can call it a loan. Anybody starting in business borrows money and pays it back out of his earnings. You surely won't fail to earn something; and it would make me happy if I could help you."

"Oh, Lanny, what a darling you are!"

"You'll do it, then?"

"How could I say no?"

"I haven't asked him, you understand; but he's never refused to do anything within reason."

"Lanny, I'll work so hard—I'll have one reason more for making good!"

"I know you'll work; the chances are you'll work too hard and do yourself up."

The road passed a wooded point, and came to an open spot with a tiny bay. "Oh, Lanny, how lovely!" whispered the girl. "Stop for a bit."

They drew up by the roadside, as young couples were doing along ten thousand rivers and streams of America. They sat looking over the water, strewn with shimmering bright jewels; and Gracyn put her hand on Lanny's and murmured: "Lanny, you are the kindest, sweetest man I've ever known."

"It's easy for me to be generous with money I don't have to earn," said he.

She answered: "I don't mean only that. I mean a lot, lot more than that."

He felt her hand trembling, and a strange feeling which he had learned to know began to steal over him. When she leaned toward him he put his arm about her. They sat so for quite a while; until at last the girl whispered: "Lanny, let me tell you how I feel."

She waited, as if it were a question; he answered: "Yes, dear, of course."

"I think you are the best person I've ever known, and I'll do anything I can to make you happy—anything in this world. You have my promise that I'll never ask anything of you, never make any claim upon you—never, never!"

So there was Lanny mixed up with the sex problem again. His father had said: "It's hard to say no." Lanny found that it was impossible.

24

The World Well Lost

I

THERE had come a post card from Sergeant Jerry Pendleton in France. "We are ready. Everything fine. Watch our smoke!" And right after that the big news began to come in. The Americans hit the spearhead of the German advance on Paris, at a little village called Château-Thierry, difficult for doughboys to pronounce. The Americans furnished two divisions for the great attack at Soissons, which caught the Germans on the flank, and cut the supply lines of their advancing armies. The same fellows that Lanny had met and talked with; they had been training for a new kind of fighting, to attack and keep on attacking, and take machine-gun nests in spite of losses—and now they were doing it! In the few days of that battle the Germans sent in seven divisions to stop the First Division of the Americans, and when they failed, their leaders knew that the tide of the war had turned.

From that time on there was one battle that went on day and night for three months. The fifty thousand sergeants led their million and a quarter men, and the machine guns mowed some of them down and left them crumpled and writhing on the ground— but others got close, and threw their hand grenades and silenced the guns. After three days of such attacks, one of the battalions from Camp Devens, a thousand strong, came out with two hundred men unwounded. But they had taken the positions.

People read about these exploits with pride and exultation, or with shuddering and grief, according to their temperaments. Lanny, who knew more about war than anybody else he met, was of two moods in as many minutes. A poet had expressed his state of mind in alternating verses:

I sing the song of the great clean guns that belch forth death at will.
Ah, but the wailing mothers, the lifeless forms and still!

At the country club Lanny had met officers who were now in France, directing this all-summer and autumn battle, and he was proud of these stern, capable men and the job they were doing. As the poet had said:

I sing the acclaimèd generals that bring the victory home.
Ah, but the broken bodies that drip like honey-comb!

A letter from Nina: "It is so dreadful, the way poor Rick has to suffer. I do not know how he can stand it. They are going to have to take out another piece of bone. Perhaps they ought to take the whole leg, but the doctors are not able to agree about it." And then one from Beauty, with words of apology for the tear stains which marred it. These were the days when she was waiting in vain for some message from Marcel; she had to pass a still longer period, clinging to the hope that he might have been captured, and that she would get word through the organization in Switzerland which exchanged lists of prisoners.

One day there came in Lanny's mail a carefully wrapped package from France, and when he opened it, there was a charming little figure of a dancing man carved in wood. M. Pinjon, the gigolo, was back in his native village and wished to greet and thank his old friend. He didn't suggest that Lanny might interest some rich Americans in giving little dancing men as Christmas gifts; but of course Lanny knew how happy the poor cripple would be if this were done. Kind-hearted persons would take duties like this upon themselves—even while they knew how pathetically futile it was.

II

Gracyn Phillipson didn't take the trip to New York; at least not right away. The morning after her understanding with Lanny she received a letter from Walter Hayden. He had meant his praise, it appeared. He was at the town of Holborn, thirty or forty miles away, about to direct a show for the Red Cross ladies there. It was a war play, and had a "fat" part for a leading lady; the committee were dubious about their local talent, and Hayden had told them about his "find" in Newcastle. They couldn't pay any salary, but would guarantee her fifty dollars' expenses for two weeks if she cared to come. It would be a chance for her to have Hayden's direction in a straight dramatic role, and the experience might be very helpful to her. The girl was wild with delight, and phoned Lanny that she was leaving by the first train.

So now the youth had another art project to be absorbed in. When he finished his study of contracts and specifications for Budd fuses furnished to the United States navy, he did not go to the country club to play tennis, but motored to Holborn and took Gracyn Phillipson to dinner—an inexpensive procedure, since she was too excited to eat. Then he drove her to the hot little "opera house" where the rehearsals were held, and watched the work, and criticized and made suggestions, and drove home late at night. On Saturday afternoon he went and stayed overnight and on Sunday took her to the beach.

This again was supposed to be "art"; and again the gossips wouldn't believe it. It was too bad that there had to be truth in their worst suspicions. There are persons who believe in the ascetic life, and when their stories of renunciation are told, as in Browning's *Ring and the Book*, they make noble and inspiring literature. But Lanny Budd had been brought up under a different code, and his leading lady also had ideas of her own. On the stage she was acting a part of conventional "virtue," and pouring intense feeling into it; but when she and Lanny were alone, she embraced him with ardor, and did not trouble to fit these two codes to each other.

Lanny felt free and happy, so long as he was in Holborn; but when he started on the long drive back to the home of Esther Remson Budd, a chill would settle over his spirit, and when he put his car in the garage and stole softly up to his room, he felt like a burglar. His stepmother didn't wait up for him, but she knew the worst—and, alas, the worst was true. She never said a word to him about it, but as the days passed, their relationship grew more and more formal. Esther saw herself justified in everything she had feared when she had let this bad woman's son into her home; he had that woman's blood and would follow her ways; he belonged in France, not in New England—at any rate not in her home, making it a target for the arrows of scandal. From that time on Esther would count the days to the latter part of September, when Lanny would be going back to school.

The thing made for unhappiness between her and her husband also. Robbie didn't feel as she did; Robbie had met the girl, and thought she was the right sort for Lanny to have at this stage of his life. He couldn't say that to Esther, of course; he had to pretend that he didn't know what was going on—at the same time knowing that Esther didn't believe him.

III

This interlude with Gracyn was a strange experience for Lanny. She was a "daughter of the people," and his acquaintance with these had been limited to servants and his childhood playmates in France. She had hardly any tradition of culture; her mother had been a clerk who had married her employer late in his life and inherited his small business. Gracyn had gone through school as Lanny was doing, bored with most subjects and forgetting them overnight. She had lived through four years of world war and it had become known to her that America was helping England and France to fight Germany; but she hadn't got quite clear about Britain and England, she didn't know which side Austria was on, and if you had mentioned Bulgaria and Bougainvillaea, she couldn't have told which was which. She was all the time pulling "boners" like that, and never minded if you laughed. "Don't expect me to know about anything but acting," she would say.

When she was a child in school she had posed in some tableaux, representing "Columbia," and "Innocence," and so on, and it had set her imagination on fire; she had discovered a way of escape from the harassments of daily life, with a mother always in debt and very rarely a good substantial meal on the table. She found that she could lose herself in a world of imagination, full of beautiful, rich, and delightful people—"like you, Lanny," she said. She had driven her childhood friends to act in stories which she made up and in which she played the princess, the endangered and adored one. She haunted the local "opera house," to which traveling companies now and then came; she learned that sometimes they would use a child to walk across the stage in a crowd scene, or to be dressed up and petted by some actress playing the mother. Thus she had watched plays from the wings, absorbed in the story, and, no matter how humble her part, she had lived it.

She was passionate and intense in whatever she did; making love to her was like holding a live bird in your hand and feeling the throbbing of its heart. Her emotions came like waves rolling on the ocean, sweeping a boat along; but they passed quickly and were succeeded by another kind of waves. Lanny would become aware that she was no longer loving him, but was thinking about love to be enacted on the stage. It would be one of the principal things she had to do, of course; and while she did it she would start to talk about it from the technical point of view. She had studied the fine points of the actresses she had been able to see; also the favorites of the motion picture screen, and Lanny found it startling in the midst of a *tête-à-tête* to be told that Gloria Swanson heaved her bosom thus and so when she was manifesting passion, and the audiences seemed to like it, but Gracyn thought it was rather overdone, and what did Lanny think?

It was unfortunate that two great crises had come piling into the life of this highstrung creature at the same time: the arrival of her Prince Charming, and the dawning of her stage career. It made too much excitement to be packed into one small female frame, and she seemed likely to burst with it. As it happened, the career part had a time-schedule that could not be altered; she had to be on hand for rehearsals, and she had to know her lines and every detail of her "business" as the exacting Mr. Hayden ordered it. So love-making had to be put off to odd moments, and food and sleep were neglected almost entirely.

Lanny had to put up with many things which his fastidious friends would have found "vulgar." He had to keep reminding himself all the time that Gracyn was poor; that she had had no "advantages"; that things which he took for granted were entirely new and strange to her. It was desire for independence which made her want to eat in cheap "joints," and to stay in a lodging-house room which not merely had no conveniences, but was dingy, even dirty. If she talked a great deal about money, that, too, was part of her fate, for money governed her chance to act, to travel, to know the world and be received by it. If she seemed ravenous for success, lacking in poise and dignity—well, as Lanny drove back to his luxurious home, he would reflect that the founder of Budd's must have had some lust for success, some intensity of concentration upon getting his patents, raising his working capital, driving his labor, finding his customers, getting his contracts signed. Because Lanny's progenitor had fought like this, Lanny himself could be gracious and serene, and look upon the still-struggling ones with astonishment mildly tinged with displeasure.

Lanny came to realize that he was not merely a lover and a

possible backer; he was a model, a specimen of the genus "gentleman" in the technical sense of the word. He was the first that
Gracyn had had a chance to know and she was making full use
of her opportunity. She watched how he ate, how he dressed, how
he pronounced words; she put him through interrogatories about
various matters that came up. What was "Ascot"? Where was "the
Riviera"? She had heard of Monte Carlo, because there was a song
about a man who broke the bank there. She knew that the fashions
came from "gay Paree," but she didn't know why it was called
that, and was surprised to be told that the French pronounced the
name of their capital city differently from Americans. Indeed, this
seemed so unlikely that she wondered if Lanny wasn't making fun
of her!

IV

The role which had been put before this stage-struck girl was
one for which her Prince Charming was oddly equipped to give
help. It was an English play, the leading lady being a war nurse
in a base hospital in France. She was a mysterious person, and the
interest of the play depended upon the gradual disclosure that she
was a lady of high station. She became the object of adoration of a
young wounded officer whom she nursed back to recovery; but
she did not yield to his love, and the audience was kept in suspense
as to the reason until the last act, when an officer who turned up
at the hospital was recognized as the husband who had deserted
her several years back. Of course her sense of duty prevailed—
otherwise the play would not have been chosen by a group of
society ladies of this highly moral town of Holborn. The handsome
young adorer went back to the trenches in sorrow, and one learned
from the play that war affords many opportunities to exhibit self-
renunciation.

"Are there really women who would behave like that?" Gracyn
wanted to know. Lanny said, yes, he was quite sure of it; nine-
tenths of the ladies who saw the play would at least think that it

was their duty to behave like that and would shed genuine tears of sympathy. He said that his stepmother would be one of them; and right away Gracyn wanted to know all about Esther Remson Budd.

Still more important, she had to have information about the manners of an English lady, a being entirely remote from her experience. Lanny was moved to tell her that he had known an English war nurse whose grandfather was an earl, and who was soon to marry the grandson of another. Straightway Rosemary began to be merged with Esther in the dramatic role—a very odd combination. Gracyn, of course, had a nose for romance, and after she had asked a score of questions about Rosemary—where Lanny had met her, and how, and what he had said and what she had said—she asked him pointblank if he and the girl hadn't been lovers, and Lanny didn't think it worth while to deny this. The revelation increased his authority and prestige.

He wouldn't let Gracyn tell Walter Hayden about this aspect of the matter. But the director knew that Lanny had lived abroad and possessed a treasure of knowledge about fashionable life. Together they pumped him and built the production on his advice—costumes, scenery, business, dialect, everything. The young society man of Holborn who took the part of the "juvenile"—that is, the wounded officer who fell in love—became Rick with his wounded leg, plus a few touches of Lanny himself. The French officer who lay in the next bed took on the mannerisms of Marcel Detaze. The comic hospital servant acquired a Provençal accent like Leese, the family cook at Bienvenu. Gracyn Phillipson received the "juvenile's" lovemaking with all the ardor of Rosemary Codwilliger, pronounced Culliver; but instead of being a "free woman" she became the Stern Daughter of the Voice of God of Wordsworth's "Ode to Duty." That part of her was Esther Remson Budd; and she was so sorrowful, so highminded, so eloquent, that some of the ladies of the college town of Holborn had tears in their eyes even at rehearsals.

So Lanny became a sort of assistant director, and gave an education as well as receiving one. He lived a double life, one lobe of his brain full of stage business, and the other full of munitions contracts and correspondence. He left the office at five, and was in Holborn by six, had supper with Gracyn and sometimes with Hayden, attended the rehearsal, and was back in bed by midnight. He saw the play growing under his hands and it was a fascinating experience, enabling him to understand the girl's hunger for a stage career. He told his father about it, and Robbie was sympathetic and kept his uneasiness to himself. He surely didn't want his son drawn into that disorderly and hysterical kind of life; but he told himself that every youngster has to have his fling and it would be poor tactics trying to force him.

V

The great day in the evening drew near. The frightened amateur players had rehearsed a good part of the previous night; but Lanny hadn't been able to stay for that, he had to leave them to their fate. He invited several of his friends to the show; Robbie promised to bring others, but Esther politely alleged a previous engagement. Rumors had spread concerning the dramatic "find," and the wealth and fashion of one Connecticut valley was on hand; the Red Cross would have another thousand dollars with which to buy bandages and medicines.

Lanny had thought he knew Gracyn Phillipson by now, but he was astonished by what she did that evening. Every trace of fright and uncertainty was left in the wings like a discarded garment; she came upon the stage a war nurse, exhausted with her labors and aching with pity, yet dignified and conscious of her social position. All the incongruous elements had been assembled into a character— it might not have satisfied an English lady of society, but it met New England ladies' ideas of such a person. They believed in her noble love for the young officer, and when she made her sorrowful renunciation their hearts were wrung.

The actress had shifted her names around, and appeared on the playbill as "Phyllis Gracyn." The director considered that better suited for the electric signs on Broadway, for which he now felt sure that it was destined. Lanny listened to the excited questions of people about him: "Who is she? Where does she come from? How did they find her?" When the show was over, they crowded behind the scenes to meet and congratulate her. Lanny didn't try to join them; she had told him to go home—all she wanted was to crawl into bed in her lodging-house room and sleep a full twenty-four hours.

When he heard from her again she was in New York. Walter Hayden had advised her to come without delay. She wouldn't have to bother Lanny for money, because she had saved the greater part of her fifty dollars. She would write him as soon as she had something to tell. As he knew, she wasn't much at letter-writing; she was always running into words that she wasn't sure about.

Lanny returned to the armaments business and found it now lacking in glamour. He had satisfied the first rush of curiosity, and had discovered that contracts are complicated and that when you have read too many they become a blur in your mind; at least that was the case with him, though apparently not with his father. Lanny kept thinking about speeches in the play, and the way Gracyn had said them. They had got all mixed up in his mind with Rosemary, Rick, and Marcel; and it made him sad.

He went back to tennis and swimming at the country club. He had become a figure of romance in the eyes of the debutantes and the smart young matrons; he had had an affair with a brilliant young actress and might still be having it. More than one of them gave signs of being willing to "cut her out," but Lanny was absent-minded. It was August, and the papers reported a heat wave in New York; how was that frail little creature standing it? She was meeting this manager and that, she wrote; hopes were being held out to her; she would have good news soon. But not a word about love! Did she think that the Stern Daughter of the Voice of God might be opening Lanny's mail?

The war kept haunting him. Every time he went home he looked for a cablegram about Marcel; but nothing came. He thought about

the monstrous battle line, stretched like a serpent across northeastern France; the mass deeds of heroism, the mass agony and
death. The newspapers fed it to you, twice every day; you break-
fasted on glory and supped on grief——

I sing the song of the billowing flags, the bugles that cry before.
Ah, but the skeletons flapping rags, the lips that speak no more!

VI

September, and there came an ecstatic letter from Gracyn. She
had a part; a grand part; something tremendous; her future was
assured. Unfortunately, she couldn't tell about it; she was pledged
to keep it a strict secret. "Oh, Lanny, I am so happy! And so grateful to you. I'd never have made the grade if it hadn't been for you.
Forgive me if I don't write more. I have a part to learn. I am going
to be a success and you'll be proud of me."

So that was that; very mysterious, and a trifle disconcerting to a
young man in love. A week passed, ten days, it was almost time
to go back to school. Lanny found that he was glad, for it wasn't
comfortable living in Esther's home when he knew that she didn't
want him and was watching him all the time, anxious when he made
the children happy, when he had too much influence over them.
He knew that he had ruined himself with his stepmother and that
nothing he could do would ever restore him to her favor.

All right; he might as well be hanged for a sheep as for a lamb;
he decided suddenly that he wanted to see the great city of New
York. He had had only a few hours there on his arrival, and only
one trip with his father the previous summer. He hadn't seen the
great bridges, the art galleries, the museums—to say nothing of the
theatrical district, where many new plays were being got ready.
He mentioned it to his father, who said all right. He sent his trunk
to the school by express and packed a suitcase and took a morning
train to the metropolis.

He had the bright idea that he would surprise Gracyn; so he

took a taxi to the address to which he had been writing. He found it was a poor lodging house—and that she had moved from there a month ago, leaving no address. Her mail was being forwarded by the post office; but at the post office they wouldn't give the address—he would have to write her a letter and wait for a reply. After thinking it over he decided to call Walter Hayden's office. The director was away on an assignment, but his secretary said, yes, she knew about Phyllis Gracyn, she was rehearsing at the Metropole Theater—she had the leading part in *The Colonel's Lady*, a new play by somebody who was apparently somebody, although Lanny had never heard the name.

He drove to the theater. You don't have to send in your card during rehearsals; one of the front doors is apt to be unlocked, and you can walk in and look around. Lanny did so. Since the auditorium was dark no one paid any attention to him; he took a seat in back and watched.

Gracyn was on the bare stage with perhaps a dozen other persons, mostly men: a director, a couple of assistants, a property boy, and so on—Lanny was familiar with the procedure by now. The place was hot, and all the men were in their shirtsleeves and mopped their foreheads frequently. Gracyn was sitting in a chair watching the work; when her cue came she would get up and go through a scene.

Another war play; the men sat at small tables and it became apparent that they were supposed to be doughboys in a wine shop somewhere behind the lines. Gracyn was a French girl, daughter of the proprietor—her father scolded her for being too free with the soldiers. When he went off she teased them and some of her lines were a trifle crude—evidently it was a "realistic" play. The doughboys sang songs, one of them "Madelon," in translation. "She laughs—it is the only harm she knows."

Gracyn was doing it with great spirit. Oh, yes, she could act! Lanny had never seen the American boys in France, but he recalled the scene with the French soldiers when he and his mother motored to see Marcel. He thought: "I could have given the director a lot of help." But they wouldn't let Gracyn tell what she was doing. And yet the secretary at Hayden's place had known about it and had told it freely. Very strange!

VII

Lanny didn't want to disturb her. He waited until the rehearsal was over and she was about to leave. Then he came down the aisle, saying: "Hello, Gracyn."

She was startled. "Lanny! Of all people! Where on earth did you come from?"

"Out of a taxi," he said.

"How did you find me?"

"Your secret appears to have leaked."

She came into the auditorium to join him. She led him back, away from the others, and sat down. "Darling," she said, swiftly, "I have something that's dreadfully hard to tell you. I couldn't put it on paper. But you have to know right away." She caught her breath and said: "I have a lover."

"A *what?*" he exclaimed. When he took in the meaning of her words, he said: "Oh, my God!"

"I know you'll think it's horrid, but don't be too mean to me. I couldn't help it. It's the man who's putting up the money for the show and giving me this part."

The youth had never been so stunned in all his life. He was speechless; and the girl rushed on:

"I had a chance, Lanny; I might never have had another. He's a big coffee merchant, who happened to see my performance in Holborn. He lives in New York and he invited me to come. He offered to take me to a good manager and find me a part—right away, without any waste of time. What could I say, Lanny?"

The youth remembered his mother's phrase. "You paid the price?"

"Don't be horrid to me, Lanny. Don't let's spoil our friendship. Try to see my side. You know I'm an actress. I told you I didn't know anything else, I didn't care about anything else—I wanted to get on the stage, and I'm doing it."

"There isn't any honest way?"

"Please, darling—use your common sense. This is New York. What chance does a girl stand? I'd have tramped the heels off my shoes going to managers' offices, and they wouldn't even have seen me. I'd have called myself lucky to get a part with three lines—and I'd have spent a month or two rehearsing, going into debt for my board while I did it. The play might have failed the first week, and I'd have twenty dollars, maybe thirty, to pay my debts with. Believe me, I've talked to show girls these few weeks, and I know what the game is."

"Well, it's all right," he said. "I wish you success, and the highest salary on Broadway."

"Don't sneer at me, Lanny. Life has been easy for you. You were born with a gold spoon in your mouth, and you've no right to scorn a poor girl."

"I'll do my best to remember it. Thanks for telling me the truth."

"I'd have told you before, Lanny; but it was so hard. I hate to lose you for a friend."

"I'm afraid you have done so," he said, coldly. "Your angel might be jealous."

"I know it's a shock, darling. But you know so little about the stage world. Somebody had to give me a start. You couldn't have done it—you surely know that."

Said he: "It may interest you to hear that I was thinking of asking you to marry me."

Did this startle her? If so, she was a good actress. "I haven't failed to consider that. But you have to go to school, and then to college—that's five years, and in that time I'd be an old woman."

"My father would have helped me to marry, if I'd asked him."

"I know, dear, but can't you understand? I don't want to be a wife, I want to be an actress! I couldn't think of settling down and having babies, and being a society lady—not in Newcastle, not even in France. I want to have a career—and what sort of a life would it be for you, tagging along behind a stage celebrity? Would you enjoy being called Mister Phyllis Gracyn?"

He saw that she had thought it all out; and, anyhow, it was too late. No good saying any unkind words. "All right, darling," he said—it was the stage name. "I'll be a good sport, and wish you all the luck there is. I'm only sorry I couldn't give you what you needed."

"No, Lanny dear," she said. "It's thirty thousand dollars!" And there wasn't any acting in what she put into those words!

VIII

The sun was going down as Lanny climbed onto the top of one of the big Fifth Avenue busses, which for a dime took you uptown, and across to Riverside Drive, and up to where the nation had built a great granite tomb for General Grant, in the shape of a soap box with a cheese box on top. Part of the time Lanny looked at the crowds on the avenue, and at sailboats and steamers on the river; the rest of the time he thought about the strange adventure into which he had blundered. He decided that he wasn't proud of it, and wouldn't tell anybody, excepting of course Robbie, and perhaps Rick or Kurt if he ever saw them again.

He told himself that he had made himself cheap. That little tart— well, no, he mustn't call her names—she had her side, she had her job to do and might do it well. But he mustn't let himself blunder like that again; he must know more about a woman before he threw himself into her arms. A man had to have standards; he must learn to say no. Lanny thought about the number of times he had said yes to Gracyn Phillipson, and in such extravagant language. He writhed with humiliation.

He didn't want to go home in that mood, and he didn't want to go to school ahead of time, so he put up at a hotel, and spent his time in the museums and art galleries. He looked at hundreds of paintings—and all the nudes were Gracyn, except those that were

Rosemary. He told himself with bitterness that they were all for sale, whether for thirty-thousand-dollar shows on Broadway, or for three dollars, the price of the pitiful painted ones who hunted on that Great White Way in the late hours of the evening. Rosemary's price would be a title and a country estate, but she was being sold just the same; it didn't matter that the bargain would be solemnized by a bishop in fancy costume, and proclaimed by pealing chimes in St. Margaret's. Would he ever meet one that didn't have her price? And how would he know her—since they were all so hellishly clever at fooling you?

There was another hot spell in New York, and he looked at the crowds of steaming people. The women wore light and airy garments and the young ones tripped gaily; but all the men who wanted to be thought respectable had to wear hot coats, and Lanny pitied them and himself. It was the time of year when "everybody" was supposed to be out of town; but there was an enormous number of "nobodies," and Lanny marveled how nature had managed it so that they all wanted to live. There were more Jews than anywhere else in the world and he might have satisfied his curiosity about that race if he had had time. There were great numbers of soldiers, and foreigners of every sort, so New York didn't seem very different from Paris. He found a French restaurant and had his dinners there and felt at home; he wished his mother were with him—what a comfort to tell her about Gracyn and hear her wise comments!

IX

The young man went back to St. Thomas's, and forgot his troubles in the pleasure of meeting his schoolfellows and hearing stories of where they had been and what they had done. He had a firm resolve to buckle down and make a record that would please his father and grandfather, and perhaps even his stepmother. It was pleasant to have your work cut up into daily chunks, duly weighed and measured, so that you knew exactly what you had to do and were spared all uncertainties and moral struggles.

The Americans had begun their attack in the Argonne, a forest full of rock-strewn hills and deep ravines thick with brush, one of the most heavily fortified districts in the war zone, and considered by the Germans to be impregnable. The doughboys were hammering there, and fifty thousand of them would be killed or wounded in three weeks. It was the greatest battle in American history, and it was a part of Lanny's life; his friends were in it, and his heart. There came now and then a post card from Jerry Pendleton—that fellow had been fighting every day and almost every night for a month and hadn't been touched. Now he was back in a rest camp, enjoying the peace his valor won. Somehow Lanny couldn't think of wounds and death in connection with Jerry; he was the wearer of some sort of Tarnhelm and would come out safe and whole to tell Lanny about it.

Also a letter from Nina. She had a brother who had been in the fighting south of the Somme and had got what the British called a "blighty" wound, one that brought him home and kept him out of danger for a while. Rick had had his operation, and this time they really hoped for better results. There were even a few lines from Rick to prove it; nothing about wounds, of course, you'd never know if Rick was suffering. "Well, old top, it looks like Fritz is really in trouble. Moving out and no time to pack his boxes. Cheerio!"

Beauty was always a dependable correspondent, and managed to smile through her tears. No word from Marcel yet. M. Rochambeau had written to friends in Switzerland, asking for information. M. Rochambeau said that Germany was cracking; discontent was breaking out everywhere inside the country. President Wilson's propaganda was having a tremendous effect; his "Fourteen Points" left the German people no reason for fighting. Baby Marceline was thriving, and all the world agreed that she was the most beautiful baby in the Midi.

Lanny knew, of course, that all this was an effort on his mother's part to hide her grieving for Marcel. What was she going to do when the war was over? He had made up his mind that his step-

father was dead; and Beauty was not a person who could live alone.
Sometimes he wondered, had he made a mistake in bringing about
that marriage? What would he have done if he had known that
Marcel was going to be a *mutilé* inside of one year and a corpse in
less than four? Maybe she should have taken the plate-glass man
after all!

X

The Allied armies continued their grinding advance. The Hindenburg line was cracked and the Germans forced to retreat. First
Bulgaria collapsed, then Turkey, then Austria; there came a revolution in Germany and the Kaiser fled to Holland—all that series of
dramatic events, culminating in the day when everybody rushed
into the streets of American cities and towns, shouting and singing
and dancing, blowing horns and beating tin pans, making every sort
of racket they could think of. The war was over! There wasn't
going to be any more killing! No more bombs, shells, bullets, poison
gas, torpedoes! The boys who were still alive could stay alive! The
war to end war had been won and the world was safe for democracy! People thought all these things, one after another, and with
each thought they shouted and sang and danced some more.

Even at St. Thomas's Academy, the place of good manners, there
was a celebration. Lanny got his father on the telephone; they
laughed together, and Lanny cried a little. He sent a cablegram to
his mother and one to Rick. People were behaving the same way in
France, of course. Even those cold and aloof beings, the gentlemen
of England, were rushing out into the streets embracing strangers.
It had been a tough grind for the people of that small island; they
hadn't been in such danger since the days of the Spanish Armada.

A couple of weeks later came Thanksgiving Day and Lanny went
home. One of the first things his father said was: "Well, kid, I
guess I'm going to have to go back to Europe pretty soon. There'll
be a lot of matters to be cleared up."

Lanny's first thought was: You can cross the ocean and enjoy it!
You can walk on deck and look for whales instead of submarines!

One needed time for that to sink in. Then he said: "Listen, Robbie—don't be surprised. I want you to take me with you."

"You mean—to stay?"

"I've thought it all over. I'll be a lot happier in France. I can get much more of what I want there."

"Aren't you happy here?"

"Everybody's been kind to me, and I'm glad I came. I had to know your people, and I wouldn't have missed the experience. But I have to see my mother, too. And she needs me right now. I don't think she's ever going to see Marcel again."

"You could visit her, you know."

"Of course; but I have to think of one place as home, and that's Juan."

"What about the business?"

"If I'm going to help you, it'll be over there. You'll be going back and forth, and I'll see as much of you one way as the other."

"You don't care about going to college?"

"I don't think so, Robbie. I've asked people about it and it isn't what I need. I was going through with it on account of the war, and to please you."

"Just what is it you want—if you know?"

"It isn't easy to put into words. More than anything else I want art. I've lived here a year and a half and I've heard almost no music. I haven't seen any good plays—of course I might see them in New York, but I haven't any friends there, all my best friends are in England and France."

"You'll be a foreigner, Lanny."

"I'll be a citizen of several countries. The world will need some like that."

"Just what exactly do you plan to do?"

"I want to feel my way. The first thing is to stop doing all the things that I don't want to do. I'm in a sort of education treadmill. I make myself like it, but all the time I know that I don't; and if I dropped it and went on board a ship with you I'd feel like a bird getting out of a cage. Don't misunderstand me, I don't want to loaf;

but I'm nineteen, and I believe I can direct my own education. I want to have time to read the books I'm interested in. I want to meet cultured people, and know what's going on in the arts—music, drama, painting, everything. Paris is going to be interesting right now, with the peace conference. Do you suppose you can manage to get me a passport? I understand they let hardly anybody go."

"I can fix that up all right, if you're sure it's what you want."

"I want to know what you're doing, and I want to help you—I'll be your secretary, run your errands, anything. To be with you and meet the people you meet—don't you see how much more that's worth to me than being stuck in a classroom at St. Thomas's, hearing lectures on modern European history by some master who's a child in comparison with you? Everything they have is out of books, and I can get the same books and read them in a tenth of the time. I'll wager you that on the steamer going across I can learn more modern European history than I'd get in a whole term in school."

"All right," said the father. "I guess it's no use trying to fit you into anybody else's boots."

XI

Lanny motored up to the school to pack his belongings, and say good-by to his masters and his fellow-pupils, who thought he was the luckiest youth in the state. Then he came home and started saying farewell to people at the country club and to the many members of the family. Most of all he wanted to see the Reverend Eli Budd; but fate had other plans about that. There came a telegram saying that the patriarch had passed away peacefully in his sleep, and that the funeral would be held two days later.

Lanny motored up to Norton with Robbie and his wife and an elderly widowed cousin who was visiting them. The Budd tribe had assembled from all over New England—there must have been two hundred of them in the little Unitarian church, where the deceased had been the minister for fifty years of his life. The Budd men were all grave and solid-looking, all dressed pretty much alike, whether they were munitions magnates or farmers, bankers or clergymen. They listened in silence while the present minister extolled the virtues of the departed, and when they came outside, where the first snowflakes of the year were falling, the older ones agreed that the Budd line was producing no more great men. When the will was opened, everyone was puzzled because the old man had left his library to his great-grandnephew, Lanning Prescott Budd. Some of them didn't know who that was, till the whisper went round that it was Robert Budd's bastard, who was now going back to France and would probably take the books with him.

Robbie had got the passports, and the steamer sailed two days later. The son went over to the office and said good-by to all the executives and secretaries who had been kind to him. He had had to see a good deal of his Uncle Lawford in the office, and he now went in and shook hands with that morose and silent man, who unbent sufficiently to say that he wished him well. Lanny called on his grandfather at his home, and the old gentleman, who had aged a lot under the strain of the war, didn't make any attempt to seem cheerful. He said he didn't know how Robbie could be expecting to drum up any more business in Europe now; they had munitions enough on hand to blow up the whole continent, and he wasn't sure but what they might just as well do so.

"There's going to be hell to pay at home," he warned. "All our workingmen have got too big for their breeches, and we've got to turn a lot of them off when we finish these government contracts. They've been watching that lunatic asylum in Russia, and they'll be ready to try it here when they find we've nothing more to give them. Better take my advice and learn something about business, so you can take care of yourself in a dangerous time."

"I'm planning to stick close to my father, sir, and learn all that he'll teach me."

"Well, if you listen to me you'll forget all this nonsense about music and stage plays. There are temptations enough in a young man's life without going out to hunt for them."

"Yes, Grandfather," said the youth, humbly. This was a rebuke, and he had earned it. "I don't think there'll be much pleasure-seeking in France for quite a while. They are a nation of widows and cripples, and most of the people I know are working hard trying to help them."

"Humph!" said Grandfather Samuel, who wasn't going to believe anything good about France if he could help it. He went on to talk about the world situation, which was costing him a lot of sleep. Forces apparently beyond control had drawn America into the European mess, and it wasn't going to be easy getting her out again. American businessmen would be compelled to sell more and more to foreigners. "We Budds have always been plain country people," declared the grandfather. "Not many of us know any foreign languages, and we distrust their manners and their morals. We can use someone who knows them, and can advise us—that is, if it's possible for anybody to live among them and not become as corrupt as they are."

"I'll bear your advice in mind, sir," replied the youth. "I have learned a great deal from my visit here, and I mean to profit by it."

That was all, but it was enough, according to the old gentleman's code. He wouldn't try to pin anyone down. Lanny had been to Bible class, and had had his chance at Salvation; whether he took it or not was up to him, and whatever he did would be what the Lord had predestined him to do. The Lord would be watching him and judging him—and so would the Lord's deputy, the president of Budd Gunmakers.

XII

There remained the partings from Robbie's own family. The two boys were sorry indeed to see him go, for he had been a splash of bright color in their precisely ordered lives. He found time for a heart-to-heart talk with Bess, the only person in Connecticut who shed tears over him. She pledged herself to write to him, and he promised to send her pictures of places in Europe where he went and of people he met. "Some day you'll come over there," he said;

and she answered that Robbie would have to bring her, or she would come as a stowaway.

As for Esther, she kissed him, and perhaps was really sorry. He thanked her with genuine affection; he felt that he had done wrong and was to blame for the coldness which had grown between them. He would always admire her and understand her; she would always be afraid of him.

Father and son went to New York by a morning train. Robbie had business in the afternoon, and in the evening Lanny had another good-by to say. Through the newspapers he had been following the fortunes of a dramatic production called *The Colonel's Lady*, which had opened in Atlantic City the beginning of October and had scored a hit; it had run there for two weeks, and had then had a successful opening at the Metropole Theater. Lanny wanted to see it, and Robbie said, sure, they'd both go. Their steamer had one of those midnight sailings which allow the pleasure-loving ones a last fling on the Great White Way.

Lanny didn't want to meet "Phyllis Gracyn"; he just wanted to see her act. He got seats for the show, for which one had to pay a premium. They were well down in front, but Gracyn probably didn't see the visitors. They followed the fortunes of a French innkeeper's daughter who was fascinated by the brilliance of an American "shavetail," but wasn't able to resist the lure of a French colonel, whose jealous wife involved him with a German spy in order to punish him. Out of this came an exciting melodrama, which was going to hold audiences in spite of peace negotiations.

Lanny was interested in two things: first, the performance of Gracyn, which wasn't finished by any means, but was full of energy and "pep"; and, second, the personality of the young American officer. Evidently the play was one of those which had been written at rehearsals, and Gracyn had had a part in it. Lanny had taught her, and she had taught the author and the young actor; so there were many touches in which Lanny recognized himself—mannerisms, phrases, opinions about the war, items about the French, their attitude to the doughboys and the doughboys' to them. There were even a few third-hand touches of Sergeant Jerry Pendleton in this Broadway hit!

"Well, you did a good job," said Robbie. "Charge it up to education and don't fall in love with any more stage ladies."

"I've made a note of it," said the dutiful son.

"Or else—note this: that if you'd had thirty thousand dollars, you might have licked the coffee merchant!"

They were in the taxi on the way to the steamer; and Lanny grinned. "There's an English poem supposed to be sung by the devil, and the chorus runs: 'How pleasant it is to have money, heigh-ho, how pleasant it is to have money!'"

"All right," replied the father. "But you can bet that poet had money, or he wouldn't have been sitting around making up verses."

On board the steamer; and one more farewell to say. Standing on the deck, watching the lights of the metropolis recede, Robbie pointed to an especially bright light across the bay and said: "The Statue of Liberty."

She had come from France, and Lanny was going home. She waved her torch to him, as a sign that she understood how he felt.

BOOK FIVE

They Have Sown the Wind

25

The Battle Flags Are Furled

I

THERE was only one steamer a week to France at this time, and those who traveled on it were carefully selected persons, able to show that they had important business, of a kind the authorities approved. In theory, the world was still at war, and it was not intended that Americans should use the peace conference as a propaganda platform, or for sightseeing tours. But Robert P. Budd knew the people at the War and State Departments; they talked to him confidentially, and when he asked for passports they arranged it at once.

The first thing Robbie did on a steamer was to study the passenger list. He was an extrovert; he liked to talk with people, all sorts, and especially those who were familiar with his hunting ground. There was no printed list in wartime, but he borrowed the purser's list, and went over it with Lanny, and told him that this man was "in steel," that one "in copper," and a third represented a Wall Street banking group. Near the top he read: "Alston, Charles T.," and remarked: "That must be old Charlie Alston, who was in my class at Yale. He's a professor now, and has published a couple of books on the geography of Europe."

"He'll have to begin all over again," ventured Lanny.

"He was a 'barb,' and I didn't know him well," added the father. "I remember him as a rather frail chap with big spectacles. He was an awful grind, and most of us considered it unfair competition. However, he's made good, I suppose."

December is apt to be a rude month on the Atlantic, and there were vacant seats in the dining saloon, and one or two at the captain's table. Robbie glanced at the place card alongside him, and read "Professor Alston." He asked the captain, and learned that his former classmate was an adviser to the peace delegation, but had been unable to sail with the presidential staff because of an attack of influenza.

The third day out, the sea was quieter, and the professor appeared on deck; the same frail little man, wearing his large spectacles. The only thing Robbie didn't recall was that his complexion was yellow with a slight tinge of green; perhaps that would change when he was able to keep food on his stomach. The professor was glad to see his classmate; it appeared that when you had known somebody in college, you felt a peculiar sentimental bond. Alston had looked up to the handsome, rich, and popular Budd as to a shining light on a mountain top; so now to have him sitting in a deckchair asking questions about the coming peace conference and listening with deference to his replies—that was a sort of promotion.

Also the professor was interested in a fresh incarnation of the handsome, rich, and popular Budd; a youth of nineteen, resembling in many ways the one whom Alston remembered. Lanny was lighter in build and faster in mind, more accessible than his father and more eager to learn. The fact that Charles T. Alston had never "made" a fraternity in college and had earned a scant living by waiting on table in a students' boarding house—that didn't mean anything to Lanny. But that he was a storehouse of vital facts, and had been chosen to help the American peace commissioners in their efforts to make Europe a saner place to live in—that made him a great personage in Lanny's eyes. He listened to the conversations between the two elders, and at other times, when Robbie was exchanging shop talk with the "big men" of steel and copper and banking, Lanny would be strolling the deck with the specialist in geography, keeping one hand under his arm to steady him when the ship gave a lurch.

II

It wasn't long before the professor entrusted the youth with his confidence; he was troubled by doubts whether his linguistic equipment—so he called it—was adequate to the task he had before him. "My knowledge of French is that of a student," he explained. "I have read it a great deal, but, as you know, it is a different language to listen to."

Lanny perceived what the shy little man wanted, and presently made the suggestion that they carry on their conversations in French. After that Lanny could have all the professor's time and all his stock of information. Once more he had found something that was better than going to college.

Professor Alston found that he could understand nearly everything that Lanny said; but would it be as easy to understand a Frenchman? Lanny knew that it was a common experience of his American friends to be able to understand American French but not French French. So he undertook to talk like a Frenchman—a matter of running his words together, taking many syllables for granted. The professor braced himself for the shock, and every now and then would ask him to stop and say it over again.

Toward this suddenly developing intimacy the older Budd felt something less than enthusiasm, and Lanny was interested to probe into his attitude. What was wrong with Professor Alston? Well, for one thing, he was a Democrat with a capital D, and his success was political. Alston was one of the crowd whom Woodrow Wilson had brought in, as part of his program to make over the world. Before the war had come along to divert his mind, the Presbyterian President had put forward a program of national reform which, if you would believe Robbie Budd, amounted to taking control of business out of the hands of businessmen and turning it over to politicians. And of course the least hint of this caused sparks to dance before Robbie's eyes.

Now the President was carrying his attitude into international affairs; he was going to settle Europe's problems for it, and to that end had picked out a bunch of theorists like himself, men whose knowledge of the world had been derived from books. The diplomats, the statesmen, the businessmen of Europe were going to be preached at and lectured and put in their places. In America this had been called "the New Freedom," and in Europe it was "the Fourteen Points," but by any other name it smelled as sour to the salesman of Budd Gunmakers.

"But, Robbie," argued his son, "a lot of the Fourteen Points are what you yourself say ought to be done."

"Yes, but Europe isn't going to do them, and it's not our business to make them."

"But what harm can it do to give them advice? Professor Alston says"—and Lanny would repeat some of his new friend's statistics regarding the economic unity of Europe, which was being crippled in so many ways by its political subdivisions. Robbie didn't deny the facts, but he didn't want to take them from a "scholar in politics." The scholar's place was the classroom, or his own cloistered study, where he would be free to write books—which Robbie wouldn't read!

III

However, the scholar was in politics—and no way to get him out until the next election. The former president of Princeton University had got the whole civilized world for his classroom, with hundreds of reporters eagerly collecting every word that he might speak, and paying fortunes to cable it to China and Peru. He had caused to be assembled a troop of his kind, a sort of general staff of peace, which, under the name of "The Inquiry," had been working more than a year to prepare for the time when the war drums throbbed no longer and the battle flags were furled.

The task of organizing this "Inquiry" had been passed on by the President to his Texas friend, Colonel House, who in turn had put the president of another college in charge. Some two hundred scholars had been selected and set to work accumulating a huge mass of data. Elaborate detail maps had been prepared, covering every square mile of Europe; statistics had been dug up, both in libraries and in the "field," as to populations, languages, industries, resources —every question which might arise during the making over of the world. Several carloads of material had been boxed and loaded onto the transport *George Washington,* together with many of the learned persons who had helped to prepare it, and all had been conveyed to the harbor of Brest under the escort of a battleship and half a dozen destroyers.

Professor Alston had been left behind, laid up with the dreadful "flu" which had come in the wake of war; a mysterious scourge which science was powerless to explain, and which many looked upon as a judgment of Providence upon the disorderly nations. The frail professor was hardly well enough to travel, but was worrying himself because of what might appear a shirking of all-important duties. Robbie Budd consoled him by saying: "You won't find all the problems settled when you get to Paris. You may not find them settled when you leave. Your learning may be saved for the next conference."

The professor didn't have his feelings hurt. "Yes, Budd," he answered, patiently. "That's what makes our task so hard—the dreadful weight of skepticism which rests upon so many minds."

I V

The curtain was about to rise upon the last act of the great world melodrama which Lanny Budd had been watching through four and a half impressionable years. During the eight days of the steamer voyage his new friend helped him to peep through the curtain and see the leading characters taking their positions. This melodrama differed from others in that it was not written, it was to be played impromptu, and only once; after that it would be precedent, and would determine the destinies of mankind perhaps for centuries. Each of the actors hoped to write it his way, and no living man could say what the *dénouement* would be.

Professor Alston talked about history, geography, and those racial and language differences which made such a complex. As a scientist, he was dedicated to the truth; he said that he had but one thought, to understand men and nations, and help to bring about a peace that could endure because it was just and sound.

That was the way Lanny wanted things to be; that was his dream, to find some method which would bring his friend Rick and his friend Kurt together, now that the war was over. For hours on end, helping the professor to practice his French, the youth asked questions, and showed himself so eager and understanding that on the last day of the voyage, when the steamer was in sight of the lighthouse of Pointe de St.-Mathieu, the frail scholar was moved to inquire: "Lanny, how would you like to have a job?"

"What sort of job?" asked the other, surprised.

"The State Department, which is my employer, has not seen fit to allow me the services of a secretary; but the nearer I get to France, the more I realize how I shall need one. It's going to be some time before I recover my full strength, and the duties before me are certain to be heavy."

"But a secretary has to know shorthand and typing, doesn't he?"

"Your knowledge of languages and of European ways would count far more with me."

"Don't you think I'm rather young for such a task?"

"You are older than you look. The main thing is that I can trust you. I couldn't pay you what you would consider an adequate salary——"

"Oh, I wouldn't let you pay me, Professor Alston!"

"I'll try to get the department to foot the bill. But in any case I would insist upon your being paid. It'll be one of those all day and most of the night jobs that one does because they're urgent, and because they're interesting. You'd meet a lot of important people, and you'd be on the inside of affairs. I should think it ought to be worth a year in college."

"It sort of takes my breath away," said Lanny. "It would be the first time I ever earned anything."

"What do you suppose your father would say?"

"He wants me to meet people; but he's all the time hoping I'll begin to take hold of the munitions business."

"Well, there's a competition between your father's business and mine right now." The professor was smiling.

"My father won't fight you," replied Lanny, seriously; "but he'll wait, feeling sure that the forces on his side will lick you."

"Perhaps I'd better be the one to put the proposal to him," said the professor. "I don't want him to think I'm trying to steal his son."

Robbie was broader-minded about it than they had foreseen. He saw the advantages which such an opening would give to Lanny. That was the way young Englishmen began their careers in politics and diplomacy; and Robbie wasn't afraid of his son's being led astray by the peace-makers. He said that the same men who made the peace would be making the next war, and Lanny would have a chance to meet and know them. "I'm going to be all over Europe during the next couple of months," added the wise father. "I'll tell you things and you can tell me things."

Lanny thought about that. "Listen, Robbie. If I'm going to be on the payroll of the government, I'll have to work for it, and there may be things I can't tell."

The other was amused. "That's O.K. by me," he said, in the slang of the day. "But this job won't last forever, and when it's done, we'll join forces again."

V

Lanny took the job. Because he liked his new boss, he became not merely secretary, but male nurse, valet, and handyman; he helped the professor to get his things packed, and to get on board the boat train, and to get to his hotel. Oddly enough, the one which Robbie had always patronized, the Crillon, had been taken by the United States government for the use of the Peace Commission and its advisers. Lanny and his professor could have rooms there, but Robbie couldn't—not for love or money. A symbol of the new order of things, under which businessmen were being ousted from the seats of authority and replaced by scholars in politics!

Lanny found himself, with hardly any warning, thrust into the midst of a beehive, or antheap, or whatever simile best indicates a great number of creatures in a state of violent activity. It has always been the practice of scholars and specialists to meet in congresses and conventions, and they always feel that what they are doing is of vital importance; but it may be doubted if any group of such persons had ever before had such good reason to hold this conviction. Some fifty American scholars, plus librarians and custodians of documents and typists and other assistants, several hundred persons in all, had been appointed to remedy the evils of Europe, Asia, Africa, and Australasia, which had been accumulating for no one could say how many hundreds of years. All the world had been told that the evils were to be remedied, and all but a few skeptical ones believed it, and waited in suspense for the promises to be kept. The fate of hundreds of millions of persons for an indefinite future might depend upon the advice which these scholars would give; so the learned ones carried in their souls a colossal burden of responsibility, and never in the history of mankind had so much conscientiousness been crowded into one structure as was to be found at the junction of the Rue Royale and the Place de la Concorde at Christmas time of the year 1918.

The first few hours for Lanny Budd were a blur of faces, names, and handshakes. He met so many persons that he gave up trying to keep them in mind. But quickly they began to sort themselves out. Professor Alston's immediate associates were eager to tell him all that had happened during the two or three weeks he had lost. Alston informed them that Lanny was to be his confidant, and so he had a front seat at the rising of the curtain upon the fateful last act of the great world melodrama.

The art work of the ages to which this production most nearly approached was the story of Daniel in the lions' den. The title role was taken by the scholar from Princeton, and the scholars from

Yale, Harvard, Columbia, and other institutions were gathered in his train, striding with bold miens but quaking hearts into an arena filled with British lions, and with tigers, hyenas, jackals, crocodiles, and other creatures whose national affiliations had better not be specified. Each of these creatures had jaws dripping with blood, and under its claws lay other creatures, equally fierce, but now torn, bleeding, and near to death.

Such was the aspect of the world at the conclusion of the greatest of recorded wars, and the task of Daniel and his associates and advisers was to persuade the victorious ones to abandon at least a part of the prey they had seized, and permit it to be hospitalized and have its wounds attended and be set upon its feet again, under solemn pledges to abandon its predatory ways and live thereafter in a millennial state of brotherhood and legality. If into this description there creeps a trace of mockery, it is due to the fact that Robbie Budd was sojourning at the Hotel Vendôme not far away, meeting his son at intervals, and hearing his description of the academic gentlemen and their activities. If it had been an assemblage of steel, oil, and munitions manufacturers meeting to apportion the trade of the world, Robbie would have taken its decisions with seriousness; but to his mind there was something inherently comical about any large group of college professors. The kindest comparison he could make was to the behavior and conversation of a flock of elderly hens in a chickenhouse when the fox comes sneaking round at night.

VI

When Lanny got to know the members of the American staff, he found that some were according to his father's imagining, but the little group of Alston's intimates had a point of view which included Robbie's far more than Robbie's included theirs. They were informed concerning munitions manufacturers and salesmen, and the part which these played in the beginning and continuing of wars. They knew it so well that they were a bit uneasy at the idea of having their intimate conversations listened to by a son of Budd's. They had to sound him out and watch his reactions for a while before they would completely trust him.

Besides academic persons the staff included a number of young men of independent means who were playing at politics and diplomacy in what they were pleased to consider the "people's cause." Lanny discovered that these fellows knew about Zaharoff, and the de Wendels, and the Briey Basin, which had come out of the war without any serious bombing. They knew about the politicians and propagandists both official and unofficial who now surrounded them. Their conversation was full of jokes about being flimflammed and bamboozled and hoodwinked, short-changed or sold a gold brick or a gross of green spectacles. They watched suspiciously every person who approached them, and received a compliment as if it might be a loaded hand grenade. Many had their wives with them, and these helped to mount guard.

The concern of many had been aroused at the outset by the fact that there was no peace conference under way, and no sign of getting ready for one. The French government had requested that President Wilson should arrive by the fourteenth of December and the President had done so. They had given him a grand reception— the people of Paris turning out and making it the most tumultuous in history. But nothing had been said about a conference; the French hadn't even named their delegates.

The more suspicious of the staff put their heads together. What did it mean? Doubtless they had wanted to get the President over here so that they could wine him and dine him and tell him that he was the greatest man in the world. They would study him, discover his weak points, and see what they could do with him. They offered to take him to inspect the war zones, and the meaning of that was obvious; they would stir up his emotions, fill him with the same hatred of the Germans which they themselves felt. Meanwhile the military men would go on weakening Germany, taking out of the country all those things which the armistice had required—five thousand locomotives, as many trucks, and a hundred and fifty thousand freight cars. Germany would be blockaded, and its remaining stocks of food exhausted—in short, those who wanted a Carthaginian peace would be getting it.

Within the Allied lines there was a struggle getting under way between those who wanted to make peace and those who wanted to wage the next war. In general the French were on one side and the Americans on the other, with the British wavering between the two. Lloyd George, who had become Prime Minister during the war, had only a faction behind him, and had seen the opportunity to cement his power by throwing the country into a general election—the "khaki election," it was called, because of the spirit in which it was carried on. Lloyd George had promised that the Kaiser should be tried, and at the hustings the cry had arisen for him to be hanged. The German people must somehow be made to suffer, as the British and French and Belgians had done. But there was a liberal element among the British representatives in Paris, especially the younger ones, who were sympathetic to the American program of peace with reconciliation. These, of course, wished to meet and know the Americans. Was it proper for the Americans to meet them? Or would that, too, be "propaganda"?

VII

Lanny had sent his mother a telegram upon his arrival in Brest, mentioning the exciting tidings that he had got a job. It meant that he could not come to Juan—at least, not until he had finished solving the problems of Europe. He wrote, suggesting that she should come to Paris.

Of course Beauty had to see her boy; and Robbie thought it would be a good thing if she left home for a while. He didn't take much stock in her efforts at rehabilitating broken Frenchmen; that was all right for women of a certain type, but not for Beauty, who was made for pleasure. Writing to Lanny, she protested that everything in Paris would be so dreadfully expensive; and Robbie answered in his usual way, by giving their son an extra check to send her. It was one of his ways of educating Lanny, helping him to realize how pleasant it was to have money, heigh-ho!

The mother was still clinging to the hope that she might hear some word about Marcel. She told herself that she could carry on her search better from Paris; if it brought no results, she could help to promote interest in his paintings, a labor of piety which intrigued her mind. Lanny could assist her, now that he was meeting so many important and influential persons. In short, life once more began to stir in the bosom of Mabel Blackless, once Beauty Budd, and now Madame Detaze, *veuve*.

She ordered her trunks packed, and oversaw the job, exclaiming over the dowdiness of everything she owned; she hadn't bought a thing for years, and would simply *have* to do some shopping in Paris! Should she give up hope and put on black for Marcel, and how would she look? Leese and Rosine of course had views which they expressed freely. Beauty would repeat her injunctions for the care of Baby Marceline, now a little more than a year old and safely weaned; the two servants would renew their pledges, and Beauty would by turns be grieved at leaving her new baby and excited at the prospect of meeting her old one.

Lanny was at the Gare de Lyon, and they rushed together; then they held each other apart, to see what twenty months had done. "Oh, Lanny, you're grand! What a great tall thing you've grown!" And: "Oh, Beauty, you've been breaking the rules! There are ten pounds more of you!"

She blushed as she admitted her sins. "But I'll soon lose it here in Paris, with the prices I'm told they're charging." They had lunch together at the hotel, and Beauty inspected the *addition*, which included fifty francs for a chicken. She exclaimed in horror, and said she would live on pear and endive salad from now on. One felt guilty to eat anything at all, with so many people starving all over Europe.

Such a myriad of things they had to talk about! Lanny had to tell about Esther and her family, and the rest of the Budd tribe, a hundred details that he had been too busy to write. He had to tell about Gracyn, that horrid creature, so Beauty adjudged her; there were women like that, and they filled a mother's heart with distress. Beauty inspected him anxiously for any signs that his life had been ruined; but he assured her that he was all right, he had learned a lot, he was wiser as well as sadder, and meant to live a strict ascetic life from now on, devoting himself to bringing peace to Europe. Beauty listened gravely; she had heard other men make such resolutions, but had rarely seen them kept.

She told him about the baby, how she looked and what she ate and the delightful sounds she made. She told him about the wounded men she had been visiting at Sept Chênes. "I don't know what I'm going to do with them, Lanny, now that the war is over—it's just like having a lot of relatives." She told about Emily Chattersworth, whose château was still given up to *mutilés*. "She's living in town now, and you must go and see her—she can be so helpful to you and your professors—she knows everybody and likes to bring people together—that's really her forte, you know."

"Don't bother," smiled the youth. "My professors are meeting several times as many people as they want to."

"Oh, but I mean the right ones, Lanny. That's the way to get things done here in France. Emily will arrange to take your Professor Alston direct to Clemenceau himself, and he can explain just how he thinks the peace ought to be settled." It was going to be as simple as that!

VIII

President Wilson and his wife went shopping in Paris. She was a buxom lady who was devoted to him and took the best possible care of him, and wore in his honor a gorgeous purple gown and a hat with purple plumes. Everywhere they appeared there were ovations; the people of Europe rushed to manifest their faith in him, their hope, their adoration. It was something entirely spontaneous, unforeseen by the politicians and not a little disturbing to them. For this man talked about Democracy, and not merely before elections;

he spoke as if he really believed in it—and these were dangerous times, when words were liable to explode, like the shells which were buried in the fields of France and went off in the faces of the peasants who tried to plow. This man talked about freedom of the seas which Britannia boasted of ruling; he talked about self-determination for those small peoples whom the statesmen of Europe were bent upon ruling.

President Wilson and his wife went to London, arriving on the day after Christmas, which the British call "Boxing Day." Enormous throngs welcomed them, and the government provided a royal banquet at Buckingham Palace, making it the most gorgeous spectacle ever seen in that land of pageantry. Britain was the only country left in Europe that could put on such a show. The empire of the Tsar was now a land of starving proletarians, and the realm of the Kaiser was ruled by a saddlemaker; but Britannia still had the money, and her field marshals and generals and admirals and lord mayors still had the costumes. Before this shining assemblage the lean Presbyterian professor stood in his plain black clothes, and talked about the rights of the people; also, he failed to tell the lords and masters of the realm that they had won the war, an offense which they wouldn't forget.

President Wilson and his wife returned to Paris, and he made a speech before the Chamber of Deputies, and failed to praise the heroism which France had displayed. It was hard for his hearers to understand that this was a peace man, who had been forced into war with bitter reluctance, and now had but one thought in his mind, to make such a calamity impossible for the future. He went to Italy, and the hungry and tormented people turned out in a demonstration which frightened the ruling classes. Everywhere it was the same throughout Europe, in defeated lands as well as in victorious ones; the peasants cut out newspaper pictures of this new redeemer and pinned them onto the walls of their huts and burned candles before them. In Vienna the children who were dying wholesale of the diseases of malnutrition smiled happily and said: "It will soon be all right; President Wilson is coming." Never had a living man held so much power in his two hands; never did a living man have so many prayers said for him and to him.

Many among the staff of advisers had considered that it was a mistake for the President of the United States to come to Europe at this time. Professor Alston was among these; he didn't say much about it, wishing to be tactful, but Lanny knew what he thought, and why. If the President had remained in Washington, and had the proposals of the peace delegates submitted to him, his decisions would have come as from Mount Sinai; but when he descended into the arena, he would be just one more contestant, and would sacrifice his prestige and authority. He who had had no training in diplomacy would be pitted against men who had had little else since childhood. They knew a thousand arts of which he was ignorant; they would find out his weak points, they would browbeat him and weary him and trap him into unwise concessions.

Reading now about the President's triumphal tour, Lanny wondered if this would alter his chief's opinion. But Alston said it was a tragic fact that these millions of people were confused in their minds and easily swayed. They wanted peace, but also they wanted national gains at the expense of others, and they could be whipped up to excitement by a venal press, and by politicians who secretly served financial interests of a selfish kind. What the outcome of these struggles would be, no man alive could foretell; but it was going to be a grim fight, and all of them would have to stand together and back their great leader to the best of their abilities. So thought and whispered the technical advisers of the American Commission to Negotiate Peace.

26

The Parliament of Man

I

THERE was not much holiday spirit in Paris that Christmas. Half the women were in mourning, and the other half doing the work of their men, who were still under arms, many of them in Germany, guarding the bridgeheads of the Rhine. The season was inclement, with cold and rain; food and fuel were scarce and disorganization general. The very rich were richer, but everybody else was poor, and anxiously peering through a curtain of fog to discern what new calamities lay ahead.

The little staff of official Americans were of course well looked after; not merely sheltered and warmed and fed, but provided with every sort of technical assistance: an elaborate courier service, a post office, a telephone and telegraph service of their own, a printing plant, a wireless station which could send a message all the way around the world in the seventh part of a second. Something like a million and a half dollars had been expended to guarantee their security and efficiency. While the President was away on his tours, the experts busied themselves preparing what was known as the "Black Book," an outline of the territorial settlements which the Americans would recommend to the President. It was highly confidential, and many persons wanted very much to know what was in it.

This had the effect of intensifying the siege being laid to the Hotel Crillon. Not a physical siege, of course, for the place was well guarded, and you couldn't get in without a pass; but a diplomatic siege, a social siege, waged with the ancient weapons of elegance and prestige, of courtesy and tact for which Paris was famed. Did anybody know a member of the American staff? And would it be possible to give the said member a dinner party, or invite him to tea, or to a salon, or to hear some music, or to see some pictures? The American professors had a hard time making excuses to all the people who wanted to tell their national troubles. The professors were disposed to be reserved, especially at the outset; bearing in mind that they were not negotiators, but advisers to negotiators.

Lanny Budd was only a semi-official person; and, besides, he had connections in Paris of a sort which few others enjoyed. Professor Alston couldn't very well expect him not to meet his own mother and father, or the friends whom he had known since childhood. And of course the effect was to constitute him a "pipeline" into the Crillon. A great many persons found out that Madame Detaze, widow of a French painter, had a son who was a translator or something to the American staff; so at once Madame Detaze became a popular hostess. "Oh, Madame, I have heard so much about that charming son of yours! So brilliant, so wise beyond his years! I'd love to meet him—couldn't you arrange it? Oh, right away, within the next few days!"

Nothing of that surprised the mother; she had always known that her son was all that! So Lanny would be asked to meet dreamers and propagandists, fortune hunters and impoverished aristocrats from places whose names he had to look up in the atlas—Kurdistan and Croatia, Iraq and Mingrelia, Cilicia which must not be confused with Silesia or Galicia, and Slovenia which must be distinguished from Slovakia. Earnest strangers would appeal in the name of President Wilson's doctrine of "self-determination of all peoples"; and Lanny would take their stories to the experts at the Crillon—and like as not would learn that these same people were busily engaged in oppressing some other people, even perhaps killing them wholesale!

II

Beauty called the hotel, saying: "Lanny, I've just met the most delightful young English officer—he's been in Arabia for years, even before the war, and tells such interesting stories about it. You know, they wear robes, and gallop across the desert on beautiful horses, and take long journeys on camels. They say he has an Arabian sheik or something with him, and he's going to bring him to Emily's for tea. Couldn't you run over?"

So Lanny, who for the last six hours had been working without a break at making abstracts of several French reports on conditions in the Ukraine, said yes, and in the drawing room of Mrs. Chattersworth's town house he met a figure out of the *Arabian Nights:* a man of thirty or so, with a mild face, long and thin, such as painters have imagined for Jesus Christ. He had a black beard and mustache and very beautiful dark eyes, and wore a robe of soft gray silk edged with scarlet, and a four-cornered turban with a hood having a flowered pattern. His father was Sherif of Mecca and King of the Hejaz—at least he said the British called his father "king," but it was silly, for the father traced his ancestry back to the Prophet, more than twelve hundred years ago, and what was any "king" in the world compared to that?

The Emir Feisal, as this young man was called, spoke no English; what he said was translated by the officer who was his companion and friend. The latter's name was Lawrence, and the two of them had been fighting the Turks and Germans all over the sun-scorched deserts of Arabia, and in the end had swept them out of the country. Colonel Lawrence was about thirty-one and seemed even younger, having the manner of a gay schoolboy. He was stocky, with sandy complexion much burned, and very bright blue eyes. He and his friend had a keen sense of humor and exchanged many jokes during the translating.

But they had a serious purpose, having come to Paris to tell the story of the heroic fight which their people had waged for freedom, and to present to President Wilson the claims they held under the terms of his Fourteen Points—Number 12, to be precise, which specified that "the Turkish portions of the present Ottoman Empire should be assured a secure sovereignty, but the other nationalities which are now under Turkish rule should be assured an undoubted security of life and an absolutely unmolested opportunity of autonomous development."

It seemed impossible to misunderstand that. The Emir put it up to Lanny Budd, having been told that he was a compatriot of the great Democrat and a member of the Crillon staff. He begged to be told what Lanny thought about the prospects, and the secretary-translator, speaking unofficially, of course, replied that he had no doubt whatever that President Wilson meant to stand by his promises. It was hard to see how any question could be raised, because the Fourteen Points, with only two reservations, had been expressly accepted by the Allies as the basis of the armistice with Germany. Having given this assurance, Lanny shook hands with the gay young warriors from the sun-scorched lands and they parted the best of friends; the youth went back to his inaccessible hotel and told his chief about it—which of course was what Feisal and his companion assumed that he would do.

Alston smiled a rather wry smile and said that this question of the Hejaz was one of the battles which had to be fought out in the Peace Conference. Lawrence had promised, and the British government had ratified the promise, that the Arabian peoples would have their independence as the price of their support against Turkey and Germany; but unfortunately there was a great deal of oil in Mesopotamia, and a pipeline was proposed to run through Syria; also the British government had promised a lot of Arab territory to the French—it was one of those "secret treaties." The French were now in possession of the land and it wasn't by any means sure that they could be got out without another war. Moreover, there was another Arab chieftain, Ibn Saud, who had driven the Turks out of eastern Arabia—and what about his claims?

All of which went to show how very inadvisable it was for a youthful translator of the American Commission to meet figures out of the *Arabian Nights* and cause them to believe that they had assurances of things which they might or might not be going to get!

III

Life does strange things to human beings. Charles T. Alston had been raised in a small farming community of Indiana, and here he was, a specialist in geography, ethnography, and allied branches of learning, helping to decide the destinies of men in lands whose very names were unknown to the people of the Hoosier state. In his village as a boy he had attended a tiny Congregational church, which could not afford a regular pastor but had the services of students from a near-by church school. One of these students had eaten fried chicken and cornmeal mush in little Charlie Alston's home, and had helped to awaken in him a longing for knowledge. Thirty-five years had passed, during which Alston had never seen him; but here he came strolling into the Hotel Crillon—having been in the interim a doctor of divinity, a professor of "Applied Christianity," a Socialist agitator, and finally one of the trusted agents and advisers of President Wilson in Europe.

Lanny watched him while he talked to his old friend, and thought he was one of the strangest-looking men he had ever known. His unusually sweet and kindly features had not merely the pallor of marble, but seemed to have its texture. His hair, mustache, and beard were jet-black. He was obviously not in good health, and his whole aspect was pain-driven, haunted not merely by his own griefs but by those of mankind; his manner was quiet, his voice low, and his language apocalyptic. He rarely smiled, and when he did so, it seemed to be reluctantly, as a concession to other people's ways. A sense of impending doom rested upon his spirit, as if he saw more of the future of Europe than any of the persons he met.

George D. Herron was his name; and later on Alston told Lanny about the tragedy which had broken his health and happiness. He had been one of the leaders of a movement called "Christian Socialist," seeking to bring justice and brotherhood in the name of the proletarian carpenter. A clergyman and professor in a small college of Iowa, Herron had been unhappily married, and had fallen in love with the dean of women of his college. He had left his wife—something not in accord with the ethics prevailing in the "corn and hog belt." The enemies of his dangerous ideas had taken this opportunity to ruin him, and he had been expelled from his job in the college, and had gone abroad with his new wife to live.

That had been a long while ago, and the unhappy professor and his great sin had been pretty well forgotten. In Europe he had come to know working-class leaders, pacifists, humanitarians—those whose spirits could not rest while their fellow-men were being butchered, mutilated, starved, frozen, drowned in mud, and fed upon hate and falsehood. Living in Geneva, he had been accessible to both sides in the war, and friends and strangers had come to him from Austria and Germany, to sound him out and use him as a means of communicating with the Allied lands. First he had reported to the American embassy in Switzerland, and later to the President direct. He had had something to do with the shaping of the Fourteen Points and had outlined a plan for the forming of a League of Nations. This Socialist agitator who had been driven from his own country in disgrace now possessed the freedom of the Crillon, and could have audiences with the President at a time when the latter was so overburdened that not even the members of his own Peace Commission could see him.

The second time that Lanny met Herron he was walking on the street toward the hotel. He walked slowly, because he suffered from arthritis. Lanny joined him, and he started talking about some of the developments of the day. When they reached the hotel, Lanny waited politely for the elder to go through the revolving doors. He had entered the moving space, when a large military man, coming the other way in haste, pushed the doors violently, and a carved wooden cane which Herron was carrying got caught in the doors and cracked in two. When Lanny came through, his friend was standing with the pieces in his hand, gazing at them and exclaiming: "My Jerusalem cane!"

"Is it valuable?" asked the youth.

"Not to anyone but me. I bought it when I was young and visited the Holy Land. It has been precious to me as a souvenir of deeply felt experiences."

"Oh, I'm sorry," said Lanny, sympathetically.

The other still held the broken pieces. "I am not superstitious," he continued; "but I will tell you a curious incident. When I was leaving home, my sixteen-year-old son asked me why I was carrying that cane, and I said, half playfully: 'I am going to Paris to set up the kingdom of heaven, and this staff from the country of Jesus is a symbol of my purpose.' 'See that they don't break it, Father!' said my son."

The professor looked at the pieces a moment or two longer and then called a bellboy and gave them to him to dispose of. "*Absit omen!*" he remarked to Lanny.

IV

It was the twelfth of January before the "Supreme Council" held its first session, in the hall of the dingy old Foreign Office on the Quai d'Orsay, just across the Seine from the Crillon. The gray stone structure kept some of the most vital secrets of France, and had high iron railings and heavy gates. Only important personages were admitted to the opening ceremony, but Lanny and his chief were among them, because some of the American delegates might need information about geography. Lanny's duty was the carrying of two heavy portfolios of maps and other data; he would take them with him to many important gatherings, but rarely would open them—instead, he would keep his ears open, and stay close behind his chief; now and then the latter would touch his knee, and Lanny would lean over and whisper what some excited Frenchman was saying. This kind of assistance was not uncommon among the American officials; neither President Wilson nor his closest associate, Colonel House, knew French, and there always had to be whisperers behind their chairs.

The council hall was splendid and impressive, having on the floor a heavy Aubusson carpet, pearl-gray with large red roses; red damask curtains at the windows, superb Gobelin tapestries on the walls. The ceilings were high, and the lights were set in enormous chandeliers. A great many tables were laid end to end in the shape of a square U, covered with green baize, and pink silk blotters which were changed every day. The chairs were gilded, with silk upholstery, and all this splendor was guarded by *huissiers* wearing silver chains.

At the bottom of the square U sat Georges Clemenceau, Premier of France, a squat little figure with a strange head, bald and flat on top. He had broad humped shoulders, a short neck, sallow complexion, white walrus mustaches, thick, shaggy eyebrows, and a long, square-tailed black coat. At his back was a fireplace with a crackling fire—you would always find that wherever he sat, for he was seventy-eight, and diabetic, and his blood was growing chilly. Over the fireplace was a figure of Peace holding up a torch—perhaps to warm his soul, which may also have grown chilly. Always he wore gray silk gloves on his hands, because he suffered from eczema.

Near him sat President Wilson, stiff and erect, with lean ascetic face and shining glasses. Beyond him was the Prime Minister of Britain with pink cherubic features and a little white mustache. Next to him was Balfour with his air of aristocratic boredom, cultivated not for this occasion but for life. The other personages tapered off down the line. In the background were generals wearing uniforms and medals, and potentates in the varicolored robes of the East. Marshal Foch was there, and General Pershing, and other military men, because the first matter in hand was the renewal of the armistice, which was for a month at a time, and each time the Marshal had thought of some new ways to tighten the screws upon the hated foe.

After that they took up the question of representation at the conference, and the future methods of procedure. It was supposed to be a deliberative assembly, but after a few sessions it became apparent that everything had been fixed in advance. Someone would make a proposal, and while he was speaking Clemenceau would sit with hands folded and eyes closed, and no one would know whether he was asleep or not. But the moment the speaker finished, the chairman would raise his heavy eyelids and say: "Any discussion?" —and then, before anybody could get his wits together to answer, he would bring down his gavel and snap out: "*Adopté!*" Said Professor Alston to Lanny: "He's fighting the next war."

V

At the head of President Wilson's Fourteen Points stood the phrase: "Open covenants of peace openly arrived at." Taking this statement at its face value, American press associations, newspapers, and magazines had sent their correspondents to Paris, and there were now a hundred and fifty of them in a ravenous condition, having waited a whole month for something to happen. The rest of the world had contributed twice as many; and now they were informed that no press representatives would be admitted to sessions of the conference, but that they would get "handouts" from a press bureau. When they got their first one they found that it contained exactly forty-eight words.

A howl went up that was heard, quite literally, all the way around the world. The hundred and fifty Americans appointed a committee and stormed the American press bureau; a war began that did not end with the Peace Conference, but was continued into the history books. Men took one side or the other—and from that choice you could know what part they were going to play, not merely in this particular melodrama, but in all the others which were to follow upon its heels.

France had been at war for four bloody years, had suffered grievous wounds, and now stood with one foot upon her deadly foe. During these four years the people of France had been under a complete censorship; officials and military men between them had decided not merely what should be done but what should be said and thought. Now suddenly it was proposed to lift this censorship and turn people loose to reveal secrets and criticize policies—in short, to say what they pleased, or what the enemy might hire them to say. "What?" cried the shell-shocked officials. "Open the sessions of the conference, and let newspaper men hear the wrangles of the diplomats, and tell the whole world about national ambitions and demands? If you do that, you will have a series of new wars on your hands—the Allies will be fighting among themselves!"

To this the believers in open covenants openly arrived at replied that the affairs to be settled by the conference were the affairs of the people, and the people had a right to know what was being planned and done. Democracy could not function unless it had information. The only way of lasting peace was to turn the conference into a means of education, an open forum where problems were threshed out in the sight and hearing of all.

So the debate raged; and like everything else with which the assemblage dealt it was settled by compromise and evasion. It was agreed that the press should be admitted to the "plenary sessions"; whereupon these were turned into formal affairs to ratify decisions already worked out by the so-called "Council of Ten." When the press took to clamoring against the secrecy of the "Council of Ten," the real work was transferred to a secret "Council of Four." Presently this became a "Council of Three," and this holy trinity not only told no pressmen what it was doing, but to make sure that they couldn't find out, it employed but one secretary and kept but one record.

VI

Of course only a small portion of the people of Paris were occupied with the Peace Conference. The common people, mostly women and elderly men, worked at their daily tasks, and gave their thoughts to getting food with prices steadily rising. The well-to-do had their cares also, for it was a violent world, exposed to sudden unforeseeable changes. Only speculators throve; and whenever

Robbie met his son he had stories to tell about what these were doing.

The munitions industry was shot to pieces, reported the salesman. Budd's had been forced to close down; all that magnificent plant which had been like a beehive—its chimneys were empty and its gates were locked. "But I thought we still had contracts with the government!" exclaimed the youth. The father answered that it didn't pay to run big plants for a few orders, and they had canceled the contracts on the basis of part payments.

"But what will all those working people do, Robbie?"

"I hope they saved their money. For us the war ended too soon. Nobody could foresee that Germany was going to collapse like that."

"We still have those fine new plants, haven't we?"

"What are plants if you can't run them? They're just a drain; upkeep, insurance, and taxes—the government soaks you as hard whether you're making anything or not."

"I never thought of that," confessed Lanny.

"Your grandfather isn't thinking about anything else very much."

Robbie was sending home long reports, mostly without a gleam of hope. There were plenty of people who wanted to go on fighting, but where were they to get the money? Who would want to finance new wars? And, anyhow, the fighting would be done with munitions already manufactured. There were mountains of it piled up all over France, and on the Italian front, and the Balkan front, and the Palestine front—everywhere you looked on the map. It could be bought for almost anything you wanted to offer.

"I've been trying to interest Father in buying some as a speculation," added Robbie. "But he says we're not going into the junk business. I can't very well do it myself while I'm the European sales agent of our firm."

In Lanny's mind was a vision of that depressing old Colonial house in Newcastle, with a worried and overworked businessman sitting at a desk piled high with papers—and having in one drawer a bundle

of pamphlets setting forth the Confession of Faith of his grandfather. "What does he expect to do, Robbie?"

"We've got to figure out ways to turn some of the plants to
peacetime uses. And that's going to cost a lot of money."

"Well, we made it, didn't we?"

"Most of it was distributed as dividends, and people aren't going
to put it back in unless we can show them new ways of making
profits."

"Surely, Robbie, there's going to be a demand for every sort of
goods! People are clamoring for them all over."

"It doesn't matter how much they clamor, unless they've got
money. The ones that have money daren't risk it when there's so
much uncertainty—and when those in authority can't make up their
minds about anything. We've got a President who spent his time
studying Latin and Greek and theology when he ought to have
been learning the elements of finance and credit."

Robbie said that Clemenceau and Lloyd George were every bit as
ignorant about economic questions; he wanted businessmen and
financiers called in to advise. With one-third of Europe in revolution, and another third hanging on the brink; with tens of millions
of people not knowing where to get their next day's bread; with
trade disorganized, railways broken down, river transport sunk,
harbors blockaded, and millions of men still kept out of production,
liable to revolt and go home, or to start shooting one another—the
man to whom they all looked for guidance had brought a shipload
of specialists in geography and history and international law, and
only a handful who knew finance, production, or trade.

VII

The telephone rang in Lanny's room, and he heard a voice,
speaking English with a decided foreign accent: "Can you guess?"
Someone in a playful mood; he kept on talking, and Lanny, who
had heard so many kinds of accents in his young life, tried his best

to think, but nothing stirred in his memory. "Five years ago," said the stranger. "On a railroad train." Lanny groped in his mind. "I got on at Genoa," said the voice; and suddenly a light dawned, and the youth cried: "Mr. Robin!"

"Johannes Robin, Maatschappij voor Electrische Specialiteiten, Rotterdam—at your service!" chuckled the voice.

"Well, well!" said Lanny. "What are you doing here?"

"A little business, which will be a secret until I see you."

"And how are the boys?"

"Fine, Lanny, fine—do I call you Lanny, even though you are grown up to a young gentleman?"

"You bet you do, Mr. Robin. I'll never forget the favors you have done me." In the course of the last four years Mr. Robin had mailed six or eight letters to Kurt in Germany, one of them only a week or two previously. That was how the trader knew that Lanny was in Paris, and his address.

Of course Lanny wanted to see that friend, even busy as he was with all the affairs of Europe. "I'm going to have lunch with my father," he said. "Wouldn't you like to join us?"

"Sure, I like to meet your father," said the dealer in electrical gadgets. Lanny told him where to come.

Johannes Robin was somewhat stouter than Lanny remembered him; he had spent money on his clothes and looked the picture of prosperity. He was the same exuberant fellow, who liked to talk about himself; but Lanny, more observant now, got the feeling that he was not entirely at ease. He wanted very much to please these two rich Americans, and was never quite sure whether he was doing it. His handsome dark eyes moved from Lanny's face to Robbie's and back again, and his smile was deprecating and hesitant, as if to say: "I hope you don't mind if I am so proud to know you."

He was genuinely glad to see the youth and exclaimed over how big he had got. Of course he wanted to tell about those two boys at home, and he had some more snapshots of his family group, which he presented apologetically—they wouldn't take up much room. They talked about Kurt Meissner; Lanny had had no answer to his last letter, and was worried about it. A captain of artillery could have been killed during the last days of the war just as well as at any other time. Robbie said that the Americans had been attacking just as hard between seven in the morning when the armistice was signed and eleven when it went into effect.

With Lanny's father Mr. Robin became the businessman, who had traveled over Europe and knew its affairs, and could tell interesting stories about money-making in wartime. From his safe retreat in the Low Countries he had made quite a lot, in spite of the British blockade; nothing to compare with Mr. Budd's affairs, he said modestly, but enough to constitute success for one who had been born in a ghetto hut with a mud floor. Robbie liked that attitude—he liked people to be what they were and not pretend to be something else; so he and the Jewish importer got along pleasantly. They agreed that business would pick up again, if only the diplomats would quit their stalling; they agreed on many things that ought to be done—and Lanny listened, picking up bits of information which he could take back to his chief, to atone for taking a couple of hours off in the middle of a busy day.

VIII

Before those two had finished their bottle of wine they knew each other well enough for Jascha Rabinowich, alias Robin, to make a confession. "Mr. Budd, I have some ideas in my head that just don't let me rest. You know the feeling perhaps: there is money to be made, so much money, and I see how it can be done at once, but later on it will be too late."

Yes, Robbie knew the feeling, and gave permission for his new acquaintance to tell him what he had in mind. It turned out to be the same thing that had been interfering with Robbie's sleep: all that mass of munitions and other supplies which had been manufactured at enormous cost, and which were now lying about—"Have you seen them, Mr. Budd?"

Robbie smiled. "My son sees them on the Place in front of his hotel." It was packed with rows of cannon of every type, howitzers, mortars, field-guns—captured German pieces with the marks of war on them, and now rusting in the rain.

"It is terrible, Mr. Budd, all those goods which cannot even be covered up: shells that they were ready to fire, boots they were going to wear. Now they do not know what to do with it all. To take things back to England—that is possible; but all the way to America—will it pay the cost of crating and shipping?"

"We have been figuring on it, and it won't," said Robbie Budd. "The army has a commission here, trying to dispose of the stuff."

"Well, Mr. Budd, I am a man who knows how to sell things. I know dealers all over Europe. And I have ideas. I wake up in the middle of the night, because one has stung me, like it might be— what is it?—*abeille*——"

"A bee," said Lanny.

"For example?" said Robbie.

"Well, hand grenades; there are millions of them——"

"We made a quarter of a million for our army."

"And now they are somewhere out in the mud of Lorraine. You know what they look like; I don't need to describe them."

"What would you do with them?"

"First I unload them. I have a mass of black powder, which I put up in bags. I know a man who supplies mining companies in Chile, Peru, all those countries. Then I cut off the handles; tomorrow I will find something to do with them. Then I have a little round metal box; it has a pretty shape, it sits up on end; I cut a slot in the top, and there you are."

"What is it?"

"It is a children's bank, where they drop their pennies, their *pfennigs*, their *sous*, their *soldi*—in every country they have little coins for the poor."

Robbie and his son couldn't keep from laughing. Such an odd idea: a hand grenade, the quintessence of destructiveness, made into a children's bank, the symbol of thrift. Swords into plowshares and spears into pruning hooks!

Mr. Robin laughed too, but only for a moment. "You don't know what a market it is, Mr. Budd. You don't know the homes of the poor, as I do."

"But they have no money now."

"They will get these small coins; and they will starve themselves and save—maybe to pay off a mortgage, maybe to buy a cow, or for a girl's dowry—such things as the peasants hope for. A bank is something sacred, it comes next to the crucifix; it teaches virtue, it is a witness and a reminder; the family that has it has something to live for. If there is peace, on next Christmas Day a million peasant women will give such banks to their children."

"Christmas is a long way off, Mr. Robin."

"You would not say that if you knew the novelty trade. Next summer we start to travel for our Christmas trade; and meantime I am finding the agents, I am sending them the samples and the circulars and the contracts; and all that I have to get ready. If I have a couple of hundred thousand banks that have cost me only a few cents each, I know I can sell them, and just where and how. And that is only one small deal, Mr. Budd. I will find a hundred bargains, and a use for each."

"Have you thought about storage costs?"

"In the old city where I live are hundreds of warehouses, and no longer will they be full of goods when ships can go directly into Germany. They are on the canals, and goods come by the rivers or the sea—there is cheap transport to every part of the world. All that is needed is cash to buy—and to do it quickly, before someone else snaps up the bargain. I am so certain of the profits that I am offering to go fifty-fifty with you; I will give all my time and experience, I will do the work, and pay you half the profits. We will form a company, and your name will be kept out of it—I know that you do not want your name in small business like this. It will be a quick thing—in a year it will be over, and I would not dare to tell you how many hundred percent we will clear, because then you would be sure that I must be a swindler."

IX

Lanny watched these two traders, smoking their cigars and knocking the ashes into the dregs of their coffee cups; he amused himself trying to guess what was going on in their minds. He himself kept silent, knowing that this wasn't his job. He personally would have been willing to trust the Jewish dealer, because he liked him. But Robbie didn't like Jews; his view was that of society people who don't want them in their fraternities or clubs. Robbie would sometimes make playful remarks based upon the assumption that Jews went into bankruptcy freely, and set fire to their warehouses and stores when the season became slack. "Fur stores burn in February" —all that sort of thing.

Would Mr. Robin be aware of that attitude? Lanny guessed that this shrewd fellow knew everything that concerned himself and his affairs; he would anticipate the attitude of fashionable gentiles listening to his business "spiel" and watching the play of his hands and shoulders.

"Look, Mr. Budd," said the dealer in gadgets. "I come to you a stranger, and perhaps I have nerve to talk money to you. But I have business connections, I have a reputation in my home city; my creditors and bankers will tell you. But more important yet is that you should know me as a man. If I may speak to you frankly, and from my heart, and not feel that I am boring you . . . ?"

"I have been interested in you ever since Lanny told me about you, Mr. Robin."

"Perhaps he told you that I come from a Polish ghetto, and that I have suffered poverty and worked bitterly hard, and paid for everything that I have gained. Now I have had some success, and if I am cautious I and my loved ones do not have to worry the rest of our lives. But I have brains and I like to use them. It is a game that we play, you and me, all of us; you know what I mean?"

"I know."

"It is a pleasure to rise in the world, to meet new people, educated people, those that have power. I know that I will always be a Jew, and carry the marks of the ghetto; I know that my accent is not right in any language, that I talk with my hands, and that I say things that are not in good taste, so I do not expect ever to shine in drawing rooms. But I expect that businessmen will recognize me, and that I will be able to do things that are worth while. And now through a chance I have met a big businessman——"

Robbie raised his hand. "Not so big, Mr. Robin!"

"I am telling you how it seems to me. You live in a world far above mine. Maybe you are not really better than me, but the world thinks you are, and I, with my ghetto memories, look up to you. I look at your son and I think: 'I would like my boys should be like him.' And if I persuade you to go into a deal with me, I have a chance to make good in a new way. If I cheat you, I will get some money quick, but then no more. You will say: 'The little kike!'— and that is the end. But if I make good, then I have your respect. You tell your friends: 'I don't care what you say about the Jews, I know one that's straight, I would trust him with the crown jewels' —or whatever it is that you value in America, the Statue of Liberty, shall we say?"

"I am touched by your confidence, Mr. Robin," smiled the American. "I will try to be worthy of your ideal."

"I will tell you something more, Mr. Budd—if I am not boring you?"

"Not at all."

"You have seen the little pictures of my two boys. How I love those boys is something I cannot tell any man. I would give my life if it would spare them unhappiness. Those boys were not born in a ghetto, and its marks are not on them. For them I imagine the finest things in the world. The little one, Freddi, is a quiet lad, and studious; he will be a professor, perhaps. But the other, Hansi, his choice is made; he lives for the violin. He will not be some obscure fellow in an orchestra; he has fire, he has temperament, and he works so hard, I know that he will be a virtuoso, a concert performer. You think, perhaps, it is a fond father's dream; and maybe so, but to me it is real."

"I understand," said Robbie, who also had a dream.

"Then one day I meet on the train a little American gentleman, and I talk with him. He is going to visit in a German castle; he has good manners, and what is more, he is kind; he plays the piano, he reads, he has traveled and met famous people, his talk is far beyond his years; it comes to me as incredible that a boy should know so much, and talk so like a man of the world. I go home and tell my boys about him, and how they wish they had been on that train and met that Lanny Budd! Then a year or two passes, and one day I get a letter, with a picture of himself and his mother in front of their home; my boys they pin it up on the wall, and all the time they are talking about that wonderful Lanny Budd. They write him little notes, and he answers, and they are saying: 'Some day we shall meet him!' They are saying: 'Do you think that he would like us, Papa? Do you think he would mind that we are Jews?' Perhaps you have never thought about how it is to be a Jew, Mr. Budd?"

"I am interested to understand," said Robbie, politely.

"If you are an orthodox Jew, you have your faith, your ancient laws and customs, and that is enough; you are not interested in anyone but Jews, because you know that the rest is accursed. But if it happens that you learn modern ideas, and decide that the Sabbath is a day like any other day, and that ham will not hurt you if it is well cooked, and that it is all rubbish that you should not eat meat and butter from the same dish—then you are done with the old religion and you are looking for something else to take its place. You wish to live in the world like other people; to be a man among men. If somebody says: 'I do not want you in my home because you are ignorant, and stupid, and you bore me'—that is all right, that may be true, and you cannot complain. But if someone says: 'I do not want you in my home because you are a Jew'—that is not fair, and that hurts. But of course every Jew hears it, and a Polish Jew most of all, because that is supposed to be a very low kind. Every Jew wishes to meet gentiles, and to live among gentiles, but no Jew is ever quite happy, or quite sure; every Jew is thinking: 'Is there something wrong here?' or perhaps: 'Have I done something

I shouldn't?' But he cannot ask, because that is not done; and when I say this to you, I have to think if it will displease you."

"Not at all," said Robbie. It was a concession on his part.

"So little Hansi is thinking: 'I will play the violin better and better, and then some day, when I meet the wonderful Lanny Budd, he will wish to play duets with me. He will really judge my music, and not as the rich boys do at school, my Jewishness.' That is what my Hansi has said to me; and now, should I smash his dream that the wonderful Lanny Budd might wish to play music with him? Shall I have to hear him say: 'No, Papa, I cannot have Lanny Budd for a friend, because his father says that you are not honest in business, that you took advantage of him when he trusted you'? So you see, Mr. Budd, I should have to go straight, even if it was against my nature."

"A new kind of business credentials, Mr. Robin!" said the other, smiling. "How much money would you say you could use to advantage in this business?"

"It is hard to know in advance. You understand that the buying will always be a spot-cash proposition. I would say a hundred thousand dollars should be in the bank. I would report to you what I am doing, and if I saw a use for further sums, you could judge each proposition on its merits."

Robbie had never told his son just how much money he had made in the last few years; so Lanny was startled when his father said: "I guess I could find a hundred thousand without too much trouble. You give me the references you speak of, Mr. Robin, and I'll look into them, and if they are what you tell me, I'll take a flier with you."

Lanny was pleased, but he didn't say so until they had dropped the dealer at his hotel. Then he chuckled and said: "You're in the junk business, Robbie!"

27

The Federation of the World

I

THE Peace Conference had begun its sessions. They had long debates as to whether they should debate in the English language or the French, and finally decided that they would use both, and have everything translated back and forth. They had a bitter controversy over the question whether they were going to try the Kaiser for his crimes; they had solemnly announced that they would do so, but the Kaiser was in Holland, which wouldn't give him up, and gradually the debate petered out—there were so many more urgent problems. Their armies were costing several million dollars a day, and so many women wanted their men back home!

President Wilson had set it as the first item on his program to establish a League of Nations and get it going. Everything else depended upon that, for without it you couldn't be sure that any arrangements you made would last a year. Premier Clemenceau had publicly sneered at the idea; what he believed in was the "balance of power"—which meant a group of nations strong enough to lick Germany. He and the President were now meeting daily, testing out each other's sparring power; meanwhile the American professors had to live upon scraps of gossip. Was it the Premier or the President who had been frowning when they emerged from the conference room that day?

The guessing grew hot when the problem of a League of Nations was assigned to a commission. That, obviously, represented Clemenceau's effort to shelve and forget it. But Wilson countered by appointing himself as one of the American members of the League of Nations Commission. Naturally he became chairman of it, since it was his idea and his hobby; when he began attending its daily sessions, he hadn't time to attend any other sessions, and so Clemenceau was left to fume and fret. The Americans rubbed their hands with delight. The Big Chief was really going to fight!

Everybody in the American staff began talking League. Even those who were supposed to be busy on other assignments couldn't keep their fingers out of the pie. Such a colossal enterprise, the most momentous in history! The poet Tennyson had sung about "the Parliament of Man, the Federation of the World," and all these professors had learned the verses in school. How much of sovereignty was each nation to part with? What representation was each to have? Should the little ones have equal power with the big ones? And what about the colonial peoples? What about the national minorities?

President Wilson had a draft of the League somewhere among his baggage. Several members of "The Inquiry" had their drafts. The British, having an "Inquiry" of their own, had prepared a layout, of which a prominent feature was that each of the British dominions should count as a separate nation and have its own delegates. The French had a plan, of which the most important feature was an international army, to make sure that Germany could never again invade France. All these plans had to be put together, in spite of their being incompatible.

II

Lanny Budd had been assigned to a room on the top floor of the Crillon, on the courtyard, along with two other secretaries. But after a couple of weeks the three were moved out to a near-by hotel, to make room for more important persons who kept arriving from America. However, Lanny still had his meals in the hotel dining room, because Professor Alston wanted him. Under the regulations he was allowed to have one guest each day. He would invite his father to meet the staff and convince himself that they were not so tender-minded as they had been imagined. He would give his mother a chance to exercise her charms upon a susceptible group of gentlemen a long way from home and not having much opportunity to enjoy feminine society.

It had been only a little more than six months since Marcel had disappeared into the furnace of war; but Beauty's grief was less, because, as she explained to Lanny, she had suffered so much of it in anticipation. This suffering had given her dignity, without depriving her of those weapons of earlier days. She was still on the good side of forty, and deducted a couple of years more in her thoughts about herself. She couldn't very well deduct more, with a son seated at her side, several inches taller than herself!

Beauty was far too much a woman of the world to pretend to knowledge before these professors; she chose the line of calling herself an ignoramus and deploring her wasted youth. "Oh, Professor Alston," she would exclaim, "do make these wonderful ideas of yours work, so that we women in Europe won't have a nightmare pouncing down on us every generation!" It was an old practice of hers, in dealing with the male sex, to ask each about his own work, listen attentively, and express admiration. This proved as effective with scholars as with those of higher station, and Beauty might have eaten all her meals at the expense of the United States government if she had cared to accept the invitations showered upon her.

She told these learned ones about her friend Emily Chattersworth, and many of them knew the name; the older ones remembered the banking scandal, back in the bad old days when pirates had sailed the high financial seas. Mrs. Emily had rented a town house, and had teas every Thursday, and a salon on a modest scale on Sunday evenings; with her permission, Beauty invited Lanny's chief, and he went, and met important people: a member of the French cabinet, or a general just returned from service in Salonika; an English statesman who had flown from London that afternoon, or a Russian grand duke who had escaped from the Bolsheviki by way of Siberia

and Manchuria. A youth who had access to social opportunities such
as these was considered an unusually good secretary.

III

One of the persons whom Lanny saw most frequently was George
D. Herron. This prophet of the new day came to see Alston, and
they talked, and Lanny listened. Herron seemed to take a fancy tu
the youth, perhaps thinking of him as a possible convert. They sat
on a bench by the embankment of the Seine, and the older man in-
terpreted the events of the time in accordance with his peculiar
ideas.

The only Socialist Lanny had met so far was that editor who had
taken such unfair advantage of a boy's indiscretion. It appeared that
Herron had called himself a Social-Democrat a couple of decades
ago, and had helped to found the Socialist party in the United
States; but the war had brought a violent reaction, and Social-
Democracy was now in his mind a part of "Germanism," the arch-
enemy of the soul of man. It based itself upon materialism, denying
freedom and respect for the personality. Herron's vision was of a
society transformed by brotherhood and love; he found those quali-
ties embodied in Jesus, and that was why he called himself a Christian Socialist, even while rejecting the dogmas of the churches.

On this subject he talked with the fervor of the prophets of old.
For him all thinking led to the basic question whether mankind
could be saved from sliding into an abyss of barbarism, a new Dark
Age of materialism and hate. The late war had brought us close to
the edge, and new wars now on the horizon might carry us over.
He pointed to the fall of empires throughout history; what was
there to save us from a similar fate? Only a vision of spiritual things
which a few great souls had caught, and for the sake of which they
had martyred themselves and must continue to do so.

To this tormented soul the League of Nations represented the one
hope of preserving justice and peace in the world, so that the higher

faculties of man might survive and be propagated. In the spring of
the previous year he had written President Wilson an urgent letter
on behalf of the project, and a considerable correspondence had
resulted. In Paris, Wilson showed him his draft of the League, and
asked his suggestions. This was known to the advisory staff, who
looked upon this strange interloper with a mingling of curiosity
and alarm. Perhaps he wasn't a scandalous person, but all America
believed him to be that—and what would America say as to the
sort of company its college professors were keeping in Paris?

It happened that Robbie Budd came to lunch and sat at table with
Herron, Alston, and Lanny. The black-bearded prophet was in his
most apocalyptic mood. Said he: "The salvation of the world from
Germanism depends upon the salvation of Germany from her ancient barbarian self. The final value of our military success, the
proof that we are worthy of it, must lie in its redemptive power.
We have won a victory over the German people and we have now
to win the German people to that victory. What we do must be
infused by such spiritual purpose as will enable the German people
to see the divine reason for it, and to enter co-operatively into the
judgments and workings of that reason."

When Lanny had been alone with his new acquaintance, listening
to such words, he had been much impressed; but now he heard them
through the ears of his skeptical father and they made him wriggle
uncomfortably. Robbie was a self-contained man, and knew how to
keep quiet when he wanted to; but when he was alone with his son,
he exclaimed: "My God, who is that nut?" When Lanny told him
that the fervid orator was one of President Wilson's trusted advisers, Robbie was ready to go home and tell America that it was
being governed from a lunatic asylum. The United States Senate—
now safely under control of the Republican party—ought to send a
committee to Europe to take charge of the peace-making!

Of course Robbie couldn't expect to keep his son in cotton wool.
Lanny was in the world now and had to meet crackpots and fanatics
along with sane businessmen. But at least he was going to have his
father's advice. In detail, and with as much conscientiousness as any

Christian Socialist, Robbie explained that the ruling class of Germany had tried to grab the trade privileges of the British Empire, and had failed. They would try again whenever they got the chance; it was life or death for one group or the other, and would continue to be that so long as men used steel in making engines, and coal and oil—not hot air—to run them with. Lanny listened, and decided that his father was right, as always.

IV

It was a time of strain and anguish, and really it wasn't easy to know what to think or do. Lanny had shared in his own soul the griefs of the people of France and could understand their dread of a wicked government which had inflicted them. For Lanny the soul of France was embodied in the memories of his stepfather; and always he tried to imagine, what would Marcel have felt about the peace-making and the various problems which kept arising in connection with it?

One thing seemed certain: Marcel would not have approved the deliberate starving of women and children. The Germans had assumed that the blockade would be lifted when they signed the armistice; but the French had no such thought. Nothing was to go into Germany until she had accepted and signed the peace terms which France meant to lay down. But the treaty wasn't ready yet, and meanwhile children were crying with hunger.

To the members of the American delegation this seemed an atrocious thing. They protested to the President, and he in turn to Clemenceau—but in vain. Herbert Hoover, who had been feeding the Belgians, wanted also to feed the defeated peoples; he did finally, as a great concession, get the right to send a relief mission to Austria —but nothing to Germany. Marshal Foch stood like a block of concrete in the pathway. Lanny saw him coming out from the conference room where this issue was fought over; a stocky little man with a gray mustache, voluble, talking with excited gestures, demanding his pound of flesh. He was commander-in-chief of the

Allied armies and he gave the orders. A singular thing—he was a devout Catholic, went every morning to mass, and kneeled to a merciful redeemer who had said: "Suffer the little children to come unto me, and forbid them not." Little French children, of course; no little German children!

This was one of the things which tormented Herron. He talked incessantly about a "Carthaginian peace," such as the Romans had imposed when they razed a great city to the ground and drove its population into exile. If France imposed a peace of vengeance upon Germany, it would mean that "Germanism" had won the war; it would mean that France had adopted Germany's false religion, and that the old France of the Revolution, the France of "liberty, equality, fraternity," was no more. The black-bearded prophet suffered so over the hunger of the blockaded peoples that he couldn't eat his own food.

He would come to the Crillon to consult with Alston, whom he trusted because he had known him as a lad. A sense of agonized impotence possessed him; to see the world drifting to shipwreck, and know what ought to be done, but be helpless to get it done; to give advice and have it accepted—but not acted upon. To see intrigue, personal jealousy, factional strife, blocking the hopes of mankind. There was all that sort of thing at the Crillon, of course; there were those who had the President's ear, and others who sought to get it, and pulled wires and flattered and fawned. There were some who were not above repeating scandals and raking up old tragedies. "Of course I'm a marked man," said Herron. "I cannot be recognized publicly; but that doesn't change the fact that I know Europe better than any of those whom the President is meeting."

V

Many times in these days Lanny had occasion to recall the words which the Graf Stubendorf had spoken, concerning "the dark cloud of barbarism in the eastern sky." In five years that cloud had spread until it threatened to cover the firmament; it was of the hue of

Stygian midnight, and its rim was red and dripping a bloody rain. No longer the Russian Tsar with his Cossacks and their whips, no longer Pan-Slavism with its marching hosts, but the dread Bolshevism, which not only formed armies, but employed a new and secret poison which penetrated the armies of its enemies, working like a strong acid, disintegrating what it touched. A good part of the secret conferences going on in Paris had to do with this peril and how to meet it. There were some who thought it made no difference what decisions the Peace Conference took, because it was all going to be swept away in a Red upheaval throughout Central Europe.

As the friends of Lanny Budd portrayed it to him, two evil creatures had been spewed up from the Russian cesspool, and had managed to seize power. They were still holding on to it—in spite of the fact that the newspapers reported Lenin as shooting Trotsky and Trotsky as poisoning Lenin about once a week. They had led the workers and peasants in a campaign of massacre, and the nobility and land owners of the Tsar's realm had fled, counting themselves lucky if they had a few jewels sewed up in the lining of their coats. Paris was full of these refugees, with pitiful and ghastly tales to tell; Lanny heard some of them, and his mother, in her incompetent way, made efforts to help the victims. It seemed to her sympathetic soul unbearable that people who had never had to work and so didn't know how to work should suddenly find themselves without money to pay for their meals. Robbie had to tell her more than once that his fortune was not equal to supporting the Russian aristocracy in the state to which it had been accustomed.

Of course Europe had to protect itself against this Red menace, said Lanny's friends; and so the Allied armies had established what they called a *cordon sanitaire* around the vast former empire of the Tsar. The Japanese and the Americans had seized Vladivostok and the eastern half of the Trans-Siberian railway. The British and Americans had occupied Archangel and Murmansk in the far North, blocking all commerce by that route. Along the European land front the Allied troops stood on guard, and French and British officers were busy organizing anti-Bolshevik Russians, and providing them with arms and money and sending them into the Ukraine, Russian Poland, and the Baltic provinces. This fighting had been going on for a year now, and each day Lanny read in the papers of "White" victories and was assured that soon the dreadful menace would be at an end.

But it was like a forest fire, whose sparks flew through the air; or perhaps a plague, whose carriers burrow underground and come up through rat-holes. The emissaries of the Bolsheviks would sneak through the sanitary cordon, and creep into the slums of some city of Central Europe, telling the hungry workers how the Russians had made a revolution, and offering to help do the same. The armies would catch many of them and shoot them; but there were always more. Even before the armistice, a Jewish "Red" by the name of Eisner had seized the government of Bavaria; in Berlin two others named Liebknecht and Luxemburg—the latter a woman, known as "Red Rosa"—were carrying on a war in the streets, seeking to take power from the Socialist government which had arisen in Germany after the overthrow of the Kaiser. In Hungary it was the same; a member of the nobility who called himself a Socialist, Count Karolyi, had given his estates in an effort to help the poor of that starving land, but now a Bolshevik Jew was leading a movement to unseat him and set up soviets on the Russian pattern.

Always it was a Jew, people pointed out to Lanny; and this kindled to flame the anti-Semitic feeling always latent among the fashionable classes of Europe. "What did we tell you?" they would say. "The Jews have no country; they are seeking to undermine and destroy Christian society. It is a worldwide conspiracy of this arrogant people." Robbie said something along this line; and Lanny grinned and replied: "Be careful, you've got a Jewish partner now!"

Robbie made a wry face. His Anglo-Saxon conscience troubled him, and his aristocratic feelings resented the odor of the junk business. But Johannes Robin had bought a couple of hundred thousand hand grenades, and had already sold the powder before he had got it extracted. The prospects looked excellent; and Robbie Budd just couldn't bear to sit on a big pile of money and not make use of it—the use, of course, being to make more money.

VI

One day when Lanny went to lunch he found at his table a young army officer, introduced as Captain Stratton; handsome, well set up, as they all were, full of smartness and efficiency. Military uniforms were plentiful in the Crillon dining room, as all over Paris; someone had counted up the soldiers of twenty-six different nations to be found in the capital at that time. Captain Stratton was connected with the Intelligence Service of the army, and it was his special task to watch out for any efforts of the Bolsheviks among the dough-boys. It was a confidential subject, but the officer was in the midst of persons who had a right to know what was going on.

He talked interestingly about his work. He said that the slum denizens were in a state close to madness, with hunger, the fever of war, and the vision of sudden power. It couldn't be said that they were without training for power, for they had a sort of discipline of their own; in fact, they had a whole culture, which they called "proletarian," and which was to replace our present culture, called "bourgeois." A truly frightening thing, said the officer, who before the war had been a rising young architect in Chicago. "I was never afraid of the Huns," he declared, "but I admit that I'm afraid of these Reds."

Just recently, he went on to tell, he had come upon evidence of the activities of a press on which had been printed leaflets addressed to the denizens of the Paris slums, calling upon them to rise against the profiteers and seize the food which was in the depots, and which the bureaucrats were refusing to release. The captain had one of these leaflets with him; it ended with a string of slogans followed by exclamation points, and was signed by the *Conseils des Ouvriers de St.-Denis.* "They don't say Soviets," remarked the officer. "But that's what the word means."

Then even more startling news: he expected to have proof that these agitators were preparing an appeal to the American troops to break ranks and go home. These troops had enlisted to oust the Kaiser, and why should they stay to hold the workers of Europe in slavery to landlords and money barons? It was a plausible argument.

"Surely you're going to stop that!" exclaimed one of the professors.

"We'll have to," replied the officer. "But it's a bit awkward, because the fellow who is most active in the matter happens to be an American."

"What difference does that make?"

"Well, my God, if you arrest an American Red in Paris, you can't keep it away from the newspapers; then all the agitators at home will be swarming like hornets."

Professor Davisson, who specialized in the Balkan languages, and had just come back from a mission to the Bulgarian front, expressed the opinion that the unprintable scoundrel ought to be dealt with by military law at once. To this Alston interposed a question: "What's the use of having licked the Germans if you have to sacrifice American free speech in the process?"

"Do you think that free speech means the right to overthrow the government which protects your free speech?" demanded Davisson.

"Free speech doesn't overthrow governments," answered the other. "It's the lack of free speech."

"You mean you'd let Bolsheviks incite our troops to mutiny?"

"They wouldn't get anywhere, Davisson—not unless there was something wrong with what the army was doing."

So they argued, and got rather hot about it, as men were apt to do these days; until one of them, wishing to dissipate the storm clouds, asked of Captain Stratton: "What sort of fellow is it that's printing the leaflets?"

"He calls himself a painter, but I don't know if he works at it. He's lived most of his life over here, and I guess he's absorbed what the Reds call their 'ideology.' "

"Budd knows a lot of painters here," said Lanny's employer. "What's the man's name?"

"I don't think I'm at liberty to tell that," replied the captain. "Perhaps I shouldn't have said as much as I have."

"It'll all be confidential," said Professor Davisson, and the others nodded their confirmation. As for Lanny, he kept up a pretense of interest in his food, and prayed that nobody would notice the blood that had been stealing into his cheeks and throat, and even, so he felt, to the roots of his hair.

VII

When the party broke up, Lanny said to his chief: "I wish you'd take me upstairs to your room for a minute. There's something important I want to tell you." When they were alone, he explained: "I can't be sure, but I think the man Captain Stratton was talking about is my uncle, Jesse Blackless."

"The heck you say!" exclaimed the startled professor.

"I thought you ought to know right away, because it might prove embarrassing if it comes out."

Lanny told briefly about this "red sheep" of his mother's family. "There aren't apt to be two American painters who are such active Reds. I know he's in Paris now, because he came to see my mother, to advise her about the best way to arrange for an exhibition of my stepfather's paintings."

"Well, well!" said the professor. "A trifle awkward, I must admit."

"It could be terribly so. I'm afraid there's nothing for me but to quit before the story breaks."

The older man smiled. "No, you don't get off so easily! I assure you, I need you too badly. We'll work out some other solution."

"But what can it be?"

"Let me think. Do you suppose you could get hold of this uncle of yours?"

"I suppose he'll have left his address with my mother."

"Well, we'll have to be quick, before the army people grab him."

"What do you want to do with him?"

"First, we'll have a talk with him and see what his ideas are, and how much he knows. Then I thought it might be well to take him to Colonel House, and possibly to the President."

Lanny could only stare, wondering if he had heard aright.

"You see," explained his chief, noting his expression, "there are two ways to deal with social discontent—one is to throw it into jail and the other is to try to understand it. The President has had to do some of the former under the stress of war, but I'm sure that in his heart he much prefers understanding. Right now, I happen to know that he's deadlocked with the French over the question of what's to be done about Russia. Can you keep a really important secret?"

"I've been keeping a lot of them, Professor."

"I had a tip this morning which I believe to be straight—that the President is thinking of moving for a conference with the Bolsheviks at some neutral place. So you see, it might be in order for Colonel House or someone who represents him to get in touch with these people, to find out what their attitude would be. Do you suppose you could find your uncle today?"

"First I'd have to get my father's consent," replied the youth. "I gave him my word that I'd not have anything to do with my uncle. That was five or six years ago, and he mayn't feel the same now."

"Tell him it's an order from the boss," smiled Alston.

VIII

Needless to say, Robbie Budd didn't like it a bit when his son brought him that proposition. Lanny couldn't tell the whole story, being under orders regarding the "Intelligence" aspect of it; he could only say that the peace experts wanted to talk with some Bolsheviks, to know what concessions they were willing to make. To the salesman of armaments it seemed an outrage that any government should be willing to do anything with such scoundrels but shoot them; however, Lanny pointed out that the Allied troops were clamoring to go home, and statesmanship required that some compromise should be worked out. So quickly was a youth of nineteen catching the official tone!

Robbie didn't smile, for he wished his son to take his duties seriously. "All right," said he. "But I want you to know, I'll be damned unhappy if I see you getting mixed up with that blatherskite Jesse."

"Don't worry," answered Lanny. "This is a job, and I want to do it as capably as I can, and maybe it'll take me to the President."

Beauty gave her brother's address, up on the Butte Montmartre, where painters and other irregular people lived. Beauty scented a mystery in her son's inquiry and it was cruel to have to put her off; but Lanny just said that one of the professors was interested in painting and might buy something. No use trusting any secrets to Madame Detaze, *veuve!*

Taking the address to his chief, Lanny said: "I've been thinking this matter over and it occurs to me that it may be awkward if I don't tell my uncle about the army people. If later they should jump on him—he'd be sure to think I'd been helping to trap him or something."

"I've thought of that also," replied the other. "I'm going with you to see him, and then I'll have a frank talk with Captain Stratton. If the Crillon is interested in the man, Intelligence will lay off, of course."

The taxis were back from the war and were being driven about the streets of Paris by homicidal maniacs. Lanny and his chief were whirled down the Rue Montmartre, and Lanny pointed out the window of the restaurant through which Jaurès had been shot. Alston said that the French authorities might have been glad to have the help of that great orator now, while their workers were seething with discontent. The cab whirled round a corner and down a crooked street—another "cabbage patch," with crowded old buildings. It was one of the rare days when the sun shone in January, and slatternly women were leaning out of windows, and swarms of children playing all but under the wheels of the taxi.

Lanny explained to his chief that Uncle Jesse didn't have to live in such a place, for he enjoyed a modest income from an inheritance. Apparently he wanted to be close to the people. Alston said there were men like that; sometimes they were saints, and sometimes a bit crazy, and sometimes both.

IX

"Entrez," called Jesse Blackless, at their knock. He was sitting in an old dressing gown by the open window, working on a manuscript. Beside him was a table, looking like the one which Lanny remembered in the cabin on the Riviera; the remains of a meal, a tobacco pouch and a bad-smelling pipe, a great quantity of books and papers which apparently were never moved or dusted. The canvas cot which served as a bed was unmade, and there was an open book on the floor beside it, as if it had been laid there when the reader was ready to go to sleep. An overcoat thrown over a chair, an umbrella on it—in short, general disorder and the absence of the feminine touch. There were unframed paintings on the walls, but no easel and no smell of paint. Apparently Uncle Jesse had given up art for politics.

He looked startled when his nephew came in, followed by a strange gentleman. He put his manuscript away in a hurried manner and his eyes moved to the door, as if he expected a couple of gendarmes might follow.

"Hello, Uncle Jesse," said the youth.

"Hello," returned the other, not rising.

"Uncle Jesse, this is Professor Alston, my chief at the Crillon."

"How do you do?" said the painter; but he didn't offer to shake hands, and he didn't say: "Have a seat"—which, indeed, would have been difficult, since the only extra chair was piled with papers. His manner said: "What's this?"

"Uncle Jesse," explained Lanny, "Professor Alston asked me to bring him to you because he has an important proposition to put and he hopes you'll be kind enough to hear it."

The painter, of course, knew that his nephew had been avoiding him for years and that this had been at Robbie's orders. He knew also that the youth had taken a job with the peace-makers. He looked over the mild and bespectacled professor, whose physical vigor hadn't improved much under the strain of hard work in damp and chilly Paris. There was no abatement of the uncle's hostile manner as he said: "All right. What is it?"

Frankly, but at the same time tactfully, the scholar explained the efforts of the American commission to bring at least a partially sane peace out of an insane war. President Wilson was being opposed, not merely by all the jealousies and greeds and fears of Europe, but by the reactionary elements at home, the big-money interests and our newly awakened militarism. Just now there was a crisis over the subject of Russia and a decision might be taken at any hour. The President wanted to get the warring factions together in a council hall; while the French and British military men wanted invasions on a big scale.

"I don't know whether you have heard it or not," said Alston, "but Winston Churchill is in Paris now, for the purpose of urging a real war to put down Bolshevism. Foch has been demanding it from the day of the armistice, and the whole French General Staff is with him. Clemenceau is beginning to waver—and of course Lloyd George wavers all the time."

"What's the use of telling all this to me?" questioned Uncle Jesse.

The professor looked about him uneasily, and asked: "May I sit down? I have not been well."

The painter knew that he hadn't been a gentleman, and he stood up. "Have my chair," he said.

"This is all right," replied the other, and sat on the edge of the cot. Lanny pushed some books aside and rested on a corner of the table.

"Mr. Blackless, nobody in our staff at the Crillon wants any more war; and there's a group of us who are convinced that concessions have to be made and an armistice brought about in Russia before there can be any real peace. That doesn't mean that we are sympathetic to Bolshevism, but it does mean that we have studied the forces which brought on the revolution, and we don't consider it possible to set back the clock of history. My own position is entirely that of a scientist——"

"What sort of a scientist?"

"I am a geographer and ethnologist, but just now I have been set the task of finding out what some of the peoples of Europe want."

"You have your hands full, Professor."

"No doubt of that; and I have the right to ask for the help of every well-meaning man."

"What leads you to think that I am well-meaning?"

"I think it of every man, Mr. Blackless, until he shows me otherwise. I assume that you don't want to see any more war in Europe."

"You assume incorrectly, Professor."

"You *do* want war?"

"I tell the workers to fight for their rights, and I hope they will do so until they have overthrown the capitalist system."

"But surely you can't think that the Russians can defeat the Allied armies, if they decide seriously to fight!"

"My answer is that if the Allied armies believed they could defeat the Russians, they'd be fighting right now. I take your visit as a sign that the Allied leaders are beginning to find out what the rank and file of their troops are thinking and saying. Lloyd George and Clemenceau will have to face it, and even Foch and the lineal descendant of the Duke of Marlborough."

So Lanny and his employer knew that they had found a real Bolshevik; one who could tell President Wilson exactly what was in the hearts of men and women who were risking their lives trying to make revolutions throughout Europe!

X

Jesse Blackless appeared to be showing the effects of mental strain. The lines around his eyes were more plentiful and those at the sides of his mouth more deeply graven. He was balder than ever, but the bare scalp wasn't so bronzed—he had, presumably, been living in cities and wearing a hat. He was even more gaunt and his voice seemed hoarse, as if he had been talking a lot. Doubtless he had much to say to proletarians, as he called them; but with bourgeois persons like Lanny and his chief he didn't care to be bothered—or so his manner seemed to say. He didn't argue, he told you, and there came that disagreeable twist of the mouth. Lanny had always disliked this strange man, and did now; but he had to admit that he had convictions and stood by them.

Just now the painter was convinced that the Bolsheviks had Central Europe in their grasp. He announced it defiantly; but Alston, who had inside knowledge, stopped him with the remark: "That is all right for a stump speech or a manifesto; but are you sure it's the attitude of Lenin? Mightn't it be that he'd like a little time to collect his forces?"

The painter eyed his visitor sharply, and decided to take a different tone. "Just what is it you propose, Professor?"

"First, that you should understand me. I know you are suspicious, and doubtless you have reason in many cases. But you waste time if you suspect me. I am a scholar who doesn't like bloodshed and has come over here to help make peace. In this visit to you I have no authority from anybody. I came on my own impulse, when Lanny told me about his uncle. Knowing the situation at the Crillon, I thought some of my superiors might like to confer with you."

"A fine time I'd have explaining to my friends if I took up with the Crillon!"

"Don't your friends trust you, Mr. Blackless?"

"A certain distance; but not that far!"

"There's no reason why you shouldn't tell them in advance that you are going, and why. There is nothing secret about my visit. You will see that I ask you no questions—who your associates are, or anything of that sort. I take it for granted that you may know where to find some persons who are in touch with the Bolsheviks and could discuss with us the basis for a conference."

"Suppose I should go to the Crillon and not come out again?"

The professor smiled. "Be reasonable, Mr. Blackless. Undoubtedly the French military authorities know your address, and can come here just as well as I can. That goes for the Americans also. I can't give you any guarantees—except that anything that happens to you won't be of my doing. On the other hand, if the Crillon should invite you to come and talk to them, it would certainly be a bonafide invitation to a conference and would confer immunity upon you for the time being."

Said Jesse Blackless: "I think the man you need to talk with is Sazonov." This was the former Foreign Minister of the Tsar, now in Paris, and the remark was, of course, a sneer.

"We don't have to go to any of the Whites," replied Alston, patiently. "They come to us in droves. They tell us they will have nothing to do with assassins and bloody-handed murderers, and so on. They demand that we give them unlimited arms and money so that they can crush the Reds. That happens to be the idea of the military men, including some of the Americans, I am sorry to say. But fortunately it is the civil authorities who have the decision. Trust me, Mr. Blackless, and help me to get your point of view before the Council of Ten, right now while the subject is up for settlement."

"You mean, it's your idea that the Bolsheviks shall come to Paris and sit down with the Whites?"

"Not in Paris—Clemenceau would never allow that. It would be somewhere close to Russia, and far from here."

"You think the Whites would come?"

"I'll put it crudely, Mr. Blackless, as you seem to prefer. The Allies are the paymasters."

Uncle Jesse smiled one of his crooked smiles. "And you imagine that we would give up to the Whites—is that it?"

"At a conference, Mr. Blackless, both sides have to give up something, unless the conference is to fail. But first there has to be a conference—that is the most difficult point."

The painter considered for a while longer. Finally he said: "All right, Professor. I'll talk to some other persons, and let you hear from me in a few hours."

28

The Red Peril

I

THERE were five members of the American Commission to Negotiate Peace. President Wilson was of course its head, and the French government had lent him a palace to stay in, the home of the Princess Murat. The second member was Mr. Lansing, Secretary of State, who did not agree with his chief about the League or anything else very much; he was a lawyer, and thought that things ought to be done according to juridical formulas which he had learned. He spent his time recording his objections in a diary; also making comical little sketches of the other diplomats. To him and his fellow members had been assigned apartments on the second floor of the Crillon, looking out on the Place and having the highest ceilings, the biggest chandeliers, and the most gilt and pink upholstery.

One of these others was General Bliss, a bluff and kindly old soldier who gave good practical advice when asked. Another was a veteran diplomat, Mr. Henry White, who owed his appointment to the fact that etiquette required that the Republican party should have representation on the Peace Commission. Mr. White was so old that the Republicans had forgotten him, but he was in the history books and nobody could question his credentials. He had been in Paris at the time of the Franco-Prussian War and the Commune, nearly fifty years back, and he liked to drive people around and show them the places and tell what he had seen; but he wasn't seeing very much now.

The fifth member was of a retiring nature, but that didn't prevent his suite from becoming the most frequented of all. Two naval yeomen in uniforms and white caps stood guard at the door, and in the anterooms you would see the great ones of the earth coming and going at all hours, and many cooling their heels, waiting in hope of an interview. The name of this commissioner was Colonel House. He was not a military man, but the kind known as a "Kentucky colonel"—although he came from Texas. He was a frail little gentleman of sixty or so, and had never enjoyed health enough to be a warrior, or even to engage in the turmoil of politics; he didn't like crowds and shrank from publicity as a mole from sunlight. What he liked to do was to consult and advise and persuade; he liked to sit behind the scenes and pull wires and manipulate the actors. Being wealthy, he could indulge in this hobby; he had made several governors of his home state, and then had picked out the head of a college as a likely "prexy" for the forty-eight states. He had promoted him and "put him over," and was now his friend and authorized agent in most of the peace negotiations.

He had come to Europe before the outbreak of the war. He had come more than once during the conflict, trying to work out ways to end it. He was gentle and unassuming, and never sought anything for himself; people compared him to a little white mouse—and right now the words of this mouse were backed by most of the money and most of the food in the world. America had financed the last year and a half of the war, and America must finance whatever peace there was to be. What did America want? What would America accept? The answer was: "See Colonel House."

So it came about that through the doors where stood the naval yeomen, polite yet impressive with their side-arms, came diplomats, and politicians and journalists from pretty nearly every nation of the earth. In those anterooms you saw uniforms worthy of the most expensive grand opera production: gold and cream and scarlet, rose-pink, sky-blue. You saw civilian costumes out of the gorgeous East, Near and Far: burnooses, mantles, and togas, turbans, fezzes, and sugarloaf hats. You saw Koreans and Malayans, Kabardians and Lezghians, Buriats and Kirghiz, Kurds, Persians, Georgians, Azerbaijan Moslems, Assyrian Christians, and all the varieties of Syrians —Moslem, Druse, and Greek Orthodox. Had ever in the history of Texas a stranger fate befallen one of its sons than to be receiving this stream of day and night callers, and to know that his smile was a matter of life and death to their peoples?

II

To this Mecca of peace-seekers now came Professor Alston, bringing the tidings that he had established contact with certain of the extremely elusive Bolshevik agents in Paris. Might it be that this would offer to President Wilson and his staff an opportunity of sounding out the revolutionaries and judging the probabilities of success for any conference?

The little white mouse found that interesting. It was the sort of thing he liked to do. He pinned his faith upon quiet talks and understandings among key people. That was the way the Democratic party was run in Texas; that was the way a college president had been nominated for President of the United States; that was the way peace was now to be brought to Europe. When the details had been agreed upon, the results would be proclaimed, and that would be "open covenants openly arrived at."

Of course these revolutionaries couldn't come to the Crillon. Where had Alston met this painter? The professor described the room, and the Texas colonel smiled and asked if it would be possible to get some extra chairs into it. He said they would go that very evening, as soon as he could get away from a reception he had promised to attend. He told the professor where and when to call for him. They would say nothing to anybody about it; they would take along Alston's translator, who already knew about it. The colonel didn't speak French, unfortunately, and it might be that the Bolsheviks wouldn't know English.

A first-class thrill for a youth just embarked upon a diplomatic career. He was going to the top right at one bound! He was going to help with the most exciting problem of the conference; to have a hand in settling the destinies of a hundred and forty million people—and incidentally to shake the gory paws of those murderers, assassins, fiends in human form, creatures whom the resources of the English language were inadequate to describe. So Lanny had been hearing, and he pictured them as pirates with bushy black whiskers, and pistols and daggers in their belts. He hurried off to tell his uncle of the appointment and make sure the little white mouse wouldn't have to sit on the cot!

Uncle Jesse said he could borrow chairs from neighbors in the tenement. "We poor help each other out," he explained, with one of his wry smiles. He added: "Keep your eyes open, Lanny, and see if you can't learn something."

"Thank you, Uncle Jesse," replied the youth. "I'm learning a lot, really."

"It won't please your father," continued the other. "I've known him since before you were born, and I've never known him to learn anything. He's going to be an unhappy man, with the world changing as it is."

Lanny wouldn't discuss his father with this uncle whom he didn't like. But he went off thinking hard, and wondering: Was Robbie really narrow-minded and set in his opinions? Or was this Bolshevik propaganda?

III

That evening Alston and his secretary strolled to the Hotel Majestic, residence of the British delegation, where a grand reception was being held. Promptly at eleven the colonel emerged, and a sturdily built man in civilian clothes fell in behind him and accompanied him to his car, and, after the others had got in, took his seat alongside the chauffeur. So far as Lanny knew, this man never spoke once, but he watched, and no doubt had a gun handy.

Huddled into one corner of the car, Lanny listened to the conversation of one of the most powerful men in the world. The youth was intensely curious about this soft-voiced and kind-faced little person. What was it that had lifted him from obscurity in a region of vast lonely plains inhabited by long-horned cattle which one saw in the movies? Lanny gathered that the Texas colonel's leading characteristic was a desire for information; he went right to work to pump Alston's mind, asking him about all the problems on which he had been specializing. Sooner or later the little white mouse might have to settle them. He had a way of shutting his eyes for a few moments when he wanted to impress something upon his memory. Presently he was asking questions about Georgia—not the state in America, whose problems had been settled long ago, but the portion of Russia in the Caucasus mountains, famed for its lovely women.

"Those people have one great misfortune, Colonel House," remarked the professor. "They are sitting on one of the world's great oil deposits."

"I know," said the other. "It may explode and blow us all to kingdom come." He asked many more questions, and then said: "Do you suppose it would be possible for you to look into this matter and let me have a report?"

"Why, I suppose so," said the professor, both surprised and pleased. "They've got me loaded up with work already, though."

"I know; but we all have to do more and more. This Georgian business complicates the Russian problem, and we'll have to find a way to settle it. What do you say?"

"I am honored, of course."

"Perhaps we'll have a committee and put you on it. I'll have to put it up to the President."

So fate gave another turn to Lanny Budd's destiny. He was going to meet the mountaineers of the Caucasus and learn about their manners and customs—but not their lovely women, alas, for they hadn't brought any of these to Paris.

IV

There were three Russians in the tenement room when the Americans entered; at least Lanny supposed they were Russians, but he discovered that one was a Frenchman and another a Lett. He had been sure they would be big, bewhiskered, and fierce; but he found that only the Frenchman had hair on his face, the black beard trimmed to a point of which you could see thousands on this Butte Montmartre; he wore glasses on a black cord and his face was abnormally pale—he was a journalist who had served a term in prison for opposition to the war. The Lett appeared to be some sort of workingman, and was smooth-shaven, blond, and quiet. The Russian was a scientist, not much bigger than the colonel from Texas; he had spent several years in Siberia and his fingers trembled as he lighted the cigarettes which he smoked with great rapidity.

Only the Frenchman knew English, so the conversation was carried on largely by him. The Russian knew French, and the Lett knew Russian; there was a good deal of whispering back and forth, and when the conversation in English was going on, the other two Bolsheviks listened with a strained expression, as if they could understand by trying harder. They were obviously anxious. They, too, knew that they were in the presence of one of the most powerful men in the world.

Lanny helped the Frenchman with a word now and then, and sometimes asked him in French just what he was trying to say. The Russian, who was apparently their "big man," became impatient at the English conversation, and moved his chair behind Jesse Blackless and whispered for him to repeat in French what was being said. So Lanny, who sat next to his uncle, would hear English with one ear and French with the other, which kept his mind on the jump. However, he got his impressions, and the first was that these seemed like decent fellows in serious trouble; it was hard for him to believe that they had been committing the crimes that his mother's fashionable friends had told about. Afterwards, when he talked over his impressions with his chief, the idea was suggested to him that in civil wars it is often the most earnest and conscientious persons who do the killing.

One thing was certain: the Bolsheviks weren't going to make any of what Professor Alston called "stump speeches." Presumably they had talked it over in advance and decided to lay their cards on the table. They had no authority to speak for their government, and no way to communicate with it quickly; but they were certain that it wanted peace, and would be willing to pay any price short of giving up their "workers' state." Just as they had gone to Brest-Litovsk nearly a year ago and given in to the power of the German armies, so now they would do so for the Allies. The Whites might keep what they held; there was land enough in the interior of Russia, and the workers would build their state and show the world what they could do; only they must have freedom to trade with the outside, so that they could get goods and repair their shattered industry.

They spoke without emotion of the sufferings of the Russian peasants and workers under the lash of the Tsar, and in the civil war now raging. They reported that Petrograd was starving; a hundred thousand persons had died in the past month, and not a baby under two was left alive. The Soviets wanted peace; they would meet the Whites anywhere, and accept any reasonable terms. They had again and again declared their willingness to pay off their debts to the capitalist nations, including the monstrous debt which the Tsar had incurred to arm their country in the interest of French militarists and munitions makers. Poor as they were now, they would pay the interest in raw materials. Lanny was surprised by this, for the French newspapers were incessantly repeating that the debt had been repudiated; this was the reason for the French clamor for the overthrow of the Soviets. "You know what our newspapers are," said the Frenchman, shrugging his shoulders; "our reptile press —I worked for it until my soul was poisoned."

V

"Well, Alston, what do you think?" asked the colonel, when they were in their car again.

"If you want my opinion," said the professor, "I think the civil war should be stopped at any cost."

"Even if it means letting these people have a chance to establish their regime?"

"If their ideas are not sound, they will fail in the end."

"Perhaps. But won't that mean another war?"

"That's a long way in the future, Colonel."

The other turned to the young translator, whose eager competence he had observed. "What do you think, Budd?"

This gave Lanny a start, and he flushed. He had sense enough to know that the great man was being kind and that it would be the part of wisdom for a youth to be brief. "What struck me was that those fellows have all suffered a lot."

"No doubt about that," replied the gentleman from Texas. "We who live under an orderly democratic government find it hard to realize what men endured under the Tsar."

Colonel House didn't tell them what he himself thought. They learned the reason later on—that he disapproved of the proposed conference and didn't think it could succeed. But the President wanted it, and he was the boss; Colonel House never gave his opinion unless and until it was asked for. He said now that he would report what the Bolsheviks had said, and they would await the decision.

What happened was soon known to all the world. The President of the United States sat down before his well-worn typewriter—it being one of his peculiarities that when he had something important in his mind he liked to type it with his own fingers. He wrote as follows:

"The associated powers are now engaged in the solemn and responsible work of establishing the peace of Europe and of the world, and they are keenly alive to the fact that Europe and the

world cannot be at peace if Russia is not. They recognize and accept it as their duty, therefore, to serve Russia in this great matter
as generously, as unselfishly, as thoughtfully, as ungrudgingly as
they would serve every other friend and ally. And they are ready
to render this service in the way that is most acceptable to the
Russian people."

The document went on to summon all groups having power in
Russia or Siberia to send representatives to a conference. President
Wilson took it to the Council of Ten next afternoon, where it became the subject of much debate. Some still demanded that an army
be sent into Russia to overthrow the Bolsheviks; but when it came
to a showdown, they wanted the soldiers of some other nation to
go. Lloyd George asked the question all around: "Would your
troops go? Would yours?" Not one statesman dared say yes, and
so in the end the program offered by Wilson was adopted unanimously.

Where should the proposed conference be held? Various suggestions were made, one being the island of Prinkipo, in the sea of
Marmora, near Constantinople. This afforded the overworked delegates a few moments of relaxation. Some refused to believe that a
place with such a musical-comedy name could actually exist; but it
was shown as a tiny dot on a map. When the council voted for it, the
august Arthur Balfour, philosopher and scholar as well as statesman,
was moved to a musical-comedy effusion:

> Oh, let us go
> To Prinkipo,
> Though why or where we do not know!

VI

This vote of the Supreme Council was one of the factors which
decided Robbie Budd to go back to Connecticut; for the proposed
war on Russia had offered about the last chance remaining for a
salesman of munitions. Robbie had his sources of information, and
had tapped them all and made certain that any money which

America might lend to the smaller nations would be hedged about with restrictions, that it was not to be spent for arms. If England and France wanted any fighting done, it would obviously be with the stocks they already had on hand. In short, the cards were stacked against Budd's, and Robbie might as well go home with the bad news.

They would have to convert the plants to the uses of peace; but what uses? Every field was already crowded; if you decided to make automobile parts or sewing machines, you entered into competition with concerns which had been making these things for some time, and knew a thousand tricks that you had to learn. Everybody agreed that Europe would constitute an unlimited market, as soon as peace was declared; but the trouble was, Europe had so many factories of its own, and they would all be seeking the same markets. It was reported that the peace treaty was going to require the demilitarization of the German arms plants; which would mean that Krupp's also would be making automobile parts and sewing machines!

In short, the manufacture of munitions was a precarious business. When danger came, public officials rushed to you for help, and expected you to exhaust yourself working in their service; but the moment the danger was over they were done with you. You heard nothing but the clamor of demagogues that you had made too much money—when the fact was that you stood to lose everything by the sudden collapse of your business. Robbie said this with bitterness, and his son, who was now meeting other men and hearing other points of view, realized more clearly the curious antinomy in his father's mental make-up. Robbie hated war, and called the people fools for being drawn into it; yet when they stopped fighting, he was without occupation, and wandered about like a boy with whom other boys wouldn't play!

It wasn't his fault, of course; he hadn't chosen to be born a Budd. Said his son: "Why can't we convert our plants for good and all, and make things that would have a steady market and not go *kaput* all of a sudden?"

What was needed was new inventions, creating new demands. Some lay in the future, but they hadn't yet come over the horizon— and meanwhile there was only the junk business. Oddly enough, the most promising deal that Robbie had been able to make since the armistice was the one with Johannes Robin, who was setting out to prove himself a first-class businessman. What he was doing and planning was going to bring in a large sum; but because it consisted of a number of small items, Robbie would never be proud of it, and to the end it would remain in his mind the sort of business for a Jew.

VII

Just before sailing, Robbie called up his son and inquired: "Would you like to meet Zaharoff again? I've an appointment with him, and he always asks about you."

The old gray wolf was still on his way up in the world. Last year he had been made a Grand Officer of the Legion of Honor, and he was soon to receive the Grand Cross, usually reserved for kings. He had invited Robbie to call, and father and son drove to the palace on the Avenue Hoche, close to where President Wilson was being housed. The duquesa served tea again; only this time, since Lanny was a grown young gentleman and budding diplomat, she did not take him out into the garden but left him to attend the business conference.

Robbie had guessed that the Greek ex-fireman was still haunted by his dream of monopolizing the armaments industry of the world; and it turned out that this guess was correct. He said that now had come the time of the seven lean years, and those whose barns were small would be well advised to make friends with those whose barns were capacious. Zaharoff had taken the trouble to accumulate a lot of information about Budd's; he knew what dividends they had paid and what reserves they had kept; he seemed to know about the different plans which the president of the concern had been considering for the conversion of the plants, and the approximate cost of such procedure. Old Samuel Budd never came to Europe, either for business or pleasure, but Zaharoff had seen a picture of him; he even knew about the men's Bible class, and spoke of it with urbanity as an original and charming hobby.

The aging Greek with the velvet-soft voice explained that Budd's was in munitions alone, whereas the several hundred Vickers companies were in everything basic in modern industry: iron and steel, copper, nickel, and all the non-ferrous metals, coal and oil and electric power, shipping and finance. "When you have such an organization, Mr. Budd, you can turn quickly from war to peace, and back again at will; you have the money, the connections, the techniques. Whereas a small concern like Budd's, off in a corner by itself, is at the mercy of the financiers, who don't do anything for love."

"I know," said Robbie; and didn't ask whether Zaharoff was going to do it for love.

The American was more cautious than he had been five years ago. He knew that his people were in a dangerous position, and he knew that Zaharoff knew it. He listened while the old man with the white imperial suavely explained that such things as family and national pride were out of date nowadays; what counted was money. The really big kind was international, and was without prejudice; it did, not what it chose, but what it had to do. In times of stress, such as lay ahead of them, little business was swept into the discard and factories went on the bargain-counter like—"Well, like field-guns right now," said Zaharoff.

The munitions king seemed actually on the way to realizing his life's dream. Vickers now completely controlled Schneider-Creusot in France, Skoda in Bohemia, and the Austrian, the Turkish, the Italian plants. Its biggest rival, Krupp, was to be put out of the trade entirely. If Lanny had ever been uncertain as to why Zaharoff was standing so valiantly by the demand for war to a finish, he had the answer now.

"How unwise for you, Mr. Budd, with your isolated small business, to stand outside the great world movement! You might come in on terms that would be both honorable and profitable"—the speaker showed his delicacy of feeling by the order in which he placed these two words. "You have done us an important service in the war, and this is a way we can show our gratitude. It had better be done at once, before the stresses of business competition begin to weaken the ties of friendship. You will understand what I mean, I am sure."

"Yes," said Robbie, "I understand." And he did. He promised to go back and put the proposition before his father and brothers. "I'd rather not attempt to guess what their reaction will be," he added.

So the tactful Grand Officer of the Legion of Honor began to talk about the Peace Conference and what it was doing. He said that President Wilson was perhaps a great statesman and certainly a high-minded gentleman, but that some of his projects were hardly in accord with the interests of either Robert Budd or Basil Zaharoff. He turned to the boy who had now grown into a statesman, and asked how he was enjoying his excursion into diplomatic affairs. When Lanny revealed that his chief was a geographer, and was engaged in preparing a confidential report on Georgian affairs, the munitions king couldn't conceal his interest. Georgia was Batum, and Batum was oil; and already Zaharoff was on the scene, and fully intending to stay!

He began telling Lanny things, hoping that Lanny would be led to tell more important things without knowing that he was doing so. When they were ready to leave, the old man insisted upon summoning his duquesa to bid them farewell, and he said in her presence that Lanny must not let the work of peace-making deprive him entirely of social life; he should come and see them some time, and meet the duquesa's two very lovely daughters. There must have been some secret signal which Zaharoff gave the lady, for she instantly joined in and pressed the invitation. Neither of them mentioned that the two young ladies were destined to divide the fortune of the richest man in the world; but Lanny knew that it was so, and knew that all the world speculated as to whether they were Zaharoff's daughters, or whether their father was the Duque de

Marqueni y Villafranca de los Caballeros, cousin of the Spanish
king, shut up somewhere in a madhouse and stubbornly refusing to
die.

When the two Americans were alone in the taxi, the father
chuckled, and said: "Look out for yourself, kid!"

"That really was a bid, wasn't it?" inquired the youth.

"A royal command," declared the other. "You can make a bigger deal than I can. All you have to do is arrange for a regiment or
two of doughboys to help the British protect Batum from the Bolsheviks!"

VIII

Lanny settled down to his new work, which was studying the
manners and customs of the Georgians. They had several delegations in Paris, and word spread, quite literally with the speed of
lightning, that Professor Alston at the Crillon had been charged
with deciding their fate. They all came at once—even though many
of them were not on speaking terms with one another. They were
large, tall men with wide mustaches, and for the most part wore their
national costumes—some because they had no others, and some because they had learned that it was good propaganda. The costumes
included long coats of hairy goatskin, high soft boots, and large
bonnets of astrakhan. Their French and English were rudimentary,
and those who spoke the difficult native tongue would become so
excited that they forgot to stop and give their translators a chance.
Their idea of persuading you was by a kind of baptismal rite; they
would put their faces close to yours and talk with such vehemence
that they enveloped you in a fine salivary spray, which went into
your eyes and which good manners forbade you to wipe away.

When they couldn't get hold of the professor, his secretary
would do, so Lanny submitted to this rite for hours at a time. He
had to meet various groups and individuals and sort them out, and
try to discover what it was which caused them to sit glowering at
one another. They all hated and dreaded the Bolsheviks, but differed

as to the way to resist them and who was to rule after the victory
had been won. There were aristocrats and democrats, land owners
and peasants, clericals and Socialist intellectuals, all the warring
groups, as in French politics. All were acutely aware of the treasure
which lay beneath the surface of their country, and some were
thinking what a noble civilization could be built with its help. But
unfortunately these were idealists who lacked experience in oil
production; on the other hand, those who had the experience were
in the pay of some foreign interest seeking concessions. All these
lied shamelessly, and Lanny, who hadn't had much experience with
liars, had to work hard for every fact he reported to his chief.

The plight of the little country was precarious. Toward the end
of the war the Germans had seized it, along with the Ukraine; the
armistice had forced them to vacate, and the French had sent a small
army into the Ukraine, while the British had taken Batum on the
Black Sea and Baku on the Caspian, and were policing the railroad
and the pipelines by which the oil was brought out. But meanwhile the Bolsheviks were swarming like bees all about them, using
their dreadful new weapon of class incitement, arousing peasants
and workers against the invasion of "foreign capitalism." They were
now driving the French out of Kiev, and literally rotting their
armies with propaganda. How long would the British armies stand
the strain? Men who had set out cheerfully to unhorse the hated
Kaiser considered that they had done their job and wanted to go
home; what business had their rulers keeping them in the Caucasus
to protect oil wells for Zaharoff the Greek and Deterding the
Dutchman?

It was that way all over Eastern and Central Europe. The soldiers and sailors of Russia had overthrown their Tsar, the soldiers
and sailors of Germany had driven their Kaiser into exile, and now
the soldiers and sailors of the Allies were demanding: "What is all
this about? Why are we shooting these peasants?" In Siberia the
American troops were meeting the Reds and feeling sorry for them,
exactly as Lanny had felt for those he had met in his uncle's tene-

ment room. The armies were disintegrating, discipline was relaxing, and officers were alarmed as they never had been by the German invasion.

So, of course, the elder statesmen in Paris were having an unhappy time; their generals in the field were pulling them one way and the great industrialists and financiers at home were pulling them the other. Coal and oil, iron and copper—were they going to let the Reds take these treasures and use them to prove that workers could run industry for themselves? There was a clamor for war in all the big-business press, and in the parliaments, and it turned the Peace Conference into a hell of intrigue and treachery. To be there was like walking on the floor of a volcano, and wherever you thrust your staff into the ground, it began to quake, and fumes shot out and boiling lava oozed up.

IX

The Georgian question, with which Lanny was occupied, was one of the hottest spots. Since the province had been a part of the old empire of the Tsar, the Georgians had been invited to send delegates to Prinkipo. President Wilson had proposed this conference, and the Council of Ten had unanimously voted it—and that had included the French. But now, what was this that the excited Georgians were stammering into the face of the shrinking Lanny Budd? They were trying to find out from him if there was going to be any Prinkipo, if the Americans really wanted it, if it was safe for the Georgians to attend. When the youth questioned them he learned that Pichon, the French Foreign Minister, had been telling them that it was all a mistake, there wasn't going to be any conference, the Bolsheviks wouldn't come and couldn't be trusted if they did.

Lanny reported this to his chief, and both of them tried to find out more. It appeared that the French were advising all the Russian Whites in Paris to oppose the proposal and refuse to attend; they were saying that the Reds had fooled Wilson into believing in their good faith; but France was not to be fooled, and would continue to support the Whites with arms and money, and if they held on they would have their estates and fortunes returned to them. More than once French agents went so far as to threaten the Georgians that, if they supported Prinkipo, they would themselves be regarded as Bolsheviks and expelled from France. So these strangers in a strange land didn't dare whisper the truth to an American until he had pledged his word not to name the source of his information. "What shall we do, Mr. Budd? Will President Wilson protect us?"

And here was Winston Churchill, powerful war minister, scholar, and orator, appearing before the Supreme Council to denounce the Bolsheviks and demand war upon them in the name of humanity, Christianity, and his ancestor, the fighting Duke of Marlborough. Here was Lord Curzon, whom his associates described as "a very superior purzon," making his appeal especially for Georgia—his lordship had visited that mountainous land in his youth, and had romantic memories of it, and didn't want these memories disturbed by dialectical materialism.

And Zaharoff! He appeared before no councils, for he was neither scholar nor orator, and had no ancestors to boast of; but he had powerful voices to speak for him. If you could believe Robbie Budd, one of these voices was that of the squat little Frenchman with the white walrus mustaches and black skull-cap who sat at the head of the conference table and choked off debate with his "*Adopté!*" Robbie said that "the Tiger" had been Zaharoff's friend for years, and both his brother and his son were directors in Zaharoff's companies. If you wanted to understand a politician you mustn't pay too much attention to his speeches, but find out who were his paymasters. A politician couldn't rise in public life, in France any more than in America, unless he had the backing of big money, and it was in times of crisis like this that he paid his debts.

X

A day or two after Robbie sailed for home, Lanny received a confirmation of his "royal command"; a little note from María del Pilar Antonia Angela Patrocino Simón de Muguiro y Berute, Duquesa de Marqueni y Villafranca de los Caballeros. She didn't sign all that, of course. She requested the pleasure of his company at tea the following afternoon; and Lanny showed the note to Alston, who said: "Go by all means and see what it's about." So, looking his best in formal afternoon attire, the youth alighted from a taxicab in front of 53, Avenue Hoche, and presented his hat and stick to the black-clad butler, and was escorted upstairs to the drawing room with the Spanish masters on the walls and the elaborate tea service on an inlaid Louis Quinze table.

The duquesa's daughters were as shy and as strictly brought up as Lanny had imagined them; they had large dark eyes and long lashes which they lowered like curtains when a handsome young American gazed too directly. They were clad alike in blue chiffon tea gowns, and blushes came and went in all four of their cheeks. It was evident that they found their visitor interesting; he had come recently from a far-off land which they saw enlarged and glorified on the motion-picture screen. It really seemed as if Lanny was considered what the French call a *parti*, an eligible person. He was expected to display his charms, and gladly did so.

He entertained three aristocratic ladies with stories of the leading personalities of the greatest show on earth. More than once it had happened that he had been waiting in anterooms when the great ones had come forth chatting, and he had heard what they said; also he knew the anecdotes which were going the rounds. Thus, Arthur Balfour and Clemenceau had appeared at some function, the former with his "topper" and all the trimmings, the latter in a bowler hat. His lordship in a spirit of *noblesse oblige* had remarked: "I was told to wear formal dress"; to which "the Tiger," with his mischievous twinkle, replied: "So was I."

Also the story of Premier Hughes of Australia, a labor leader who had fought his way up in a rough world; a violent little man who had become deaf, and carried with him a hearing machine which he set up on the table. He defied President Wilson, declaring that what his country had got it meant to keep. This delighted Clemenceau, for if Australia kept what she had got, it would mean that France might keep hers. So when they were arranging for another session, Clemenceau remarked to Lloyd George: "Come—and bring your savages with you!"

XI

Presently the master of the house came in, and tea was served; he too was interested in the stories, and it was like a family party. Until finally the ladies arose and excused themselves, and Lanny was alone with the old gray wolf.

It was really a fascinating thing to watch; most educational for a young man with a possible future in the diplomatic world. The perfection of a Grand Officer's technique: the velvety softness of manner, the kindness, the cordiality, even affection; the gentle, insinuating voice; the subtle flattery of an old man asking advice from a young one; the fatherly attitude, the strong offering security to the weak. Won't you walk into my parlor? It is warm, and the cushions are soft, and there is no sweeter honey provided for any fly.

What the munitions king wanted, of course, was for Lanny to become his spy in the Crillon; to circulate among the staff, ask questions, pick up valuable items, and bring them quickly to his employer—or should we say his friend, his backer, perhaps his father-in-law? Nothing was said about this directly; it is only in old fairy stories that the king says: "Go out and slay the seven-headed dragon, and I will give you my daughter's hand." In the modern world men have learned to convey their meaning with a glance or a smile.

Lanny had read of the Temptation on the Mount in two synoptic narratives. In that ancient trial Satan had shown all the kingdoms of the earth, but had overlooked the greatest treasure of all. Perhaps the high mountain had been a bad choice and it would have been wiser to invite his victim to the home of one of the rich and mighty of the kingdom, and let him see dark eyes peering seductively from behind the curtains of a seraglio.

Lanny had inspected what Zaharoff had to offer and he knew that it was good. These young women had been brought up in a convent and were unspoiled by the world; their hearts were in a susceptible state, and Lanny could have made himself agreeable and stood a chance at either. He had only to bring his daily meed of news and the way would have been made smooth for him; he would have been left alone with the one of his choice and they would have looked at engravings together, played music, strolled in the garden, and whispered the secrets of eager young hearts.

Of course Zaharoff may not have meant it seriously; but why not? He might have done worse. A youth who was pleasing and intelligent, who had got himself a start in the great world, and with a fortune behind him, could have gone to the top in diplomacy, politics, finance. And what more could the youth have asked? Either one of the young women would have made him a good wife. He was sure they were Zaharoff's daughters, and therefore the taint of insanity was not in their blood. He had seen that the old man was fond of them, and would make a helpful father-in-law; it wouldn't be long before Lanny would be in control of the greatest fortune in the world.

All he had to do was to be as tactful as the munitions king himself. He didn't need to say: "I accept your offer and will betray my trust." No, no; his speech would have been: "I appreciate your position, and how greatly you are inconvenienced by the blundering of the diplomats. If at any time I have information that will be of use to you, I'll be most happy to bring it—of course purely as an act of friendship, and without any thought of reward." That was the way Robbie hired his agents—those of the high class, who got the biggest pay.

XII

Such things were being done all the time in the great world; and why didn't Lanny accept? Was it because he knew how his father despised Zaharoff? Not entirely; for Lanny's father despised President Wilson, yet Lanny had come to think that President Wilson was in many ways a great man; not equal to his present tasks, perhaps, but far better than the politicians with whom he was dealing. Lanny was coming to think highly of many of the Crillon staff; he had even permitted himself to have good thoughts about the Bolsheviks he had met, although his father couldn't find words enough to denounce them.

Was it because he wasn't impressed by the young ladies? He couldn't say that, because he hadn't seen enough of them; and young ladies are always interesting to investigate, at the least. You met them everywhere you turned here in Paris, where so many of the young men were in the ground with white crosses over them, or else living in barracks along the German frontier, or in Salonika and Odessa and Syria and Algiers—so many places you couldn't keep track of them.

Was it perhaps because Lanny had in his heart an image of an English girl with broad brow and smooth, straw-colored hair and a gentle manner reminding him of his mother? That girl was married now to the young nobleman in the British War Office. Did she love her husband? Was she going to be a true and faithful wife? Or would she continue getting her ideas from "free women"? Lanny knew that the women had at last got the ballot in Britain, so Rosemary wouldn't have to carry any more hatchets into the National Gallery. When she wrote, it was one of her brief, uncommunicative letters; he would have to go and see her, before he would know how to think about her in the future.

Nobody could have been more polite than Lanny to his elderly host. He said that nobody really knew whether there was going to be any Prinkipo conference; the French were working against it—

Lanny smiled inwardly, well knowing that Zaharoff was one of the hardest of the workers.

"There's no doubt," the youth added, "that President Wilson means what he says, the American troops are going to find a way to withdraw from the fighting." And when Zaharoff brought up another subject, he replied: "I really don't know what's going to happen at Batum. The British can't seem to make up their minds. Have you heard the bad news as to the troubles of the French in the Ukraine?"

All that was sparring, of course; and Zaharoff knew it. He knew what it meant when Lanny explained that, unfortunately, on the few occasions when he did get advance news of the Crillon's intentions, it was always confidential, and so his lips were sealed. The munitions king realized that he had wasted his afternoon. He didn't show any signs of irritation, but brought the interview politely to a close and parted from the youth on terms which would make it possible for the duquesa to invite him again.

But she didn't; and Lanny didn't see those shy and well-bred young ladies for quite a while—until he met one of them as the wife of an English ship owner who was said to be helping Zaharoff secretly re-arm Germany. He learned that the other one had married a nobleman and gone to live in Constantinople, where she had become celebrated for the protection she offered to the pariah dogs of that city. The wheel of fate had made a circle, and a portion of Zaharoff's fortune had returned to the place from which it had made its not so creditable start!

29

A Friend in Need

I

THE Supreme Council was now going ahead under full steam.
They were hearing the claims of the small nationalities, and it was
proving a tedious process. As the Americans reported it, Dmowski,
presenting the case of Poland, began with the fourteenth century at
eleven o'clock in the morning, and reached 1919 at four in the
afternoon. Next day came Beneš to present the claims of the Czechs,
and he began a century earlier and finished an hour later.

Professor Alston had to be there, for no one could say at what
moment an American commissioner might beckon to him and ask
some question; Lanny had to be there, because of the heavy portfolios, and also because the professor's French couldn't cope with
the outbursts of Clemenceau, who used not merely the slang of the
boulevards, but that of the underworld—many of his ejaculations
being so obscene that Lanny was embarrassed to translate them and
the recorders of the proceedings had to be told to expurgate them.

A weary, weary ordeal! You couldn't lounge or tilt back in a
frail gilded chair a couple of hundred years old; you had to sit stiff
and motionless and tell yourself it was a history lesson. But did you
want to know all that history? Lanny would close his eyes and remember the beach at Juan, the blue water sparkling in the sunshine,
and the little white sailboats all over the Golfe. He would summon
up the garden with the masses of bougainvillaea in bloom; he would
remember the piano, and yearn over those boxes of books which
he had had shipped from the home of Great-Great-Uncle Eli and
which some day he was going to have the delight of unpacking. Did

he really want to be a person of distinction, live in the *grand monde*, and submit to endless, unremitting boredom?

He would open his eyes and watch the faces of the old men who were here deciding the destinies of the nations. Clemenceau sat shrunken into a little knot, the hands with the gray gloves folded over his stomach, the heavy lids covering his weary brown eyes. Was he asleep? Maybe so, but he had an inner alarm clock, for the moment anyone said anything against the interests of his beloved *patrie* he was all alert, bristling like the tiger he was named for. The pink, cherubic Lloyd George quite frankly dozed; he told one of the Americans that two things had kept him alive through the ordeal of the war—naps were one and the other was singing Welsh hymns.

Woodrow Wilson was unsparing of himself, and as the weeks passed his health caused worry to his associates. He was attending these Council sessions all day, and in the evenings the sessions of the League of Nations Commission. He was driving himself, because he had to sail on the fourteenth of February to attend the closing sessions of the Congress, and he was determined to take with him the completed draft of the Covenant of the League. A thousand cares and problems beset him and he was getting no sleep; he became haggard and there began a nervous twitching of the left side of his face. Lanny, watching him, decided never to aspire to fame.

The oratory became intolerable, so the Council picked out the talkers, and appointed them on what was called the "Clarification Commission," where they could talk to one another. Altogether there were appointed fifty-eight commissions to deal with the multiplicity of problems, and these commissions held a total of 1646 sessions. But that didn't remedy the trouble, because all the commissions had to report—and to whom? Where was the human brain that could absorb so many details? Hundreds of technical advisers assembling masses of information and shaping important conclusions —and then unable to find a way to make their work count!

All the problems of the world had been dumped onto the shoulders of a few elderly men; and the world had to crumble to pieces while one after another of these men broke down under the strain. There was that terrible influenza loose in Paris, striking blindly, like another war. It was the middle of winter, and winds came storming across the North Sea, tempered somewhat by the time they got to Paris, but laden with sleet and snow. It would cover the mansard roofs and pile up on the chimney pots; it didn't last many hours, and then the streets would be carpeted with slush, and the miasma that rose from it bore germs which had been accumulating through a thousand years of human squalor.

II

Early in February the Bolshevik government announced its willingness to send delegates to the Prinkipo conference. That put it up to President Wilson to act, if he was going to stand by his project. A few days later Alston told his secretary an exciting piece of news: the President had decided to name two delegates, one an American journalist, William Allen White, and the other Alston's old-time mentor, George D. Herron!

The official announcement was made a day or two later and raised a storm of protest from the "best" people back home. The New York *Times* led off with an editorial blast exposing the Socialist ex-clergyman's black record; the Episcopal bishop of New York followed suit, and the church people and the women's clubs rushed to the defense of the American home. It was bad enough to propose sitting at a council table with bloody-handed thugs and nationalizers of women; but to send to them a man who shared their moral depravity was to degrade the fair name of Columbia the Gem of the Ocean. All this was duly cabled and printed in Paris, and reinforced the efforts of the Quai d'Orsay to torpedo the Prinkipo proposal.

Herron, who had gone back to his home in Geneva, now returned to Paris, deeply stirred by the opportunity which had come to him. No longer would he have to sit helpless and watch the world crumble. He saw himself arbitrating this ferocious class war which had spread over one-sixth of the globe and was threatening to wreck another huge section of Europe. He was busy day and night with conferences; the newspaper men swarmed about him, asking questions, not merely about Russia and the Reds, but about free love in relation to the Christian religion, and whatever else might make hot news for the folks at home.

The Socialist prophet was all ready to go to work. But how was he to do it? He had never held an official position, and came to Alston for advice. How did one set about working for a government? Where did one go? If he was to set out for Prinkipo, presumably he would have a staff, and an escort, and some funds. Where would he get them?

Alston advised him to see Mr. Lansing. That was easy, because the Secretary of State didn't have much to do in Paris. Formal and stiff, his feelings had been mortally wounded because so few persons paid attention to him. But he didn't want the attention of Socialist prophets; he looked on Herron as on some strange bird. He was as cold as the snowy night outside, as remote as the ceiling of his palatial reception room with the plaster cupids dancing on it. He had received no instructions about the conference, didn't approve of it, and was sure it would prove futile.

President Wilson was driven day and night trying to get ready for his departure, and Herron could find nobody who knew or cared about the musical-comedy place called Prinkipo. The Supreme Council had passed a resolution, but unless there was someone to fight for it and keep on fighting, it would be nothing but so many words. Alston explained the intrigues of the French as he knew them. Herron, a simple man to whose nature deception was foreign, was helpless against such forces. People fought shy of him, perhaps because of the scandal freshly raked up, but mainly because he was believed to sympathize with the Reds. In a matter like that it was safer to lie low—and let Marshal Foch and Winston Churchill have their way.

III

Over at the Hotel Majestic was the British staff, almost as large as the American; and from the outset they had been coming over to make friends. The Americans did their best to keep on their guard, but it was difficult when they found how well informed and apparently sincere the Englishmen were. They had such excellent manners and soft agreeable voices—and, furthermore, you could understand what they said! A Frenchman, or a European speaking French, talked very rapidly, and was apt to become excited and wave his hands in front of you; but the well-chosen words of a cultivated Oxford graduate slid painlessly into your mind and you found yourself realizing how it had come about that they were the managers of so large a portion of the earth. If a territory was placed in the hands of such men, it stood a chance to be well governed; but what would happen if the Italians got it—to say nothing of the Germans or the Bolsheviks!

The British members of commissions of course had young secretaries and translators carrying heavy portfolios, and Lanny met them. They reminded him of Rick and those jolly English lads with whom he had punted on the Thames. One of them invited him to lunch at their hotel, an ornate structure which seemed to be built entirely of onyx; the dining room was twice as big as the Crillon's, and in it you saw the costumes of every corner of the empire on which the sun never set. The English youth, whose name was Fessenden, had been born in Gibraltar, and was here because of his fluent Spanish and French. He was gay, and had the usual bright pink cheeks, and Lanny exchanged eager confidences with him; each was "pumping" the other, of course, but that was fair exchange and no robbery.

What was this business about Prinkipo? Lanny told how anxiously Dr. Herron was trying to find out. The English youth said his government hadn't appointed any delegates, so presumably they thought it was going to fizzle. One more of those "trial balloons." Fes-

senden's chief had said that the only way it might be made to work
would be for President Wilson to drop everything else and go there
and put it through. But of course he couldn't do that. "Don't you
think perhaps he's a bit too afraid of delegating authority? One man
just can't make so many decisions by himself."

That was the talk all over Paris; three of the peace commissioners
were figureheads, and Colonel House had been weakened by an
attack of flu. That was no secret, and Lanny admitted it.

"All of us," said the Englishman, "at least all the younger crowd,
were hoping Wilson could put it over. Now we're a bit sick about
it."

Lanny answered cautiously. "One hears so many things, one
doesn't know what to believe."

"But there are definite things that you can be sure of. It seems as
if your President just doesn't know enough about Europe; he does
things without realizing what they mean. At the outset he agreed
to let the Italians have the Brenner! Shouldn't he have asked somebody about that before he spoke? Of course it's important for the
defense of Italy; but if you're going to distribute the world on the
basis of strategic needs, where will you stop?"

"I don't know much about the Brenner," admitted Lanny.

"It's a pass inhabited almost entirely by German people; and what
is going to happen to them when the Italians take them over? Will
they be compelled to send their children to Italian schools, and all
that sort of rot?"

Lanny smiled, and said: "Well, you know it wasn't we who
signed that treaty with the Italians."

"True enough," admitted Fessenden. "But then it wasn't we who
brought up those Fourteen Points!"

That was why it was a pleasure to meet the English; you could
speak frankly, and they didn't flare up and deliver orations. It was
true they wanted the Americans to pull some chestnuts out of the
fire for them, but it was also true that they would meet you halfway in an effort to be decent. The best of them had really hoped
that the American President was going to bring in a new order and

were saddened now as they discovered how ill equipped he was for the tremendous task.

Lanny didn't tell his English friend an appalling story which Alston's associates were whispering. The Supreme Council was planning to recognize a new state in Central Europe called Czechoslovakia, to consist principally of territories taken from Germany and Austria. The Czechs, previously known as Bohemians, had a patriotic leader named Masaryk, who had been a professor at the University of Chicago and a personal friend of Wilson. An American journalist talking with Wilson had said: "But, Mr. President, what are you going to do about the Germans in this new country?"

"Are there Germans in Czechoslovakia?" asked Wilson, in surprise.

The answer was: "There are three million of them."

"How strange!" exclaimed the President. "Masaryk never told me that!"

I V

Lanny was worried because he hadn't had any letter from Kurt. After he had been in Paris a month, he wrote again, this time to Herr Meissner, asking that he would kindly drop a line to say how Kurt was. Lanny assumed that whoever the mysterious person in Switzerland might be who had been remailing Kurt's letters to Lanny, Kurt's father would be able to make use of him. Lanny followed his usual practice of not giving his own address, for fear the letter might come into the wrong hands; he just said that he was to be addressed at his mother's home.

Lanny sent his letter in care of Johannes Robin, in Rotterdam, and there came in reply one from Hansi Robin, saying that his father had forwarded the letter as usual. Hansi was now fourteen, and his English was letter-perfect, although somewhat stilted. He told Lanny how his work at the conservatory was progressing, and expressed the hope that Lanny's career in diplomacy was not going to cause him to give up his music entirely. He said how happy he was that his father had become a business associate of Lanny's father and that they all hoped the adventure was going to prove satisfactory. Hansi said that his brother joined in expressing their high regard and sincere good wishes. Freddi, two years younger, added his childish signature to certify that it was true.

Lanny put that letter into his pocket, intending to forward it to his father the next time he wrote; and maybe that was the reason why for the next two or three days his thoughts were so frequently on Kurt Meissner. Lanny was sure that he would get a reply, for the comptroller-general was a business-like person, and it would be no trouble for him to dictate to his secretary a note, saying: "My son is well, but away from home," or: "My son is ill," or whatever it might be. Every time Lanny called for his mail he looked for a letter with a Swiss stamp.

And of course he thought about Schloss Stubendorf, and Kurt's family, and Kurt himself, and wondered what four and a half years of war had done to him. What would he be doing now, or planning? Would he be able to go back to music after battle and wounds, and the wrecking of all his hopes? Around him Lanny saw men who had become adjusted to war and couldn't get readjusted. Some were drinking, or trying to make up for lost time by sleeping with any woman they could pick up on the streets—and the streets were full of them. Would Kurt be like that? Or was Kurt dead, or mutilated as Marcel had been? What other reason could there be for his failure to communicate with the friend to whom he had pledged such devotion? Could it be that he now hated all Americans, because they had torn Germany's prey from out of her jaws?

Such were Lanny's thoughts while taking a walk. Such were his thoughts while he sat in the stuffy, overheated rooms at the Quai d'Orsay, attending exhausting sessions whenever a geographer was likely to be needed. While furious and tiresome quarrels were going on over the ownership of a hundred square miles of rocks or desert, he would turn his thoughts to the days when he and Kurt were diving and swimming off the Cap d'Antibes; or the holiday at the Christmas-card castle, which he saw always as he had seen it the first morning, with freshly fallen snow on its turrets shining in the newly risen sun. There were so many beautiful things in the world—oh, God, why did men have to make it so ugly? Why did they have to rage and scream and bluster, and tell lies so transparent that a geographer and even a secretary were made sick to listen.

Kurt was only a year older than Lanny, but he had seemed much more; he was so grave, so precise in his thinking, so decided in his purposes, that Lanny had honored him as a teacher. For nearly six years the American had kept that attitude; and now, when Kurt didn't write to him, he was worried, puzzled, hurt. But he kept telling himself that he had no right to be. There was bound to be some reason, to be explained in good time.

V

The streets of Paris were full of picturesque and diverting sights: dapper young officers in Turkey-red pants, looking as if they had just stepped out of bandboxes; poilus trudging home from the front, unshaven, mudstained, bent with weariness; elegant ladies of fashion tripping from their limousines into jewelers' and coiffeurs'; pathetic, consumptive-looking grisettes with blackened eyebrows and scarlet lips. The glory of La Ville Lumière was sadly dimmed, but there had to be ways for the foreigners to enjoy themselves. There were always crowds of them in the fashionable restaurants, no matter how often the prices were raised; always lines of people trying to get into every place of entertainment. So many had made money out of the war—and they had to have pleasure, even though their world might be coming to an end.

The strolling youth would note these things for a while, and then again be lost in thoughts about the problems of the peace. What was the conference going to do with Upper Silesia? That territory was full of coal mines and many sorts of factories; the French wanted to take it from Germany and give it to Poland— so that in the next war its coal would serve the purposes of France, and not of her hereditary and implacable foe. There was a commission to decide all that, and Professor Alston had been asked to attend it; when Lanny finished his walk he would hear arguments concerning the destiny of the Meissner family! A translator, of course, could take no open part, but he might be able to influence his chief by a whispered word, and his chief might influence the higher-ups in the same way.

So thinking, Lanny strolled on—into what was to prove the strangest adventure of his life up to that time. He had come to a street intersection and stood to let the traffic by. There came a taxi, close to the curb, and as it passed it was forced to slow up by another vehicle ahead. In the taxi sat a single passenger, a man, and at that moment he leaned forward, as if to speak to the driver. His profile came into clear view; and Lanny stared dumfounded. It was Kurt Meissner!

Of course it was absolutely impossible. Kurt, an artillery captain of the Germany army, riding in a Paris taxicab while the two countries were still formally at war! It must be somebody else; and yet from the first moment Lanny knew it wasn't. It hadn't been merely a physical recognition, it was some kind of psychic thing; he knew that it was Kurt as well as he knew that he himself was Lanny Budd. Could this be another apparition, like the one he had seen of Rick? Did it mean that Kurt was dead, or near to death, as Rick had been?

The cab was moving on, and Lanny came out of his daze. His friend was in Paris, and he must get hold of him! He wanted to shout: "Kurt! Kurt!"—but the traffic was noisy, and Lanny's training kept him from making a public disturbance. He began to run, as fast as he could, dodging the pedestrians, and trying to keep his eye on that cab. Perhaps he could catch it at the next crossing; but, no, it was going on faster. Lanny was despairing, when he saw a vacant cab by the curb. He sprang in and cried: "Follow that cab! Quick!"

Taxi drivers have such experiences now and then. It means a pretty girl, or perhaps a fashionable married lady—anyhow, some sort of adventure. The driver leaped into action, and presently they were weaving their way through the traffic, Lanny peering ahead, to pick out one cab from all the others. He made sure he had it, because he could see through the rear window the passenger's gray fedora, which had been a part of the image stamped upon his mind in one quick flash.

VI

They had turned onto the Boulevard Haussmann, with much fast traffic, so there was nothing to do but follow; meanwhile Lanny had a chance to think, and get the aspects of this problem sorted out in his mind. Kurt in Paris, wearing civilian clothes! He couldn't be on any official mission, for there were no enemy missions in France; there had been a lot of talk about having the Central Powers represented at the Peace Conference, but the talk had died down. Nor could Kurt be here on private business, for no enemy aliens were being given passports into France. No, his presence could mean only that he was here on some secret errand, with a false passport. If he were detected, they would try him before a military court and stand him against a wall and shoot him.

Lanny's next thought was that he, a member of the Crillon staff, had no business getting mixed up in such a matter. He ought to tell his taxi driver that it was a mistake, and to turn back. But Lanny hadn't learned to think of himself as an official person, and the idea that he couldn't speak to Kurt just didn't make sense. Whatever his friend might be doing, he was a man of honor and wouldn't do anything to get Lanny into trouble.

Kurt's cab turned off the boulevard, into the Neuilly district. "I can drive up alongside him now," said Lanny's driver; but Lanny said: "No, just follow him." He would wait until Kurt got out, so that they could meet without witnesses.

Watching ahead, Lanny saw the passenger turn round; evidently he discovered that he was being followed, for his cab began turning corners rapidly, as no sane taxicab would have done. Lanny could imagine Kurt saying: "Ten francs extra if you shake off that fellow behind us." Lanny said: "Ten francs extra if you don't let that fellow get away from us."

So began a crazy chase in and about the environs of Paris. Lanny's driver had been a dispatch rider on the upper Meuse front, so he called back to his passenger; he looked like an *apache*, and behaved like one. They turned corners on two wheels, and Lanny leaned out of the window to balance the cab. They dashed through cross-wise traffic—and they held onto the other car. More than once Lanny saw the passenger in front turning round to look—always holding his gray fedora below the level of his eyes. Lanny took off his hat and waved it, to give his friend every opportunity to recognize him. But it had no effect.

However, Lanny's *apache* was better than the other one. Kurt's taxi stopped suddenly in front of a department store, and Lanny's came up with screeching brakes behind it. Kurt got out, paid his driver, and turned to go into the store; Lanny came running, having also paid quickly. He realized the need of caution, and didn't call out; he came up behind the other and whispered: "Kurt, it's me—Lanny."

A strange thing happened. The other turned and gazed into Lanny's face, coldly, haughtily. "You are mistaken, sir." Lanny had spoken in English, and the answer was given in French.

Of course it was Kurt Meissner; a Kurt with features more care-worn, stern, and mature; his straw-colored hair, usually cut close, had grown longer; but it was Kurt's face, and the voice was Kurt's.

Lanny, having had time to think matters out, wasn't going to give up easily. He murmured: "I understand your position. You must know that I am your friend and you can trust me. I still feel as I have always done."

The other kept up his cold stare. "I beg your pardon, sir," he said, in very good French. "It is a case of mistaken identity. I have never met you."

He started away again; but Lanny walked with him. "All right," he said, his voice low. "I understand what is the matter. But if you get into trouble and need help, remember that I'm at the Crillon.

But don't think that I've turned into an official person. I'm doing what I can to help make a decent peace, and you and I are not very far apart."

One of the clerks of the store came forward with inquiry in his manner, and Kurt asked for some gloves. Lanny turned and started to leave. But then he thought: "Maybe Kurt will think it over and change his mind." So he waited, just inside the door of the store. When the other had completed his purchase and was going out, sure enough, he said: "You may come with me, sir, if you wish."

VII

The two of them went out to the street, and walked in silence for quite a while, Kurt looking behind them to make sure they were not being followed. Then they would take a glance at each other. More than four years had passed since their last meeting in London; they had been boys and now they were men. The German officer had lines in his long thin face; he walked as if he were bowed with care—but of course that might have been because he was trying not to look like a military man. It was plain that he was deeply moved.

"Lanny," he exclaimed, suddenly, "may I have your word of honor not to mention this meeting to any person under any circumstances?"

"I have an idea of your position, Kurt. You can trust me."

"It is not merely a matter of my own life. It might have extremely unpleasant consequences for you."

"I am willing to take the risk. I am sure that you are not doing anything dishonorable."

They walked on; and finally Kurt broke out: "Forgive me if I am not a friend at present. I am bound by circumstances about which I cannot say a word. My time is not my own—nor my life."

"I promise not to misunderstand," replied the other. "Let me tell you about my job, and perhaps you can judge about trusting me." He spoke in English, thinking it would be less likely to be caught by any passer-by. He told how he had come to be at the Crillon, and gave a picture of the Peace Conference as it appeared to a translator-secretary.

Kurt couldn't bear to listen to it. He broke in. "Do you know what is being done to my people by the blockade? The food allowance is one-third of normal, and the child death-rate has doubled. Of course our enemies would like them all to die, so there wouldn't be any more of us in the world. But is that what President Wilson promised?"

Lanny replied: "There isn't a man I know in the American delegation who doesn't consider it a shame. They have protested again and again. Mr. Hoover is in Paris now, wringing his hands over the situation."

"Wringing Mr. Hoover's hands won't feed the starving babies. Why doesn't President Wilson threaten to quit unless Clemenceau gives way?"

"He can't be sure what that would do. The others might go on and have their way just the same. It's hard to get a sane peace after a mad war."

Said the captain of artillery: "Are you aware that our people still have some of their gold reserve? They don't ask anybody to give them food, they ask merely to be allowed to buy it with their own money. And there's plenty of food in America, is there not?"

"So much that we don't know what to do with it. The government has agreed to take it from the farmers at fixed prices, but now there's no market. There are millions of pounds of pork that is going to spoil if it isn't used."

"But still our people can't spend their own money for it!"

"The French say they want that gold to restore their ruined cities with."

"Don't you know that we have offered to come and rebuild the cities with our own hands?"

"That's not so simple as it sounds, Kurt. The people here say that would throw their own workers out of jobs."

"Maybe so; and again maybe it would let them find out how decent our people are—how orderly and how hard-working."

The two strolled on, arguing. Lanny guessed that his friend was sounding him out; and presently Kurt said: "Suppose it became known to you that there were some Germans in Paris, working secretly to try to get this wicked blockade lifted—would that seem to you such a bad thing?"

"It would seem to me only natural."

"But you understand that in the eyes of military men they would be spies, and if they were discovered they would be shot?"

"I realized that as soon as I saw you. But I don't see what you can possibly accomplish here."

"Hasn't it occurred to you that you can accomplish something anywhere in the world if you have money?"

A light dawned on Lanny. So that was it! He had heard his father say many times that you could get anything you wanted in Paris if you had the price.

Kurt went on: "There are people here who won't let our babies have milk until they themselves have gold. And even then you can't trust them—for after they have got the gold they may betray you for more gold. You see, it's a complicated business; and if one happened to be in it, and to have a friend whom he loved, it would be an act of friendship to be silent. It might be extremely inconvenient to know about these matters."

Lanny didn't hesitate over that. He declared with warmth: "If that was all that was being done, Kurt, I should think that any true friend would be willing to know and to take a chance at helping. Certainly I would!"

VIII

The walk prolonged itself to several miles. Lanny decided that his duties at the conference could wait. His friend was questioning him as to persons who might be interested in helping to get the blockade of Germany lifted. There were two kinds whom a secret

agent might wish to know: journalists and politicians who might
be bought, and idealists and humanitarians who might be trusted
to expend money for printing or other such activities. Lanny told
about Alston and others of the staff—but they were doing all they
could anyhow. He told about Herron, who was being called a Red
because he wanted a truce with the Bolsheviks, and a pro-German
because he didn't want the French to keep the Rhineland. He told
about Mrs. Emily, who was kind and charitable, also influential;
too bad that a German officer couldn't come to her home and be
properly introduced and invited to set forth his case! Kurt hinted
that perhaps she might be useful as a distributor of funds. It was
hard to give much money without having the French police make
note of the sudden increase of spending power of some group. But
if a wealthy American lady were willing to furnish funds to help
make known the plight of the starving babies of Germany . . . ?

Presently Lanny, racking his mind, mentioned another person
who was an idealist and propagandist of a sort, however perverted.
That was his uncle. "I never told you about him, because I've been
taught to be ashamed of him. But it appears that he's a personage of
a sort here in Paris." Kurt was interested and asked many questions.
Just what were Jesse Blackless's ideas? What group did he belong
to? Was he an honest man—and so on.

Lanny answered: "Really, I hardly know him at all. Most of my
impressions have come from my father's calling him names. Robbie
thinks his ideas come from the devil, and the fact that he really
believes them only makes it worse."

"How much money has he?"

"He lives like a poor man, but he may give money away. I suppose he'd have to, believing as he does."

"Do you suppose I could trust him with my secret?"

"Oh, gosh!" Lanny was staggered. "I wouldn't dare to say,
Kurt."

"Suppose I were to go to him and introduce myself as a musician
from Switzerland, interested in his ideas: how do you suppose he'd
receive me?"

"He'd probably guess that you were a police agent, and wouldn't trust you."

They walked on, while Kurt pondered. Finally he said: "I have to take a chance. Can you do this for me? Go to your uncle and tell him that you have a friend who is interested in pushing the demand for the lifting of the blockade throughout Europe. Tell him that I have money, but there are reasons why I do not wish to be known. Tell him that you know me to be a sincere man— you can say that, can't you?"

"Yes, surely."

"Tell him someone will come to his room at exactly midnight and tap on his door. When he opens it the person will say the word 'Jesse,' and he will answer the word 'Uncle,' and then a package will be put in his hands. He will be under pledge to spend the money in the quickest and best way, for leaflets, posters, meetings, all that sort of thing. I'll watch, and if I see signs of his activity, I'll bring more money from time to time. Would you be willing to do that?"

"Yes," said Lanny, "I don't see why I shouldn't."

"You understand, both you and your uncle have my word that never under any circumstances will I name you to anyone."

"How much money will it be?"

"Ten thousand francs should be enough to start with. It will be in hundred-franc notes, so it can be spent without attracting attention. You will be able to see your uncle before midnight?"

"I don't know. I'll try."

"You know the park of captured cannon in the Place in front of the Crillon?"

"I see them every day."

"There is a big howitzer, directly at the corner as you enter the center lane of guns. It happens to be one that I had charge of; I know it by the marks where it was hit. It's directly across from the main entrance of the hotel, so you can't miss it."

"I think I know it."

"Can you be standing in front of it at exactly eleven tonight?"

"I guess so."

"If you lean against the gun, it means that your uncle says all right. If you walk up and down, it means that he says no, and the deal is off. If you're not there, it means that you haven't been able to find him, or that he wants more time before he gives his answer. In that case I'll look for you at the same hour tomorrow evening. Is that all clear?"

"Quite so. Isn't there any way I can get hold of you again?"

"Your mail at the hotel comes without censorship?"

"Oh, surely."

"I'll write you some time, a note in English, just saying, meet me at the same place. I'll sign an English name—shall we say Sam?"

"All right, Sam," said Lanny, with a grin. It promised to be great fun. Lanny's mother would be dancing tonight in behalf of charity, and Lanny would be conspiring in the same cause!

IX

The conspirator paid another call on his Uncle Jesse. This time no one answered his knock, so he poked a note under the door, saying he would return at seven. He had pressing duties, and the only time he could get free was by skipping his dinner; he bought a couple of bananas and ate them in the taxi, donating the dinner to the German babies. On his second call the uncle was waiting; Lanny, explaining that he had to attend a night session of one of the commissions, got down to business at once. "Uncle Jesse, do you agree that the blockade of Central Europe should be lifted?"

"I am an internationalist," replied the other. "I am opposed to every such interference with human liberty."

"You know people who are working to have it lifted—I mean they are writing and publishing and speaking in support of that demand, aren't they?"

"Yes; but what—?"

"I have a friend, who for important reasons cannot be named. It's enough that I know him intimately, and trust him. He feels about this blockade as you do, and it happens that he has a great deal of money. He asked me to suggest some way that he could put money into the hands of someone who would spend it for that purpose. I took the liberty of naming you."

"The devil you did!" said Uncle Jesse. "What then?"

"You realize that I don't know you very well—I haven't been allowed to. But I have the impression that you have real convictions, and wouldn't misapply funds that you accepted for such a cause."

"You have guessed correctly in that."

"No doubt you have friends who are trying to raise money for promoting your party, or whatever it is?"

"We get it by persuading poor workingmen to cut down on their food. We don't have rich people coming and dropping it into our laps."

"Well, this is one time it may happen—if you say the word."

"How much will it be?"

"The first payment will be ten thousand francs, in bank notes of small denominations."

"Jesus Christ!" said Uncle Jesse. Lanny had heard that these Reds were nearly all hostile to the accepted religion, but they still had one use for its founder.

"You have to pledge your word to spend it in the quickest and most effective way to promote a popular demand for the lifting of the blockade throughout Europe. If there are signs that you are spending it effectively, more will come—as much as you can handle."

"How will I get it?"

"Someone will knock on your door at midnight tonight. When you open the door the person will say 'Jesse,' and you will answer 'Uncle,' and a package will be put into your hands."

The painter sat eying his young nephew. "Look here, Lanny," said he. "The police and military are busy setting traps for people like me. Are you sure this isn't a scheme of some of the Crillon crowd?"

"I can't tell you whose scheme it is, but I assure you that the Crillon knows nothing about it, and neither do the police. They'll probably take notice as soon as you begin spending the money. That's a risk you have to run."

"Naturally," said Uncle Jesse, and pondered again. "I suppose," he remarked, "this is some of the 'German gold' we read about in the reptile press."

"You mustn't ask any questions."

"I'm free to spend the money according to my own judgment?"

"For the purpose agreed upon, yes."

The painter thought some more. "Son, this is wartime. Have you thought what you're getting in for?"

"You take risks for what you believe, don't you?"

"Yes, but you're a youngster, and you happen to be my sister's son, and she's a good scout, even if her brains don't always work. This could get you into one hell of a mess."

"If you don't mention me, there's no way it can get out. Wild horses couldn't drag it out of my friend."

Again a pause; and the bald-headed painter smiled one of his crooked smiles. "Perhaps you read in the papers how Lenin was in Switzerland when the Russian Revolution broke out, and he wanted very much to get into Russia. The German government wanted him there and sent him through in a sealed train. They had their reasons for sending him and he had his reasons for going. His reasons won out."

Lanny got the point and smiled in his turn. The uncle thought for a while and then told him how, many years ago, there had been a big fuss in America over the fact that multimillionaires who had corrupted legislatures and courts were trying to win public favor by giving sums of money to colleges. It was called "tainted money," and there was a clamor that colleges should refuse such donations. One college professor, more robust than the rest of the tribe, had got up in a meeting and cried: "Bring on your tainted money!" The painter laughed and said: "That's me!"

30

Out of the Depths

I

On the fourteenth of February the Supreme Council ratified the Covenant of the League of Nations at a stately ceremony; and immediately thereafter President Wilson took the night train for Brest, to return to Washington for the closing sessions of Congress. He and his purple-clad lady walked on red plush carpets spread all the way to the train, between rows of potted palms set out by a polite government. All official France attended to see him off; and thereafter it was as in a barn when the cat has departed and the mice come out to devour the stores of grain. The diplomats of the great states began helping themselves to German and Russian territory, and the reactionary newspapers of Paris declared with one voice that the foolish and utopian League was already dead and that the problems of Europe were going to be settled on a "realistic" basis.

Professor Alston said that this was the voice of Clemenceau, who controlled a dozen newspapers of the capital and could change their policies by crooking his finger. Alston and his friends were greatly depressed. What was the use of meeting all day and most of the night, wrestling over questions of fair play and "self-determination," when it was evident that those who held the reins of power would not pay the least attention to anything you said? The French delegates now wore a cynical smile as they argued before the commissions; they had their assurance that their armies were going to hold the Rhineland and the Sarre, and that a series of buffer states were to be set up between Germany and Russia, all owing

575

their existence to France, all financed with the savings of the French peasants, and munitioned by Zaharoff, alias Schneider-Creusot. France and Britain were going to divide Persia and Mesopotamia and Syria and make a deal for the oil and the laying of pipelines. Italy was to take the Adriatic, Japan was to take Shantung—all such matters were being settled among sensible men.

Lanny continued to attend sessions and listen to tedious discussions of imaginary boundary lines. His chief was called in to advise the American delegates on the commission which was trying to pacify the Italians and the Yugoslavs, who for a month or two had been taking pot-shots at one another. The revolting Yugoslav sailors had seized the Austrian war vessels, and the Italians wanted them, but the Yugoslav sailors wanted the Americans to take charge of them. The Italians were trying to seize Fiume, a city which hadn't been granted to them even in the secret treaty. They were like the man who said he wasn't greedy for land, he just wanted the land adjoining his own. They made a fuss, they interrupted proceedings, they blocked decisions on other questions—and how execrable was their accent when they tried to speak French!

A pathetic victim of this system of muddle was George D. Herron. He had been formally appointed a member of a delegation to travel to Prinkipo; but now President Wilson had set out for America without even taking the trouble to let him know that the project was dropped. The poor man, whose arthritis made moving about an ordeal, was left to spend his money and time holding preliminary consultations with various Russian groups in Paris; he would convince them one day and the French would unconvince them the next. The first hint he got that he had been laid on the shelf was when his friend Alston brought him a report that the President had appointed a mission which was already on its way to Moscow, to find out the situation and report.

Watching Herron and listening to him, Lanny learned how dangerous it was to have anything to do with unpopular ideas. The prophet was called a Red, when in truth he looked upon Bolshevism as his Hebrew predecessors looked upon Baal and Moloch. He had heard about Jesse Blackless and was worried for fear Lanny might be lured by the false faith of his uncle. He told the youth, in his biblical language, that dictatorship was a degradation of the soul of man, and that anyone who took that road would find himself in the valley of the shadow of death. Either Socialism must be the free, democratic choice of the people, or it would be something worse than the rule of Mammon which it sought to replace. Lanny promised very gravely that he would remember this lesson. Privately, he didn't think he was going to need it.

II

The conspirator for charity expected every day to have a note from Kurt, but none came. He spent some time trying to figure out what Kurt would be doing, and wondering if it would be possible for a German spy in Paris to be apprehended and shot without anything getting into the papers. There were great numbers of persons of German descent living in Switzerland, in Holland and the Scandinavian countries, so it was possible for Germans to pass as citizens of these countries. All through the war German spies had been doing this, and there was no reason to imagine that they had all gone home when the armistice was signed. Kurt must be a member of such a group; and being young, he would have a superior who told him what to do.

When the weather was decent and Lanny had time, he liked to walk, to get the air of the overheated conference rooms out of his lungs. One of his walks took him to Montmartre, and he climbed the musty stairs of the old tenement, and found his uncle covered up on his cot to keep warm, absorbed in the reading of a workers' newspaper. The first thing the uncle said was: "Well, by God, from now on I believe in Santa Claus!"

It really had happened: the knock on his door, the exchange of passwords, the package placed in his hands! He chuckled as if it was the funniest thing that had occurred to a Red agitator since the birth of Karl Marx. "Every sou has been honestly spent, so tell your friend to come again—the sooner the better!

"Did you notice the *affiches?*" continued the painter; and Lanny said he hadn't seen any referring to the lifting of the blockade against Germany, but on the kiosks he had noticed in big red letters a call for a *réunion* that evening, to demand government action against the rise in food prices. "That is ours," said the uncle. "We couldn't post anything on behalf of Germany—the *flics* would be down on us before we got started. But they can't prevent our defending the rights of French workers and returned soldiers."

"As a matter of fact, Uncle Jesse," asked the youth, "if they allow food to be exported into Germany, won't that make it scarcer in France?"

"The Germans don't want any food from France," replied the other. "They can buy it from America. What we want the French government to do is to get after the middlemen and speculators who are holding food in warehouses and letting it spoil because they can make more when prices are high."

Jesse Blackless launched upon an exposition of his political views. He had been a "syndicalist," which meant that he supported the left-wing labor unions, whose aim was to take over industry for the workers. But recent events in Russia had convinced him that the Bolshevik program represented the way to victory, even though it might mean the surrender of some liberties for a time. "You have to have discipline if you expect to win any sort of war," said the rebel painter. It was practically the opposite of what Herron had said.

Lanny really wanted to oblige his father; but how could he hold his present job without giving thought to the ideas of these Bolsheviks? In the Crillon people talked about them all the time. You couldn't discuss the problems of any state or province of Central Europe without their being brought up. "If you don't lend us money, if you don't give us food, our people will go over to the Bolsheviks. . . . If you don't give us guns, how can we put down the Bolsheviks? . . . If you take our territory away from us, we will throw ourselves into the arms of the Bolsheviks." Such were the utterances in every conference room. Often it was a form of blackmail, and the French would resent it with fury. The ruling classes of Germany, Austria, and Hungary were playing up this fear in order to get out of paying for the ruin they had wrought in Europe. "All right!" the French would answer. "Go to Moscow or go to hell, it makes no difference to us."

But this was a bluff. As soon as they had said it, the French would look at one another in fear. What if the Red wave were to spread in Poland, as it had spread in Hungary and Bavaria? If the Reds got the upper hand in Berlin, with whom would the Allies sign a treaty of peace? The Americans would ask this, and French and British diplomats didn't know what to answer, and took out their irritation on the persons who asked the questions. They must be Reds, too!

III

"Would you like to come to the *réunion* tonight?" asked Uncle Jesse; and Lanny said he would if his duties left him a chance. "I won't offer to take you," said the other. "It'll be better for the Crillon if you're not seen with me."

It happened that the staff at the Majestic was giving a dance that evening, and Lanny had a date with a fair-haired English secretary who reminded him of Rosemary. He thought she might find it romantic to take in a Red meeting, and do the dancing later. Lanny could call it a matter of duty, for he had told his chief about it and Alston had said: "Let me have a report on it."

The *salle* was in a teeming working-class quarter, and apparently not large enough for the thousand or two who wanted to get in. Lanny and his young lady were among the fortunate ones, because they were recognized as foreigners, and people made way for them. The place was hazy with tobacco smoke, and up on the platform, among a dozen other men and women, Lanny saw his uncle. He saw no one else whom he knew, for these were not the sort of persons one met at Mrs. Emily's teas. There was a sprinkling of intellectuals, art students, and others whom you could recognize by their garb, but for the most part those present were workers and returned soldiers, their faces haggard from long years of strain.

Lanny would be in a position to report to his chief that the workers of Paris were bitterly discontented with their lot. Hardly had the speakers got started before the shouting began, and he was a poor speaker indeed who could not cause some auditor to rise and shake his clenched right hand in the air and shout "*à bas*" somebody or something. There were no poor speakers, by that standard; they all knew their audience and how to work it into a fury, how to bring first murmurs and then hoots and jeers against bureaucrats and bemedaled militarists who feasted and danced while food was rotting in the warehouses and the poor in their dens were perishing of slow starvation.

Especial object of their hatred appeared to be Georges Clemenceau. Traitor, rat, Judas, were the mildest names they called him; for the "tiger of France" had been in his youth a *communard*, one of themselves, and had served a term in prison for his revolutionary activities. Now, like the other politicians, he had sold out to the capitalists, now he was a gang leader for the rich. Lanny was interested to discover that these workers knew most of the facts about Clemenceau which his father had been telling him. One of the speakers mentioned Zaharoff—and there was booing that might have brought a shudder to the Grand Officer. They knew about Clemenceau's control of the press; when the speaker said that journalists were bought and sold in Paris like rotten fish the crowd showed neither surprise nor displeasure.

Lanny was surprised to discover that his uncle was an effective orator. The sardonic, crooked smile became a furious sneer, his irony a corroding acid that destroyed whatever it touched. The painter was there to see to it that the real theme of the evening was adequately covered; he pointed out that the workers of France were not the only ones who were being starved, the same fate was being deliberately dealt to the workers of Germany, Austria, Hungary. All the workers of Europe were learning that their fate was the same and their cause the same; all were resolving that never again would they fight one another, but turn their guns against the capitalist class, the author of their sufferings, the agent of their suppression, the one real enemy of the people throughout the world. The English girl, of course, didn't know he was Lanny's uncle, and after she had listened to his tirade for a while, she exclaimed: "Oh, what a vicious person!"

IV

Lanny told himself that he was observing this *réunion* professionally; he was going to make a report. Every day for seven weeks and more he had been translating reports, revising reports, filing reports. And now he was going to report on the sentiments of the working classes of Paris. Should he say that they no longer had any feelings of enmity against the *sales boches*, but that all their fury was turned against Clemenceau and his government? Hardly that—for it was obvious that this was a special group, who had come to listen to the sort of speeches they enjoyed. And even they were not unanimous. Every now and then there were cries of dissent; a man would leap up and shout contradictions and others would howl him down. More than once there was uproar and confusion, men seizing the impromptu orator and pulling him into his seat; if he resisted, there would be fist-fighting, and perhaps chairs wielded as a convenient weapon. It appeared that much of the opposition was organized; there were groups of protestants looking for trouble. They were the *Camelots du Roi*, the royalists of France; their inspirer a raging journalist named Maurras, who in the paper which he edited did not hesitate to call for riots and murders.

Lanny, as he listened, kept thinking of the French revolution. Jean Marat, "friend of the people," living in the sewers of Paris to escape his enemies, had come forth to deliver just such speeches, denouncing the aristocrats and demanding their blood. Here too one saw the *tricoteuses*, grandmotherly-looking old women who sat knitting, and at the same time listening attentively; every once in a while one of them would open her mouth and scream: *"Mort aux traîtres!"*—and without missing a single stitch.

Lanny watched the faces. Sinister and dark they seemed, but full of pain, so that he was divided between fear and pity. He knew there were whole districts of Paris which were vast "cabbage patches," in which the poor were housed in dingy, rotting buildings centuries old. They had suffered privations so that Zaharoff and his friends might have their war to the finish; and now, with production almost stopped and trade disorganized while diplomats and statesmen wrangled—could it be expected that they would not complain?

Among those packed against the walls of the *salle* was a youth whose violent gestures caught Lanny's attention. You could know that he was a workingman by the fact that he wore a corduroy suit and a cotton shirt with no collar or tie. His face was emaciated, unshaven, and unkempt, but there was a light in his eyes as of one seeing visions. He was so wrought up by the oratory that his lips kept moving, as if he were repeating the phrases he heard; his hands were clenched, and when at the end of a climax he shouted approval, he shook not one but both fists in the air.

Lanny tried to imagine what life must seem to a youth like that. He was about Lanny's age, but how different in his fate! He wouldn't know much about the forces which moved the world; he would know only suffering, and the fact that it was caused by those in authority, the rulers and the rich. Maybe that wasn't the truth, but he would think it was, and Lanny would have a hard time contradicting him. The well-educated young Englishwoman, whose father was a stockbroker at home, had called Jesse Blackless a "vicious person"; and maybe he was that, but all the same, Lanny knew that what his uncle was saying was true. When he raged at the Clemenceau government because it had stopped in Berne a shipment of Red Cross medical supplies intended for the ailing children in Austria, Lanny knew it had happened, and that Mr. Herbert Hoover, most conservative of businessmen, was uttering in the Hotel Crillon censure fully as severe—and far more profane.

When the meeting was over, Lanny saw the young workingman

elbowing his way to the front. He went onto the stage and grabbed Jesse Blackless by the hands and shook them. The painter patted him on the back, and Lanny wondered, was this unkempt youth a friend of his uncle's, a member of his group, or just a convert, or a prospect? Lanny continued to reflect upon it, only half hearing the shocked comments of Penelope Selden, his lady friend.

They got into a taxi to drive to the Majestic, and on the way she forgot politics and put her hand in his. They danced together in the onyx-lined ballroom; a gay and festive scene, with half the men and many of the women wearing uniforms. They too had suffered, and been under strain; they too needed relaxation from heavy duties, and it wasn't fair to blame them for dancing. But Lanny was haunted by the faces of the angry workers; he was haunted by the millions of children who were growing up stunted and deformed, because of things which these dancing ladies and gentlemen had done and were still doing.

The young English girl, with soft brown hair and merry eyes and disposition, was pleasant to hold in your arms. Lanny held her for an hour, dancing with no one else; she made plain that she liked him, and he had got the impression that she would be his for the asking. So many of the women were in a reckless mood, in these days of deliverance from anxieties too greatly prolonged. Lanny couldn't very well say to her: "I've had an unhappy love affair, and I've sworn off the sex business for a while." What he said was: "Don't you think maybe your chief could do something with Lloyd George, if he told him about this meeting, and what a fury the people are in? Really, you know, it's a very bad state of affairs!"

V

Lieutenant Jerry Pendleton showed up in Paris, having got a week's leave. He had won promotion in the Argonne Forest by the method of being luckier than other sergeants of his outfit. In his new uniform he looked handsome and dignified, and Lanny at first thought he was the same gay and buoyant red-head from whom he had parted back at Camp Devens. But soon he noticed that Jerry had a tendency to fall silent, and there would come a brooding, somber look. Apparently going to war did something to a man. Lanny had been expecting to be entertained with accounts of hairbreadth 'scapes i' the imminent deadly breach; but his former tutor said: "Let's not talk about it, kid. All I want is to go home and try to forget."

"Aren't you going down to see Cerise?"

"I haven't enough time."

Lanny knew that wasn't true, for Jerry could have taken the night express and been in Cannes in the morning. The youth let the subject drop; but later, after he had told about his misadventure with Gracyn in Connecticut, the lieutenant warmed up and revealed what was troubling his mind. "The plain truth is, I just don't like the French. I'm sore at the whole damn country."

"What have they done to you?"

"It's just that we're so different, I guess. I'm always stumbling on things I dislike. I realize I don't know Cerise very well, and I'm never going to be allowed to know her until I've married her; and then what will I find out?"

"My mother married a Frenchman, and they were very happy."

"Your mother lived here a long time and probably knew how to choose. I've seen so many things in France that I want to get away from. Manure-piles!"

Lanny laughed. Having spent nearly all his life in France, he assumed that this national institution was necessary to the agricultural process. But Jerry said they ordered things differently in Kansas; everything there was clean and agreeable, even the hogs. Lanny was amused, because when Jerry Pendleton had first made his appearance on the Riviera he had described his home state as a dull, provincial place, and had earnestly desired not to go back and help run two drug stores.

But now what a change! "I fought to save these people," said the lieutenant of a machine-gun company, "and now I have to bite every franc to see if it's made of lead."

"That can happen anywhere in Europe," replied his friend.

"It doesn't happen in Koblenz," declared the other, emphatically. He was part of the army which had gone into the Rhineland to guard the bridgeheads pending the signing of a treaty. Jerry's brigade was covering a semicircle of German territory, some forty miles in diameter on the far side of the river, and his company had been quartered for three months in a tiny village where they had every opportunity to know the population. The lieutenant himself was billeted in a farmhouse where everything was so neat, and the old couple so kind, so patient and humble, grateful for the tiniest favor—it was exactly as Kurt had told Lanny it would be, the dough-boys had learned that the Germans were not the Huns they had been pictured. More and more the Americans were wondering why they had had to fight such people, and how much longer they were going to have to stay and blockade them from the rest of the world.

The Rhineland is a rich country and produces food and wine in abundance; but it had been just behind the fighting front for four years and the retreating German armies had carried off all they could. Now the people were living on the scantiest rations and the children were pale and hollow-eyed. The well-fed Yanks were expected to live in houses with undernourished children and preg-nant women and never give them food. There were strict orders against "fraternizing with the enemy"; but did that include stuffing half a load of bread into your overcoat pocket and passing it out to the kids?

And what about the Fräuleins, those sweet-faced, gentle creatures with golden or straw-colored braids down their backs, and white dresses with homemade embroidery on the edges? Their fellows had been marched back into the interior of Germany, and here were handsome upstanding conquerors from the far-off prairie states, with chocolates and canned peaches and other unthinkable delicacies at their disposal. Lieutenant Pendleton chuckled as he told about what must surely have been the oddest military regulation ever issued in the history of warfare; the doughboys had been officially informed that entering into intimate relations with German Fräuleins was not to be considered as "fraternizing" within the meaning of the army regulations!

"Is that why you've lost interest in Cannes?" asked Lanny, with a grin.

"No," said Jerry, "but I'll tell you this. If somebody doesn't hurry up and make up his mind about peace terms, a lot of our fellows are just going to take things into their own hands and go home—and their Fräuleins with them. What's the matter with these old men in Paris, Lanny?"

"I'll introduce you to some of them," answered the youth, "and you can find out for yourself."

VI

Jerry Pendleton having lunch at the Crillon; a piece of luck that rarely fell to the lot of a "shavetail," even one who had fought through a war! It would be something to tell at the officers' mess in the Rhineland; it would be something to tell to his grandchildren in Kansas, in days when all this was in the history books—the "First World War."

Lanny sat at table with his chief, because meals were times for confidential chats and informal reports, and perhaps for helping to translate the excited French of somebody who wanted more territory for his tiny state. A young officer on leave from the front might hear things that would give him a jolt—for these college professors had opinions of their own, and did not hesitate to bandy about the most exalted names.

The young lieutenant was asked to what unit he belonged and what service he had seen. When he said that he had been through the Meuse-Argonne—well, it was no great distinction, for more than a million others could say the same, not counting fifty thousand or so who would never speak of that, or anything else. The conversation turned to that six weeks' blood-bath, hailed as a glory in the press at home. What was the real truth about it? Had Foch wished to set the Americans a task at which no army could succeed?

Had he been punishing General Pershing for obstinacy and presumption?

The young lieutenant learned that from the hour when the first American division had been landed in France there had been a war going on between the American commander-in-chief and the British and French commands, backed by their governments. It had been their idea that American troops should be brigaded in with British and French troops and used to replace the wastage of their battles; but Pershing had been determined that there should be an American army, fighting under the American flag. He had declared this purpose and hung onto it like any British bulldog. But the others had never given up; they had used each new defeat as an excuse for putting pressure; they had pulled every sort of political wire and worried every American who had any authority or influence.

So, by the summer of 1918, they had managed to acquire a pretty complete dislike of the jimber-jawed Missouri general. When Baker, Secretary of War, had visited England, Lloyd George had tactfully suggested that President Wilson should be requested to remove Pershing; to which the secretary had replied coldly that the American government was not in need of having anyone decide who should command American troops. Clemenceau had written a long letter to Foch, insisting that he should appeal to President Wilson to remove Pershing, on the ground that he had proved himself incompetent to handle armies in battle. Alston said he had seen a copy of that letter, though he wasn't at liberty to tell who had shown it to him. What more likely than that the generalissimo of all the Allied forces had said to himself: "Well, if this stubborn fellow is determined to have his own way, we'll give him something to do that will keep him busy."

After listening to such conversation, Lanny and his friend strolled down the Champs-Élysées, between the mile-long rows of captured cannon, and for the first time and the last the lieutenant was moved to "open up" to his friend. "My God, Lanny!" he exclaimed. "Imagine fifty thousand lives being wiped out because two generals were jealous of each other!"

"History is full of things like that," remarked the youth. "Ten thousand men march out and die because the king's mistress has been snubbed by an ambassador."

The ex-tutor went on to pour out the dreadful story of the Meuse-Argonne, a mass of hills and rocks covered with forest and brush. "Of course that's all gone now," said Jerry, "because we blasted every green thing from a couple of hundred square miles; we even blew off the tops of some of the hills. The Germans had been working for four years making it a tangle of wire, with machine guns hidden every few yards, and dugouts and concrete shelters. We were told to go and take such and such places, no matter what the cost, and we took them—wave after wave of men, falling in rows. I saw a man's head blown off within three feet of me, and I wiped his brains out of my eyes. We had whole regiments that just ceased to exist."

"I heard about it," said Lanny.

"You might, because you met insiders; but the folks at home haven't the remotest idea, and won't ever be told. Military men say that troops can stand twenty percent losses; more than that, they go to pieces. But we had many an outfit with only twenty percent survivors and they went on fighting. There was nothing else you could do, because you were in there and the only way out was forward. The hell of it was that the roads ran crossways to our line of advance, so there was never any way to get in supplies except on men's backs. You took a position, and flopped down into a shell hole, and there you lay day and night, with shells crashing around you and bullets whining just over your head. The rain drenched you and near froze at night, and you had no food, and no water but the rain you caught in your tin hat; all around were men groaning and screaming, and nothing to do but lie there and die. That's modern war, by God, and if they give me any more of it, I'm going to turn Bolo."

"Be careful how you say it, Jerry," warned his friend. "There really are Bolos, you know, and they're working in our army."

"Well, tell those old fellows at the Crillon to hurry up and settle it and send us home, or my outfit will turn Bolo without anybody having to do any work at all."

VII

Next morning Lanny had his light French breakfast and went to Alston's office. He was standing by the latter's desk, going over their schedule for the day, when in came Professor Davisson; the big, stout man was hurrying, greatly excited. "Clemenceau's been shot!"

"What?" exclaimed Alston, starting up.

"Anarchist got him as he was on his way here to see House."

"Is he dead?"

"Badly hurt, they say."

Others of the staff came in; the building was like an ants' nest when something upsets it. Everybody's plans were bowled over; for what was the use of holding conferences and making reports, when the whole thing would have to be done over? If the Tiger died, Poincaré would take his place; and the professors who had been scolding Clemenceau now had a sickening realization that he was a man of genius and a statesman compared with his probable successor, a dull pasty-faced lawyer who came from Lorraine, and therefore had drunk in hatred of Germany with his mother's milk. If Poincaré got the reins of power in his hands there would be no more talk of compromises, but a straight-out campaign to cripple Germany forever.

Clemenceau had been driving from his home, and as his limousine turned into the Avenue du Trocadéro, a young worker wearing corduroy clothing had stepped from behind a kiosk and fired eight or ten shots at him. Two had struck the elderly premier, one in the shoulder and one in the chest; it was believed that a lung had been penetrated, and there seemed little chance of life for a man of seventy-eight, a diabetic, weakened by four years of terrific strain.

"Well, that's the end of peace-making," said Alston. The staff agreed that it would mean a wave of reaction in France and the suppression of left-wing opinion.

But the old man didn't die; he behaved in amazing fashion—with a bullet hole in his lung he didn't want even to be sick. Reports came in every few minutes; the doctors were having a hard time persuading him to lie down; he could hardly speak, and a bloody foam came out of his mouth, but he wanted to go on holding conferences. The Tiger indeed; a hard beast to kill! Of course he became the hero of France and people waited hour by hour for bulletins as to his fate.

A messenger brought in newspapers with accounts of the affair. The assassin had been seized by the crowd, which mauled him and tried to kill him; the papers gave pictures of him being held by a couple of gendarmes who had protected and saved him. His name was Cottin, and he was said to be a known anarchist; the photographs showed a frail, disheveled, frightened-looking young fellow. Lanny studied them, and a strange feeling began to stir in him. "Where have I seen that face?" As in a lightning flash it came to him: the youth whom he had watched in the *salle* while Jesse Blackless was making his speech! No doubt about it, for Lanny had watched the face off and on for an hour, taking it as a symbol of the inflamed and rebellious masses.

Lanny's last glimpse of the young worker had been on the platform, with Uncle Jesse patting him on the back. Lanny had wondered then, and wondered now with greater intensity, did that mean that he was a friend of the painter, or merely an admirer, a stranger moved by his speech? Was this attempted killing the kind of political warfare that Uncle Jesse favored, whether publicly or secretly? Lanny remembered what his father had said, that syndicalism was for practical purposes the same as anarchism. Now Uncle Jesse had said that he had adopted the theories of the Bolsheviks. Did this by any chance include taking pot-shots at one's opponents on the street?

Decidedly a serious question for a youth getting launched upon a diplomatic career! To be sure, his chief had told him to go to the meeting and report; but nobody had told him to go secretly to the home of a syndicalist-Bolshevik conspirator and arrange for him to receive ten thousand francs of German money to be used in stirring up the workers of Paris to commit assassinations. Of course nobody at the meeting had directly advised the killing off of unsatisfactory statesmen, but it was an inference readily drawn from the furious denunciations poured upon the statesmen's heads. The orators might disclaim responsibility, but certainly they must know the probable result of such speeches.

Lanny's thought moved on from his uncle to his intimate friend. How much had Kurt known, and how far was he responsible for what had happened? It had become clear to Lanny that Kurt's money was being used for a lot more than the lifting of the blockade of Germany. Uncle Jesse had explained by saying that the police wouldn't allow a meeting on behalf of Germans, so the subject had to be brought in under camouflage. Lanny hadn't thought about the matter long before realizing that he had been extremely naïve. The obvious way to relieve French pressure on Germany was to frighten France with the same kind of Bolshevist disturbances that were taking place throughout Central Europe. Kurt and his group were here for that, and they were using camouflage just as Uncle Jesse was.

VIII

A lot of complications to occupy the thoughts of a secretary supposed to be marking for his chief's attention a dozen conflicting reports on the proper boundary between the city of Fiume, inhabited by tumultuous Italians, and its suburb Susak, on the other side of a creek, inhabited by intransigent Yugoslavs! Lanny sat with a stack of .documents before him: American, British, and French recommendations, and translations of Italian charges and Yugoslav countercharges. He sat with wrinkled brows, but it wasn't over these problems. He was saying to himself: "What does Kurt think about assassination of statesmen as a means of influencing national

decisions? And would he be willing to use me for such a purpose?"
Lanny's sense of fair play compelled him to add that Kurt had given
him warning. Kurt had said: "Forgive me if I am not a friend at
present. My time is not my own, nor my life."

Of course the attempt on Clemenceau would rouse the French
police and military to vigorous action. They would begin a round-up
of the associates of the anarchist youth; they would subject them
to inquisition, trying to find out if there had been a conspiracy, and
if there was danger to other statesmen. No doubt they had spies
in Uncle Jesse's movement and must know of his sudden appearance
with a large sum of money. Perhaps they had him already and were
questioning him about the source of those funds! Lanny was sure
that his uncle wouldn't "give him away"; but still, he got a sudden
realization how close to a powder magazine he had been walking.
Yes, modern society was something dangerous and insecure, and a
youth who strolled blandly along, feeling safe because he was well
dressed and his father was rich—such a youth might see the earth
open up in front of him and masses of searing flame shoot out into
his face. Lanny decided that for the present he would repress his
curiosity as to the relationship between his uncle and the anarchist
Cottin; also that if he should meet his friend Kurt Meissner again
he would be extremely reserved and cautious.

IX

Two days passed, and Clemenceau didn't die, but on the contrary
was announcing that he would be back on the job of peace-making
in half a week. Then one afternoon in Lanny's mail he found a note
reading: "Meet me at the same place, same time. Sam."

Professor Alston was to advise some American delegates on the
Fiume problem that evening. They probably wouldn't get through
by eleven o'clock; but Lanny had been working faithfully, and felt
justified in asking to be excused at five minutes before the hour.
Wrapped in his warm trench overcoat, which had a detachable
sheepskin lining, and wearing a waterproof hat against the driving

rain, the youth strolled out of the hotel, across the wide avenue, and past the great gun which Kurt had once used to blow entrenchments and poilus to Kingdom Come. The German officer came from the other direction and fell in beside him, and they walked between the rows of monstrous engines rusting in the rain. "Well, Kurt?" said Lanny, seeing that his friend didn't speak at once.

"I have no right to call on you," said the other, at last. "But I'm in danger, and I thought you might wish to know it."

"What is it?"

"The police have raided the group with whom I have been working. I went last night to the place where I stay. I always make it a practice to walk on the other side of the street, looking for a window signal indicating that everything is all right. I saw a police van drawn up in front and they were taking people out of the house. I walked on, and I've been walking the streets most of the time since. I don't know any place to go."

Lanny didn't need to be told how serious this danger was. "Have you any reason to think the police know about you?"

"How can I tell what they know? I'm sure my leader won't talk, and we never kept any papers in the place. But one can never be sure what has happened in this business."

"I've been watching the newspapers. There's been nothing in them."

"The police would surely not make anything public about spies."

"How long have you been at this work, Kurt?"

"Only since the armistice. I got into it because of you."

"Of *me?*"

"My father has a friend in Switzerland—the man who used to forward my letters to you. After the armistice he asked me to come and see him. He told me he had been doing government work, and offered me an important duty to help the Fatherland. I accepted."

"How many others of your people know about you?"

"I don't know for certain. The other side may have had a spy among us. It's the attempt on Clemenceau that has stirred them up, of course."

"You must tell me the truth about that, Kurt. It's been worrying me a lot."

"What do you mean?"

"Whether you had anything to do with that attack."

"Oh, my God, Lanny! What put that idea into your head?"

"Well, I have realized that you are trying to stir up revolt here. And it's fair to assume that some of your agents would be in touch with people like that anarchist."

"I don't know whether they are or not, Lanny, but, granting it, we have nothing to gain by such an attempt. It has set us back, it may have ruined everything. I assure you my associates are not fools. Would they want to put Poincaré in power?"

"I can have your word of honor, Kurt, that you and your people had nothing to do with that attack?"

"You have that absolutely."

"It's a mighty serious matter for me, you know."

"I understand that fully. That's why I walked the streets all day, trying to make up my mind to call upon you. I'm not sure that I have the right to, and if you decline to touch the matter, I'll not blame you."

"I want to help you, Kurt, and I will."

"You know what would happen if you were caught aiding an enemy agent."

"I'm willing to take a chance on that—provided I know that neither you nor your friends have been destroying life or property."

"The truth is, Lanny, I have no idea what they did before the armistice. I suppose they were doing everything they could to help the Fatherland. But now they are trying to soften the French government by promoting political opposition. We have such troubles to deal with at home, and why shouldn't the French have their share?"

"That's all right with me," said the French-American, with a grin.

X

They had come to the embankment of the Seine, and were walking along the *quais*, close together, talking low, with wind and pelting rain to absorb their voices. When a passer-by came, they fell silent until he was gone. Lanny was thinking busily: "What shall I do? Kurt can't stay out on a night like this." Already the rain was turning to sleet.

"Let's get down to the problem," he said. "I can't take you to my rooms, because I share them with two other fellows. I can't take you to my uncle, because the police may have him already."

"That is true."

"Wherever we go, we'll have to take somebody into our confidence. It wouldn't be decent to introduce you under a false name. One can't play a trick like that on one's friends."

"I suppose not."

"I believe Mrs. Chattersworth would be sympathetic, but she has so much company, and you'd have to meet people, otherwise the servants would think it strange."

"The servants will make trouble anywhere."

"I might get a car and drive you down to Juan; but the servants know you, and have heard my mother and me talking about you during the war."

"That's out."

"I thought of Isadora Duncan, who's in Paris. She's an internationalist and has queer people around her all the time. But the trouble is, she's irresponsible. They say she's drinking—the war just about drove her crazy."

There was a pause while he thought some more. "I believe our best guess is my mother. She's not very good at keeping secrets, but she'd surely keep this one because it means danger for me also."

"Where is she?"

"In an apartment in a small hotel. Most of the time she's invited out to meals, but she has breakfast sent to her rooms. She has no servant except a maid, and could find some excuse to get rid of her. That's the one way I can think of to get you hidden."

"But, Lanny, would your mother be willing to have a strange man in her apartment?"

"You aren't a stranger; you're my friend, and my mother knows how dear you are to me. It would be inconvenient, of course; but it's a matter of life or death."

"But don't you see, Lanny—the hotel people would be sure that she had a lover. There couldn't be any other assumption."

"They don't pay so much attention to that in Paris; and Beauty knows what it is to be gossiped about. You see, she lived with Marcel for years before they were married. All her friends know that story, and you might as well know it too."

"I only saw your mother for a few hours, Lanny, but I thought she was a wonderful person."

"She's been through a lot since then, and it's left her sort of distracted and at loose ends. She's only recently got reconciled to the idea that she's never going to see her husband again. Now she's figuring how the world may be persuaded to recognize his genius. He really had it, Kurt."

The gusts of icy rain were blowing into their faces from across the river, and Lanny turned into a side street. "The hotel is up here," he said.

"You mean to take me there without telling her?"

"I'll phone and make sure she's alone. She won't want you left out in this rain, that I know. Tomorrow the three of us will have to figure out some way to get you out of France."

31

In the Enemy's Country

I

PRESIDENT WILSON was back in the United States, taking up the heaviest of all his burdens, that of persuading the American people to accept his League of Nations. He had wrought them into a mood of military fervor, and the war had ended too suddenly. In the November elections, a few days before the armistice, they had chosen a majority of reactionary Republicans, determined to have no more nonsense about idealism but to think about America first, last, and all the time. President Wilson invited the opposition chieftains to a dinner party, and they came, but neither good food nor moral fervor moved them from their surly skepticism. Wilson had, so he told the world, a "one-track mind." Now he was traveling on that track, and the Senate leaders were digging a wide and deep ditch at the end of it.

Of course the election results were known in Paris, and were one of the factors undermining the President's position. Both Lloyd George and Clemenceau had consulted their people and had their full consent to the program of "making Germany pay." Their newspapers were taunting the American President with the fact that his people were not behind him; now they printed the news about his failures in Washington, and on that basis went ahead to remake the world nearer to their hearts' desire.

Already they had fourteen little wars going—one for each of the Fourteen Points, said Professor Alston, bitterly. They were getting ready for the really big war, the Allied invasion of Russia. The blockade was screwed down tighter than ever; the Allies refused to lift it even from Poland and the new state of Czechoslovakia, for fear that supplies might get into Germany, or that Red agents might get out through the *cordon sanitaire*.

Clemenceau got out of his sick bed and resumed his place in command of the conference. He sat slumped in his chair, a pitiful, shrunken figure—but try to take anything from under his claws, and hear the Tiger snarl! This statesman aged in bitterness had performed a strange mental feat, transferring all that he had of love to an abstraction called *la patrie*. Individual Frenchmen he despised, along with all other human creatures; he humiliated and browbeat his subordinates in public, and poured the acid of his wit upon the pretense of idealism in any person in public life. But France was glory, France was God, and for her safety he was willing to destroy everything else in Europe and indeed in the world.

Colonel House was representing the President. The "little white mouse" didn't have a one-track mind, and hadn't come to Europe unprepared; he knew the age-long hatreds which made life a torment on that continent. He was trying to placate and persuade, and was sending long cablegrams to his chief about his great failures and his small successes. The staff at the Crillon watched and whispered, and the hundred and fifty registered newspaper correspondents from America hung about on the outskirts, gathering rumors and sending long wireless messages about secret covenants being secretly arrived at.

II

Meanwhile Lanny was taking all the time his chief could spare to run over to his mother's hotel and try to solve the embarrassing problem of his German friend. First he had the bright idea that Jerry Pendleton was the trustworthy person who would take this charge of dynamite off his hands. Jerry was going back to his regiment; surely he could take with him a Swiss musician friend, and find some pretext, a concert or something, to get him into Koblenz. Let him entertain the regiment! After that it would be easy for him to disappear into Germany, for the American lines were loosely held and peasants and others came freely into Koblenz.

Lanny even worked up a likely story for the lieutenant to tell about how he had met this musician; he phoned to the Hotel du Pavillon—one of the "Y" shelters, where Jerry had been staying— and to his vexation learned that his friend had departed, leaving no address. Next morning came a post card marked Cannes. After all that scolding at the French, and all those doubts and fears, Jerry had gone running off to his girl!

Lanny's mother wasn't surprised. Lovers were like that, she declared: full of agonies and uncertainties, embarrassments and extravagances, impulses and remorses; quarreling bitterly, parting forever, and making it up next day. You just couldn't tell what unlikely sort of partner anyone would pick, or what crazy thing he or she would do. Lanny could understand that a man who had been drilled and disciplined for a year and a half, and had fought through one of the greatest battles in history, was apt to be restless and moody—and very much in need of feminine society.

Lanny sent his friend a telegram: "Don't fail to see me before you return to duties." A couple of days later he was bowled flat by a letter from the lieutenant, saying that he was never going to return to his duties, and that Uncle Sam could come and get him if and when he could find him. Jerry was going to marry his Cerise, and settle down to helping run a boarding house without boarders. "Tell those old buzzards to hurry up and sign the peace," said the ex-tutor from Kansas, "so that tourists can begin coming back to the Riviera!"

Lanny was much worried about this, for he knew that desertion in wartime was a serious matter. He took occasion to bring up the subject with one of the military men at the Crillon, and learned that the army had been severe with the A.W.O.L.'s at the outset, but was becoming less so every day as a matter of sheer necessity. Men who had submitted cheerfully to the draft now considered that their duty was done, and wanted to go home before some other fellow got their girls and their jobs; there were so many deserters in Paris that the M.P.'s couldn't bring them in nor the guardhouses hold them. Lanny wrote his friend for heaven's sake to take off his uniform and not show himself in public places until after the peace was signed. Then, presumably, the army would go home and forget him!

Lanny and his mother had also discussed Johannes Robin, prosperous speculator in cast-off armaments. He journeyed frequently to Paris and other places; surely he must know persons at the border, and could arrange to import a competent Swiss musician to play duets with his son! Lanny composed a nice sociable letter, telling the news about himself and his parents, and saying that he hoped to see Mr. Robin when he came to the city, and did he have any plans to come? So tactful was this letter that Mr. Robin missed the point and replied even more sociably, telling how happy his whole family was to hear from Lanny, and all about what they were doing and thinking. Only at the end did he mention that he had no plans to come to Paris just now, but that when he did, Lanny would be sure to hear from him. What Lanny said was: "Damn!"

III

On account of her secret "house guest," Madame Detaze was compelled to receive her friends in the parlor of the hotel, a circumstance which sooner or later was bound to awaken their curiosity. Only two persons, her brother and her son, were accustomed to come up unannounced; the next afternoon, when Lanny entered his mother's drawing room, he found his Uncle Jesse seated there. Kurt wasn't visible, so Lanny assumed that he must be hidden in Beauty's boudoir. The youth couldn't get away from the feeling that he was playing a part in a stage comedy. Suppose the German captain of artillery should happen to be seized by a fit of coughing or sneezing—there would be quite a job of explaining to Beauty's brother!

But this calamity did not befall. With more than one of his twisted smiles the brother told about his adventures with the agents of the Sûreté Générale, who had descended upon him within a couple of hours after the attack upon Clemenceau. Jesse hadn't heard about the incident, and was caught with a letter half-written on his table—fortunately it dealt with American affairs! The police took him to the Préfecture and gave him a grilling, threatening among other things to expel him from the country. The painter had taken a high stand, declaring that this would make more propaganda than he could achieve by a hundred speeches.

"They wanted to know about my sister and my nephew," added Jesse. "I gather that few things would please them more than to be able to tie the Crillon up with the attempt on Clemenceau."

"They all think we're pro-German," replied the youth. "Or at any rate they say they do."

Beauty had been told about the *réunion*, so Lanny was free to ask his uncle: "Do you know that fellow Cottin?"

"Never heard of him," was the reply. "I don't go much with anarchists. It's my judgment they nearly always have a screw loose."

Lanny had been taught by his father that all varieties of Reds were in that condition. Said he: "Do you remember a young workingman who came onto the platform at the meeting and shook hands with you?"

"There were several who did that."

"This one talked to you and you patted him on the back."

"Probably he was praising my speech," said Uncle Jesse. "If so, I liked him."

"Don't you remember one who wore corduroys?"

The painter searched his memory. "I believe I do. A rather frail chap, looking as if he'd been sick?"

"That was Cottin."

Jesse exhibited astonishment—and his nephew watched him closely. Was it genuine, or was it good acting? No doubt many comrades

of the young anarchist were forgetting him just now. Distrust of
his uncle had been so deeply ground into Lanny's mind that he was
never sure if any of the painter's emotions were genuine.

Beauty interrupted the drama with some remark about the wickedness of shooting that poor old man who was doing so much for
France. This caused her brother to turn upon her with what certainly seemed a genuine emotion. He said that attempts at assassination were foolish, because they didn't accomplish the purpose desired; but so far as wickedness was concerned, how about statesmen
and diplomats who had caused the murder of ten million innocent
persons and the destruction of three hundred billions of dollars'
worth of property? And what were you going to say about bureaucrats and politicians who left the poor to stand in line for hours
waiting for a chance to buy a few scraps of half-spoiled food at
twice the prices charged before the war?

Jesse Blackless was started on the same speech he had made at the
meeting. He told about food rotting in warehouses at Le Havre and
Marseille, about freight cars rusting idle—and all because speculators
reaped fortunes out of every increase in prices. "What does it mean
to you that the cost of living in Paris has doubled, and that some
foods cost five or six times as much? All you have to do is to ask
Robbie for another check."

"I assure you you're mistaken," said Beauty, spunkily—for she
had had plenty of practice quarreling with her brother. "I've lost
ten pounds since I came to Paris."

"Well, it's probably due to dancing all night, not to going
hungry. I don't go into the smart restaurants, but I pass them and
see they're crowded all night with bemedaled men and half-naked
women."

"That's because Paris is so full of strangers. People sit packed at
the tables so that they haven't room to move their elbows."

"Well, they manage to get the food. But the people I know
haven't tasted a morsel of sugar in four years, and now they stand
in the rain and snow for hours for a loaf of bread or a basket of
fuel. Is it any more wicked to kill a cynical old politician than to

starve a million women and children so that they die of anemia or pneumonia?"

IV

Jesse Blackless went on in this strain until he saw that he was hurting his sister without helping his cause. Then he remembered that he had come to advise her on the subject of the exhibition of her late husband's paintings. He calmed down, and said that he had been thinking the matter over, and it would be better to wait until peace had been signed, when the newspapers would have more space to devote to painting. June would be a good month; the elderly vultures could hardly take that long to pick the bones of the German carcass. When Beauty answered that she couldn't stay away from Baby Marceline, Jesse advised her to go home and come back. When she said she wanted to be with Lanny, her brother said that her problems were too complicated for any man to solve.

He arose to take his departure, signing to Lanny to follow him. In the passage he said: "My comrades have got the habit of coming to me for funds, and I don't know what to tell them. Is your friend coming again?" What a sensation Lanny could have made if he had said that the friend had been in the adjoining room!

Having seen his uncle out of the building, Lanny went back and found Kurt talking to his mother. Kurt had heard the conversation, and made up his mind that he was no longer going to impose upon Beauty's too great kindness. "You try to hide your fears," he said; "but I know what a scandal it would make if the police were to arrest me here. I'm ashamed of myself for having stayed so long."

"You may be going to your death," protested Beauty.

"The worst of the storm has blown over. And anyhow it's wartime, and I'm a soldier."

There was another reason, which Lanny could guess. Kurt had written a letter to Switzerland and Lanny had mailed it for him. Now it was time for a reply to be at *poste restante*, and there was no keeping Kurt from going for it. "The letter will tell me a new place to report," said he, "and no one else must take the risk of getting it."

He thanked his two friends, and it was the old Kurt speaking, the man of conscience and exalted feelings. "I told you, Lanny, that life is a dedication; but neither of us knew how soon we'd have to prove it."

There were tears in Beauty's eyes. The poor soul was sending another man away to death! She was living again the partings with Marcel; and the fact that Kurt was fighting on the other side made no difference whatever. "Oh, God!" she exclaimed. "Will there never come a time on this earth when men stop killing one another?"

She tried to keep Lanny in the apartment, and he knew what that meant. The police might be waiting in the lobby of the hotel, and would get both of them! Lanny said: "I won't go very far; just escort him outside and make it respectable!"

What Lanny wanted was to deliver his uncle's message to Kurt; also to follow him at a safe distance and make sure of what happened at the post office. He watched his friend receive a letter and put it into his pocket and walk away. Lanny went to a telephone and told his mother that all was well. Then he returned to his safe job of trying to stop the fourteen little wars and one big one.

V

The Supreme Council decided to go ahead and complete the treaty with Germany, and ordered all the various commissions to deliver their reports and recommendations within a few days. That meant rush times for geographers, and also for secretaries and translators. Professor Alston's French was now equal to all demands, and Lanny's geography had improved to such an extent that he could pretty nearly substitute for his chief. There was work enough for both, and they hurried from place to place with briefcases and portfolios. A fascinating game they were playing, or rather a whole series of games—like the chess exhibitions in which some expert keeps a dozen contests in his head at the same time. In this case the chessboards were provinces and the pawns were national minorities comprising millions of human beings. Some games you were winning and some you were losing, and each was a series of surprises. At lunchtime and at dinner you compared notes with your colleagues; a busy chatter was poured out with the coffee, and human hopes were burned up with the cigarettes.

On the whole it was exhilarating, and contributed to the sense of importance of gentlemen whose domains had hitherto been classrooms with a score or two of undergraduates. Now they were playing parts in the great world. Their names were known; visitors sought them out; newspaper reporters waylaid them in lobbies and begged them for news. What a delicious thrill it gave to the nineteen-year-old Lanny Budd to say: "Really, Mr. Thompson, I'm not supposed to say anything about that; but if you will be careful not to indicate the source of your authority, I don't mind telling you that the French are setting their war damages at two hundred billion dollars, and of course we consider that preposterous. Colonel House has said that they play with billions the way children play with wooden blocks. There's no sense in it, because the Germans can never pay such sums."

When Lanny talked like this he wasn't being presumptuous, as you might imagine; rather he was following a policy and a technique. Over a period of two months and a half the experts had observed that confidential information leaked quickly to the French press whenever it was something to French advantage; the same was the case with the British—and now the Americans also were learning to have "leaks." Trusted newspapermen had found out where to come for tips, and would carefully keep secret the sources of their treasures.

Lanny didn't even have to have explicit instructions. He would hear his chief say to some colleague: "It mightn't be a bad thing if the American people were to know that one of the great powers is proposing to get rid of a large stock of rancid pork by selling it to the Germans and replacing it with fresh pork from America." Go-

ing out for a walk Lanny would run into Mr. Thompson of the
Associated Press, and they would stroll together, and next day a
carefully guarded secret of state would be read at twenty million
American breakfast tables. A howl of protest would echo back to
Paris, and Lanny's chief would remark to his colleague: "Well, that
story got out, it seems! I don't know how it happened, but I can't
say I'm sorry."

VI

In such ways the youth was kept so busy day and night that he
had little time to think about his German friend. Beauty called up
to ask if he had any news, and Lanny understood that his tender-
hearted mother had taken another human fate into her keeping and
had a new set of fears to mar her enjoyment of fashionable life in
La Ville Lumière. Lanny made note how little politics really meant
to a woman. Beauty had been an ardent pacifist so long as she was
hoping to keep Marcel away from the fighting; she had been a
French patriot so long as that seemed the way to get the war over;
now, tormented by the image of Lanny's friend being stood against
a wall and shot, she was for letting bygones be bygones and giving
the German babies food.

The youth didn't have time to call upon his uncle, but he got a
little note saying: "Your friend called again. Thanks." That seemed
to indicate that Kurt had got in touch with his organization and
was carrying on as usual.

At one of the luncheons in the Crillon, Lanny met Captain Stratton, and brought up the subject of the spread of discontent in Paris.
The intelligence officer said it was a truly alarming situation: a suc-
cession of angry strikes, and protest meetings every night in the
working-class districts; incendiary speeches being made, and the
city plastered with *affiches* containing all the standard Bolshevik demands—immediate peace, the lifting of the blockade, food for the
workers, and the suppression of speculators.

"Aren't those all reasonable demands?" asked Alston; and so came
another installment of the controversy among the staff. The young

captain said the demands might be reasonable enough, taken by themselves, but they were mere camouflage for efforts to overthrow the French government and seize the factories and the banks.

"But why not grant the reasonable demands?" asked Lanny's chief. "Wouldn't that weaken the hands of the agitators and strip off their camouflage?"

"That's outside my province," replied the other. "My job is to find out who the agitators are and keep track of what they're plotting."

The stoutish and pugnacious Professor Davisson broke in. "My guess is you'll find they're operating with German gold."

"That's what we assume," replied the other. "But it's not easy to prove."

Said Alston: "My opinion is, you'll find that German gold in the eye of Maurras and his royalists. The French masses are suffering and they have every reason in the world to complain and to agitate."

Lanny smiled to himself. His chief called himself a "liberal," and Lanny had been trying to make up his mind just what that meant. He decided that a liberal was a high-minded gentleman who believed the world was made in his own image. But unfortunately only one small part of it was deserving of such trust. He had been looking for such a spot, and the only one he had found was the tiny country of Denmark, whose delegates had come to the conference determined not to take on any racial minorities. Others were trying hard to persuade them to accept a chunk of Germany down to the Kiel canal; but they would have no land of which the population was not preponderantly Danish—and they would insist upon a plebiscite before they took even that. If only the whole of Europe had been "liberal" according to that formula, how simple all the problems would have been!

VII

President Wilson returned to Paris in the middle of March, one month after his leaving. There were no tumultuous receptions this time; the various peoples of the world had learned that he wouldn't give them what they wanted, and couldn't if he would. He came a beaten man; for the expiring Congress had left unpassed three vital appropriation bills, in order to make certain that he would have to summon a special session of the new Congress. He arrived at a Peace Conference which had laid all his Fourteen Points on the shelf, and also its own resolution of seven weeks earlier, whereby the Covenant of the League of Nations was to become a part of the peace treaty.

Wilson set his long Presbyterian jaw and went into a three-hour conference with the two head malefactors, Clemenceau and Lloyd George. When he came out from it he gave out a statement to the effect that the Covenant was a vital part of the treaty and would remain in. Then what a steaming and stewing, a bubbling and boiling of diplomatic kettles! Pichon, French Foreign Minister, issued a declaration to the effect that the Covenant would not have any place in the treaty; and when the reporters asked him about President Wilson's statement, he said he hadn't heard of it. There was a great scandal, and Clemenceau was forced to "throw down" his foreign minister and stop the publication of his communiqué. Then Lord Robert Cecil gave out a statement supporting Wilson's side, and the clamor of the Tories forced Lloyd George to throw him down. So it went, back and forth; those elderly gentlemen met and argued until they were sick of the sound of one another's voices. The shrill clamor penetrated to the attachés outside, and caused them to look at one another with anxious faces, or perhaps with mischievous grins.

The "Big Four" were meeting by themselves now, resolved to push things through and get done. A more oddly assorted quartet of bedfellows had rarely been chosen by political fate. Woodrow Wilson was a stiff and grave person, of principles which he held as divinely ordained. He kept his sense of humor for his private life; in public it was his function to deliver eloquent discourses in favor of righteousness, and at this there was no one in the world to rival him. He brought his great talent to every session and exercised it upon Georges Clemenceau, who sat hunched in his chair with eyes closed, the picture of agonized boredom; every few minutes the Tiger would open his heavy-lidded eyes and reply with any one of half a dozen French words, the equivalent of four-letter English words which every guttersnipe knew, but which few had ever seen in print.

This form of political argument was something hitherto inconceivable to the Presbyterian professor. He had been brought up to the idea that scholar and gentleman formed an inseparable combination; but here was a scholar who was perfectly content to be a blackguard and a rascal. His political career had been that of a Tammany Hall boss—so Robbie Budd had told his son. As Lanny didn't know much about New York City's political history, the father explained that forceful men of the people went into politics, their hearts bleeding for the wrongs of the poor; so they collected votes and built up a political machine, which they used to blackmail their way to fortune.

The Tiger, now seventy-eight, had seen a great deal of the world, but here was a phenomenon the like of which he had never encountered: a politician who in the presence of other politicians pretended to mean what he said in his speeches! At first Clemenceau had found it absolutely infuriating; he had raged and stormed, and there was a dreadful story going the rounds that he had struck the President in the face and that Lloyd George had had to separate them. You met people who declared that they knew this story was true; but how did they know it? Others reported that as the battles of the Big Four went on, the Tiger began to take a humorous attitude; at the end he had actually grown fond of this odd phenomenon, as one might of some human freak, a man with two heads or four arms.

The mediator in the battle was Lloyd George, one of those superpoliticians who could be on both sides of every question. Lloyd George had begun as "a little squirt of a Welsh lawyer," friend of the people and a terrifying demagogue. When he got power he had kept it by the device of selling titles of nobility to beer barons, press lords, and South African diamond kings. In his recent "khaki election" he had become the slave of a Tory majority, and he swung back and forth between what they told him to do and what he thought would please the public. He was gay and personally charming, and possessed what was called a "mercurial temperament"— meaning that he didn't mind saying the opposite of what he had said yesterday, if in the meantime he had found that he was in danger of losing votes. In this he was the twin brother of Orlando, the Italian Premier, a good-looking and amiable old gentleman whose one thought in all issues was to gain some advantage, however tiny, for his native land.

VIII

A terrifying world in which this duel of wills went on. The war upon the Soviets was continuing on a dozen fronts, but without notable success. A Red Hungary had been added to a Red Bavaria and an almost Red Berlin. The Poles were fighting the Ukrainians for the possession of Lemberg. The Italians were threatening to withdraw from the conference unless they were permitted to fight the Yugoslavs for the possession of Fiume. The Armenians were in Paris demanding freedom from the Turks, and the Turks were trying to settle the problem by killing the last Armenian before a decision could be reached. Not one, not a dozen, but a hundred problems like that, all being dinned into the ears of four bewildered and exhausted old men.

They wrangled over the question of Danzig and the proposed Polish Corridor to the sea. They decided it, and then, when the clamor rose louder, they undecided it and referred it back to the commission. So geographers and ethnographers and their assistants were summoned once more, and Lanny Budd lugged his portfolios into the high-ceilinged, overheated conference rooms at the Quai d'Orsay, and stood behind his chief for hours—there being not enough chairs for secretaries and translators. Lanny couldn't help but feel grave, for there was a consensus among the American experts that here was where the next war would start.

The real purpose of that corridor had by now become clear to all; the French were determined to put a barrier between German manufacturing power and Russian raw materials, which, if combined, might dominate Europe. So give the Poles access to the sea by driving a wedge through Germany, with Danzig for a port. But the trouble was that Danzig was a German city, and the proposed corridor was inhabited by more than two millions of that race. When this was brought to President Wilson's attention, he produced a report from Professor Alston, pointing out that this district had been Polish, but had been deliberately "colonized" by the Germans, by the method so well known in Europe of making the former inhabitants so miserable that they emigrated. At a conference with his advisers President Wilson said that this appeared to be a case where one principle conflicted with another principle.

Alston reported this remark to Lanny, and the youth asked questions of his chief. Could two principles be principles when they contradicted each other? Apparently it was necessary for men to have such moral maxims; but there would seem to be something wrong when they betrayed you in an emergency. The highly conscientious gentlemen at the Crillon racked their brains for some way to prevent fighting in that corridor. Most of the scholars were inclined to sympathize with the Poles—perhaps on account of Kosciuszko, and because in their youth they had read a novel called *Thaddeus of Warsaw*. But, alas, their sympathies were weakened by the fact that the Poles were carrying on dreadful pogroms against the Jews; and if they were that sort of people, what were the chances for the two million Germans of the corridor? The time was out of joint: O cursèd spite, that ever college professors were born to set it right!

They Shall Reap the Whirlwind

BOOK SIX

They Shall Reap the Whirlwind

32

I Have Seen the Future

I

PARIS was dancing. It was a mania that had seized all "society"; in hotels and cafés, in private drawing rooms, wherever men and women met, they spent their time locked in one another's arms, swaying and jiggling this way and that. These modern dances seemed to have been invented to spare the necessity of any skill, any art; if you knew how to walk, if you were sober enough so that you could stagger, then you could dance, and you did.

Lanny didn't have much time for diversion, but his mother went out now and then, and when he called on her, she would tell about her adventures. More than once she had left the room because of disgusting things she had witnessed. Beauty's world seemed to be coming to an end; that world of grace and charm for which she had spent so many years equipping herself. She had learned all the rules—and the result was she was out of date. Men no longer wanted coquetry or subtlety, elegance, even intelligence; they wanted young females to hug, and that was too cheap and easy, in the opinion of Beauty. She said that apparently the real horrors of war didn't begin until it was over.

Her old friends were scattered. Sophie, Baroness de la Tourette, had lost her lover in the last dreadful fighting on the Marne, and had gone back to visit her relatives in Ohio. Margy Eversham-Watson was at her country place in Sussex, his lordship having been struck with a bad attack of gout. Edna Hackabury, now Mrs. Fitz-Laing, was on the Riviera, waiting for her husband to return from a military expedition in the Near East. All these persons were unhappy in one way or another, and Beauty, who craved pleasure as a sunflower craves the light, seemed as if trying to flee from her world. A horrible world! She told Lanny how, sitting at dinner next to Premier Orlando, that genial statesman had declared himself displeased that so lovely a woman had waited eighteen years between children. In his family it was different, he gravely assured her; his wife never got up from her accouchement bed without being pregnant again.

More and more she was coming to rely upon Emily Chattersworth, a tower of strength in times such as these. Emily had money enough and force of will enough to make a world of her own. Emily had learned the rules, and persons who didn't know them and obey them got no share of her hospitality. In her home you met intellectual people and heard serious talk of the problems of the day, as well as of literature and art and music. Beauty would remark sadly that she was coming to an age where it was necessary for her to be intellectual; she would go to one of Emily's soirees, and listen while more brilliant persons talked, and come home and tell Lanny whom she had met and what compliments they had paid her.

Lanny accompanied her when he could find time. He realized that Mrs. Emily was performing an important service in bringing people together in gracious ways. When the American delegates and advisers met the French, it was always for business, and too frequently the discussions ended with bitterness. But in the drawing room of a woman of the world they could discuss the same problems with urbanity and humor; their shrewd hostess would be watching, ready to help the conversation past a dangerous corner. Here the women came; and the Americans found it easier to like the French when they met their women.

Mrs. Emily was fond of Lanny Budd, who from childhood had learned to behave in a drawing room. She considered him extraordinarily fortunate in his present role, and permitted him to bring members of the staff to her affairs without special invitation, an honor she granted to few. She came to have lunch with his friends at the Crillon, and this too was a distinction. Professor Alston remarked that many women had money, but few knew how to use it;

if there were more persons like Emily Chattersworth in the world there wouldn't be so many like Jesse Blackless.

II

The British and the French were taking unto themselves those portions of Asia Minor which had oil, phosphates, and other treasures, or through which oil pipelines had to travel to the sea. Since the Fourteen Points had guaranteed the inhabitants of these lands the mastery of their own destinies, the subtle statesmen had racked their vocabularies to find some way of taking what they wanted while seeming not to. They had evolved a new word, or rather a new meaning for an old word, which was "mandate." The scholars at the Crillon had an anecdote with which to divert their minds from sorrowful contemplations. Some diplomat newly arrived in Paris had inquired: "What's going to be done about New Guinea and the Pacific islands?" and the answer was: "They are to be administered by mandatories." "Who is Mandatories?" inquired the newcomer.

Mister Mandatories—or was it Lord Mandatories?—was going to take over Syria and Palestine and Iraq, the Hejaz and Yemen and the rest of those hot lands which had been promised to the people of the young Emir Feisal. The brown replica of Christ had taken off his multicolored silk robes, his turban and veil, and put on the ugliest of black morning coats, in the hope of impressing the Peace Conference with his civilized condition—but all in vain. Behind the scenes Grand Officer Zaharoff had spoken, and Clemenceau was obeying; Henri Deterding, master of Royal Dutch Shell, had spoken, and Lloyd George was obeying.

One portion of the former Turkish empire had no oil or other mineral treasures of consequence; it had only peasants, who were being slaughtered daily by Turkish soldiers, as they had been off and on, mostly on, for ages. To stop this slaughter there was needed another Mandatory—a kind, idealistic, high-minded Mandatory, who cared nothing about oil nor yet about pipelines, but who loved

poor peasants and the simple life. The British and French brought
forward a proposal in the name of humanity and democracy: an
elderly gentleman named Uncle Samuel Mandatory was to take
charge of Armenia, and doughboys singing "Onward, Christian Soldiers" would drive out the Turks and keep them out.

This proposal was sprung, and President Wilson promised to consider it and give his decision promptly. There was a rush call to the
staff for everything they had on Armenia, and a hundred reports
on history, geography, language, population, resources, production,
trade, government, had to be dug out and read, digested, summarized,
headlined, so that a busy statesman could get the whole thing in his
mind in ten minutes' reading. Professor Alston had to do his part,
and Lanny had to help—which was the reason he missed a musical
evening at Mrs. Emily's town house.

Beauty attended; and shortly before midnight she telephoned her
son at the hotel. "Lanny, the most amazing thing has happened."

He knew from the tone of her voice that she was upset. "What
is it?"

"I can't tell you over the phone. You must come here."

"But I'm not through with my job."

"Isn't it something that can wait till morning?"

"It's for the Big Boss himself."

"Well, I must see you. I'll wait up."

"Any danger?" His first thought, of course, was of Kurt.
"Don't try to talk now. Come when you can."

III

So Lanny rather stinted the Armenians, and maybe let more of
them die. So many poor peasants were dying, in so many parts of the
world—there came a time when one just gave up. He omitted from
his report some of the Armenian charges and some of the Turkish
admissions, and slipped into his big trench coat, ran downstairs, and
hopped into a taxi.

His fair blond mother was waiting in one of those bright-colored silk dressing gowns from China—this time large golden dragons crawling clockwise round her. She had taken to smoking under the strain of the past year, and evidently had done it a lot, for the air in the room was hazy and close. Beauty deserved her name almost as much as formerly, and never more so than when tenderness and concern were in her sweet features. After opening her door she looked into the passage to see if anyone had followed her son, then led him into her boudoir before she spoke.

"Lanny, I met Kurt at Emily's!"

"Oh, my God!" exclaimed the youth.

"The first person I saw, standing at her side."

"Does she know who he is?"

"She thinks he's a musician from Switzerland."

"Who brought him?"

"I didn't ask. I was afraid to seem the least bit curious."

"What was he doing?"

"Meeting influential Frenchmen—at least that's what he told me."

"You had a chance to talk to him?"

"Just a moment or two. When I went in and saw him, I was pretty nearly bowled over. Emily introduced him as M. Dalcroze. Imagine!"

"What did you say?"

"I was afraid my face had betrayed something, so I said: 'It seems to me I have met M. Dalcroze somewhere.' Kurt was perfectly calm—he might have been the sphinx. He said: 'Madame's face does seem familiar to me.' I saw that he meant to carry it off, so I said: 'One meets so many people,' and went on to explain to Emily why you hadn't come."

"And then?"

"Well, I strolled on, and old M. Solicamp came up to me and started talking, and I pretended to listen while I tried to think what to do. But it was too much for me. I just kept quiet and watched Kurt all I could. By and by Emily called on him to play the piano and he did so—very well, I thought."

"Whatever he does he does well."

Beauty went on to name the various persons with whom she had observed their friend in conversation. One was the publisher of one of the great Paris dailies; what could a German expect to accomplish with such a man? Lanny didn't try to answer, because he had never told his mother that Kurt was handling money. She continued: "Toward the end of the evening I was alone with him for just a minute. I said: 'What are you expecting to accomplish here?' He answered: 'Just meeting influential persons.' 'But what for?' 'To get in a word for our German babies. I pledge you my honor that I shall do nothing that can bring harm to our hostess.' That was all we had time for."

"What do you mean to do?"

"I don't see what I can do. If I tell Emily, I am betraying Kurt. If I don't tell her, won't she feel that I've betrayed her?"

"I'm afraid she may, Beauty."

"But she didn't meet Kurt through us."

"She met him because I told him about her, and he found some way to get introduced to her under a false name."

"But she won't ever know that you mentioned her."

"We can't tell what she'll know. We're tying ourselves up in a knot of intrigue and no one can guess what new tangles may develop."

A look of alarm appeared on the mother's usually placid features. "Lanny, you're not thinking that we ought to give Kurt up!"

"Telling Mrs. Emily wouldn't be quite the same as giving him up, would it?"

"But we promised him solemnly that we wouldn't tell a soul!"

"Yes, but we didn't give him permission to go and make use of our friends."

A complicated problem in ethics, and in etiquette too! They discussed it back and forth, without getting very far. Lanny said that Mrs. Emily had expressed herself strongly against the blockade of Germany; she would, no doubt, be deeply sympathetic to what Kurt was doing, even while she might disapprove his methods.

The mother replied: "Yes, but don't you see that if you tell her you make her responsible for the methods. As it is, she's just a rich American lady who's been deceived by a German agent. She's perfectly innocent, and she can say so. But if she knows, it's her duty to report him to the authorities, and she's responsible for what may happen from now on."

Lanny sat with knitted brows. "Don't forget," he remarked, "you're in that position yourself. It ought to worry you."

Said Beauty: "The difference is that I'd be willing to lie about it; but I don't believe Emily would."

IV

When in doubt, do nothing—that seemed to be the wise rule. They had no way to communicate with Kurt, and he didn't make any move to enlighten them. Was he arguing the same way as Beauty, that what they didn't know wouldn't hurt them? It was obvious that in trying to promote pro-German ideas among highly placed persons in Paris he was playing a desperately dangerous game, and the fewer dealings he had with friends the better for the friends.

Many ladies in fashionable society become amateur psychologists, and learn to manipulate one another's minds and to extract information without the other person's knowing what they are after—unless, perchance, the other person has also become an amateur psychologist. Beauty went to see her friend in the morning; and of course it was natural for her to refer to the handsome young pianist, to comment on his skill, and to ask where her friend had come upon him. Emily explained that M. Dalcroze had written that he was a cousin of an old friend in Switzerland who had died several years ago, and that he had come to Paris to study with one of the great masters at the conservatory.

"I asked him to come and play for me," said the kindly hostess. "He's really quite an exceptional person. He plans to be a composer and has studied every instrument in the orchestra—he says that you have to be able to play them if you are going to compose for them."

"How interesting!" said Beauty, and she wasn't fibbing. "Where is he staying?"

"He tells me he's with friends for a few days. He's getting his mail at *poste restante.*"

Said the guileless friend: "I only had a chance for a few words with him, but I heard him talking with someone about the blockade of Germany."

"He feels deeply about it. He says it is sowing the seeds of the next war. Of course, being an alien, he can't say much."

"I suppose not."

"It's really a shocking thing, Beauty. The more I hear about it the more indignant I become. I was talking to Mr. Hoover the other day; he has been trying for four months to get permission for a small German fishing fleet to go out into the North Sea—but in vain."

"How perfectly ghastly!" exclaimed Lanny's mother.

"I am wondering if I shouldn't get some influential French people to come here some evening and hear Mr. Hoover tell about what it means to the women and children of Central Europe."

"I've thought of the same idea, Emily. You know Lanny talks about that blockade all the time. The people at the Crillon are so wrought up about it."

"Our French friends just can't bring themselves to realize that the war is over."

"Or perhaps, as Professor Alston says, they're fighting the next one. We women let the men have their way all through, but I really think we ought to have something to say about the peace."

"I know just how you feel," said the grave Mrs. Emily, who had had Beauty weeping on her shoulder more than once during the days of Marcel's long-drawn-out agony.

"Let's you and me take it up, Emily, and make them let those women and children have food!" It was farther than Beauty had meant to go when she set out on this visit; but something in the deeps of her consciousness rose up unexpectedly. A woman with a loving nature may try her best to dance and be merry while other women are bearing dead babies, and while living babies are growing up with twisted skeletons; but all of a sudden comes a rush of feeling from some unknown place and she finds herself exclaiming, to her own surprise: "Let's do something!"

V

The discussions among the four elder statesmen were continuing day and night and reaching a new pitch of intensity. They were dealing with questions which directly concerned France; and the French are an intense people—especially where land or money is involved. There was one strip of land which was precious to the French beyond any price: the left bank of the river Rhine, which would save them from the terror which haunted every man, woman, and child in the nation. They wanted the Rhineland; they were determined to have it, and nothing could move them; they could argue about it day and night, forever and forever, world without end; they never wearied—and they never gave up.

Also they demanded the Sarre, with its valuable coal mines, to make up for those which the Germans had deliberately destroyed. The French had suffered all this bitter winter; other winters were coming, and who were going to suffer—the French, or the Germans who had invaded France, blown towns and cities to dust and rubble, carried away machinery and flooded mines? The French army held both the Sarre and the Rhineland, and General Foch was omnipresent at the Peace Conference, imploring, scolding, threatening, even refusing to obey Clemenceau, his civilian chief, when he saw signs of weakening on this point upon which the future of *la patrie* depended.

The British Prime Minister very generously took the side of the American President in this controversy. Alston said it was astonishing how reasonable Lloyd George could be when it was a question of concessions to be made by France. England was getting Mesopotamia and Palestine, Egypt and the German colonies; Australia was getting German New Guinea, and South Africa was getting

German Southwest Africa. All this had been arranged by the help
of the blessed word "mandatory," plus the word "protectorate" in
the case of Egypt. But where was the blessed word that would
enable the French to fortify the west bank of the Rhine? That was
not to be found in any English dictionary.

Lanny got an amusing illustration of the British attitude through
his friend Fessenden, a youth who was gracious and likable, and
infected with "advanced" ideas. Lanny had been meeting Fessenden
off and on for a couple of months, and they had become one of
many channels through which the British and Americans exchanged
confidences. Among a hundred other questions about which they
chatted was the island of Cyprus, which Britain had "formally"
taken over from Turkey early in the war. What were they going to
do with it? "Self-determination of all peoples," ran the "advanced"
formula; so of course the people of Cyprus would be asked to whom
they wished to belong. Young Fessenden had been quite sure that
this would be done; but gradually he became less so, and the time
came when he avoided the subject. When it became apparent that
the island was "annexed" for good, young Fessenden in a burst of
friendship confessed to Lanny that he had mentioned the matter to
his chief and had been told to stop talking nonsense. If the British
let the question of "self-determination" be raised, what would become of Gibraltar, and of Hong Kong, and of India? A young man
who wanted to have a diplomatic career had better get revolutionary catchwords out of his head.

VI

Such was the atmosphere in which Mrs. Emily Chattersworth and
her friend Beauty Detaze set out to change French opinion on the
subject of the blockade. They had resolved upon getting persons
influential in French society to gather in Mrs. Emily's drawing room
and hear an appeal from Mr. Herbert Hoover, who had been in
charge of Belgian relief and now had been put in charge of all relief
by the Supreme Council. The persons whom Mrs. Emily planned to

invite were many of them intimate friends, frequenters of her salon for years; but when she broached this proposal to them, they were embarrassed, and certain that it couldn't be done.

They would start to explain to her, and it would turn into an argument. The blockade was cruel, no doubt, but all war was cruel, and this was part of the war. The Germans hadn't signed the peace, and the blockade was a weapon to make them sign; so the army chiefs said, and in wartime a nation took the advice of its general staff. Yes, it might be that German babies were dying; but how many French babies had died in the war, and how many French widows would have no more babies as a result of the German invasion? The famous critic who had been Mrs. Emily's lover for a decade or more told her that every German baby was either a future invader of France, or else a mother of future invaders of France; and when he saw the look of dismay on her face he told her to be careful, that she was falling victim to German propaganda. It didn't make any difference whether one got this propaganda direct from Germans, or from Americans who had been infected with it across the seas.

Such was the mood of the people of France. Those two or three friends who were sympathetic told Mrs. Emily that her action would be misunderstood, and that her future career as a *salonnière* would be jeopardized. As soon as the treaty was signed something would doubtless be done; but few French people, unless they were tainted with Bolshevist ideas, would attend an assemblage where pro-German arguments were to be voiced. The French were grateful for American help, but people who lived in safety three thousand miles away shouldn't presume to give advice about the problems which France faced every day and every hour.

The fact was that the French regarded the Peace Conference as an intrusion, and they watched all foreigners suspiciously. One of Mrs. Emily's friends asked her: What did she really know about the tall and severe young musician who looked so much like a German and spoke with a trace of German accent? He had been discussing the blockade in her drawing room, and more than one person had made note of it. "Enemy ears are listening!" Mrs. Emily mentioned this warning to her friend Beauty, as an example of the phobias which tormented people in Paris. Beauty said, yes, it was really pitiful.

VII

The four elder statesmen met in the morning in President Wilson's study and in the afternoon at the headquarters of the Supreme Council at Versailles. Members of their staffs accompanied them and waited in anterooms; sometimes they were summoned to the presences, but most of the time were forgotten for hours on end. The proceedings of the Big Four were supposed to be completely secret; only one secretary was present. The meeting place became a whispering gallery, with awe-stricken subordinates pricking their ears for every sound, watching the expressions and gestures of those who emerged from the holy place.

The slightest anecdotes spread like wildfire among the staff. Marshal Foch had come rushing out of the chamber, his face red, his eyes dark with storm. He would never go back there, never, never! —so he shouted. Frightened members of his staff whispered to him, begged him, implored him; finally he went back. Professor Elderberry, whose specialty was Semitic dialects, and who had been on a "field commission" to Palestine, had witnessed Lloyd George and Clemenceau in a near fracas. Wilson had interposed, his outstretched arms between them, exclaiming: "I have never seen two such unreasonable men." Lanny, waiting outside for his chief, saw Clemenceau coming out in a rush and being helped into the big gray fur-lined overcoat which protected his chilly old bones. "How are things going?" someone asked, and the Premier of France replied: "Splendidly. We disagreed about everything."

Professor Alston, summoned to one session, described to his colleagues the curious spectacle of four elderly gentlemen who had spread a big map on the floor and were crawling round on their hands and knees, looking for bits of territory which they were going to assign to one nation or another. They were ignorant on many points of geography, and invented names for foreign places when they couldn't remember the right names; when the right ones were given they forgot, and went on using their inventions. Alston was violating no confidence in telling this, for Lloyd George had asked in Parliament: "How many members ever heard of Teschen? I don't mind saying that I never heard of it." Now, having heard of it, he took it from Austria and divided it between the Czechs and the Poles.

For ten days they had wrangled over the French and German boundary and got nowhere. They were exhausted, their tempers badly frayed. The peoples too were becoming hysterical; for where news was lacking rumor took its place. All parties continued to whisper the things they wanted to have believed, and the dozen Paris papers which Clemenceau controlled were denouncing the American President, lampooning him, cartooning him with shocking bitterness. Wilson was ill equipped for a struggle such as this; he was gentle, courteous, anxious to oblige people, and could hardly be brought to realize the nature of the forces being mobilized against him.

Clemenceau had his formula, from which he never varied: "This —or France has lost the war." Of course the President didn't want France to lose the war; he didn't want the responsibility of causing it to happen. He just hadn't realized what an inferno he was coming into. Many of his staff now urged him to go home; others begged him to take the American people into his confidence, telling them the real situation. He might not get what he wanted, but at least he would save his ideals intact and give the peoples of the world a glimpse of the forces that were wrecking Europe.

VIII

George D. Herron, distressed over these developments, left his home in Geneva and returned to Paris. He saw the President and afterwards told Alston and Lanny about it. Wilson was a sick man, paying the penalty of his temperament. As Herron explained it, he was lacking as an executive. "He knows how to judge himself, but not others; he knows how to drive himself, but not others; he can't trust anyone to write his speeches and memoranda, or even to type-write them. The result is that he's overwhelmed. He and he alone is the American Commission to Negotiate Peace, and the number of matters he has to consider and decide are more than can be got into one human brain."

What troubled the President in this crisis was the fear of seeing Europe fall prey to Bolshevism. The French assured him that this would happen; and might it not be true? The American staff had prepared a map, with terrifying large red arrows pointing into Lithuania, Prussia, Poland, Hungary, the Ukraine, Georgia. If Wilson were to break off negotiations and take the American army home, the Germans might refuse to sign the peace treaty, the war might start again, and revolts might follow in Paris and even in Britain.

A young member of the Crillon staff had been picked by the President and sent to Moscow. "Bill" Bullitt was his name, and he had taken with him a journalist friend, once famous as a "muck-raker." In the days when Lanny had been a toddler on the beach at Juan, this man had been traveling over the United States probing into political corruption, interviewing "bosses" and their big-business paymasters. Latterly his work had been forgotten, and Lanny had never heard the name of Lincoln Steffens until he was told that the "Bullitt mission" had set out for the land of the Reds.

They had come back with surprising news. Lenin wanted peace, and was ready to pay almost any price for it. He would give up all Siberia and the Urals, the Caucasus, Archangel, and Murmansk, even most of the Ukraine and White Russia. He would recognize all the White governments. But, alas, President Wilson had a severe headache that evening, and Colonel House also was ill. Bullitt saw Lloyd George first and told him the terms; Wilson, on the verge of a nervous breakdown, was so angry at this slight that he wouldn't see Bullitt, he wouldn't hear of peace with wicked Bolsheviks. And Lloyd George stood up in the House of Commons and denied that he had ever known anything about the Bullitt mission!

All this suited the French, who didn't want peace under any circumstances. They were being beaten, but dared not admit it. They were having to back out of the Ukraine; their armies were becoming unreliable—this dreaded new kind of war, fought not merely with guns but with ideas. War-weary soldiers listened, and began to whisper that maybe this was the way to end matters. There were mutinies in the French fleet in the Black Sea, and when Colonel House was asked by newspapermen about Odessa, he replied: "There's no more Odessa. The French are clearing out." British troops, ordered to embark at Folkestone for Archangel, refused to go on board. No use to look for such events in newspapers, whether British or American; but the staff at the Majestic knew, and Fessenden gossiped to Lanny with wide-open startled eyes. "For God's sake, what's going to happen next?"

IX

Lanny kept thinking he ought to hear from Kurt; but no word came. He wondered about his Uncle Jesse, whether he was getting more money and what he was doing with it. Having a couple of hours off one afternoon, Lanny yielded to the temptation and turned his steps in the direction of Montmartre.

It was the first day of April; bright sunlight, blue sky, fleecy white clouds; crocuses blooming in the gardens, daisies in the grass of the parks; the trees just far enough in the bud to show a pastel green. The poor frightened world was coming out of the winter of war; Lanny, climbing the hill, carried a thought which by now had become his familiar companion: Why, oh, why did men have to make their lives so ugly? What evil spell was upon them that they wrangled and scolded, hated and feared?

He climbed the stairs in the dark hallway which hadn't yet learned that winter was over. He knocked on his uncle's door, and a voice called: "Come in"; he did so, and saw there was a visitor, seated in the extra chair from which a load of books and papers had been dumped. He was a short, compactly built man with brown hair and

small gray imperial and mustache trimmed neatly; a rather square face
with glasses, and small blue-gray eyes with many wrinkles around
them, giving him a quizzical appearance. The visitor was plainly but
neatly dressed, and you would have taken him for a small businessman, or perhaps a college professor. Said Uncle Jesse: "This is
Lincoln Steffens."

Lanny was surprised, also pleased, and showed it. "I've been hearing about you at the Crillon!"

"Indeed," said the other. "I've been trying to figure out a way to
let them know I was in town."

When Lanny knew him better he would understand such teasing
remarks. As it was, he decided to be frank, and said: "You know
how it is—they're a bit afraid of you."

"That's why I came to see your uncle," replied the journalist.
"One man who might be interested to hear about the future."

"Stef has spent a whole week in the future," explained the uncle,
with one of his twisted smiles.

Lanny took his seat on the cot, which had become familiar to
him. Because it sank down in the middle it cut his knees, so presently he stretched out on it, leaning on one elbow. In this position
he listened for an hour or more to an account of one of the great
events of human history.

For a matter of seventeen months now Lanny had been hearing
about the Bolshevik Revolution. Again and again he had been told
how one-sixth of the earth's surface had been seized by bloodthirsty ruffians, more cruel and cunning than any that had ever
before plagued the earth. He had seen all the policies of his own
country and a number of others based upon that certainty. The
fact that his Uncle Jesse believed in and supported these devilish
creatures merely meant that his uncle was "cracked" in some serious way, and must be dealt with as you would with an inmate of a
home for mental patients.

But here sat this correct-looking middle-aged gentleman, who
had been sojourning among these Reds, and not merely hadn't had
his throat cut or his watch stolen, but apparently hadn't even got

his clothes wrinkled. He had an unusually pleasing voice and poured out the details of what he so oddly called "the future." Apparently this wasn't one of his jokes; he really thought the world was going to be like that. Lanny, who was going to live in the future, naturally wanted to know about it.

He learned that in this new world everybody would have to work. That didn't trouble him so much as it would have done three months earlier, for now he was working. As it happened, he was being paid by the state, so it didn't worry him to hear that this was the way among the Soviets. When he heard that the state was preparing and serving meals to workers in factories, it sounded very much like what was happening to him and the rest of the staff at the Crillon. In Russia, to be sure, they had only one meal a day, and that scanty; but "Stef" said that was due to five years of war and revolution, and to civil wars now going on over a front of ten thousand miles. What there was, all shared alike; that being the first principle of "Communism."

What, then, was the difference between America and Moscow? The "muckraker" said it was a question of who owned the state. In America the people were supposed to own it, but most of the time the big businessmen bought it away from them. "It is privilege which corrupts politics," was his phrase. He explained that among the Soviets it was soldiers and sailors, workers and peasants, who had seized power; capitalists had been abolished. Now there was war between these two kinds of states, and it looked as if it was going to be a war to the finish.

X

Lanny Budd was interested in this news, and no less in the envoy who brought it. What an eccentric little man, he thought. Why should a scholarly person, of breeding and presumably of means, take the side of those underworld figures against his own class? He took it only partly, as Lanny soon began to understand; there appeared to be a war between his heart and his head, and you could almost watch this conflict going on. Stef would become eager and excited, and then would check himself. "If I go too fast," he would say, "people won't listen to me. And, besides, I may be wrong." He would proceed to put some "ifs" and "buts" into his discourse.

Steffens was like Herron, a pacifist and a moralist first of all. He wanted a revolution, but one of the mind and spirit; he was pained by the thought that it might have to be bloody and violent. Did we want such an overturn in western Europe? Could we pay the price?

Jesse Blackless, for his part, was sure that we were going to pay it, whether we wanted to or not. There developed an argument between the two men, to which Lanny listened with close attention. The painter foretold how the Allied armies would continue to decay, and the Red movement would spread to Poland and Germany, and from there to Italy and France. The painter knew it was coming; he knew the very men who were preparing to do the job. Stef looked at Jesse's nephew with a twinkle in his little blue-gray eyes and said: "It's nice to have a religion, Budd. Saves all the trouble of having to think."

A curious experience to Lanny to hear Bolshevism referred to as a "religion," even in jest. But he understood when the reporter described the wave of fervor which had seized upon the people of Russia, victims of many centuries' oppression, sunk in unspeakable degradation—and now suddenly finding themselves masters of a mighty empire, and setting to work to make it into a workers' and peasants' co-operative. People were hungry, they were ragged, half-frozen all winter, but in their eyes was a feverish light and in their hearts was hope, vision, a dream of the future. From the unformed, unregarded mass, from soldiers and sailors and factory workers and peasants, had come new leadership, new statesmanship. . . .

Steffens had talked for hours with Lenin: that studious, shrewd little man who had watched the storm gathering and seized the proper hour to strike. "From now on we proceed to build Socialism," he had said quietly, the day after the coup. As Steffens described him, he knew more about the Allied statesmen than they knew about themselves. He understood the forces confronting the

Soviets; and while the bourgeois world sent armies against him, he would send fanatics, men and women who hated capitalism so much that they were willing to give their lives to undermine and destroy it. "Men like your Uncle Jesse," said Stef, with his sly smile; and Lanny understood, even better than Stef could have imagined.

Lanny was sorry that he had to leave. He summoned his courage and asked if Mr. Steffens would have lunch with him at the Crillon. The other advised him to think it over for a day and then call him. "Colonel House is the only other member of the staff who would have the courage to invite me just now!"

XI

The young fellow who had attempted to kill Clemenceau had been tried and sentenced to death, but the Premier had been persuaded to commute his sentence. The one who had killed Jaurès had been held in prison for nearly five years, because the authorities were afraid to try him during wartime. Now the trial was held, and the lawyers who defended him did so by seeking to prove that Jaurès had been disloyal to his country. So it became in effect a trial of the Socialist leader, and he was found guilty, while the assassin, whose name, oddly enough, was Villain, was acquitted.

The result was a mighty demonstration of protest by the workers of Paris, culminating in a parade in which the red flag was carried for the first time since the armistice. Lanny stood on the street corner and watched it go by, in company with his new friend Steffens. Each of them had his thoughts and did not say them all. Lanny saw his Uncle Jesse marching in the front ranks, looking very determined—but doubtless quaking inside, because no one knew if the police would try to stop the parade, and it might be a killing matter if they did. The nephew thought: "Kurt had something to do with this"; and again: "I wonder if he's watching."

The same crowd that Lanny had observed at the *réunion;* the same sort of persons, and in many cases no doubt the same individuals: men and women, hungry, undernourished from childhood,

with pale faces set in grimmest hatred. Lanny knew more about
them now; he knew that they meant blood, and so did their opponents. The submerged masses were in revolt against their masters
and sworn to overturn them. A few weeks ago Lanny would have
thought it was a blind revolt, but now he knew that it had eyes and
directing brains.

He noticed how few of the marchers looked about them, or paid
any attention to the watching crowds. They stared before them
with a fixed gaze. Lanny remarked this to his companion, who replied: "They are looking into the future."

"Do you really want it, Mr. Steffens?" Lanny asked him.

"Only half of me wants it," replied the muckraker. "The other
half is scared." He meant to say more, but his words were drowned
by the menacing thunder of the "Internationale":

> Arise, ye pris'ners of starvation,
> 　Arise, ye wretched of the earth;
> For justice thunders condemnation,
> 　A better world's in birth.

33

Woe to the Conquered

I

THERE was another question which the Big Four had to settle, and which they kept putting off because it contained so much
dynamite. The problem of money, astronomical sums of money,
the biggest that had ever been talked about in the history of man-

kind. Who was going to pay for the rebuilding of northeastern France? If this peasant people had to do it out of its own savings, it would be crippled for a generation. The Germans had wrought the ruin—a great deal of it quite wanton, such as the cutting of vines and fruit trees. The French had set the cost of reparations at two hundred billion dollars, and thought they were generous when they reduced it to forty. The Americans were insisting that twelve billions was the maximum that could be paid.

What did it mean to talk about forty billion dollars? In what form would you collect it? There wasn't gold enough in the world; and if France took goods from Germany, that would make Germany the workshop of the world and condemn French industry to extinction.

This seemed obvious to an American expert; but you couldn't say it to a Frenchman, because he was suffering from a war psychosis. You couldn't say it to a politician, whether French or British, because he had got elected on the basis of making Germany pay. "Squeeze them until the pips squeak," had been the formula of the hustings, and one of Lloyd George's "savages," Premier Hughes of Australia, had come to the conference claiming that every mortgage placed on an Australian farm during the war was a part of the reparations bill. Privately Lloyd George would admit that Germany couldn't pay with goods; but then he would fly back to England and make a speech in Parliament saying that Germany should and would pay. The Prime Minister of Great Britain had Northcliffe riding on his back, a press lord who was slowly going insane, and revealing it in his newspapers by clamoring that the British armies should be demobilized and at the same time should march to Moscow. Lloyd George pictured the Peace Conference as trying to settle the world's problems "with stones crackling on the roof and crashing through the windows, and sometimes wild men screaming through the keyholes."

The time came when Clemenceau lost his temper and called Woodrow Wilson "pro-German" to his face. It may have been a coincidence, but right after that the President was struck down by influenza and retired to his bed under doctor's orders. When next he saw the Premier and the Prime Minister it was in his bedroom, and they had to be considerate of an invalid. Once more the fate of the world waited upon the elimination of toxins from the blood-stream of an elderly gentleman whose powers of resistance had been dangerously reduced.

Everybody quarreling with everybody else! General Pershing in a row with Foch, because he wouldn't obey Foch's orders as to the repression of the Germans on the Rhine; Americans wouldn't treat a beaten foe as the French demanded. The Marshal was in a row with his Premier, and Poincaré, President of France, was at outs with both. Wilson was snubbing his Secretary of State, who agreed with none of his policies, yet didn't choose to resign. There was open conflict with the Senate opposition, which now had couriers bringing news from Paris, because it didn't trust what President Wilson was telling the country. There were even rumors among the staff to the effect that a coolness was developing between Wilson and his Texas colonel. Had the latter made too many concessions? Had he taken too much authority? Some said yes and some said no, and the whispering gallery hummed, the beehive quivered with a buzz of gossip and suspicion.

II

The question of the blockade had narrowed down to this: was America willing to sell the Germans food on dubious credit, or would she insist on having some of the gold which the French claimed for theirs? A deadlock over the issue, while mothers hungered and babies died of rickets. The American government had guaranteed the farmers a war price for their food, and now the government had to have that price. At least, so the Republicans clamored—and they controlled the new Congress that was going to have no more nonsense about "idealism."

Lanny listened to controversies among members of the staff. What would our government do with the gold if we took it? Already we had an enormous store which we couldn't use. Alston insisted that when it came to a showdown the French wouldn't dare to take Germany's gold, because that would wreck the mark, and if the mark went, the franc would follow; the two currencies were tied together by the fact that French credits were based upon the hope of German reparations.

Lanny was finding out what a complicated world he lived in; he wished his father could be here to explain matters. But the father wrote that he expected to be busy at home for quite a while. Budd's had been forced to borrow money and convert some of the plants to making various goods, from hardware and kitchen utensils to sewing machines and hay rakes. For some reason Robbie considered this a great comedown. Incidentally he was in a fresh fury with President Wilson, who had failed to repudiate the British demand that increases in the American navy, already voted by Congress, should be canceled and abandoned.

Mrs. Emily hadn't heard again from "M. Dalcroze," and an invitation addressed to him in care of *poste restante* had been returned. Lanny said: "He must have gone back to Germany," and Beauty said: "Thank God!" But Lanny was only half convinced, and was troubled by imaginings of his friend in a French prison or a French grave.

One hint Lanny picked up. At luncheon the professors discussed the amazing change in the attitude of one of the great French dailies toward the subject of reparations and blockade. Actually, it appeared that light was beginning to dawn in French financial circles. A Paris newspaper pointing out editorially that Germany couldn't pay unless she acquired foreign exchange, and that to do this she had to manufacture something, and to do this she had to have raw materials! A miracle, said the hardheaded Professor Davisson—who ordinarily didn't believe in them.

Lanny got a copy of the paper, and did not fail to note that the publisher was the man with whom Kurt had been getting acquainted in Mrs. Emily's drawing room. Lanny hadn't forgotten what his father had told him concerning the method by which "miracles" were brought about in the journalistic world. Before the war the Russians had sent gold to Paris and paid cash for the support of French newspapers; and now the Germans were trying to buy mercy! Could it be that Kurt had moved into those higher regions where a man was safe from both police and military authorities?

III

One couldn't talk about such matters over the telephone, so Lanny went that afternoon to call upon his mother. He rode up in the lift unannounced and tapped on her door. "Who is it?" she called; and when he answered she opened the door cautiously, and after she had let him in, whispered: "Kurt is here!"

The German officer gave no sign until Beauty went to the door of the inner room and called him. When he emerged, Lanny saw that he had adopted fashionable afternoon garb, in which he looked handsome. He wore a little mustache, trimmed close in English fashion, and his straw-colored hair, which had been perhaps a quarter of an inch long when Lanny first met him at Hellerau, was now of a length suited to a musician. Kurt was pale, but easy in manner; if the life of a secret agent was wearing on his nerves, his friends were not going to be troubled with the fact. "I thought I owed it to you both to let you know I'm all right," he said to Lanny.

"Isn't it dangerous to come here, Kurt?"

"Things are all right with me so far as I know. Don't ask more."

The other held up the newspaper, saying: "I was bringing my mother a copy of this." There was a flash of the eyes between the two friends, but no more was said.

They seated themselves, and Kurt drew his chair close, so that he could speak in a low tone. He asked first what Lanny knew about the intentions of the Peace Conference regarding the district of Stubendorf; Lanny had to tell him the worst, that it was surely going to the Poles. Then Kurt wanted to know about the blockade; Lanny outlined different projects which were being discussed, and the attitude of various personalities he knew or knew about. Kurt repaid his friend by talking about developments in Germany, information which might be valuable to the Crillon staff.

This talk went on for quite a while. When there came a lull, Beauty remarked: "Kurt has told me something that I think you ought to know about, Lanny—his marriage."

"Marriage!" exclaimed Lanny, dumfounded. The smile went off the other's face.

Another of those tragic tales of love in wartime—*amor inter arma*. The affair had begun when Kurt lay in hospital after his second wounding, some pieces of his ribs torn out by a shell fragment.

"It was a small town near the eastern border," said the officer. "The front had shifted back and forth, so there was a lot of wreckage and suffering. The nurse who took care of me was about a year younger than I, a fine, straight girl—her father was a schoolteacher, and poor, so she had been obliged to work for her education. I'd got a touch of gangrene, so I had a long period of convalescence and saw a great deal of her, and we fell in love. You know how it is in wartime——"

Kurt was looking at Beauty, who nodded. Yes, she knew! Lanny said: "The same thing happened to Rick. Only it wasn't a nurse."

"Indeed! I must hear about that. Well, I was going back to duty and the time was short, so I married her. I didn't tell my parents, because, as you know, we pay a good deal of attention to social status in Germany, and my parents wouldn't have considered it a suitable match. My father was ill with influenza and my mother was under heavy strain, so I just sent my father's lawyer a sealed letter, to be opened in the event of my death, and I let the matter rest there until the war was over. Elsa wouldn't give up her duties as nurse, even though she was pregnant; and in the last weeks of the war she collapsed from undernourishment. So you see this blockade meant something personal to me."

Kurt stopped. His face was drawn, which made him look old; but he gave no other sign of emotion. "There wasn't enough food for anybody, unless it was speculators who broke the law. Elsa kept the truth from me, and the result was the baby was born dead, and she died of hemorrhages a few days later. So that's all there was to my marriage."

Beauty sat with a mist of tears in her eyes; and Lanny was thinking a familiar thought: "Oh, what a wicked thing is war!" He had lived through the agony of France with Marcel and his mother, and the agony of Britain with Rick and Nina; now in Germany it was the same. The younger man, thinking always of patching matters up between his two friends, remarked: "Nobody has gained anything, Kurt. Rick is crippled for life and is seldom out of pain. He crashed in a plane."

"Poor fellow!" said the other; but his voice sounded dull. "At least that was in a fight. His wife hasn't died of starvation, has she?"

"The British had their food restrictions, don't forget. Your submarine campaign was effective. Both sides were using whatever weapons they had. Now we're trying to make peace."

"What they call peace is to be just another kind of war. They are taking our ships and railroad stock, our horses and cattle, and saddling us with debts enough to last a century."

"We are trying to make a League of Nations," pleaded the American; "one that will guarantee the peace."

"If it's a league that France and England make, it will be a league to hold Germany down."

Lanny saw that it wouldn't do any good to argue. For a German officer, as for a French one, it was still war. "We Americans are doing everything in our power," he declared. "It just takes time for passions to cool off."

"What you Americans should have done was to keep out of it. It wasn't your fight."

"Maybe so, Kurt. I wasn't for going in, and now most of our men at the Crillon are doing their best to reconcile and appease. Do what you can to help us."

"How can we do anything when we're not allowed near your so-called 'conference'?"

A hopeless situation! Lanny looked at his watch, recalling that there would be an Armenian gentleman waiting for him at the hotel. "My time isn't my own," he explained, and rose to go.

Kurt rose also. But Beauty interposed. "Kurt, you oughtn't to go out until after dark!"

"I came before dark," he replied.

"I don't want you to go out with Lanny," she pleaded. "Why risk both your lives? Please wait, and I'll go with you." She couldn't keep the trembling out of her voice, and her son understood that for her too the war was still being fought. "I want to talk to you about Emily Chattersworth," she added; "she and I are hoping to do something."

"All right, I'll wait," said Kurt.

IV

The deadlock among the Big Four continued; until one day came a rumor that shook the Hotel Crillon like an earthquake: President Wilson had ordered the transport *George Washington* to come to France at once. That meant a threat to break off the conference and go back to his own country, which so many thought he never should have left. Like other earthquakes, this one continued to rumble, and to send shivers through many buildings and their occupants. Denials came from Washington that any such order had been received. Then it was rumored that the British had held up the President's cablegram for forty-eight hours. Had they, or hadn't they? And did Wilson mean it, or was it a bluff?

Anyhow, it sufficed to send the French into a panic. Clemenceau came hurrying to the President's sickroom to inquire, and to apologize and try to patch matters up. Even though he had called the stiff Presbyterian "pro-German," he couldn't get along without him, and his departure would mean calamity. A whole train of specters haunted the French: the Germans refusing to sign, war beginning again, and revolution spreading to both countries!

They resumed meeting in the President's room, and patched up a series of compromises. They decided to let the French have the

Sarre for fifteen years, during which time they could get out the coal and keep their industries going until their own mines were repaired. Then there would be a plebiscite, and the inhabitants would choose which country they preferred. The Rhineland would go back to Germany after fifteen years, permanently demilitarized. Marshal Foch went on the warpath again, and it wasn't long before he and his friends were trying to start a revolt of the French population in the Rhineland, to form a government and demand annexation to *la patrie*.

It was easy to understand the position of a man who had spent his life learning to train armies and to fight them. Now he had the biggest and finest army ever known in the world; troops from twenty-six nations, and more races and tribes than could be counted. Two million Americans, fresh and new, magnificent tall fellows, utopian soldiers, you might call them—and now they were being taken away from their commander, he wasn't going to be allowed to use them! The generalissimo had worked out detailed plans for the conquest of Bolshevism in Russia, and in Central Europe, wherever it had shown its ugly head; but the accursed politicians were turning down these plans, demobilizing the troops and shipping them home! The voluble little Frenchman was behaving like one demented.

Three subcommissions had been studying the question of reparations, but all in vain; so finally they decided to dodge the issue of fixing the total amount. Germany was to pay five billion dollars in the first two years, and after that a commission would decide how much more. Another job for the League of Nations! Woodrow Wilson was having his heart's desire, the League and the treaty were being tied together so that no one could pry them apart. But Clemenceau had his way on one basic point—Germany was not to be admitted to the League.

This last decision filled the American advisers with despair. They had been working day and night to devise an international authority which might bring appeasement to Europe, and now it was turning into just what Kurt had called it, a League to hold Germany down! There were rumors that the President was going even farther and granting the French demand for an alliance, a promise by England and America to defend her if she was again attacked. President Wilson had given way on so many points that Alston and others of the "liberal" group were in despair about him. All agreed that any such alliance would be meaningless, because the American Senate would never ratify it.

V

All day long and most of the night Lanny listened to arguments over these questions. He was not just a secretary, carrying out orders; he was concerned about every step that was being taken, and his chief dealt with him on that basis, pouring out his hopes and fears. Lanny had the image of Kurt Meissner always before him, and he pleaded Kurt's cause whenever a chance arose. He couldn't say: "I have just talked with a friend who lives in Germany and has told me about the sickness and despair." He would say, more vaguely: "My mother has friends in Germany, and gets word about what is happening. So does Mrs. Chattersworth."

These, of course, were grave matters to occupy the mind of a young man of nineteen. With him in the hotel suite were two other secretaries, both college graduates and older than he. They also carried portfolios, and filed reports, and made abstracts, and kept lists of appointments, and interviewed less important callers, and whispered secrets of state; they worked overtime when asked to, and when they grumbled about low pay and the high cost of cigarettes, it was between themselves. But they didn't take to heart the task of saving Europe from another war, nor even of protecting Armenians from the fury of Turks. They enjoyed the abundant food which the army commissary provided, mostly out of cans—and found time to see the night life which was supposed to be characteristic of Paris, but in reality was provided for foreign visitors.

Lanny listened to the conversation of these roommates, which

was frank and explicit. To them the sight of a hundred women
dancing on the stage stark naked, and painted or enameled all the
hues of the rainbow, was something to stare at greedily and to
gossip about afterwards. To Lanny, who had been used to naked-
ness or near it on the Riviera, this mass production of sex excitement was puzzling. He asked questions, and gathered that these young
men had been raised in communities where the human body was
mysterious and shocking, so that the wholesale exposure of it was a
sensational event, like seeing a whole block of houses burn down.

To these young men the need for a woman was as elementary as
that for food and sleep. Arriving in a new part of the world, they
had looked about for likely females, and exchanged confidences as
to their discoveries. They wanted to know about Lanny's love life,
and when he told them that he had been twice jilted and was nursing a broken heart, they told him to forget it, that he would be
young only once. He would go off and ponder what he had heard
—in between his efforts to keep the Italians from depriving the
Yugoslavs of their one adequate port.

"Take the good the gods provide thee!"—so had sung an English poet in the anthology which Lanny had learned nearly by
heart. That seemed to apply to the English girl secretary, Penelope
Selden, who enjoyed his company and didn't mind saying so.
Lanny found that he was coming to like her more and more, and
he debated the problem: what was he waiting for? Was he still in
love with Rosemary? But that hadn't kept him from being happy
with Gracyn. It was all very well to dream about a great and permanent love, but time passed and there was none in sight. Was he
hoping that Rosemary might some day come back to the Riviera?
But she was expecting a baby, the future heir to a great English
title. Lanny had written to her from Paris, and had a nice cool
friendly reply, telling the news about herself and their common
friends. All her letters had been like that, and Lanny assumed it was
the epistolary style of the English aristocracy.

He reviewed all over again the question of his sexual code, and
that of his friends of the *grand monde*. The great and permanent

love theory had gone out of fashion, if indeed it ever had been in fashion with anybody but poets and romancers. Rich and important persons made what were called marriages of convenience. If you were the son or daughter of a beer baron or diamond king, you bought a title; if you were a member of the aristocracy, you sold one, and the lawyers sat down and agreed upon what was called a "settlement." You had a showy public wedding, as a result of which two or three new members of your exclusive social set were brought into the world; then you had done your duty and were at liberty to amuse yourself discreetly and inconspicuously.

Was Lanny going to play second fiddle in some fashionable chamber concert? The invitation had been extended and never withdrawn. Assuming that he meant to accept, what about the interim? Live as an anchorite, or beguile his leisure with a refined and discreet young woman secretary? He was sure that if Rosemary, future Countess of Sandhaven, ever asked questions about what his life had been, it would be with curiosity as friendly and cool as her letters. Such were the agreeable consequences of that "most revolutionary discovery of the nineteenth century," popularly know as "birth control."

VI

The Big Four were deciding the destiny of the Adriatic lands and finding it the toughest problem yet. President Wilson had traveled to that warm country and been hailed as the savior of mankind; he had thrown kisses to the audience in the great Milan opera house, and had listened to the roaring of millions of throats on avenues and highways. He had got the impression that the emotional Italian people really loved him; but now he learned that there were two kinds of Italian people, and it was the other kind which had come to Paris: those who had repudiated their alliance with Germany and sold the blood and treasure of their land to Britain and France, in exchange for a signed and sealed promise of territories to be taken in the war. Now they were here, not to form a League of

Nations, not to save mankind from future bloodshed, but to divvy the swag.

The British and French had signed the Treaty of London under the stress of dire necessity, and now that the danger was over they were not too deeply concerned to keep the bargain—on the general principle that no state ever wants to see any other state become more powerful. But they lacked an excuse for repudiating their promises, and regarded it as a providential event when a noble-minded crusader came from overseas, bearing aloft a banner inscribed with Fourteen Points, including the right of the small peoples escaping from Austrian domination not to be placed under some other domination. The British, who had repudiated the idea of self-determination for Cyprus, and the French, who had repudiated it for the Sarre, were enthusiastic about it for the Adriatic—only, of course, it must be President Wilson who would lay down the law.

The crusader from overseas did so; and Premier Orlando, that kindly and genial gentleman, wept, and Baron Sonnino scowled, and the whole Italian delegation stormed and raved. They said that Wilson, having lost his virtue on the Rhine and in the Polish Corridor, was now trying to restore it at the expense of the *sacro egoismo* of Italy. There were furious quarrels in the council halls, and the Italians packed up their belongings and threatened to leave, but delayed because they found that nobody cared.

In the early stages of this controversy the hotels and meeting places of the delegates had swarmed with charming and cultivated Italians whose pockets were stuffed with banknotes; anybody who had access to the Crillon might have expensive parties thrown for him and enjoy the most delicate foods and rarest wines. The Hotel Édouard VII, where the sons of sunny Italy had their headquarters, kept open house for the diplomatic world. Later, when the thunder clouds burst, they didn't sever friendships, but were heartbroken and made you understand that you and your countrymen had shattered their faith in human nature.

The dispute broke into the open in a peculiar way; the Big Three agreed that they would issue a joint statement opposing the Italian demands, and the American President carried out his part of the bargain, but Lloyd George and Clemenceau didn't, so the Americans were put in the position of standing alone against Italy. Wilson's picture was torn from walls throughout that country, and the face which had been all but worshiped was now caricatured *sub specie diaboli*. The Italian delegation went home, and the French were greatly alarmed; but the Americans all said: "Don't worry, they'll come back"; and they did, in a few days.

VII

Lively times for experts and their secretaries! Professor Alston would be summoned to President Wilson's study, where the elder statesmen were on their hands and knees, crawling over Susak or Shantung. There would come a call to Lanny, asking if he could hurry over to the Quai d'Orsay to bring an important document to some associate who was assisting in the final revision of the League of Nations Covenant. An extremely delicate situation there, because the American Congress had insisted upon a declaration that the League was never going to interfere with the Monroe Doctrine; this provision had to be slipped in as quietly as possible, for there were other nations having "regional understandings" which they would have liked to put into the Covenant, and there was danger of stirring them up.

A group of the professors would meet at lunch, and Lanny would hear gossip about arrangements being made for the reception of the German delegation, now summoned to Paris to receive the treaty. The Germans were to be regarded as enemies until the document had been signed; they were not allowed to wear uniforms, and all intercourse with them was forbidden under military law. They would have the Hotel des Réservoirs, and building and grounds were to be surrounded with a barbed-wire stockade. This, it was explained, was to keep the mob from invading the premises; but it would be difficult to keep the Germans from feeling that they were being treated like wild beasts.

The delegation arrived on the first of May, the traditional holiday of the Reds all over Europe. A general strike paralyzed all Paris that day: métro and trams and taxis, shops, theaters, cafés—everything. In the districts and suburbs the workers gathered with music and banners. They were forbidden to march, but they poured like a hundred rivers into the Place de la Concorde, and the staff of the Crillon crowded the front windows to watch the show. Never in his life had Lanny seen such a throng, or heard such deep and thunderous shouting; it was the challenge of the discontented, a voicing of all the sufferings which the masses had endured through four and a half years of war and as many months of peacemaking.

Lanny couldn't see his uncle in that human ocean, but he knew that every agitator in the city would be there. It was the day when they proclaimed the revolution, and would create it if they could. Captain Stratton had told how Marshal Foch was distributing close to a hundred thousand troops at strategic points. The Gardens of the Tuileries were a vast armed camp, with machine guns and even field-guns, and commanders who meant business. But with the example of Russia only a year and a half away, could the rank and file of the troops be depended on? Fear haunted everyone in authority throughout the civilized world on that distracted May Day of 1919.

VIII

Lanny Budd had come to be regarded by the Crillon staff as what they called half-playfully a "pinko." It amused them to say this about the heir of a great munitions enterprise. The rumor had spread that he had a full-fledged Bolshevik for an uncle; and hadn't he brought that avowed Red sympathizer, Lincoln Steffens, into the hotel dining room? Hadn't he been observed deep in conversation with Herron, apostle of free love and Prinkipo? Hadn't he tried to explain to more than one member of the staff that these wild men and women, marching and yelling, might be "the future"?

What the Crillon thought of the marchers was that they wanted to get into the streets where the jewelry shops were. The windows of these shops were protected by steel curtains for the day, but such curtains could be "jimmied," and doubtless many of the crowd had the tools concealed under their coats. None knew this better than the commander of the squadron of *cuirassiers*, in sky-blue uniforms decorated with silver chains, who guarded the line in front of the hotel. The cavalrymen with drawn sabers were stretched two deep across the Rue Royale, blocking the crowd off; there was a milling and moiling, shrieks of men and women mingled with sounds of smashing window glass. Lanny watched this struggle going on for what seemed an hour, directly under the windows of the hotel. He saw men's scalps split with saber cuts, and the blood pouring in streams over their faces and clothing. It was the nearest he had come to war; the new variety called the class struggle, which, according to his Uncle Jesse, would be waged for years or generations, as long as it might take.

The Crillon staff took sides on the question as to the seriousness of the danger. Of course if the Reds succeeded in France, the work done by the Peace Conference would be wiped out. If it succeeded in Germany, the war might have to be fought again. The world might even see the strange spectacle of the Allies putting another Kaiser on the German throne! But apparently that wasn't going to happen, for Kurt Eisner, the Red leader of Bavaria, had been murdered by army officers, a fate that had also befallen Liebknecht and "Red Rosa" Luxemburg in Berlin. The Social-Democratic government of Germany hated the Communists and was shooting them down in the streets; and this was rather confusing to American college professors who had been telling their classes that all Reds were of the same bloody hue.

Strange indeed were the turns of history! A government with a Socialist saddlemaker at its head was sending to Versailles a peace delegation headed by the Imperial Minister of Foreign Affairs, Count von Brockdorff-Rantzau, member of the haughty old nobility who despised the German workers almost as much as he did the French politicians. He and his two hundred and fifty staff members were shut up in a stockade, and crowds came to look at them as they might at creatures in the zoo. The count hated them so that it made him physically ill. When he and his delegation came to the Trianon Palace Hotel to present their credentials, he became deathly pale, and his knees shook so that he could hardly stand. He did not try to speak. The spectacle was painful to the Americans, but Clemenceau and his colleagues gloated openly. "You see!" they said. "These are the old Germans! The 'republic' is just camouflage. The beast wants to get out of his cage."

34

Young Lochinvar

I

THE tall and stately Mrs. Emily Chattersworth was going shopping, and called at her friend Beauty's hotel rather early in the morning. "Such a strange thing has happened, my dear," said she. "Do you remember that young Swiss musician, M. Dalcroze?"

"Yes, very well," said Beauty, catching her breath.

"I had a visit last night from two officials of the Sûreté. It seems that they are looking for him."

"What in the world for, Emily?"

"They wouldn't tell me directly, but I could guess from the questions they asked. They think he's a German agent."

"Oh, my God!" exclaimed Beauty. Almost impossible to conceal the surge of her emotion. "How horrible, Emily!"

"Can you imagine it? He seemed to me such a refined and gentle person."

"What did they ask you, Emily?"

"Everything, to the remotest detail. They wanted to know how I met him and I gave them the letter he had written me. They wanted a description of him, height and weight and so on, which it's so difficult to remember. They wanted a list of the persons he had been introduced to at my home; they were much disturbed because I couldn't remember them all. You know how many persons I entertain—and I don't keep records."

"Did you give them my name?" asked Beauty, quickly.

"I'm happy to say I realized in time how that might point the finger at the Crillon."

"Oh, thank you, Emily—thank you! Lanny's whole future might depend on it!" Beauty got herself together, and then rattled on: "Such an incredible idea, Emily! Do you really suppose it can be true?" A woman doesn't spend many years in fashionable society without learning how to conceal her emotions, or at any rate to give them a turn in a new direction.

"I don't know what to think, Beauty. What could a German be trying to do now? Blow up the Peace Conference with a bomb?"

"Didn't you tell me that M. Dalcroze talked a great deal about the evils of the blockade?"

"Yes; but it's no crime to do that, is it?"

"It would be for a German, I suppose. The French would probably shoot him for it."

"Oh, how sick I am of this business of killing people! I hear there were several hundred killed and wounded in those May Day riots. The papers don't give us the truth about anything any more!" The kind Mrs. Emily, whose hair had turned snow-white under the stress of war, went on to philosophize about the psychology of the French. They were suffering from shellshock. It was to be hoped that when this treaty was signed they would settle down and become their normal selves. "If they have the League of Nations to protect them—and surely it can't be possible that the American Congress will reject such a great and beneficent plan!"

Beauty controlled her trembling and added a few reflections, derived at second hand from Lanny's professors. After a decent interval she said: "You haven't any idea what's become of that young man?"

"Not a word from him since he left my house that night. I thought it very strange."

"I'll ask Lanny about him," suggested the mother. "He knows many musical people, and might find him. Do you suppose he's related to Jaques-Dalcroze?"

"I asked him that. He told me no."

"Well, I'll see if Lanny can find him."

"But why, Beauty? Isn't it better not to know, under the circumstances?"

"Then you wouldn't want to give him up?" inquired the devious one.

"Surely not—unless I knew he had committed some serious crime. The war is over, so far as I am concerned, and I've not the least interest in getting anybody shot. Let the Sûreté find him if they can."

"Are you satisfied that they believed your story, Emily?"

"It hadn't occurred to me that they wouldn't," was the great lady's reply. She was a most dignified person, and did not have to assume this role. "Apparently they knew all about me, and they talked as if they were gentlemen. They are high officials, I am sure."

"Of course they'd find out how to approach you, Emily. But they probably don't tell anybody all they know, and they might take it for granted that you wouldn't either."

"What on earth are you driving at, Beauty?"

"Well, Lanny keeps telling me how the French are always calling the Crillon staff 'pro-German'; and if there should be German agents in Paris trying to make propaganda on behalf of lifting the blockade, wouldn't it please the French to be able to tie them up with us?"

"What a witch you are!" exclaimed her friend. "You look so innocent and trusting and then you talk like a Sherlock Holmes!"

"Well, Lanny told me the other day that since I have no money I have to develop brains."

"I wonder what Lanny is thinking about me!" reflected the *salonnière;* and in their laughter Lanny's mother found a chance to hide the nervous tension under which she was laboring.

II

Beauty declined to have lunch with her friend, saying that she wasn't feeling well and wouldn't dress. As soon as the visitor had departed, she called the Crillon, and said: "Come at once, Lanny. Tell the professor your mother is ill."

The youth had no trouble in guessing what that meant. He made the necessary excuses and reached the hotel as quickly as a taxi could bring him. He found his mother weeping uncontrolledly, and he guessed the worst, and was both relieved and puzzled when he learned that the Sûreté hadn't yet got hold of Kurt, so far as Beauty knew. "Certainly they didn't have him last night," he argued. "And he may be out of the country after all."

"I just know he isn't, Lanny! Something tells me!" Beauty sobbed on; her son hadn't seen her in such a state of distress since the days when she was struggling with Marcel, first to keep him alive, and then to keep him from plunging back into the furnace of war.

Suddenly she looked up, and the youth saw a frightened look in her eyes. "Lanny, I must tell you the truth! You must manage to forgive me!"

"What do you mean, Beauty?"

"Kurt and I are lovers."

Those were the most startling words that Lanny Budd had heard spoken up to that moment of his life. His jaw fell, and all he could think of to say was: "For God's sake!"

"I know you'll be shocked," the mother rushed on. "But I've been so lonely, so *distraite* since Marcel died. I've tried to tell myself that my baby was enough, but it isn't so, Lanny. I'm just not made to live alone."

"I know, Beauty——"

"And Kurt is in the same state. He's lost his wife and baby, he's lost his war, and his home—the Poles are going to have it, and he says he'll never go back to be ruled by them. Don't you see how it is with us?"

"Yes, dear, of course——"

"And did you think that Kurt and I could be shut up here in three rooms, and not talk about our hearts, or think about consoling each other?"

"No, I must admit——"

"Oh, Lanny, you were such a darling about Marcel—now you must manage to be it again! Kurt is the best friend you have, or he will be if you'll let him. I know what you think—everybody will say it—that I'm old enough to be his mother; but you've always said that Kurt was older than his years, and you know that I'm much too young for mine. Kurt is twenty-two, and I'm only just thirty-seven—that's the honest truth, dear, I don't have to fib about it——"

Lanny couldn't keep from laughing, seeing this good soul! desperately defending herself against all the gossips she had ever known. And taking a year or so from her own age and adding it to Kurt's!

"It's all right, dear. I was a little taken aback at first——"

"You don't have to feel that you've lost either your mother or your friend, Lanny. We will both be to you just what we were before, if you will forgive us and let us."

"Yes, Beauty, of course——"

"You mustn't think that Kurt seduced me, Lanny!"

The youth discovered himself laughing even more heartily. "Bless your dear heart! I'd be a lot more apt to think that you seduced Kurt!"

"Don't make fun of me, Lanny—it's deadly serious to both of us. You must understand what a gap there's been in my life ever since your father left me—or since I made him leave me. You'll never know what it cost me."

"I've tried to guess it many times," said the youth, and put his arm about her. "Cheer up, old dear, it's perfectly all right. Come to think of it, it's a brilliant idea, and I'm ashamed of my stupidity that I didn't think of it. Are you two going to marry?"

"Oh, that would be ridiculous, Lanny! What would people say? I'd be robbing the cradle!"

"Does Kurt want to marry you?"

"He thinks it's a matter of honor. He thinks you'll expect it. But tell him that's out of the question. Some day soon I'll be an old woman, and then I'd be ashamed of myself, to be a drag on his life. But I can make him happy now, Lanny. He's been coming here nearly every day, and we've both been embarrassed to tell you."

"Well, I don't think this was a very good time for you to turn into a prude," said the youth, severely. "But anyhow, that's done, and the question is how we're going to get you two sinners out of the country."

III

Beauty was like a person in a nightmare in which one is possessed by an agonizing sense of helplessness. She had no way to reach Kurt; he had given no address; he was under pledge, so he told her. He would come again—but when? And would he find police agents waiting for him in the hotel? Lanny must go downstairs and see if any suspicious-looking men were sitting in the lobby. Of course there are often men sitting in hotel lobbies, and how are you to say whether they look suspicious? Are police agents chosen because they look like police agents, or because they don't?

Beauty had to have help; and who was there but her son? She was terrified at the thought of involving him. Not on account of the Crillon—she didn't care a sou for them, she said, let them look out for themselves! But if the police were to take Lanny with Kurt? If he were to be punished for her guilty love—so she persisted in regarding it, being a woman who had been brought up respectably, a preacher's daughter, knowing the better even while she followed the worse!

Somebody must stay in the room, to be there when Kurt came, to warn him and hide him until night. Then they must get him out of Paris, and the safest way seemed to be by car. Beauty would go out and buy one, hers having been commandeered in the spring of the previous year. She supposed it would now be possible to get one if you had the price. Gasoline was still rationed, but that too could be arranged with money. She had only a little in the bank, she always did; but Lanny had a supply, and could draw on his father's account in an emergency. He offered to go out and attend to these matters; but the mother's terror took a leap—the police might trace all this, and Lanny would be guilty of helping a spy! No, let him wait here; she would run the errands.

Where would they go, he asked, and when she didn't know, he suggested Spain. If you went to Switzerland you were traveling toward Germany, and the authorities would be on the alert; but Spain was a neutral country, a Latin country, and a natural place for a rich American lady to be motoring with a lover. Or had it better be a chauffeur? They discussed the problem. A lover would appeal to Latin gallantry, but probably a chauffeur in uniform would be passed by the guard at the border with fewer questions.

Beauty had no passport, that evil device having been invented during the war, and she hadn't been out of France all that time. She would have to apply for one, and have a little picture made. She decided she would go back to the name of Budd, a powerful name, and foreign, more suitable to a tourist. Kurt doubtless had a passport, forged or genuine; if it was under the name of Dalcroze, it would have to be changed. No use to discuss that until he came.

In the meantime Beauty's heart would be in her mouth every moment. Oh, why, why did the life of men have to be an affair of danger, of obsessing and incessant terror?

Lanny promised to wait in the room, and positively not to leave it unless the hotel burned down. If a German officer were to arrive, what should be done with him? Hide him in the boudoir? Or send him out to walk in the parks? Lanny argued for the former. What chance was there of the Sûreté connecting Kurt with them? But Beauty was ready with an answer. Emily had named the other guests at that musicale. The agents would interview them, and ask the same questions they had asked Emily; surely some of them would remember Beauty! Perhaps already the police had her name and were on the way to question her! If her son were in the room, that would be all right; but Kurt must go out into the Parc Monceau, take a book, sit on a bench, and look like a poet; watch the rich children playing, and flirt with the *bonnes* like a Frenchman. "All right, all right," said Lanny.

IV

He wrote his mother a check, and while she dressed they discussed makes of cars, probable prices, and routes to Spain; also the possibilities of Kurt's evading the police or soldiers at the border, by paying a guide and climbing through the mountain passes. It would be the Basque country, which Beauty had traveled in happier days; but no day ever so happy as that one, if she lived to see it, when she and her new lover would be free in Spain. Again Lanny remembered his anthology. Young Lochinvar had come out of the east this time, and the steeds that would follow were swifter than any hero of Sir Walter Scott could ever have dreamed: sixty miles per hour on the roads and a hundred and fifty through the air— to say nothing of messages that traveled round the earth in the seventh part of a second.

Beauty telephoned; she was making progress; was there any news? Lanny said no, and she hung up. Another hour, and she

tried again; more progress, but still no news. So it went through
the longest of days. She came back late and reported she had a car
safely stored in a garage. All the formalities had been attended to;
she had paid, five francs here, ten francs there, and petty func-
tionaries had hastened to oblige her. She had a passport in the name
of Mabel Budd. That had been arranged through an influential
friend to whom she had explained that she didn't want to be a
widow any more; he had smiled, and offered to relieve her of the
handicap forever. Many matters could be arranged in France if
you were a beautiful woman and able to have clothes which did
you justice.

She had had the passport visaed for Spain, and had bought a map.
With her to the hotel came a man carrying a large package containing a uniform for a tall chauffeur. They stowed it under the
bed, where perhaps the Sûreté Génerale would overlook it. That
completed everything that Beauty and her son could think of; all
that was needed now was a chauffeur to put inside the uniform.

Lanny, having done his part, must return to the Crillon and
forget this dangerous business. If anyone questioned him, he was
to say that he knew nothing about it whatever. The mother sat
at the escritoire and wrote a note on hotel stationery: "Dear Lanny:
I have gone away on a short trip; will wire you soon. Have a chance
to sell some of Marcel's paintings. Adieu." That would be his alibi
in case he should be questioned. When she got into Spain, she would
wire him. If she or Kurt got into trouble, he must go to Emily
Chattersworth and make a confession of the whole affair and beg
for her help with the French authorities. Beauty kissed him many
times, and told him he was a darling—no news to him.

He went back to the question of Shantung, which now was
destroying the peace of mind of the Crillon staff. His mother went
to packing her belongings, and then to pacing the floor and smoking one cigarette after another. She couldn't eat anything, she
couldn't think anything but: "Kurt! Kurt!" She saw him in a score
of different places with the hands of French police agents being
laid upon his shoulders. She saw herself weeping in Emily's room,

pleading for forgiveness, explaining how she had kept this dreadful secret from her friend for the friend's own good. She saw herself on her knees before French officials, weeping, begging for mercy which they wouldn't or couldn't grant. Always she saw herself hating war, going to live in some part of the world where it wasn't —but what part was that? Why had God made so many wretched creatures, born to trouble as the sparks fly upward? Because of a pious upbringing, Beauty had phrases like this in her mind.

V

All through the proceedings of the conference the little Japanese delegates had sat listening, polite but inscrutable. They had tried to get into the Covenant of the League a provision for "racial equality," intended to get them access to California and Australia. That proposal having been turned down, they waited, studying the delegates and learning all they could. Which meant what they said and which could be bluffed or cajoled? Japan had taken the rich Chinese province of Shantung and meant to keep it unless it meant war with somebody. Would it, or wouldn't it?

The American staff was agog over this problem. If the Japanese had their way, it meant that the Fourteen Points had gone up in smoke. The patient, ever-smiling Chinese delegates haunted the Crillon corridors, morally and intellectually when not physically. Would "Mister Wilson" stand by them, or wouldn't he? The staff couldn't guess. They knew that "Mister Wilson" had been harried by seven unbroken weeks of wrangling, and was a badly exhausted man. Did he have one more fight left in him? Everybody speculated; and Lanny heard them as if in a dream. An absentminded and far from satisfactory secretary, he was excused because he was so worried about his mother's illness. Every hour he would go to the phone. "How do you feel, Beauty?" She would say: "Not very well."

In the middle of the evening the mother called: "Come at once, please." He went, and found her in a state of tension. Kurt had come, and now had gone to interview someone who had authority over him, to get permission to leave. He had said no more, except that he was sure he could get a passport into Spain. "He says he has friends there," Beauty explained.

Lanny hadn't thought of that. Of course the Germans would be working through Spain as well as through Switzerland, and if they could buy or manufacture passports in one country, they could do it in another.

Beauty was to meet Kurt at an agreed place on the street. "In one hour," she said. "But let's get out of here at once."

Her bags were packed and ready. Lanny paid the hotel bill, explaining that his mother had been called back to her home on the Riviera. The car had been phoned for and was at the door; the bellboys stowed the luggage, and Lanny tipped them generously. The couple stepped in, the car rolled away—and Beauty put her face into her hands and burst into sobbing. So much she had feared in that well-appointed family hotel; and nothing of it had happened!

They drove slowly about the boulevards, still unlighted, as in war days. After a while Beauty told him to drive to the spot where Kurt was supposed to come. "Draw up to the curb," she requested, and when he did so, she said: "Please go quickly."

"I don't like to leave you here," he objected.

"I'll lock the car. And I have a gun."

"I wanted to wait and see you off."

"Don't you understand, Lanny? The police may be following Kurt! They would want to get his associates, too."

He had to admit that this was reasonable. Since she didn't know how to drive, he asked: "What'll you do if he doesn't show up?"

"I'll lock the car and find some place to telephone you."

Lanny had hoped to see Kurt and give them both his blessing; but the most important thing was to calm his tormented mother. He got out, and said: "Tell him that if he isn't good to you I'll turn him over to the Sûreté."

She gave a little broken laugh. "Good-by, darling. Go quickly, please. Don't hang around."

VI

It was late, but Lanny returned to his desk, because documents were piling up and he was a conscientious secretary; also, he doubted if he could sleep. His mind was traveling the Route Nationale that ran south by west from Paris to the Bay of Biscay. He had never traveled it, but knew it would be good, for the safety of *la patrie* depended upon her roads. The distance was some five hundred miles, and if all went well they would cover that during the night and part of the next day; probably the border would be closed at night. There was a little town called Hendaye, and a bridge, and not far on the Spanish side was a popular resort called San Sebastián. Early in May it might be chilly, but those two had means to warm their hearts. No use thinking about possible mishaps—better to see Alston and work out the next day's schedule.

It was the day of a strange ceremony, the formal presentation of the peace treaty to the German delegation, taking place in the great hall of the Trianon Palace Hotel. The Allied delegates were received with drums and trumpets, which made more awe-inspiring the deathlike silence when the Germans were ushered in. Upon the table in front of their seats had been placed copies of an elaborate printed volume of close to a hundred thousand words, the Treaty about which the whole world had been talking and writing for half a year. The official text, in both French and English, was supposed to be the inspired word; but the Crillon heard strange rumors to the effect that numerous changes agreed upon at the last moment hadn't been got in, and even that the French had fixed up some things to read the way they wanted them. Whose business had it been to study the document line by line and compare it— with what? How could there be any checking up when three elderly gentlemen had met in the bedroom or study of one of them and kept no record, except for notes made by a trusted friend of Mr. Lloyd George who himself was not always to be trusted?

Anyhow, there was the volume, and Clemenceau arose and made

a brief speech to the Germans, informing them that they would have fifteen days in which to make their written observations. Said he: "This second treaty of Versailles has cost us too much not to take on our side all the necessary precautions and guarantees that the peace shall be lasting."

When it came the turn of Count von Brockdorff-Rantzau to answer, he did not rise, but sat motionless in the big leather chair. Perhaps this was because he was ill; but in that case he might have said so, and it appeared that his action was a studied discourtesy. The Allies had put into the treaty a statement to be signed by the Germans, assuming sole responsibility for the war. This filled the count with such fury that his voice shook and he could hardly utter the words: "Such a confession on my part would be a lie."

At the same time the Crillon gave out the news that President Wilson had made an agreement, jointly with Britain, to guarantee France in the event of another attack by Germany. The great master of words had searched his vocabulary once more, and this was not to be an "alliance," but an "understanding"; and of course that made it different. Many of the advisers were in a state of excitement about it, and wherever two of them met there were arguments. "If the treaty were just," declared Alston, "the whole world should help to defend it. But this treaty is going to cause another war; and do we want to obligate ourselves to be in it?" He pointed to the news from Germany, where the government had declared a week of national mourning in protest against the war-guilt declaration.

Lanny Budd wasn't supposed to have opinions; so he ran errands among the excited advisers who had stopped speaking to one another. He noted black looks and listened to angry words, and was unconcerned—because all the time his thought was: "Why don't I get that message?" He knew that the telegraph service of the French government was shockingly disorganized. Why hadn't he thought to tell Beauty to telephone? But he hadn't; so maybe they were safe in Spain, or maybe they were in jail in Tours, or Bordeaux, or Hendaye. Lanny couldn't keep his mind on his work.

Until late the next day, when the telegram arrived. Short and sweet it was: "Lanny Budd, Hotel Crillon, Paris: Peace love beauty." Highly poetical—but the important point was that the message was marked from San Sebastián!

VII

How was that oddly assorted couple going to make out? Lanny tried in his spare moments to imagine it. He had learned that you never could tell about other people's guesses in love; you just had to let them guess. Kurt would find that he had taken into his life a woman who hadn't much real interest in his ideas—only in him. Whatever he believed would be the truth and whatever he did would be important. Beauty would be loyal to her man; would take up his cause and fight for—not it, but him.

She talked a great deal and would certainly bore him while motoring over Spain. But she had sense enough to let a man alone if he asked it. If Lanny said he wanted to read, all right, he could go off in a corner of the garden and stay half a day. If Marcel had wanted to paint, or Robbie to play poker, that too was all right. If Kurt could only realize that the war was over, and get his musical instruments together and go on with his work, Beauty would be content to hear him tootling and tinkling all day. She had learned her formula from Emily: Kurt was a composer, and in order to write for any instrument you had to know its range, what fingerings were easy, what were impossible, and so on.

The day that Kurt produced his Opus 1, he would become for Beauty the greatest composer in the world; she would take up that composition and fight for it as she had fought for Marcel's art, and for the selling of munitions. She would inquire around and find out who was the topmost conductor of the hour, and somehow she would manage to be in his neighborhood and have him invited to tea. Maybe he would know what was up or maybe he wouldn't, but, anyway, he would hear Kurt's Opus 1, and soon it would be performed by a great symphony orchestra, and Beauty would see to it that all the critics were there, and that they met the *crème de la crème* of Paris or London society. Kurt would be dressed for the occasion, and presented to everybody—or would he? Maybe he'd be eccentric, like Marcel, despising smart society, wanting to hide himself! If so, Beauty would fall on her knees and tell him that she was a crude and cheap person, that he might have it his way—any way in the world, so long as he didn't go to war again! (Lanny, living over those days of anguish with his stepfather at Juan-les-Pins!)

Now it was Kurt who was going to be stepfather. What an odd thing! Of course Kurt had always taken the attitude of an elder and Lanny had thought of him as a mentor. As they grew older, fifteen months' difference in their ages would matter less; but probably Kurt would always know what he wanted to do, whereas Lanny might never be sure. Lanny had imaginary whimsical conversations with his friend, in which they adjusted themselves to the trick which fate had played upon them. Anyhow, they wouldn't be jealous of each other; and they would have lots of music in the house! Lanny began to reflect that he ought to concentrate upon that great art and try to make something of himself with Kurt's help.

VIII

The German delegation was bombarding the conference with notes, protesting against the terms of the "monstrous document," as the treaty was called by the President of the German Republic. They said that it was impossible of fulfillment; that in failing to fix the amount of the indemnity the Allies made it impossible for Germany to obtain credit anywhere; that in taking all her colonies and her ships, and requiring her yards to make new ships for the Allies, they were making it impossible for her to have any trade and so condemning millions of people to starvation. The better to continue this bombardment, the Germans brought in a special train with linotype machines and printing presses, and set about preparing a volume of their own, a "counter-proposal." Clemenceau replied with cold rejection of most of the German notes, and the experts and secretaries and translators worked at preparing ammunition to repel this new kind of bombardment.

It became Lanny's duty to take the files referring to Upper Silesia, and help the staff to digest them all over again, and prepare answers to the strenuous arguments of the German delegation, that this province was overwhelmingly German, and that giving it to the Poles was merely a move of power politics, to deprive Germany of coal and manufacturing power. A lot of extra work fell upon Lanny's shoulders, because Alston was giving so much time to discussing whether it was his duty to resign his position as a public protest against what he felt was a breach of faith with Germany.

There were signs of wavering among those responsible for the drastic terms of the treaty, and Lanny had the exciting idea that by some stroke of superdiplomacy he might be able to save the castle and district of Stubendorf for Kurt and his family. At any rate, Lanny would make special mention of it in the data he got together; he would underscore the name if it occurred; he would make notes on the margin of reports. When he had a chance to talk with his chief he told how he had visited that beautiful country— and assuredly every man, woman, and child that he had seen was German.

Professor Alston shook his head sadly. Lanny wasn't telling him anything new; it was just such blunders which were tormenting the conscience of the Americans, and of some Britons, too. But what could they do? It might be possible to persuade the Big Four to grant a plebiscite for the bulk of Upper Silesia, but Stubendorf lay too far to the east, and was surely going to the Poles. Paderewski, President of the new Polish Republic, had come to Paris, to fight for every foot of territory he could get, and the French were backing him. As Robbie had so carefully explained, this new republic was a French creation, to be armed with weapons manufactured by Zaharoff.

Lanny had been too busy to return to the mansion on the Avenue

Hoche; but every now and then he would come upon another strand of the web of that busy old spider. Right in the midst of the bright dream of saving Kurt's home came news that gave everybody at the Crillon a poke in the solar plexus: a Greek expedition had landed at Smyrna and taken the city, with British and French warships supporting them, and—here was the part which the Americans could hardly believe—the battleship *Arizona* and five United States destroyers lending aid! The French took the harbor forts, the British and Italians held the suburbs, while the Greeks invaded the center of the city and slaughtered the Turkish inhabitants.

Turkey was going to be dismembered, of course. The British and French were going to quarrel over the oil. The Italians were going to hold some of the islands. The Greeks were going to get Smyrna, as a reward for sending troops to Odessa to help fight the Bolsheviks. But what was America getting out of it, and why were American warships assisting against Turks, upon whom we had never declared war?

These developments had been foreseen by Robbie Budd, and Lanny now passed his information on to Alston and others of the staff. Zaharoff was a Greek, and hatred of Turkey was, next to money-making, the great passion of his life. Zaharoff controlled Lloyd George through the colossal armaments machine which had saved Britain. Zaharoff controlled Clemenceau through Schneider-Creusot—to say nothing of Clemenceau's brother and son. The Grand Officer of the Legion of Honor had practically an official status at the Peace Conference, and was now getting himself a port for the future conquest of Turkey and the taking of its oil. America was to accept a mandate for Constantinople, which meant sending an army and a navy to keep the Bolsheviks shut up in the Black Sea; also a mandate for Armenia, which meant blocking them off from the Mosul oil fields. Lloyd George had a map showing all this—young Fessenden had revealed the fact to Lanny without quite realizing its importance.

One fact Lanny failed to grasp—what he was doing to himself

by talk such as this in the Crillon. His mother was fondly imagining that he might have a diplomatic career, something so distinguished and elegant. He himself was finding it thrilling to be behind the wings and at least on speaking terms with the great actors. But he forgot about the whispering gallery, the busy note-takers and filers of cards. Zaharoff had tried to hire him as a spy. Did he imagine that Zaharoff had failed to hire others? Did he imagine that one could sit in with the Alston malcontents and discuss the project of resigning, and not have all that noted down in one or many black-books?

35

I Can No Other

I

LANNY BUDD was in a state of mental confusion. He had absorbed, as it were through the skin, the point of view of his chief and the latter's friends, the little group who called themselves "liberals." According to these authorities, the President of the United States had muffed a chance to save the world and that world was "on the skids"; there was nothing anybody could do, except sit and watch the nations prepare for the next war. George D. Herron went back to his home in Geneva, sick in body and mind, and wrote his young friend a letter of blackest depression couched in the sublimest language. Uncle Jesse, on whom Lanny paid a call, had the same expectations—only he didn't worry, because he said it was the nature of capitalism on its way to collapse. "Capitalism is war," said the painter, "and what it calls peace is merely time to get ready. To try to change it is like reforming a Bengal tiger."

A very young secretary listened to these ideas, bandied back and forth among the staff. He tried to sort them out and decide which he believed; it was hard, because each man was so persuasive while he talked. And meanwhile Lanny was young, and it was May in Paris, a beautiful time and place. Rains swept clean the streets and the air, and the sun came out with dazzling splendor. The acacia trees in the Bois, loaded with masses of small yellow blossoms, were bowed in the rain and then raised up to the sun. Children in bright colored dresses played on the grass, and *bonnes* with long ribbons dangling from the backs of their caps chatted together and flirted impartially with doughboys, Tommies, Anzacs, and chocolate soldiers from Africa. The beautiful monuments and buildings of Paris proclaimed victory, the traffic hummed and honked, and life was exciting, even though it might be on the way to death.

Lanny, walking on the boulevards, thought about his mother and Kurt, safe in Spain, and having a magical time. A letter had come from his friend, full of needless apologies, signed by that oddly unsuitable name of "Sam" which he had chosen without a moment's thought. Beauty had written also; no more about the past and its perils, but personal and happy news. A rugged and inspiring coast—the Bay of Biscay, O! Fascinating old towns, picturesque inns, sunshine and white clouds floating; peace and safety, heavenly anonymity, and, above all, love.

Lanny understood each of these words in its secret inner meaning. Voices told him that he was missing something in his life. Other people were finding it, but he was alone; no mother, no father, no girl—only a group of middle-aged and elderly gentlemen looking at the world through dark glasses, no two of them able to agree as to what they wanted to do—and powerless to do it anyhow!

II

"Society" was reviving. The fashionable folk were coming out of their five years' hibernation, hungry for pleasure as the bears for

food. The Grand Prix was to be run at Longchamps, and President
Wilson would attend, the first holiday that harassed man had allowed
himself in a couple of months. Lanny resolved to attend, and to do
it in style—with the help of the complaisant little army officer who
had charge of the nice big open Cadillacs with army chauffeurs who
took people on "official business" to the races or anywhere else in
or near Paris.

His thoughts turned to that agreeable lass at the Hotel Majestic.
She could get time off, and so could young Fessenden and the female
member of the staff who was his special friend. The English are a
sporting people, and the severe chaperon who looked after the
welfare of the young ladies of their delegation would regard watching horses race under the eyes of President Wilson as a form of
social duty. It is amazing how young women on very small salaries
can manage to look as gay and new as the richest ones; they don't
tell you how they do it, and Lanny had no means of guessing, but
he saw that the *toilettes* of the professional beauties which were
featured in the newspapers could hardly be distinguished from those
of girls who worked all day typing letters and keeping files. It was
democracy.

To look at that racetrack and its throngs of people, you would
have had a hard time realizing that Paris had been in deadly peril
less than a year ago; that long-range cannon had been peppering
her streets and houses with shells, and that hundreds of thousands
of her sons had given their lives to save her. The women who wore
mourning did not attend the races; only those fortunate ones whose
men had made profits out of the war. Now they wore hats full of
flowers, and the most striking ensembles that dressmakers had been
able to invent at short notice; they flaunted striped parasols and
waved handkerchiefs which represented a month's wages for one
of the working girls who made them. The beautiful sleek horses
strained and struggled for their entertainment and roars of cheering
swept over the stands and around the track.

In short, life had begun again for the leisure classes. The mood
was to spend it while you had it, and Lanny's father had it. So the

youth drank in sunshine and warm spring air and felt his soul expanding. He strolled among the smiling, chattering throngs, bowed to distinguished persons whom he knew, and told his friends who they were. The *grand monde* at its very grandest was here: important persons not merely of Paris and London and Washington, but of Greece and Egypt, Persia and India, China and Japan, Australia and New Zealand—and back to Paris by way of San Francisco and New York.

Penelope Selden was slender and quick-moving, with hair that glinted without dye and cheeks that were bright without rouge. Certainly she was happy without any effort that afternoon; they all made jokes, and bubbled with laughter at the poorest of them, and no shadow of the world's trouble crossed their souls. They bet no more money than they could afford to lose, and oddly enough they won, and enjoyed the delight of getting something for nothing.

Fessenden had an engagement for the evening, so they were driven back to town. Then, because all the restaurants of Paris would be packed to the doors on the evening of the Grand Prix, Lanny and Penelope took a taxi to the suburbs and found a little inn, having outdoor tables in a garden, an obliging moon to provide the right amount of light, and a host who was not obtrusive. The cooking was good, the wine tolerable, and afterwards they strolled in the garden and sat on a bench. Someone in the inn was playing a concertina—not the highest type of music, but it sufficed.

Lanny reflected upon the dutiful life he had been living these past five months or so; and also that in places such as this were rooms which could be hired with no questions asked. He had already made up his mind that he would take the good the gods provided him. He permitted the conversation to become personal, and when he put his arm on the top of the bench behind the girl, and then about her shoulders, she did not withdraw. But when he began to whisper his feelings, she exclaimed, in a voice of pain: "Oh, Lanny, why did you wait so long?"

"Is it too late?" he asked.

"I've gone and got myself engaged!"

"Oh, damn!" thought Lanny—to himself. Aloud he replied: "Oh, dear! I'm sorry!" Then, after a pause: "Who is it?"

"Somebody in England."

She didn't tell him more. Did that mean that she wasn't altogether pleased with her choice? They sat for a while, watching the tree shadows in the moonlight, which had become suddenly melancholy; the concertina was playing *adagio lamentoso*.

"What was the matter, Lanny? Did you think I was a gold digger, or something horrid?"

"No, dear," said he, truthfully. "I was afraid I mightn't be fair to you."

"Couldn't you have left that to me?"

"Perhaps I should have. It's hard to be sure what's right."

"I wouldn't have made any claims on you—honestly not. I've learned to take care of myself, and I mean to." They were silent once more; then she put her hand on his and said: "I'm truly sad about it."

"Me too," he replied; and again they watched the wavering shadows of the trees.

III

They talked about the relationship of the sexes, so much in the thoughts of young people in these days. They had thrown overboard the fixed principles of their forefathers, and were groping to find a code which had to do with their own happiness, the thing they really believed in. If you were going to have babies, that was another matter; but so long as you couldn't afford to have babies, and didn't mean to—what then?

Lanny told about his two adventures; and Penelope said: "Oh, those were horrid girls! I would never have treated you like that, Lanny."

"There's something to be said for both of them. The English girl belongs to a class and she owes a duty to her family. Don't your parents feel that way?"

"A stockbroker isn't so much in England—unless he's a big one, and my father isn't. He has other people to take care of besides me; that's why I went out on my own. So long as I earn my way, I think I've a right to run my own life. At any rate, I'm doing it."

"Have you ever had an affair?" he made bold to inquire.

She answered that she had loved a youth in the business school she had attended. His parents were well-to-do, and wouldn't let him marry. "I guess we didn't really care enough for each other to make a fight for it," she said. "Anyhow, we didn't. It messes things all up when one has more money than the other. That's why I was afraid to let you know that I liked you so much, Lanny. A girl can generally start things up if she wants to."

"I haven't much money," said he, quickly.

"I know, you say that. But you have what looks like it to a girl on the salary our Foreign Office pays. I waited, hoping you would speak, but you didn't."

It was a dangerous conversation. Their hearts were bared to each other and their feelings were stirred; it wouldn't have taken much to "start things up." But something like an alarm bell was ringing in the young man's soul. This was a lovely girl, and she was entitled to a square deal. It might be that she would call off her engagement and take a chance with him; from vague hints he guessed that the man in London was in business, and was not glamorous to her. But to break with him would be a serious step. If Lanny caused her to do it, he would be under obligations—and was he prepared to keep them? The Peace Conference was drawing to its close and their ways would part. Did he want to invite Penelope to Juan? If so, what would become of her job and her boasted independence? On the other hand, would he follow her to London?

No, he hadn't intended anything so serious. He had been thinking about a little pleasure, in the mood of these days, when men and women had the feeling that life was cheating them. Penelope said something like that; she was leaning closer to him, practically in his arms, and all he had to do was to close them.

"Listen, dear," he said; and his tone forecast what he was going to say: "If we do this, we'll get fond of each other, and then we'll be unhappy."

"Do you think so, darling?"

"You may be thinking you can go back to that chap at home. But perhaps you'll find you don't care for him any more, and you'll make yourself miserable, and him too."

"I've thought about it a lot, Lanny. We do what we think is right—and then we go off and spend many a lonely hour wondering if we didn't make a mistake."

"I'm judging by the way I am with that English girl I told you about."

"You can't forget her?"

"I've tried to, and I ought to, but I just don't."

"I suppose that's what's the matter between us," reflected Penelope. "There's a German poem that tells about a youth who loved a maiden who had chosen another."

"I know—Heine. And whom it just touches, his heart breaks in two."

"I don't suppose there'll ever be a remedy for that," said the girl.

They sat listening to the concertina player, who was evidently a returned poilu; he played their songs, which Lanny knew from Marcel and the other *mutilés*. Many of them dealt with love, and as a rule were sad; the toughest old campaigner would sit with a mist of tears in his eyes, hearing about the girl he had left behind him and wouldn't see again. Lanny told Penelope what was in these songs, and with echoes of them in their ears they strolled to the car and drove back to the city. Afterward, it was just as she had said—they both wondered if they hadn't made a mistake.

IV

The Germans were continuing their bombardment of the treaty, and were getting the help of liberal and "radical" groups all over the world. The statesmen in Paris who had pledged themselves to "open covenants openly arrived at" were now doing their best to keep the terms of this treaty from reaching the public; the text was unobtainable in America, and even in France, but you could buy a copy for two francs in Belgium, and protests against it arose more loudly every day in the neutral lands. The British Labour Party denounced it, which meant many votes and had a disturbing effect upon the "mercurial" Prime Minister. He began wobbling again and caused an amusing situation.

Through all the battles, it had been the Presbyterian President against the cynical Tiger, with Lloyd George holding the balance of power, and generally giving the decision to the Tiger. But now, here was the little Welshman fighting the Tiger, and President Wilson having the decision—and he too giving it to the Tiger! This amazed the people at the Majestic. One of the staff, Mr. Keynes, said that Lloyd George had set out to bamboozle the American President and had succeeded too well; now, when he set out to "debamboozle" him, it couldn't be done. The agile-minded little Welshman was helpless before the stiff "Covenanter" temperament, which had to convince itself that what it did was divinely inspired, and then, having acquired that conviction, had to stand by it, no matter how many votes it might cost.

Lanny heard the President's side from Davisson and others who were defending him in hot arguments with Alston. At the time when Wilson had needed Lloyd George's help it had been refused. Now the treaty had been presented to the enemy, and it was a question of making him sign it. What time was this for the Allies to start weakening? Clemenceau couldn't give way, for he had Foch on his back, and Poincaré watching for the moment to trip him. All that could be brought about was another deadlock, such as they had had two months ago, and starting the whole weary wrangle all over again.

One aspect of the problem could be mentioned only in whispers. General Pershing wasn't sure how long he could control his troops. His armies were melting away. All over France, Belgium, Switzerland, were not merely doughboys but also officers who had quit in disgust. No need for Jerry Pendleton to hide, or for Lanny

to worry about him any more! And if the Germans should refuse
to sign the treaty, would the men still under arms consent to march
and fight? Congress had been summoned in special session, and
there was a resolution before the Senate declaring that a state of
peace existed with Germany. Just as easy as that!

Clemenceau and Marshal Foch wouldn't yield an inch; no, not
an inch; but having said that and sworn it, they began to yield,
a fraction of an inch here and a fraction there. Germany was going
to be admitted to the League of Nations after all. And there was
going to be a plebiscite for a part of Upper Silesia—not the part
containing Schloss Stubendorf, alas, but the part with the coal
mines, which the Poles wanted so badly, and which the French
wanted to use against Germany the next time. So it went, and each
small concession was a bite out of the body and soul of France;
the screams were loud and terrifying—and Lanny, most of whose
life had been lived among the French, couldn't make up his mind
whether to listen to his boyhood friends, or to these new ones who
talked so impressively about justice, chivalry, democracy, and other
abstractions.

It was a complex problem that taxed the mental powers of the
ablest minds in the world, and would continue to be argued about
by historians. Professor Davisson and others to whose arguments
Lanny listened declared that these were not questions of right and
wrong, of morality or immorality, but of statesmanship. Of course
it wasn't just that Germany should be shut off from East Prussia;
but wouldn't it be equally unjust if Poland should be shut off from
the sea? The real question was, which course would provide for
international security. Said Davisson: "The main lines of this settlement have been established by the processes of history. It is fighting
against these processes not to recognize the successor states, especially Poland and Czechoslovakia, and give them the territory and
resources to maintain and defend themselves."

There were those who went even farther, driven by the mood
of war; they insisted that the Allied armies should have marched
to Berlin, to let the Germans know what war is really like, and

cure them of their fondness for it. The peace terms should now provide for the dividing of Germany into a number of small states, as in the days before Bismarck. The Prussians were a tribe incapable of understanding any ideal save that of conquest, and it should be made impossible for them to use the peace-loving Germans of Bavaria and the Rhineland in their adventures. Lanny didn't associate with persons who held such views, because Alston and his group considered them outside the pale; but he met them among his mother's friends, and among those who came to Mrs. Emily's. They seemed to know a lot of history.

V

Bullitt and Steffens had journeyed to Russia on a mission, of a sort contrived by statesmen who wish to keep themselves free either to accept the results, in which case it was an official mission; or to reject the results, in which case the statesmen had nothing to do with the mission and didn't even know about it. In the case of the expedition to Russia, Wilson and Lloyd George had chosen the latter course; and now what were the expeditioners going to do?

Lincoln Steffens had already had his experience of martyrdom, and was having it still. He had written too sympathetically about various "radicals" in trouble, and as a result no magazine of any circulation was willing to have his name appear in its pages. Here he was, a highly trained journalist in Paris, enjoying contacts such as no other had; every day he collected marvelous stories—and could do nothing with them but hand them over to less competent men.

Lanny sat in Stef's room, listening to some of these tales, when in came Bill Bullitt; bouncing, eager young newspaper fellow, now being suddenly matured and sobered. His was an old and wealthy family of Philadelphia, and young men of exalted social position perhaps have their own way too easily, and are impatient of neglect and frustration. Also, they can afford the luxury of moral scruples. It made young Bullitt furious when Lloyd George would send for

him, and pump his mind of everything he had seen and heard in
the land of the Soviets, express deep appreciation of the service
which Bullitt had performed—and then get up in Parliament and
officially lie about him. The young aristocrat was like a man who
strolls in a lovely garden, picking the fruit and tasting it, and suddenly falls through the sod and discovers that the garden is made
over a charnel pit. When Lanny first met him, Bill had just scram-
bled out, his eyes and mouth full of horrors. He was hating it in a
blind fury, and determined to expose it to the world.

And here was Stef, middle-aged, sad, and accustomed to the odors
of charnel pits; they were ancient institutions, all the national gardens of Europe were built over them. If any young fellow wanted
to go on a crusade against lying and cheating in diplomacy, all
right, but let him know what he was fighting. It was nothing less
than the property system, which was the foundation of modern
western culture; and were you prepared to scrap it? If not, why
all this fuss about a few of its by-products?

Stef told about two French journalists who had come to him
at the outset of the Peace Conference, obviously sent by Clemenceau or one of his agents, putting up to the Americans the question:
Just how much of his Fourteen Points did President Wilson really
mean, and how far were the Americans ready to go in support of
these exalted principles? Did they mean to apply them to India,
to Hong Kong, Shanghai, Gibraltar? Of course they didn't; of
course they meant to let the British Empire keep on going—so why
not a French empire? This put the Americans in a hole, as it was
meant to do. The whole world saw, the first thing President Wilson
did when he reached London was to begin hedging on his "freedom of the seas," making plain that it didn't mean what everybody
but statesmen had supposed it meant.

"All right," said Stef, "go in and fight; but don't start until you
know who your enemy is, and have some idea of his strength. The
war on Russia which we denounce, and the peace treaty, are parts
of the same imperialist program. The Polish Corridor, the new

Baltic states, and all the rest of it, are meant to keep Germany and
Russia apart, so that the British Empire and the French Empire
can deal with them separately. That's what empires do, and must
do if they are to go on existing. What we Americans have to get
clear is that the same forces are building the same kind of empire
at home, and we'll be doing the same thing as the British and
French, because we have to have foreign trade, and outposts like
the Panama Canal and Hawaii. So why not start reforming ourselves, Bill?"

Young Bullitt didn't see that; and Lanny only half saw it. He
listened to the muckraker talking in his quizzical fashion, teasing
people with paradoxes, often saying the opposite of what he really
meant; Lanny decided all over again that these radicals were damned
irritating. But at the same time he was embarrassed to discover how
much they knew, and how often their unpleasant predictions came
true. He decided that maybe he'd agree with them after they were
able to agree among themselves.

VI

In a private dining room of the Crillon a small group met to
choose their future course. They were in a painful situation, and
some were wishing they had never crossed the seas. They had to
choose whether to let their names and reputations be used in support of what they believed to be falsehoods and blunders, or to get
themselves called unpatriotic and eccentric, to be looked upon as
unreliable, perhaps touched with the poison of "radicalism."

It was a not too luxurious dinner, for most of them were not well
off. Even for those who had private fortunes it was a grave decision, for they didn't want to live idle lives—they had come with a
fond dream of helping to make the world better, and the course
they now contemplated might put them on the shelf for a long
time, perhaps for life. Their wives came with them, and over a
dinner table decorated with yellow jonquils and red roses they

talked more solemnly and frankly than Lanny had ever heard from persons of their clever sort. Were they going to ride along on the bandwagon, or climb off as a gesture of protest?

It was a young people's party; the only middle-aged ones were Steffens and Alston. Bullitt was twenty-eight, and Adolf Berle, acting chief of the Russian Section, was only twenty-four; there were others of that age, and their wives were still younger. You could feel the spiritual wrestling going on; but they all tried, in the modern fashion, to take it lightly and not look or act like martyrs, or heroes, or anything that was bad form. Over the liqueurs and coffee everyone had his say, and heard what the others thought about his arguments, and even about his moral status.

Those who were not resigning built themselves a defense mechanism. They were members of a team and had to stand by their captain. He had done the best he could, and they had to exclude from their minds all arguments against his many surrenders. Or else they declared that they were subordinates, employed to furnish information, not to make decisions. Certainly they weren't signing any treaties. Some were in the army, and for them to resign would mean courtmartial!

Those who were resigning were none too patient with these excuses. Being young, their judgments were harsh; black was black and white was white, and no half-tones between. "Oh, yes!" they said. "Be a good boy and do what you're told! Feather your own nest and let the world go to hell!" One of the group had decided at the last minute not to attend; it was rumored that he had been promised a job on the Secretariat of the new League of Nations, which seemed the way to a glamorous European career. "He has his thirty pieces of silver!" exclaimed the resigners.

They had been sold out; that was the general sentiment of the rebels. Each had his own department, about which he knew, and on which he contributed information. Samuel Morison of the Russian Section was furious because the Allies were trying to use his favorite Baltic states as a springboard for White Russian interventions. Bullitt's anger was because the French General Staff had a mandate to run Europe. Berle was indignant because the Allied and associated powers remained untouched by the high moral principles which they were applying to their enemies. Said Alston: "It is not a new order in Europe but a piece of naked force." Because of his age his words carried weight.

The non-resigners fought back, and their wives helped them. They talked about "futile gallantry"; one woman compared them to a group of mosquitoes charging a battleship. It was an old, old question, which Lanny had confronted in talks with Kurt and his father. What part do moral forces play in history? Is there any real use in making yourself uncomfortable for a lot of people who will never hear about it, and wouldn't appreciate it if they did? "It's going to be a long, long time before the verdict of history is rendered on this treaty," said one; and when Alston appealed to the public at home, another said: "All they are thinking about is to punish the Germans; if you try to stop it, you're 'pro-German,' and that's the end of you."

When it came Lanny's turn, he said that Alston was his chief, and he meant to follow him. Alston answered that it might be better if Lanny stayed, because he knew the files and the contents of many reports, and could be of help to whoever took over the job. But Lanny said: "I joined on your account. If you go, I'm sick of the whole business." When the voting was over, one guest reached out and took some of the flowers which decorated the table and, pulling the blossoms off the stems, tossed one to each person—red roses to the resigners, and yellow jonquils to the "good boys" and their girls. It was highly poetical.

When they broke up, close to midnight, Lanny and young Berle walked twice around the Place de la Concorde, in the blue fog and between the rows of looming guns. The acting chief of the Russian Section reminded his still more youthful companion of the saying of Count Oxenstjerna, Swedish diplomat of nearly three hundred years back: "Go forth, my son, and learn with how little wisdom the world is governed!"

VII

The few protestants were in the mood of Martin Luther at the Diet of Worms: "God help me, I can no other!" Carefully and conscientiously each one composed a letter to the State Department, setting forth the reasons which impelled him to the grave step. These letters were duly handed in, and copies were given to the press representatives. Having fired the shot which was supposed to be heard round the world, each patriot held his breath and waited for the echoes.

Alas, they had things to learn about the world they lived in. One of the great New York papers gave an inch or two to the report of some resignations, naming no names; the rest of the press gave not a line to the matter. And then—a pathetic sort of anticlimax— the tactful secretary-general of the American Commission sent for each of the resigners separately and said that their objections had been duly recorded on the books of history; so their honor must now be considered to be satisfied. Wouldn't they kindly consent to stay on and perform their duties during the short time still remaining? No one else knew what they knew; they were really indispensable. Amateurs in diplomacy, they could hardly evade this trap. A couple of days later the department in Washington gave to the press a denial that anyone had resigned except Bullitt, and one professor who was returning on account of pressing duties at home.

Lanny parted from his friend Alston, who was going to teach summer school—a humble professor once more, with no presumptuous ideas of guiding the destiny of states. He had had a great influence upon his secretary, and would not be forgotten. That is the consolation of professors.

Lanny stayed resigned, and so was loose and alone in Paris. He no longer had the use of a room, paid for by the government; no more free meals, and no more honors. The doormen of the Crillon knew him, and would still let him in, but he became aware that persons who talked to him were a bit uneasy. It wasn't quite the safe thing to do.

More to his surprise, Lanny found the same sense of discomfort when he went to see his friend Fessenden. The American had understood, of course, that he was being used as a source of information, but he had assumed that the friendship was real, even so. Now the young Englishman wanted him to understand that it was really real, but Fessenden was dependent upon his career for a living— he wasn't a playboy like Lanny, and couldn't afford to get himself marked as a "pinko." He was very busy now; but when the conference was over there would be time for sociability.

Mrs. Emily invited the homeless youth to be her guest, and he was glad to accept. Here was a comfortable place to stay, and quiet friendship to smooth his ruffled plumage. His hostess was nearing sixty, and with her white hair was a dignified and impressive figure. In her home he met mostly French people; and oddly enough, cultivated Frenchmen paid very little attention to his revolt. The French are a well-insulated people, and seldom bother to know what is going on outside their own world unless it is forced upon them. Disputes and disagreements among the American staff? Yes, they are a rather violent people; their cinema reveals it; they still have wild Indians, don't they? The French would shrug their shoulders.

Lanny was a man of leisure, with time to stroll on the boulevards and watch the sights of a great city and reflect upon them. He himself didn't realize to what extent his point of view had changed; how different his reflections from what they would have been a year ago. For example, the painful spectacle of the women of Paris. In the early days of the Peace Conference you hardly saw a spot on the Champs-Élysées where a person could sit that didn't have a doughboy with a French girl in his lap; now, when the doughboys were disappearing, the competition among the women had become ravenous. Three or four would sight Lanny at once, and come to him swiftly, each looking ready to tear the eyes out of her rival; when he politely told them in good French that he was living a chaste life, their enmity to one another would vanish, and they would gaze mournfully after him, saying: "Oh, but life is hard for the women!"

Six months ago, Lanny would have attributed all this to natural depravity, of a sort peculiar to the Gallic race; he would have recalled some phrases which M. Rochambeau had quoted from Tacitus, censuring the moral code of that race in its then barbaric state. But now Lanny had the phrases of Stef and his Uncle Jesse in his mind. His attention had been called to the fact that municipal authority under the stress of war had set the wages of French workingwomen at six francs per day; whereas to go into a restaurant and have a poor dinner would cost one of them at least seven. Yes, it was the stark, simple fact that hunger was driving them to sell their bodies; hunger was driving the poor of Europe to madness, and making the ferocious class struggles.

What about the women of more prosperous classes, so many of whom were selling themselves for silk gowns, fur coats, and jeweled slippers? "Well," Lanny could hear his uncle saying, "aren't these the tools of their trade?" The gentle and refined scholars whom Woodrow Wilson had brought to Paris were appalled at the behavior of females who wore the clothes of ladies and had been expected to behave that way: females of all nations, American included, some of them in Red Cross costumes. In the Crillon order was maintained, but in other hotels they peddled themselves from door to door like book agents. The shocked professors repeated a story about the American Ambassador to Belgium, who was lodged in the ultra-magnificent Palace Hotel of Brussels, owned by the King of Spain. Said the ambassador to his friends: "It is the custom in European hotels to leave your boots outside the door, to be gathered up by the porter and polished in the early morning hours. So I have bought myself a pair of ladies' shoes, and every night I place them outside my door along with my own boots!"

VIII

There were other aspects of life in Paris less depressing. There were theaters with more to show than troupes of naked women. There were concerts, to remind one that the life of the spirit still

continued. Most interesting to Lanny was the spring salon in the
Petit Palais. To think that in the midst of the last desperate agony
of war, with several "Big Berthas" dropping shells into the city
every twenty minutes, with food scarce and fuel unobtainable, more
than three thousand men and women had sat at easels and maintained their faith that art could not be destroyed, but was and
would remain the supreme achievement and goal of life!

Lanny went to this show day after day. There were many kinds
of paintings, many subjects, many techniques; he studied them, and
tried to understand what the artist was telling him. Beauty had had
three of Marcel's last works brought to Paris, and they had been
hung; Lanny now compared them with the work of other men,
and confirmed his opinion that there was nothing better being
shown. You could see how the crowds felt, for there were always
people looking at Marcel's work, and asking questions concerning
the painter. Not many knew about him, but they were going to;
that would be one of Lanny's tasks, and his mother's—when she
came back from her new honeymoon.

Lanny knew many of the artists at this show. Some came to the
Cap and worked; for others Beauty had posed in her very young
womanhood. They came to see how their work was being received,
and to compare it uneasily with work that might be better. Lanny
talked with them, got their addresses, and went to visit their studios
and talk shop. They were glad to welcome a rich young man who
might be a customer, or could send others. As a stepson of Marcel
Detaze and nephew of Jesse Blackless, he was an insider; they talked
freely, and it was like old times. He had expected to find them all
starving and was happy to hear that art activities had come back
with an astonishing rush. The bourgeoisie had money and wanted
portraits of their beautiful ladies and their eminent selves; they were
planning palaces and villas and wanted them made elegant. Artists,
eternal enemies of the bourgeois, spoke of them with condescension;
another form of the class struggle.

Beautiful things, always touched with sadness. Lanny would stop
before a certain painting, and the thought would come to him:

what would Marcel think of this? His stepfather's spirit hovered at his shoulder, and would do so at every exhibition for the rest of his life; pointing out brushwork, atmosphere, composition, meaning, all the things that painting conveys to the trained intelligence. If Lanny was puzzled, he would wait and Marcel would tell him; if Lanny had a conclusion to announce, it would take the form of a dialogue with Marcel. So it is with impressions which form our childhood, and which we pass on to others in their turn.

Kurt Meissner was here in Lanny's thoughts, because they had attended a salon the year before the war; Rick, too, because they had attended the one of 1917. With these two friends Lanny was hoping to resume the life of art, in London, on the Riviera, all over Europe—when finally the statesmen had settled their squabbles and men could begin to think about the things that mattered. Lanny was in a mood of intense repugnance toward politics and everything that had to do with it. He had been on the inside, and never again would he believe in a statesman, never would a stuffed shirt or a uniform decorated with medals produce the slightest stir in his mind. Lanny's dream was to build himself an ivory tower and invite his chosen friends; they would live gracious lives, such as you read about in the days of the Medicis, and the Esterhazys, and other patrons of the arts.

The future patron had in his pocket a letter from Rick, begging him to come to England for a visit. Lanny had replied that he would do so as soon as he could arrange it. He had written to both his mother and his father, telling them about his resignation and asking as to their plans. From Robbie the reply came in the form of a cablegram—the old familiar kind that had made life such an adventure: "Sailing for London steamer Ruritania meet me Hotel Cecil Monday."

36

The Choice of Hercules

I

WHEN Lanny left Paris, at the beginning of June, the Allies and the Germans were still exchanging notes about the treaty, and all the world was waiting to know, would they sign, or wouldn't they? The railwaymen of France were threatening to tie up the country with a strike against low wages, long hours, and the high cost of living; so Lanny took his departure by plane, a new and adventurous way of traveling, if you had the price. This was one good thing that had come out of the war; air travel had become quick and easy, and top members of the British delegation found it swanky to fly to London in the morning, have lunch and a conference, and return to Paris in the afternoon.

Private passengers paid eighty dollars for a one-way trip. You were bundled up in a heavy sheepskin coat and robe and wore a helmet with goggles. A marvelous sensation to feel yourself being lifted off the ground and see the earth falling away. What hath God wrought! The wind roared by at a hundred miles an hour, and the noise of the engine made it necessary to write a note to the pilot if you had anything to say. Down below were the farms of France, little checkerboards of green and brown and yellow. Then the Channel, made safe for traffic, the submarines having been surrendered to the English fleet. Fishing boats were tiny specks on the smooth blue and the heavy coal lighters trailed streamers of black smoke.

When Lanny got off the train at the station near The Reaches, Rick and Nina were waiting in a little car, Nina driving; Rick could never drive because of his leg. He had it in a steel brace, but even with this support it pained him to walk, and now and then he would go white and have to lean against something. But he didn't want anybody to help him; it was his own trouble and he would attend to it. Just oblige him by going on with the conversation, quietly and indifferently, English fashion.

Lanny had expected to find his friend emaciated, but he was stouter than he had been. That was on account of the lack of exercise; he couldn't go into the water, and the only form of work he could perform was to lie on his back and wave his arms, or raise himself to a sitting position—all of which was a bore. He couldn't play the piano very well, because of the pedals. Most of the time he read, and he was exacting of his authors, also of people who came to talk with him. Nina said he had fretted himself near to death, but gradually he was learning to get along with what fate would allow him.

A little more than two years had passed since Lanny had seen him, strong and confident, hopping into a railway car with a load of cigarettes and chocolate for the "corps wing." Now you'd have thought ten times as many years had passed; his face was lined and melancholy and there were touches of gray in his wavy dark hair. But inside him was the same old Rick, proud and impatient, critical and exacting for himself as well as for others, yet warm-hearted in his reserved way, generous and kind in actions even when he was fierce in words. He was pathetically glad to see Lanny, and right away on the drive began asking questions about the Peace Conference, what it had done, what it was going to do.

Lanny could talk a lot about that and he found himself an important person, having been on the inside, and knowing things which the papers didn't tell. Even Sir Alfred wanted to hear his story. In the twilight they sat on the terrace of that lovely old place, and friends came, young and old, whom Lanny had met five years ago. What strange things they had been through—and how little they had been able to guess!

A basic question which they discussed at length: Could you by any possibility trust the Germans? Would they be willing to settle down, let bygones be bygones, take their part in a League of Nations, and help to build a sane and decent world? Or were they incurable militarists? If they got on their feet again, would they start arming right away, and throw the world into another Armageddon? Manifestly, the way you were going to treat them depended upon the answer to these questions. Lanny, having heard the subject debated from every possible angle, was able to appear very wise to these cultivated English folk.

Some had had experience with Germans, before and during the war, and had come to conclusions. Sir Alfred Pomeroy-Nielson, pacifist and radical of five years back, had now become convinced that Germany would have to be split up, in order to keep her from dominating Europe. On the other hand Rick, who had done the fighting and might have been expected to hate the people who had crippled him, declared that the dumb politicians on both sides were to blame; the German and the English people would have to find a way to get rid of these vermin simultaneously. With his usual penetration, Rick said that the one thing you couldn't do was to follow both policies at the same time. You couldn't repress Germany *à la française* with your right hand, and conciliate her *à l'américaine* with your left. That, he added, was exactly what the dumb politicians were attempting.

II

Next day they went punting. Rick spread himself on cushions on the bottom of the boat, with Nina at his side, and Lanny took the long pole and walked them up the Thames. They recalled the boat races, which had been postponed for five years, but would be held again next month. They stopped under an overhanging tree and ate lunch, while Lanny told about his stay in Connecticut, and the great munitions industry and the trouble it was in; he told about Gracyn, whose play had run all winter in New York.

Lanny thought how much better it would have been if he'd had the luck to find a girl like Nina, who so obviously adored Rick, and watched over him and waited on him day and night. They had a lovely little boy toddling about on the green lawns and Nina was expecting another. That was all Rick was good for, he said; to increase the population and make up for the losses of war. It wasn't any fun making love without a kneejoint, but he could manage it as a patriotic duty. Nina didn't make any objection to this form of conversation; it was the fashion among these young people, who went out of their way to say exactly what they meant.

Rick told about his family's affairs. When Lanny went for a walk he would discover that those old cottages which had shocked him had been razed and the ground planted to potatoes. A part of the estate had been sold to pay war taxes, and they might have to part with the whole thing if government didn't let up on them. The poor fools who imagined they were going to make Germany pay for the war would pretty soon begin to realize that Germany had nothing to pay with, and wouldn't do it if she could. Lanny agreed with that; he reported that the Crillon expected the Germans to sign with their fingers crossed and begin every possible method of evasion.

They drifted back with the current. While Rick lay down to rest, the other two sat under a tree on the lawn, and Lanny made friends with the baby while Nina told about her life. She didn't have to say that marriage and motherhood had agreed with her; her frail figure had filled out and her eager, intense manner had changed to one of repose. Rick's exacting ways didn't trouble her too greatly; she had learned to understand him, and managed him as an expert would a problem child. She counted herself fortunate, because she had love, which so many others had lost or had never found.

"At least they can't take him to war," she said, and added: "Now that we women have got the vote, if we allow any more wars, we'll deserve the worst that comes to us. Do you think women will get the vote in America?"

Lanny answered that President Wilson had been strongly against it, as a federal measure; but it had been shown that he could be made to change his mind. "I have seen that happen," said the youth, with a touch of malice.

"What are you going to do with yourself?" Nina wanted to know. When he told her that he was trying to make up his mind, she said: "You can't just drift around; if you do, some woman will get hold of you and make you miserable. Why don't you come and live near here, and let Rick and me find you a wife?"

He laughed and said he'd have to find a way to earn his living first; he didn't want to live on his father indefinitely. "Why don't you and Rick come to the Riviera next winter, and let him stay outdoors in the sunshine?"

"I don't believe we'll be able to afford any travel, Lanny."

"You'll be surprised how cheaply you can live, if you don't put on side. There are lots of little villas, and food will be cheap again when Europe settles down." Lanny was figuring on bringing Kurt and Rick together again. Such a clever intriguer he was!

III

He had asked Rosemary if he might come to see her. She answered that she was expecting a baby in a couple of months, and was "a sight," but if he could stand her she'd be delighted. Sir Alfred lent him the small car, and he drove for a couple of hours through the lovely English countryside, now at its best, and so peaceful you would think there had never been a war in the world: soft green meadows and fields of ripening grain, villages with broad commons and sheep grazing, great estates with parks, villas with well-kept hedges full of blossoms and singing birds. In most of those houses there would be gracious and kindly people, good to know; yes, maybe he would come to England—and learn to drive on the wrong side of the road without so much effort of mind.

Rosemary was now the Honorable Mrs. Algernon Armistead 'rougham, pronounced Broom, and she lived in what was called 'lodge," a fairly large house on the estate of her husband's grandfather. She enjoyed the scenery of a beautiful park without the trouble or expense of keeping it; an ideal environment for the incubating of a future member of the ruling class. The visitor was ushered into a sun parlor full of flowers and the song of a canary; presently Rosemary came in, wearing an ample robe of pink silky stuff, and looking so lovely that Lanny felt the blood start in warm currents all over him.

A strange thing to see the woman he loved carrying another man's child! But then, stranger things had happened to Lanny already; and in this part of the world, whatever you felt you didn't show it. Certainly the future mother of a future earl was going to show no signs of worry. "The sons of Mary seldom bother, for they have inherited that good part"—and the daughters the same. Rosemary was gracious, she was kind, and for the time being she was an elder sister to this youth who had had the good fortune to please her.

She wasn't much interested in politics, and he didn't even bother to mention his resignation from the Crillon. What she wanted to hear about was the members of the British delegation he had met; she knew some of them, and had heard talk about others. She wanted the latest news about Nina and Rick and their common friends. She asked politely about Lanny's mother, and when he said that she was traveling in Spain, that sufficed; for the leisure class went traveling when the mood took them, and no other reason was required. Nor had she much curiosity about his visit to America—a remote and provincial place that people came from but didn't go to.

Most of all she wanted to know about Lanny himself; what was the state of his heart, and what was he planning to do with himself? He didn't tell her about Gracyn, being ashamed of it. When she asked the direct question whether he had fallen victim to the lures for which La Ville Lumière was famous, he answered that he had lived a well-disciplined life, but had been sorely tempted by the charms of a stockbroker's daughter on the British staff.

"Poor darling Lanny!" said she. "He's going to be meat for some designing woman!" She was not to be persuaded that any man could ever see through the wiles of her sex.

The advice she gave him was the same as Nina's—to come and live in England. Rosemary, also, would like to find some "nice girl" to take care of him! "They can't fool us with their tricks, you know."

She had given him an opening, and he said: "Tell me—are you happy with your husband?"

"Oh, we get along," was the reply. "He's a very good boy—not vicious at all, only a bit soft." Her frank blue eyes met Lanny's. "He had a love affair, too."

"I see!" replied the youth. He had lived in France most of his life and wasn't naïve; but all the same, he was in revolt against the property marriage. Perhaps it was because he had read so many novels and dramas—impractical inventions which attempted to maintain the rights of the heart over those of great estates and family fortunes! Few indeed among the heroines of these works had been able to take the complications of their sex life with the serenity of the future Countess of Sandhaven.

"Lanny, darling," said she, "I feel for you just what I used to; and maybe some day things will be so that we can be happy again. But don't be silly and try to wait for me. It may be a long time. Take things as they are and don't wear yourself out trying to change them all at once."

IV

Lanny went up to town early on Monday morning, and was waiting in the hotel lobby for his father. It amused him to sit in the same chair which he had occupied under the same circumstances almost exactly five years earlier. In that far-off time people had been wont to complain that life had become commonplace, that civilization had taken all the romance and excitement out of it. But very certainly Lanny hadn't found it so during those five years!

Robbie came in, looking prosperous and well cared for as always. His son gave him a hug and some pats on the back, and they went upstairs, and after Robbie had unpacked his whisky bottle and got his ice and soda, he said: "Now what the dickens is this about Beauty going to Spain?" Lanny had written cryptically, for he couldn't give any hint about Kurt in France, and he thought it better not to allude to a love affair which would require a lot of explaining.

Now he told the story, and Robbie sat astonished, forgetting his drink. The younger man wasn't at liberty to tell the part about Uncle Jesse and the money, even to his father; but he told about the duel with the Sûreté, and the father said: "Look here, kid, did all this happen, or did you dream it?" When Lanny began to picture Kurt's life in Beauty's apartment, Robbie exclaimed: "You left those two people shut up together for a week?"

So the "love interest" in the story didn't require as much explaining as the younger man had anticipated. Robbie knew his former mistress from top to toe, as he said, and he had never imagined that she could live without a man. "Even if she tried, the men wouldn't let her," said he.

What he was interested in was trying to guess the chances of her finding happiness in this oddest and most unexpected of liaisons. He had met Kurt only a few times, in London five years back; what had he turned into, and what could Beauty have to offer him, apart from the arts of love? Lanny, of course, defended his friend ardently, and read his father the brief letters which had come from his mother in Spain, indicating her perfect happiness. Robbie said: "Of course, if they can hit it off together, it's all right with me. But don't count on it for too many years."

The father gave some of the news from home. Esther and the children were well and sent messages of affection; they lived uneventful lives over there. As happens in all large families, one or two old Budds had died and several new ones had made their entrance upon the scene. The family was having the devil's own time making over the plants. They had had to go into debt; but

Robbie was hopeful, for the world was half a decade behind in every form of production except guns and shells, and there was sure to be a terrific boom as soon as order was restored.

"Then we're not going to sell out to Zaharoff?" said Lanny; and his father authorized him to bet his boots that it would not happen.

V

Of course Robbie wanted to hear about the Peace Conference. Nearly three months had passed since he had left, and Lanny hadn't been able to put the confidential things into letters. The father plied him with questions about those aspects which were important to a businessman. Was Wilson really going to stand by that preposterous guarantee which Clemenceau had wangled out of him? Were we really going to get ourselves tied up with Constantinople and Armenia? Were France and Britain likely to get anywhere with the scheme they had been trying to work from the outset, to tie up German reparations with the money they had borrowed from America for the prosecution of the war? To make the paying of their own just and lawful debts dependent upon their collections from Germany—and thus, in effect, get America to do their collecting for them!

Lanny replied that a lot of people at the Crillon were questioning whether either form of debts could ever be paid. Even if the Allies took all the livestock and the movable wealth out of Germany, they couldn't get more than a billion or two; the gold reserve was much less than anyone believed, and to take it would mean to destroy Germany as an industrial power, and hence her ability to pay anything more. Lanny quoted what Steffens had said, that every dollar the Allies collected would cost them a dollar-five. He talked a lot about Steffens and Bullitt, in many ways the most interesting men he had met.

Gradually the younger man began to notice a shift in the conversation. The father stopped asking what the Peace Conference had done, and began asking about what Lanny thought. Lanny, who wasn't slow-witted, caught the meaning: his father was worried about the sort of company he had been keeping. Lanny was in the position of a man who has been out in the woods or some place where he hasn't had the use of a mirror; now suddenly one was held up before him and he saw the way he looked. To put it plainly, the way he looked was pink with red spots—a most unpleasing aspect for a young gentleman of leisure and good family.

The change had happened so gradually—a little bit one day and next day another little bit in another part of his mind—that Lanny hadn't had time to become aware of it, and now couldn't believe it, wouldn't admit it. He imagined that his father must be misunderstanding him, and tried to explain himself—thereby making matters worse than they were before. He would cite things that Robbie himself had told: what the big businessmen had done to cause the war and to prolong it and to get advantages out of the settlement. The Crillon was full of talk about *concessionnaires* from every nation who were in Paris, pulling wires more or less openly, telling statesmen what to do to protect these coal mines or that oil territory. Grabbing this and threatening to grab that—surely Robbie must know that as well as anybody! Surely he must realize that these were the things which had wrecked the conference!

Yes, Robbie knew all that. Robbie knew that right now Britain and France were squabbling behind the scenes over the oil in Mesopotamia. Robbie knew as well as the Crillon that nothing in the world but fear of Germany would keep Britain and France from turning against each other in that dispute. Robbie knew that the two nations were still trying to hold on to Baku with its oil, and had even succeeded in having a vessel flying the American flag in the Caspian Sea, in the effort to overawe the Bolsheviks and keep them out of their own country's oil fields. And knowing all that— why was Robbie so disturbed when his son named the big oil promoters among the enemies of a sane peace?

There was a very special reason, which had to do with Robbie's crossing the ocean. Perhaps he had made a mistake in not mentioning it earlier in the conversation. An oil geologist whom he had known for many years, and who had worked for the big companies in the Near East, had come to Newcastle on purpose to interest him in a project for getting a concession in Eastern Arabia. After hearing his story, Robbie had got together a group of his friends, men who had made money out of Budd dividends and were looking for a place to invest it; they had formed a syndicate, and Robbie was here to work on the project, to interview representatives of the Arabs and pull wires with the British and French officials, as he knew so well how to do. Some Americans were going to get more than paper promises out of all the blood they had poured into the soil of France, and the billions of dollars' worth of food and clothing, oil and machinery, guns and shells and what not which they had ferried across the ocean to France and England!

VI

Robbie behaved like the battalion chief of a fire department who arrives on the scene and discovers that he has a dangerous conflagration on his hands; he sent in a second and a third alarm, brought up all his apparatus, and started to flood his incandescent son with arguments. Surely Lanny couldn't have watched modern war without realizing that oil was vital to a nation! Not a wheel in a Budd plant could turn without it; and what was going to become of America, what would be the good of dreams about liberty, democracy, or other sorts of ideals, if we failed to get our share of a product for which there was no substitute? All over the world the British were grabbing the territories in which there was any chance of oil; they were holding these as reserves and buying our American supply for immediate use—it was their deliberate policy.

"Look at Mexico!" exclaimed the father. "Right at our own doors they are intriguing, undermining us, freezing us out. Every official in the Mexican government is for sale and the British are there with the cash. That is 'law and order,' 'freedom of trade,' 'peace'—all those fine phrases! Everywhere an American businessman goes his British competitor is there with his government behind him—and we might as well quit and let them have the world. Fine phrases make pleasant week-end parties, Lanny, but they don't lubricate machinery."

"The Crillon is hoping to adjust such matters through the League of Nations," argued the son.

"Did anybody at the Crillon ever persuade the British to give up anything in the final showdown? And if you had an insider to advise you, you'd see that one demand after another is to protect the oil they have or to get more."

"But what's to be done about it, Robbie? The British and French are begging to continue the Supreme Economic Council, but the Americans insist upon ending it and going back to unrestricted competition."

"That's because we know the British are bound to dominate the Council. Imagine the nerve of them—each of their dominions to have a vote in the League, while the United States has only one!"

"One vote will be enough for a veto," countered Lanny, who knew that League Covenant pretty nearly by heart.

"That's the silliest thing in the whole scheme," declared the father; "it means that the machine will be stalled from the outset. I read somewhere that they had such an arrangement in old-time Poland—any knight could rise in the assembly and veto any measure and kill it. A nation couldn't survive on such a basis, and neither can a League of Nations."

Lanny had heard all these arguments; he knew his father's mind inside out. Nor was he conscious of any disagreement. What Robbie said was true, and likewise what Lincoln Steffens said; it was just that they drew different conclusions from the facts. But Lanny had better not say that, because then the father would repeat his arguments all over again. Better agree with him as far as you could, and keep the rest of your ideas to yourself. That was the course which Robbie had recommended during the years that Lanny had lived in France at war; and now Lanny would apply the method to its teacher.

VII

Robbie told all about his business project: who was backing it in America and who was to be approached in London. It wasn't a big one, as oil projects went; only about eight million dollars, but there would be more where that came from if Robbie continued to be satisfied about the prospects. It was a fast game they were going to break in on; in telling about it the father used the language of sport, of gangsters, of war—it was all of those things. Zaharoff had gone into oil; no munitions people could stay out, for it was oil that had won the last war. Did Lanny realize why the German armies had so suddenly begun clamoring for an armistice? It wasn't because they couldn't fall back and defend a new line; it wasn't because of revolts at home; it was because the Rumanian oil field had been destroyed, and the surrender of Bulgaria had cut them off from the southeast, and there was no more oil to run the tanks and trucks without which armies were stalled.

Lanny perceived that the money his father had made was burning a hole in his pocket. The idea of settling back and resting hadn't occurred to him, and it would do no good to suggest it. The purpose of having money was to get more. Money was power, the ability to do things. Money was patriotism, also. Robbie told about a Dutch bank clerk of the name of Henri Deterding who had forced his way into the oil industry and now was the master of Royal Dutch Shell; it was he who had kept the British fleet supplied with fuel all through the war. The British had had to meet his terms, and, as a result, little Holland was one of the most prosperous countries in the world—and with hardly any army or fleet of its own!

American money had made it possible for the British to take Mesopotamia from the Turks and keep it. Said Robbie: "If we hadn't sent our men and supplies, the Germans would be getting that oil right now. So why shouldn't our country have a share? We'll take in some influential Britishers and give them a chance to

co-operate; but if they won't we'll use the power of the government and make them give up."

"You mean you'll threaten them?" asked Lanny.

"Not even an argument," said the father, smiling. "Just a little
understanding among gentlemen."

"You'll have to get a new administration in Washington," ventured the youth; and Robbie said he hadn't overlooked that.
Wilson's peace treaty was going to be dumped into the ashcan, and
his fool League with it. There would be a Republican President,
and a State Department that would understand businessmen and
back them up.

"Believe me," said Robbie, "the haughty gentlemen of this 'City'
know how to give up when they have to. Some day you'll see
them make Robbie Budd a Knight Commander of the Bath—as I'm
told they're planning to do for a Greek ex-fireman who's got hold
of their munitions industry!"

VIII

Hitherto in the life of this father and son the younger had been
bubbling over with interest in the elder's affairs, eager to go with
him and share what he was doing. And here was another chance.
Lanny would only have to say: "Can I help you with this, Robbie?"
and his father would let him attend the conferences, would give
him a block of stock in the enterprise, and make him, in effect, a
partner. Perhaps Robbie had been counting upon it—for now,
having been trained in the duties of a secretary, the son could be
of real help. But the father was too proud to ask; he waited for his
son to speak—and Lanny didn't speak.

Only six months had been needed to make that difference; to fill
Lanny's mind, not merely with doubts and questionings, but with a
distaste which startled him when he came face to face with it. He
just didn't want to be in the oil business! The very thing which
made it so important to Robbie had made it in the eyes of the

Crillon liberals the arch-malefactor of the time. Five years ago it had been possible for Lanny to think of intrigues and battles over the selling of guns and cartridges as romantic and exciting; but now it was impossible to get up such feelings about an oil concession and pipeline.

So, while the father went to keep the first of his appointments, Lanny walked on the Embankment, watching the traffic on the river and saying to himself: "What is it that I really want to do?" He pictured his life if he should become Robbie's London representative. He would have a sumptuous office and meet the important men of the City, also of Whitehall; Rosemary, Margy Petries, and others of the ladies would put him into the social whirl; they would find him a rich wife, and his father would see that he made all the money he wanted. He would spend his time figuring how to outwit Zaharoff and Deterding and lesser men of that sort; he would be in a game, or racket, or battle, in which there was no rest, no let-up— it was dog eat dog, and if you didn't get your grip on the other dog's throat, he would get his grip on yours, and that would be your finish.

Lanny's fancy moved on to that peaceful Côte d'Azur, with sunshine and blue water, and air always warm, except at night, or when the mistral blew. There were a lot of fashionable goings-on, noise and distraction, gambling and vice, and doubtless it would be worse since the war; but you didn't have to bother with it, you could go your way and let the wasters go theirs. In the living room was a piano, good enough when it had been tuned, and a great stack of music which Lanny had played through and would like to tackle again. He had been to concerts, and heard new music which he would try out. In the storeroom of the studio were all but a few of Marcel's paintings; and now, fresh from an exhibition, Lanny would view his stepfather's work all over again and compare it with what he had seen. Also there were a score or so of wooden cases, containing the books which his Great-Great-Uncle Eli had willed to him; Lanny promised himself an adventure unpacking these and having shelves made for them. He hadn't liked New

England any too well, but he thought he might come to know it better through its poets and sages than through its country club gentry and munitions makers.

He had it planned out in detail. His mother and his new step-father would come back from Spain as soon as it was safe, and they would build another studio for Kurt on the other side of the grounds—if both of them were going to tootle and tinkle they would want as much distance between them as possible. Some day Rick and Nina would come to visit them; and—still farther in the future—Rosemary would come. Lanny remembered the spot where they had sat in the darkness and watched the lights over the water and listened to the distant music from the casino orchestra; the thought of it sent little shivers coursing up and down his nerves. *"Ein Jüngling liebt ein Mädchen, Die hat einen Andern erwählt!"*

IX

A delicate situation between a devoted father and an equally devoted son: one calling for a lot of tact—and fortunately Lanny had been in the polite world long enough to acquire it. Never would he say a word against the oil industry; never would he argue, but let Robbie have his say. Lanny would think his own thoughts— one of the great privileges of man. He would lunch or dine with his father and meet some of the "big" men—interesting personalities, provided you entered into their world and didn't expect them to enter into yours. An oil magnate discussing the market prospects or the international situation might be an authority; but discussing a book or a play he wasn't so hot. Lanny would say that he had a date, and would go look at an art show or hear a concert.

He had told about these plans before they crossed the seas, so there could be no complaint. Robbie was a fair man, and wouldn't try to compel his son; Robbie's own father had made that mistake, with results which Robbie would never forget or forgive, and he was not going to repeat the offense. He had promised Lanny an allowance, what he would have had if he had been going through college. So long as he was improving himself and not wasting his life, he was free to choose his own course. Lanny did really mean to make something of his opportunities—even though he wasn't sure just what it was going to be. The world was so big, and there were so many things he wanted to see and to understand; so many interesting people, to start new ideas going in his mind!

He accepted an invitation to a week-end with Beauty's old friends, the Eversham-Watsons, and practiced riding and jumping some more, and learned about the gout from his lordship, and had an amusing time fencing off the efforts of Margy Petries to find out what his blessed mother was doing in Spain. No use trying to fool that eager chatterbox and manipulator of men—she knew it was a "romance"—she knew that Beauty Budd wasn't going to remain a widow—and who was it, some grandee of that land of castanets and cruelty? Lanny would just smile and say: "Beauty will tell you some day. Meanwhile, be sure that anything you guess will be wrong!"

He walked, and saw London at the beginning of the peace era. He knew what he was looking at now; he could recognize the signs of that poverty in the midst of luxury which was the plague of the modern world, and perhaps, as Stef thought, the seed of its destruction. He walked in Piccadilly and saw hordes of women peddling themselves, as in Paris—only they lacked the *chic* and *esprit* of the French. In the fashionable shopping streets he saw returned soldiers, hundreds of them, wandering listless and depressed; England had needed them, but now they peddled pencils, boxes o' lights, any trifling objects that would keep them from being beggars within the meaning of the law. Prosperity was coming back, everybody insisted—but for these men it was a marshlight, flitting out of reach.

As in Paris, all the smart forms of play had been resumed with a rush. A horde of people had got money, and the newspapers assured them that the way to help the poor was to spend it fast. Benevolent souls, they labored hard to do their duty. They acquired new outfits of costly clothing, thus making work for seamstresses and tailors; they motored to the racetracks, thus making work for jockeys and trainers, for salesmen and chauffeurs of automobiles; they swarmed into the expensive restaurants, ordered lavishly, and tipped the waiters generously. To assist their efforts were shows and pageants, balls and festivals, events with historic names— "Wimbledon" and "Henley," a "Peace Ascot" and a "Victory Derby," a Cowes regatta coming for the first time in six years. There would be no "Courts," but there were six Royal Garden Parties at Buckingham Palace, gay and delightful affairs at which the ladies were forbidden to wear *décolleté* in the afternoons. In the days of Jane Austen it would have been proper, but the present Queen considered female arms and bosoms improper until after sundown.

Pearls were the gems of the day, and fashions were "anarchical"; dresses might be anything so long as skirts were short and waistlines nonexistent. Capes had come back; they were pleated, and large at the waist—built in imitation of barrels, so Margy Petries declared. The keynote of a day costume was plumes; not the curled ones, but lancer plumes, glycerined plumes, plume fringes, plume cascades, plume rosettes. Because of the great number of gas cases, which healed slowly if ever, many entertainments were given and costumes worn for the benefit of the crowded hospitals.

Lanny missed his mother, or some girl to enjoy the society game with him. He persuaded Nina and Rick to motor to town, and put them up at the hotel, and took them to see the Russian dancers— not Bolsheviks, but good, old-time Russians, doing *La Boutique Fantasque*, enacting can-can dancing dolls. Nina managed to persuade her husband to forget his pride and look at the spring exhibition of art from a wheel-chair. Lanny, having read what the critics had said in Paris, was able to talk instructively about the relative merits of the two displays. Altogether he managed to pass the time agreeably, until one day his father said: "I have to go to Paris for a while."

"That's on my way home!" answered Lanny.

37

Peace in Our Time

I

THE day that Lanny and his father arrived in France was the
last day of the last extension of time allowed to the Germans, to
say whether or not they were going to accept the terms imposed
upon them. At least so the Allies declared, and at each of their
outposts, fifty kilometers beyond the Rhine bridgeheads, their
motorized columns were packed up and ready to start. They were
going to advance thirty-five miles per day into Germany, so it was
announced; and meanwhile in every drawing room and *bistro* in
France the leading topic of discussion was: Will they sign or
won't they?

An Austrian peace delegation had come, and a Bulgarian one,
and were submitting with good grace to having their feathers pulled
out while they were still alive. Not a squawk from them; but the
Germans had been keeping up a God-awful clamor for six or seven
weeks; all over their country mass meetings of protest, and Clemenceau remarking in one of his answers that apparently they had
not yet realized that they had lost a war. Their delegation was kept
inside their stockade and told that it was for their safety; some of
them, traveling back and forth to Germany, were stoned, and for
this Clemenceau made the one apology of his career.

The Social-Democrats were ruling the beaten country. It was
supposed to have been a revolution, but a polite and discreet one
which had left the nobility all their estates and the capitalists all
their industries. It was, so Steffens and Herron had explained to
Lanny, a political, not an economic revolution. A Socialist police
chief was obligingly putting down the Reds in Berlin, and for this

the Allies might have been grateful but didn't seem to be. Stef said they couldn't afford to let a Socialist government succeed at anything; it would have a bad effect upon the workers in the Allied lands. It was a time of confusion, when great numbers of people didn't know just what they wanted, or if they did they took measures which got them something else.

In the eastern sky the dark cloud continued to lower; and here, also, what the Allies did only made matters worse. The Big Four had recognized Admiral Kolchak as the future ruler of Siberia—a land whose need for a navy was somewhat restricted. This land-admiral had agreed to submit his policies to a vote of the Russian people, but meanwhile he was proceeding to kill as many of them as possible and seize their farms. The result was that the peasants went into hiding, and as soon as the admiral's armies moved on they came out and took back their farms. The same thing was happening all over the Ukraine, where General Denikin had been chosen as the Russian savior; and now another general, named Yudenich, was being equipped to capture Petrograd. They didn't dare to give these various saviors any British, French, or American troops, because of mutinies; but they would furnish officers, and armaments which were charged up as "loans," and which the peasants of Russia were expected to repay in return for being deprived of the land.

At any rate, that was the way Stef described matters to Lanny Budd; and Lanny found this credible, because Stef had been there and the others hadn't. The youth had gone to call on this strange little man, whose point of view was so stimulating to the mind. Lanny didn't tell his father about this visit, and quieted his conscience by saying, what use making Robbie unhappy to no purpose? Lanny wasn't ever going to become a Red—he just wanted to hear all sides and understand them. Robbie seemed to have the idea that the only way to avoid falling into the snares of the Reds was to refuse to have anything to do with them, or even to know about them. The moment you started to "understand" them—at that moment you were becoming tainted with their hateful infection!

II

There came a letter from Beauty, now viewing the art galleries and cabarets of Madrid. She was so, so happy; but her conscience was troubling her because of Baby Marceline, left motherless on the Riviera for so many months. To be sure, the servants adored her, and Beauty had asked friends to go and look her over; but still the mother worried, and wanted Lanny to run down and take her place. "You know my position," she pleaded. "I dare not leave our friend alone." Always she used the tactful phrase, "our" friend. If a woman wrote *mon ami*, that had a special meaning; but *notre ami* was chaste, even Christian, and took Lanny into the *affaire*.

There was much to be done at their home, Beauty informed him. The house needed very much to be redecorated, and it was fortunate that Lanny had such good taste; his mother would leave it to him, and be interested to see what new ideas he had acquired in two years of journeying about. Lanny decided that he would surprise her by building that extra studio. The many relatives of Leese would be summoned *en masse;* they were slow, but Lanny knew them and liked them, and they would work well for him.

This was something the youth could present to his father as a plausible substitute for a job in the oil industry. Robbie believed in buildings, as something you could see, and if need be could sell; he said to do the studio right, and he would pay for it. He added that Baby Marceline would probably be better off if Beauty would stay in Spain, or go back to Germany with Kurt; all she could do with a child was to spoil it. She would have done that with Lanny if Robbie hadn't put his foot down many times. Lanny said maybe she had anyhow.

The youth wanted to remain in Paris until his father was through. He was seeing the Crillon and all its affairs through a new pair of eyes. The men with whom Robbie was dealing were not the statesmen, but those who told the statesmen what to do. Yes, even the stiff-souled Presbyterian, the reformer to whom big business had been anathema—even he had become dependent upon the masters of money. A whole procession of them had been called over to Paris: prominent among them Lamont of the House of Morgan, whom Wilson had refused even to receive at the White House before the war. A score of such men had now become the President's confidential advisers on questions of reparations and the restoring of trade and finance.

Of course these businessmen were telling him to do the things which would enable them to go on making money, as they had been doing so happily before the war. The railroads were to be handed back to private management, and government controls over industry were to be abandoned. The Supreme Economic Council was to be scrapped, so that the scramble for raw materials could be resumed and Wall Street speculators could buy up everything in sight. To Robbie Budd all this was proof that the world naturally belonged to vigorous, acquisitive persons like himself. He was here to consult with others of his sort, and make certain that American diplomatic and naval authorities would co-operate with American oil men endeavoring to obtain their share of a product for which there was no substitute.

III

Johannes Robin came to Paris to consult his business associate. He brought with him a suitcase full of letters, contracts, and financial statements, and Lanny had lunch with the two, and listened while the Jewish enterpriser explained the various affairs in which he had been using Robbie's money. Things hadn't gone so well as he had hoped, because the delays in the peace settlement had held up transportation and credit. Meanwhile storage charges were eating up a share of the profits; but still, there would be goodly sums left, and Robbie professed himself as satisfied with what had been done.

They went upstairs to their suite, and Robbie settled down to look over the documents, with his associate explaining them. Lanny went along, because Mr. Robin said he had brought more snapshots of his family, also a present, a copy of Hansi's "Opus 1," a violin étude; the copy made by the fifteen-year-old composer's own hands. Lanny sat down to study it and became absorbed; he had heard so much about that talented and hard-working lad who wanted to be his friend and adorer. He could see right away what had happened: Hansi had learned to perform a number of difficult technical feats on the violin, and in his composition he had been concerned to give himself an opportunity to do them all. But then, most performers' compositions are like that; you take it for granted, as you do the make-up and mannerisms of a "professional beauty."

Mr. Robin was so interested in Lanny's interest that he could hardly keep his mind on the business documents. When Lanny said: "That's a lovely theme just after the cadenza," the fond father turned pink with pleasure. "Can you really get it without hearing it?" he exclaimed; and of course Lanny was pleased to have his musical accomplishments admired. Perhaps the Jewish businessman knew that Lanny would be pleased—thus human relationships are complicated by the profit motive! Anyhow, Lanny promised to take the composition home with him and master the piano part, in preparation for the day when he and the young composer would play their first duet.

Robbie told his new associate about his plans to break into the oil game, and the latter said he would like to put his profits into that venture. Living in the land of Henri Deterding, he knew quite a lot about the oil business, and the two of them talked as equals in the fascinating game of profit-hunting. To Lanny they resembled two sleek and capable panthers which have met in the jungle and decided to work together for the quicker finding and bringing down of their prey. One had been born in a mud hut in Poland and the other in an aristocratic mansion in New England, but modern standardization had brought them to a point where they talked in shorthand, as it were—they understood each other without the need of completing a sentence. Lanny had a lot of fun teasing his father about it afterward, and trying to decide whether the new firm was to be known as Robbie and Robin, or Robin and Robbie. A delicate point in verbal aesthetics—or was it in social precedence? Of course, said the youth, when they had conquered the world and possessed its oil, they would be known as "R. & R."

The Dutch partner in this combination said that as soon as peace was certain he was planning to move his office and family to Berlin. Hansi had learned about all he could in Rotterdam; and for the father there would be extraordinary opportunities of profit in Germany in the next few years. He would keep his Rotterdam office, and turn all his money into guilders and dollars. With the reparations settlement as it was, the mark was bound to lose value; the only way, short of repudiation, for Germany to reduce her internal debts. Incidentally, by inflation, she could collect large sums from foreigners, who believed in the mark and were buying it now. Johannes Robin said there was much argument among Dutch traders on this point, and of course fortunes would be made or lost on the guess. Robbie was inclined to agree with his new partner, but advised him that it would be safer to buy properties and goods, which would be thrown on the market for almost nothing in a collapse of the German money system.

IV

The ministry of the Socialist Scheidemann resigned; he wouldn't sign the treaty. Brockdorff-Rantzau wouldn't sign. But somebody had to sign, for it was clear that Germany had no other course. The new ministry sent word that it would bow to the inevitable; but still they didn't send anybody. President Wilson was impatient to return to Washington, where a special session of the new Congress had been waiting for him for more than a month. But the ceremony of signing had to be put off day after day. It was most annoying, and offensive to the dignity of the victorious Great Powers.

Lanny went to call on Lincoln Steffens at his hotel. After listening to his father and his father's new business associate, the youth wanted someone to tell him that the world wasn't created entirely to have money made out of it. Sitting in his little hotel room, con-

fined by a cold, Stef said that the money-makers were having their
own way everywhere; but the trouble was they couldn't agree
among themselves, and kept flinging the world into one mess after
another. So there were revolts; and the question was, would these
revolts be blind, or would they have a program?

Stef told what had just happened to an artist friend of his, a
brilliant cartoonist of Greenwich Village, the artists' quarter of
New York. Robert Minor had gone in a fine state of enthusiasm to
look at the new revolutionary Russia, and had then come to Paris.
He visited the headquarters of the railwaymen, then threatening
their strike, and told them what the Russians were doing. As a
result, a couple of French *flics* had picked him up at his lodgings
and taken him to the Préfecture and grilled him for half a day; then
they had turned him over to the American army authorities at
Koblenz, who had held him prisoner in secret for several weeks.
They had talked about shooting him; but he had managed to smug-
gle out word as to his whereabouts, and the labor press of Paris
had taken up the case. It happened that "Bob's" father was a judge
in Texas and an influential Democrat; so in the end the army authorities had turned their prisoner loose.

Lanny mentioned how his Uncle Jesse likewise had been questioned by the police, and had threatened them with publicity. Jesse
had been sure they wouldn't jail an American just for making
speeches.

"This was a special kind of speech," answered Stef. "Bob advised
the railwaymen how to stop the invasion of the Black Sea by calling a strike on the railroads to Marseille."

"Yes, I suppose that's different," the youth agreed.

The muckraker asked whether Lanny hadn't been spied on himself. Lanny was surprised, and said he hadn't thought about it.
Stef replied: "Better think!" He imparted a piece of news—that two
of those members of the Crillon staff who had tried to resign had
had dictographs put in their rooms—presumably by the Army Intelligence. This news worried Lanny more than he cared to let his
friend know.

"How do you know a spy when you meet him?" he asked, and the other answered that often you didn't until it was too late. It was generally somebody who agreed with your pinkest ideas and went you one or two better. Lanny said he hadn't met anyone like that as yet—unless it was Stef himself!

This world observer, whose ideas were so hard to puzzle out, told some of his own experiences since his return from Russia. The Intelligence had thought it necessary to dog his footsteps continually. "There is a Captain Stratton——"

"Oh, yes!" broke in the youth. "I saw a lot of him at the Crillon."

"Well, he and another officer took the trouble to get the next table in a restaurant where I was dining with a friend. I saw that they were listening to our talk so I invited them over, and told them all about what I had learned in Russia, and had reported to Colonel House. I tried my best to convert them."

"Did you succeed?" asked Lanny, delighted.

"Well, they stopped following me. Maybe the reason was what President Wilson did a day or two later. I suppose he had heard that I was being shadowed, and he chose a tactful way to stop it. You understand, he has refused to see me and hear what I have to report on Russia; having made up his 'one-track mind' that he's not going to stop the war on the Soviets, he doesn't want to be upset by my facts. But he knows how I came to go to Russia, and he has no right to discredit me. I was one of a crowd of newspapermen waiting in the lobby of the hotel, when he passed through and saw me, and he came and bent over me and pretended to whisper something into my ear. He didn't say a word that I could make out; he just made murmurs. Of course his purpose was to tell everybody that I still had his confidence."

"So now you can be as pink as you please!" chuckled the other.

V

The German delegation arrived, and the much-postponed signing was set for the twenty-eighth of June. The signers were two subordinates, but the Allies were determined to make a ceremony of it. The setting was the great Hall of Mirrors of the Versailles palace, where the victorious Germans had established their empire forty-eight years earlier, and had forced the French to sign the humiliating peace surrendering Alsace-Lorraine. Now the tables were turned, and with all pomp and circumstance the two distressed German envoys would put their signatures to the statement that their country alone had been to blame for the World War.

Every tourist in France visits the Versailles palace, and wanders through the magnificent apartment where once the Sun King ate his meals and the population had the hereditary right to enter and stare at the greatest of all monarchs gulping his *potage* and at his queen and princesses nibbling their *entremets*. Lanny had been there with his mother and Kurt, motored by Harry Murchison, nearly six years back; that lovely October day stood out in his memory, and as he recalled it he had many strange thoughts. Suppose that on that day he had been able by some psychic feat to peer into the future and know that his German friend, adoring his mother, was to become her lover! Suppose that Beauty had been able to perform the feat and foresee what was going to happen to Marcel—would she have married Harry Murchison instead? Or suppose that the Germans, at the signing of the first Peace of Versailles, had been able to foresee the second!

Only about a thousand persons could be admitted to witness the ceremony, and Lanny Budd was not among the chosen ones. If he had cared very much he might have been able to wangle a ticket from his Crillon friends, whom he still met at Mrs. Emily's and other places. But he told himself that he had witnessed a sufficiency of ceremonies to last the rest of his days. No longer had he the least pleasure in gazing upon important elderly gentlemen, each brushed and polished by his valet from the tips of his shoes to the roof of his topper. The colonel from Texas wore this symbol of honorificabilitudinitas on occasions where etiquette required it, but he carried along his comfortable Texas sombrero in a paper bag, and exchanged head-coverings as soon as the ceremony was com-

pleted. Nothing so amusing had happened in Paris since Dr. Franklin
had gone about town without a wig.

The important thing now was that the much-debated document
would be signed and peace returned to the world. Or would it? On
the table in his hotel room lay newspapers in which he could read
that the treaty to be signed that day left France helpless before the
invading foe; and others which insisted that it was a document of
class repression, designed to prepare the exploitation of the workers
of both Germany and France. Lanny had read both, and wished
there was some authority that would really tell a young fellow
what to believe!

VI

The telephone rang: the office of the hotel announcing "Monsieur Zhessie Bloc-léss"—accent on the last syllable. Lanny didn't
want to have his uncle come up, because that would look like intimacy, so displeasing to Robbie if he should happen to return. "I'll
be down at once," he said.

In the lobby of the marble-walled Hotel Vendôme he sat and
exchanged family news with his relative who didn't fit the surroundings, but looked like a down-at-heels artist lacking the excuse
of youth. Uncle Jesse wanted to know, first, what the devil was
Beauty doing in Spain? When Lanny answered vaguely, he said:
"You don't have to hide things from me. I can guess it's a man."

But Lanny said: "She will tell you when she gets ready," and
that was that.

More urgently the painter was interested to know what had
become of that mysterious personage who had paid him three silent
midnight visits. At the risk of seeming uncordial, Lanny could only
say again that his lips were sealed. "But I fear he won't visit you
any more," he said. "You know about the public event which is to
happen today."

"Yes, but that isn't going to make any difference," insisted the
other. "It doesn't mean a thing." They were speaking with caution,

and the painter kept glancing about to be sure no one was over-hearing. "Your friends are still going to be in trouble. They are going to have to struggle—for a long, long time."

"Maybe so," said Lanny; "and it may be they'll call on you again. But as matters stand, I'm not in a position to inquire about it, and that's all I can say."

The uncle was disappointed and a trifle vexed. He said that when the owners of hunting forests put out fodder for the deer in winter, the creatures got the habit of coming to the place and thereafter didn't scuffle so hard for themselves. Lanny smiled and said he had observed it in the forests of Silesia; but when it was a question of scuffling or starving, doubtless they would resume scuffling.

"Well," said the painter, "if you happen to meet your friend, give him these." He took a little roll of papers from the breast pocket of his coat. "These are samples of the leaflets we have printed. I've marked on each one the number of copies distributed, so he can see that none of his fodder has been wasted."

"All right," said Lanny. "I'll give them to him if I see him." He put the papers into his own pocket, and sought for another topic of conversation. He told of visiting Stef and how Stef had a cold. He repeated some of the muckraker's stories about espionage on the Reds.

"I, too, have tried the plan of chatting with the *flics*," said the painter. "But I've found no idealism in their souls."

Lanny repeated the question he had asked of Stef. "How do you recognize a *flic?*"

"I wouldn't know how to describe them," replied the other. "But when you've seen a few you know the type. They are always stupid, and when they try to talk like one of us it's pathetic."

There was a pause. "Well, I'll get along," said Jesse. "Robbie may be coming and I don't want to annoy him. No need to tell him that I called."

"I won't unless he asks me," replied the nephew.

"And put those papers where he won't see them. Of course you can read them if you wish, but the point is, I'm not giving them to you for that purpose."

"I get you," said Lanny, with a smile.

VII

The youth saw his visitor part way to the door and then went to the apparatus you called a "lift" when you were talking to an Englishman, an "elevator" to an American. At the same moment a man who had been sitting just across the lobby, supposedly reading a newspaper but in reality watching over the top of it, arose from his seat and followed. Another man, who had been standing in the street looking through the window, came in at the door. Lanny entered the elevator and the first man followed him and said to the operator: "*Attendez.*" The second man arrived and entered and they went up.

When they reached Lanny's floor he stepped out, and so did the other two. As soon as the operator had closed the door, one man stepped to Lanny's right and the other to his left and said in French: "*Pardon, Monsieur.* We are agents of the Sûreté."

Lanny's heart gave a mighty thump; he stopped, and so almost did the heart. "Well?" he said.

"It will be necessary for you to accompany us to the Préfecture." The man drew back the lapel of his coat and showed his shield.

"What is the matter?" demanded the youth.

"I am sorry, Monsieur, it is not permitted to discuss the subject. You will be told by the *commissaire.*"

So, they were after him! And maybe they had him! Wild ideas of resistance or flight surged into his mind; it was the first time he had ever been arrested and he had no habit pattern. But they were determined-looking men, and doubtless were armed. He decided to preserve his position as a member of the privileged classes. "You are making a very silly mistake," he said, "and it will get you into trouble."

"If so, Monsieur will pardon us, I trust," said the elder of the two. "Monsieur resides in this hotel?"

"I do."

"Then Monsieur will kindly escort us to his room."

Lanny hesitated. His father's business papers were in that room and Robbie certainly wouldn't like to have them examined by strangers. "Suppose I refuse?" he inquired.

"Then it will be necessary for us to take you."

Lanny had the roomkey in his pocket, and of course the two men could take it from him. He knew that they could summon whatever help they needed. "All right," he said, and led them to the room and unlocked the door.

The spokesman preceded him and the other followed, closed the door, and fastened it; then the former said: "Monsieur will kindly give me the papers which he has in his pocket."

Ah, so they had been watching him and Uncle Jesse! Lanny had read detective novels, and knew that it was up to him to find some way to chew up these papers and swallow them. But a dozen printed leaflets would make quite a meal, and he lacked both appetite and opportunity. He took them out and handed them to the *flic*, who put them into his own pocket without looking at them. "You will pardon me, Monsieur"—they were always polite to well-dressed persons, Lanny had been told. Very deftly, and as inoffensively as possible, the second man made certain that Lanny didn't have any weapon on him. In so doing he discovered some letters in the youth's coat pocket, and these also were transferred to the pockets of the elder detective. Lanny ran over quickly in his mind what was in the letters: one from his mother—fortunately she had been warned, and wrote with extreme reserve. One from Rosemary, an old one, long-cherished—how fortunate the English habit of reticence! One from his eleven-year-old half-sister—that was the only real love letter.

Lanny was invited to sit down, and the younger *flic* stood by, never moving his eyes from him. Evidently they must be thinking they had made an important capture. The elder man set to work to search the suite; the escritoire, the bureau drawers, the suitcases—he laid the latter on the bed and went through them, putting everything of significance into one of them. This included a thirty-eight automatic and a box of cartridges—which of course would seem more significant to a French detective than to an American.

If Lanny had been in possession of a clear conscience, he might have derived enjoyment from this opportunity to watch the French police *chez eux,* as it were. But having a very uneasy conscience indeed, he thought he would stop this bad joke if he could. "You are likely to find a number of guns in my father's luggage," he remarked. "That is not because he shoots people, but because he sells guns."

"*Ah! Votre père est un marchand d'armes!*" One had to hear it in French to get a full sense of the *flic's* surprise.

"*Mon père est un fabricant d'armes,*" replied Lanny, still more impressively. "He has made for the French government a hundred million francs' worth of arms in the past five years. If he had not done so, the boches would be in Paris now, and you would be under the sod, perhaps."

"*Vraiment, Monsieur!*" exclaimed the other, and stood irresolute, as if he hadn't the nerve to touch another object belonging to a person who might possibly be of such importance. "What is it that is the name of your father?" he inquired, at last.

"His name is Robert Budd."

The other wrote it down, with Lanny spelling the letters in French. "And Monsieur's name?"

The youth spelled the name of Lanning, which a Frenchman does not pronounce without considerable practice. Then he remarked: "If you examine that gun, you will see that it has my father's name as the *fabricant.*"

"*Ah, vraiment?*" exclaimed the detective, and took the gun to the window to verify this extraordinary statement. Evidently he didn't know what to do next, and Lanny thought that his little dodge had worked. But when the detective took the bundle of leaflets from his pockets and began to examine them; and so of course Lanny knew that the jig was up. He hadn't looked at the papers, but he knew what would be in them. "Workingmen of all countries, unite! You have nothing to lose but your chains; you have a world to gain!"

The *flic* put the papers back into his pocket, and went on piling Robbie's papers into a suitcase. "It is a matter which the *commissaire* will have to determine, Monsieur."

38

Battle of the Stags

I

RIDING in a taxi to the Préfecture de Police, Lanny thought as hard as he had ever done in his life. Had these agents been following him because they had learned about his connections with a German spy? Or had they been following the notorious Jesse Blackless and seen him hand papers to Lanny? Everything seemed to indicate the latter; but doubtless at the Préfecture they would have Lanny listed in connection with Lincoln Steffens, and with Herron, and Alston—who could guess where these trails might lead? Lanny decided that he had talked enough and would take refuge in the fact that he was not yet of age. Even in wartime they could hardly shoot you for refusing to answer questions; and, besides, the war was coming to an end this very afternoon! Many, many times in five years he had heard Frenchmen exclaim: *"C'est la guerre!"* Now, for once, he would be able to answer: *"C'est la paix!"*

The Préfecture is on the île de la Cité, the oldest part of Paris, having as much history to the square meter as any other place in the world. Like most old buildings it had a vague musty odor. They booked him, and took away his billfold, his watch, his keys; then they put him in a small room with a barred window high up, and an odor of ammonia, the source of which was obvious. The younger of the two detectives sat and watched him, but did not speak. In half an hour or so he was escorted to an office, where he found no less than three officials waiting to question him. All three were polite, grave, and determined. The eldest, the *commissaire*, was dressed as if he were going to have tea at Mrs. Emily's. At a second desk sat a clerk, ready to begin writing vigorously—the so-called *procès verbal*.

"Messieurs," said Lanny, "please believe that I intend no discourtesy; but I consider this arrest an indignity and I intend to stand upon my rights. I am a minor and it is my father who is legally responsible for me. I demand that he be summoned, and I refuse to answer any questions whatsoever until that has been done."

You would have thought that the three officials had never before in their lives heard of anyone refusing to answer questions. They were shocked, they were hurt, they were everything they could think of that might make an impression upon a sensitive youth. They demanded to know: was it the natural course for an innocent man not to tell frankly what was necessary to secure his liberty? They wished him no harm; they were greatly embarrassed to have to detain him for a moment; the simple and obvious thing would be for him to tell them for what innocent reason he had come into possession of documents inciting to the overthrow of *la république française,* the murder of its citizens, the confiscation of their property, and the burning of their homes. The three officials had the incendiary documents spread out before them, and passed them from hand to hand with exclamations of dismay.

Was all that really in the documents? Lanny didn't know; but he knew that if he asked the question, he would be answering a very important one for the officials—he would be telling them that he didn't know, or at least claimed not to know, their contents. So he said again and again: "Messieurs, be so kind as to send word to my father."

Never had courteous French officials had their patience put to a severer test. They took turns arguing and pleading. The oldest, the *commissaire*, was paternal; he pleaded with the young gentleman not to subject himself to being held behind bars like a common felon. It was really unkind of him to inflict upon them the necessity of inflicting this embarrassment upon a visitor from the land to which France owed such a debt of gratitude. In this the *commissaire*, for all his lifetime training, was letting slip something of importance. They took him for a tourist; they had not connected him with Juan-les-Pins, and probably not with Madame Detaze, *veuve*, and her German lover now traveling in Spain!

The second official was a man accustomed to dealing with evildoers, and his faith in human nature had been greatly weakened. He told Lanny that *la patrie* was at war, and that all men of right feeling were willing to aid the authorities in thwarting the murderous intrigues of the abominable Reds. It was difficult for anyone to understand how a man would have such documents in his pocket and not be eager to explain the reason. And what was the significance of the mysterious figures penciled upon each sheet? If a man refused to perform the obvious duty of clearing up such a mystery, could he blame the authorities for looking upon him as a suspicious character?

The third official was younger, wore glasses, and looked like a student. Apparently he was the one whose duty it was to read incendiary literature, classify it, and take its temperature. He said that he had never read anything worse in his life than this stuff which Lanny had had in his pocket. It was hard for him to believe that a youth of good manners and morals could have read such incitements without aversion. Was Lanny a student, investigating the doctrines of these Reds? Did he know any of them personally? Had he been associated with them in America? Lanny didn't answer, but listened attentively and asked questions in his own mind. Were they just avoiding giving him any clues? Or had the two *flics* really not known who it was that gave him the papers?

Certainly Lanny wasn't going to involve his uncle unnecessarily. To all attempts to trap him he replied, as courteously as ever: "Messieurs, I know it is tedious to hear me say this; but think how much trouble you could save yourselves if you would just call my father."

"If you refuse to answer," said the *commissaire*, at last, "we have no recourse but to hold you until you do."

"You may try it," said Lanny; "but I think my father will manage to find out where I am. Certainly if an American disappears from the Hotel Vendôme, the story will be in the American newspapers in a few hours."

The official pressed a button and an attendant came and escorted Lanny down a corridor and into a room that was full of apparatus. In the old days it might have been a torture chamber, but in this advanced age it was the laboratory of a new science. Lanny, to complete his education, was going to learn about the Bertillon system for the identification of criminals. The operations were carried out by a young man who looked like a doctor, wearing a white duck jacket; they were supervised by a large elderly gentleman wearing a black morning coat and striped trousers, and with a black spade beard almost to his waist. They photographed their prisoner from several angles; they took his fingerprints; they measured with calipers his skull, his ears, his nose, his eyes, his fingers, his feet. They told him to strip, and searched him minutely for scars and spots, birthmarks, moles—and noted them all down on an elaborate chart. When they got through, Lanny Budd could be absolutely certain that the next time he committed a crime in France, they would know him for the same felon they had had in the Préfecture on the twenty-eighth of June 1919.

II

Lanny Budd sat on a wooden stool in a stone cell with a narrow slit for a window, and a cot which had obviously been occupied by

many predecessors in misfortune. Perhaps the police were trying to
frighten him, and again, perhaps they were just treating him impartially. For company he had his thoughts: a trooping procession,
taking their tone-color from the dismal clang of an iron door. Impossible to imagine anything more final, or more crushing! So far,
emotions such as this had been communicated to Lanny through the
medium of art works. But the reality was far different. You could
turn away from a picture, stop playing music, close a book; but in
a jail cell you stayed.

Lanny had no idea how old this barracks was. Had it stood here
in the days when Richelieu was breaking the proud French nobility, and had some of them paced the floor of this cell? Had it stood
when the Sun King was issuing his *lettres de cachet?* Had the Car-
dinal de Rohan been brought here when he was accused of stealing
the diamond necklace? It seemed a reasonable guess that some of
the aristocrats had sojourned here on their way *à la lanterne;* and
doubtless a long string of those poisoners and wife stranglers who
provided the French populace with their daily doses of thrill. All
through the Peace Conference Paris had been entertained by the
exploits of a certain Landru, who had married, murdered, and buried
some eight or nine women. Every now and then the authorities
would dig up a new one, and the press would forget the problems
of the peace. This happened whenever the situation became tense,
and it was freely said at the Crillon that it was done to divert attention from what the delegates were doing.

The jailers brought Lanny food and water; but he didn't like the
looks of the former, and was afraid the latter might be drugged. He
spent most of his time walking up and down—five steps one way
and five the other—thinking about his possible mistakes and regret-
ting them. Almost surely the bureau would be digging in its files,
and coming upon the name of Lanning Budd as a nephew of Jesse
Blackless, revolutionary. Would they find him as son of Beauty
Detaze, mistress of Kurt Meissner, alias Dalcroze, much wanted
German agent? Phrased in the language of police files, it was certainly most sinister. Lanny recalled the melodramas he had seen on

the screen, with the hero lined up before the firing squad and res-
cuers galloping on horses, or rushing madly through automobile
traffic. Invariably they arrived just before the triggers were pulled;
but Lanny had been told that the movies were not always reliable.
Ride, Robbie, ride!

The father was supposed to be in conference with some "big"
men. Sooner or later he would return to the hotel and find that his
belongings had been rifled. He would learn from the elevator boy
that Lanny had gone away with two strange men. Would he think
that his son had been kidnaped, and apply to the police? That,
indeed, would be funny. But Robbie had a shrewd mind, and he
knew about his revolutionary brother-in-law, also about Kurt
Meissner, alias Dalcroze. He wouldn't fail to take these into his cal-
culations. He had friends in high position in the city, and Mrs. Emily
had still others. The *commissaire* of the Sûreté Générale would
surely get a jolt before many hours had passed!

The trouble was, the hours passed so slowly. Lanny's watch was
gone, so he couldn't follow them. He could only observe the slit
of light; and at the end of June the days linger long in Paris. Lanny
recalled that at three o'clock the treaty was to be signed, and he
occupied his mind with picturing that historic scene. He knew the
Galerie des Glaces, and how they would fix it up with a long horse-
shoe table, and gilded chairs for the delegates from all the nations
of the earth. Most of them would be black-clad; but the military
ones would be wearing bright-colored uniforms with rows of
medals, and there would be silk-robed pashas and emirs and maharajas and mandarins from where the gorgeous East showers on her
kings barbaric pearl and gold. He could picture the equipages rolling up the great avenue, lined with cavalry in steel-blue helmets,
with red and white pennants fluttering on their lances. He visioned
the palace, with the important personages ascending the great flight
of steps, between rows of the Gardes Républicaines, clad in brass
cuirasses, white pants, and high black patent-leather boots; on their
heads the shiniest of brass helmets with long horsetails stuck in the
tops. There would be two of them to each step, their shining sabers

at present arms. Inside, the hall would be crowded, and there would
be a babel of whispering, the polite chit-chat of the *grand monde*
which Lanny knew so well. How everlastingly delightful to be in
places where you were assured that only the really important could
come!

The treaty would be bulky, printed on vellum sheets decorated
with numerous red seals. Presumably somebody would have checked
it this time and made certain it was right. The enemy signers would
be escorted by those *huissiers* with silver chains who had been the
bane of Lanny's life, because they were forever trying to stop a
secretary-translator from entering rooms where his chief had told
him to go. Lanny had seen pictures of the two unhappy Germans:
one big and beefy, like the proprietor of a *Bierstube*, the other lean
and timid-looking, like a private tutor. They were the scapegoats,
carrying the sins of their people, and signing a confession on two
dotted lines.

The *huissiers* would command silence, and a hush would fall
while the pens scratched. A tedious ceremony, for the plenipoten-
tiaries from all over the world had to fall in line and sign four documents: the treaty proper, the protocol with modifications extracted
by the German clamor, an agreement regarding the administration
of the Rhine districts, and an agreement with Poland regarding the
treatment of minorities—she would keep the minorities but not the
agreement, Professor Alston had remarked while helping to draft
this document.

Lanny's imaginings were interrupted by the thunder of cannon.
So! It was signed! Those would be the guns on the Place d'Armes;
and then a booming farther away—that would be the old fort at
Mont Valérien. Shouts from the crowds in the near-by streets—
Lanny knew how people would behave, he had done it himself on
Armistice day at St. Thomas's Academy in Connecticut. The biggest
banker in that state had warned him that he might get into jail if he
didn't mend his ideas; and sure enough, here he was! He got up and
began to pace the floor again.

Better to go on thinking about the treaty. He had been told by some of the insiders that General Smuts, head of the South African delegation, was going to sign under protest, stating that "We have not yet achieved the real peace for which the peoples are looking." So, after all, the little group of liberals had not protested in vain! Alston had said that this treaty would keep the world in turmoil for ten years, twenty years, whatever time it took to bring it into line with the Fourteen Points. Was he right? Or was that French general right who had announced to the company at Mrs. Emily's: "This treaty is turning loose a wounded tiger on the world. He will crawl into a hole and nurse his wounds, and come out hungrier and fiercer than ever"?

Lanny couldn't make up his mind about it; nothing to do but wait and see. Some day he would know—provided, of course, the French army didn't shoot him at sunrise tomorrow morning.

III

The sun's rays do not linger very long in any place, and the light faded quickly from Lanny's cell. He sat in twilight, and thought: "Surely Robbie must have returned by now!" His stomach was complaining, and in many ways he was tiring of this bad joke. When at last he heard a jailer approaching his cell he was glad, even though it might mean a court martial. "*Venez,*" said the man; and escorted him to the office of the *commissaire* again.

There were the same three officials, and with them, not Robbie, as the prisoner had hoped, but Uncle Jesse! So once more Lanny had to think fast. What did it mean? Doubtless his uncle had been brought in, like himself, as a suspect. Had he talked? And if so, what had he said?

"M. Budd," said the *commissaire*, "your uncle has come here of his own free will to tell us the circumstances by which you came into possession of those documents." He paused as if expecting Lanny to speak; but Lanny waited. "Will you be so kind as to answer a few questions in his presence?"

"*Monsieur le Commissaire,*" said Lanny, "I have already told you that I will answer no questions until my father has come."

"You mean that you don't trust your uncle?" A silence. "Or is it that the gentleman is not your uncle?"

"It would be such a very simple matter to telephone to my father's hotel, Monsieur!"

"We have already done that; but your father is not there."

"He is quite certain to arrive before long."

"You mean you intend to force us to keep you in this uncomfortable position until we can find your father?"

"No, Monsieur, I haven't the least desire to do that. I am willing for you to release me at any time."

There was a long silence. Lanny kept his eyes on the *commissaire,* whose face wore a stern frown. The prisoner wouldn't have been entirely surprised if the man had said: "Take him out and shoot him now!" He was really surprised when he perceived a slow smile spreading over the features of the elderly official. "*Eh bien, mon garçon,*" he said, finally. "If I let you have your way, will you promise to harbor no ill feelings?"

"Yes, sir," said Lanny, as quickly as he was able to take in the meaning.

"Don't think that we are naïve, M. Bloc-léss," said the *commissaire* to the painter. "We have investigated your story. We knew most of it before you came."

"I was quite sure that would be the case," replied Uncle Jesse, with one of his twisted smiles. "Otherwise I might not have come."

"You are playing a dangerous game," continued the other. "I don't suppose you wish any advice from me; but if we are forced to ask you to leave the country, it will not be without fair warning—now repeated for the second time."

"If that misfortune befalls me, Monsieur, I shall be extremely sorry, for France has been my home for the greater part of my life. I shall be sorrier still for the sake of the republic, whose reputation as a shelter for the politically persecuted is the fairest jewel in her crown."

"You are a shrewd man, M. Bloc-léss. You know the language of liberty and idealism, and you use it in the service of tyranny and hate."

"That is a subject about which we might argue for a long while, *Monsieur le Commissaire*. I don't think it would be proper for me to dispute with you in your professional capacity; but if at any time you care to meet me socially, I'll be most happy to explain my ideas."

There was a twinkle in the elderly Frenchman's eye. *Esprit* is their specialty, and he knew a good answer when he heard it. He turned to Lanny. "As for you, *mon garçon*"—taking Lanny into the family—"it appears that you have been the victim of persons older and less scrupulous than yourself. Next time I would advise you to look at papers before you put them into your pocket."

"I assure you, Monsieur," said the youth, respectfully, "I intended to do it as soon as I got to my room." This too had the light play of humor in which the French delight; so the *commissaire* said he hoped his guest hadn't minded his misadventure. Lanny replied that he had found the experience educational, and that stories of crime and detection would be far more vivid to him in future. The suitcase containing Robbie's papers was restored to Robbie's son, and the three officials shook hands with him—but not with Uncle Jesse, he noticed. "M. Bloc-léss" was one of the "older and less scrupulous persons."

IV

Nephew and uncle stepped out into the twilight; and it seemed to Lanny the most delightful moment he had spent in Paris. Very certainly the île de la Cité with its bridges and its great cathedral had never appeared more beautiful than in the summer twilight. Flags were out, and the holiday atmosphere prevailed. To everybody else it was because of the signing of the treaty, but there was nothing to prevent Lanny Budd's applying it to his emergence from the Préfecture.

The moment was made perfect when a taxi came whirling up the Boulevard du Palais, and there was Robbie Budd peering forth. "Well, what the devil is this?" he cried.

"You got my note?" inquired Jesse, as Robbie jumped out.

"That—and your telegram."

"I wanted to be sure of reaching you. I was afraid they might hold me, too."

"But what is it all about?"

"Get back into the cab," said Uncle Jesse. "We can't talk about it here."

The two got in, and Lanny handed in the suitcase, and followed it. When the Préfecture was behind them, the painter said: "Now, Robbie, I'll tell you the story I just told the *commissaire*. You remember how, several months back, Professor Alston sent Lanny to me to arrange for a conference between Colonel House and some of the Russian agents in Paris?"

"I was told about it," said Robbie, with no cordiality in his tone.

"Don't forget that it was United States government business. Lanny did it because it was his job, and I did it because his chief urged me to. I have made it a matter of honor never to force myself upon your son. I have done that out of regard for my sister. Lanny will tell you that it is so."

"It really is, Robbie," put in the youth.

"Go on," said Robbie, between his clenched teeth.

"Well, this morning a French labor leader came to me. You know the blockade of Germany is still going on, the war on the Soviet government is still going on—and both are products of French government policy."

"You may assume that I have read the newspapers," replied the father. "Kindly tell me what the police wanted with Lanny."

"This labor man of course would like to have American support for a policy more liberal and humane. He brought me a bundle of leaflets presenting the arguments of the French workers, and asked if it wouldn't be possible for my nephew at the Crillon to get these into the hands of Colonel House, so that he might know how the workers felt. I said: 'My nephew has broken with the Crillon, because he doesn't approve its policies.' The answer was: 'Well, he may be in touch with some of the staff there and might be able to get the documents to Colonel House.' So I said: 'All right, I'll take them to him and ask him to try.' I took them, and advised Lanny not to read them himself, but to get them to the right person if he had a chance."

Lanny sat rigid in his seat, his mind torn between dismay and admiration. Oh, what a beautiful story! It brought him to realize how ill equipped he was for the career of an intriguer, a secret agent; all those hours he had spent in the silence of his cell—and never once had he thought of that absolutely perfect story!

"My friend told me how many of these leaflets had been printed and distributed in Paris, and I jotted down the figures on each one, thinking it might help to impress Colonel House. It appears the Préfecture found those figures highly suspicious."

"Tell me how it happened," persisted Robbie.

"When I left the hotel I got a glimpse of a man strolling past the window and looking into the lobby. He happened to be one of the *flics* who had picked me up several months back. I saw him enter the hotel, and I looked through the window and saw him and another man go into the elevator with Lanny. I waited until they came down and put him into a taxi. Then I set out to find you. I was afraid to go into the hotel, so I used the telephone. When I failed to find you, I sent you a note by messenger, and also a telegram, and then I decided to go to the Préfecture and try my luck. It was a risk, of course, because Lanny might have talked, and I couldn't know what he had said."

"You might have guessed that he would have told the truth," said the father.

"I wasn't that clever. What I did was to fish around, until they told me Lanny had confessed that he was a Red——"

"What?" cried Lanny, shocked.

"The *commissaire* said that himself; so I knew they were bluffing and that Lanny hadn't talked. I told them my story and they held

me a couple of hours while they 'investigated.' What they did, I
assume, was to phone to Colonel House. Of course they consider
that most everybody in the Crillon is a Red, but they can't afford
any publicity about it. That's why they turned us loose with a
warning."

Robbie turned to his son. "Lanny, is this story true?"

The next few moments were uncomfortable for the younger
man. He had never lied to his father in his life. Was he going to do
it now? Or was he going to "throw down" his Uncle Jesse, who
had come to his rescue at real danger to himself—and who had invented such a beautiful story? There is an old saying that what you
don't know won't hurt you; but Lanny had been taught a different
moral code—that you mustn't ever lie except when you are selling
munitions.

Great was the youth's relief when his uncle saved him from this
predicament. "One moment, Robbie," he put in. "I didn't say that
story was true."

"Oh, you didn't?"

"I said I would tell you what I told the *commissaire*."

The father frowned angrily. "I am in no mood for jokes!" he exclaimed. "Am I to know about this business, or am I not? Lanny,
will you kindly tell me?"

"Yes, Robbie," replied the youth. "The truth is——"

"The fault is entirely mine," broke in Uncle Jesse. "I brought
Lanny those papers for a purpose of my own."

"He is going to try to take the blame on himself," objected
Lanny. "I assure you——"

"He can't tell you the real story, because he doesn't know it!"
argued the painter.

"Nobody really knows it but me," retorted Lanny. "Uncle Jesse
only thinks he knows it."

Robbie's sense of humor wasn't operating just then. "Will you
two please agree which is going to talk?"

Said Lanny, quickly: "I think we'd all three better wait until
we get back to the hotel." He made a motion of the finger toward

the taxi driver in front of them. To be sure, they were speaking English—but then the driver might have been a waiter at Mouquin's on Sixth Avenue before the war. The two men fell silent; and Lanny remarked: "Well, I heard the guns. Has the treaty really been signed?"

V

When they were safely locked in their suite, Robbie got out his whisky bottle, which the *flics* hadn't taken. He had been under a severe strain, and took a nip without waiting for the soda and ice; so did the painter. Lanny had been under a longer strain than either of them, but he waited for the ginger beer, for he wasn't yet of age, and moreover he thought that his father was drinking too much, and was anxious not to encourage him. Meanwhile the youth strolled casually about the suite, looking into the bathroom and the closets and under the beds; he didn't know just how a dictograph worked, but he looked everywhere for any wires. After the bellboy had departed, the ex-prisoner opened the door and looked out. He was in a melodramatic mood.

At last they were settled, and the father said: "Now, please, may I have the honor of knowing about this affair?"

"First," said Lanny, with a grin, "let me shut Uncle Jesse up. Uncle Jesse, you remember the Christmas before the war, I paid a visit to Germany?"

"I heard something about it."

"I was staying with a friend of mine. Better not to use names. That friend was in Paris until recently, and he was the man who came to call on you at midnight."

"Oh, so that's it!" exclaimed the painter.

"I gave him my word never to tell anybody. But I'm sure he won't mind your knowing, because you're likely to become his brother-in-law before long—you may be it now. Beauty and he are lovers, and that's why she's gone to Spain."

"Oh, my God!" exclaimed Jesse. And then again: "Oh, my

God!" He was speaking English, in which these words carry far more weight than in French.

"I told Robbie about it," Lanny continued, "because he has a right to know about Beauty. But I didn't tell him about you, because that was your secret. May I tell him now?"

"Evidently he's not going to be happy till he hears it."

Lanny turned to his father. "I put my friend in touch with Uncle Jesse, and my friend brought money to help him stir up the workers against the blockade. I thought that was a worthy cause and I still think so."

"You knew you were risking your life?" demanded the shocked father.

"I've seen people risking their lives for so long, it has sort of lost meaning. But you can imagine that I felt pretty uncomfortable this afternoon. Also, you can see what a risk Uncle Jesse took when he walked into that place."

Robbie made no response. He had poured out the drinks for the red sheep of his former mistress's family, but not an inch farther did he mean to go.

"You see how it was," continued Lanny. "When my friend stopped coming, Uncle Jesse wanted to know why; he brought me some literature so that this friend might see what he had been doing. He asked me to pass it on if I got a chance, and I said I would. He suggested that I didn't need to read it. I didn't say I wouldn't—I just said that I understood. Uncle Jesse has really been playing fair with you, Robbie. It was my friend and I who planned this whole scheme and brought it to him."

"I hope you don't feel too proud of it," said the father, grimly.

"I'm not defending myself, I'm trying to set you straight about Uncle Jesse. If I've picked up ideas that you don't like, it hasn't been from him, for he's avoided talking to me, and even told me I couldn't understand his ideas if I tried. I'm a parasite, a member of the wasting classes, all that sort of thing. What I've had explained has been by Alston, and Herron, and Steffens——"

"Whom you met in Jesse's room, I believe!"

"Well, he could hardly refuse to introduce me to his friend when I walked in. As a matter of fact I'd have met Steffens anyway, because Alston's friends talked a lot about his visit to Russia, and he was at the dinner where they decided to resign. So whatever I've done that was wrong, you must blame me and not Uncle Jesse. I don't know whether he hasn't any use for me, or whether he just pretends that he hasn't, but anyhow that's the way things have been between us."

Said Robbie, coldly: "Nothing alters the fact that he came to this hotel and brought a swarm of hornets down on both of us. Look at my room!" Robbie pointed to his effects strewn here and there. "And my business papers taken by the police, and copies made, no doubt—and sold by some crook to my business rivals!" Robbie knew how such things were done, having done them.

"You are perfectly right," said the painter. "It is my fault, and I am sorry as can be."

"All that I want to know is that I don't have to look forward to such things for the rest of my life. You are Beauty's brother, and if you decide to behave yourself as a decent human being, I'm ready to treat you that way. But if you choose to identify yourself with the scum of the earth, with the most dangerous criminals alive—all right, that's your privilege, but then I have to say: 'Keep away from me and mine.' "

"You are within your rights." Uncle Jesse spoke in the same cold tones as his not quite brother-in-law. "If you will arrange it with your son to keep away from me, you may be sure that I will never again invade his life, or yours."

VI

That was a fair demand and a fair assent; if only those two could have let it rest there! But they were like two stags in the forest, which might turn away and walk off in opposite directions—but they don't! Instead they stand and stare, paw the ground, and cannot get each other out of their minds.

The painter was moved to remark: "You may hang on to your dream of keeping modern thought from your son; but I assure you, Robbie, the forces against you are stronger than you realize."

To which the man of business was moved to answer, with scorn: "Leave that to my son and me, if you please! When Lanny learns that 'modern thought' means class hate, greed, and murder, he may decide to remain an old-fashioned thinker like his father."

"The fond father's dream throughout the ages!" exclaimed the other, in a tone of pity, even more exasperating than one of ridicule. "Let my son be exactly like me in all things! Let him think exactly what I think—and so he will be perfect! But the world is changing, and not all the fathers leagued together can stop it, or keep the sons from knowing about it."

"My son has his own mind," said the father. "He will judge for himself."

"You say that," answered the revolutionist, "but you don't feel nearly as secure as you pretend. Why else should you be so worried when someone presents a new idea to Lanny's mind? Don't you suppose he notices that? Don't you suppose he asks himself what it means?"

That was touching Robbie Budd on the rawest spot in his soul. The idea that anybody could claim to know Lanny better than his father knew him! The idea that the youth might be hiding things, that doubts and differences might be lurking in his mind, that the replica of Robbie's self might be turning traitor to him! In the father's subconscious mind Lanny remained a child, a budding youth, something that had to be guarded and cherished; so the feelings that stirred the father's soul were not so different from the jealous rage of the forest monarch over some sleek and slender doe.

"You are clever, Jesse," said he; "but I think Lanny understands the malice in your heart."

"I'm sorry I can't call you clever," retorted the other. "Your world is coming to an end. The thousands of your wage slaves have some other purpose than to build a throne for you to sit on."

"Listen, Uncle Jesse," interposed Lanny. "What's the use of all this ranting? You know you can't convince Robbie——"

But the stags brushed him aside; they weren't interested in him any more, they were interested in their battle. "We'll be ready for them any time they choose to come," declared Robbie. "We make machine guns!"

"You'll shoot them yourself?"

"You bet your life!"

"No!" said the painter with a smile. "You'll hire other men, as you always do. And if they turn the guns against you, what then?"

"I'll be on the watch for them! One of them was fool enough to forewarn me!"

"History has forewarned you, Robbie Budd, but you won't learn. The French Revolution told you that the days of divine right were over; but you've built a new system exactly like the old one in its practical results—blind squandering at the top, starvation and despair at the bottom, an insanity of greed ending in mass slaughter. Now you see the Russian revolt, but you scorn to learn from it!"

"We've learned to shut the sons-of-bitches up in their rat-holes, and let them freeze and starve, or die of typhus and eat their own corpses."

"Please, Robbie!" interposed the son. "You're getting yourself all worked up——"

Said the painter: "Typhus has a way of spreading beyond national boundaries; and so have ideas."

"We can quarantine disease; and I promise you, we're going to put the right man in the White House, and step on your Red ideas and smash the guts out of them."

"Listen, Robbie, do be sensible! You're wasting an awful lot of energy."

"Stay in France, Jesse Blackless, and spit your poison all over the landscape; but don't try it in America—not in Newcastle, I warn you!"

"I'm not needed there, Robbie. You're making your own crop of revolutionists. Class arrogance carries its own seeds of destruction."

"Listen, Uncle Jesse, what do you expect to accomplish by this? You know you can't convert my father. Do you just want to hurt each other?"

Yes, that was it. The two stags had their horns locked, and each wanted to butt the other, drive him back, beat him to the earth, mash him into it; each would rather die than give an inch. It was an old, old grudge; they had fought like this when they had first met, more than twenty years ago. Lanny hadn't been there, Lanny hadn't been anywhere then, but his mother had told him about it. Now it had got started again; the two stags couldn't get their horns apart, and it might mean the death of one or both!

"You and your gutter-rats imagining you can run industry!" snarled Robbie.

"If you're so sure we can't, why are you afraid to see us try? Why don't you call off your mercenaries that are fighting us on twenty-six fronts?"

"Why don't you call off your hellions that are spreading treason and hate in every nation?"

"Listen, Uncle Jesse! You promised Robbie you'd let me alone, but you're not doing it."

"They don't let anybody alone," sneered the father. "They don't keep any promises. We're the bourgeoisie, and we have no rights! We're parasites, and all we're fit for is to be 'liquidated'!"

"If you put yourself in front of a railroad train, it's suicide, not murder," said the painter, with his twisted smile. He was keeping his temper, which only made Robbie madder.

Said he, addressing his son: "Our business is to clear the track and let a bunch of gangsters drive the train into a ditch. History won't be able to count the number they have slaughtered."

"Oh, my God!" cried Uncle Jesse—he too addressing the youth. "He talks about slaughter—and he's just finished killing ten million men, with weapons he made for the purpose! God Almighty couldn't count the number he has wounded, and those who've died of disease and starvation. Yet he worries about a few counter-revolutionists shot by the Bolsheviks!"

VII

Lanny saw that he hadn't accomplished anything, so he sat for a while, listening to all the things his father didn't want him to hear. This raging argument became to him a symbol of the world in which he would have to live the rest of his life. His uncle was the uplifted fist of the workers, clenched in deadly menace. As for Robbie, he had proclaimed himself the man behind the machine gun; the man who made it, and was ready to use it, personally, if need be, to mow down the clenched uplifted fists! As for Lanny, he didn't have to be any symbol, he was what he was: the man who loved art and beauty, reason and fair play, and pleaded for these things and got brushed aside. It wasn't his world! It had no use for him! When the fighting started, he'd be caught between the lines and mowed down.

"If you kill somebody," Uncle Jesse announced to the father, "that's law and order. But if a revolutionist kills one of your gangsters, that's murder, that's a crime wave. You own the world, you make the laws and enforce them. But we tell you we're tired of working for your profit, and that never again can you lead us out to die for your greed."

"You're raving!" said Robbie Budd. "In a few months your Russia will be smashed flat, and you'll never get another chance. You've shown us your hand, and we've got you on a list."

"A hanging list?" inquired the painter, with a wink at the son.

"Hanging's not quick enough. You'll see how our Budd machine guns work!"

Lanny had never seen his father in such a rage. He was on his feet, and kept turning away and then back again. He had had several drinks, and that made it worse; his face was purple and his hands clenched. A little more and it might turn into a physical fight. Seeing him getting started on another tirade, Lanny grabbed his uncle by the arm and pulled him from his seat. "Please go, Uncle Jesse!" he exclaimed. "You said you would let me alone. Now do it!" He kept on, first pulling, then pushing. The uncle's hat had been hung on a chair, and Lanny took it and pressed it into his hand. "Please don't argue any more—just go!"

"All right," said the painter, half angry, half amused. "Look after him—he's going to have his hands full putting down the Russian revolution!"

"Thanks," said Lanny. "I'll do my best."

"You heard what I had to say to him!"

"Yes, I heard it."

"And you see that he has no answer!"

"Yes, yes, please go!" Lanny kept shoving his exuberant relative out into the hall.

A parting shot: "Mark my words, Robbie Budd—it's the end of your world!"

"Good-by, Uncle Jesse!" and Lanny shut the door.

VIII

He came back into the room. His father was staring in front of him, frowning darkly. Lanny wondered: was the storm going to be turned upon him? And how much of it was left!

"Now, see here!" exclaimed the elder. "Have you learned your lesson from this?"

"Yes, indeed, Robbie; more than one lesson." Lanny's tone was full of conviction.

"You put yourself in the hands of a fanatic like that, and he's in a position to blackmail you, to do anything his crazy fancy may suggest."

"Please believe me, Robbie, I wasn't doing anything for Uncle Jesse. I was trying to help a friend."

"How far will a man go to help a friend? You were bucking the French government!"

"I know. It was a mistake."

"A man has to learn to have discretion; to take care of himself. You want friends, Lanny—but also you want to know where to draw a line. If people find out they can sponge on you, there's no limit to it. One wants you to sign a note and bankrupt yourself. One gets drunk and wants you to sober him up. One is in a mess with a woman, and you have to get her off his neck. You're a soft-shell crab, that every creature in the sea can bite a chunk out of. Nobody respects you, nobody thinks of anything but to use you."

"I'll try to learn from this, Robbie." Lanny really meant it; but his main thought was: Soothe him down; cool him off!

"You have a friend who's a German," continued the father. "All right, make up your mind what it means. As long as you live, Germany's going to be making war on France, and France on her. It doesn't matter what they call it, business or diplomacy, reparations, any name—Germany's foes will be trying to undermine her and she will be fighting back. If Kurt Meissner is going to be a musician, that's one thing, but if he's going to be a German agent, that's another. Sooner or later you've got to make up your mind what it means to have such a friend—and your mother's got to make up her mind what it means to have such a lover."

"Yes, Robbie; you're right. I see it clearly."

"And those Reds you've been meeting—I don't doubt they're clever talkers, more so than decent people, perhaps. But think what must be in the minds of revolutionists when they waste their time upon a young fellow like you! You have money, and you're credulous—you're their meat, laid out on the butcher's block! Maybe those Russians are going to survive awhile; maybe the Allies are too exhausted to put them down. They can live as long as they can plunder other people's wealth. And you have to make up your mind, are you going to let them use you, and laugh at you while they play you for a sucker? What else can you be to them—a parasite, the son of Robbie Budd the bloated capitalist, the merchant of death! Don't you see that you're everything in the world they hate and want to destroy?"

"Yes, Robbie, of course. I've no idea of having anything more to do with them."

"Well, for Christ's sake, mean that and stick to it! Go on down to Juan and fix up the house and play the piano!"

The youth couldn't keep from laughing. "That's the program!" He put his arm about his father—knowing him well, and realizing how ashamed of himself he would be for having lost his temper and roared at a man who wasn't worth it.

Lanny was beginning to feel gay. A great relief to be out of jail— and also not to have to take any worse scolding than this. "The treaty's signed, Robbie!" he exclaimed. "And we've a League of Nations to keep things in order!"

"Like heck we have!" replied the father.

"Pax nobiscum! E pluribus unum! God save the king! And now let's get this room in order!" Lanny took the suitcase which he had brought from the Préfecture, and put it on the bed and began sorting out the precious papers, like the good secretary he had learned to be. "Tomorrow night I leave for the Côte d'Azur, and lie on the sand and get sunburned and watch the world come to an end!"